Only then did Comrade notice the trees encircling them.

Their trunks had been stripped bare to a man's height, carved with druidic runes. Some gleamed with lacquered wood in the firelight; others were streaked in ritual paints—blue, red, yellow. One tree stood apart. It jutted a thick limb over the clearing like an accusing arm, its bark worn smooth by rope.

The execution tree.

Typical. Primitive. Effective. The Shadow Circle had no need for mercy.

"This meeting of the Shadow Circle has convened," Fox said.

"She will take it back someday," they replied.

"We will take it back someday," they answered in unison.

Comrade's skin prickled. He did not share their vision. Let them speak of rot and rewilding—the Wizards of Arcana sought power, not prophecy. These druids were zealots in decay, poisoning land and mind in equal measure. Civilization had given them language and tools—they offered blood.

Fox turned toward him. "Before our first order of business with Comrade, we must punish failure. Bring him forth."

Two masked druids dragged a prisoner into the ring—naked, bound, beaten. A sack hood covered his face; muffled cries fought through the gag. The message was clear: this was no ceremony. It was a demonstration.

The man was hoisted onto the gallows branch. The rope pulled taut.

Comrade did not flinch, but he listened for the sound.

A hollow crack. The body sagged. Silence followed, broken only by the creak of rope.

The druids called it justice.

He knew it as control.

"The One Tree did not rise by chance—it was planted in silence, beneath ash and ruin, when the world had forgotten what green even was."
— Grand Druid Ellisar, AR5

"Elves speak of roots not as boundaries, but as bridges—every tree a whisper, every grove a memory. And Vaer'Elaril'Thalien listens to them all."
— Archdruid Thalendil of *Elarien Taldras*, AR17

"I have studied ley-lines, Mage-maps, and relic trails. They all vanish near Druid's Glen. Either we have been deceived, or The One Tree hides more than shade."
— Scholar Olven Thray, *Library of Second Light*, AR42

"The Mages built fortresses. We regrew the forests they destroyed. They commanded the world until they answered for their heresy. A new tree grows from the seed of Elaril. Its roots will go deep into the marrow of the earth. Never again will we be misled into betrayal."
— Grand Druid Ellisar, AR3

"The druids claim The One Tree hears all, remembers all, and connects all life. I've seen it. It's a very large tree. That's all."
— Scholar Merrow Keff, *Library of Gilded Thought*, AR61

"The druids named their city Arboretum, which means 'tree-home.' Really? Thousands of Elvish words? That's it?"
— Scholar Merrow Keff, *Library of Gilded Thought*, AR63

The One Tree

Paul Heisel

ISBN: 978-1-969376-09-2
Cover design and illustrations © 2025, generated using AI under the direction of the author, Paul Heisel.
Map illustrations by: Ryne Callahan
https://www.rynecallahon.com/commission
Manufactured independently via print-on-demand.
First Edition

Visit www.books.by/books-by-paul
For more works by Paul Heisel, visit: www.paulheisel.com
For Collector's Editions and Merchandise, visit
www.paulhbooks.etsy.com

The One Tree

Keeper of the Deer
Book Two

Also by Paul Heisel

First Frontier

Tale of the Catstaff

<u>An Emperor's Fury Series</u>

Book One—Most Favored
Book Two—The Frayed Rope
Book Three—Warlord of Pyndira
Book Four—Legion

<u>Keeper of the Deer Series</u>

Book One—The Servant
Book Two—The One Tree

We have many inspirations in our lives—people, you know who you are, but there is an artform that must not be overlooked.

Music.

I listen to Alan Parsons while I write.

The entire catalogue, start to finish.

It is soothing.

Familiar.

Stimulating.

Remember, there is *No Future in the Past* and *You're Gonna Get Your Fingers Burned.*

Pelt
NORTHERN REALMS
Thalraya
DARRIEN
TANN
STORM
ISLANDS
COLLETH
City of Colleth
Kaldaraya
City of Haddensack
HALST
Abyssal Bastion
Tralina
HADDENSACK
Withering Pass
Leafhold
Caliss
WICKTON
ATARIN
NOREMBEL
Golden Wood
THARIE
Sigin
Tower of Knekora
Arboretum
CANTER
ICHING
Mist
DAWN
GRENN
Bacani
SMYTHE
BONNER
ORNST
THROM
DAWN
City of Ornst
PENDLETON
Rasmus
City of Throm
BIGGS
Cheris
GRELSHORE
BUCK
Grew Ocean
Saltfell
RICHARDSON
The Great Sea
Veilrock

Sea of Ice
Kaldaraya
HALSTEAD
addensack
Tralina
Veilspire
SACK
FAUS
hold
STENGA
Gold'n Wood
Needle Forest
Mallin
THARIEL
Arboretum
Mist Fen
Wintermourne
Bacani
SMYTH   SONNER
JECLEN
Rasmus
Curow
GGS
Cherish
PEHRONE
ATRUA
Shadowfang Citadel
Pehrone City
reat Sea
FLAUX SMYA
Virdaya
Hollowkeep
TROASIA
Gatebreaker
Lyrom
SCURIA
Boundless
Aridaya

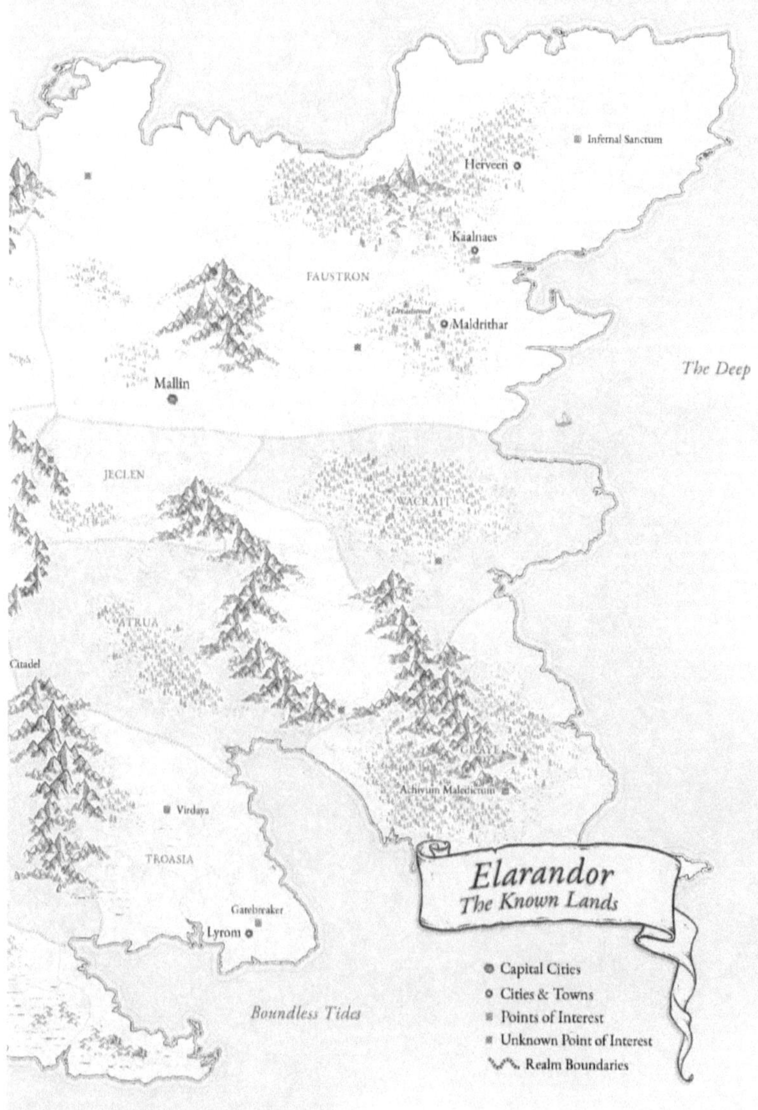

Infernal Sanctum
Herveen
Kaalnaes
FAUSTRON
Dreadwood
Maldrithar
The Deep
Mallin
JECLEN
WACRAIT
ATRUA
Citadel
KRAIL
Achivum Maledictum
Virdaya
TROASIA
Gatebreaker
Lyrom
Boundless Tides
Elarandor
The Known Lands
Capital Cities
Cities & Towns
Points of Interest
Unknown Point of Interest
Realm Boundaries

CHAPTER ONE

∞

Spring Council

Heather picked up the pace, not knowing how far ahead her siblings were along this streamside path. The twelve-year-old girl rounded the corner and suspiciously, her three older brothers were waiting for her. Whatever they were up to, a knot of frustration tightened in her chest. If she couldn't run with them now, how would she survive the druid trials in the autumn?

Cedric, the eldest of the Manawove children, pointed toward the stream and said, "Hey Sissy, look what we found. You better keep up with us—can't be a novice forever."

Heather clenched her jaw. "You found you brain in the mud?"

Her other two older brothers, Aaron and Eric, laughed.

Cedric smirked and said, "A tree fell over, *Sissy*. It's jutting into the river. Look."

Heather gritted her teeth and gazed at the dying white willow, likely brought down by the winds that tore along the stream. The roots were still intact, which made her pause, and the rest of the trunk stretched into the water. The first fifteen feet were bare of branches, clean as if swept by force.

"I see," she said. "Woodworms got it. And you call yourself a druid apprentice. Novice sounds more appropriate for you."

"You're the novice," Cedric said, his voice cool.

Heather tightened her grip on her staff. It was the same word her instructors used—'novice'. She hated it. Every time she heard it, she was reminded how far she still had to go before her trials.

Cedric pointed with his staff to the stump of rotted pulp. "You're right Sissy, woodworms feast on white willows."

Heather tapped her staff against the mud on her boots and looked around. The forest was slow to stir, with tiny shoots of green peeking through the dead leaves and the first buds clinging to bare branches. By autumn, those leaves would be full-grown, and so would she. Or so she hoped. "So what? Everyone knows woodworms prefer white willows."

Cedric bowed, his voice mocking. "Her esteemed title is '*Novice Sissy*.'"

Aaron and Eric laughed.

Heather clenched her teeth.

"We should burn it," Cedric said. "We can't let the woodworms spread to any of the other white willows."

"Fire, in a forest?" Heather asked. "Are you crazy? Didn't find your brain, did you? You're the novice."

"She's actually correct," Aaron said. "You didn't find your brain."

The siblings laughed.

"Laugh it up," Cedric said, tilting his head toward the woodworms. "It's not amusing, no matter what you think. They're serious and destructive. Fire is the best way to eradicate them. We'll need to be cautious and keep it under control."

"I have a better idea," Aaron said with a dismissive wave. He tilted his staff to Heather, extended a hand, and uttered a cantrip. The air chilled as the stump froze solid, the woodworms falling still.

"Brilliant idea," Cedric said, eyes alight. "I'll have to remember that one. Do you think the frost killed them?"

"Certain," Aaron answered. "The first frost in the winter kills woodworms. It also kills insects; this should be no different."

"Let's keep moving," Heather said as she handed the staff back to Aaron. "I'm bored with these woodworms, I'm bored with you three idiots. Plus, I'm getting hungry, and father is waiting for us."

"You're always hungry," Aaron said.

"I'm growing!"

Cedric pointed to the log jutting out into the stream and said, "We'll get moving in a minute and you can have your breakfast, Sissy. You've been bragging about how good you've gotten with your staff. Let's spar on the fallen tree. It will be a test of skill, balance, and who doesn't want to get soaking wet. You up for the challenge Sissy?"

Heather hesitated, her eyes darting between the slippery log and Cedric's grinning face. It was another one of his stupid games, but it could also be practice—a way to prove that she was making progress. Balance. Skill. If she couldn't stay steady on the log today, how would she stay steady through two weeks alone in the forest when the time came for her trials?

She gritted her teeth. "Stop calling me Sissy."

"I'll call you what I want, Sissy. *Novice Sissy.*"

She took a calming breath. "First one to hit the water loses?" she asked. "Is that the rule?"

"First one in the water loses. Which will be you." Cedric twirled his staff, alternating sides, spinning it so fast the cool air hummed, stirring stray leaves at his feet.

Heather's fingers tapped her staff while she decided. "All right, I accept your challenge. Let's shake for who goes onto the log first."

"Deal."

Cedric stopped twirling his staff and tipped it to Aaron.

Heather tipped her staff to Eric, who fumbled with it, stopping it by letting it hit the side of his head. He muttered a curse that his siblings didn't hear.

"One, two, three, shake!" Heather and Cedric said in unison.

Heather signaled blade which cut Cedric's leaf.

Heather grinned, Cedric always picked leaf.

"No matter," Cedric said. "You're going to be soggy and freezing on your walk back to the house. I will have victory!"

"We'll see about that. I've gotten faster and stronger."

Cedric climbed onto the fallen tree, stepping carefully on the unstable trunk and shuffling further over the stream. The bark was slippery with moisture, so he slowed a bit. He turned his head toward the bank and said, "Come on Sissy, your fate awaits!"

Cedric was out as far as he could go without running into the branches being pulled by the flowing water. The log swayed under his feet as he pivoted to face his sister. He maintained his balance and got good footing. Despite the instability, he looked ready and dangerous.

"Get out here Sissy. The water is cold, cold, cold as you will soon find out. Quit stalling."

Heather's gaze went toward the fallen tree, her keen blue eyes bright and mischievous. Testing her balance against Cedric wasn't the best option this morning. She jammed her staff beneath the trunk and heaved upward.

If she couldn't beat Cedric with balance, she'd beat him with brains.

The smirk vanished from Cedric's face as the log lurched beneath him.

The Needle Forest sat at the center of the known world, a place where humans, druids, and scattered families lived in quiet villages beneath the trees. At its heart lay the capital city of Arboretum, named for the Elvish word for tree—*arbo*.

Animal life was abundant in this area nestled within the protected borders of the Kingdom of Haddensack. Crops were tended to for foodstuffs and tobacco was harvested by the druids, and the most famous, respected member of these druids was Gideon Manawove. He was a druid of the highest order, the Grand Druid, attaining it at a young age and holding the honored position for two decades.

In that time, he had fathered four children with his wonderful wife. His lovely Emma, though, had died seven years ago to the day. He remembered it with aching clarity: the air had been thick and cold, like the forest was suffocating alongside her. The room smelled of herbs and old wood, but no spell or elixir could save her. Her muscles failed, one by one, until her lungs refused to work. The magic only gave them a little more time together—a few more stolen moments, for which he was grateful. Every second with her had been precious.

Gideon was sitting in his worn wooden rocking chair, moving it back and forth on the smoothed planks of his front porch. Unlike the day his wife died, today was clear and bright with the morning sun streaming in through the great canopy of trees.

He had already dressed in his green druid robes. It was comfortable clothing with pockets for magic powders, healing roots, and more importantly, his tobacco and pipe.

He was tempted to light a smoke, but it was early, and he could hear his darling Emma scolding him for smoking in the morning. It was a guilty pleasure, and as he thought of her wonderful smile and amazing blue eyes, he was so thankful his daughter Heather looked so much like her.

When Heather laughed, he could almost hear Emma in her voice. Some days it made his heart ache; today it just made him grateful. He would never take his children for granted—not while he could still see pieces of Emma in all of them.

They behaved, mostly, and worked hard at their studies and chores. Yes, they had fun and got into small bits of trouble—what child didn't? They weren't like some of the other village children who would fight each other and steal from merchants or vandalize farmer's crops to get attention.

His oldest was Cedric, named after Gideon's father. He was tall and lanky, a runner, and could handle himself in any situation. He was eighteen and apprenticed to be a druid, though he was impatient and unwilling to take the time to study his surroundings for any length of time.

That would change as he continued to walk the druid's path. Cedric had a penchant for growing things—trees, crops, tobacco—he had a way of coaxing the plants to life. Saying he had a 'green thumb' was an understatement.

Next was Aaron, a patient young man of sixteen who noticed *everything*. He remembered *everything*. He wasn't shy about pointing out mistakes and correcting anyone who needed correcting, an annoyance to those who were around him.

He was the smartest of the Manawove family, Gideon thought he was smarter than him, the Grand Druid. He was apprenticed to be a druid as well, and in truth, was more advanced than Cedric. He often corrected Cedric, and at first that was irritating to his brother, but Cedric turned that into a positive. He had a built-in consultant, a reliable, smart partner that would gladly fix his mistakes and not worry about recognition or seek any credit.

Aaron was happy to point out the flaws or comment on a better way to do something. Aaron simply didn't care about those things; he cared about getting things right. It was a strange dynamic, and he could see Cedric becoming the Grand Druid one day and naming his younger brother as his second in command. Or perhaps Aaron would take Finola's spot on the Druid Council when she moved on to a different phase of her life. The future possibilities were promising for those two.

Their third child was Eric. He was as smart and as driven as his older brothers, yet he was quiet and reserved. He was fourteen years old, and Gideon thought fourteen was also the number of words he had said since birth. It wasn't that he was disinterested or aloof or arrogant, Eric was a listener.

Like Aaron, he noticed everything and everyone around him. Eric was the person you asked who someone was, because somehow, he knew everyone. He knew the families in the villages, he knew the children's names, he knew who they were and what they did.

The most intriguing thing about Eric was his love for books. Gideon had never seen anyone so devoted to the written word. He felt fortunate, too—Eric never complained about the limited collection in the Arboretum Library, though Gideon was fairly certain he had read and re-read nearly every volume it housed. His birthday was approaching, and Gideon had the perfect gift in mind: a trip to the most renowned library in Eldor—the Ornst Library.

Last was his precious Heather, a young girl of twelve. She had shot up in height and was all arms, legs, knees, and elbows. She was like Emma, and Gideon knew in the coming years she would be a tall, striking young woman not fully matured but close to it.

She had long blonde hair, like his Emma, and those striking blue eyes. Heather loved all the creatures of the forest and had a talent for taming them, or calming them, and Gideon didn't understand how she could do it. It was a gift, and he wasn't sure where it had come from, and now he didn't think it odd when he would see her talking to a horse or the occasional cow.

She was quite athletic and strong for a gangly girl, always carrying her staff with her. She could outrun Eric and best Aaron with a staff— she would only get better as she got older. Gideon figured she would follow in his footsteps as well and join the Order of Druids, or The Circle as it was called. It was spring, and after the summer, Heather would have her druid trials in the autumn.

Aaron and Cedric had passed the trials without incident. Eric, not so much—but to his credit, he endured, like a sapling bent by wind. Gideon was proud that Eric had thanked him for the opportunity to pursue druid-hood and had declined an official apprenticeship in the Circle. He would find another career, and he was determined to work with books one day.

The rocking chair creaked, and Gideon vaulted forward in a smooth motion to a standing position, flexing his strong legs. He could hear his children coming toward their modest home, making too much noise, more than they should.

Heather was in the lead with her blonde hair streaming behind her as she outdistanced the boys with her gangly legs churning up the ground. Eric and Aaron were not far behind, laughing more than they were running—the source of the noise. Cedric brought up the rear, his face red apparently from exhaustion. As he got closer, Gideon could see that Cedric was soaking wet and without his staff.

They had been down by the stream which was swollen by the winter runoff, and Cedric had fallen in.

Or had been pushed in.

Heather came to an abrupt halt and handed her staff to her father, then put her hands on her knees to catch her breath. She was laughing too. The two boys arrived, both laughing as well, and their hands went onto their knees.

"He's going to kill you," Aaron said.

"No one is killing anyone," Gideon said before any other words spilled out.

Cedric slowed to a walk, his body dripping with cold water. He was thoroughly soaked. The coolness of the spring morning made him shiver as he came to a halt. His normally pleasant face was tense and red with embarrassment.

"You no-good animal-loving weirdo!"

Eric and Aaron laughed.

Gideon took a step forward, as he had never seen his son this angry at his sister.

"Did you say 'hello' to the fishes for me?" Heather asked, her tone mocking him. Her voice was like music, clear and vibrant.

"I lost my staff! You freak! I'll get you for this!"

Gideon held his son at arm's length, keeping him from Heather. He noted Eric and Aaron were still laughing at their brother's expense, and Heather hadn't backed away an inch. She was tall and gangly for her age, not nearly as strong as her brothers, but she had courage and grit that couldn't be ignored.

"What happened?" Gideon asked. "Before I punish all of you!"

"She cheated! And I lost my staff!"

Gideon guided the tense Cedric to the side. The young man was shivering. "It seems to me that your pride is hurt more than anything.

What happened? Aaron? Do you want to explain this to me? Be quick about it before I lose my patience with the four of you! I can hand out four punishments just as easily as one."

"We were down by the river, a quarter mile downstream," Aaron said. "We were walking our normal trail for the morning. Around the bend, by the stands of cedar, a trunk of white willow fell over into the water. It had woodworms. One end was lodged in the lower bank and the rest of it was out in the river. Like a finger."

"I see where this is going," Gideon muttered. "What happened?"

"Cedric challenged Heather to spar while on the trunk. They shook for who would go out first."

Gideon nodded, familiar with the game of 'shaking', where you picked one of three options with your hand, and each option beat one other. Leaf, rock, blade. Blade cuts leaf, leaf covers rock, rock crushes blade. You would 'shake' your hand three times and declare your choice.

"I lost the shake so I went onto the log first," Cedric said, shivering. "She cheated!"

Aaron continued, "Heather jammed her staff under the log and levered it off the bank. The whole thing rolled into the water before Cedric could make it back. It was hilarious."

They burst out laughing.

Cedric's scowl softened a bit. "She cheated! I lost my staff!"

"I won, you went into the water first," Heather said. "That was the challenge. You said whoever goes in the water first loses. Rules are rules."

"You've had your fun," Gideon told his children before this escalate. "No harm in learning a valuable lesson. Get cleaned up and get ready for breakfast."

"It was my best staff!"

"You can carve another one while you think about how your little sister outwitted you."

Heather stepped forward and tipped her staff toward her older brother, who caught it with a scowl.

"Take mine," she said, her tone smug. "I'll find another one. It'll be fun to make myself a better one while I savor this *glorious* victory. I think I will call my staff, *Cedric's Bane.*"

Cedric glared at her, gripping the staff like he wanted to snap it in half.

"Thanks, Sissy," he muttered, though his voice was thick with irritation rather than gratitude. He paused, his knuckles whitening around the wood. "But I'm not apologizing. Not to you."

Heather raised an eyebrow. "Oh, still mad I bested you? Don't worry, Cedric, I'll try not to bring it up *too often*. Maybe just every day. Morning, noon, and night."

"I said I'm not apologizing," Cedric said. "You didn't win. You cheated."

Heather gasped, clutching her chest and falling to her knees. "*Cheated?* I can't believe you'd say that, big brother. I *earned* that victory. I bet if we ask the Poussin's cow, she'd say the same thing."

Cedric's pale face turned an alarming shade of red.

"Don't," he warned, his voice low. "Don't even start."

"*Oh, Cedric,*" she said in a higher pitched voice.

"Don't," he said, face still red.

Heather stood up and dusted off her trousers. "I think you want to know what the Poussin's cow told me."

Cedric clenched his teeth so hard it looked like his jaw might crack.

"What did the Poussin's cow tell you?" Gideon asked, his tone light. His gaze was sharp as it flicked between his children.

"Father, it's nothing," Cedric said, his voice strained and pleading. "It's *nothing*. We're friends."

Gideon's attention shifted. "Heather?"

"Nothing important, really. Just something about Beatrice. *Oh Cedric…*"

Cedric's composure snapped. "Heather, I swear—"

"More than just a friend," Heather said as she took a step toward the house. "*Oh Cedric. Oh Cedric,*" she cooed again.

Gideon crossed his arms, assessing Cedric with the weight of fatherly suspicion. "Beatrice, hmm? Is there something you'd like to share, son?"

Cedric opened his mouth, but no sound came out. His face burned as red as the leaves of The One Tree.

"Father, there is *nothing* for you to be concerned about. Let's go inside, it's cold out here."

Gideon's eyes narrowed when Cedric changed the subject. "I wasn't concerned. But now I am."

"*Oh, Cedric*," Heather said again in the higher pitched voice. She made kissing noises.

Cedric growled, "You're *dead*, Heather."

Heather bolted for the house, laughing as she hit the edge of the porch and opened the front door.

Cedric took a step after her, but Gideon held him back.

"You need to forget this," Gideon said, his tone edged with authority. "Your sister outwitted you, learn from it. Now, what is going on with Beatrice?"

"Nothing," he replied. "We're just friends."

Cedric stormed after Heather, muttering under his breath, *this isn't over.*

Aaron and Eric, grins on their faces, followed behind, tipping their staves into the decorated rack at the front and vanishing inside.

"Boots!" Gideon yelled at them, gazing at the trail of mud and dirt on the porch. "Boots," he muttered.

Gideon shook his head, chuckling under his breath. Even now, his children managed to surprise him in ways he never expected. A deep breath of the morning air soothed him, and he wondered if he should be worried about Cedric and Beatrice Poussin.

The sound of his children's laughter drifted from inside, warm as the morning sun.

How did he get so lucky?

And why wasn't Emma here to share it?

Gideon swallowed against the lump in his throat and rubbed his face, thinking it was time to trim his winter beard. With a deep breath, he went inside to join his family.

It was going to be a long day.

After chores, Cedric and Aaron disappeared into the forest to join the other apprentice druids. They carried their staffs and tomes, eager to learn the art of casting spells and crafting potions.

Eric stayed behind, content to pore over history books in the quiet of the house.

Heather set off to the woods with the younger novices, determined to memorize every berry, root, and leaf she could find.

Gideon gripped his gnarled staff and set off down the well-worn path. His steps were sure and steady—he had traveled this route thousands of times. Druid's Glen wasn't far, nestled in a majestic clearing deep within the Needle Forest, where The One Tree stood tall and ancient. It was called The One Tree because its roots went deep into the marrow of the earth, and it was connected to all living plants on earth. This was how the druids traveled great distances and moved unseen through the forests—The One Tree.

Druid's Glen was protected by rings of tall evergreen trees, thick intertwined briars, and choking vines. Only an experienced druid could pass unhindered.

As he approached, Gideon began the incantation to tree-stride. It was a simple enough spell, but only a skilled druid could master the proper application of the spell to navigate the formidable protections of Druid's Glen.

The cadence, the words, the auxiliary phrase, and the inflections had to be perfect. Gideon could do it without thinking, as could the other members of the Druid Council.

Other magic, like teleportation, could bypass the protections. With wizards it seemed nothing was secure if they were clever enough using their magic, spells, or underlings. Yet, since he had become Grand Druid, no one to his knowledge had tried to get inside Druid's Glen. He wondered, though, perhaps no one had been caught yet.

He melded into the tangle, vanishing as he was allowed passage by the protective vines. He instantly emerged on the inside of Druid's Glen beyond the tangle. Druid's Glen opened wide before him, a circular meadow carpeted with soft grass, tangled underbrush, and wild flowers.

At its heart stood The One Tree—a red oak with fiery leaves that blazed against the dark backdrop of towering evergreens. Gideon inhaled deeply; the air was thick with the scent of oak and earth, as if the ancient tree itself was breathing alongside him.

The One Tree was over one hundred feet tall, soaring high into the clear spring sky. At the base it was ten feet in diameter, and the gnarled roots had burst through the surrounding ground in uneven undulations. Its bark had shiny ridges, stripes, that went from the base to the top. At ten feet up, the branches began, stretching up and out. Boughs were laden with acorns, and many of them had fallen to the ground. It was a favorite food of squirrels and birds, and as Gideon walked forward, he could see the small denizens of Druid's Glen grabbing what they could before scattering.

In the open, next to the tree, was a round table made of wood, stained and lacquered to withstand the ravages of the weather. There were cuts of wood they used for seats, and Gideon knew the reason their meetings were so short was because the chairs were uncomfortable.

Others of the druidic order would arrive soon. The Druid Council was the most misunderstood ruling body in Eldor—everyone believed that the members lived in the Needle Forest. They didn't need to, because as Archdruids, they could travel from place to place through the interconnected network of living things made possible by the ancient magic of The One Tree.

The Druid Council consisted of nine members, an odd number so there were no tied votes. The Grand Druid lived in the Needle Forest and was the caretaker of Druid's Glen and The One Tree, while the others lived throughout the lands in their groves. Gideon figured he would have all members of the Druid Council in attendance today, as it was the first part of spring, and everyone would want to hear news.

First to arrive was Ilimitar, the Elf from the Golden Wood, Archdruid of The Greenwood Circle, or *Elarien Taldras* as the Elves called it. His slim frame stepped from the bark of The One Tree as though the tree itself had spit him out.

Gideon stifled a grin—the image was amusing every time he saw it.

"Greetings, Grand Druid," Ilimitar said, his accent sharp and unmistakably Elven.

Ilimitar was of slight build with pale skin and golden hair, his pointed ears were partially hidden by his green felt hat. He had a mahogany staff, and he carried a short bow and quiver of deadly elven-made arrows with him. His forest cloak was magical, and it blended with his surroundings, red near The One Tree. The crest of his light leather armor bore the image of a blue spruce tree, the symbol of Halamar, the Elven god of nature and forests.

The proud Elf strode forward, his steps light and silent. Gideon read the expression on his face; there was news from the Elven world.

Gideon greeted Ilimitar and motioned toward the cooking stoves, kettles already steaming. "Ilimitar, welcome to Druid's Glen. You are the first to arrive. Please, make yourself at home."

"*Arboras Taldorien*," Ilimitar corrected, his voice smooth and measured. "So much better than 'Druid's Glen.'"

He placed his weapons on a wooden rack near the meeting area, every movement deliberate.

"I forget how musical the Elven names for Druid's Glen and our circles are," Gideon replied, then bowed his head slightly and added with a smile, "Welcome to *Taldras Arbo Solien.*"

Ilimitar cringed, as if the words scraped against his ears.

"*Lathren vëa taldorin,*" he muttered. Then louder, in Common: "Please—call it *the Circle*, to spare my ears."

Gideon chuckled and gave the tea a slow stir. "May his leaves rot inward," he translated under his breath, shaking his head.

"Do not even attempt *Vaer'Elaril'Thalien*," the elf said. "All the leaves might fall from The One Tree at the cut of your voice."

Gideon clenched his teeth. Ilimitar was… on edge.

"I hoped to arrive before the others did so I could have a word with you. It seems I have accurately anticipated the exact time to arrive."

Gideon nodded and thought, *this is odd.* Discussions outside the Druid Council were never about official matters, only personal concerns. Ilimitar was no friend of anyone on the council, including himself. *Curious…*

"You have me intrigued," Gideon said, his arms crossed. "You could have sent me a message via green-speak."

"*Aras'Lir*," Ilimitar said in Elvish. "*Leafsong.* Sounds better than your human slang."

Gideon's teeth clenched. "What news do you bring that you can't share with the rest of the Council or send via *root-tongue*?"

The Elf's thin lips formed the slightest smile. "A jab back at me or my people?" He sighed. "Of the Grand Druids I have known through the decades, I like you the least Gideon."

Gideon watched the Elf closely. "Why do I feel that's meant to be a compliment?"

Ilimitar's lips curved into the barest hint of a smile. "The others before you were… simpler. Their interests lay solely with the Needle

Forest and Haddensack. Yours, however, wander farther north and east. It makes your judgment difficult to trust."

"I don't recall interfering with the Golden Wood or its denizens, which is what you're implying."

"Interference, not directly. You have your way of *indirectly* pushing your human ideals upon us. Ideals we will not accept. Or tolerate."

Gideon drew a deep breath, and as he did, he studied Ilimitar's demeanor.

He looked worried.

What news was he bearing?

"Spit it out before the others arrive. I will not repeat anything you say. You have my word as Grand Druid. What is so unnerving to the elves that you must speak to me in secret, and in person?"

"Two things," he answered. "We have concerns with *Talthrien Mor'vany.*"

"Dreadwood?"

"It is not our responsibility, but we exist in harmony with forest and groves alike through our connection with The One Tree. We hear of evil things roaming *Elar'andoré na Tharaniel araneth* to the east, where Hexenfold once ruled from Dreadwood. That evil place grows strong once again. It would be tragic if Hexenfold regained strength and returned their evil magic to the lands."

"The Hexenfold are extinct," Gideon said. "You're worried about shadows. Evil creatures turn up everywhere, not just in Dreadwood."

Ilimitar stiffened, his voice was a hiss, and he said, "We are not slouches when it comes to using druid magic and understanding where the creatures might be coming from. Evil is there, and it's growing. I am sure of it. It must be Hexenfold."

"Your concern is noted. I will send word to the Stairwell."

"If you feel it is that important, please do so. The Stairwell needs direction these days."

Gideon considered the Elf in front of him, noting how he brought forth a concern and so easily shuttled it to him for investigation, but only after he dismissed the seriousness. That meant it was his decision, his concern, and directed by the Grand Druid, not a request by the Elves from the Golden Wood.

"The second thing?" Gideon asked. He hoped Dreadwood wasn't the good news so to speak.

"*Galanor Sylas* is peaceful and pristine," he began, "and we continue to guard our borders and have sentries on our bridges over the *Lirwen Ithiloras*. Despite our vigilance, we have encountered odd creatures from time to time. They originate from her sister, *Lirithil Vaenor*, and *Haloth Vaenor*. Powerful magic is at work. Coincidence that there are evil things coming from *Talthrien Mor'vany* and *Haloth Vaenor*?"

Gideon acknowledged the comment with a nod, yet Dreadwood and the Mist Fens were separated by a thousand or more miles. The connection was tenuous at best. The sister streams Ilimitar was referring to—Narrow Iris and Lost Reed—started from the same mountain range and joined together to form the Thalos River. The Elven name escaped him for a fleeting second—*Liraethar*, meaning The Great Vein.

"The shifting fog in *Haloth Vaenor* is confusing for anyone who enters. I can also confuse what people see. What odd creatures have been reported from the Mist Fens?"

"*Narthtunel* - devils," Ilimitar said flatly as if he was saying 'raccoons.'

"Preposterous." Gideon realized the haste of his response.

Ilimitar brow furrowed and he glared.

"Apologies for my dismissal of your concern," Gideon said. "Devils—the magic to summon devils is rarer than that to summon demons. Do you have additional details you can share?"

He muttered something inaudible in the Elven tongue, a curse perhaps. "Few," he answered. "As you know we keep to *Galanor Sylas*, and creatures, trolls and other ilk, coming from *Haloth Vaenor* along the *Lirithil Vaenor* are dealt with swiftly. One of our scouts, before he perished, said there was a *Kel'Saevren*, its touch as cold as ice. And *Thulven Gaathir* have been sighted that are made completely of bone, akin to fleshless undead."

"Devils are shut off from the Material Plane," Gideon said. He was certain Ilimitar knew this. "The same is for the demons trapped in the Abyss. Sightings are rare, and it takes special magic, knowledge, and training to summon such creatures."

"Yet here we are talking about sightings of devils near the Golden Wood. Perhaps there is a rift between the planes, or a wizard with that knowledge is using it. The Mist Fens has numerous human fortifications, small towns and villages that go unchecked. That could be your source."

"*My source?*" Gideon asked, noting that Ilimitar had switched to only the Common tongue.

"The source."

Ilimitar leveled a finger at Gideon. "We haven't seen incursions of devils and demons in hundreds of years, if not a thousand. Not since the times of the Mages. It makes me… uneasy. Will you send a message to the Stairwell to look at this disturbance as well?"

"I will," Gideon answered.

There was a low *whoosh*, and Krik stepped from the bark of The One Tree with the smell of pine clinging to him. His red hair and beard blazed as fiercely as the crimson leaves above. Krik was druid more suited for combat than being in harmony with nature. He carried twin battle axes on his back, sharp implements he knew how to use well. An array of knives was strapped across his light leather armor, and there were two longer knives sheathed at his waist.

He came from the western parts of Eldor, where there were small duchies loyal to Haddensack, and he represented the sparse forests in those areas. There were three druids under his command, who watched over the coastal, plains, and mountain regions. *Gorvan'dar* was the ancient name for his circle, commonly known as The Ironwood Circle.

"You two are getting started early," Krik boomed as he strode forward. "I heard you talking."

"Just pleasantries," Gideon said, holding to his promise to Ilimitar. "It is good to see you Krik. Welcome to Druid's Glen."

Krik grunted. "Greetings Grand Druid." He paused. "By the way, the word 'disturbance' isn't a pleasantry."

Two more druids came out of The One Tree, their tree-stride spell ending at the same time. One was Lillia, the mysterious dryad with druidic powers. In body, she was the perfect form of a human woman. To say she was beautiful was an understatement, and Gideon never let his guard down for a moment while around her.

True to her nature, she was barefoot and without clothing, her long green hair swept around her left shoulder. At least that covered one of her round breasts. Around her neck was a leather throng tied around a magical acorn. Her eyes were emerald green and piercing, chilling though, and with a glance she could penetrate a person's soul.

She came from the southern parts of the lands, where the climate was warm nearly the year round and snow was but a dream. She arranged her hair with tiny white roses and took up her normal seat. The dryad scanned her surroundings with intelligent eyes, crossed her bare legs, and raised an eyebrow in Gideon's direction.

Right behind her came Aurora, a tall, lean woman in her later years. She had been on the Druid Council longer than anyone, and Gideon considered her to be the wisest of the assembled Archdruids. The north was her realm, among the evergreens and constant snow, and the fur-lined leathers underneath her cloak told everyone it was still cold where she had come from.

Her face was burned by the cold, wind, and sun—she was as leathery as her worn clothes. Her gray hair was shorn short for convenience, and any sense of style had been forgotten long ago. She had a black staff that glinted in the light, it looked lacquered and untarnished. Her strides were confident as she tipped her staff into the weapons rack. Aurora went straight for the kettles, predictable, to get a cup of hot herbal tea to warm her old bones despite the pleasant temperature of Druid's Glen.

Nightshade arrived next, probably the oddest member of the Druid Council. She was Fey, one of the ancient wood-folk who lived in the deepest and inaccessible forests. Where she came from was unknown to Human and Elf alike, and the fairies kept their realm's exact location a secret. She was diminutive, a replica of an Elf only two feet tall, slender, with iridescent wings. The Archdruid wore a white dress that was partially hidden by her plentiful black locks. She wore a crown of ivy that had been woven into her hair.

After arriving, she fluttered for a moment then darted through the air—it wasn't like flying, it was like she moved from point to point in the blink of an eye. She hovered near Krik, who greeted her with a hug, and he belted out a laugh after she whispered in his ear.

A minute later, Wilmund arrived. He was from the far east and carried with him a scythe. He was adorned in all blacks, a purveyor of death, and was known to the council as the Dark Archdruid.

His black beard was streaked with gray, his dark eyes pools of intense wonder. The part of the world he came from was vast, and he had little time for council meetings as there was too much work to do, too many concerns. Gideon figured this would be the only meeting he would attend until winter, and not until they threatened expulsion, would he return.

At last count, Wilmund had twelve druids serving under him managing the areas of Faustron and eastern Halstead, along with the sparsely settled Jeclen and Wacrait—areas so vast he often commented about needing to recruit more. The Circle of Farreach had countless groves under their protection.

He placed his scythe next to the other weapons and went for a cup of tea as well.

Finola arrived next, a fair-haired druid with enormous brown eyes and eyebrows as slender as her fit body. She looked frail but wasn't. Her light blue robe was cinched tight by a golden rope around her slight hips, accentuating her figure. The Archdruid placed her staff among the others and glided to her seat. She looked around the table and set her eyes on Gideon.

She was from the Needle Forest as well, two villages over, and had studied with Gideon in their youth. In truth, she could have been the Grand Druid had Gideon not earned the position years ago. She would be his successor until Cedric or Aaron showed they could lead the Druid Council. The Circle of Heartwood was her domain, the Midlands of Haddensack in and around the Needle Forest and stretching to the Leafy Forest. In truth, Druid's Glen was part of The Circle of Heartwood.

She tapped her fingers on the table, noted they were waiting for one more person, stood up, glanced around as if deciding on a course of action, and went to get tea.

They spoke among themselves, chatted about families, children, villages, and things of no importance to the Druid Council. Gideon was about to call the meeting to order when the last member arrived out of The One Tree.

It was Buvic, a man from the northwest who often dealt with the Black Storm and barbarian tribes. The Circle of Frosthall was aptly named as the northwest climes never relinquished its cold grip on the lands. He was a solidly built man with square shoulders and a square jaw to match, tousled brown hair that was the same color as his staff.

The Archdruid hurried forward and tipped his staff with too much energy and knocked over the other weapons leaning there.

The clatter brought all conversations to a halt.

As he picked up the weapons and righted them, the druids took their assigned seats. Nightshade zipped across the table and hovered over her seat, sitting only when Buvic finally approached the table.

Everyone was present.

Gideon rapped a polished crystal shard onto the table, the sharp sound cutting through the chatter. He opened one of many volumes of the Druid Histories to the next empty page and noted the date with his quill and ink.

"I call this council to order," he said, his gaze sweeping the gathered Archdruids. "Wilmund, let's hear your report."

The Dark Archdruid leaned back in his chair, boots thudding onto the table. He cradled his tea in both hands, his dark eyes fixed on the liquid as if it held the answer to an unspoken question. For a moment, he sipped slowly, savoring the taste—not out of leisure, but as though fortifying himself for what was to come.

"Where should I begin?" he murmured, his lips pressing into a grim line.

The humor in the room faded as the other druids shifted in their seats. Nightshade's wings fluttered in agitation. Krik, usually unfazed, leaned forward, his hands resting on his knees.

Wilmund exhaled, the steam from his cup rising between them like smoke before a storm. "There's news from Farreach," he said at last, his voice low and deliberate. "It's not good."

Chapter Two

∞

Mage-Gate

Heather had found six varieties. Baneberries gleamed bright red, as dangerous to Humans as they were beautiful. Bluebeads shone cobalt-blue beneath their waxy coating, another deadly temptation. Fairy-apples, orange at the base and red at the top, were edible for Humans but fatal to animals. Huckleberries and blueberries both promised sweetness, perfect for pies, while the black dewberries clustered together in tangled brambles.

She knew she had done well. She tucked the blueberries into her pouch—these would be for her father. With the right magic, he could turn them into druid-berries, powerful enough to keep someone alive for days in the wilderness, heal a wound in moments, or stop poison from spreading. Heather always kept a few in her own pockets when she could. They had saved her brother Eric's hand once when he cut it on a fishing hook.

The other novices were standing near their instructor and showing their berries, explaining the varietals and their properties. Heather recited the properties in her head as she watched them present them.

The instructor, a druid named Lana, came over the Heather.

"What have we found?" she asked.

"I know these well enough, you know that," Heather answered.

"Just because your father is the Grand Druid doesn't mean you can skip tests, Heather." Lana crossed her arms, her expression sharp with disapproval.

Heather was twelve, but already eye level with her instructor. Lana was pleasant enough—a patient teacher who knew how to keep the other novices engaged. Heather shifted on her feet and bit the inside of her cheek. She wasn't the rebellious type, not really. But today, focus felt like a waste of time.

She should've been in the forest, searching for the perfect tree to shape into her new staff—not trudging through the underbrush collecting berries like a half-trained forager. She already knew this lesson. If she said as much, though, word would get back to her father. And that wasn't worth the lecture.

"No Lana," she said. "I apologize, my mind is elsewhere. I need to replace my staff, and I want to go hunting for the perfect piece of wood. This is what I found." Quickly and with precision, she described each berry; the shape, color, places they grew, properties, and deadliness or not of them.

"Well done," Lana said. "After the midday meal you can go search for your staff. We'll be turning rocks near the Druid's Glen to see what insects have been hibernating."

"Lady bugs, snow bugs—but they are a crustacean, black-stone bugs, millipedes, and black widows."

"There are more," Lana said.

"But not around here. Anyone knows that."

Lana's lips twitched with amusement. "For that comment, you get one hour to find your staff, no more."

Heather clenched her jaw so tight it hurt.

Why couldn't she keep her mouth shut?

An hour wasn't nearly enough time, and they both knew it—but now she'd have to make it work.

"That should be plenty," Heather said with confidence, though both she and Lana knew it wasn't. Still, she'd find a way. She had to. The perfect piece of wood was out there waiting for her—and she wasn't going back without it.

Wilmund clanked his teacup against the table, the sound unnervingly loud in the still morning. He let the silence stretch, savoring the weight of his words. Finally, he said, "I found a Mage-Gate."

Gideon pressed his fingers into his thighs beneath the table, the muscles knotting painfully. He forced his expression to remain neutral, though the cold weight in his chest threatened to crush him.

This cannot be happening.

"Are you certain it's a Mage-Gate?" Gideon asked, keeping his voice steady despite the cold knot forming in his chest.

"It can't be anything else," Wilmund said, his voice tinged with excitement and a trace of fear. "It's dormant—nonfunctional. At least, as far as I can tell."

Gideon pursed his lips into a frown. *A Mage-Gate might be dormant, but it can be activated.*

Ilimitar's sharp eyes narrowed; Lillia's green brows furrowed in deep thought, while Nightshade's wings twitched uneasily. They, at least, understood the full weight of the discovery. Across the table, Aurora shifted uncomfortably.

"I've never heard of a Mage-Gate," she admitted as she tapped her teacup with her silver ring. "What exactly are we dealing with?"

"Nightshade," Gideon said, "your people and the Elves saw more of that era than any of us. Would you explain?"

The graceful fairy fluttered to the center of the table, her wings trailing soft light.

"After the Age of Expansion, long ago, before even the eldest trees of Druid's Glen took root, *Elarandor* was ruled by the nine Mages— chief among them, the Yholl brothers, Dergan and Mikal. Their reign was one of shadow and fire, built on fear and domination. Thankfully their reign was cut short, and lasted only a hundred years."

Ilimitar scoffed. "The Elves survived, barely."

Nightshade nodded. "Yes. The Elves endured, as did the Fey, Gnomes, and a few others. But the rest were enslaved, corrupted, or destroyed. Wizards, warlocks, and druids alike fell to the Mages or were forced into servitude. The Mages created Mage-Gates, allowing them to move armies, weapons, and assassins without detection by spell, seer, or ward."

Krik scratched his beard, unimpressed. "It's a door. Lock it, bury it—done."

"The problem," Gideon said, "is that anything connected to the Yholl brothers is dangerous. These gates operate outside any magic that we understand. The gate, in theory, could be activated. We have no idea what the consequences of that would be."

"And we don't know what reactivation could unleash," Nightshade added grimly. "It connects to other Mage-Gates. It may awaken dormant guardians left behind by the Mages. Or activating one activates all of them. We don't know."

"Then destroy it," Finola snapped.

"It may not be that simple," Gideon said. "It may not be vulnerable to any magic or weapon we possess. My concern is if someone finds it later, they could unleash magic not seen in a thousand years."

Wilmund leaned forward. "The site is protected by enchantments that block magical access—no tree-striding or teleportation, I'm guessing. It's part of a larger ruin—likely Mikal Yholl's stronghold. The Mage-Gate is inside the keep, and the only way in is on foot. We stopped exploring once we found it. I decided the matter should be for the Council. I cannot take on this burden myself."

"And now you want us to help you explore this *burden*?" Lillia asked, brushing a strand of green hair from her face. Her usually warm complexion was pale.

Wilmund lifted his chin. "This is a great opportunity to recover lost knowledge. Not all magic is evil—it's how it's used that determines its nature. We as druids know this!"

"That's foolish," Lillia shot back. "If there's even a chance of discovering dangerous artifacts, we should bury it under a mountain of ruble."

Nightshade nodded in agreement. "No good will come from stirring the ghosts of the past."

Krik grunted. "We can mask it with druid magic, bolster the barrier Wilmund says is there. It's stayed hidden for a thousand years, it can stay hidden for a thousand more."

"It's only a matter of time before someone else finds it," Wilmund said.

"Then we hide it better—or figure out how to destroy it," Krik said.

Buvic shifted. "We shouldn't destroy what we don't understand. There could be magic there that could help us. Magic that could help our druidic causes. Our Circles can benefit from these relics of the past."

Gideon stood, brushing his hands along the fabric of his robe. "This is not a decision we can make lightly, but we must decide."

Finola glared. "You're rushing us, Gideon. You'd like us to vote now, wouldn't you—before anyone can suggest another way? We need to discuss this."

"We need a plan," Gideon replied, not answering the question. "Not endless discussions without proper context or information."

Aurora leaned forward, her hands clasped tightly. "I think we should gather more information before we decide. This is quite surprising, and intriguing."

"I agree with Aurora," Gideon said after a moment of contemplation. "Ilimitar and Lillia will help me review the druidic histories—there may be useful references."

Both gave him sour looks.

Nightshade's wings twitched from an unseen chill. "What if there is a *Librum*?" she whispered. "Hidden in the keep? The Mage-Gate would be the least of our worries."

Silence fell over the council.

The breeze stirring the leaves of The One Tree above paused.

Gideon's stomach sank. It was a possibility he had hoped no one would speak aloud.

"Those tomes are steeped in more legend and myth than truth," Gideon said, his voice challenging the Council. "So little is written about them, and there is so much speculation on their uses, let alone their whereabouts. They were destroyed when the Mages turned upon themselves, if they even existed in the first place."

"Don't be naïve. We know they exist," Ilimitar said. The Elf tapped an elegant finger on his temple. "The Elves may not be as long-lived as the Fey like Nightshade, but we have good memories. Legends of the books have been passed down from generation to generation, so we won't forget human folly and the misguided efforts of the Mages."

Gideon gave a half smile and said, "Then indulge us with a history lesson. Tell us of these *Librums*—I'm sure we ignorant *humans* could use the education."

Ilimitar stood, addressing the assembled Archdruids with an intense focus. "The *Librums*, these books of power, were created by the Mages for wondrous and terrible purposes. Though much has been lost, we know they summoned creatures from other planes, manifested spells so powerful they frightened the gods, and they controlled life and death."

"They are dangerous relics," Nightshade added, her voice soft and matter of fact. "They cannot be destroyed, not by any magic or force. When the Mages fell, the *Librums* were fought over by their followers. Entire civilizations were leveled, erased from existence, consumed by forests and deserts. Eventually, these books were gathered, scattered, buried, and hidden, so they would not be found. We can only hope these books remain protected—or that their guardians haven't turned."

Aurora, who had been quiet, coughed and said, "Then we must be wary and cautious. The discovery of the Mage-Gate—it may be the first flake of snow in the avalanche."

Gideon scanned the faces of his Archdruids, each expression revealing more than words could.

Ilimitar sat rigid, arms crossed, his gaze distant and impenetrable— a wall no one would breach.

Krik slouched lazily in his chair, his rugged face unreadable, as if the weight of the discussion had already bored him.

Lillia and Nightshade, however, wore their fear openly—Lillia's lips pressed into a thin line, her fingers fidgeting with her acorn necklace, while Nightshade's wings twitched with unease.

Aurora and Buvic shifted in their seats, their eyes darting from one face to another, trying to gauge the mood of the group before deciding where to plant their own opinions.

Finola sat stiffened, her jaw clenched, an unspoken frustration simmering beneath her composed exterior, ready to boil over at any moment.

Across the table, Wilmund drummed his fingers on his empty teacup, the rhythmic *tap-tap-tap* suggesting he already knew what was coming and was prepared for it.

The diverse reactions troubled Gideon.

This wasn't a disagreement over policy—these were deep fractures forming in the foundation of their Council, and the decisions made today would carry monumental consequences.

"Well said Aurora," Gideon spoke. "We have additional work to do." He tapped the crystal on the table, signaling the transition of discussion. He made a single note in the journal next to Wilmund's name. "For now, we move on to your reports. Lillia, what news do you bring from your grove?"

Lillia squared her shoulders, though unease lingered beneath the surface. "It will seem mundane compared to a Mage-Gate, but it's worth sharing. A force, hidden, is stirring in the southern forests—unfamiliar magic. I can't yet determine what it is, but the trees are uneasy. I'm disheartened to hear of Wilmund's discovery and this unfamiliar magic…"

She trailed off, brushing her hair back nervously, as if sensing that the winds of change were already sweeping through her grove, whether she liked it or not.

The council shifted, sensing the weight of her words. Gideon exchanged a glance with Nightshade, who gave a slight nod, confirming that the forest's unease was more than superstition.

"This may be connected to the Mage-Gate in ways we don't yet understand," Gideon murmured, though the thought offered little comfort. If the *Librums* were somehow involved…

He pressed the heel of his hand against his temple, trying to fend off the cold ache spreading behind his eyes.

One ancient problem was bad enough.

Two would be catastrophic.

Heather was in the workshop next to their home, rummaging through her father's tools, looking for a suitable axe. She felt rushed—Lana had already started her hour of searching, and time was slipping away. The other novices were out turning over rocks near Druid's Glen, while she was here, scrambling through cluttered shelves and drawers.

Finally, she found a small, sharp axe and sprinted out of the workshop, her feet pounding the packed dirt path as she made for the forest.

It was moments like these that made Heather feel free.

The world blurred around her as she ran, every step carrying her closer to her goal. Druid's Glen loomed ahead, and she slowed to a walk as the protective brambles came into view, thick and menacing.

She knew the best trees would be near the tangled barrier that surrounded Druid's Glen.

Just one sapling—four inches in diameter—that was all she needed. She could plane it down and shape it into the perfect staff. A thicker piece of wood would take longer to prepare, but Heather didn't mind. She wanted this one to be perfect.

The path ended at the thorns—a wall of twisted bramble, black as night, with thorns long and sharp as spearheads. Her father could walk through it without trouble and enter Druid's Glen, but she knew the stories—those who weren't welcome were caught, immobilized, or worse, left to die among the vines.

Heather stayed back, careful not to touch the wicked thorns. She zigzagged along the forest edge, scanning the saplings with a critical eye. Too tall, too short, too crooked—none of them felt right.

Then she saw it; a lone, elegant sycamore sapling, rising from within the tangle. It was perfect—slender and straight, like an elf's arrow.

She moved closer, heart racing. The sapling was caught in a knot of vines, its branches starting high above her head, the bark smooth and unblemished beneath the thorns. She'd have to cut it free from the bramble, but she didn't care.

This was the one.

She knew it.

Heather gripped the axe and began to chop.

The first strikes came easy, the axe biting into the thorny vines with a satisfying *thunk*. But soon, her muscles began to ache, her arms heavy with effort. Sweat beaded on her brow as she kept swinging, determined to finish. She chipped away at the bramble, clearing the right side to reach the base of the trunk. All she had to do was cut through the last section—and the sapling would be hers.

"Heather!"

The sharp voice startled her mid-swing. The axe slipped from her grip, glancing off the bramble and embedding awkwardly into a cluster of thorns.

Heather spun around, frustration evident.

"Father! You made me miss!"

Gideon stepped into the clearing, his expression stern but puzzled. "What in the name of Thatara are you doing?"

"I found a sycamore sapling for my staff!" Heather said, panting but smiling. "Lana gave me an hour—and I'm almost out of time! I'm running out of time!"

Gideon's gaze swept over the bramble, then back to Heather, his expression one of puzzlement.

It should have attacked her, he thought. *It should have wrapped around her the moment she came close.*

"I'm certain Lana didn't tell you to pull saplings from the protections surrounding Druid's Glen," Gideon said, his voice sharp and scolding. "This isn't a safe place for novice druids, regardless of who your father is. The bramble only knows intruders."

Heather blinked, confused.

She glanced at the vines wrapped around the sapling, then she understood.

They should have seized her the moment she approached.

"I… I didn't think about that," she muttered, brushing a strand of hair from her eyes.

"This shouldn't have happened," Gideon murmured. His thoughts churned—luck didn't explain it. "The bramble…"

The air shimmered nearby, and a soft scent of flowers drifted on the breeze.

A sweet, melodic voice followed.

"I felt it too. What is it?" Lillia asked.

Heather stiffened.

The dryad appeared without warning, stepping out from the bramble like a shadow slipping into light.

Lillia's naked form glowed faintly, her flawless skin the color of honey. A swirling orb of ruby-red magic floated above her hand, spinning dangerously.

Gideon stepped between his daughter and the dryad, his expression darkening.

"Put that away," he commanded. "Now."

Lillia smiled, but the red orb remained in her hand. "Do you think I conjured it for no reason?"

Her voice was light, but there was danger in the way she held herself—like a cat watching a bird too slow to fly away.

When Lillia didn't dismiss the spell, Gideon muttered words of power and made a quick gesture with his hands.

The orb fell from Lillia's hand, landing with a wet splash on the forest floor. Acid hissed as it consumed the broken bramble, reducing the plant matter to steaming mush. Lillia stepped back, her delicate bare feet skimming over the spreading puddle of acidic pulp.

"This is my daughter, Lillia." Gideon's voice was low but tight with anger. "There was no need for that."

Lillia's smile never wavered. "The disturbance worried me. You remember what we spoke of earlier—about what lies beyond these forests to the distant east." She tilted her head toward Heather. "How long have you been here, child?"

Heather crossed her arms. "Long enough to find my staff."

Gideon exhaled. "Run along now, Heather. We'll talk about this later."

"But Father! I need my staff!" Heather protested. "I gave mine to Cedric this morning—this one is perfect!"

Gideon's expression softened slightly, though his eyes remained wary. "You can collect it later. It's not going anywhere."

The dryad laughed, the sound like warm wind through sunlit leaves—soft, beckoning, and laced with a sweetness that unsettled the heart.

"Let the child have it, Gideon. She's earned it."

Lillia sauntered forward with fluid grace, the white roses in her hair bouncing with every step. One slipped loose, and without stopping, she caught it and tucked it back into place.

Heather grinned. "I like her. She needs clothes, though. Cedric and Aaron would be blushing. Eric… "

Gideon scowled. "Cedric and Aaron will never meet her, nor will Eric. That, I promise you."

Lillia brushed past Heather, her bare hand resting on the girl's shoulder. She squeezed, the gesture affectionate.

A jolt shot through Heather's body, spreading warmth from her shoulder to her limbs. Her knees became weak, and the world slowed around her. An unfamiliar sensation, warm and tingly, welled up inside her. For a moment, it felt like pure happiness, so overwhelming it was almost frightening. Unsteady, Heather grabbed her father's arm for support.

"Lillia!" Gideon stepped forward, pulling Heather close, his voice sharp with alarm. "This is not one of your… subjects. This is my daughter! You will—"

Lillia's piercing green eyes flicked to him, her expression amused. "I will what?"

The words were soft, but the challenge behind them was unmistakable. She raised a single brow, waiting, daring him to continue.

Gideon's jaw tightened. He knew better than to push the dryad further. Lillia was powerful—more powerful than most of the council knew—and she enjoyed mischief too much for comfort. A single misstep could provoke her, and Gideon had no illusions about the chaos she could unleash if she chose.

After a long pause, he spoke. "You will not touch my daughter again, nor will you enchant her."

Lillia's smile was slow and unreadable, the sort that said she was listening—but not agreeing. She shrugged and turned away, her attention drifting to the trapped sycamore.

The thorny brambles shifted as she approached, slithering out of her way like obedient snakes retreating from their master. With surprising strength, Lillia gripped the eight-foot sapling and yanked it free from the tangled vines. The wood groaned as it came loose, thorns falling away in clumps.

The sapling's trunk, though straight, was marked with scars—knife-like thorns that had pierced and embedded in the wood over time. Lillia muttered a quiet incantation, her hand gliding over the bark. The outer layer peeled away, revealing pale, marbled wood beneath. It reminded Heather of freshly baked bread, twisted with doughs from different grains.

"This will make a unique staff," Lillia mused, running her hand along the raw wood. "White, with black thorn patterns from the tangle.

How interesting… " She closed her eyes, fingers lingering on the wood as if feeling something no one else could.

Heather's knees buckled again, and she sagged against her father's side.

"She's beautiful… " Heather murmured dreamily, her voice soft and distant. "Those green eyes… "

Lillia chuckled, low and musical. "Yes, child. Look at my eyes and nothing else. My eyes are my best feature, don't you think?"

The dryad adjusted her posture—shoulders back, chest forward, and one leg lifted to show the curve of her toned thigh. It was an effortless, deliberate pose, one meant to captivate.

Heather nodded, her lips parted but unable to form words.

Gideon pressed his lips into a thin line, inhaling through his nose to keep his temper in check. He had seen this enchantment before.

"What did you do to my daughter?" he said, his voice demanding, dangerous.

"Harmless enchantment," Lillia replied. "A little spell to help her relax. You are so tense, Gideon, it made her tense." She gave him a sidelong glance, as if daring him to challenge her further. "I know you were only protecting her but let me give you some advice; I don't take kindly to being shouted at."

Without ceremony, Lillia hefted the bark-stripped sapling and tipped it toward Gideon. The heavy log swung in the air, forcing him to release Heather and catch the eighty-pound trunk before it could slam into them.

While Gideon struggled with the weight, Lillia leaned closer to Heather, slipping her arm around the girl's slender frame. Heather sagged into the dryad's embrace, her body relaxing.

"Enchantments aren't harmless," Gideon grunted as he shifted the sapling into a more manageable grip. "No matter the intent." He straightened, eyes dark with warning. "This is my Glen, Lillia. It responds to my will—and even a dryad as powerful as you can't overstep that. You've gone too far. Let her go—release her from your enchantment. Now."

Lillia gave a soft sigh, as if bored, but there was a flicker of sharpness in her eyes. Reluctantly, she released Heather from her grasp and nudged her back toward Gideon.

The moment Lillia let go, the brambles stirred at Gideon's silent command. A wave of thorny vines surged forward, rising and twisting with sudden aggression. They wrapped around the dryad in an instant, their razor-sharp talons slicing into her skin.

Lillia didn't scream. She stood perfectly still, her expression tight, but not pained. The only sign of discomfort was the faint flush on her cheeks. She muttered an incantation under her breath and vanished, slipping into the tangled maze of Druid's Glen as if she had never been there.

Heather blinked, her head clearing slowly as she turned toward her father.

"I felt happy and scared at the same time," she said. "Her skin is… so warm. Like a blanket fresh from the drying fire." She hesitated, as if the memory were slipping away. "She smelled like cinnamon… I love cinnamon."

Gideon muttered a quiet spell under his breath, his hand brushing over Heather's head. A faint shimmer of magic flickered and vanished, dissolving the remnants of Lillia's lingering enchantment.

Heather blinked again, clarity returning to her eyes. She squeezed her father's arm tighter.

"Let's get this wood to the workshop," Gideon said. "Working on your staff will help take your mind off Lillia. You'll forget her soon enough."

Heather frowned. "What about Lana? I was supposed to look for bugs. I'm probably in trouble."

"You've had enough lessons for one day," Gideon said with a wry smile. "I'll talk to Lana. This is… more important."

He hugged her, inhaling as if to center himself. No matter how hard he tried, he couldn't protect his children from every danger. There were spells, enchantments, and lessons he could teach, guards he could hire—but it was the unknown threats that worried him. The ones he couldn't predict.

Dryads were enchanting creatures, able to ensnare men and women alike with magic and beauty. The effects were rarely permanent—most victims were tasked with simple errands or kept for companionship—but that didn't make them less dangerous.

Lillia was… different.

Men had fallen in love with her without ever falling under her spell. That made her far more dangerous than most realized.

"She's so beautiful… Why does she need spells to charm people?" Heather asked, frowning in confusion. "It doesn't make sense."

"It's in her nature," Gideon answered, his voice soft. *How else could he explain the unexplainable?* "Dryads are solitary creatures by design. Their beauty makes them approachable, but even the wisest of us can be caught off guard by their magic. Lillia is the only dryad I know who can travel so far from her grove—and she's more powerful than she lets on. Be careful around her, Heather."

Heather nodded.

"I think you'd have to be stupid to trust a naked woman in the forest."

Gideon chuckled despite himself. "Spoken like a true Manawove." He ruffled her hair affectionately. "For your age, you've got more sense than your brothers."

"Do you think I'll make a great druid one day?"

"I'm certain of it. You'll pass your trials splendidly."

Mention of the trials sent a wave of anxiety crashing through Heather, erasing the last traces of Lillia's enchantment. Moments ago, her muscles had felt loose and light, but now they stiffened as if a heavy weight had settled on her shoulders. The warmth and tingle from the dryad's touch were gone, replaced by the familiar tightness in her chest—the same feeling she always got when she thought about the trials.

She bent down to lift the eight-foot sycamore sapling, wrapping her hands around the smooth, newly-exposed wood. The trunk was heavier than she expected. It pressed awkwardly into her hands, and the weight shifted as she tried to heave it up alone, her fingers slipping on the damp wood.

"Careful," her father said, grabbing the other end with ease. "It's too much to carry on your own. We'll do it together. Come on, on three."

Heather gave a curt nod, frustrated with herself.

The trials would be a solo endeavor—no one would be there to catch her if she faltered.

The thought lingered at the edge of her mind as she adjusted her grip. If she couldn't carry a log by herself, how would she survive two weeks alone in the wild?

Her father counted. "One, two, three."

On three, he hefted his side smoothly, but Heather struggled. The log shifted, and for a moment she nearly lost her balance. She staggered, but with a grunt, she managed to stabilize the weight.

The wood dug into her palms, and for a moment, it felt like it might slip out of her grip.

"Cradle it against your hip," her father instructed, his voice calm and steady. "Grip your belt with your hand. That's it, you've got it."

Heather did as she was told, feeling the log settle and stabilize.

"Walk forward. You lead, I'll follow," Gideon said.

Heather pulled her father along, the log awkward but bearable. Moving in harmony with him proved harder than she thought. Each step felt off-balance, as if the slightest misstep might topple them both.

"Don't hurry," Gideon said. "Be strong and steady. We'll be home before you know it."

His calm, measured tone was meant to encourage her, but instead it only deepened her frustration. It reminded her of the many times her brothers had made things look easy while she struggled to keep up. The knot in her stomach tightened.

Her thoughts drifted back to the trials.

Cedric had breezed through them, his natural confidence carrying him forward.

Aaron's exact nature made him a perfect fit—every task precisely planned, every detail accounted for.

Even Eric, quiet and bookish, had made it through, though barely.

But what if she failed?

What if she wasn't ready?

What if the forest swallowed her whole?

A cold breeze drifted through the trees, stirring loose strands of her hair, but Heather barely noticed. All she could think about was autumn. Two weeks alone in the wilderness, surviving on whatever skills she could muster. No help, no second chances. Just her, the forest, and the weight of everyone's expectations.

She exhaled, forcing herself to focus on the path ahead and the log carried between them.

Step by step.

Just get through this first.

Her father's voice broke the silence.

"Heather, don't tell your brothers about what happened with Lillia," he said quietly. "This is something for us to talk about—just you and me."

Heather nodded solemnly, the sapling chafing against her hip with every step.

"Did the brambles hurt her?" she asked.

"She's fine," Gideon muttered. "She left before they did any real damage." He shifted the log in his grip, his jaw tightening. "I wanted her to feel uncomfortable—that's all."

I wanted to remind her who's in charge. Who commands Druid's Glen.

Gideon glanced back toward the Glen, unease prickling at the edges of his thoughts. An unfamiliar pit formed in his stomach. The chill of the spring air and the cold ground told him something was wrong.

Besides the Mage-Gate discovery.

"Lillia's not to be trusted?" Heather asked.

"That remains to be seen," Gideon replied. His eyes scanned the forest as though it held the answer to his unease. "But stay on your guard. I don't know why she showed up where you were today—and that worries me."

Gideon returned to Druid's Glen to find the Archdruids finishing their impromptu break. Lillia stood slightly apart, one hand on her hip, sunlight weaving through her green hair and lighting her honey-toned skin like silk through leaves. She was not scowling so much as radiating impatience.

Ilimitar lingered nearby, arms crossed, his expression unreadable— though Gideon knew that among Elves, such stillness often meant agitation.

"Join me in *Haron Talathien*," Gideon said, gesturing toward the northern slope of Druid's Glen. "There are a few tomes we should examine. The first is *The Sundering Testament*."

They followed him toward what appeared to be a natural barrow—an unremarkable rise at the edge of the meadow, overgrown with wildflowers. But as Gideon approached, he raised his hand and spoke a word of shaping in the druidic tongue.

The wildflowers shivered, then parted—petals folding back like obedient servants, revealing a narrow stairwell of carved stone. Moss clung to the edges, and the scent of old earth drifted up. With a small gesture, Gideon kindled the lanterns that lined the passage, one by one, igniting soft blue druidlights—cool and smokeless.

They descended into the ground, footsteps echoing in the curved, root-ribbed corridor. The walls seemed to breathe with age, earth pulsing faintly with the heartbeat of the Tree. At the tunnel's end stood a lone door: thick, ancient wood, painted with faded runes in ochre, cobalt, and gold.

Gideon pressed his fingers to the doorframe, whispering words too low to catch. Then he touched the runes in sequence—red, yellow, blue. There was a soft click… then a hiss of ancient air escaping.

The door opened inward on a breath of stillness.

Magical lights stirred awake, blooming along the curved ceiling like clusters of glowing seedpods. The chamber beyond was wide and cool, the air dry, preserved. Shelves sagged under the weight of old knowledge. No flame was allowed within *Haron Talathien*—only light born of will and root.

"You predecessors never let me see *Haron Talathien*," Ilimitar said, his tone quiet but pointed. "I do not know what to think of this."

Gideon led them deeper. "Several of the older volumes are written in Elvish. Both you and Lillia speak it fluently. I'd be a fool not to ask your help."

"I didn't think it was because you wanted to be alone with me in the dark," Lillia murmured, trailing one hand along the wall. "Let's begin, then. The sooner, the better. I don't enjoy stone over my head."

Ilimitar stepped into the chamber with quiet confidence, his boots silent on the stone. As he passed beneath a dangling cluster of seedpods, he raised one hand and flicked his fingers in a graceful gesture. The druidlight responded—pulsing once, then brightening with a soft breath of golden-green glow. Other pods followed, casting the chamber in warm, living light that shimmered across the shelves like sunlight through a canopy.

All but one.

A pod in the far corner flickered and dimmed, pulsing weakly before going still.

Gideon sighed and moved to it, placing his hand gently against the thick root it clung to. He whispered an old phrase and closed his eyes. A heartbeat later, the pod swelled with new light, blooming softly to life.

"Don't get down here often?" Lillia asked, arms crossed, a faint smirk playing at her lips.

Gideon straightened, brushing bark dust from his palm. "Haven't had the need."

He returned to the central table as the archive settled into a hush— lit by breath, not flame, and watched over by memory rather than locks.

"Ah," Ilimitar said, a smile just barely visible. "*Vaernil Harondras.* I never thought I'd see this with my own eyes. There is a rumored copy of this in Ornst, but I believe this is the only copy in *Elarandor.* Our archives were destroyed long ago by the Mages."

"It must remain here," Gideon said before Ilimitar formed any notions.

"I prefer it to be here," Ilimitar said. "Safe in this underground vault. With only one idiot having access to it who can barely read Elvish."

Gideon let the insult slide off, but he did catch the titter from Lillia.

"I'll take this one," Lillia said hefting a tome. "*Nuin'Kelharon. Beneath the Chains of Memory* in the common tongue. For you Gideon."

"Thank you," he said. "I would be lost without you two. I'll take *The Sundering Testament.* If you need to take notes," he added, "there's parchment and ink on the desk."

Neither Lillia nor Ilimitar moved toward it.

Gideon exhaled. "Right," he muttered. "Forgot who I was talking to."

Ilimitar tapped a slender finger against his temple—no smirk, just that same infuriating look of elven superiority.

The chamber was silent save for the rustle of parchment and the soft breath of druidlight.

Ilimitar sat with *Vaernil Harondras* open across his knees, one hand hovering over the yellowed page. He read aloud, just above a whisper—more to himself than to the others:

"The gates are not keys but wounds. They open because they remember being torn. Only the old magic keeps them together."

He turned the page with care.

"Mikal Yholl built the first Mage-Gate. He oversaw the creation of the gates that followed. No one asked why he was so involved, when each Mage was capable of crafting lesser versions. He was the architect, and Master."

His brow furrowed.

"Three Librums remain lost. One was buried beneath a root that will never die."

He glanced around the chamber, eyes drifting over the sagging shelves and the soft-lit walls. Could one of the *Librums* be here, hidden among the Druid Histories? Was *this* the root the manuscript spoke of?

He said nothing further. But when he closed the book, his gaze lingered on the rows of ancient volumes. He wondered.

"Narae'loth taldren vaerun," he whispered. "Do not stir the roots that drink in silence."

The soft rustle of parchment gave way to silence as Lillia leaned over her chosen volume, *Nuin'Kelharon*. The cover was old bark-backed leather, its title carved rather than inked—worn by centuries, but still clear beneath her fingers.

She opened it without ceremony. The pages exhaled dust and memory.

"The Librums are not books but bindings even the gods do not understand."

Her fingertip paused on the script. She read on, silently.

"Each was born at a hinge-point between realms, cast not by mortal hand alone but with the shaping of will across planes. To unmake one is to strike through more than paper and binding—it is to unravel the stitches between worlds."

She turned the page slowly, reverently.

"Only the First Druid touched a Librum and remained unbroken. He bound it in silence and gave no name to the tree above it."

Her breath caught—not at the words, but at the weight they carried. As if remembering something she had never spoken aloud.

She lingered there, the quiet pressing in.

"If ever the Council seeks to unearth what was meant to be buried, the Circle will split. Not by war or vote, but by instinct."

She closed the book, her touch gentle.

That last line—she knew it wasn't metaphor.

"Let them lie," she murmured, eyes distant. "Let the roots grow around them and forget the shape of power."

Gideon stood before the pedestal.

Unlike the other tomes, *The Sundering Testament* did not rest openly on a shelf. It was cradled within a cradle of rootlike stone, its surface wrapped in a thin shimmer of air that bent the light—an old ward, subtle and complex. He extended his hand toward it, fingers hovering just above the surface. The air prickled.

He whispered three names—each one a Grand Druid of old—then pressed his palm forward, pausing at each resistance, unraveling the threads of the enchantment one by one. It was a ward meant to protect, not repel. A ward meant to remember who had the right to read.

The light dimmed around it.

The final tether faded, and the cover was his to touch.

He opened it with care.

"The Magefall did not begin with fire, but with silence and indifference."

He frowned. He had expected accounts of war—battles, confrontations, betrayals. Not this.

"One by one, the towers fell quiet. Their magic dimmed. Their gates closed. And when they rose again, it was not to speak, but to judge."

He turned a page, rough with age.

"The One Tree was planted not only to connect—but to conceal. Its roots do not just bind life, but bury truths too dangerous for the surface."

He paused.

No one had ever said this aloud—not to him.

"When the Librums fell into mortal hands, the balance cracked. It was not wizards who first opened them, but druids who believed they could resist what was written."

He closed the book softly, fingers still resting on the cover.

And then—quietly, more to himself than anyone—

"So that's the part we never tell."

He didn't look at the others when he stepped away. He just nodded once and said, "Let's go."

They emerged from *Haron Talathien* as the sun slanted westward, casting long gold shadows across the glen. None of them spoke at first. The stone steps behind them closed with a sigh of old air, and the wildflowers crept back over the mound, sealing the archive from view as if it had never opened.

Lillia brushed dirt from her palms and gazed at her soiled hands.

They walked in silence a few steps more before she spoke.

"So," she said softly, "we bury what must not be found. We remember what we dare not use."

Gideon nodded, eyes ahead. "And we forget just enough to keep walking forward."

Ilimitar gave a faint hum, neither agreement nor dissent.

As they neared the council's gathering place, the quiet changed. Wind stirred. Birds sang. Squirrels darted among the roots. Rabbits scampered through the Glen. Lillia's gaze swept across the meadow, noting the soothing rhythms of the wild.

Among the movement, her eyes lingered on a brown hare near one of the twisted roots of The One Tree. It sat very still, ears tilted, not startled—but present.

She went straight to the water font adjacent the Council table, dipping her hands into the cool water. After cleansing her hands, she drank fresh water and soothed her flushed cheeks. She rubbed her hands dry on her hips, turning toward the table.

Gideon let Lillia move ahead, watching as she cleansed her hands at the font. Ilimitar veered off without a word, heading for the outer edge of the glen where the long roots of The One Tree sprawled like great serpents through the grass.

The others were scattered.

Krik and Nightshade leaned together against one of the shattered roots, their conversation hushed. Krik's arms were folded; Nightshade was munching on a honeycomb, her favorite food.

Near the kettle table, Aurora braced herself, both hands gripping the edge. Her back was arched, face pale, as if nausea had taken hold. Her short hair clung to her brow. She hadn't noticed their return.

Wilmund sat alone in the meadow, robe discarded beside him. His eyes were closed, spine straight, breathing steady. The grass around him shifted subtly with his presence—as if it too waited.

At the Council table, Buvic had also shed his robes, sitting heavily on one of the carved chairs that never quite seemed built for comfort. He had a cup in hand but wasn't drinking.

Finola paced in the open meadow, staff in hand. She moved through a flowing sequence of strikes and sweeps—disciplined, elegant, purposeful. A dancer in armor no one else could see.

Gideon turned toward the center table where the polished crystal sat nestled in its wooden stand.

He didn't hesitate.

He raised his hand and brought it down in a sharp strike. The crystal rang out—a single, clear note that pierced through chatter and motion alike.

The Archdruids stilled.

Lillia and Ilimitar returned to their seats, wordless.

Gideon remained standing.

"We've all had time," he said. "Now let's speak."

The evening breeze stirred the leaves of The One Tree, carrying the scents of roasted pheasant, spiced plums, and fire-roasted potatoes. Druidlights flickered at the edges of the glen, casting restless shadows on the Archdruids' faces—as if the forest itself was unsettled by the day's debate.

They were gathered around the supper table—a smaller, more intimate setting beside the great meeting table where decisions were forged. Nearby, a modest firepit crackled gently, its flames low and steady. The cooking fires scattered around the glen had begun to wane, their warmth fading into smoke. The meal was slow, quiet, the air laced with the soft clink of dishes and the burn of *Andy's Fireside Brandy*, a rare indulgence Krik had brought to share.

Gideon kept his gaze moving, reading the table like a battlefield. Something was off. A current of unease ran beneath the surface, subtle but tightening with each passing moment.

Finola, usually a wellspring of stories from the Needle Forest, sat in uncharacteristic silence. She nudged her food with the tip of her fork, prodding it like a child faced with an unwanted vegetable.

Ilimitar swirled his brandy, the glass turning slowly between his long fingers. He'd eaten only the spiced plums and kept glancing down at his drink, as if it might yield the answers. When his eyes met Gideon's, the Elf looked away too quickly, retreating into his glass with a flicker of unease.

Krik tore into his second pheasant with gusto, seemingly oblivious to the tension—but Gideon caught the flicks of his eyes toward Lillia. Wary. Measuring. Krik had little patience for subtlety, and the way he tracked the dryad suggested he expected trouble.

Lillia sat stiffly, her usual ease replaced by a rigid stillness. She had draped her shoulders with a shawl woven from the red leaves of The One Tree—simple and functional, to ward against the evening chill. She rolled a blueberry between her fingers with idle precision, as if crushing an invisible plan. The air around her felt cold—unnaturally so. If a dryad could become ice, Lillia had done so tonight.

Lillia's presence nagged at him. She was cold, distant—and too quiet. What had happened with Heather still troubled Gideon, a knot of unease he couldn't untangle. Why would a dryad—creatures so often detached from human affairs—take such interest in his daughter? Why had the brambles granted Heather safe passage? The question wasn't *if* he should be worried. It was *how much.*

Aurora, a lifelong vegetarian, was finishing off the roasted potatoes. She had sprinkled her own herbs over them—fragrant and sharp—and Gideon wondered, as he often did, whether they were meant to aid her lingering illness. He doubted she had many seasons left. The thought gnawed at him. Yet her resolve remained unshaken. She had been among the fiercest voices urging investigation of the Mage-Gate and the ruins of Mikal Yholl's keep.

Nightshade sat in silence, nibbling at honeycombs and licking the sweetness from her fingers. Her wings fluttered with unease, a faint tremor that cast restless shadows against the table. The ancient fairy carried the weight of the Yholl brothers' reign in her fragile frame. A thousand years had passed, but some horrors didn't fade. Gideon met her gaze—sharp, wary—and gave her a small, knowing frown.

Buvic, like Aurora, had stuck to the roasted potatoes and plums, but he'd added green shoots—harsh, pungent willow onions from the coastal marshes. An acquired taste, long associated with vitality—which Buvic could certainly use. Aloof and clumsy as he often appeared, it remained a mystery how he'd retained such high standing within the Council. But there was strength beneath that sluggish exterior. Gideon couldn't shake the feeling that Buvic's slow manner masked a sharper mind than most realized.

Wilmund sat in perfect stillness, his tea untouched. He never partook of alcohol—*fortified refreshment*, as he called it—and Gideon had no doubt where the man's thoughts were. The Mage-Gate. Wilmund would go to the ruin, regardless of the Council's vote. If they chose to destroy or bury it, they would have to move quickly—before Wilmund uncovered a relic that couldn't be buried again.

Gideon finished his second glass of brandy—a rare indulgence, but the day had earned it. He reached for his pipe and a jar of precious tobacco, cultivated with care by his own children. It was a family tradition—each leaf picked by hand, aged for three years, and stored in sealed jars that opened with a soft, satisfying gasp.

He broke the seal with a faint hiss, the earthy aroma rising like memory. Scents of soil, ash, and sun-warmed leaves wrapped around him—echoes of his father, his grandfather, and all that had been lost. He passed the jar around the table. Those who smoked took a pinch; those who didn't held it briefly, inhaling the scent before passing it on.

As expected, the tobacco paired perfectly with *Andy's Fireside Brandy*. Pipes were lit. Laughter flickered at the edges. More brandy passed from hand to hand.

Gideon poured himself a third glass, intending to make it last.

As he drew from his pipe, Gideon's thoughts drifted to Emma. She would have known how to lift the mood with a story or a well-timed joke, disarming even the most stubborn among them. How he missed her. In moments like this, her absence felt like a boulder against his chest.

If only his children could grow in a world free of ancient threats—a world without Mage-Gates, cursed tomes, or looming conflict. But that was not the world they had inherited. All he could do now was guide them through the storm to come.

He missed her more than words could hold.

Gideon tapped the stem of his pipe against his glass. The sharp clink echoed through the glade like a bell of finality. One by one, the druids turned toward him, their expressions guarded, unreadable.

Even as he raised his glass, a chill stirred beneath his skin.

The tapestry was coming undone, thread by thread.

He lifted his glass.

"I'd like to offer a toast. Few of you knew my Emma—my best friend, the heart of my family. She would've loved a night like this. I want to celebrate our friendship, despite our differences. Food and drink shared as kin—let it remind us that we are still allies, even in disagreement. May Thatara keep us safe."

Brandy, tea, and water were raised. No one spoke. The leaves of The One Tree stirred in the breeze, their rustling a soft, ominous whisper.

Wilmund set his cup down with deliberate care, the firelight catching in his steady gaze. "The sun is nearly gone," he said, his voice low but firm. "We've read the old truths. The *Librums* are bindings—volatile, dangerous. The Mage-Gate is no mere ruin. The histories confirmed what we feared—and more. No more waiting, Gideon. We choose a path tonight. Or someone else will choose it for us."

Gideon stared into the fire for a breath longer, dread tightening in his chest. Calling the vote would make it real. Saying the words aloud would strip away the illusion that this was still a debate—that it wasn't already a fracture in the making. He had hoped, perhaps foolishly, that such days would fall to another Grand Druid. That this crisis—this unraveling of balance—would be faced in a different era, by a different hand.

But it had come for them. For him.

He looked up and met Lillia's gaze across the table.

She held it.

Her expression was unreadable, cool and composed. Then, almost imperceptibly, her eyes flicked toward The One Tree. Her posture shifted—not in alarm, but in response. A faint lean. A narrowing of focus. As if the air itself had changed, and she alone could feel its texture bending.

She didn't speak. But Gideon knew she had sensed a turn in the current.

And whatever it was—it had begun.

The vote ahead was more than a decision about the Mage-Gate. It was a test of trust, a measure of loyalty. Betrayal waited to take root, threatening to fracture the Council at the moment they most needed unity. A sharp pang of dread settled in Gideon's gut—cold, certain. His intuition, long-honed and rarely wrong, whispered what he dared not say aloud.

This is going to be my end.

Chapter Three

∞

The Shadow Circle

It was unnaturally dark, the shadows pooling beneath the tall spruce, smothering the fire that crackled softly, starved of proper fuel. The coals glowed orange and every so often, the wood popped and sent an ember into the slight breeze rustling through the evergreens.

The hoot of a boreal owl penetrated the night, the quick hollow calls were from a male looking for a mate. The clearing was small, surrounded by tall spruce.

The stranger noted the pine needles on the forest floor were cleared to the edge of his vision—he assumed for safety.

His dark cloak covered him and kept him nearly invisible. He knew they were here, but he didn't see them. He would exercise his patience and not worry about their tardiness.

Without a sound, he squatted down and sat on the ground, took a deep breath, and closed his eyes. The cold ground bit through his robes, the chill seeping into his bones, amplifying the discomfort of the tense stillness around him.

A pinecone tumbled from a tree, spinning along the ground across the clearing. It came to an auspicious stop next to where he was crouched. He reached out, grasping the rough object in his hands.

With a gentle squeeze he tested its strength, and he was surprised how sturdy it was. As Comrade held the pinecone, it pulsed with potential, a small token of the primal strength that surrounded him—untamed, relentless, and unpredictable. He slipped it into a pocket, and rocked on his heels, feeling for his balance.

With a soothing breath, he calmed his insides.

There was nothing to fear here, yet he experienced a twinge of apprehension because they were consorting with these Shadow Druids. His hand lingered near the satchel concealed under his robes, and he rubbed the worn leather.

This was the price they had to pay.

He was eager to be rid of it—its necessary creation was against his order's basic laws, although fully supported by those who sat high in the Towers. He adjusted the mask on his face, the rough fabric chafing against his skin, its damp interior making each breath feel stifled. This was the third time he had met the group in secret; this was the first time at this spot. This location not only looked different than the others but felt different. There was importance to this place. He sensed… death on the night, yet not his own.

There was a subtle disturbance in the air.

An elegant fox emerged from a tree and trotted toward him, red fur and bright eyes, black tips on her ears. This was the leader of the Shadow Circle, the Shadowmaster.

The Shadow Druids only appeared to him in animal form, shapechangers, to conceal their identity. He nodded in the direction of the fox, acknowledging her presence. That was the only thing that couldn't be concealed—the gender of the shapechanger. Her name was simply, Fox. He was known as Comrade.

"Comrade, welcome," Fox said. "I trust your travels were safe."

"Indeed," Comrade replied. The slight smile was hidden behind his mask—how odd it looked seeing an animal talk. "Teleportation is a bit easier than your greenstep."

"A necessary abuse of magic," Fox said.

"It suits my needs," he said. "And that of my superiors. You would be wise to hold your critical tongue."

Like Fox, a deer with a broken antler popped out of a tree and trotted to the side of the smoldering fire.

An imposing grey wolf with broad shoulders followed.

A wild boar arrived next, muscled and brawny, and greeted the grey wolf with a headbutt.

A massive polar bear arrived, followed by a darting red squirrel.

The last to arrive was a hawk that settled on a carved perch that Comrade had not noticed before.

The deer trotted forward and, with deliberate purpose, nudged small logs into the fire. The flames responded hungrily, flaring up as the fuel caught, casting a brighter glow across the clearing.

Only then did Comrade notice the trees encircling them.

Each trunk had been stripped of branches up to ten feet high and marked with druidic runes. Some bore exposed, lacquered wood, smooth and gleaming in the firelight. Others were painted in vivid strokes of blue, red, and yellow—ritual colors layered with care.

A solitary tree stood near the edge of the clearing, its single thick branch jutting out over the open space like an arm. The bark had been stripped away, worn smooth by the friction of countless ropes.

Comrade recognized it at once.

The execution tree.

He regarded it with cool detachment. Typical. Primitive, but effective. The Shadow Circle had little need for subtlety—or mercy.

"This meeting of the Shadow Circle has convened," Fox said, addressing the attendees. "She will take it back someday."

"We will take it back someday," they answered in unison.

Comrade felt the hair on his neck rise. He did not share their vision. The Wizards of Arcana had merely struck a bargain—arcane power exchanged for influence, information, and favors the Shadow Circle claimed it could deliver.

To him, their mission bordered on absurdity. Anonymous druids poisoning the land to subvert the very society that gave them language, tools, structure—it was almost laughable. A contradiction so stark he often wondered if the entire Shadow Circle wasn't teetering on the edge of madness.

He thought of them as anti-druids. They despised the expansion of cities, loathed the softness civilization bred, and longed to drag the world back to its primordial roots. A purity of purpose, perhaps. But wrapped in rot.

He noted, with mild irritation, that he was encircled—surrounded on all sides by the Shadow Druids.

Comrade rose and moved to an open space in the ring, settling near the hawk perch. The bird watched him with intelligent eyes but said nothing. He was certain the initial silence was for his benefit. The Shadow Circle did not conduct business in front of outsiders, not even useful ones like himself.

Of all the secret societies, criminal networks, and sinister factions he had encountered, this one remained among the strangest. Their rites were rooted in decay, not ambition. He found it easier to understand those who worshipped demons or devils—their cruelty was at least consistent. But the rituals of such cults… they reveled in brutality, crossed into depths so vile that even he, a seasoned wizard well acquainted with horror, found them difficult to endure.

"Before our first order of business with Comrade," Fox said, "we must punish failure. Bring him forth."

A commotion stirred to one side of the circle.

Two masked figures in dark robes with golden sashes dragged a prisoner forward. Comrade recognized them—the same guards who had blindfolded him and led him to this hidden grove.

The captive was naked, filthy, and bloodied—already beaten. His limbs were bound, and a sackcloth hood concealed his face. Beneath it, muffled cries rose, the words lost behind a gag. Comrade assumed the display was staged for his benefit—to remind him who held the power in this exchange.

He didn't need the reminder.

The Shadow Circle was formidable. Cunning. They had remained hidden for decades, perhaps longer, and their numbers were growing. This execution changed nothing in his estimation—it was expected.

A demonstration.

A warning.

The guards hoisted the man onto the execution tree, looping the rope over the scarred, branchlike gallows. Dark stains marked the ground beneath it—mute witnesses to previous failures. This clearing served two purposes: it welcomed new initiates to the Circle… and eliminated those who had disappointed it.

The figure thrashed, a frantic, convulsive dance as the rope dug deep. Then came the sharp, hollow crack of his neck snapping—a sound that cut through the glade with finality. Silence followed, save for the slow creak of the rope and the lifeless sway of the body.

Even Comrade, hardened as he was, felt a cold edge slip through him.

The druids called it justice.

He knew it as control.

"Second order of business is at hand," Fox said, her voice grim. "Do you have the magic? We have fulfilled the first part of the contract."

From beneath his robe, Comrade drew out the book. Small, leather-bound, and sealed with a metal buckle, it radiated restrained power. The magic within had been crafted by the Wizards of Arcana—power rarely entrusted to outsiders.

Handing it over came at great risk. The act breached foundational covenants of his order. But rules, he reflected, were often bent—especially by those in the Towers—whenever their goals demanded it.

Comrade cleared his throat and said, "I have it. The magic in these pages will do as you asked. It will create talismans imbued with spell-like abilities that can be transferred from a scroll containing spells, or a spellbook." He held the book for Fox to see.

"Demonstrate."

He drew a breath, his fingers lingering on the buckle of the tome.

He didn't move.

The weight of her command pressed against him like a stone to the chest. His jaw clenched tight, the muscles twitching beneath his skin. A dull buzz filled his ears, the pressure rising.

Fox stared at him—expression unreadable, patience dwindling. The tension between them coiled tighter with every second.

Comrade raised the book slightly, his grip precise.

"You would waste a single use of this tome as a demonstration?" he asked. "I can instruct you on its use without wasting a charge. It does not operate infinitely."

"Indulge me. We can spare one charge."

"Once the magic from the page has been transferred to the talisman, the ink on the page is consumed. There are one hundred pages. If I use one, there will only be ninety-nine pages remaining. Think carefully on this."

Fox said nothing. She stared at Comrade.

"Do as I command."

"I would not waste one of these on a demonstration," he replied. "The instructions are simple. Even a novice can transfer the spell to the talisman."

Fox circled him, kicking up dirt with her paws. She scraped the ground once, then stilled—settling back on her haunches. Her eyes locked on the wizard, tail twitching in irritation. The look she gave him was not one of curiosity, but calculation. A predator assessing its prey—cautious, cold, and unimpressed.

This was what she despised about the Wizards of Arcana: their arrogance, their shifting loyalties, their obsession with outcomes no one else asked for. The most powerful magical organization in the world—and yet, they accomplished so little. In truth, she was surprised they had delivered at all. This alliance was brittle from the start.

Fox let her gaze linger on Comrade a beat too long, her disdain laid bare.

Their arrogance would cost them. And she would be there when the debt came due.

"Do as I command," she repeated.

Comrade had seen enough over the years to know how fragile alliances could be—especially ones forged in shadows. Here, surrounded by masked zealots, every move felt like navigating a brittle web. One misstep, one ill-chosen word, and the execution tree behind him could serve again—this time for *his* neck. The druids' magic, though wild and primitive, held power he did not fully understand.

His mind cycled through possibilities—routes of escape, contingencies, costs. He calculated his odds of survival if he defied Fox. Teleportation was possible. He could vanish before they ensnared him… but not without injury. And not without consequences. These zealots were unpredictable, and he had no illusions about their appetite for blood.

The trees around them twisted in the wind, unnaturally so, as though the forest itself leaned in to listen—aware, observant, old. Branches swayed above, dislodging pinecones that thudded softly into the clearing. Every sound, every word from Fox, was a reminder that he stood alone here. Every glance from the druids was weight. Every rustle of the leaves whispered: *You are outnumbered.*

With reluctance, he said, "Very well. I will need a talisman—an object that can be worn and touched easily. A simple ring, necklace, hat… anything common you won't mind destroying."

Fox raised a paw.

One of the guards stepped forward and handed him a lacquered leaf, strung on a leather throng. It was a brilliant, fiery red. As soon as it touched his palm, Comrade felt the pulse of residual magic. The leaf had come from a powerful tree.

For a moment, he stared at it.

The One Tree.

This was a leaf from The One Tree.

A being worthy of study—perhaps the most extraordinary living entity in the realm. Yet the Wizards had never been invited to examine it. Not once.

He set the thought aside and reached into his robe, pulling free his own worn, voluminous spellbook. Flipping to a dog-eared page, he caught movement—several of the shapechangers inching closer, eager for a better view of what he was doing.

Comrade cleared his throat and raised his voice. "To enchant the talisman, you must speak a word of power, recite the spell, read the page in the tome, recite the spell once more, and then close the loop with a final word of power."

He sat cross-legged on the ground, placing his spellbook to his left, the lacquered leaf in the center, and the enchanted tome to his right. He selected a basic spell for the demonstration.

Then, with measured care, he spoke the first word of power.

He recited the spell. Read the words from the tome. Recited it again. And closed the loop with the final word of power.

The magical ink vanished from the page.

Comrade leaned forward, the charm now active, and fastened the throng around Fox's slender neck.

"Touch it to activate," he said.

She did so with her paw. The air responded—a soft buzz, faint but unmistakable.

"I've placed a simple shield spell on the leaf," he continued. "May I demonstrate further?"

As the magic enveloped her, Fox's eyes flickered—curious, but not convinced. A slow, nearly imperceptible nod followed. She acknowledged the power, though her skepticism remained intact. The Wizards of Arcana were powerful, yes—but unreliable when it mattered most. They over-promised. Under-delivered. Still, she hoped this alliance would serve her ends, not complicate them—especially when the world began to shift.

"Proceed," she said.

"Move back. I need space."

Fox circled left, her movement smooth, unhurried. She came to rest ten feet away, settling on her haunches with a low wiggle of satisfaction. The talisman swayed gently from her neck, catching the light.

With a flick of his wrist and a sharp word of power, Comrade unleashed a volley of magic. A dozen blue darts streaked from his outstretched hand, crackling as they tore through the air toward her.

Gasps rippled through the gathered druids.

The darts struck the barrier—and vanished. A burst of sparks and fizzles lit the clearing, swallowed harmlessly by the shield.

Comrade's heart pounded—not from the spell, but from the waiting. The stillness that followed.

He could feel their stares, heavy and sharp. Too many eyes. Too many risks.

Fox's ears twitched. Her gaze locked on him, unblinking. No flinch. No recoil. Just the slow swish of her tail, cutting the air like a pendulum—precise, measured, watching.

"Halt," Fox said, raising a paw to still the druids advancing behind her. She stepped forward and fixed her gaze on Comrade.

"I can appreciate your dramatic demonstration," she said. "You could've thrown a rock. Instead, you unleashed a volley of magical darts. I can't help but feel that was a veiled threat."

"Threat or no," Comrade replied evenly, "the tome performed as requested."

Fox's eyes narrowed. "How many uses?"

Comrade hesitated. The question caught him off guard. Ninety-nine pages remained in the enchanted book, but that wasn't what she meant.

Then it clicked.

"The number of uses a talisman holds is finite—but unknowable. It varies. Randomly limited," he said. "You'll know when it's spent. The talisman is consumed at the end of its life. I suggest you don't use any precious heirlooms… or favored clothing."

Comrade chuckled, hoping to ease the tension. Silence followed. His attempt at levity fell flat.

Unmoved, the Shadow Druids stared back.

With a quiet sigh, he slipped his fat spellbook back into the folds of his robe, then presented the magical tome to Fox. One of the guards stepped forward to take it on her behalf.

"Now that it is in your possession," Comrade said, "you must honor our request."

"We will honor our second part of the bargain," Fox declared. "Now, we have additional business to attend to—business not for outsiders. You may take your leave."

Comrade tilted his head, acknowledging the dismissal. His eyes swept the gathered circle—measuring, memorizing.

"I will remind you it must be done by summer. Other... things... are in motion and cannot be undone. Your failure, I also remind you, will not be tolerated."

"Failure means death," Fox said flatly. "It will be done before summer. One way or another, you will have what you want. I remind *you*—if we succeed, you will owe us more."

"I'm aware of the... consequences... of your success."

"You are glib," Fox said, stepping closer. "Our success will bring both our orders new opportunities. Tell your superiors—opportunity comes at a cost. And our expectations will be met."

Her voice dropped, sharp as a fang.

"I know what you think of us. Freaks. Nature-lovers. Backward wielders of forgotten magic. But do not underestimate us. You may reside in your high Towers... but we can crumble the earth beneath them—and bring them down."

"Your threats aren't so subtle," Comrade said, his voice cracking despite himself. "We understand your power—but we also understand your limitations. You may be able to crumble our towers, but we can unleash a firestorm that will turn this forest into a smoldering wasteland. The flames will rise so high, the smoke and ash will be seen for hundreds of miles."

Fox's fur bristled.

"Do not mistake this alliance for friendship," she said, each word cold and carved. "Our patience wears thin. And our roots go deep."

She paused, her gaze locking onto Comrade's. The fire's reflection danced in her eyes. She let the silence stretch, let the weight of her warning settle like falling ash.

"Cross us," she said at last, "and those towers will fall—stone by stone."

"Just as well," Comrade replied. "Our flames know no mercy. Let's see which burns brighter—your resolve or our hellfire."

The silence that followed felt sentient. Heavy. Pressing in from all directions.

Only the fire's crackle and the wind in the branches dared to move.

Finally, Fox spoke. "Now that we have an understanding, you may take your leave."

One of the masked guards stepped forward, guiding Comrade away from the circle—past the hanging body that swayed gently in the dark.

A reminder. Grim and clear.

These were not people. These were druids who had buried mercy to let something far older grow in its place.

Their ruthlessness would serve the Wizards of Arcana well— whether they realized it or not. The key was impeding the living network—stalling its flow just enough to expose the arcane residue left behind by ancient relics. Only then could they hope to locate the *Librums*, tomes of unimaginable power penned by the Mages.

It was a masterstroke of strategic imagination.

Comrade bowed to his escorts and dismissed them with a flick of his fingers. They departed without a word, returning to the clearing where the Shadow Druids continued their murmured deliberations.

The wind stirred, and the trees groaned in response. In the hazy moonlight, pinecones fell from above with heavy, deliberate thuds. He fingered the one he had taken earlier. It sat like a stone in his pocket—a keepsake of the alliance, a token of power cloaked in silence and bark.

It would rest on his shelf as a reminder: beneath nature's quiet beauty lay a force capable of leveling civilizations.

Several owls called out overhead, their hoots sharp and sudden. Comrade flinched. The sounds of the forest unsettled him more than he cared to admit. Every branch creak felt too precise. Every leaf's rustle, a whisper he wasn't meant to hear.

Then came the smell—wet soil and charred moss, like a battlefield sealed beneath centuries of rot. He wrinkled his nose. The stench felt wrong, almost ritualistic.

The magic swirled faintly around him, preparing his departure. But the night's cold clung to his robes like a second skin, a memory of Fox's eyes and the quiet menace in every masked gaze. He could still hear them behind him—voices low, speaking in the druidic tongue, foreign and unsettling.

As he vanished, the creaking branches gave way to a distant, low howl—long, hollow, and not quite wolf. It echoed through the trees like a sentient thing, chasing after him as he slipped from the clearing.

It followed him, that sound.

An omen.

It reminded him that true allies were few.

And enemies were watching.

- 58 -

Chapter Four

∞

The Vote

The Manawove children ate bowls of buckwheat porridge sweetened with blueberries and raw honey. As a rare treat, they were allowed a mug of ale with supper. Heather sipped hers reluctantly. She didn't find it particularly enjoyable.

Eric, by contrast, downed his in one gulp. She couldn't tell if he was trying to get it over with—or showing off. Probably both.

She'd overheard conversations in the village tavern, The Hound and Shrew, about drinking contests—men and women bragging over who could drink the most, the fastest.

If there were a contest for slowest drinker alive, she thought, *I would win. Desert palms drink faster than me.*

Cedric and Aaron were halfway through their mugs, following their usual pattern—two big gulps, then slow sips to finish.

The conversation shifted easily, settling on the spells they were learning. Cedric described one that let them see in the dark as clearly as day, while Aaron explained another that hardened their skin into bark-like armor.

Not wanting to be left out, Eric began reciting passages from the book he'd been reading, his voice animated.

Heather stayed quiet.

She still felt the ghost of Lillia's touch on her skin. It clung to her—unshakable, strange. Exciting, yet revolting. The feeling lingered like a whispered secret, just out of reach, and left her unsure of what to make of it.

"What happened to you today?" Aaron asked.

"What?" Heather blinked, startled out of her thoughts.

"You're lost in thought," Aaron said, eyeing her curiously. "What happened?"

"I think the word you're looking for is *pensive,*" Eric offered without glancing up from his bowl.

"You are lost in pensive?" Aaron deadpanned, raising an eyebrow.

"No!" Eric shook his head and sighed. "*You are pensive.* It's a shorter way of saying the same thing."

Aaron scoffed and leaned back in his chair. "Half the world doesn't know what that means. Communication needs commonality, not big fancy words."

Cedric chuckled, shaking his head as he drained the last of his ale.

Eric smiled—it wasn't often he bested Aaron at anything.

Heather finally gathered herself. "I found a sapling for my staff," she said. "Worked on it a little today. Found it near Druid's Glen."

Cedric gave her a sidelong glance. "Is that why you're so quiet? Did you get too close? The brambles didn't get you, did they?"

Heather shook her head quickly, recalling her father's warning not to mention what had happened with Lillia. "No. I didn't get that close."

Aaron pushed up his sleeve to reveal a pale scar on his forearm. "The brambles will grab you if you're within ten feet of the perimeter of Druid's Glen. I've measured it. Exactly ten feet." He tapped the scar with pride.

Cedric leaned in, more serious now. "You didn't get hurt, right? You sure?"

"I'm fine," Heather said—too fast.

Her thoughts snagged on the memory. She *had* been within ten feet. Closer than that. Yet the brambles hadn't stirred. No vines had snapped toward her. No thorns had touched her skin. The protections hadn't stopped her at all.

Only when she'd started chopping—only then had anything responded.

The axe.

Her breath caught.

I left it there. It's Father's axe!

"What kind of sapling did you find? Ash?" Cedric asked, leaning forward with interest.

"Sycamore," Heather replied.

"Sycamore?" Cedric wrinkled his nose. "Too soft. Not as good as ash. Ash has the best grain for staves—strong, straight, reliable. Satisfying *crack* when you smack someone with it."

"Sycamore is great for furniture," Eric chimed in, eager to contribute. "I read that in a book about… furniture."

Aaron scoffed. "It's lighter. She can swing it faster. She's not as stout as we are—it's a good choice, all things considered." He held up a finger. "Three—no, *four*—extra layers of lacquer should stiffen it up."

"Sycamore doesn't hold enchantments as well," Cedric added. "The grain's too open. You'll have to etch the runes deeper or they'll fray."

"Unless she burns them in," Eric said quickly. "Charred runes last longer. That's in the…" He looked to the ceiling. "*Runic Manual of Wands*. Haven't thought about that book in a long time."

"You've never even held a wand," Aaron muttered.

"I've read about *plenty* of wands."

"Books don't count."

Heather let them go for another breath before cutting in, her voice sharp enough to slice through the chatter.

"Let me finish." She leaned forward, lowering her voice slightly as if she had a secret. "It's not only sycamore. The bramble grew into it, or the tree grew around the bramble. It looks… weird."

"Weird?" Aaron repeated, intrigued.

"Weird how?" Cedric asked. "Like knotted? Diseased?"

"Or cursed?" Eric offered, a little too cheerfully.

Aaron cocked his head. "Or do you mean like, *weird* like the miller's daughter?"

Cedric laughed. "Or weird like you talking to animals."

Heather rolled her eyes and silently mouthed, *Beatrice*.

Cedric stiffened.

Eric snorted.

Aaron grinned.

Heather searched for the right word. *Weird* wasn't it.

The staff was unlike anything she'd seen—half sycamore, half bramble, as if the two had fused over time. And not just any bramble—the bramble. The one that guarded Druid's Glen and The One Tree. The same living barrier that should have stopped her…but hadn't.

"The bramble grew into it," she said quietly.

The scrape of chairs against the floor startled her.

Her brothers were already on their feet, excitement charging the air between them.

"What's going on?" she asked.

"You said it looks weird?" Cedric exclaimed. "We have to see it!"

Aaron's face lit up. "Yeah! Come on!"

Eric pushed back his chair, a sly grin spreading across his face. "I read about pirates today, one of Merrow Keff's best works," he muttered with a chuckle. "If anyone gives a hoot."

Heather sprang to her feet and bolted, her heart pounding in her chest.

She didn't want them touching the staff before she could work on it properly—or worse, *before Cedric got any ideas*. What if he was still mad about the river? What if this was about payback?

They burst into the woodshed, the door slamming open against the wall.

Cedric snapped his fingers. A cantrip flared to life, casting a soft golden glow from a plank of oak nailed to the far wall. The workshop lit up, shadows dancing across stacked timber and dull tools.

Heather's staff rested on a pair of ancient gray sawhorses—half-shaped, waiting for the lathe. The boys crowded around it, drawn like moths.

Their fingers hovered, then touched, tracing the strange fusion of sycamore and bramble, where pale wood met black vine in a seamless, living grain.

Cedric ran his hand down the streaked wood, slow and reverent.

"It's warm," he whispered. His eyes closed, both palms resting on the staff now. "It's humming… Heather, this isn't just a staff."

He opened his eyes, voice quiet with wonder.

"This thing is *alive*. It's got the magic of the tangle. The same tangle that guards Druid's Glen."

Heather's heart swelled with pride. Cedric wouldn't lie about something like that.

Her staff was infused with magic—*real* magic.

She could hardly wait to show their father.

But that thought pulled her back to earth. The axe.

She had to retrieve it before he returned from the council meeting. Sundown was minutes away.

"I'm going to work on it for a little bit," she said quickly, glancing toward the window to gauge the fading light. "How long will your spell last?"

"An hour," Aaron replied, holding up one finger—just beating Cedric to the answer.

"You three clean up from dinner," she said, already nudging them toward the door. "Go."

Aaron grinned as they filed out. "That staff is going to be amazing. I can't wait to see it finished."

Heather waited until their footsteps faded, giving them enough time to get back to the house. Then she moved fast.

She grabbed the glowing wood Cedric had enchanted, snuffed it out with a cloth, and slipped through the door.

Cool evening air met her like a warning.

Her pulse quickened.

She had no time to waste.

The axe was still out there—waiting. And no one could know she'd gone back to Druid's Glen.

The vote had gone worse than Gideon anticipated.

Only he, Nightshade, and Lillia opposed investigating the Mage-Gate and the ruins of Mikal Yholl's stronghold.

Despite her icy demeanor, Lillia held firm—her fear of magic beyond druidic understanding had not lessened.

Nightshade had pleaded with the others, her wings fluttering with distress, but her warnings had gone unheard.

Curiosity had triumphed over caution. The remaining Archdruids were eager to unearth what should have stayed buried. Ilimitar was an enigma—so vehemently against Mages and *Librums*, yet the Elf had sided with the *Humans*.

Gideon had made peace with hard decisions before. But this one felt different. This was no fork in the road—it was the pebble before the landslide.

Or maybe the snowflake Aurora had warned of.

Now, as twilight deepened over Druid's Glen, preparations for the expedition were already underway.

It was agreed that Gideon would lead the group—his magic was essential for long-distance travel. Aurora had volunteered to accompany him, and Wilmund, ever eager to explore the ruin within his own domain, had confirmed his place without hesitation.

No one else from the Council offered to join them. Despite the risk. Despite the warnings.

Wilmund insisted his own followers could handle the exploration. The Stairwell rangers Gideon had recommended would provide additional protection—two seasoned forest-warriors, discreet and dependable.

They set the departure for one week's time, beginning at Wilmund's grove, where supplies and transport would be waiting.

Each Archdruid touched The One Tree, vanishing into its branches to return to their groves.

Gideon remained.

A cold dread settled in his chest, heavy and immovable—as if the vote had cast a shadow he couldn't shake. He stood alone beneath the ancient trunk, one hand resting on its rough bark, seeking…

Guidance.

Clarity.

Reassurance.

He wielded formidable power, but the truth pressed in like a tight band across his ribs—he didn't know enough. Not about the Mage-Gates. Not about the ruins of Mikal Yholl.

For a fleeting moment, he considered the unthinkable: contacting the Wizards of Arcana.

But wisdom—older than fear—whispered *no*.

Involving the Towers would bring scrutiny. Secrets like these never stayed buried once the Wizards started asking questions.

The Stairwell rangers were the better choice—quiet allies, unbound by council politics. He made a mental note to reach out to Dhallphkin soon. Not tonight. He needed time to plan—what to say, what to *withhold*. He could offer tree-stride in exchange for the short notice.

A breeze stirred the canopy above, rustling the leaves with a whisper like breath on water.

He turned toward the sound.

Nightshade appeared, gliding out of shadow, her wings catching the dim light in a shimmer of silver and violet. She hovered close, her eyes narrow, her expression drawn.

"You know you must destroy it," she whispered, voice urgent. "Nothing good can come from anything the Mages left behind—especially not relics tied to the Yholl brothers."

Gideon exhaled and rubbed his temple. "It's crossed my mind. I've been working through a few ideas. But that's not the only reason you're here, is it?"

Nightshade's wings flickered.

"No," she said. "Watch your back, Gideon."

She scanned the glade, her eyes darting through the shifting shadows. "I fear someone on the Council wants you gone. It would be easier for another to ascend if you... weren't around. Accidents happen. And missions like this?" Her wings gave a slow beat. "They have a way of becoming fatal."

Gideon tilted his head, watching her closely. "How do I know *you're* not the one with such ambitions?"

Nightshade gave a soft, mirthless laugh. "If I wanted to be Grand Druid, I would have claimed the title centuries ago. That chair holds no appeal. My only concern is the Mage-Gate—it must be destroyed. That's my agenda. But Gideon... not everyone on the Council sees the danger as you do."

"I'll need allies to survive this," he said, frustration tightening his voice. "I can't watch my back alone."

Her gaze softened, but the steel behind it didn't fade. "I won't endanger my people by standing openly beside you. Anything tied to the Yholl brothers could unravel the protections I've worked to preserve. But if you call, I'll come. And if anything stirs in the dark, I'll send word."

She began to rise, wings catching the last of the light.

"Take care, Gideon. I would mourn you... but not all on the Council would shed a tear."

Before Gideon could respond, Nightshade flitted toward The One Tree, her wings catching the moonlight.

In a blink, she vanished into the ancient bark, leaving him alone in the glade.

He lingered a moment longer, waiting—half-hoping another Archdruid might return, offering a scrap of solidarity.

But no one came.

With a weary sigh, he turned toward the path that wound to the bramble's edge, where Druid's Glen met the wider world.

His thoughts drifted to his children, and for a moment, a rare flicker of longing warmed his chest. He needed them—a hug, a laugh, *something* to remind him why this burden was worth carrying.

As he walked, a thought crept in and quietly took root.

Maybe I should bring Cedric and Aaron.

They weren't full druids yet—just apprentices—but he trusted them. Trusted their loyalty. Their instincts.

They would watch his back without question.

The two Stairwell rangers would provide protection.

But his sons?

They would give him strength.

It was a risky decision, but what choice did he have?

If something happened to them… could he bear the weight of knowing it was *his* decision that put them in harm's way?

Bringing them was madness.

He knew that.

But leaving them behind?

Who else could he truly trust to stand with him when it mattered most?

The thought didn't sit well. It gnawed at him as he walked, quiet and persistent. He would sleep on it. Pray to Thatara. Hope that the dawn would bring clarity.

Gideon stepped toward the living bramble that guarded Druid's Glen.

As he neared, a sharp tingle pulsed through his fingertips—like the crackle of distant thunder before a storm.

The hairs on the back of his neck rose.

He froze mid-step, a prickle of apprehension settling between his shoulders.

The brambles whispered—not disturbed but frenzied. Their magic shivered through the air, agitated and wild.

A vile presence was caught in their grasp. Evil that should never have breached the protective weave.

A cold knot twisted in Gideon's gut.

Heather's sapling.

The disturbance was coming from the same place. The same clearing. The brambles writhed like restless serpents, their whispers urgent—insistent—almost frantic.

His pulse surged.

His mind raced.

Staff in hand, the Grand Druid murmured a protective incantation and broke into a sprint, boots thudding against the ground like the first beats of a war drum.

- 68 -

Chapter Five

∞

Wizard

The path ahead felt both familiar and strange in the dim light—every root, every branch cast into alien shape by the shadows. Heather kept the cloth-wrapped light close, her steps careful along the narrow trail. She didn't want anyone thinking she was sneaking around Druid's Glen. All she needed to do was grab the axe, get back to the woodshed, and work on her staff for a few minutes.

No one would know she'd left.

She pulled back the cloth, letting the glow spill out just enough to see where she walked.

The clearing looked the same as they'd left it.

Chopped brambles lay scattered like rusting blades, and a pulpy mess marked where Lillia's acid had eaten through the vines. A hollow patch remained where the sycamore sapling had stood.

But the axe was gone.

What she *did* see was a hare meandering through the brambles, the way small creatures did at night—careful, slow, and deliberate.

Heather knew animals like that could slip through the tangle if they moved gently enough. The hare's deep brown fur shimmered in her soft light, its white tail flicking as it stepped between the thorny roots. It was beautiful.

"Hey there, little one," Heather whispered. "Where are you going?"

The hare paused and looked at her. Its ears twitched.

There was something about the way it watched her—too still, too focused. Heather found herself on the verge of speaking again, a strange compulsion rising in her chest. Normally the little ones answered…

Then a voice behind her made her jump.

"You shouldn't be out here by yourself."

Heather whirled around, heart pounding.

Lillia stood at the edge of the clearing.

The dryad's normally supple skin had gone rough and ridged—*barkskin*. Her green hair was swept to one side, and the usual flicker of mischief in her eyes was gone.

What remained was intensity.

Dangerous, focused intensity.

"You scared me!" Heather hissed. "What I'm doing here is none of your concern! I'm old enough to go where I please. Stay away from me! My father told me what you are—what you *do* to people."

"That's not important right now," Lillia said, her voice clipped and urgent. Her posture was tense, coiled. "Did you see a rabbit?"

Heather scowled. "It's a *hare*," she snapped. "How can *you*, an Archdruid, not know the difference?"

Lillia growled, flipping her hair over her shoulder in frustration. "The mistake was for expediency. Where is it? *Show me. Now.*"

Heather turned and raised the cloth-wrapped light, casting it toward the moving shape.

The hare was still there—hopping in slow, stilted motions, pausing now and again to glance back.

It wasn't fleeing.

"It's acting weird," Heather muttered, unease curling up her spine. "It didn't talk to me. It should have bolted by now."

"Get behind me," Lillia commanded, her voice sharp and unyielding.

Heather moved before she had time to think. She bent to grab the axe lying at her feet—*how had she missed it earlier?*—just as Lillia's hand clamped down on her shoulder.

The world blurred into a twisting swirl of green and brown light.

Every nerve in Heather's body tingled as they slipped through the trees, her vision fracturing into stars. When they emerged, she stumbled, breath catching in her throat.

They now stood ten feet ahead of the hare.

The creature had frozen, its small black eyes fixed on Lillia.

"Get behind me," Lillia repeated, this time a whisper.

She spoke a word of power.

A flaming scimitar appeared in her hand with a burst of heat and light, casting flickering shadows across the bramble floor.

Heather took a step back, heart slamming in her chest.

The hare rose on its hind legs—and in the blink of an eye, it twisted into a man.

A wizard.

He wore brown robes threaded with gold buckles and chains. His cloak fluttered in the breeze as he pulled a vial from his belt, his lips already moving.

Foul, ancient words spilled from his mouth, tainting the air with their weight.

He hurled the vial to the forest floor.

It shattered—*and darkness rippled outward in a wave.*

From the spreading gloom, six bloated demons clawed their way into the glade. Their gray flesh sagged, leaking filth, and their diseased claws tore furrows into the dirt.

"Drav'korath," the wizard whispered, his voice low and soaked in malice, the meaning clear enough: *destroy them.*

Before Heather could even breathe, Lillia was gone—*a blur of motion.*

The flaming scimitar carved through three demons in a single, fluid arc. Fire consumed them as they crumpled, dissolving into clouds of black smoke.

Lillia turned the blade on the wizard—but the scimitar struck an unseen barrier and skidded off in a spray of sparks. Both combatants staggered, thrown off balance by the blow.

The remaining demons lunged for her, shrieking.

Heather knew she had to act—*anything* to help.

Without thinking, she hurled the axe at the sorcerer with all her strength. Pain ripped through her shoulder as it left her hand, and she watched in dismay as the blade ricocheted off the wizard's magical shield.

Bright blue darts of energy flared from his fingertips.

Most of them streaked toward Lillia.

The rest veered toward Heather.

Two slammed into her chest, knocking the wind from her lungs and driving her to her knees. The pain was searing—like fire burrowing deep between her ribs.

Lillia fought desperately, scimitar flashing as she cut down another demon—but one flanked her, slipping past her defenses.

Heather's mind raced.

The bramble.

It hadn't stopped her before. What if it *recognized* her? What if it would obey?

She shut her eyes and reached for it—not with her hands, but with her will. She pictured the vines slithering forward, angry, wild, *alive.*

The ground stirred.

Four thorned branches shot through the clearing.

One drove through a demon's skull with brutal finality.

Another missed the sorcerer by inches.

A third pierced a demon's belly, slamming it into the earth.

The last coiled tight around the final beast and *crushed* it, the sound a wet, bone-snapping crunch.

Despite the odds, the wizard pressed his advantage.

A ghostly sword materialized beside him, sweeping through the air toward Lillia. She blocked it with her scimitar, but the blow staggered her—her barkskin cracked, flickering once before vanishing entirely.

Lightning cracked overhead as Lillia summoned a storm.

Bolts rained down from the darkened sky—searing flashes of raw power. The sorcerer dodged the first few strikes, retreating toward the edge of the clearing where the canopy thinned and shadows pooled.

Heather's chest still burned from the earlier spell, but she forced her legs to move. Her brothers had taught her one rule when facing a spellcaster: *close the distance, get in their face.*

She sprinted.

Screaming, she slammed into the sorcerer with all her strength.

The vial in his hand shattered as they fell, its dark contents splashing onto the dirt. He twisted away from her grasp, and Heather hit the ground hard, rolling into scorched soil.

The stench of demon ichor filled her nose—*sour, burning*—and she gagged, retching violently.

Then—*a pulse.*

A silent wave of magic rippled through the clearing.

Heather froze, her body going still.

This is it, she thought. *This is how it ends.*

The ghostly sword lunged for Lillia—only to vanish mid-strike, snuffed out as if it had never been.

"*Gideon,*" the sorcerer spat, rising slowly. His voice curled with disdain. "I wondered when you'd arrive."

Her father stood at the edge of the clearing, staff raised, magic coiled at his fingertips.

The sorcerer snarled a word of power.

The air shimmered—warped—like ripples across a pond. His form blurred, turned translucent… and vanished.

Gone without a trace.

Gideon surged forward, reaching into the space the wizard had occupied. His spell unraveled in his hands, magic bleeding away before it could find purchase.

For a heartbeat, frustration burned across his face.

Then it was gone.

Heather mattered more.

He dropped his staff without hesitation and knelt beside her, pulling her into his arms.

She was trembling violently, her smaller frame locked tight with shock. He could feel her heart pounding against his chest like a drum of panic, and for a long moment, he simply held her—grounding her, quieting the terror that radiated off her in waves.

Lillia stirred nearby, rolling onto her knees with effort. Her barkskin armor had been dispelled, leaving her exposed and raw. Burns streaked her arms and chest; shallow cuts oozed blood. Dirt clung to her tangled green hair, and the once-proud flowers woven through it lay crushed and wilted.

"He teleported," Gideon muttered, eyes still on the place the wizard had vanished. His voice was tight, edged with frustration.

He shifted slightly, brushing a steadying hand along Heather's back as she shivered in his arms.

"I suppose I have you to thank for keeping her alive," he added, glancing at Lillia.

Lillia shook her head and wiped dirt from her face. Her expression softened, exhaustion pressing into every movement as she rose unsteadily and limped toward them. Her eyes never left Heather.

The dryad—so often aloof, so often untouchable—stood before the trembling girl.

With quiet reverence, she cupped Heather's face in her hands.

Her touch was feather-light, but the tenderness in it felt almost foreign coming from Lillia.

"You saved both of us," she whispered, her voice hoarse but steady.

Then she leaned in, and with a gentleness that surprised them both, kissed Heather's brow.

"For that," she said, "I am forever in your debt, Heather. *Forever.*"
She drew a ragged breath, the word itself seeming to cost her.
Then she said it again—softer this time, but no less true.
"*Forever.*"

The aftermath of the attack left more questions than answers.

The intruder's identity remained unknown, and though he had spoken Gideon's name with unsettling familiarity, that didn't mean Gideon knew him in return. Being Grand Druid meant many knew *of* him—but only a handful should have recognized him on sight, let alone dared to speak his name so directly.

That alone gnawed at Gideon.

They reconstructed the encounter, step by step. The hare had either come from within Druid's Glen… or had been trying to infiltrate it. Gideon suspected the former. If it had slipped in earlier—during the Council—it could have witnessed everything spoken beneath the boughs of The One Tree.

If so, it knew *far* too much.

Lillia confirmed his fears. She explained that she had sensed a disturbance earlier in the day—a wrongness that had set her on edge. Now, she suspected that presence had been the hare entering, not leaving. She remembered it clearly: a lone animal among the dozens frolicking freely within the Glen, indistinguishable from the rest—until it lingered too long by the roots of The One Tree.

After the Council adjourned, Lillia had returned to the Glen, her instincts unsettled. She'd tracked the hare in secret, quietly following its trail until her path had crossed with Heather's.

Then came the fight—brief, but telling.

The wizard had summoned lesser demons, creatures bloated with filth and rot—hallmarks of Abyssal magic. That kind of knowledge wasn't easily come by, even for seasoned practitioners. The magic darts were more familiar—basic combat spells meant to incapacitate quickly—but the translucent, dancing sword?

Gideon had never seen its like in all his years of study.

More troubling was what *didn't* happen.

Lillia's flaming scimitar should have felled him outright. That weapon cleaved through armor, flesh, and bone with ease. Yet the wizard had blocked it—*survived* it—and recovered as though it were a glancing blow.

Then came the lightning.

Lillia's storm had been powerful enough to devastate a grove, to split trees and leave the earth scorched black. But he'd moved through it with uncanny precision, slipping past bolts that should have cooked him alive.

Any other man would have been dead twice over before the second spell left Lillia's lips.

But not this wizard.

Gideon rubbed his temple, the knot of unease tightening in his chest.

This wasn't the work of some hedge mage dabbling in forbidden arts.

No.

This was the hand of a master—well-instructed, highly skilled, and dangerous.

A sorcerer with purpose.

He poured Lillia another measure of Peak Estate brandy. The bottle clinked against the rim of her glass, the sound sharp in the quiet room.

She accepted the pour with a nod, her fingers brushing the edge of the cloak draped over her shoulders—bandages peeking out beneath the folds.

When she brought the glass to her lips, she hesitated. The sharp bite of the brandy curled her nose before she drank.

"I will inform the other members of the Council," Gideon said. His voice was low, but the words hung heavier in the air than he intended.

"No," Lillia replied, her tone edged and unflinching. "We need to be careful—about what we reveal, and when."

Gideon's brow knit. "Why? They deserve to know what we're dealing with."

Lillia stepped closer, her expression sharp but not without empathy. "Think, Gideon. The Council may trust one another—but trust is not the same as control."

When he didn't answer, she continued, her voice softening.

"The moment they know, the course is set. There will be arguments, delays, layers of politics. Every move will become ceremony. And this wizard—he's already ahead of us. If we act too soon, or too loudly, he'll vanish into the wind."

Gideon exhaled, considering her words. "So what?" he said. "We just let this wizard run free without alerting anyone?"

"No," Lillia replied. "But for now, the fewer who know, the better."

She glanced toward the shadows, her gaze sharp, as if expecting eyes to materialize from the dark.

"We're dealing with a dangerous unknown—a wizard who conjures demons without effort and managed to spy on the Council without triggering so much as a whisper of alarm. Until we know who he is and what he wants, any move could expose us… or alert watchers we can't see."

Gideon's voice dropped. "You think there's a spy on the Council?"

Lillia gave him a small, tight smile—though there was no joy behind it. "I don't believe there is. But others are always listening, whether we invite them or not. If word of this encounter spreads, it won't just be our Council paying attention. Wizards. Scholars. Treasure hunters. The Mage-Gate is too dangerous to ignore. And if they learn a rogue wizard was involved, they'll come. And when they come… they'll bring trouble with them."

Gideon rubbed his beard, eyes narrowing in thought. She was right. Even if the Council kept its silence, the mere *existence* of the wizard— and the Mage-Gate—was tinder for the wrong kind of fire. There were always those eager to exploit ancient magic, to dig up what should remain buried. Whispers of a sorcerer summoning demons would spread faster than they could contain.

"If the Council is aware," Lillia continued, her voice softer now, "they'll be honor-bound to act. That means involving more people— ones we may not be able to guide or contain. And the more movement, the more notice we draw. He'll see us coming."

She looked him in the eye. "For now, we keep this between us. Once we know more, we can decide what to share. But not yet."

Gideon closed his eyes, the weight of her logic pressing down. "You're asking me to lie by omission. To keep secrets from the Council. They won't thank me for it."

"They'll forgive you," Lillia said, calm and certain. "*They will forgive you,*" Lillia said, "if it means we succeed. But if we step from shadow before the sun is ready, we may never get another chance to stop him."

He didn't like it. He never liked keeping things from the Council. But her reasoning was sound. The risks were too great, the wizard too dangerous. Even wise minds could stumble when forced to act on half-truths.

And right now, the advantage wasn't theirs.

"Fine," Gideon muttered at last. "For now, we keep it quiet. But the moment you learn anything—anything—you tell me."

"Of course." Lillia inclined her head, the glint in her green eyes unreadable. "If he reappears, you'll be the first to know."

A beat passed—just long enough for the implication to settle.

"But until then," she continued, "we move in silence. Trust me, Gideon—things like this are better dealt with in the shadows."

She glanced away, her voice flattening. "I'll try to find out who he is. Though it will likely be a wasted effort."

Across the room, Aaron tapped his fingers against the table, clearly trying not to stare at the dryad.

Cedric paced, his eyes bouncing between Heather's bedroom door and Lillia, like he was waiting for an explanation that would make the day make sense.

Eric stepped into the room, a damp cloth in hand.

"She's still warm," he said quietly, worry pulling at his brow. "Fever won't break. No matter what I do, she's burning up."

"It's from the demons," Lillia said, her voice calm but edged with fatigue. "It will pass by morning. They secrete fungal spores and toxins—she must have inhaled them. But she's strong. It will break with rest."

She paused, her gaze lingering on Eric. "Only the weak perish from such exposure."

Gideon's jaw tightened. He couldn't tell if her words were meant as comfort or a veiled warning.

"Anything else you remember?" he asked.

Lillia shook her head, eyes narrowing in thought. "The wizard was there all day. Listening. Watching. He heard everything—the full council meeting. He knows what we know."

Gideon gave a slow nod. That kind of knowledge, in the wrong hands, could tilt the world.

Lillia finished her brandy in a small, slow sip. "If anything else surfaces, I'll return to Druid's Glen and tell you myself. But for now, there's no use lingering over what we've already turned."

Her gaze drifted toward the boys—unreadable, unread.

"Agreed," Gideon said. "You may go whenever you're ready. There's no reason for you to remain here. We'll care for Heather."

Lillia's eyes softened, though her expression stayed guarded. "May I see her before I leave? Just to say thank you—and goodbye? It's the least I can offer for her bravery."

Gideon took the glass from her hand and motioned toward the bedroom door.

"Just this once," he said, his voice edged with finality. "You are not welcome in this home after tonight. Do you understand?"

Lillia gave a faint, knowing smile—more habit than warmth. "Understood."

As she rose, the cloak slipped from one shoulder, revealing the smooth curve of her collarbone, her honey-hued skin bare beneath the folds of fabric. Only the bandages clung to the worst of her wounds. She moved with effortless grace, unbothered by the blood and dirt—as if her injuries hadn't truly happened to her.

The door closed behind her with a quiet, deliberate click, sealing her into the still room where Heather rested.

Aaron leaned forward the moment she disappeared from sight, his voice an urgent whisper. "Why can't we talk to her? I have so many questions."

"She's a dryad, Aaron," Cedric muttered, pinching the bridge of his nose like his brother's excitement physically pained him.

"But this is a rare opportunity!" Aaron pressed on, undeterred. "She's a reclusive Archdruid. We could learn so much—her magic, her culture, how she thinks. This is—" he threw up his hands— "a once-in-a-lifetime chance!"

Gideon leveled a steady look at his son, his voice calm but edged with warning. "Lillia is not to be trifled with. She is dryad-born, shaped by the fairy world and its strange, tangled magic. She may be charming, but she does not think or act like a human—or an elf. The dryads live by no laws we understand. What they consider normal, we would find… disquieting."

He let the silence hang, then added, "Let your curiosity run wild, and you might not come back the same."

Aaron opened his mouth, then shut it again, frustration simmering just beneath the surface. "We could learn so much," he muttered, more to himself than to anyone else.

"You need to let this go," Cedric said, nodding toward the closed door. "Lillia's nothing but trouble. We've had enough excitement for one day—let's not invite more."

Aaron exhaled sharply, but relented, slumping back in his chair. "Fine. But it's a missed opportunity."

Eric, quiet as ever, looked up from where he sat twisting the damp cloth in his hands. "She's… beautiful," he said softly. "I read a story about dryads once. Does her hair really change color with the seasons?"

"Yes," Gideon said, rubbing his temple, weariness creeping into his voice. "In spring and summer, it's green—like now. In autumn, it turns red, like a maple. In winter, it darkens to brown. Their eyes change too. Green, then blue, then brown."

Eric nodded slowly, his expression somewhere between wonder and awe. "She's… amazing."

Gideon shook his head.

How easily they fall under her spell.

"Boys," he said, his voice low and steady, but edged with steel. "Listen to me."

Aaron straightened.

Eric looked up, still holding the twisted cloth.

"The allure wears off quickly," Gideon continued. "Once you understand what she truly is."

Aaron frowned. "What do you mean? What is she?"

Gideon took a breath, weighing his words. He could soften the truth—but that would serve no one.

"She's a predator," he said at last.

The word landed with finality, cold and unmistakable.

Silence fell.

Aaron glanced toward the closed door, unease creeping into his posture.

Eric's dreamy expression faltered, replaced by a furrowed brow and a quiet wariness.

Gideon drained the last of Lillia's brandy and set the glass down with a sharp, deliberate clink.

"Remember that," he said. "It might save your life someday."

Heather sat with her head propped against a pillow and the wall, her simple pallet cradling her weakened body. She was comfortable here. This room was her refuge—a place to retreat when the world became too much.

The wooden walls bore familiar carvings of forest animals and painted druidic symbols in red, blue, and yellow. Those colors always grounded her.

A lantern flickered between her bed and Eric's, its warm light casting restless shadows that rippled across the floor and walls. She shut her eyes to still the spinning in her head and clutched the blankets until her knuckles went pale.

Her insides were… wrong.

She couldn't explain it—only feel it. Hollow. Off. Like a part of her had been scraped away and left behind.

Her father had done what he could—soothing spells, teas steeped with forest herbs, quiet reassurances that her strength would return by morning.

But she didn't feel better. She felt worse.

Untethered.

The attack clung to her like smoke, impossible to wash off. That wizard—he had tried to kill them.

Despite the fear, her thoughts kept returning to the same place— what could she have done differently?

No answer came. Only one truth remained clear: she needed a weapon.

A real one.

Carrying a staff and knife wasn't frowned upon. No one would question her if she began training. If a wizard could infiltrate Druid's Glen, what was stopping others? The thought settled like stone in her chest—a threat she couldn't yet name, but one she could no longer ignore.

But it wasn't just about protection.

The brambles.

Her command over them haunted her more than the pain or the fear. How had she done it? Why had they obeyed?

Her father had offered an answer—that the Glen's magic had responded to her instinctively, that she was attuned to it. But she knew it had been more than that. She hadn't been saved.

She had shaped them.

And even after she told him so, he'd dismissed it. Said she was confused.

But she remembered.

She would prove it to him.

And when she did, he'd have no choice but to help her understand what she truly was… and what she was becoming.

The door creaked open, then eased shut with a soft click. Bare feet padded across the wooden floorboards. Heather opened one eye, brushing strands of hair from her face.

Lillia stood in the lantern's dim glow, her silhouette haloed by flickering light. She moved like mist through the underbrush—fluid, soundless. The cloak over her shoulders hung loosely, slipping as she stepped forward. Bandages wrapped parts of her body, but the shifting fabric revealed glimpses of smooth skin—her stomach, her legs, toned and unbothered by injury.

Her green hair was pulled up tonight, exposing the sharp symmetry of her features. Eyes large and bright, lashes long, brows arched in soft composure.

The dryad was beautiful—unsettlingly so.

Without speaking, Lillia knelt beside the bed and lowered her head to Heather's chest, listening to the thrum of her heartbeat. When she lifted her gaze, their eyes met.

Those brilliant green irises held her still, as though peering into truths Heather hadn't yet uncovered—truths buried deep within her, waiting to rise.

"Thank you," Lillia whispered. "I survived because of you. You are a brave woman, Heather."

Her voice was soft, almost hypnotic. Heather's breath hitched. The praise warmed her, though it felt strange—unreal—coming from a dryad like Lillia, a being not quite mortal.

"You rushed that wizard without a thought for your own safety," Lillia went on. "If he'd made it farther, he would have unleashed spells meant to kill us both. The demons were only a distraction—to keep us busy while he prepared worse. But he underestimated you." Her smile appeared, fleeting and joyless. "That's why we lived. You turned the fight."

She leaned closer, her tone darker now. "If he returns, he will bring the Abyss down upon us. If you see him again—run."

The words hit Heather like a cold wind. She hadn't considered that he might return—but now, the thought burrowed deep, planting seeds of fear.

Lillia lifted her head from Heather's chest and whispered words in a language older than the Glen. Her hands moved with delicate precision, tracing invisible lines over Heather's skin. The air shifted. Magic stirred—soft, potent, alive.

A warm, humming energy flooded Heather's limbs, setting every nerve alight. It was overwhelming—uncomfortable and intoxicating all at once. She gasped as the warmth spread through her, her blood quickening, her cheeks flushed. Her whole body tingled, as though waking from a deep, enchanted sleep.

Lillia smiled—not with mischief, but with quiet understanding. She reached into the space between them, her fingers plucking at nothing—and revealed a leather thong, a single perfect acorn bound within its woven strands. It gleamed in the lantern light, smooth and flawless, untouched by time.

"This is a precious thing," Lillia said, her voice low, reverent. "It carries part of my domain—my world, and my soul, if that makes sense."

Heather stared at the acorn, trying to grasp what it meant. Her gaze flicked upward as Lillia touched a similar one hanging between her breasts, nestled just above the edge of her cloak.

"I don't understand," Heather admitted.

"You don't need to understand for it to work," Lillia replied, brushing her fingers across the acorn's smooth shell. "Keep it with you. If you are ever in mortal danger, crush it underfoot, and I will come. Once. No matter where you are, I will find you."

Her tone shifted—more serious now, each word carved with purpose.

"But use it wisely. Once you summon me, all debts between us will be paid. Until then, I will treat you and your family with… neutrality."

"And after?" Heather asked, her voice edged with suspicion. "What happens after the debt is paid? Will you turn on us?"

Lillia laughed—light and lyrical, almost too perfect. The kind of laugh village girls practiced when they wanted boys to notice them. Heather had heard it before, but never from anyone quite like Lillia.

"No, dear," Lillia said, her voice smooth and unreadable. "I will simply do what is in my nature. Men and women, young and old, have succumbed to my kind for centuries. They always will."

She leaned in, her eyes holding Heather's. "But I respect you, Heather. That may be enough to keep your brothers safe from me."

Heather's heart stilled at those words, a cold dread creeping in. Of her brothers, it was Eric she feared for the most. The village girls teased him mercilessly, always finding ways to make him blush. He was too easily swayed by their charms. Perhaps he would grow out of it… perhaps not.

Aaron and Cedric were different—stronger, sharper, nearly full druids now. They would soon have magic of their own to protect them. But Eric... Eric worried her.

Heather clenched the acorn necklace in her fist, her knuckles whitening. "If you try to charm my brothers, you'll have me to deal with. And my father. Don't think it will be easy."

Lillia stood with fluid grace, each movement deliberate. She reached out and patted Heather's head, her touch soft and cool, like dew on early spring leaves.

"Remember," Lillia murmured, her voice low and melodic, "summon me only when it is truly dire. I would be... disappointed if it were wasted—crushed beneath a careless step." Her smile was gentle, but her words were heavy with hidden promise. "But when you call, I will come. I will fight for you. Defend you."

She paused.

"Die for you, if I must."

Heather nodded, her fingers tightening around the acorn. She wouldn't waste this gift. She already knew what she'd do with it.

Lillia lingered a moment longer, her green eyes gleaming—unreadable. Then, without another word, she turned and sauntered to the door. The cloak swayed around her bare legs as she moved, and with a soft click, the door closed behind her, leaving Heather alone with her thoughts—and the strange weight of the acorn resting in her palm.

Eric shot to his feet, alarm flashing across his face. "What do you mean she's a predator? And you left Heather alone with her?"

"Sit down," Gideon ordered, waving him down with a firm hand. "Lillia may be a predator, but she also has a sliver of honor. She won't harm Heather—not after what she did today. The debt is owed, and until she repays it, we have nothing to fear from her."

Eric didn't move. His jaw tightened, eyes darting to the closed bedroom door.

"What... exactly did Heather do today?" he asked slowly, his voice barely above a whisper.

Gideon hesitated, then let out a sigh. "She fought beside Lillia."

Eric's breath caught. "Fought?"

"A wizard," Gideon said quietly. "And demons. She saved Lillia's life."

Eric stared at him, the words sinking in like stones. "Heather fought demons?" He shook his head, trying to make sense of it. "A wizard?"

Gideon gave him a sharp look. "This doesn't leave this house. No one outside this family is to know what happened. The fewer people who know, the better. Lillia will search for the wizard's identity, and if she succeeds, we'll find him and learn what he's after."

A heavy silence settled over the room as they waited for Lillia's return. When she finally emerged, she gave them a parting glance and, with deliberate grace, let the cloak slip from her shoulders. It fell to the floor without a sound. She stepped through the doorway and vanished into the night, leaving the men in stunned silence.

Eric, his face flushed crimson, shifted awkwardly. "She doesn't wear clothes? Ever?"

"Never," Gideon said flatly, his tone dry.

He caught their dumbfounded expressions and allowed himself a faint smile. Let them have their moment. Today, at least, they'd earned it.

Heather felt better the next morning, though the haze of sleep still clung to her like cobwebs. She stayed in bed well past breakfast, nearly slipping into the noon hour. Her muscles ached from the skirmish the night before, and it took a few tentative steps to confirm she wouldn't be confined to bed all day.

The kitchen smelled of herbs and fresh bread. On the table, her family had left a simple plate: cheese, sliced fruit, and a wedge of soft bread. She savored the creaminess of the cheese and the tart bite of the fruit, though her appetite hadn't fully returned. The cup of water beside the plate was warm, but welcome, easing the dryness in her throat.

After finishing her meal, she wandered over to her father's desk. There, resting atop a tiny note scribbled on a leaf, was a single blueberry. Parchment wasn't used for simple messages—leaves served that purpose. She plucked up the note, which said only one word:

EAT

No further instructions.

Heather popped the berry into her mouth.

A pleasant warmth spread through her as the druid magic took hold, easing the last traces of fatigue. Druid-berries were prized for moments like these, able to heal injuries, counteract poison, or provide nourishment when none was available.

She leaned against the desk, thinking. There were things she could do—lessons to study, training exercises to practice—but none of them appealed to her. Maybe she'd just crawl back into bed and rest a little longer.

Then something nudged at the back of her mind—a small itch of curiosity.

Her staff.

The sapling hybrid of sycamore and bramble. It was still in the workshop, waiting for her.

The thought stirred her from her sluggishness. She pulled on her boots and headed for the back door, her steps gaining purpose. She shut the door firmly behind her and jogged toward the workshop, excitement bubbling just beneath her weariness.

Gideon let the day unfold as usual for his sons, though he knew the conversation waiting at supper was anything but routine. What he planned to ask would change everything—setting them on a path lined with danger. But if he couldn't trust his own children with the truth, then who could he trust?

Earlier that day, Gideon had traveled hundreds of miles via tree-stride, crossing the wilds in minutes to reach the Leafy Forest. There, he met with Dhallphkin, commander of the Stairwell. The ranger leader had listened in silence, then agreed to send two seasoned Swordarm rangers to accompany the expedition. As promised, Gideon would return to fetch them—tree-stride made such distances trivial to one who knew the forests well.

His sons, Cedric and Aaron, would join him—and he planned to cast every protective enchantment he could muster to shield them. Trinkets and magical objects from his adventuring days would bolster their defenses. With the two rangers, plus two swords pledged by Wilmund, they would have ample protection.

Aurora had also promised to join them, and Gideon expected her arrival any day now. With her and Wilmund's magical abilities combined, they would have a formidable team.

The one missing piece was a cleric—someone with divine magic, capable of healing wounds and warding off dark forces. A temple of Thatara lay not far from his grove, and he recalled a priestess named Chefera from a previous visit. As a devoted servant of Thatara, she would be trustworthy—and, more importantly, affordable. Gold crowns would seal the agreement. He'd stop by the temple tomorrow with an offer.

As the expedition solidified in his mind, the memory of the wizard lingered like a thorn. The man's identity remained unknown—his motives, even more so. When Gideon had mentioned the Wizards of Arcana to Dhallphkin, the ranger had dismissed the notion. This didn't match their methods. The Wizards of Arcana were obsessed with knowledge—spells, relics, natural phenomena—but they weren't cruel. They weren't kind, either. They walked the line between order and chaos, but they didn't summon demons. That suggested a purpose far darker than mere curiosity. For now, he would have to wait for Lillia's investigation, though the weight of the unknown pressed heavy on his thoughts.

He pushed those thoughts aside as there was the Mage-Gate to focus on now.

He traveled through the tangle surrounding Druid's Glen to gather supplies.

In the heart of Druid's Glen, Gideon uncovered his hidden cache. He kept it buried here to deter prying eyes, though the value of these secret items were not significant. Those who frequented the Glen wouldn't think to search for it, and few outside the forest could reach it in the first place.

He found the white marker stone and rolled it aside. Using a small spade, he unearthed a storage space—a wooden box, weathered but intact. Gideon lifted the hinged lid, revealing a smaller, unadorned chest within. Plain, without locks or seals, the chest gave no hint of the minor treasures it contained. He carried it tenderly to a nearby table to sort through its contents.

Inside, memories and magic greeted him. His fingers brushed over two enchanted necklaces—long forgotten, but still potent. These would go to Cedric and Aaron. A ring caught his eye next, and he slipped it into his pocket without hesitation. He had forgotten about that one.

Then his gaze landed on a brooch shaped like a beetle, and a grin crept across his face.

Mischievous, that little thing. Tapping its shell summoned a swarm of ordinary beetles to defend the wearer—not dangerous, just unbearably annoying.

He chuckled, remembering the day he accidentally triggered it while asking Emma's father for her hand in marriage. The memory was vivid: her father sprinting through the vineyard, swatting at the cloud of beetles chasing him.

Yes! Yes! You can have her hand! Take her! Just stop these cursed bugs!

Emma had come running from the house, doubling over with laughter as her father flailed and shouted promises. That year's vintage had been labeled *Beetle Wine*, and Gideon still had a bottle tucked away somewhere in the house.

The memory warmed him, but the ache for Emma soon followed, as it always did. He longed for her presence now, more than ever. Tough times lay ahead, and he would have to face them without her steadying influence. His children would have to be enough.

Returning to the chest, Gideon sorted through the rest of the items. He set aside scarves, coins, and gemstones—useful, but not what they needed. The gnarled wand he pulled free pulsed with latent power.

This would do nicely.

Satisfied with his selection, he replaced the chest in its hiding spot, covering it once more with soil and the white stone marker.

He grinned, thinking fondly of the prank that could unfold if he tapped the beetle again—but now wasn't the time for such antics.

He slipped the ring onto his finger. It adjusted itself with a subtle tightening, as though recognizing its wearer once more. A faint hum pulsed through the band, syncing with the rhythm of his heartbeat. He could feel the protective enchantment settling in—comforting, grounding. Not overwhelming, but present, like a steady hand at his back.

He fastened the beetle brooch to his robes, its tiny legs clinging to the fabric as if alive, then tucked the wand into an accessible pocket, ready for whatever lay ahead.

Gideon stepped carefully over the sprawling roots of The One Tree, pausing as the wind stirred through the upper branches, sending a fresh scatter of fiery red leaves across the Glen. He brushed his hand along the bark with gentle reverence, fingers tracing the ancient ridges as one might touch the shoulder of an old friend. Then, with a whispered word, he vanished.

He reappeared just beyond the village boundary, choosing a secluded grove near the east path—close enough to Arboretum to be convenient, but far enough not to alarm any of the locals with sudden magic.

His errands were quick. The baker handed over five steaming meat pies filled with thick stew and root vegetables, wrapped in parchment and tied with twine. On his way out of town, he stopped by a nut vendor, a stout woman named Milna with bright eyes and calloused hands.

"Afternoon Milna," Gideon said. "The honey hickory nuts. Wrap them up for my children."

She measured two heaping scoops into parchment and tied it into a plump sack.

Gideon snapped down a silver.

"For your little druids," Milna said with a wink, passing him four twists of candied ginger wrapped in large leaves. "Still the best cure for nerves if you ask me."

Gideon accepted the gift with a grateful nod and a soft smile, tucking the sweets and nuts into his satchel.

He walked the rest of the way home on foot, arms full and cloak tugged by the wind, content to enjoy the quiet rhythm of his steps.

Back in the kitchen, he unpacked the pies, nuts, and treats. He sliced purple carrots and small red potatoes, tossed them in duck fat with salt and rosemary from the garden, and left them to simmer in a clay pot beside the fire.

Two fresh pitchers of ale were already on the table. As the rich scent of roasting vegetables filled the house, he poured himself a small measure of *Andy's Fireside Brandy*—the bottle nearly empty now, thanks to Krik's generosity—and took a slow sip.

Gideon took his time setting the table, letting the familiar task steady his thoughts. He arranged the honeyed hickory nuts neatly beside each plate, tucking a twist of candied ginger at every setting. It was a small gesture, but tonight, comfort mattered.

It would be difficult. He wasn't just telling his children about the expedition—he was placing them in harm's way. Cedric and Aaron would join him, but Heather and Eric would stay behind, safe at home.

For a fleeting moment, the irrational thought of taking Heather and Eric along crossed his mind. He dismissed it. They would be protected here. Bringing them would be madness, and yet... leaving them behind didn't sit well with him either.

The front door creaked open.

Eric entered, clutching an armful of books as always. Gideon paused, setting aside his tasks to help him. The boy looked up with a grateful nod as his father took the weight from his arms and placed the books carefully on the table.

"Where did you find these?" Gideon asked, lifting one with a worn cover and dogeared pages. "These aren't from the library."

"The butcher, Mister Mesqindil, found them in a crate and gave them to me!"

Gideon smiled, encouraged by his son's enthusiasm. "What kind of books are they?"

"I don't know yet, but I'll start reading them tonight. One's about the adventures of a bandit. It's missing a few pages, though. I hope that doesn't leave too many holes for me to fill in."

"Well, that was gracious of Freese to let you borrow them."

"He said I could keep them. I don't have to give them back. I can add them to my collection. One day I'm going to start my own library."

Gideon chuckled. "When you're finished, take them back and offer to return them—just to be sure. Maybe write him a thank you note, too. Deliver it in person. It'll show your appreciation."

Eric grinned. "Yes, I'll do that."

"Go ahead and put the books in your room," Gideon said, gesturing toward the hallway. "And when you're finished, I want to talk to you about your upcoming birthday. I've got a surprise for you."

"Yes!" Eric grinned, clutching the nearest stack to his chest.

Gideon watched as his youngest son made two trips, carefully carrying the precious volumes to his room where they would join the growing collection he was so proud of.

It gnawed at him—Eric's birthday was fast approaching, and it was likely he, Cedric, and Aaron would be gone. Investigating the Mage-Gate—and hopefully destroying it—would take weeks, perhaps longer if they encountered trouble. He told himself it wouldn't take more than a month.

But deep down, Gideon knew better than to make such promises.

The responsibility pressed hard against Gideon's shoulders, a weight from all sides—his duty as a father, his duty as Grand Druid, and the harsh truth of the world they lived in. If he failed to destroy the Mage-Gate, the world would face dangers beyond imagining. And if the world was in peril, so too was his family.

He understood he could never shield them from every threat—no one could—but he would do what was necessary, even if that meant standing alone against his fellow druids. The Mage-Gate had to be destroyed, or the site made so inhospitable that no sane soul would attempt to reclaim it. Years, if not decades, of digging would be required to uncover what he intended to bury.

He had a spell for that—an obscure, complex working bound within an old scroll. A spell that would reduce the keep and everything inside it to rubble. The components were simple enough. The magic was anything but. It would scar the land, collapse the buildings, shatter the Mage-Gate, and erase the threat.

And yet… it concerned him. The Council had voted for investigation, not destruction. By plotting otherwise, he was breaking his word.

But what was a promise weighed against the safety of the world?

Eric returned, quiet as always, respectful and patient.

Gideon glanced at him, amused. "You're not going to ask me about your birthday present?"

Eric tilted his head. "You seem preoccupied. Pensive. I've been standing here a while… you didn't notice me."

Gideon chuckled softly. "Lots on my mind." He leaned back. "Your birthday present?"

"I figured you'd bring it up," Eric replied, his tone calm. "I didn't want to seem too eager."

Gideon smiled. "It's alright to show a little enthusiasm. We're family. We understand each other's ways. You are patient, Eric—that's a rare thing for your age, and it'll serve you well. But you can still be excited about your birthday."

Eric's expression remained steady. "Father, don't mistake patience for lack of courage. I have courage. I just believe… everything has its moment. That's how I think."

Gideon regarded him with pride. "Fair enough. Point taken." He let the pause linger, then said, "Well, since you've been so patient—and courageous—I'll tell you. The gift I have for you is a journey. You're going on an excursion that I think you'll find fascinating… and perhaps, enlightening."

"I don't want to go to the Stairwell or visit the capital of Haddensack," Eric said, his tone careful, almost apologetic. "I don't mean to sound ungrateful. I'm sorry."

Gideon studied him, appreciating the honesty.

Aaron had gone to the Stairwell for his fifteenth birthday. Cedric had journeyed to Haddensack to see the capital's bustling markets and towering spires. But neither destination suited Eric. Gideon knew why—neither held what his youngest son treasured most. Books.

"As it happens," Gideon said with a smile, "I've arranged something different. A month-long excursion to Ornst. You'll study with the librarians at their great library. They say the Ornst Library holds more books, scrolls, and tablets than there are people in the world."

Eric's face lit up. He leapt into his father's arms, squeezing him tight. "I don't know what to say—I've always dreamed of going to the Ornst Library! The Ornst Library! Merrow Keff was a librarian there. Or an assistant one."

"Well, your dream is coming true," Gideon said, his smile widening. "On your birthday, you'll set out for Ornst. The head librarian has agreed to host you for one month as a special guest. You'll assist with restoring damaged tomes, cataloguing new arrivals, and helping however they need. They even offered to pay you a modest wage for your efforts." He gave Eric a playful look. "But there's one condition—you must come back home. You can't stay there forever, even if you try."

"I'll get to read! And get paid?" Eric's face shone with wonder.

"Yes, you'll read and earn some coin," Gideon chuckled. "Every young man's dream."

"This is the most incredible news! I can't wait." Eric broke the hug, stepping back with a rare, radiant grin. But the joy flickered, giving way to hesitation. "Why are you telling me now? My birthday isn't for a couple of weeks."

Gideon sighed, bracing himself for the harder truth. "I must set out on a mission for the Druid Council. I may… I *will* be gone when your birthday comes." He rested a hand on Eric's shoulder, squeezing gently. "But everything is arranged. Cipher is heading to Ornst with his merchant caravan. You'll travel with them, and the Library will handle your return when your time there is done. They've committed to a month, though I wouldn't be surprised if they ask you to stay longer." He smiled, though it felt heavy in his chest. "You may accept, if you wish. Just not forever."

"Thank you so much," Eric said, his face glowing. "This is a dream come true! I'm so excited I want to pack my things right now!"

"To be truthful, it *is* a good idea to get things ready. Ornst is in the south—warmer than here. You won't need much. Go on, start organizing your trip."

Eric darted off toward his room, his enthusiasm leaving an echo of energy behind.

Gideon remained where he was, drawing in a slow, deliberate breath. He let it out through his nose, trying to settle the knot of tension twisting in his chest.

This business with the Mage-Gate… it worried him. Deep down, he feared it would be the end of him. And yet, he was sending Aaron and Cedric to stand beside him in the thick of it. Was it the right thing? He couldn't say with certainty.

But his gut told him it had to be done.

The dinner table buzzed with talk of Eric's trip to Ornst. Gideon welcomed the distraction, letting Eric ramble on about everything he planned to see, read, and explore at the great library.

The meat pies and roasted vegetables had vanished quickly—duck fat had a way of turning even simple fare into a worthy, savory delight. Gideon nursed another glass of *Andy's Fireside Brandy*, the bottle now tipping toward empty. Finishing it no longer seemed an impossible task.

When Eric finally ran out of plans and possibilities, a hush settled over the table.

It was time.

Gideon struck the table with the butt of his dinner knife, the sharp crack slicing through the quiet. All eyes turned to him. He took one last sip of brandy and set the glass aside, steadying himself.

"I need to speak with you, as a family, about an urgent matter. What I'm about to tell you stays within this house—within this room. You are not to speak of it outside this table, not to friends, not to neighbors, no one. Only with each other, and only when you are certain no one else is listening. Do you understand me?"
Gideon let the silence stretch, ensuring they felt the weight of his words. When each of them nodded, he remained still. "Say it aloud."

One by one, they answered in turn.

"I understand," Cedric said first.

"I understand," Aaron echoed, his brow furrowing.

"I understand," Eric added quietly.

"I understand," Heather finished, her gaze steady.

Gideon clasped his hands, his tone shifting to something heavier. "Far to the east, buried beneath ancient ruins, we have discovered an artifact. It's called a Mage-Gate."

Aaron blinked. "A what? I've never heard of that before."

"Isn't it just a portal?" Eric asked. "I read about… I don't remember where."

"A Mage-Gate is a physical portal, yes," Gideon replied, "but it's imbued with celestial magic beyond the comprehension of ordinary men. In the old days, when the Mages ruled, it was how they moved from place to place—hidden, undetected."

"Why didn't they just teleport?" Cedric asked. "Weren't Mages basically wizards?"

"Not exactly," Gideon said, shaking his head. "Mages had abilities far beyond even the most powerful wizards—some say godlike. And while wizards can teleport, that kind of magic leaves traces. Others can sense it, track where you came from or where you're going. Mage-Gates left no such trail."

"Why did they need such secrecy?" Heather asked, her brow tightening.

Gideon paused, his gaze lingering on each of them before he answered.

"The Mage-Gate can move armies, supplies—anything—from one gate to another without anyone knowing," Gideon explained. "During the Rise of the Mages, there were thought to be dozens scattered across Eldor, hidden in key places and guarded by terrible things. Imagine stepping through a Mage-Gate in the far east of Faustron and appearing… in the Ornst Library."

"You could rootwalk," Aaron said, tilting his head. "What, fourteen hops?"

Gideon allowed himself a small smile. "Sounds about right. As long as there are forests near the Ornst Library, of course."

"Weren't there two brothers?" Eric asked, snapping his fingers as if the names hovered just beyond reach.

"Yes. The Yholl brothers—two powerful Mages who ruled with terror. These gates were their tools of domination—"

"Dergan and Mikal Yholl," Eric cut in with a triumphant snap. "That's them. I read about them. They were monsters. Wanted to kill everyone. They worshipped devils and demons, right?"

"They did," Gideon answered grimly, his mind drifting to the putrid demons Heather and Lillia had faced.

"But… didn't they also chronicle knowledge?" Eric pressed, his brow furrowed. "That was when all the ancient texts were written, wasn't it?"

"They were obsessed with cataloguing everything—physical, metaphysical, things even the gods might not have wanted recorded."

Gideon waved off the next question before it could form. "It's an unfortunate part of our history. When the Mages ruled, the lands were in chaos. Strife, endless war, cruelty beyond imagination. Creatures, men, women… slaughtered by the thousands. During that time, the lesser races were nearly wiped out."

"Lesser races?" Heather asked, tilting her head. "I've never heard that term before."

"It's an old term Humans used," Gideon explained, his tone careful. "It referred to Gnomes, Dwarves, Elves, and the Fey. I don't use it to suggest they're lesser—but that's how they were labeled back then. No disrespect is meant."

"It was meant as disrespect," Eric said quietly, meeting his father's gaze. "I read that in a book about Dwarves. Humans used it to elevate themselves above the other races. The Mages—they were human, weren't they?"

Gideon allowed himself a small nod, glad to see Eric challenging him. "As far as we know, they were human. I think otherwise. There are mentions of 'celestial blood.' And you're right, Eric. The Mages ruled with such brutality that they nearly drove those races to extinction. That's why the Fey, the Elves—they stay hidden even now. Their societies never truly reopened. They remember. They fear what those Mages did, and they remain wary of humans… especially humans who wield magic."

"A Mage-Gate was found," Aaron muttered, his brow furrowing. "A network of hidden gates… What are you planning to do with it? Study it? Open it and see where it leads?"

"Absolutely not," Gideon said, firm. "We will *not* activate it. That's why I've called you together. I will be going east with other druids, rangers of the Stairwell, warriors, and a cleric to investigate the Mage-Gate."

The room erupted into protest. His children spoke over each other—voices rising, pleading, insisting he couldn't leave them behind, that it was too dangerous. Gideon let them vent, waiting until the flurry of words softened into frustrated silence. He tapped the butt end of his dinner knife against the table until their attention returned to him.

"I will be taking Cedric and Aaron with me," he said evenly.

The outcry shifted. This time it was Eric and Heather's turn to protest, while Cedric and Aaron beamed, clearly thrilled at the prospect of an adventure alongside their father.

Again, Gideon let them speak, giving them space to feel heard before tapping the knife against the table once more, restoring order.

"I'm not going to make excuses for why Eric and Heather aren't coming with us," Gideon began, his tone calm but weighty. "You're both capable. Heather, you've proven yourself resourceful and tough—Lillia herself said as much. Eric, you know more about this world than most adults I know."

He paused, swirling the last of the brandy in his cup before taking a slow sip.

"But this one time, I need to leave you both behind. And I promise you—*if the time comes when you're needed, you will go. But not yet.*"

He let the words hang in the stillness before continuing.

"The reason Cedric and Aaron are coming is because I trust them. I need two people at my side whose loyalty is beyond question. There will be others with us—but they are there to investigate, to assess if the ruins or the Mage-Gate hold any value. Cedric, Aaron—*we are not going there to study the Mage-Gate.*"

His voice sharpened.

"We are going there to destroy it—or bury it under enough stone and earth that no one will ever find it again. Gates like that lead to dark places, to evils that could tear this world apart if left unchecked. I won't risk that. Not for treasure, not for knowledge, not for anything."

Cedric nodded. "Understood."

"Destroying it seems harsh," Aaron said. "Are you sure we need to do that? We could learn more about magic."

Gideon had expected Aaron to push back. The boy's thirst for knowledge mirrored his own at that age. He only hoped his explanation would carry enough weight to curb that instinct—for now.

"No good will come from letting anyone near it," Gideon said, his voice firm. "The Mage-Gates were crafted by men who sought domination, not discovery. And those two—Dergan and Mikal Yholl—when they turned on each other, the world was nearly torn apart. It's been a thousand years, Aaron. We're still cleaning up their mess."

He hesitated, then added quietly, almost more to himself than his children, "And there are worse things than the Mage-Gate itself. *If it's still linked to places of legend, it could lead to… things best left buried. Relics that were never meant to be found. The Librums. You've heard the name, Aaron. You know what they could do in the wrong hands.*"

A silence fell over the table. Even Aaron looked sobered by the weight in his father's voice.

"I will do as you ask," Aaron said at last. "But I want it understood—I intend to study the Mage-Gate. I'll learn whatever I can, if the opportunity presents itself."

Gideon nodded. "Fair enough. Learn what you can—but the priority is destruction. We leave in one week. Which means… yes, we'll miss Eric's birthday."

Aaron kept his face neutral, but inside, a quiet war had begun. *Destroy it. Bury it. Seal it away.* It all made sense, but a part of him bristled at the idea that knowledge—any knowledge—shouldn't be hidden forever.

They feared the ancient magic, but wasn't it more dangerous not to understand it? Wasn't ignorance the seed of fear?

He clenched his hands under the table, forcing the thought down for now. *Yet… if an opportunity presented itself—one he couldn't yet see—he would be ready.*

"I'm going to Ornst in two weeks, so Heather will be here by herself," Eric said. "Maybe I should stay and go later. I don't want her to be alone."

"Finola has agreed to watch over Heather," Gideon replied, his tone leaving little room for argument. "She'll check on you daily, but she won't be staying in the house. Heather, that means you'll need to handle things after Eric leaves. And no wandering near Druid's Glen or the tangle. You stick to the house, the village, or the river. Understood?"

"Understood," Heather said, though her voice carried a thread of stubbornness. She squared her shoulders, unwilling to let it go without one last try. "But wouldn't it make more sense if I went with you? I proved I can handle myself. You said it yourself—Lillia said it, too. I wouldn't slow you down."

Gideon's expression hardened. "It's been decided. You will stay. That's final."

Heather clenched her jaw but forced herself to nod. She would obey—but she wouldn't forget. Not this.

"What about the wizard who came to the Glen?" she asked, pressing once more. "Lillia said he might return. What if he does while you're gone?"

"He may," Gideon admitted. "He was spying on us, and we still don't know what information he gathered. But Finola will be here, and she's more than capable if he dares to return."

Heather nodded, the weight of the acorn heavy in her pocket. If trouble came, she had a weapon no one else possessed—Lillia's promise. It was a big *if*, but enough to calm her worries, for now. Though part of her still longed to see the Mage-Gate with her own eyes, she accepted her place would be here. Once Eric left for Ornst, the house would be hers alone. The thought stirred a quiet thrill. Yes, she would miss them—but she would also prove to her father that she could manage the home, keep up her studies, and finish her staff.

"I'll be fine," she said, more confidently this time.

Gideon's expression remained hard. "I need to reiterate the seriousness of this mission. It will be dangerous—more dangerous than you can imagine. Cedric, Aaron… you'll be under my command, and you will do as I say without hesitation. No questioning my orders, no second-guessing. Is that clear?"

"Yes," they replied together, their voices steady.

Gideon reached beneath the table and brought forth a worn wooden box. He opened it, the hinges creaking. Inside rested the two enchanted necklaces from the Glen's hidden cache. He handed one to each of his sons.

"Wear these always," he said, his voice softer now but no less firm. "They will protect you—for as long as you wear them."

"What does it do?" Cedric asked as he accepted the gold chain.

He unclasped it, slipped it over his head—and froze.

A subtle hum of magic coursed through him, spreading like warmth beneath his skin. It filled him with a fleeting calm, a sense of security that made his breath catch. Then the feeling faded, settling into the background of his senses.

"Oh," he breathed, fingertips brushing the charm. "I feel it."

Beside him, Aaron turned the necklace over in his hands, his sharp eyes studying the fine links as if they might reveal secrets to him. He set it on the table and whispered a simple divination cantrip. Faint glyphs shimmered over the chain for a heartbeat, confirming what his instincts had already told him.

"Magical protection," Aaron confirmed, glancing at his father. "Does it have other properties? Anything hidden?"

"No," Gideon said. "Only protection." His gaze hardened. "But that will only be part of what keeps you alive. Before we depart, I'll make sure we have every spell and weapon we need for what's ahead. I know you've been practicing, but this will be different. Starting tomorrow, you'll train with me. Each day until we depart, you'll learn a set of spells that may—will—save your life."

"What about me and Eric?" Heather asked, her voice firmer than Gideon expected. "Can we study with you? I'd love to learn one spell. Just one."

Gideon shook his head. "Normal studies for you two. Your routine doesn't change. In one week, we leave. In two weeks, Eric travels with Cipher to Ornst. While I'm gone, I expect both of you to be where you're supposed to be and see to your duties. No wandering. No shortcuts. Finola will check on you, and you'll respect her authority. Understood?"

Both nodded, though Heather's was slower, more reluctant.

He sighed, leaning forward. "I need to hear you say it."

"Understood," they said together, though the word sat heavy on Heather's tongue.

Gideon let the moment stretch as he studied them—Cedric devouring his meat pie, oblivious to the tension. Aaron still studying the necklace, eyes narrowed, already dissecting its enchantment as if it were some relic of lost days. Eric nibbled at his crust, quiet as ever. Heather sat with her face half-hidden in her hands, staring at him with those blue eyes—her mother's eyes.

"What's troubling you, Heather?" he asked, keeping his tone soft.

She hesitated, her fingers tightening. "I was thinking… what if the wizard we fought and the Mage-Gate are connected? What if he's not coming back here because… he's already where he wants to be?" Her gaze flicked to him, searching. "What if he's already at the Mage-Gate?"

Gideon blinked, surprised despite himself.

That was sharp. Sharp and dangerous thinking. She was as quick as her mother, maybe quicker. And certainly quicker than him.

"I've considered that," he admitted after a pause, his voice lower now, the truth heavier for it.

Chapter Six

∞

Into the Trap

The week passed quickly. Heather lingered on the edge of the clearing, pretending to be unobtrusive but taking in every detail. She wanted to remember everything about this moment—her father checking packs, the warmth of the clearing, and the sound of the wind in the fiery leaves of The One Tree—because once they were gone, everything would feel a little emptier.

She and Eric were there with Finola, waiting for the party to depart. Druid's Glen was beautiful, full of woodland creatures and meadows of grass and flowers. The One Tree was imposing, and she found that she couldn't stop staring at it. It was the widest tree she had ever seen, and it had the prettiest fiery, red leaves.

Near The One Tree, her father, Cedric, and Aaron were checking their packs for the final time. They had enough supplies to last several days, various weapons, material components for different spells, and warm clothing to endure the colder climes in the northeast.

Next to them were two rangers from the Stairwell, Val and Sarif. They were broad, strong looking men, with furtive, watchful eyes. Both carried longswords and small shields, hand axes, broadaxes, knives, and bows. They wore leather armor that wasn't the best protection in battle but would allow them freedom of movement.

A priestess from the Temple of Thatara had joined the expedition. She was an expert in healing, curative spells, and caring for wounds. Her name was Chefera, and she was as distracted as Heather was by the beauty of The One Tree.

Aurora arrived, as Gideon expected, to accompany them to the ruins. She looked pale and was coughing, mentioning curtly that her ailment was temporary and would pass.

Gideon knew the truth—she was dying, of what he didn't know, and he could see that she wasn't long for this world. He had seen too many friends march through life with that same hollow cough—the kind that starts small but ends in silence.

He wondered if she would make it back alive.

The assembled companions inside Druid's Glen checked their supplies for the last time. Their destination was Wilmund's grove, where he was waiting for them. From there, they would go to the ruins and begin the investigation.

Gideon wondered if Aurora already suspected the truth—that when this was over, he would destroy the Mage-Gate. Deep down, he believed she did.

Once the Council learned what he had done, it would tear them apart. He had agreed to investigate, to study the ruins and report back. To defy that mandate would be seen as betrayal. What the Council might do to him afterward… he would face that when the time came.

For now, his path was clear. He would investigate the Mage-Gate, keep his sons and their companions alive, and, when the moment came, ensure the gate was destroyed—whatever the cost.

Gideon had the group gather close around The One Tree. They would travel the great distance using tree-stride and numerous waypoints.

The common folk thought druids spent time walking the forests, visiting with animals and tending to plant life. That was true, yet what was not widely known was the real reason druids familiarized themselves with forests far and wide was being able to use the tree-stride spell.

Less experienced druids, such as Aaron and Cedric, could only rootwalk several miles to places they had been before. He, the Grand Druid, could travel hundreds of miles in a single incantation. Using his waypoints and the forests he knew, he could travel to Kaalnaes in hours—a journey by horse would take two months. He had mapped out twelve waypoints to get to Kaalnaes, even though he figured he could do it in eight if pressed. It would be tiring to take the entire party with him, so he shortened the tree-strides for his and their sakes.

Gideon conjured the tree-stride spell, murmuring the word of power. Their first waypoint was Sonner, a small barony near the southern edge of the expanse of the Needle Forest, but just north of the Upper Skelk River. It was the shortest hop they would make—

meant to ease the group into the disorienting pull of the network of living things.

He finished the incantation, placed a steadying hand on Cedric's shoulder, and the world folded around them as they stepped into The One Tree.

Heather and Eric watched their father and brothers disappear.

Finola was by their side and reassured them, "They'll be fine. They'll be safe."

"I know," Heather said. "Father is the greatest druid ever."

"Indeed. Now, do you two have studies today?" Finola asked.

"I'm supposed to classify trees," Heather said.

"I'm researching pirates," Eric said. "My father did mention to you that I'm not on the traditional druid path, didn't he?"

"Yes, he did mention that." Finola laughed. "I know your education is not traditional, and I'm not saying that is unacceptable. Different that's for sure. Books are a distinct sort of wisdom, I suppose. But nature has its own truths, and that's the kind I know best."

Eric noted a hint of sarcasm in her tone. "You think I should be studying the druidic ways? I'd make a terrible druid."

"As a druid, I think everyone should study nature regardless, the strength of the earth, and the power of the air we breathe. I don't see the appeal of books, these pirates you want to learn about, brigands on the seas—rubbish. But I'm not your parent. Do as you wish."

"That is true, you aren't my mother," Eric said, his tone was not friendly.

Heather backhanded him. She didn't want Finola to get worked up on the first day within the first minute of their father being away.

"Enough talk about that," Heather said. "Our studies are our studies. When will we see you next?"

"I'm staying in Arboretum proper, so I will come around in the evening to make sure you two are settled. If you need anything, I will be staying at The Shrew and Hound until your father returns. Do you know of it?"

"It's the other way around," Eric said. "The Hound and Shrew. Don't worry about us, we know how to take care of ourselves."

"Good, I'm counting on it. Babysitting is not an endeavor I want to be known for. In fact, it's embarrassing that I agreed to do this. I should have trusted an underling with this… chore. Yet, you are the children of the Grand Druid, and he asked for my help."

Eric crossed his arms and said, "If it's such a burden, then you can go back to the Midlands. We'll be fine. Our father doesn't have to know."

"Tempting, but when you agree to a task for the Grand Druid, even something this trivial, you must follow through on your promise. Understood? I'm watching you whether *we* like it or not. And I don't like it that much, but I will do it because I promised the Grand Druid."

"We don't like it either," Heather said. A knot tightened in Heather's stomach, an instinct she couldn't quite name. It wasn't Finola's words—it was the way she stood, like she was waiting for a door to open. "We will behave if you promise to not mess with our lives."

"I accept your proposal." Finola motioned to The One Tree. "Take one last look. It may be years, or never, when you get to see this wondrous tree again. Come now, I'll guide you through the tangle, unless you want to test the defenses yourself and spend the week tending to your wounds. I will not be helping you with that."

Heather and Eric trudged back from Druid's Glen, the absence of their family leaving a strange quiet in the forest that surrounded their home. It wasn't quite lonely, but Heather felt the weight of their departure. She glanced sideways at Eric, who was lost in thought.

"I wish we could've gone with them," Heather muttered, kicking a loose pebble from the path. Normally, the trail was scattered with pinecones to kick, but today it was bare. "Where are all the pinecones?"

Eric raised an eyebrow, but didn't comment, his focus elsewhere. After a pause, he finally said, "It could be worse. Lillia could have volunteered to watch over us."

Heather stopped mid-step and her face lit up. "Oh, *that* would be worse for me, huh? Not you?" She elbowed him hard in the shoulder.

"You've already seen *way* too much of her, haven't you? You, Aaron, and Cedric!"

Eric's ears turned bright red, and he looked away, rubbing his aching shoulder. "That was… unfortunate… what happened to you."

"Oh please, you'll only remember that a bare-butt dryad pranced through our house."

"You're *never* going to let that go, are you?" he asked, his tone serious.

"Nope."

Eric groaned but managed a nervous laugh. "Anyway, we'll stay out of Finola's way. As long as *you* don't cause trouble."

"Me?"

"Yes, you! You're always defying Lana and getting in trouble. How is this going to be any different?"

"I don't defy her," Heather said, protesting. "I point out all this stupid stuff I already know."

"Maybe you should volunteer to help her then," Eric said. "If you're so smart."

"I know Finola will find a reason to mess with us," Heather grumbled, changing the subject. "She's trouble, not me. I just know it. At least you get to go to the Ornst Library. I get to stay here with Miss Prickly Cone."

When they reached the front porch, neither bothered to remove their boots. Eric had his studies waiting for him at the kitchen table, while Heather would spend her time outdoors with Lana and the other novices. As they opened the door, the familiar smells of home greeted them—ash from the hearth, porridge from breakfast, and the lingering sweetness of maple syrup. But there was another scent, sharp and fresh.

"Do you smell that?" Heather asked, wrinkling her nose.

Eric moved toward the table and picked up a leaf resting in the center. "This is for you," he said, holding it out.

Heather snatched it, a bit too forcefully, tearing off the corner that Eric still held between his fingers. She unfolded it and read the message scrawled in Cedric's unmistakable handwriting:

Sleep well, Princess of the Pines.

She cocked her head to the side. "What is this supposed to mean?"

Eric shrugged. "Cedric's handwriting. You might want to check our room."

Heather groaned. "Ugh." She stormed toward the hallway, the leaf still clenched in her hand. "If he messed with my stuff, I swear—" Her voice cut off as she reached their shared room and swung the door open.

She froze.

Her bed—and her entire side of the room—was buried in pinecones. They were everywhere. Piled on her pillow, spilling out from under her blanket, balanced on the windowsill, and tucked into her spare boots and shoes by the bed. The air was thick with the earthy scent of pine resin.

A single pinecone sat perched atop the mound, and beneath it, another folded leaf. Heather grabbed it and unfolded it with a snap. Two words stared back at her in Cedric's neat scrawl:

We're even.

Her hands tightened around the note as her mouth fell open. "Even? This is even?"

Behind her, Eric peeked around the doorframe and let out a low whistle. "Wow. He really got you. That's…a lot of pinecones."

Heather spun around, glaring. "Even? *Even?*" She grabbed the nearest pinecone and hurled it at Eric's head.

He ducked and grinned. "Hey, at least he kept it on your side of the room."

"Get out," Heather growled, snatching another pinecone.

"Gladly," Eric said, retreating quickly as another pinecone sailed over his shoulder and smacked against the overflowing bookcase. "Good luck cleaning that up. Try not to be late for your studies!"

Heather fumed as he disappeared, tossing one last pinecone after him for good measure. She looked back at the crumpled leaf in her hand, her expression softening into a sly grin.

"It's not over until *I* say it's over," she muttered under her breath. She smoothed out the note and placed it on the bookcase before turning back to the sea of pinecones with a glint of mischief in her eyes.

A week passed and it was Eric's fifteenth birthday. They had no word from their father about what was going on in the east. Finola wasn't forthcoming with anything she had heard. That morning Heather made a breakfast for Eric of wheat pancakes with real syrup she harvested from local trees, along with fresh farm eggs from the market. She messed up the pancakes, they turned out tough as bark, but Eric was gracious and ate them anyway.

Cipher showed up as promised, the numerous wagons of the caravan full of durable goods to be taken to Ornst for sale. There was barely room for Eric to accompany them.

Heather said her goodbyes and lingered watching them leave, hoping Eric would enjoy his time in Ornst. She had no concept of the city other than what she had heard—that it was as big as the entire Needle Forest with structures taller than The One Tree. She couldn't imagine buildings and buildings for as far as the eye could see. It amazed her too that each structure had a purpose.

She kept up with her studies despite the inclination to skip. What she found is, without the family, she had too much time on her hands. Yes, there were basic chores and she had to eat, but taking care of herself was easy. So much so, that she had oodles of time to spend completing her staff.

The length was perfect, the diameter was comfortable in her hands, and the mottled look of it, alternating white sycamore and black bramble, was mesmerizing. The only unnatural look to it were the lines she etched on it, as druids did, to measure a tree's diameter, and the druidic runes she had burned into the length of it.

It felt good in her hands, and she felt invincible when she was practicing with it. Now that she had a serious weapon, she always kept it with her along with a long knife.

Though it had been weeks ago, the memory of the wizard was fresh in her mind and kept her suspicious of anything unusual. Thus far, the unusual hadn't materialized into anything.

The Archdruid Finola was effective as a 'babysitter', preferring to spend five minutes talking to Heather then moving on to whatever else she was doing that day.

Another week passed without word from her father. It didn't worry her as he said they may not be able to communicate with each other.

She did want to know what was going on with the Mage-Gate and she wanted to know that her family was safe.

This morning's studies were about mosses and grasses that grew in the forest. She knew lichens well, understanding they covered trees—some were harmful, others weren't. Three types existed; leaflike lichens that adhered to the trees loosely, crusty lichens that tightly attached, and round lichens that had no distinct top or bottom.

Grasses were numerous and categorized into sedges, reeds, rushes, and traditional grass often identified by stalks, seeds, or what it looked like—like purple oat grass.

She sped out of her home, running down the path toward where the lesson would begin for the morning. Full of energy, she sprinted as fast as she could, pretending hell hounds were snapping at her heels, breathing fire with every step.

The path went by in a blur, as did the trees lining the path. Her footfalls were sure and true. The gangly girl slowed when she reached the clearing, certain she had outrun the devilish beasts again if she had to. She wasn't winded, and she thought, *I could run all day if I had to.*

Lana, their instructor, was already there organizing pieces of parchment for the lesson. She had specimen bags with different grasses and lichens that she was setting on tables for the students to inspect, touch, and smell.

"Need any help?" Heather asked, remembering Eric's idea.

Lana looked up from her task, surprised to hear a voice before class. "Heather, you are early today, why so eager?"

"Hell hounds were chasing me, so I had to run here. Didn't have a choice."

Lana scanned the edges of the clearing and said, "I didn't know hell hounds were native to the Needle Forest. Did you catch one of these hounds for study? We must understand their species."

"Nope, just outran them. Next time I'll subdue one and bring it to you. Maybe it'll make a good pet."

Lana scoffed. "Probably not. Can you match the species with the correct bags?"

Lana held up a bag and a piece of parchment with the name of the plant, almost as if it were a challenge.

"What order would you like it in?"

"Lichens to the left, then grasses to the right."

Heather presented her hands and took the stack of parchment. As instructed, she put the ten lichens on the left and the twelve different grasses on the right. She put them in alphabetical order as well. Then she took the bags and matched them up.

"Done," Heather announced.

"That quickly? Are you sure?" Lana asked in that teacher's voice.

"Positive."

Lana checked Heather's work. All twenty-two subjects were correctly organized. She sighed.

"I suppose you could teach this class," she muttered.

"Probably not. You're good at teaching, I'm good at learning. Just because I learn well doesn't mean I can teach it."

"Well said. I suppose I owe you a reward of sorts? Yes?"

Heather shrugged her shoulders. There wasn't much to do now that Eric was gone. Wandering the forest by herself wouldn't be allowed. She would love to go exploring. Then she was reminded of the wizard, the innocent looking hare that turned into a vile person who tried to kill her and Lillia.

"I'm fine staying here today. I can help with the lesson if you want."

"That makes me curious. Weeks ago, you would have jumped at the chance to bypass a lesson, and now you are willing to help me teach it. What's changed?"

"Nothing. I'd prefer to be around people while my father is away. It's safer."

Which was the truth. Being alone, as refreshing as it seemed, wasn't that much fun. It wasn't companionship she needed, it was strength in numbers—she didn't think the wizard would return if he knew she was around others and had druids to protect her.

"Safer? And where did you say your father went?"

"I didn't say," Heather replied coolly. "And stop prying. If you must know, they're looking at a special tree they found in the Leafy Forest."

"Oh, certainly," Lana said, her tone thick with sarcasm. "That explains why two Stairwell rangers, a cleric, and both your brothers went with him. And Finola, skulking in the woods to keep an eye on you. I do have eyes, girl—don't forget that. But enough of this. No good will come of it. I'm sure your father made you promise not to speak of it, and I won't be the one to tempt you into breaking your word."

Heather clenched her jaw, biting back the retort burning on her tongue. *You have a mouth—now keep it shut for once.*

It was exhausting, the way everyone expected her to have all the answers. Even if she did know more than most, she wasn't about to prance around like a peacock.

So she smiled thinly and said nothing, running her fingers along her staff.

Rumors swirled, as they always did—none of them close to the truth.

They all thought she was just a kid.

But she knew exactly what her family was doing.

Additional days passed with no word from Faustron. Heather was getting restless, longing for information about her family. Finola checked on her each day as promised, she studied with Lana on the prescribed days, and practiced her fighting forms with her staff.

It wasn't the same without a training partner, even the disinterested Eric.

It was a warm spring day, and she was down by the swollen stream with a net trying to catch trout. Silver ones were the tastiest, and she thought she could catch one, clean it, and cook it for dinner. Dip netting wasn't too difficult, but it did take skill to find the right spot.

She was knee deep in the stream with her trouser legs rolled up. She waded farther out so she could get to a place where the fish might be lurking under the surface. It would take patience.

"What are you doing?"

The voice startled Heather, and the net slipped from her grip. She fumbled it, barely catching it by the tethered safety float before it hit the surface.

Her heart raced.

It was Finola.

"Fishing," Heather said, hiding her panic. "You scared me."

"Apologies, that wasn't the intent. So, fishing are you? Is this how you were taught to fish? Interesting."

"I don't have a second net, but you're welcome to try with my net if I don't catch anything. It takes patience, the key is finding a good spot—I think there are some fat ones around here."

Heather turned toward the Archdruid.

Finola wasn't in her robes today. She was in light leather armor that looked supple and comfortable. A curved sword was attached to her back, and in her left hand was her brown, gnarled staff. She had numerous pouches along her weapon's belt and a light pack that wouldn't hamper movement. She looked ready for travel.

"I was wondering, would you like to train today?" Finola asked. "I'm getting restless, and I'm sure you are too. We need to keep our bodies as active as our minds."

Heather almost tossed the net aside—training sounded far better than fishing. But if she didn't catch dinner, the cupboard would be bare.

"I need to catch fish first. It may take me a while. Can we go later? I don't want to have to scrounge scraps for dinner."

Finola motioned with her hand, causing the water to shift and swell. The stream diverted into the air, bringing with it several trout who were none the wiser. She directed the water toward the bank, where the trout swam until Finola released the spell.

The water splattered on the ground, along with the trout.

There were four fat ones and two smaller ones flopping around.

Heather made her way to the bank and put two fat ones in her basket, then tossed the remaining fish back into the water before they suffocated.

Heather's expression turned dark. "Father wouldn't approve of that. Not very sporting."

"Your father doesn't need to know. Our little secret."

Finola put an upraised index finger to her mouth, shushing Heather, then flashed her brown eyes in the direction of Druid's Glen.

"Take your fish home and do what you need to do. Meet me outside Druid's Glen when you're ready, but don't get too close to the tangle. I'll show you how to use that lovely staff of yours."

Heather didn't hesitate, she ran back to her home, basket, boots, and staff nestled in her arms. She killed the two fish, thanked them for the sustenance they would give her for two days, and put them in a bucket of water. They would stay fresh if she kept them in the shade.

She was excited to train with another druid. Finola knew what she was doing, and it intrigued Heather as well to learn more about combat. Her brothers only bested her because of their strength, not because of technique. Finally—something interesting to break the monotony of the day.

She was wearing more appropriate attire for training—sturdy boots, thicker trousers, and a leather jerkin that acted somewhat like armor. Though she lacked the protective gear Finola wore, the outfit made her feel prepared, or at least closer to it.

On her belt was her knife, and in her hands, the mottled staff. She liked the way the wood felt against her palms—solid, grounding—but she wondered if it would be enough to carry her through what lay ahead.

As she walked the narrow path through the woods, the late morning sun warmed her back, a reminder that the upcoming summer would soon fade into autumn—and with it, her druid trials would finally arrive.

The thought made her stomach churn.

The trials weren't just a test—they were everything. Two weeks alone in the wilderness with nothing but her wits, her staff, and her knife.

Surviving wasn't enough.

She had to demonstrate understanding, connection, mastery.

The forest would demand as much from her as her instructors would, and if she failed… well, she didn't want to think about what that would mean.

But she did think about it—too often.

What if she wasn't good enough?

What if she came back failed, or worse, didn't come back at all?

What if she made it halfway through and realized that no matter how many plants she could identify or staves she could wield, she simply wasn't cut out to be a druid?

What if everyone found out she was… ordinary?

Her brothers made everything look so easy—Cedric with his quick thinking and action, Aaron with his stubborn confidence—and he knew everything.

It didn't help that they treated her like their little sister who was always one step behind. No matter how hard she practiced, how many times she drilled the same forms, that nagging voice whispered in the back of her mind: *You're going to fail.*

And then there was Eric.

He'd passed his trials—not because he wanted to, but because their father had asked him to. *Two weeks,* Eric had grumbled, *just to get it done.*

And he had.

He went into the woods, did everything he was supposed to, came back with the right results, and told their father, *No thanks. No druid life for me.* As if the whole thing had been a mild inconvenience, like shoveling snow off the front porch.

That's what made it worse. Not that Eric had succeeded—she was proud of him, she loved him—but that he'd passed without caring. He wasn't a druid, he didn't want to be one, and yet he'd managed to finish the trials.

And if *he* could do it and still walk away, what did that say about her if she failed?

What excuse would she have?

None!

The thought made her tighten her grip on the staff until her knuckles turned white.

Maybe training with Finola would help—maybe the Archdruid could teach her skills her brothers hadn't. If she could learn a new technique, it might give her an edge when the time came. More than anything, she wanted that edge. She wanted to prove to her father that she wasn't just a tagalong on this path.

Yet… there was another part of her—quieter but persistent—that wondered if no amount of training would be enough.

What if she simply wasn't meant to be a druid?

What would happen if she failed the trials, came back with nothing, and her father—her brothers—looked at her with the kind of disappointment she dreaded most?

Her throat tightened at the thought.

Maybe Finola could help or maybe not. It was better to try than to spend another day tangled in her own fears, waiting for time to run out.

As promised, Finola was waiting for her outside Druid's Glen.

The fair-haired woman was leaning on her staff and smiling.

"That was fast," Finola said.

"I killed the fish and put them in a bucket of water for later. Keeps them fresh. Where do you want to train? There is a clearing not far from here where Lana teaches us. You know of it?"

"Now that I have been here for many weeks, I have become familiar with the surrounding territory. Yes, I do know it, but I thought we would find a more exotic place to train. We're going to have fun and I'm going to find out what strong stuff you're made of. We might break a rule or two."

"I don't like breaking rules," she said, trying to keep the edge from her voice. This had to be a test, or worse—a trap. Finola would hold this over her head when her father came home. *Blackmail,* that's what the criminals in Eric's books called it.

Finola arched an eyebrow. "That's not what I hear from Lana. She says you know as much as she does—and you don't always keep that to yourself."

Heather flushed but said nothing.

"Don't worry," Finola added with a small smile. "I won't tell your father. Today stays between us. We'll work on your staff forms, and if you behave, maybe I'll show you a spell or two. More exciting than snaring fish for dinner."

She gave Heather a wink. "What do you say to that?"

Heather hesitated, still thinking this was a trap, a test. It would be like the druids to devise a tempting plan to teach her a lesson. Maybe her father put Finola up to this, to see if she would follow the rules he had set forth when he left.

"I'll train with you if we don't break any rules. This is my father's forest. He knows everything that goes on here. If we break the rules, he'll know."

"Oh, I doubt he knows everything that goes on. Let's be real. He's engaged far away and is probably too busy to monitor what's going on here. Now, shall we? I'm not going to get you into trouble, far from it. We'll train in Druid's Glen until noon, have a wonderful lunch at The Hound and Shrew, and I'll send you back to your home so you can cook your fish for dinner."

A flutter stirred in her stomach—part excitement, part unease.

"I'm not sure now about this. My father would disapprove of us going into Druid's Glen. He only let us in to say goodbye."

"Here, take my hand. It's alright. I'm a member of the Druid Council, an Archdruid of good standing. We can go into Druid's Glen. You have my permission to enter."

Heather hesitated.

Never did her father take them into Druid's Glen—the first time was weeks ago when she watched them depart.

"I don't know about this," she muttered.

"It'll be fun. You won't get in trouble. It's between us. No one will see, and no one will know—not your brothers, not your father. Inside Druid's Glen, we'll have privacy like nowhere else. Take my hand."

Heather paused as she worked through what Finola was saying.

"*Take my hand.* Silly girl, I will not offer it again."

Heather, against her instincts, grasped the outstretched hand.

With a word of power and the secret incantation, the tree-stride spell was activated by the Archdruid.

Heather's stomach knotted, and nausea swept over her. Her vision blurred as if her entire body were being stretched to the breaking point. The sensation subsided and she was walking out of a massive tree— The One Tree. It was a red oak with fiery leaves, towering one hundred feet tall.

She was inside Druid's Glen for the second time in her life.

She noted nothing had changed—there were cuts of wood and a table nearby, a place to hang cloaks and a weapon rack, and an open grassy area that was so beautiful it looked like an artist's painting. There were rabbits and squirrels bounding away, taking with them huge acorns that The One Tree dropped. In the distance was a small mound covered in wildflowers.

It was glorious.

"Welcome once again to Druid's Glen," Finola announced, twirling her staff in lazy figure eights as she strolled toward the open grassy area. She stretched her limbs, then slipped into a fluid warm-up routine with her staff, as if this were just another day, another lesson.

Heather's stomach sank. She whispered under her breath, "I'm in so much trouble."

"You worry too much," Finola said without looking back. "No one will be the wiser. This stays between us women."

But Heather's mind was racing. The problem wasn't just being seen—it was getting out. The tangle's magic worked both ways. It kept the world out… and trapped the unwary inside. She didn't know how to rootwalk, not yet, and the only other way was to slip through the brambles—*only if* it still obeyed her.

And if it didn't? It would be a painful lesson.

"You won't be in trouble as long as you're with me," Finola said. "Get a drink of water, then meet me over there. We'll go over today's rules while we limber up."

Heather was here now—there was no changing that—so she pushed down any lingering hesitation and did as instructed, already bracing for the punishment she would face later.

The water in the font was fresh and crisp, the basin magically refilling as she drank cup after cup, the coolness settling her nerves.

When she turned, Finola was already in the clearing, twirling her staff in smooth, precise arcs, her body flowing like water in a dance with an unseen partner.

Heather froze at the edge, mesmerized.

These weren't the clumsy drills she practiced—these were forms, polished and perfected, every strike an elegant blur of balance and power. Finola moved with the ease of a warrior who had drilled the patterns a thousand times until they lived in her bones.

Heather's heart swelled with excitement as she stepped forward. She had to learn this. She wanted it more than anything.

"What form is that?" Heather asked, unable to keep the awe from her voice.

"This one is called *Dance of the Phoenix.*" Finola paused, letting the name linger. "It's a bit advanced for you. That will have to wait for another day."

Dance of the Phoenix, Heather mouthed the words under her breath, committing them to memory.

"Rules are simple," Finola continued, her tone shifting into instruction. "You will hold back your strikes to the body—no strikes to the head, under any circumstance. We'll start with basic defending forms. I will attack, and you will focus only on defense. Then we'll switch—you attack, I defend. After that, we'll test each other a bit more freely, and if I'm satisfied, I'll teach you one form of my choosing."

She planted her staff in the earth, her sharp gaze appraising Heather from head to toe. "With three brothers and being the Grand Druid's daughter, I imagine you've had your share of sparring? You're good with that staff, yes?"

Heather squared her shoulders, gripping her staff tighter. "You'll see."

While Heather was confident, she wasn't about to let herself fall into overconfidence. Her brothers used that trick often—flatter her, bait her, try to soften her guard. She'd learned to counter it by reminding herself of the truth: she was younger, smaller, and not as strong. That stung more than any blow, and it made her angry every time she thought about it.

"My forms are decent—for a little girl," Heather said, narrowing her eyes. "But I can't promise you won't feel the sting of my staff once or twice."

"Fair enough. Same applies to you. It wouldn't be proper training if we didn't collect a few bruises," Finola replied, her tone light but steady.

Heather planted her feet, gripping her staff tighter. "Then let's begin."

Finola gave a slight shake of her head, the faintest smile touching her lips. "And one more thing—no crying when it gets tough."

Chapter Seven

∞

Ensnared

By the time midday approached, Heather was worn out. Finola was masterful with a staff and had taken time to fix her errors exploited by the training. Her gloved hands were sore, the callouses nearly torn free of her palms. Her arms were dead weight, and her legs were just as tired.

Heather relaxed next to the font and drank cup after cup of water. She was so thirsty.

Finola was winded as well and took water once Heather had her fill.

"Are you ready to learn a form?" Finola asked.

Heather perked up. Energy came back. "Yes!"

"There are two basic forms you would benefit from learning. One is *Serpent's Coil*. There is a lot of twisting, coiling to strike from different angles with great precision. The other is *Crashing Waves*. It alternates between fluid and powerful strikes, like waves lapping against the shore."

"Which do you think I should try?" she asked.

Finola paused and looked at the gangly girl, then she answered, "*Crashing Waves*. You already have great fluidity; it is a matter of generating power in the rhythm of your strikes. Let's try that one. Watch me—it always begins with the footwork."

Heather took a step back and watched Finola dance forward with her staff moving hypnotically, then brought it slamming down through an invisible target. She demonstrated the movements one more time.

"Do it quarter speed, slowly."

Finola came behind Heather and adjusted her shoulders. "Don't hit me with your staff. Be aware of where I am."

The two moved in tandem, with the instructor correcting the student many times over. While not perfect, Heather was starting to get the footwork right at full speed. Had her arms not been so tired, she would have been able to progress further.

"You know, Heather, if you spent more time with me, I could teach you more staff forms. You should visit me in my grove after your father returns. We could train every other day—alternate staff work with basic spell practice. I could prepare you for your trials. They must be coming up soon, yes? You could even become my apprentice."

Heather blinked, caught off guard. "I… I don't know what to say. I'd love to learn more and be better prepared for the trials. And… I'm not very good at spells. I struggle with cantrips. My father would have to approve."

"Of course," Finola said with a warm chuckle. "The decision wouldn't be made in isolation. I'll speak to him when he returns. It would be a pleasure to have you learn with me. And don't worry about your spellcasting. Manifesting magic is different for everyone. You just need the right path. I can help you find it."

Heather hesitated. The mention of her trials settled in her stomach like a stone. She wasn't ready—not yet. The thought of being alone in the wilderness, with no one to help her, filled her with a creeping dread she didn't want to admit, even to herself.

She swallowed hard, forcing the words out. "Tell me about your trials. Were they… hard?"

Finola smiled, tilting her head. "Interesting question. In retrospect, it wasn't too difficult. But at the time, I thought it was the end of the world. My master took me far outside Haddensack—no chance of finding my way back home. That's what your father will do, too. Rootwalk you far away, leave you with the essentials—staff, knives, basic gear, a tent if you're lucky. Enough to survive, if you use your head."

Heather shifted uncomfortably, imagining it already.

Her brothers didn't get a tent…

"The first thing I did was a safe spot. I made camp near a brook. Water was easy, and there were wayward pines for shelter if I needed it. I foraged what I could, took notes, observed the forest around me. I even managed to snare a few rabbits, though dressing them is… not my favorite task. And bird eggs. Spruce grouse, I think. Not exactly a feast, but enough to get by."

"Spruce grouse lay their eggs in late spring," Heather said. "It must have been another species."

Finola blinked, then chuckled. "You're right, now that I think about it. How careless of me. You are a sharp one, Heather. You do enjoy correcting your instructors, don't you?"

Heather shook her head, a faint frown tugging at her mouth. "Not really. It just… slips out. I always end up in trouble for it. I should probably just learn to keep my mouth shut."

"Well, not with me. It's refreshing to meet someone who… pays attention."

"Your trials were successful?"

"Of course. If they hadn't been, I wouldn't be here now."

"That's not what I meant," Heather said, her voice dipping lower. "Did they make you want to be a druid even more?"

"Oh, certainly. It cemented my purpose—to protect nature, to nurture its growth. I've wanted that all my life."

"That's what I figured."

Finola tilted her head, studying Heather's face. "Any other questions about the trials? I'm happy to share advice. But judging by how you handled yourself today—you'll pass your trials without much fuss."

Heather blushed, heat creeping up her cheeks. She wasn't as certain as Finola made it sound. "What were those other forms you used against me earlier?"

Finola's smile widened. "I showed you *Whispering Shadows* and *Frost Bite*. *Shadows* is about speed and unpredictability—darting in, striking hard, slipping away before they can counter. *Frost Bite* is similar, but you mix in a cantrip—ice magic, meant to freeze your opponent's hands so they lose grip on their weapon. Of course, I didn't actually cast the spell on you. You would have noticed."

Heather straightened. "Thanks. I want to learn all of them."

"And you will. Mastering the staff comes first, then we'll talk about blades. It's a different kind of discipline. Ever held a sword?"

"No. Just the staff. And my knife—but not for fighting." She tapped the hilt at her belt. "I keep it with me since…"

"Since what?"

"Since I've been on my own. Well… not exactly alone. You're here. But, you know. At home."

Finola arched an eyebrow. "Yes, Heather. I'm aware you're here by yourself."

The admission left Heather feeling oddly exposed, and she swallowed hard, trying to shake it off. The long hours of training were starting to catch up to her—her limbs heavy, her stomach hollow and grumbling loud enough that Finola surely heard it.

The cool water helped, but it wasn't enough. She kept stealing glances toward the edge of the Glen, wondering when Finola might finally release her for the promised trip to The Hound and Shrew. But as the sun arced overhead and the drills dragged on, the promise of pies and ale began to feel like a cruel trick, dangling just out of reach.

From her pouch, Heather snuck out one of the blueberries reserved for emergencies and ate it quickly before Finola could see her. The sweet berry burst across her tongue, warmth spreading through her tired limbs. It was such a small cheat, but guilt sank into her belly almost as quickly as the relief. This wasn't an emergency. Her father's voice echoed in her mind—*Only when you truly need it.* But what was *need* if not this moment, when she felt both hungry and exhausted?

The wind kicked up, rustling the fiery leaves from The One Tree, and sending them spiraling to the ground. Rabbits scampered away, as did the lingering squirrels who were braver and more mischievous than the rabbits.

There was a distinct chill in the air, like winter had returned for one fleeting moment.

Heather gripped her staff.

Her instincts called out in warning.

The air was wrong.

The wind swirled again, kicking up the leaves into a small dust devil.

"Something amiss?" Finola asked.

"There was a change in the air, I can feel it. The rabbits are scattering. The squirrels are departing—they wait until that last moment to run away, even from a predator."

"We are safe in Druid's Glen, believe me. I would know of any danger before it arrived. Archdruids are attuned to this grove when we're inside it. Besides, no one can get inside, either through the tangle or through the magic of The One Tree. It is not easily accomplished, believe me. Many have tried, none have succeeded."

"What about the wizard? How did he get in here?" Heather asked.

Finola had a puzzled look. "What wizard do you speak of?"

Heather's insides tumbled. She looked at the ground. "Nothing."

"No one speaks of wizards in passing. A wizard in Druid's Glen? When did this happen?"

Heather forced her mouth shut.

Shades! What else can I mess up?

"If you know of a wizard, then tell me. Why would a wizard cause you such distress? Did an acolyte of the Wizards of Arcana visit here? Is your father talking with them in secret? Tell me!"

Heather remained silent.

No good could come from this conversation, as her father must not have told the Council what happened. Only Lillia knew—until now. Now, Finola knew too, because she couldn't keep her mouth shut.

What else would slip out before the day ended?

The only thing that interrupted the silence was the rustling leaves in the breeze and a sudden dust devil that scattered more leaves.

She looked up and held Finola's gaze, those large brown eyes were insisting that she talk. She wouldn't say one more word.

"I see this is going nowhere," Finola said, her voice calm and even. "I won't pester you about it anymore. We will have one last lesson and we'll go to The Hound and Shrew for meat pies and ale. You've earned both. And we'll talk more about an apprenticeship in my grove. The more I think about it, the more I'm convinced you should learn beside me."

Heather felt relieved that Finola wasn't going to push her for answers about the wizard.

"That sounds wonderful. I'm famished. Meat pies and ale! But I don't know if I can do anything more training. You worked me hard. I don't think I can endure another lesson. My legs feel like dead weight and my arms—I can't lift my staff."

"This lesson isn't physical. It is magical—I told you that I would show you magic. Let me see your staff. It hardly has a nick on it. Is this new?"

Heather handed over the mottled staff. "I made it. The wood came from a sycamore tree near here. The black streaks are from the tangle—it grew right into the tree I picked. My brother Cedric says that makes it magical."

Finola turned the staff over in her hands, studying the grain, the bramble's twisting marks. "I see you've carved druid runes into it. And druid marks. Measuring trees already?"

"Not yet," Heather admitted. "I wanted it to look like a real druid's staff. Like yours. I'll be ready for my trials in the autumn—and whatever comes next."

Finola nodded, her expression softening just a fraction. "Have you heard the word 'tempering'?"

"I heard the blacksmith mention it once. It's… good for metal? I'm not sure what it does."

"Tempering makes metal stronger. Without it, a sword might shatter the first time it strikes something hard. Tempering toughens it, removes its flaws." Finola paused, tapping the staff against her palm. "I know this because my father—Thatara rest his soul—was a blacksmith. He made the sword I carry now. It's as tough as he was. Tough to the end."

More than once, Heather had seen staves snap against stone or harder wood. That was why most druids lacquered theirs—to harden the outer layer, to guard against splinters and cracks. She had done the same, adding half a dozen coats, just as Aaron had advised.

"Is there a way to temper wood?" Heather asked, curiosity pushing past her hesitation. "To make it tougher like steel? Can that even be done with a staff?"

"There is," Finola said, her tone shifting, more serious now. She ran her fingers along the grain, pausing where the bramble streaked through the sycamore. "It's a rare spell I know. But I'll warn you, it's not without risk. The magic could destroy your staff if the wood rejects the tempering. But if it survives…" She smiled faintly. "It'll be tougher than steel. You could parry a sword with it and the blade would break before your staff did."

Heather's heart thudded. She thought of the way the tangle had fused into the sycamore, how the staff still felt warm in her hands, humming with that quiet, restless energy. It was part of the tangle now, part of her.

"Before I decide… what exactly will you do to it?" Heather asked.

"I'll hold it like this," Finola said, shifting the staff to demonstrate, "and cast a spell called shadow flame. It'll make the wood unnaturally strong—resistant to the bane of all staves: fire. If the spell takes, it won't break, won't burn, and no sword or axe will splinter it. My own staff is tempered. It's never failed me." She gave Heather a sidelong glance. "But a word of advice? Swords are always better than staves."

Shadow flame? Heather rolled the unfamiliar words in her head. She'd never heard of such a spell. Her brothers might know it, or her father certainly would, but it was beyond her knowledge.

Doubt trickled in. This staff wasn't just a tool—it was a discovery, a rare gift she might never find again.

What if the spell failed?

What if it ruined the bramble-fused wood?

Maybe it was better to wait. Let her father decide. He was more powerful than Finola, more experienced. He would know if it was ready.

Her fingers flexed, as he wanted the mottled shaft back in her hands. She felt a pang of reluctance, a creeping sense that she was about to lose everything.

Maybe… maybe I'll wait. Let her father temper it. When he gets back from the Mage-Gate.

"Perhaps another time," Heather said, holding out her hand to take back her staff. "I'd like to think about it. Maybe when my father returns, he can advise me on what's best. He knows about shadow flame, I'm sure. He's the Grand Druid, after all. He can temper it for me when he gets back."

"Of course," Finola replied smoothly. "No sense rushing into something you're not ready for. Shall we head to The Shrew and Hound for our meal? You said you were hungry."

Hound and Shrew, Heather thought. *How can she get it right then get it wrong?*

"I'm starving! I'd like that. I'm not much of an ale drinker, but it sounds good right now. Meat pie—I think I could eat two!"

She exhaled, relieved that Finola wasn't pressing the issue. Heather motioned with her hands to receive her staff.

But Finola didn't hand it back.

The Archdruid took a step back and lifted the staff overhead.

A leather throng Heather hadn't noticed before twisted near Finola's neck, revealing a bright red leaf pendant. Without a doubt, the leaf came from The One Tree.

She muttered words of power—guttural and low.

Flame spread up and down the staff, and it burst into magical fire, charring as it burned. She flung the burning wood to the dry grass, where the flames grew in intensity. The mottled wood was burning. So was the grass.

"What are you doing?!"

Heather dropped to her knees, frantically swiping dirt over the fire with both hands, but it was no use. Her eyes darted around the glade and locked onto the water font.

She needed water.

Finola struck—a quick, precise jab to Heather's unprotected head. The blow wasn't lethal, but it dropped her to the ground in a heap.

Finola stepped over her.

"To answer your question," she said, "I'm not doing anything. You have potential, Heather. You'll pass your druid trials—of that I've no doubt. But your father made sure it would come to this. And for that, I'll carry regret."

Heather's ears rang, and stars danced across her vision. Her body wouldn't respond to her brain's commands. She wasn't even sure what Finola had said.

Tendrils coiled around her legs, pinning her to the ground before she could rise. No matter how hard she yanked, the grasses were relentless.

Her senses returned in a rush. She pulled her knife free and moved to slash the tendrils—only for the quick-handed Finola to knock it from her grasp with the butt of her staff.

Pain exploded through her hand, adding to the throb in her head.

More tendrils curled around her thighs as she sat up. Though her hands were free, she was helpless. No matter how hard she tore or tugged, the grasses held fast.

Heather growled, "You have no idea what my father will do to you for this. You've made the worst mistake of your life."

Finola's smile was thin and sharp, like a blade sliding between ribs. "We all pay for our mistakes, Heather. Your father is no different—he must pay for his."

The tendrils kept wrapping, encasing Heather's lower half. She gripped a patch of ground, tore out a clump of dirt, and hurled it at Finola's face.

An invisible shield deflected it harmlessly aside.

Finola brushed herself off and touched the leaf talisman, reactivating the shield. Her scowl deepened. She took a step forward and jabbed the butt of her staff into Heather's chest, knocking the wind from her.

Writhing on the ground, Heather tried to catch her breath but couldn't. She was in agony. Her head, hands, and chest hurt.

Finola, irritated, stood over her. "Have we learned our lesson? You continue to defy me, and I will continue with your physical punishment. I only need you alive until your father arrives—your condition will be up to you."

Heather gulped for air. She could breathe again, but it did little to stem the pain, and she was beginning to lose feeling in her legs from the constricting grasses.

"Now, tell me about this wizard. Be quick about it, or I'll jab you again."

"He was spying on the Council," Heather said, staring up into the blue sky. "The meeting. The Mage-Gate."

"Your father told you about the Mage-Gate? Who was this wizard, and how did he escape Druid's Glen?"

"Don't know."

Finola struck her ribs with the staff.

Heather cried out, pain flaring. It took a moment for her to catch her breath.

"Tell me!"

"I don't know! He tried to kill me and Lillia when we found him, then he teleported when my father arrived. I don't know, I don't know!" She was crying now. "I don't know!"

She braced for another blow—but it didn't come.

Gingerly, she sat up, pain blooming. Finola was near The One Tree, her hand pressed to the bark, muttering words Heather couldn't hear.

Suddenly, Finola took a step back—then leapt aside.

Two armed warriors stepped out of The One Tree.

Then four.

Then six.

They were coming in waves.

Heather noted a druid or two among the intruders, helping to organize the effort. Some wore masks of animals. They were cloaked in green, wearing armor of all kinds, and armed for battle with swords, spears, staves, and bows.

More poured from The One Tree, small barrels clutched in their arms. Heather stopped counting. The men and women kept arriving, fanning out to fill Druid's Glen. They were organizing into platoons.

Was this an attack on Druid's Glen? Why?

More invaders followed, carrying bundles of crude spears—eight feet long, sharpened at both ends. When the flood of arrivals slowed, two teams set to work. One ringed the tree with barrels in three tiers, securing each level with stout rope to keep them from toppling. Ten feet away, the second team began planting spears in the ground, all pointed inward *at* The One Tree.

Heather watched as archers established stations at the cardinal points. Each position had racks of arrows, containers of oil, and braziers for flame.

They were preparing to burn it.

The barrels were oil. If The One Tree caught fire and was left to burn freely, it wouldn't survive. Heather couldn't believe what she was seeing.

"You would destroy The One Tree?" she asked.

She repeated it, louder this time, to pull Finola's attention from her lieutenants.

"It is a means to an end," Finola replied, handing the charred remains of Heather's staff to a nearby druid. "Go, DeCa. Take this as proof. Gideon is in Heerveen—most likely at a place called The Stately Potato. Go quickly. Bring him here."

The druid slipped past the ring of spears, touched a leaf talisman around his neck, and vanished into The One Tree.

Heather's heart sank into depths she never knew existed.

It wasn't just the tree or the Glen at risk—*she* was the key to the whole thing. Finola was counting on her father's fury, knowing he'd rush back the moment he learned Heather was being held. Her safety was the perfect lure, a lever to pry open her father's composure. Once he charged in to rescue her, he'd be caught too.

She wasn't only a hostage—she was the bait in a trap set for the Grand Druid.

The grasses continued their work, locking Heather in a sitting position.

Finola wanted her to see this.

Heather calmed herself with deep breaths, willing the panic to subside. Around her, the warriors were setting up temporary camps, establishing perimeters, maintaining readiness. It was done with military precision.

She imagined her father stepping through The One Tree—only to impale himself on the waiting spears. Then the hail of arrows. Then spells from the dozen druids. And if that failed, they would burn the tree—with her father inside it.

She had to act. Anything. But how could she warn him?

Heather let her body go slack, testing the strength of the grasses. Her legs were pinned, but her torso and arms had more give. She twisted at the waist, slowly easing herself onto her side. It was more comfortable—and it gave her a better view.

From here, she could see just how many intruders had arrived. Fifty, maybe a hundred.

But with her back to The One Tree, she could no longer see what was happening at the center of the glade.

"Keep away from the tangle!" Finola yelled. "I can't protect you if you get too close!"

Heather closed her eyes and reached out to the tangle, asking it for help. She imagined it snaking outward, striking at the enemy. A yelp. Then a scream. Then the sound of axes chopping.

"Keep away!" Finola shouted again. "Stay at least ten or twenty feet from the perimeter! Do as I command!"

Calmer now—knowing she could draw on the tangle for help—Heather focused, repeating the same plea over and over: *help me, help me, help me, please.*

Heartbeats later there was another commotion. Heather opened her eyes.

Voices barked orders. Feet scrambled. She wriggled inside her grass coffin, trying to restore feeling to her legs. The effort brought pain—but also warmth. The blood was flowing again.

She closed her eyes and pleaded for help once more.

If only I had the acorn necklace, she thought. She could crush it and summon Lillia.

Her gut twisted. No—she couldn't. That would only bring about Lillia's death. Anyone, druid or otherwise, who came to Druid's Glen uninvited would face a violent, formidable force.

Heather opened her eyes and blinked against the brightness, noting the chaos she must have caused. It gave her hope. Amid the temporary disarray, she spotted forest animals darting from hiding places, fleeing toward the edges of Druid's Glen.

At the edge of her vision, she noticed a cottontail rabbit lingering in the grass. It disappeared—then reappeared.

It stopped, moved again, stopped—then moved once more.

Bit by bit, it was drawing closer, taking a meandering path in her direction. She closed her eyes and pleaded again for help from the tangle.

She felt a warm nose nudge against her cheek. The cottontail had arrived.

"Hey, little one," she whispered. "Can you help me? Please."

The rabbit gave a series of muttering sounds.

"Really? Get Albic Fang. Yes, the other side of the village. Go. As fast as you can."

The cottontail hopped away—slow at first, then bolting out of sight, spraying dirt from its paws as it fled.

There was a commotion, and then she saw one of the warriors speaking with Finola. The Archdruid approached and dropped the dead cottontail beside her, a bloody arrow still lodged in its body.

The sight stole the breath from her lungs. Its small, soft form lay crumpled, the arrow an ugly wound that stained the fur red. Her insides broke—sharp and bitter—as if the arrow had pierced her hope as well. She clenched her jaw against the sob rising in her throat.

No more mistakes.

No more hope wasted on things she couldn't control.

"Nice try," Finola said. "We'll have no more of that." She motioned toward the grasses and spoke a word of power.

The vines coiled around Heather's chest, then her neck, then her mouth. The blades of grass bit into the corners of her lips, gagging her. The coppery taste of blood was instant and unavoidable. She went slack, not resisting—afraid further struggle would make it worse.

Minutes passed. Then ten. Then twenty. Then an hour.

She could no longer feel her hands or feet. There was nothing she could do to change her situation—nothing she could do to warn her father.

Heather squeezed her eyes shut and clung to a final, flickering hope—that Thatara, god of the forest, might still hear her.

Please, she prayed. *Help me. Help my father. I can't do this alone.*

But as the prayer left her, a sliver of doubt curled around her heart.

What if Thatara didn't answer?

What if no one came?

Chapter Eight

∞

Judiciar

The sun was bright, the air chill, and Gideon was tired—worn from hours of physical, mental, and magical exertion. They followed a path that would lead them to Kaalnaes, a town deep in the Wilds of Faustron, where they would begin the final leg of their journey to Wilmund's grove.

With him were Cedric, Aaron, Aurora, Val, Sarif, and Chefera.

Aurora was pale—death not far off, Gideon assumed. She masked her illness with healing potions and bitter herbs, but they only dulled whatever was eating her from the inside. He admired the older woman's refusal to yield, though he suspected he'd be burying her before the journey ended. Despite her frailty, she kept pace without complaint, even when pain tightened her features.

He wished he could help her.

Val, a broad-shouldered ranger from the Leafy Forest, had greasy red hair and dark eyes, his freckled face half-hidden by a goatee flecked with gray. His leather armor had seen battle and been repaired many times. He looked comfortable taking orders. His weapons of choice were a longsword and a broadaxe, though he also carried a shortbow.

Sarif was a fair-haired fellow with long, flowing blonde hair—he reminded Gideon of the Elves. Lively-faced and friendly, he was a Master of the Sixth Step, a mid-level Ranger in the Stairwell. Since the journey began, Sarif hadn't stopped talking—mostly about nature, asking every question that popped into his head. He was armed similarly to Val but carried a longbow with his kit.

Chefera was a short woman with silver hair—not old, but always looking worried. She was a cleric from the Temple of Thatara, a master of healing and skilled in curing spells. Her weapons weren't especially interesting, as she reminded Gideon more than once that she wasn't a "frontline warrior." She carried a mace—the traditional weapon of clerics—and wore light chainmail. Of everyone assembled, Chefera had the best armor, and it amused Gideon that she was likely the most protected, yet least willing to enter a fight.

He, Cedric, and Aaron wore light leather armor that didn't hamper their movements. It wasn't the strongest—barely enough to stop a poorly swung blade—but it suited their needs. They needed to move quickly, to cast spells freely. Out in the wild, that's where they shined.

Each carried a staff, knives, swords, and supplies. They were a formidable group, and they would see to the investigation of the ruins.

Gideon still intended to destroy the site when they departed—and that wouldn't change, no matter what they discovered.

In centuries past, Kaalnaes had been a thriving Elven city—vast, radiant, and full of life. It was said that spires of white stone had once gleamed here, shaped by magic and craftsmanship long forgotten. Now, little remained but earth-covered bones.

As they approached, the ruins grew more apparent—swells in the land where structures had once stood tall, now reduced to buried mounds beneath grasses, weeds, and creeping brambles. Here and there, a broken foundation jutted from the soil like a fractured tooth. Vines choked the base of a derelict column, half-intact, the delicate etchings on its surface nearly worn away by wind and time. Bits of glazed tile peeked from the ground where a grand walkway might once have curved through a plaza. Hollow depressions, long filled with silt and moss, hinted at once-fountain-fed pools.

It was clear a great city had once lived here—and that its fall had not been swift. Nature had not just claimed it; it had buried it gently, mournfully, as if trying to preserve what it could.

Much like the Elves themselves, Gideon thought.

Directly south, a hundred miles away, lay Dreadwood—an evil place steeped in the ruin of Eldor and the downfall of Elven civilization. Gideon cast a glance toward that distant horizon, wondering if Ilimitar's warning had been true. Perhaps the witches and warlocks had returned.

Hexenfold.

The name alone made his skin crawl.

In the age of the Mages, the witches and warlocks of Dreadwood had forged a dark order and named it Hexenfold. Their deeds were vile—devil-worshippers whose magic thrived on deceit and domination. Children were stolen from their families, raised in brutal isolation, and shaped into agents of corruption.

They had stood against the Mages, and the bitter irony was that the Elves found themselves trapped between two fronts, battling powers they could scarcely comprehend.

If Hexenfold lived again, Gideon feared it would not be only the Mage-Gate at risk. The price could be far greater.

The town structures came into view, nestled in a lush forest not yet exploited by industry. Gideon noted where the townsfolk had made great effort to preserve the trees near the village. Still, the roads bore deep ruts from the heavy wagons that carried logs—there was likely a sawmill or two near the river.

He caught the scent of soot from afternoon cooking fires, strong enough to overpower any food aromas. That struck him as odd.

Even stranger were the people. They gave the group a wide berth in the streets, as if instinctively avoiding them. It puzzled him—there was no mistaking who he was. He wore the cloak and breastplate bearing the crest of The One Tree. He was the Grand Druid. No threat to anyone. Even the common folk would know that.

And yet, they crossed the street to avoid him. Suspicious glances followed.

He told the others to watch their steps and mind their words—until they figured out what was really happening in Kaalnaes.

They continued toward the town center, where taverns and businesses clustered together. Up ahead, a crowd had gathered outside a large building.

"Stay hidden," Gideon whispered, gesturing the others back beneath the shadow of an overhang. He moved into the crowd.

Ahead, Gideon saw a man being dragged through the dirt street. His clothes hung in tatters, soaked with grime and blood. One eye was swollen shut, his lip split, and he barely had the strength to keep his feet. With every stumble, the man dragging him gave a cruel yank, grinning with satisfaction.

That man was lean, sharp-faced, and wore fitted black leather armor. His aquiline features were etched with something mean— delight, even—as if the prisoner's suffering was his reward. He looked too clean, too well-kitted for a thug. This was no simple guard. He *enjoyed* his work.

Behind them walked a nobleman untouched by the filth of the street. He wore black trousers, a red silk shirt, and a black cloak lined with red silk that caught the light when he moved. He walked with the ease of a man who expected the world to move aside for him. His face was calm. Unreadable.

Flanking him were soldiers bearing the heraldry of Duke Graystone—a crimson rearing horse with silver eyes on a black field, crowned with a silver coronet. Their armor was polished, their weapons sharp. They carried themselves like men used to being obeyed.

Gideon's gaze returned to the noble. There was no heraldry on his cloak. Nothing to identify him.

But Gideon had met Duke Graystone years ago. The bone structure, the bearing—it was unmistakable. This had to be one of his sons.

The scene—the brutality of it—made Gideon wonder.

In Faustron, there was a Judiciar: a singular man with absolute power. He was not bound by oversight, nor answerable to anyone. He was an extension of the Duke's will, empowered to pass judgment and carry it out without appeal or delay. Some called it justice. Others whispered of darker intentions.

The sight chilled Gideon to the core.

This was no inspection. This was no passing visit.

This man was about to die, and more than one life might hang in the balance if Gideon wasn't careful.

He motioned to the others. At his command, they slipped away from the town's center and headed for the trees.

For now, Gideon would wait—just long enough to be sure his companions were hidden beyond the city outermost structures.

"I swear I don't know anything!" the beaten man cried, his words slurred from a face battered beyond recognition.

"It is too late for that," the nobleman said.

The sharp-faced man bound the prisoner's hands with cruel efficiency. He dragged him to a post once meant for tethering horses, leaned him against it like a makeshift gallows, drove a fist into his gut, and shoved him over the rail.

"Make it clean," the nobleman said.

The sharp-faced man obeyed without hesitation. With a single swipe of his thick short sword, he took the man's head clean off—much to the horror of the assembled men, women, and children.

They stared in stunned disbelief at the brutal display.

As the body crumpled and blood spilled across the dust, a heavy silence fell over the town center.

Gideon kept his face still, unreadable, but the stench of blood and the suddenness of death twisted his spirit. The forest was no stranger to violence—but this was inhuman cruelty, delivered with precision and ceremony.

"Is there anyone else who wants to lie to me?" the nobleman asked, his voice rich and smooth—almost amused.

"I can question every person who ever spoke to this criminal piece of filth. If you insist on protecting known criminals—which, apparently, is the way of things here in Kaalnaes—then you will share his fate. That sword," he said, gesturing toward the bloodied weapon, "won't need sharpening until it's taken a hundred heads. And I *will* take a hundred heads if I must."

He paused, letting silence stretch.

"All I want is the truth." A heartbeat. "Now."

Though Gideon didn't know what this was about, he knew better than to interfere.

He was the Grand Druid. He held respect—support even—from the kingdoms, duchies, baronies, and earldoms that made up these lands. But that didn't mean he could meddle in matters of state. This was Faustron. And this had the look of justice, however grim.

He hoped, for the crowd's sake, that this would be the only life taken today.

Whether the nobleman's cause was righteous or not—whether the dead man had been a criminal or a scapegoat—Gideon had made his decision.

He melted deeper into the crowd and slipped toward the edge of the square.

A woman stepped forward. She wore a simple green dress with a white blouse, her sleeves stained with dirt. A bonnet covered her hair, and she stood firmly in black boots.

"Jymmie Cratz is who you're looking for," she said. "He lives near the broken bridge. Saw him pack up and leave for Gorath two days back. Stopped by the tavern for an ale before he left. Said he was meeting some folk. Bragged about finding some elf treasure."

"How do you know this?" the nobleman asked.

"I served him the ale. His tongue was wagging. Men like to talk when they're drunk."

"You chose to remain silent while this man died. What do you say to that? You could have prevented this bloodshed."

She spat into the street toward the decapitated body. "Good riddance to that bastard."

Gideon saw the nobleman's expression shift—he was weighing her fate. The sharp-faced man began moving toward her, ready to act on his master's slightest word.

The brutality…

"That'll be enough," the nobleman said at last.

His manservant returned to his side without a word.

The woman in the green dress gave a half-curtsy in the muddy street.

The nobleman turned to the crowd. "I have what I require—for now. Unless anyone else has information to grant me, I suggest you scatter."

No one moved.

He growled, "Go. Scatter, before I decide I need more heads to dull his sword."

The crowd fled, breaking apart in a rush. Within moments, only the nobleman, the sharp-faced man, the host of well-armed guards, and the headless body remained.

Gideon began to withdraw, hoping to slip away unnoticed.

Then the nobleman spoke.

"Druid! I didn't see you there among these simpletons." The nobleman smiled, his voice rich with false warmth. "I recognize your sigil. A member of the Druid Council, no doubt? You *must* be—I see the mark of The One Tree! *Thatara be blessed!*"

"I am," Gideon replied calmly. "My name is Gideon Manawove, Grand Druid, Protector of Druid's Glen, and Head of the Druid Council. At your service."

He inclined his head—just enough to be courteous, but not enough to suggest deference.

"Well, isn't this serendipitous," the nobleman said. "Ah, titles—we do love to drape ourselves in them, don't we?"

He smiled, gesturing with one gloved hand. "I am Hanlock Kull, Marquess of Graystone, eldest son of Dordar Kull, Duke of Faustron, and heir to the duchy. You may also know me by another title: *Judiciar of Faustron*. I *am* justice."

He inclined his head faintly. "With me is Gam Ritawn—my manservant of many talents."

Hanlock's eyes gleamed. "Tell me, why is the Grand Druid in backwater Kaalnaes?"

"Passing through," Gideon replied evenly. "I could ask the same of you."

"Indeed," Hanlock said, as if amused. "Will you take refreshments with me? I should very much like to hear of the Grand Druid's comings and goings through Faustron. You've piqued my interest—and your presence merits further discussion. I would like to hear what is going on in greater Tora."

Gideon noted Hanlock's choice of words—Tora, the easterners' clipped and dismissive name for *Elarandor*. It was no surprise. Those in the east had long resented the west, and even the naming of the lands had become a point of contention. Eldor was the favored term in the west, a shortened, Human version of the Elvish name, *Elar'andoré na Tharaniel araneth*—*Elarandor*. Tora had taken root in the east, and Randor was spoken in the deeper southern reaches. A single land, divided even by what it was called.

"It would be my pleasure," Gideon said, even as his intuition screamed caution.

He couldn't divulge their mission, nor could he let Hanlock know he was traveling with rangers from the Stairwell. Though the Stairwell served Faustron through formal treaties, it was well known that the duchy and the ranger order rarely saw eye to eye. At the heart of it was the power of the Judiciar—authority that often interfered with Stairwell investigations.

It wasn't uncommon for the Stairwell, an organization respected for its integrity and trustworthiness, to make enemies of the very states it served. It was an unfortunate dynamic. Kingdoms wanted the added manpower to police their lands—but not the prying eyes that came with it, nor the accountability that followed.

"I fear there may not be a suitable tavern in Kaalnaes," Hanlock said, his voice dramatic—over-melancholic, almost theatrical. "We may have to travel to Gorath together to find satisfaction. Oddly, you seem alone. It's settled. You'll travel with us to Gorath. It's but a few days away. We'll have time to get to know each other better on the road."

"If I may," Gideon said, trying to recall the only tavern he knew in this dismal place, "The Double Weasel is one of my favorites. It should be suitable for a nobleman such as yourself. I've never favored the fare, but the ale is acceptable—particularly if you've been on the road for many days. No need to go out of our way and travel to Gorath for refreshments when we have a venue right here."

"Spoken like a true, confident leader," Hanlock replied. "But we both know The Double Weasel serves goat piss for ale. *Goat piss.* We go to Gorath."

"Then The Double Weasel must have declined since I was last here," Gideon said mildly. "What a shame. I was rather hoping for a good brandy to celebrate this first meeting of the Grand Druid and the Judiciar."

"And when was that? When were you here last?" Hanlock asked. "Recently?"

Gideon laughed. "You have a curious way of making small talk, *Marquess.*"

"I call it conversation. Others call it interrogation. Gorath awaits."

"The Double Weasel has a wonderful brandy, as I recall," Gideon said. "Nutty, sharp—everything you want in a good nip. What do you say, comrade?"

Hanlock Kull smiled.

He was a handsome man with a delightful smile.

It made him chilling.

"Grand Druid," Hanlock said, "I enjoy the company of a man who can play the game. Let's go drink this wondrous spirit. I bet it tastes like goat piss regardless."

He smiled. "And I'd like to hear what news you bring from the Druid Council. I'm not interrupting anything important, am I, *comrade?*"

Gideon knew every word was a test—an attempt to make him slip. Hanlock was trying to find out whether he was traveling alone, whether he had a timeline, whether he was on a mission, and where that mission might lead.

Fortunately, they had prepared for this. The cover story had been concocted with the party in advance. Val, ever the seasoned veteran, would get everyone clear of Kaalnaes. The rangers knew how to follow orders.

Gideon nodded. "I have as much time as you need. The errand I'm on isn't urgent. Yet."

"Curious," Hanlock said. "You're armored, and your pack is heavy with supplies. An errand? I think it's a mission. A mission in my homeland. Now do you understand *why* I'm curious?"

"Indeed," Gideon said smoothly. "I travel this way because one can't be too careful. After all, we are in Faustron—*your* homeland. Even a simple errand for a druid can be fraught with danger. Lawlessness and such… around every corner. Every tree, as it were."

Hanlock Kull smiled. "I like you. No wonder you're the Grand Druid. It takes guts to slight the safety of my homeland—fortitude, even, to say it in front of the Judiciar. I could detain you indefinitely. Few would say such a thing to me and live."

"You're too kind to spare my life," Gideon replied. "Shall we venture to The Double Weasel? I promise the brandy will surprise you. No goat piss today—for the Judiciar *and* the Grand Druid."

Hanlock breathed deeply, clearly savoring the tension. "Grand Druid, if you manage to impress me in this backwater town, I'll let you go without a proper interrogation."

"That's fair. Though I suspect you'll be disappointed. I know my drink better than I know trees."

"Disappoint me."

Hanlock surveyed the modest city, his expression a blend of disdain and boredom.

"This is a backwards village if I've ever seen one," he said. "Disappoint me—so I'll need to interrogate someone else. Perhaps Jymmie Cratz, down by the broken bridge."

He smiled faintly.

"My men can hold him until I'm ready. Truth be told, he'll likely confess everything just to avoid speaking with me directly. Believe what you've heard about me, Grand Druid. It's all true."

The Double Weasel smelled of stale ale and damp wood, its warped tables and lopsided chairs leaned in mutual surrender. A faded mural of two cartoonish weasels—half-rubbed from the wall—grinned over the bar like ghosts of better days. The place had long since given up trying to impress anyone.

Since word had spread that the Judiciar was in town, most of the regulars had stayed away. Those few brave enough to sample the local goat piss made a quiet exit when the nobleman stepped through the door.

Gideon noted how Hanlock Kull could empty a room with nothing but his presence. There was intimidation in every step, yes—but it went deeper than that. He wasn't armored, yet he was more dangerous than any man in full plate. His fine attire—a nobleman's wardrobe, was perfectly tailored. The air shifted when he entered, as if even the tavern itself recognized it was out of its depth.

He was healthy, handsome, and poised. He moved with the assurance of a man born to command. His voice could charm, his smile could soothe, and both were deadly.

There was a chiseled elegance to him—refined, magnetic. If charisma had a shape, it wore Hanlock Kull's face.

Even Gideon, who distrusted the man instinctively, found him disarming. That, more than the guards, more than the sword at his side, was what made him dangerous.

Anyone who let their guard down around Hanlock Kull would pay for it. Sooner or later.

The Double Weasel emptied out moments later as the last patron downed his ale and dropped a copper on the table. Within minutes, only Hanlock Kull, Gideon, and the workers remained. Two of Hanlock's guards took up station outside to keep others from entering. Gam Ritawn and the rest, Gideon guessed, had gone to detain Jymmie Cratz.

The owner stood near the bar, wringing his hands, eyes flicking from Gideon to Hanlock in nervous rhythm.

Near him, three serving women clustered in silence, debating with glances and frowns who would be the unfortunate soul to approach the Marquess of Faustron—the Judiciar.

This was not a man to be trifled with. Not bothered. Not interrupted. And certainly not disappointed.

Gideon gestured to the servers.

When none of the three moved, he raised his hand again—this time pointing directly to the woman in the middle. She was younger than the others, with more weight to her frame, and her serving dress strained across her ample chest.

He had noticed Hanlock Kull admiring her when they first entered.

"I'll order for us," Gideon said.

The server stopped short of the table, nerves plain on her face.

Hanlock Kull stared at her. "Do you know who I am?"

She nodded.

"Do you know what happens when I'm disappointed?"

She nodded again, slower this time.

"Don't disappoint me."

Another nod.

"Do you speak?"

"Yes, milord."

Hanlock tapped the tabletop. "Good. Now listen to the Grand Druid. Impress me. Impress me. This is going to be delightful. I'm actually *anxious* to interrogate you, Gideon—to find out the real reason you're in my homeland."

"Could you ask the owner to come over for a moment?" Gideon said to the server. "I need his assistance finding a particular bottle."

Relieved, the server turned and scurried off. Moments later, the owner hurried over, wiping his hands on his apron.

"My fine gentlemen," he said. "What can I do for you today? I do hope you're feeling generous—you've driven off my other patrons."

"We'll be generous," Hanlock said, his voice laced with irritation, "if we aren't disappointed."

"I was here three or four years ago," Gideon said, his tone light. "Was this your place then?"

"Yes, it was my place then—as it is now. Not much has changed," the owner said.

"You had a liquor," Gideon continued, "a brandy, in fact. You kept it in the back, in crates. Brown bottles with a mountain peak on the label. *Peak Estate.*"

The owner hesitated, then shook his head. "I think I may have sold out of that."

"See what you can find. If you don't mind."

The man looked uneasy. "It may take some time."

"Take the time you need. Find that bottle."

"Indeed," Hanlock Kull added, a flicker of interest crossing his face. "Go fetch this *Peak Estate.* It will give me time to begin my interrogation."

When the owner still didn't move, Hanlock said, "Off with you."

The man scurried away.

Hanlock turned back, eyes bright with amusement. "So—*esteemed* Grand Druid—why are you here in this backwater town? What brings you here? Certainly not the rustic charm. Certainly not the goat piss the locals drink."

"News of a blight," Gideon answered, tapping the table. "Terrible business. I've come to assist my fellow Archdruid, Wilmund. If we can stem the spread of the disease, we may yet save an entire forest from destruction."

"And the others you travel with?"

"Druids, like me," he said without hesitation. Gideon was confident Hanlock Kull hadn't seen the full party. "I sent them ahead. They're already in route to Wilmund's grove. Rest assured—they should be there by now."

Hanlock's voice dripped with authority, his tone laced with condescension and inherited entitlement.

"What about permission? Protocol?" he asked, as if humoring a child. "My dear Grand Druid, such matters are *my* concern. These lands"—he gestured expansively—"fall under the dominion of my father, subject to his rule, and by extension, to *my* authority as Judiciar."

He smiled thinly.

"All in this land bend to my will. And I act upon necessity."

"Never do we ask permission. Anywhere," Gideon replied, his voice steady. "The Druid Council is autonomous and answers to no one. We discuss concerns as a group and act as a group. We don't consult regimes, kingdoms, organizations, or individuals.

"There are times when we notify others—as a courtesy—if the matter is grave enough. This is not one of those times. Stopping the spread of the blight will benefit Faustron. Why would you want to prevent us from doing that?"

Hanlock Kull's expression didn't waver. His confidence was undisturbed by the Grand Druid's pointed question.

"You contradict yourself," he said. "A blight isn't grave enough to warrant notification? A blight sounds *terrible!*"

"Do you answer questions with questions?" Gideon asked. "We're not going to get far if we only ask and never answer."

Hanlock chuckled—low, amused. "Ah, clarity emerges from the fog. Yes, I do answer questions with questions. It keeps things lively."

Then, more directly: "To answer yours—no, I don't wish to prevent you from protecting Faustron. I simply desire the courtesy of being notified when powerful agents enter my lands. A reasonable request, don't you think?"

"I understand your perspective," Gideon said. "It's not my intent to operate in secrecy, but to safeguard nature—wherever we're needed."

"Yet here you are, operating in secrecy." Hanlock's smile was thin. "Another admitted contradiction."

"It's no secret that the Druid Council operates independently, free of politics. We've never reported our activities to outside powers. It's never been warranted. And we make no exceptions—not even for the Judiciar of Faustron."

"And this blight—what will you *secretly* do?"

Gideon gave a low snort. "First, we'll take samples and study it, of course. Then we'll destroy the infested wood to prevent the spread. If we can eradicate it, more trees will be saved. It's one less problem for the Duchy to handle. You should be grateful we're managing it without drawing on your resources."

Hanlock's expression tightened—a flicker of annoyance flashed across his sharp features. "Your wit is sharp, Grand Druid. But let's not twist the discovery of this blight into absurdity."

He leaned forward, his eyes narrowing.

"I'm no purveyor of blights, nor do I possess the power to start them."

He let the silence stretch, then added—softly, coldly—

"But *you* could, couldn't you? A druid with your extraordinary skill… could spread blight just as easily as you claim to purge it."

"That is true of any disease, is it not?" Gideon replied, unflinching. "A plague could be unleashed upon a population—just like blight. When sickness spreads through your towns, do you hunt for those who caused it? Or do you accept that disease often moves without intent, and focus instead on healing the sick, quarantining the well?"

Hanlock Kull's expression softened. His posture eased, shifting into something more contemplative.

"Indeed," he said. "Plague and blight are distinct—each with their own nature and consequence. Blight, a corruption that stains the land. Plague, an affliction that consumes its people."

"You didn't answer my question."

"I don't need to."

"*Indulge me,*" Gideon said.

The words hung in the air—gentle, but heavy. A reminder of station. Of authority. Of resolve.

Hanlock met the Grand Druid's gaze, and for a moment, the glint in his eye shifted—less predator, more peer.

"I see," he said at last. "This is a delicate dance. You compare guardianship of nature to the preservation of my people. But the weight is not the same. And yet… here you are, justifying your investigation of this so-called blight."

The Grand Druid, expressionless, met Hanlock Kull's gaze. "Druids know nature well enough to spread disease—if we wished to. Or if we must."

Gideon sighed.

"We don't take sides, Marquess Graystone. We exist between mankind and nature. And there are times when we must stand with nature, even if it is against mankind. This blight, it will cost you."

"Cost?"

"We're standing with *your* people—eliminating a blight that must be contained. If you lose the forest, you lose timber. The sawmills close. Jobs vanish. People leave. Those who remain may starve. Cost."

"Dramatic. Simplistic," Hanlock said, waving a hand. "My people won't starve over a bit of blight."

Gideon gave a small shrug. "It was an illustration, not a prophecy. The threat may not be famine—but blight never comes without consequence. Or cost."

Hanlock leaned back, his tone sharpening. "And yet, you are still men and women. Corruptible. You *can* be influenced—coerced into acts that betray your so-called neutrality."

He narrowed his eyes.

"Or perhaps persuaded to overlook criminal acts… if committed by organizations you favor. You *claim* neutrality, Grand Druid—but I know you conspire with the Stairwell. Don't deny it. Rumors abound that your Council holds allegiances in more than one region."

Gideon suppressed a frown. "Allegations of corruption, while potent, lack substance. I assure you—our dedication to nature and neutrality is unwavering. We are guided by principles that transcend the external influences you suggest."

Hanlock Kull's fingers began tapping against the table—faster now. Each tap echoed a flicker of growing impatience. For a moment, his charming veneer slipped, and irritation flashed in his dark eyes.

"So I'm expected to believe the Grand Druid himself is above such meddling?" he asked. "That your Council and the Stairwell aren't two sides of the same coin?"

He leaned back, smoothed his cloak with slow precision, and his composure returned. His voice, once more, was calm.

"Of course you'd say that. How convenient."

Gideon paused, weighing his next words with care.

"Collaboration, when warranted, often extends beyond appearances. The Stairwell may form alliances outside our control, but our interactions with them are borne of necessity—not servitude. We serve nature. No others."

Hanlock's gaze held steady.

"I beg to differ," he said smoothly. "Your engagements, while cloaked in mutual interest, compromise your neutrality. You do not serve nature—you serve the Haddensacks. You serve the Stairwell."

He leaned in, voice lower, more deliberate.

"These broad collaborations align with alliances woven across the land… alliances that do *not* include Faustron. You conspire with our adversaries."

"If by *conspire* you mean our efforts to maintain the health of the forests and uphold nature's balance—then yes, we collaborate," Gideon said. "We share common concerns with the rangers. We engage with the Elves, the Fey, the Dwarves—and yes, we occasionally cross paths with the Black Storm or Leskaré. Our focus is nature's welfare, fostering harmony among all races—humans, beasts, and even deities.

"We interact with rulers across the territories we serve, but our priority remains preservation. I maintain a positive relationship with Haddensack because it is necessary. After all, my home is in Haddensack."

"Of course," Hanlock said smoothly. "You claim necessity—because necessity so often dictates our interactions. Then tell me: why don't you have a *positive* relationship with my father, the Duke?"

Gideon measured his response.

"As for your father—the Duke—relationships are intricate webs, woven by many threads. Alignment of priorities has not yet been established. And even if I had the opportunity to engage your esteemed father, it would not guarantee a positive rapport.

"You seem to think we druids sit around tending gardens and composing poetry. We haven't the time for political maneuvering, which is what you're implying."

Hanlock Kull paused, staring at the Grand Druid.

"I see we are both focused on our duties—irrespective of personal affiliations and preferences. Or so we claim," he said. "Your commitment lies in the preservation of the natural world, which may not always align with the ambitions or strategies of ruling figures. Including the Duke. Including me."

"I won't seek misguided assistance," Gideon replied. "I owe you no favors, and our interests will not align into mutuality. So tell me, Hanlock—what is it you *really* want?"

Hanlock didn't answer immediately. When he did, his voice was calm, almost agreeable.

"You've indirectly made me an interesting offer," he said. "One day, I may conspire with you. And when our paths converge—you will not refuse me. You will not refuse my request, regardless of circumstance. Is that clear?"

Gideon's laughter filled the air.

"Neither I nor the Druid Council owe such debts. Seeking ill-advised assistance in Druid's Glen will yield you nothing. You'll find no joy in Druid's Glen."

Hanlock remained composed. "Then let us embark on this journey together—where the truth of the blight will be revealed, and your observations may serve both our causes. In *that*, we are aligned… are we not?"

"Most assuredly."

"For the good of my people," he said, smiling faintly. "I admire your passion for neutrality. For not taking sides. And when our endeavor is concluded, we will travel to meet my father. The Duke will be most interested in the comings and goings of the Grand Druid."

The owner interrupted their debate, returning with a dusty brown bottle of brandy in one hand—and, unexpectedly, two large bulbous snifters in the other.

"They're mine," he said, a bit sheepish. "Not from the tavern's stock. But important men like you deserve proper glasses."

It was the bottle Gideon had requested. At his nod of approval, the man uncorked it and poured what remained evenly into the snifters, coaxing out every last drop. He set the empty bottle on the table and quickly withdrew.

Gideon said nothing, keeping his thoughts to himself. He understood the tactic behind Hanlock's insistence on joining him at the blight—recognized it as a ploy, a veiled effort to provoke objection and dig deeper. But Hanlock was bluffing. Gideon saw no real intent behind the offer, no true interest in Wilmund's grove. And so, he held his ground.

"You're welcome to join me in eradicating the blight," Gideon said, lifting his glass and swirling the amber liquid. "You may visit

Wilmund's grove as well, help with the preparations. If you think Kaalnaes is a backwater town, wait until you see Heerveen."

Hanlock Kull paused—genuinely taken aback. For a moment, surprise flickered across his features. He lifted his snifter and examined the contents with a practiced eye.

"This is interesting… swill."

"This is a wonderful brandy," Gideon replied, calm and quiet. "Made by my late wife's family."

Hanlock Kull's expression softened. "I'm sorry for your loss."

It was the first thing he'd said that felt genuine—unshaped by pretense, free of posturing.

He nodded slowly. "I lost my mother years ago. My father never recovered from the tragedy. Her name was Frieda." He paused, gaze distant. "I'm truly sorry for the loss of your wife."

Gideon swirled the brandy, his hand tightening slightly around the glass. "Emma," he said softly, almost to himself. Then he looked up and added, "Sorry for your loss. To Emma and Frieda."

"Emma and Frieda," Hanlock echoed.

They raised their glasses. The quiet clink marked a shared tribute—simple, sacred, and silent.

Gideon breathed in the aroma. He closed his eyes. "This will impress you," he murmured, "and I'll be on my way with no further questions."

Then, opening his eyes, he met Hanlock's gaze.

"Hanlock Kull, Marquess Graystone, one final toast—with a druid's axiom: *May the wind ever be at your back.*"

Hanlock lifted his glass higher, his steeled eyes fixed on Gideon.

"Regardless," he said, "the next time we meet, you will tell me the truth about your dealings in Faustron. No veiled excuses about blights. I expect candor—none of this blight bullshit."

Gideon took a sip, savoring the brandy. It was rich, nutty, potent—filling his mouth with layered warmth. That was what he appreciated about the Peak Estate brandies: they knocked you on your arse.

With deliberate composure, he took another sip, letting the flavors wash over him again. He closed his eyes and let it linger.

When he opened them, he watched Hanlock Kull lift the glass, inhale the scent.

For a moment, the hardened Judiciar looked almost… content. At peace. Joyful.

Hanlock took a measured sip, savoring the taste, his eyes shut. A faint, unguarded smile threatened to surface—betraying a deeper appreciation of the drink's subtlety.

Then he took a longer pull, closed his eyes once more, and in a smooth motion, drained the last of it.

Hanlock Kull placed the snifter gently on the table. "You may depart, Grand Druid. I'm not easily impressed, and I am a man of my word. While this isn't the elite brandy I'm accustomed to, it is… slightly better than goat piss."

Gideon downed the rest of his brandy with enthusiasm. "Just slightly. I agree—it's barely drinkable. A pleasure, Hanlock Kull. Until we meet again?"

"Indeed. I look forward to visiting Druid's Glen."

The two men stood and shook hands, their strength matched in silent measure.

The Grand Druid turned from the table, his pack in one hand, his staff in the other. He was relieved—and eager to rejoin his companions and his sons.

"One more thing, Grand Druid," Hanlock called. "Before you depart to eradicate this blight."

Gideon stopped, drew in a breath, turned. "Yes? How may I serve you?"

"Who do I need to speak to," Hanlock asked, "to find a case of this Peak Estate brandy? If one were interested in sampling more?"

"Peak Estate brandy and wine? You'll find them in Meadowhollow, deep in the Needle Forest. Fine vineyards, a proper carriage house— worth the trip." Gideon offered a wry smile. "And if you do visit, tell them I sent you—the soil will be soft beneath your feet."

Hanlock gave a slight nod. "Soft soil beneath my feet? I'll take that as an invitation of sorts… perhaps. If I'm ever that far west, I may pay them a visit. And when I do, I'll stop by Druid's Glen."

"Please do. I'm sure my wife's family would be delighted by your company. They welcome any friend of mine."

"And Druid's Glen? Will I get the same sincere, heartfelt reception?"

"That is for The One Tree to decide."
Gideon turned and walked away.
He didn't look back as he departed The Double Weasel.

Chapter Nine

∞

The Cost of Curiosity

Gideon found the others outside town, well-hidden and patient. They had waited without error. At first, they asked many questions, and he answered what he could as they walked—thanking them for doing exactly as instructed.

As they made their way toward Wilmund's grove, anticipation hung heavy in the air, thick with both hope and unease.

Outside Kaalnaes, Gideon came upon a familiar cluster of pines. There, he invoked the tree-stride spell—transporting the group across the wilds in a motion as jarring as it was swift.

When they emerged, they were surrounded by the quiet, sacred stillness of Wilmund's grove. Familiar sights greeted them, grounding and reassuring, though the bite of winter's chill still lingered here.

Wilmund himself stood among his followers, draped in somber black. His weathered face—etched by seasons and sorrow—softened with a rare smile as he welcomed each newcomer personally.

Gideon watched the interactions with quiet relief, the tension in his shoulders finally easing as his companions were welcomed into the fold of Wilmund's grove. The chill in the air was soon overcome by camaraderie and the promise of shared purpose—their mission to investigate the Mage-Gate.

He felt renewed. Not only by the prospect of exploring Mikal Yholl's stronghold, but by the knowledge that he had bested the Judiciar of Faustron at his own game. He knew he might not be so fortunate the next time they met—but a victory was a victory.

Silently, he thanked Thatara for strength.

Then he stepped forward and embraced Wilmund—not as a formality, but as a friend, a fellow druid.

This city was known as Heerveen. It stood as a testament to the passage of time and the intricate dance between civilization and nature.

The grove surrounding it was a dense, twisting stand of black ash trees, their dark branches crowding the sky like the spindly fingers of giants.

Marshes hugged the edges of the grove—remnants of the swamp that once ruled this land before villagers drained it, forcing the water to meander away through a network of dams, dikes, and channels. The black ashes were heavy with ebony winter buds. When warmth returned, those buds would unfurl into leaves.

The village itself had grown into a sprawl, with huts organized in wheels—groupings of five or six residences clustered around shared, multipurpose spaces. The main thoroughfare served as the trunk of a tree, while these wheeled communities formed its branching limbs.

Farther out, just beyond Gideon's line of sight, lay the heart of the settlement: the markets, inns, taverns, and businesses that marked its evolution. As he studied the layout, he saw a reflection of order, growth, and quiet ambition. What once had been a village had become, unmistakably, a small city.

He reflected on the history Wilmund had shared: Heerveen was founded long ago by immigrants from the Duchy of Ornst—one of many such settlements formed by refugees and migrants seeking space, land, and freedom. The Duchy of Faustron was vast, expansive enough to be a kingdom in all but name.

But it lacked the recognition.

And the Haddensacks would never allow it.

Meeting Hanlock Kull had confirmed what Gideon feared—Faustron was a kingdom in all but name, and its ambitions wouldn't stay chained forever. If it ever broke free from Haddensack's grip, conflict would be inevitable. He prayed to Thatara that day would never come.

"Welcome to Heerveen, old friend!" Wilmund, normally more reserved, surprised Gideon with an uncharacteristically warm embrace.

"Thank you for your welcome," Gideon said. "It's needed."

"Did your travels go without incident? What happened?"

"One thing." Gideon's tone darkened. "We encountered Hanlock Kull in Kaalnaes. He was interrogating bandits, searching for an elven treasure. I couldn't avoid him, and of course, he took an interest in my presence."

He paused. "Before I say more—did you send your druids to deal with the blight?"

"I did," Wilmund replied, frowning. "Though my followers are confused—and rightly so. Sending them to combat a blight that doesn't exist has raised more questions than I care to answer."

Their conversation unfolded against the quiet hum of Heerveen's daily life—villagers moving, children laughing, smoke curling from cookfires. As they walked, Gideon recounted the encounter at The Double Weasel. Wilmund listened closely, his expression steady as Gideon explained the strange nature of their debate: neutrality, nature, blights, and politics.

"I'm grateful you've kept the ruse intact—it's been invaluable," Gideon said quietly. "We'll speak of the details later. Have the preparations been made?"

"Yes," Wilmund nodded. "Everything is ready. Come, I've arranged lodgings for you."

He gestured toward a path leading deeper into the grove. "We leave for the ruins at first light."

Gideon chuckled at the sight of the dark yet whimsical sign above the inn: The Stately Potato. Beside the bold lettering was a lumpy potato with human eyes, wearing a tall black hat. One stick arm held a bloody axe; the other, the decapitated head of a carrot—its eyes marked with little *x*'s.

The common room inside was dimly lit, its sparse decorations dominated by paintings of the same ridiculous potato in increasingly outlandish scenes.

There it was as a sea captain.

Then a knight.

Getting married to a sweet potato.

Riding an eggplant shaped like a horse.

Dressed as a sorcerer, casting spells.

And seated on a golden throne, wearing a crooked crown.

It was absurd—and it made Gideon chuckle all over again.

They were ushered upstairs by the innkeeper and promised a full dinner later. The group was given two rooms, each cramped with four pallets laid over thin mattresses. Water basins stood in the corners beside chamber pots, and little else adorned the space.

At Gideon's direction, he, Cedric, and Aaron took one room, while Aurora, Val, Sarif, and Chefera were settled in the other.

They unloaded their supplies, packs, and weapons. Light armor was unbuckled and set aside. Once things were in order, Gideon gave Wilmund a nod—it was appropriate to speak freely here.

The Archdruid shut the door behind them and turned to address Gideon's companions.

"These are my sons, Cedric and Aaron," Gideon said.

Wilmund gave a short bow. "A pleasure. Though their presence does stir my curiosity."

"You need not be curious," Gideon replied. "For an endeavor this delicate, I thought it wise to have family by my side. Both are advanced in their studies—apprentice druids, if you must assign them a rank. What is the status?"

Wilmund folded his arms. "The ruins are fifty miles from here, deep in the forest wilds. We can rootwalk forty-five miles. The last five, however, are protected by ancient enchantments—woven into the land itself. As far as I know, neither tree-striding nor teleportation can breach that final stretch."

"That may serve us well," Gideon muttered. "No one can follow us using magical transportation."

Wilmund gave a slight nod. "I've established a temporary camp where the spell travel ends—just outside the invisible boundary. There are supplies waiting there with two trusted mercenaries and two of my most capable apprentice druids."

Gideon did the math—twelve. That would be sufficient to investigate the ruins and provide enough support.

"What about the ruins?" he asked.

"The ruins lie at the center of a forested valley," Wilmund replied. "There's a stream for fresh water, trees if we need wood. An ancient road—crumbling, but still traceable—follows the stream. When we arrive, you'll see open fields now choked with devilclubs and tangle. Long ago, those were cultivated farmlands watered by two canals."

"Will we need to ford the stream? The canals?"

"No, there are two stone bridges span the canals. Only one remains intact. Half the city is in ruins. The central square has been torn apart, save for a single, headless statue. Perhaps symbolic—Mikal Yholl being decapitated for his crimes against the world?"

"Seems logical to me," Gideon said. "What else can you tell us?"

Wilmund continued. "The outermost structures were destroyed. We found signs of habitation from long ago, but no evidence of recent activity. They appear to be what you'd expect—shops, trades, things to support a small city.

"Across the bridge, it's much the same—ruined buildings, the remains of businesses and residences. But as you move toward the keep, the architecture changes. Larger structures—places of worship, laboratories, barracks."

"You've done a lot of work already," Gideon said.

"No in depth… searching." He paused. "The outer walls of the keep are intact, draped with gold glory vines. If the place weren't so… oppressive, I'd call it beautiful. The courtyard before the keep is worse. There are stone gallows and upright pillars where prisoners were once chained. The keep itself descends into subterranean levels we haven't yet explored."

"And the Mage-Gate?"

"Inside the keep, front and center. Once we discovered the Mage-Gate, I halted the investigation and brought the matter to the Druid Council."

"What are your suggestions?" Gideon asked.

"We need to explore the subterranean levels of the keep and investigate the Mage-Gate," Wilmund replied. "We'll catalog any discoveries and make an inventory of anything useful. I suspect the levels beneath the keep may contain traps—and long-lived or undead guardians."

"What makes you say that?" Gideon asked, his head cocked to one side.

"The dungeon entrance is warded with ancient runes. Powerful ones. I could feel the magic crawling over my skin before I even approached the threshold. Once I sensed it, I went no further."

"Undead?"

"Perhaps. I've studied a little necromancy—an old acquaintance sparked the interest. Dabbled in it when I was younger, curious about magic's boundaries."

"That doesn't explain why you feel there are undead there."

"These would be things that don't need food or shelter," Wilmund explained. "Creatures with standing orders, still following their master's command. To them, time is meaningless. Undead make perfect guardians."

Gideon nodded. "Mikal Yholl had a taste for devils. I expect some infernal forces may oppose us. Dergan was demons."

Like the ones that attacked Lillia and Heather.

He gave a grim smile.

Whatever was buried beneath the keep would be powerful—dangerous beyond measure. He was grateful they had time, that they didn't have to rush this investigation.

And he was relieved Heather and Eric had stayed behind.

Still, he worried.

They had no wizard accompanying them.

An arcane practitioner might have proved invaluable, despite the risks. But the Wizards of Arcana had a knack for chasing power over prudence. If they'd been involved, their first instinct wouldn't be to seal the Mage-Gate—it would be to activate it.

"You said none of the lower levels were explored?"

"None," Wilmund confirmed.

"Even with protections in place… you weren't curious?"

"Of course I was," Wilmund said. "But when I figured the potential for deadly guardians, I chose caution. And once I identified the object in the main keep as a Mage-Gate, I knew it was time to contact the Druid Council."

He gave a half-shrug.

"I enjoy adventure as much as the next man—glory has its appeal. But not at the cost of my life. I'm cautious, and I'm no fool."

"Understood. We depart at first light, then?" Gideon asked.

"Better under the cover of darkness," Wilmund said. "Two hours before sunrise."

"Before sunrise works. A good night's rest is essential."

Gideon motioned toward the common room. "Will you dine with us tonight? The innkeeper hasn't stopped talking about his lamb stew."

"Sadly, I can't. I have affairs to settle before we leave. We could be at the ruins for months. But do order the stew. It's worth the praise."

"You could always commute back here every week or two," Gideon offered. "There's no shame in stepping away for a day or so. Family is important."

"I'll see this through to the end," Wilmund replied. "I'll be with you as we uncover whatever lies beneath. My second, Uthorim Dorra, will attend to the grove."

"That's a name I haven't heard in some time. How is that old half-elf?"

"Well," Wilmund said with a faint smile. "He's the best recruiter I have. His ranks grow steadily—he's as good with people as he is with trees."

"We'll meet you at your grove tomorrow," Gideon said. "Do you need anything else?"

"No, I think we're clear on the schedule. In fact, I'll head there now—to make sure my team is ready to receive us. They've been waiting patiently for word of the expedition."

"Thanks, Wilmund. We appreciate your cooperation—and your hospitality."

Wilmund gave a courteous nod and stepped out, leaving the door ajar.

Gideon followed, then quietly closed it. He spoke a word of power and passed his hand over the wood, sealing it with a simple ward.

He had trusted Wilmund once—back when the man's ambitions hadn't yet sharpened to a point. But now, every smile, every gesture, felt too measured. Too controlled.

Wilmund masked his intentions the way a fox hides in tall grass—silent, watchful, waiting for the right moment to pounce.

If he suspected their true purpose, it wouldn't take long before that cunning turned into interference.

Gideon turned to his sons and said, "He doesn't trust us. He's keeping us close enough to watch—but not close enough to move freely."

"My assessment as well," Aaron replied. "He must suspect our secondary objective."

"Regardless," Gideon said, "our plan remains unchanged. We'll deal with the friction—and the fallout—when it comes."

Aaron leaned forward slightly. "And if we find relics? Magic that could strengthen the druid cause—won't we keep it?"

Gideon gave him a faint smile, reached out, and shook his shoulder. "Even if we find riches fit for a million kings, we're going to destroy the Mage-Gate—or make certain it's never used again."

He could see the flicker of doubt in Aaron's eyes. It wasn't surprising. His son was endlessly curious, always seeking knowledge, always wanting to understand. The thought of obliterating ancient magic without studying it first must have felt like burning a library to the ground.

Aaron would've liked to question Lillia. He'd want to know more about dryads, their lore, their link to The One Tree. Being here—on the edge of the ruins—had only deepened his curiosity.

Cedric, in contrast, stood silent. Steady. He would do what needed to be done. He wouldn't let wonder distract him from duty.

Gideon cleared his throat. "This is a rare chance—to work with the Stairwell, with other druids, and maybe even make lasting friendships. If you stay sharp, keep your wits about you, and follow my lead, you'll come through this just fine."

"Understood," they said in unison.

"Good," Gideon said, allowing himself a quiet moment of pride. "Go grab a seat downstairs. One ale each—no more. I'll check in with the others and join you shortly."

As Gideon and his companions arrived at the designated spot, they were met with a scene of quiet, organized activity. The spacious clearing was free of clutter, marked by the orderly scattering of sizable tents. The soft crackling of nearby fires blended with the faint rustling of the surrounding forest. A cool breeze whispered through the camp, carrying the damp scents of wood and pine.

The orange glow of the embers danced against the darkening sky, casting long shadows across the canvas walls—shadows that stretched like the forest itself was leaning in, listening.

Members of Wilmund's grove greeted them upon arrival, guiding the party toward the central tent where the expedition personnel waited. Inside, Wilmund's followers stood assembled and alert, already geared for the task ahead.

Introductions circled the tent.

There were two mercenaries—brothers named Doud and Garret. Both were weighed down with weapons and wore the hardened look of men accustomed to battle. They weren't twins, but the resemblance was unmistakable: rectangular faces, jutting jaws, patchy facial hair, and cold, steady brown eyes. Garret was missing part of his ear, the hair around it shaved to showcase the old wound. They moved like experienced fighters—strong, quick, and quiet—clad in light chainmail and wary silence.

Two lesser druids accompanied them—a young man and woman, both about Cedric's age.

Wellsey was lean and wiry, dressed in light leather armor fitted with straps for easy access to an array of knives. A curved sword hung across her back alongside a compact crossbow. She had auburn hair and a round, attractive face, her almond-shaped gray eyes gleaming with sharp intelligence.

Her companion was called Spider—a stout druid marked by a web-shaped tattoo on the left side of his face. His olive skin was pitted with acne scars, and he wore leather from head to toe. Twin curved blades hung at his sides, matched by an assortment of throwing knives. His deep-set brown eyes, bushy eyebrows, and crooked nose (clearly broken more than once) gave him a hardened, almost feral appearance.

Where Wellsey radiated wit and precision, Spider radiated brute strength and grit.

Wilmund stood in front of the group, gesturing toward the tent's entrance.

"After we take nourishment in the mess tent, we'll cross into the enchanted zone and hike to the ruin. It's about five miles—not a treacherous path."

"We can't rootwalk within the enchanted area?" Aaron asked.

Wilmund's brow twitched at the interruption, though he quickly covered it with a tight-lipped smile. His voice, however, carried a trace of irritation he didn't quite manage to hide.

"I didn't try. I tree-strode into the barrier once, and… it wasn't pleasant. Imagine being tossed into a barrel of prickled cones, then dragged out by devilclubs. It spat me out like a cherry pit. Took me a day to recover. So, we walked to be sure."

Aaron stood and addressed the group, his voice steady. "If it's a three-dimensional barrier—likely a sphere centered on the ruins—tree-striding *within* it should still be possible. I'm willing to test it. I'll just need someone who knows the trees near the site."

Wilmund glanced to Gideon, curiosity overtaking his annoyance.

"He doesn't need my permission," Gideon said. "If he wants to volunteer, that's his choice."

"I'll go with him," Wellsey said, flashing a grin. "Better to volunteer before I'm voluntold."

Aaron cleared his throat, visibly thrown by her voice—low, melodic, confident. "Uh, thanks. I guess we'll find out soon enough if the theory works."

Wellsey adjusted the strap across her shoulder, her smile sharp with amusement. "It'll work. Or we'll come back with a wicked case of bark rash and regret."

Aaron chuckled, uncertain whether she was joking or serious—but already hoping for more time in her company.

Wilmund grinned and nodded. "It's worth a try. Wellsey can rootwalk with Aaron to the site. If it works, the rest of us can follow—aside from a few who'll travel with the supply wagons. If it doesn't… well, you two will need time to recover. Are we in agreement?"

"Agreed," Gideon said.

"The mess tent awaits," Wilmund continued. "Let's eat and talk more over breakfast. We have fresh sweet rolls, dried fruits, and hot herbal tea."

Aaron raised his hand. "I have a question about the camp."

Wilmund forced a polite smile, masking his irritation. "Of course. What is it?"

Aaron's eyes flicked toward the camp perimeter. "Wouldn't it be smarter to set up camp a few hundred yards *inside* the barrier?"

Wilmund blinked. "The barrier stops any magical transportation."

Aaron shook his head, his annoyed expression plain to see. "Let me rephrase. If you move the camp to the *inside* of the barrier, no one can rootwalk or teleport in. The enchantment becomes a shield. They'd hit the barrier and get expelled—like you described. It gives us an extra layer of protection. All you need to do is move this camp a few hundred feet that way."

Wilmund scratched the back of his head, a sheepish grin spreading. "You know… I could pretend I'd thought of that, but I'd be lying. That makes too much sense." He laughed softly, half in disbelief. "Sometimes it takes a fresh mind to see what the rest of us miss. We'll scout a spot and shift the camp at first light. Splendid thinking."

Gideon smiled, pride warm behind his eyes. Aaron was brilliant— and moments like this reminded him just how much.

As the group turned toward the mess tent, Cedric reached out and held his brother back for a moment.

"Remind me to never go anywhere without you," Cedric said. "Honestly, you've got enough brains for both of us."

Aaron shrugged.

To him, it was just another day of solving problems.

Chapter Ten

∞

The Infernal Sanctum

Once the camp was established beyond the magical barrier, they loaded supplies into two draft-horse wagons. A second camp would be raised near the ruins—assuming the tree-stride succeeded. Half the group would rootwalk; the others would ride the five miles alongside the wagons.

Aaron and Wellsey, already prepared, walked to a pitch pine on a ridge above the stream. The steady gurgle of water and occasional birdsong offered a peaceful backdrop.

Wilmund approached and said, "If it doesn't work, you'll know. Good luck."

They stood beneath a drooping branch. Wellsey muttered the incantation, drawing power from the earth. Aaron placed a hand on her shoulder. She glanced at him but didn't pull away. She touched the branch—and they vanished into the tree.

The sensation was familiar—being stretched thin between two points, tingling cold from head to toe. The old queasiness was gone, replaced by a new bitterness that coated his tongue.

They stepped out onto another ridge—this one overlooking the ruins. The ground beneath them was slate and eroded earth—perfect for pitch pines.

To the right, an enormous plain sprawled with thorny groves, devilclubs, and massive, gnarled oaks. Some trees looked ancient— perhaps as old as The One Tree—while others stood lifeless, strangled by vines.

Aaron surveyed the land. Beneath the wild overgrowth, he recognized the remnants of old farmland.

To their left, the stream had been diverted into a stone sluiceway that ran parallel to the ruins. Beyond the twin bridges, long-forgotten structures sagged and crumbled, overtaken by tangles of devilclubs and thick webs of vine.

But Aaron's gaze was fixed on the keep.

The outer walls loomed high—forty feet at least—swallowed in gold glory vines. Their bright blooms flared like torches against the ruin's gloom. Triangular bastions jutted from the walls at even intervals, each capped with a vine-wrapped guard tower. Beneath the golden canopy, a living mesh of green vines pulsed against the stone, adding a second layer of defense.

Aaron realized his hand was still resting on Wellsey's shoulder.

She tensed and gave him a look. "I normally don't let anyone put their hands on me," she said. "It's... a rule I have."

He didn't move. "I have rules too. And I'm breaking one right now. You're the worthy exception."

She smirked. "You can move it now."

"I'm not ready."

"Well, you'd better get ready."

Aaron counted to five—then finally pulled his hand away.

"Well, that wasn't so hard, was it?" she asked, her voice light and teasing.

"Did you taste that bitterness?" Aaron asked, spitting into the dirt. "Like horseradish that's gone off."

"Well, you pinpointed it." Wellsey laughed. "Eating a lot of spoiled root vegetables lately?"

"Not recently. What do you think it is?"

"These trees are alive, but something's... off." She frowned. "It's not blight—blight has a different taste. I tree-strode through a blighted ash once. It wasn't like this."

"They feel tainted," Aaron said. "Spoiled by exposure to magic. Like they're dead, but still living. Does that make sense?"

"Well, I've never heard of undead trees—if that's what you're getting at. But sure, why not?" She chuckled. "Druidic necromancy. That'd be a first."

Aaron grinned. "Or maybe a wizard's spell gone wrong."

"Or gone right," she said with a shrug. "Either way, it's beyond my expertise."

Aaron's gaze returned to the ruins below. The keep wrapped in gold glory vines held a strange kind of beauty, mesmerizing in its ruin.

"We should head back," he said. "Let the others know it's safe."

"Well, you can go," she replied with a teasing glint. "I'll wait here. Unless you always follow the rules?"

Aaron shook his head. "Not when it comes to touching the shoulder of a beautiful woman. I break those rules all the time."

"Well, now that I know." She smirked and, to his surprise, slipped her hand into his. "This is so you don't have to break any more rules—no shoulder grabbing required. And don't get any ideas."

Aaron gave her hand a light squeeze. "Not even one?"

"Not... a... one," she said, drawing out the words, playful and firm. "Now focus—we've got work to do."

She touched the branch and murmured the spell again. In a blink, they vanished into the pitch pine.

They established camp in the open courtyard beside the keep, surrounded by the quiet menace of the gold glory vines. The vines had overtaken the walls but hadn't crept into the courtyard proper—held back, it seemed, by unseen forces. Gideon suspected the old magic laced through the area kept them at bay.

The remnants of the gallows stood like grim sentinels, marking the keep's dark history. Deep notches scarred the stone beneath, worn by time and countless executions.

Nearby, the crumbled remains of a hanging platform had all but turned to sawdust beneath their boots. Grim as it was, Gideon saw its potential—a place to consolidate their findings and stage supplies.

The rusted portcullis, frozen in the open position, was a stroke of luck—though in places like this, luck always came at a cost. Its immobility spared them the trouble of scaling the walls, granting them entry to the keep's inner sanctum. But with no way to close it, the gate left them vulnerable.

The keep itself rose two stories high, a rectangular structure with a steep, broken roof and a sense of purpose long since faded. Time had worn away portions of the upper floor, the missing roof sections allowing centuries of rain to seep in. Gideon noted how exposed it was—and yet, it stood in better condition than it should.

The main doors, however, were untouched by time.

Twin slabs of dark, ancient wood stood tall and defiant. The massive doors looked heavy enough that giants might've crafted them. They bore intricate devilish carvings, and the gold leaf inlaid across their surface gleamed—untarnished, preserved by magic that felt neither passive nor kind.

Gideon approached with caution, his senses alert. Power pulsed through the doors like a heartbeat in stone.

The first story loomed at twenty feet high, built with a scale and strength that bespoke formidable construction. The second story, twelve feet above, was scarred and shattered. Every window was broken, each one a gaping wound that bled cold air and shadow.

The whole of the keep felt like a monument to something terrible—forgotten, but not dormant.

Once their camp was established, Wilmund led them to the front doors of the keep. Despite their pristine appearance, the massive hinges screamed in protest as he pushed them open, the sound echoing through the stone like a warning.

Inside, the keep exuded slow decay. Damp air clung to the skin, thick with the scent of mold and rot. Darkness pooled in corners where the light barely reached.

Without prompting, the group lit lanterns and cast spells of illumination, revealing more of the vast interior.

The flagstone floor was cracked and worn, the gaps between stones filled with slime and tangled patches of moss. Water dripped from above, each splash a sharp note in the otherwise dead silence. It must have rained recently—everything here felt damp, as if the keep itself were sweating.

To the left of the entryway rose a monumental vertical ring of black stone: the Mage-Gate. Twelve feet in diameter and mounted on a pedestal, the gate was inscribed with runes of gold and silver, glimmering faintly in the lanternlight. It dominated the space, its size alone demanding a vaulted ceiling nearly twice its height.

A wide ramp, flanked by shallow, worn steps, led up to the gate— broad enough for several people or even a wagon to pass. Gideon followed the line of sight from the Mage-Gate to the front doors, noting the straight, purposeful path.

He imagined long caravans passing through here, guided by Mages to unknown lands, strange cities, and otherworldly places. Perhaps even stranger destinations than that.

At the center of the chamber sat a raised black basalt dais, where an elaborately carved marble throne waited—embellished with the same eerie devilish imagery that adorned the keep's front doors. Its presence made Gideon's skin crawl.

To the right of the room stretched what appeared to be a reception hall, now shadowed and hollow. Toward the rear, walls and sealed doors hinted at deeper secrets—corridors waiting to be opened, chambers not yet explored.

"There are kitchens, the larder, and pantries beyond this great hall," Wilmund said. "Upstairs are the common quarters, Mikal Yholl's personal chambers, a study, and a library. After a thousand years of exposure, the upper floor is an absolute mess." He pointed toward the ceiling, where water still dripped through wide cracks. "Care must be taken. The floor is unstable. Much of the debris you see here has fallen through from above."

Gideon stepped toward the Mage-Gate.

It stood like a wound in the world—massive, deliberate, and steeped in the kind of magic that outlives kingdoms. Bathed in the soft glow of lantern light, the gate shimmered darkly, its surface forged from obsidian veined with streaks of pale, unknown stone. The white rock gleamed faintly—not quite inert. Almost watching.

Twelve runes, arranged across the top arc of the circle, were set at equidistant points. Each one was delicate, intricate, etched in gold and silver with masterful precision. None were familiar.

That alone unsettled Gideon. He considered himself well-read in ancient runecraft—yet these symbols eluded him entirely. They didn't just look foreign. They looked… personal. As if invented by Mages who had moved beyond the world's known languages of magic.

Beneath the upper ring of runes were six additional markings—three on each side. These were not delicate. They were bold and unforgiving, carved deeper into the obsidian and inlaid with thick bands of gold and silver.

They pulsed.

Even dormant, they thrummed with restrained energy.

Elder Runes.

Gideon swallowed. Crafting even one functioning Elder Rune took years of mastery. They didn't merely store power—they were power, bound to no single source. They fed from across the planes, pulling magic from wherever it could be found.

They endured.

He stepped closer. The air changed around him—charged, but not warm. There was no heat here, only pressure. As if the gate might wake if touched too long or spoken to in the wrong tongue.

Upon closer inspection, he saw that the bottom symbol on the left was incomplete. A section of the inlaid silver was missing—cleanly, as if cut or pried out. Gideon mused that this might be the reason the gate lay dormant. The indestructible rock near the broken rune bore subtle signs of damage—stress fractures, a faint warping of the surface. From what force, he couldn't tell. But it looked as though the missing silver could be extracted—if enough pressure was applied.

His arcane senses whispered of power in each Elder Rune. Even the broken symbol radiated potential. It wasn't dead—it was waiting.

That was the problem.

It didn't feel dormant. It felt paused. Patient. Like a breath held in the dark.

Gathering his nerve, Gideon reached out and ran his fingertips along the obsidian ring. The surface was cool, smooth as glass. Beneath it, he felt a faint vibration—a pulse, steady and slow. The pale white veins threading through the stone caught the lantern light and shimmered faintly, as if aware of his gaze.

The runes, for all their beauty, felt sharp beneath his hand.

Sharp like teeth.

He drew his hand back. This was a Mage-Gate. A relic of an older, darker age. It was not meant to be touched—not casually, not without cause.

Before curiosity carried anyone too far, Gideon turned and gathered the others.

He climbed to the top of the ramp, letting the full height of the Mage-Gate rise behind him like a silent sentinel. When they were assembled, he addressed them.

Cedric stood near the ramp, leaning on his staff, calm and ready for instructions.

Aaron was counting—runes, most likely, or a hidden pattern within the Mage-Gate that only he could see. His keen mind never rested.

Beside him was Wellsey, the young druid who hadn't strayed far from Aaron since their scouting trip to the ruins. Something had passed between them, quiet but unmistakable.

Behind them stood Val, arms crossed, his sharp ranger's eyes fixed on the gate. Concern tugged at his features, mingled with confusion.

Chefera stood wide-eyed, transfixed. She recognized what she was looking at, even if she didn't understand it.

Aurora leaned heavily on her druid staff, her pale face tight with dread. Gideon knew the look well—it wasn't just the sickness within her. The gate unnerved her too.

Doud and Garret stood shoulder to shoulder, both warriors frowning at the structure as if trying to measure its threat. Their hands hovered near their weapons.

Spider and Sarif exchanged uneasy glances. Neither spoke, but their expressions said enough—they felt the wrongness here.

Wilmund lingered at the edge of the group, arms folded. His face was composed, but Gideon didn't trust the look in his eyes. Awe, perhaps. Or something colder. Hungrier.

Gideon took in the room, the light dancing on the gate behind him. Then he spoke.

"This is a Mage-Gate."

The silence deepened.

"This is an ancient device, crafted by the Mages and perfected by the wild magic of Dergan and Mikal Yholl. As Wilmund has suggested, this may be Mikal Yholl's lost stronghold."

He let that thought settle.

"A Mage-Gate, when active, links to others like it. Travel is instantaneous. Undetectable. Silent. That is why the Mages created them—so they could go where they pleased without interference. This is no mere artifact. This is power.

"Our task is to investigate the gate and the keep. Study what we can. Catalog every finding. No one is to act alone."

Gideon gestured toward the obsidian ring. "I need to make this clear. No one is allowed to be alone with the gate. And no one is to explore this keep without a partner. We move in pairs or groups—always."

He pointed as he assigned teams.

"Chefera, you're with me. Cedric, you and Garret are together. Aaron, take Wellsey and Sarif. Aurora, you'll go with Doud and Spider. Wilmund, you'll work with Val."

There were no objections Gideon could detect. The groups shifted together, organizing as instructed. Chefera climbed the ramp slowly, joining Gideon near the Mage-Gate, her eyes lingering on the carved runes before turning to face the others.

"Anything we find gets catalogued," Gideon said. "What it is, where it was found, and what condition it's in. All discoveries will be brought to the gallows platform for evening inspection. I want discussion—ideas, theories, questions. Nothing is too far-fetched."

He motioned toward Cedric. "You and Garret—clear the outer wall. We need full access around the perimeter."

He turned next to Aaron. "You, Wellsey, and Sarif—start with rune rubbings. You'll need to build a ladder. Once that's done, begin clearing the main hall."

Then to Aurora. "Take Doud and Spider—clear the gallows platform, repair what you can, then help outside if you finish early."

Lastly, he looked at Wilmund. "You and Val will sweep the rest of this level. Chefera and I will handle the upstairs."

Gideon continued, "Don't wear yourselves out. Take frequent breaks, and don't overlook any detail. Take your time. If you find something that seems significant, let everyone know. We're working together toward the same goal. Once we've finished investigating the keep, we'll turn our attention to the levels below—and whatever might remain in the ruins."

He paused, letting the silence stretch just long enough to become uncomfortable.

"Remember," he said at last, "Mikal Yholl was a powerful Mage—and a wicked man. We don't know what he left behind. Traps, creatures… worse. Don't work alone. And if you encounter anything—run."

Val stepped forward. "What about perimeter defenses? Should we assign patrols?"

"If we reinforce the magic feeding the gold glory vines, they'll provide all the defense we need," Gideon replied. "Anything unfamiliar that gets close won't make it far."

"I can do that," Aurora said. "Once I'm finished, you can all leave your armor off if you like—you'll need full range of motion to work efficiently."

"Very well," Gideon said. "You have your assignments. Aurora, I'll join you outside."

As the others dispersed, Gideon lingered on the platform. His gaze drifted back to the Mage-Gate. In the quiet, its runes shimmered under lantern light—faint and flickering, like they were whispering promises only the dead could hear.

That evening, Gideon examined the rubbings of the runes, frowning at their imprecision. The renderings were too crude to reconstruct the symbols with any accuracy. They would need to be redrawn by a practiced hand. He made a mental note to ask if anyone among them could draw or paint.

The twelve runes along the upper arc of the Mage-Gate remained a mystery. Intricate in design, they had an organic quality—like flowery handwriting, grown rather than crafted. They weren't arranged with any obvious logic, which unsettled him. Most runes followed a structure, drawing from known schools of magical thought. These were special, but wild.

He reminded himself that all runes served as magical switches, pulling energy from specific sources—some divine, some arcane, some utterly alien. Perfected runes could draw power from other planes entirely, and Gideon suspected that was the case here.

The six Elder Runes—three on each side—were likely the gate's power source. That much made sense. But the twelve above? That was where his understanding faltered. How was the destination chosen? Was it keyed to a spell, an incantation? An object? A phrase?

It was logical to assume the gate connected to other open, powered Mage-Gates. But how a user accessed or activated them remained a mystery.

He glanced out toward the courtyard, satisfied with their progress. The outer keep, blanketed in gold glory vines, had been further secured by bramble spells conjured by Aurora and himself. Nothing on foot would breach it. The thorns functioned much like the living wall that guarded Druid's Glen.

There was only one entrance left unwarded—a narrow, hidden door along the city-facing wall. Well concealed, it would elude any casual observer. And Gideon felt confident no one would stumble on it by accident. Or at least, not live to report it.

Though Gideon was confident no one would find the hidden passage—neither by design nor by accident—the thought still lingered. Its secrecy gave him comfort. No signs of recent activity, no footprints or disturbances. But in the back of his mind, a quiet worry stirred. If the wizard showed up… Perhaps it wasn't a question of *if*, but *when*.

Upstairs, the living quarters of Mikal Yholl lay in ruin. Gideon had expected as much. Time and weather had ravaged everything—furniture, parchment, shelves, even the bones of the structure itself. Most of the books were long rotted, little more than pulp. A few had survived in part.

One tome, a journal, had endured. Its leather cover warped but intact, its pages filled with daily accounts from the keep's final days. Tucked between its pages was a torn scrap of parchment, likely pulled from another book—its script magical, unfamiliar. Gideon didn't recognize the language, nor did he expect anyone else here to. He added it to their growing collection of findings and moved on.

The main keep had offered few obvious clues. Mold coated the walls, and rainwater had pooled and spread across the floors. But here, Aaron's ingenuity had shone.

Using a simple cantrip—one typically used for conjuring large chunks of ice—he found a clever workaround. Aaron cast the spell again and again, pulling moisture from the flagstones and forming neat three-foot cubes of ice. The blocks were heavy, dense, and clean. Together, the team rolled and hauled them outside, stacking them near the broken wall to melt in the sun.

By day's end, the interior was dry. And thanks to Aaron, their investigation could continue without slipping through slime.

The gallows platform was finished, and their meager discoveries were laid out for all to see. Everyone had taken a turn studying the mysterious parchment Gideon had found, but no one recognized the language—not even a hint of its origin.

Among the other finds: a ceremonial knife, untouched by time and clearly magical in nature; several ancient books written in the common tongue; and a set of platinum jewelry etched with devilish markings.

As the sun dipped low and shadows stretched long across the courtyard, the expedition huddled around the campfire. The chill came on quickly in this place, creeping in with the twilight.

The companions had spread out, each lost in their own thoughts and rhythms.

Aaron was chatting with Wellsey and Spider, the three of them deep in conversation, interrupted now and then by shared laughter. Cedric had fallen in with the mercenary brothers, swapping stories that earned broad grins.

Chefera sat with the rangers, while Aurora meditated in silence, her staff resting against her knees.

Wilmund was alone, poring over a dog-eared book lit by magical glow. When he finally snapped it shut, he crossed the camp and joined Gideon.

"We could move into the keep now that it's dry," Wilmund suggested. "It would give us another layer between us and the weather, if things turn."

"Perhaps," Gideon said, patting his robes in search of his pipe. After a long day, a smoke sounded welcome. "But I'd rather we stay out here, away from the Mage-Gate. And if the rains return, everything inside will be soaked again. Not unless we fix the roof."

Wilmund chuckled, gesturing toward the looming keep. "We'd need a month just to patch it—if we could find enough wood. Maybe enchantments could cover the roof, or brambles."

"I'd rather not cast anything directly on the keep," Gideon said. His tone was mild, but firm.

Wilmund nodded. "Understood." He looked around the camp. "Seems like everyone's getting along. You've chosen well."

"That's a bonus," Gideon said. "We'll see how cheerful they are in two weeks, when they're tired, sore, and longing for home."

He nodded toward their organized cache of supplies—the barrels, sacks, and stores.

"We'll need to make a run back to Heerveen at some point."

"Agreed," Wilmund said. "No wildlife out here to hunt."

"Not a one," Gideon replied. "I've seen a few birds, but no squirrels, no rabbits, no deer. It's the magic—this place is tainted. Corrupted. Animals know better than to feed where corruption has taken root."

Wilmund gave a grim smile. "I felt it when we tree-strode. Like a rotted vegetable on the tongue."

"Care for a smoke?" Gideon asked, drawing out his pipe. "I brought the good stuff."

Wilmund declined with a wave. "No thank you."

He stood for a moment, surveying the camp with a thoughtful gaze. "Your boy, Aaron—he's quite the thinker. The ice block trick to dry the keep? Inspired. And having Chefera move the debris with her spells? Smart. I think you may have a rival for Grand Druid living under your own roof."

Gideon smiled, pride unhidden. "Truth be told, he's smarter than all of us."

"As long as he doesn't figure out how to turn that thing on," Wilmund said, nodding toward the Mage-Gate.

"Indeed."

Gideon struck a flame and lit his pipe from the campfire, taking a slow draw and savoring the tobacco. It grounded him, reminded him of home.

"The brothers," he said, exhaling a curling thread of smoke, "they worked with you before?"

Wilmund followed his gaze to the mercenaries speaking with Cedric. "They're loyal, if that's what you're asking. Helped me out in the past. Never let me down."

"Good to know." Gideon puffed again. "I don't need to tell you how sensitive this discovery is."

Wilmund didn't answer right away. His lips drew into a tight frown, then he gave a single nod.

"I'll let you enjoy your smoke," he said, patting the worn journal tucked beneath his arm. "I've got some writing to do."

The next morning, camp stirred to life as the group assembled for their meal and daily briefing. Gideon was pleased to see that a night's rest had eased the weariness in their faces. He sipped from a steaming cup of tea and bit into a sweet, dense biscuit—the kind favored by travelers for its longevity, not flavor. Around him, companions stretched, chatted, and gathered in loose circles to break their fast.

"Cedric," he asked, brushing crumbs from his robe, "have you seen Aaron this morning?"

"Not yet. He wasn't in the tent when I woke up."

"He went into the keep with Spider," Chefera offered. "I'd just returned from morning prayer. They had parchment with them."

"Spider can draw," Wellsey added, nodding.

"Ah," Gideon said, chewing thoughtfully. The biscuit was dry enough to demand a quick slurp of tea. "Makes sense. I'll check on them—I'm curious what they're working on."

He rose, casting a glance toward the gallows as he crossed the courtyard. The execution platform stood silent, its presence more accusation than relic. He couldn't help but wonder what horrors had taken place there. A Mage like Mikal Yholl didn't need gallows to kill— but he'd likely used them anyway.

The massive, devil-carved doors to the keep stood ajar, the weight of their imagery still unsettling. Gideon stepped inside.

The interior swallowed him in gloom. Morning light filtered through the fractured ceiling and shattered upper windows in thin, trembling shafts. It wasn't enough to banish the darkness—only to sketch long shadows that shifted as the wind stirred above.

He walked carefully, boots clicking on the damp stone as he made his way toward the Mage-Gate.

Near the base of the ramp, he found them—Aaron and Spider— working by the light of simple cantrips cast from their staves. Spider hunched over a spread of parchment, sketching with swift, practiced movements. Aaron stood nearby, arms folded, eyes fixed on the arcane structure before them.

Whatever he was thinking, it ran deep.

"Getting a step ahead today?" Gideon asked as he approached.

"Couldn't sleep," Aaron said, not looking away from the runes. "Too excited."

"Same," Spider added without glancing up, focused on his parchment. "Figured I'd sketch before the crowd showed up."

"We're nearly done with the upper runes," Aaron said. "Then we'll move to the side ones."

"Good," Gideon nodded. "Those side runes are Elder Runes. I recognize the structure, though not the function. They're powerful—unstable if handled improperly. Be cautious casting spells near them. Even a simple light spell could trigger disaster. I should've warned you sooner."

Spider paused, pulling back a little. "Not that I was planning on casting anything at the ancient death circle."

Aaron grinned. "You don't strike me as the cautious type. Might be worth trying—see if we can destroy the rest of this keep."

Spider smirked. "If it turns on, I'm stepping through."

They both chuckled. Gideon gave a tight-lipped smile, less amused.

"Gideon," Aaron said, "how many Mages were there? Including the Yholl brothers?"

"Historically? Nine," Gideon answered. "Chief among them were Mikal and Dergan Yholl. The most powerful—and the most monstrous. That's why we remember their names and not the others. Truth is, I couldn't name a single one of the others anymore."

Aaron pointed toward the Mage-Gate. "I've been studying it. The twelve runes across the top—those aren't just decorations. They're destinations."

He stepped closer, tapping his finger in the air just below one of the runes.

"If there were nine Mages, and this gate belonged to Mikal, then eight of these probably point to the other Mages' gates. Makes no sense to have a rune for where you already are. That leaves four for… something else. Places he set up personally. Or maybe safe havens."

Gideon folded his arms. "You don't think all Mage-Gates are identical?"

Aaron shook his head. "Not at all. For all we know, this could be the master gate. That's what I've been calling it in my notes. From here, Mikal could've gone to see his brother," he pointed at a different symbol, "or the other seven, and four other key sites he built. If we understood more about the others, maybe we could guess where the last four lead."

Gideon allowed himself a small smile, watching Aaron's mind work. The boy saw patterns where others saw only puzzles. It reminded him of what Emma used to say—that Aaron thought with both heart and head. Equal parts curiosity and logic. Always seeking the truth hidden in the edges.

"Secret places?" Gideon asked.

"Unlikely," Aaron replied. "They're not disguised. Anyone who knows how to read a Mage-Gate would spot the additional destinations immediately. If we knew more about the other Mages, we might guess where the remaining four runes lead. But if I had to wager—one could be a neutral place. A meeting ground, maybe. Like Druid's Glen. The other three?" He shrugged. "No idea."

"Write down everything," Gideon said. "Every theory, even the mad ones. I want a full stream of thought. No idea is too wild."

"Understood."

Gideon stepped toward the Mage-Gate again and raised a hand toward the thick runes along the sides. "These Elder Runes... they must power the gate. That much seems clear. But why six? Why not one? Or six of the same? Each one takes years to master. This isn't efficient. It's... overdesigned."

"Would they take years to activate, too?" Aaron asked.

Gideon shook his head. "No. That's the problem. They store energy—they don't require the caster to be powerful. Even a simple cantrip—like light—could trigger one, if it's the correct match."

"Then why six?" Aaron pressed.

Spider paused his sketching. "Could be a safety measure. Like a lock. Six runes could mean hundreds of combinations. Thousands. I can't do the math, but... it's a lot."

Aaron nodded. "Exactly. It could require activating all six in a sequence—or just two, or three. Without knowing the code, we'll never open it. Not without blowing ourselves up."

Gideon stared at the gate, his brow furrowed. "They didn't trust each other, that is obvious."

"Or they feared what was on the other side," Aaron added quietly.

"Millions of combinations," muttered Gideon. "It's strange, though, why make it this complicated? If this was intended to be a network for the Mages, why not simplify it? Six Elder Runes is excessive for a safety mechanism." He tapped his chin, his brow furrowed.

"Then we should be safe and not worry about activating it with our light spell," Aaron offered.

Gideon gave a slow nod. "If we're right that it needs a specific sequence to function, then yes, we're safe. Even if we fixed the damaged rune, we'd still need the proper combination. So perhaps we're doubly protected."

"Regardless, I won't be casting any spells near this," Aaron said, then added with a grin, "But Spider will."

Spider glanced up, smirking. "Obviously."

They shared a quiet laugh, tension momentarily forgotten beneath the flicker of cantrip light and the silent bulk of the Mage-Gate behind them.

"Aaron, Spider—you've both done good work today. And it's only the second day." Gideon rested a firm hand on his son's shoulder. "If we keep this pace, we'll uncover more than we ever imagined before the fortnight's end."

He glanced once more at the runes glowing faintly in the lantern light—so ancient, so precise, so patient.

"I'm proud of you both," he said. "Now let's hope we can stay one step ahead of whatever secrets this place is still hiding."

Chapter Eleven

∞

Leverage

By the second week, they had begun exploring the levels beneath the keep—only to discover that the protections in place were too powerful, even for Gideon. Reluctantly, he deemed them off-limits, unwilling to risk triggering wards whose purpose and power remained uncertain.

By the third week, they had cataloged most of the rubble within the keep and turned their focus to the surrounding city. Beyond the keep's walls stood the remnants of Mikal Yholl's forgotten dominion—structures ranging from storefronts and temples to sprawling homes and workshops. The layout had once been orderly, city blocks arranged in clusters of four to fifteen buildings. Now, it was a shattered shell of its former self.

Though many of the buildings remained partially intact, they had been stripped bare long ago. Occasionally, they unearthed a rusted weapon or a tarnished piece of jewelry buried in the dirt—trinkets without magic, legacy, or meaning. Gideon suspected that the city had been plundered in the wake of Mikal Yholl's fall. If the stories were true, his loyal followers were slaughtered to the last man, woman, and child. And those who turned against him fared no better. No one had survived.

The party was growing restless. Days spent around the Mage-Gate from sunup to sundown had dulled their morale, and Gideon knew they needed a meaningful breakthrough—or a reason to leave. Without a wizard, the deeper layers of the keep remained sealed. The expedition was nearing its end.

Though the Mage-Gate was inert, it remained dangerous. And while Gideon knew he could not destroy it, he could still bury it—collapse the keep, seal the levels below, and erase the path to Mikal Yholl's legacy with stone and fire.

He didn't relish the thought. But it had to be done.

Still, his mind drifted to something lighter. Perhaps it was time to call for another day of rest. A return to Heerveen—just for the evening—might lift their spirits. A night of ale, warm food, and soft beds at The Stately Potato sounded wonderful. They had earned it.

He needed to send a message to Finola and Heather regardless, something brief through plant-speak. Just enough to reassure them they were well. But the magic had limits. The vast distance between Faustron and the Needle Forest meant his words would need to be few and carefully chosen. Even with the deep-rooted power of The One Tree, longer messages risked unraveling before they reached their destination.

He took a breath, about to call the group together and make the announcement, when Aaron approached—his steps quick, his face lit with curiosity. Gideon could see that familiar spark in his eyes. Besides the countless ways Aaron had used small spells to make their work easier, his insights into the Mage-Gate had become invaluable.

There were always ideas turning in that boy's mind.

"Good morning, Aaron." Gideon pulled his son into a brief embrace, gripping his shoulders with affection. "I thought maybe today we'd gather everyone and head back to Heerveen. A proper rest. The Stately Potato should have good food, strong drink, and dry beds. We've earned a break from these ruins."

Aaron considered it for only a breath before replying. "As wonderful as that sounds, I'd like to start exploring the levels beneath the keep. That's the only area we haven't thoroughly investigated."

Gideon nodded, though it was an absent motion. It had been more than a week since they'd even looked at the dungeon entrance. He was confident nothing had changed—the wards had been too strong.

"It's still off-limits," Gideon said. "Triggering the enchantments down there could be catastrophic. The web is layered, interlocking—too complex to untangle. Only a wizard could dismantle it properly. Besides, we don't want to invite disaster."

Aaron didn't flinch. "I was talking with Wellsey—she's super smart. We came up with an idea. We don't need to break the wards… we can trick them."

Gideon raised a brow. "I'm listening," he said, not the least bit surprised that Aaron had a theory.

"I need to know exactly what the wards are designed to protect against. What triggers the magic? Motion? Heat? Life?"

Gideon exhaled, gathering his thoughts. "What Chefera and I determined," he said slowly, "is that any *living flesh* crossing the threshold activates the ward. We believe inanimate objects can pass through unhindered, but it hasn't been tested. Like I said, we didn't want to provoke disaster. Curiosity alone isn't a good enough reason to breach ancient protections. And we don't have a wizard to help us."

"What if we sent an object through that wasn't living flesh?" Aaron asked.

Gideon chuckled, folding his arms. "Ready to dabble in necromancy, are you? Summon a ghoul or two to do your bidding, my young Master of Death?"

Aaron grinned. "Not yet. But I have a different idea."

"I figured."

"What if we used one of Chefera's invisible servants to carry vines through the threshold? If we can create a continuous mass of living plant matter on the other side, even briefly, we could rootwalk into the vines before they completely die. You've said it yourself—when we tree-stride, we *become* part of the trees, the roots, the plants. Maybe that's enough to mask our presence—our flesh—from the wards."

Gideon's expression grew thoughtful. "It's a clever theory," he admitted. "But even cleverness can't outwit old magic without risk. These wards are powerful, ancient. They've endured for a thousand years. Once triggered, there's no telling what might happen."

Aaron pressed on. "What about Wilmund's idea? He said he could summon crows, have them fly through. If the wards trigger, we know for certain they're still active."

"We'd just end up with dead crows," Gideon said bluntly. "And runes set off. It would confirm what we already suspect—that anything living triggers the magic."

"So... maybe the vines would work?"

"They might," Gideon said slowly. "But these protections weren't meant to keep birds out. They were crafted to keep *us* out. They're not just defenses—they're warnings. Still... your idea has merit. Inventive. But we must tread with caution."

"I know it's dangerous," Aaron said. "But that's why we should try. Whatever's down there—it has to be important. That much protection doesn't guard empty rooms. I'll volunteer."

"No," Gideon said flatly. "You won't."

"Father—"

Gideon held up his hand. "I can only promise this—I'll discuss your theory with the other druids and Chefera. Beyond that, don't get your hopes up."

"If those protections are that strong, they must be guarding incredible relics," Aaron said. "This risk is worth it. Imagine what we might find."

"Your life is not worth that risk," Gideon said, voice firm. "We're not desperate enough to gamble with those protections just to satisfy our curiosity... your curiosity."

Aaron nodded slowly, his enthusiasm dimming. "I understand. But you *will* speak with them?"

"I will," Gideon confirmed. "Because you asked me. But I'll bring it up in my own time. It may not be today or tomorrow. You'll be patient."

He paused, then Gideon softened his tone. "Now—how about a day or two in the village? We need time away from this place."

Aaron managed a crooked smile. "That's not a bad idea."

"Good. After a proper ale or two and restocking supplies, we'll give your theory the attention it deserves." Gideon laid a hand on his son's shoulder. "Aaron... we're nearing the end of this expedition. And you know what we must do before we leave. We have to make sure the Mage-Gate can never be used—ever."

Aaron hesitated, then said, "I understand the mission. But I can't help feeling we're locking a door without ever learning what's on the other side. Even if someone repaired the rune, they'd still need to know how to activate it. And that's not easy—it's practically impossible."

He glanced toward the keep and smiled faintly. "So... when do we leave for the village?"

"Soon," Gideon answered. "We'll go in pairs or threes. I've got assignments for everyone to gather supplies, and once that's done, we'll meet at The Stately Potato for a day or two of relaxation. We've earned it, that's for sure."

"Would it be all right if Wellsey and I worked together? I mean—for the supply run?"

Gideon raised a brow, though he already knew the answer. "I've noticed you enjoy spending time with her. And as the leader of this expedition, I'll say this—you two make a good team."

He hid a smile. It wasn't just teamwork Aaron was hoping for—he recognized the look in his son's eyes. He'd seen it before, long ago, when he first laid eyes on Emma. Young love was a strange thing—exciting, consuming, and wildly confusing. Amusing, and just a little terrifying.

"We do," Aaron said, half-grinning. "She's easy to talk to. Smart. Funny. She was kind of standoffish at first, but…"

"But?"

"You know… she's more agreeable now. Willing to talk. I'm just…" Aaron frowned, clearly groping for the right word. "I'm—what's the word…?"

"Tongue-tied?"

Aaron nodded.

Gideon chuckled. "Then she must mean something to you. Take it slow. You and Wellsey are still young—no need to rush. If what you feel is real, it'll last."

Aaron's smile was sheepish. "It might take us a while to gather everything. You know, in case we get… sidetracked. So if we're late to The Stately Potato, don't wait up."

Gideon raised a brow. "The word you're looking for is *smitten.*"

Aaron lit up. "That's it! *Smitten!*"

"Run along, then. I won't make your list too long—you can spend as much time as you want with her. We'll rootwalk to the camp, then again to the village once were beyond the magical shield."

Gideon watched his son walk away, a spring in his step and hope in his eyes.

He shook his head, smiling. Young love—and all the joy, trouble, and mystery that came with it.

At least the boy had good taste.

As far as Gideon was concerned, Wellsey was a keeper.

The Stately Potato was bustling. With the addition of the druid expedition, the common room was packed to the rafters—voices loud, tankards clinking, the scent of stew and spiced ale thick in the air. Early evening light slanted through the windows, golden and lazy, casting long shadows over the crowd.

Gideon sat near the hearth, nursing an ale and recounting the progress they'd made. Supplies had been secured and delivered to Wilmund's grove. One by one, his companions had trickled in throughout the afternoon, gathering to celebrate a hard-earned day of rest. Nearly everyone was present now—spread around crowded tables, leaning against doorframes and pillars, flushed with drink and laughter.

The message he'd sent to Druid's Glen via The One Tree had gone unanswered. That didn't trouble him—Finola would collect it when she reached the network. He'd check the living web again in the morning. Messages always found their way, eventually.

What did trouble him, though, was the absence of Aaron and Wellsey.

He tapped his fingers against the tankard, brows furrowed. He'd given them space, even anticipated their late return. But dusk had settled, and they still hadn't appeared. Teenagers, perhaps distracted by the novelty of freedom—or by each other. He was just about to call Cedric over and ask if he'd seen them when the room shifted.

It was subtle at first—voices thinning, laughter faltering. A hush rippled outward like wind through tall grass. Heads turned. Chairs scraped back. The crowd parted.

Not for Aaron and Wellsey.

Two figures stepped into view, walking with purpose.

The first, Gideon recognized at once—DeCa. A younger druid from the Midlands, fiercely loyal to Finola. He was dressed for conflict, leather armor scuffed, a curved blade at his hip, and in his hands… the charred remains of a staff.

Gideon's breath caught.

The second man was unfamiliar, but not a stranger. There was tension in his bearing—the way he scanned the room, appraising every soul in it—that suggested danger wrapped in velvet. Another of Finola's, no doubt. A weapon with a name.

Gideon stood slowly. The weight of unease settled on his shoulders like a heavy cloak.

"Heather…" he muttered under his breath, eyes locked on the ruined, mottled staff in DeCa's hands.

Something had gone terribly wrong.

DeCa stopped a few feet from Gideon and offered a curt bow, holding out the burnt staff for him to see.

"Outside," DeCa said, his voice low and deliberate. "I have a message from Druid's Glen."

Gideon's eyes locked onto the ruined wood.

Heather's staff.

Mottled and distinct—now blackened, warped, nearly unrecognizable from the charring.

His heart stopped.

Then started again, harder, thudding with cold dread. His jaw clenched until his teeth ached. Without a word, he turned and followed DeCa through the door and out into the street.

"Out with it," Gideon snapped the moment the door shut behind them.

DeCa didn't flinch. His expression was stone. "You are to come at once to Druid's Glen to discuss the conditions for the release of your daughter. She remains unharmed—for now. You will accompany me back. Alone. And you will not alert the others."

The words hit like a blow to the gut.

Gideon staggered, not in body, but in soul. That hollow, helpless feeling—the one he thought buried with Emma—came rushing back.

Finola.

This was her move. She wanted him gone. She wanted him to abdicate his role, to hand her the mantle of Grand Druid. Now, she had the leverage to force it.

He knew it was a trap. The only question was whether he was clever enough to spring it without being caught in it.

The tavern door creaked open behind him.

Cedric stepped out, Wilmund at his side. Concern etched both their faces. Wilmund's hand drifted toward the ornate dagger at his belt.

"What's going on?" Cedric asked.

Gideon's glance flicked to the two druids watching him. He gave a slow nod, calm returning like armor. Wilmund, reading the shift, eased his hand away from the blade.

"A bit of trouble in Druid's Glen I must attend to personally," Gideon said. "Wilmund, you'll remain in charge until I return. Cedric, look after your brother, and keep him close. In fact—he's overdue. Would you mind finding him and Wellsey? I imagine they've lost track of time." He forced a wry smile. "Teenagers."

Cedric narrowed his eyes. "Is Heather all right?"

Gideon gave DeCa a pointed glance. "Yes. Sound and safe as can be."

He turned back to Wilmund. "After you've gathered the group, I suggest you take another day of rest. Head back to the site the following morning. I'll rejoin you in two days—three at the most."

"It'll be done," Wilmund said. His eyes were shadowed, his face worn. Sleep, it seemed, had not been kind to him lately.

Gideon watched as Cedric and Wilmund slipped back into the tavern, the din of conversation rising up to swallow them.

"Let's go," DeCa said.

"It'll be suspicious if I leave without my things," Gideon replied. "If there's trouble in Druid's Glen, Wilmund will expect me to be prepared for it."

DeCa hesitated, then gave a short nod. "I'll go with you."

Gideon returned to the inn, DeCa shadowing his every move. He retrieved his armor, staff, sword, and pack, watching for any sign of suspicion. Wilmund's expression remained neutral. He wasn't part of this—thank Thatara. Not because he was an ally, but because he wasn't an enemy. Not among the two sons Gideon was leaving behind.

Cedric looked puzzled, but said nothing. He would do as asked.

The second druid—silent all this time—would be the messenger. He'd be tree-striding back to Finola, confirming that Gideon had taken the bait. But it would take time. These weren't master druids. Covering that kind of distance wasn't easy, not without training.

Still, they'd found him. That meant they'd been watching—waiting for him to come to town. Days, maybe longer. They'd used plant-speak, or a relay of short tree-strides, to coordinate this. He did the math in his head. It didn't add up. There wasn't enough time for this to unfold naturally.

Were other forces helping them?

Wizards?

That made it worse. Far worse. If the Wizards of Arcana were involved…

His mind flicked to the one Heather had encountered outside Druid's Glen—the one with the demons.

Could he be part of Finola's scheme?

Gideon didn't ask. He didn't speak.

Without a word, they left The Stately Potato.

Their strides were swift, cutting down the main avenue toward the nearest thicket of mature trees. The sun had dipped below the rooftops, casting long shadows between buildings. As they reached the edge of the forest, the world darkened beneath the thick canopy. Dappled light gave way to near-night as the trees swallowed them whole.

Behind him, DeCa's sword nudged his back.

"Keep moving."

Gideon felt the spell forming in his throat—an incantation that would paralyze DeCa long enough to escape.

But the magic faltered.

Died.

They broke into a clearing.

Two tents stood near a smoldering fire.

Three warriors waited.

One stood motionless, a bow drawn, arrow already nocked and trained on his heart. The other two stepped forward, blades out, gleaming with purpose. Their movements were slow. Deliberate. As if they knew exactly what they were there to do—and fully intended to enjoy it.

This wasn't a warning.

It was reinforcement.

They were here to make sure he tree-strode with DeCa—and that he didn't try anything clever.

"This way," DeCa said, sheathing his sword with a whisper of steel on leather.

He reached beneath his armor and pulled out a leather throng. Hanging from it was a single red leaf—lacquered and preserved. A leaf of The One Tree.

Gideon's stomach turned. A talisman. How had DeCa come by such a sacred object? Had Finola allied with the Wizards of Arcana? Or worse—what had she traded for such favors?

"Move," DeCa ordered, gesturing toward the nearest tree.

As they approached, Gideon whispered a spell under his breath, quiet enough to be lost in the crunch of leaves beneath their boots.

"Touch my shoulder," DeCa said.

Gideon complied, placing his hand on the man's shoulder. DeCa began his incantation.

But Gideon finished first.

He slapped his palm against the bark, and the tree swallowed them whole.

They emerged not where DeCa intended, but just outside Wilmund's grove—exactly where Gideon had aimed.

The moment his boots touched soil, Gideon pivoted and cracked DeCa across the back of the head with his staff. The blow staggered him. A second shove sent him to his knees.

With a word of power, virulent grasses erupted around DeCa's limbs, snagging and binding him to the ground. He struggled once, twice—and was caught fast.

"You just killed your daughter," DeCa growled. "They expect me any moment."

Gideon didn't believe him. That kind of timing was too tight—even for Finola.

Without hesitation, Gideon spun the staff and struck DeCa again, this time across the temple. The crack echoed through the trees. DeCa collapsed, unmoving.

The grasses held him fast. Whether he was unconscious or dead, Gideon didn't check. There wasn't time.

They had his daughter.

His Heather.

The rage hit him like a hammer—hot, immediate, and all-consuming—driving out every other thought. He couldn't afford rage.

Not now. But it simmered beneath the surface, waiting for the moment it could be unleashed.

When it did, there would be no mercy.

He reached down and snatched the talisman, fingers closing around the lacquered red leaf. He meant to destroy it, to crush it between his hands and snuff out whatever connection it held to The One Tree.

But instinct, or a whisper of caution stayed his hand.

Destroying it now might close a door he would need later.

With grim resolve, he slipped the leather throng over his neck.

If Finola meant this talisman to be his leash, his noose, then he'd turn it into her downfall. Maybe it still had uses. Maybe it would bring him close enough to finish this.

He muttered the first incantation, placed his hand on the nearest tree, and vanished.

He'd go as far as the talisman—and his own magic—would carry him. Alone, he could make at least eight strides before exhaustion set in. That might be enough.

His hope rested with a fickle dryad druid who might not help him. But if she did…

He would find Heather.

He would get her to safety.

And then he would deal with Finola.

Chapter Twelve

∞

Dungeon

aron held Wellsey's hand, her permission granted after some teasing negotiation. With the supplies staged at Wilmund's grove, they had the rest of the day to themselves. No oversight. No duties. Just time.

Time to explore the keep.

If luck was on their side, they'd slip into the dungeon beneath Mikal Yholl's stronghold, uncover whatever secrets lay below, and return in time for dinner at The Stately Potato. If they couldn't bypass the protections, no one would be the wiser. They'd show up late, blame the village crowds, and let the others think nothing of it.

They held hands until they reached the keep, where they began hacking through the thick gold glory vines, twisting them into a rope of living-dead plant matter. The key to Aaron's plan. He was certain it would work. It *had* to.

Once the path was cleared, they rechecked their armor, packs, and weapons. Then, without a word, they pushed open the towering doors and stepped inside.

"What do you think we'll find?" Wellsey asked as the double doors thudded behind her. "Treasure? Magic?"

"I think perhaps…" Aaron's voice trailed off. He had turned toward the Mage-Gate—and stopped cold.

The Elder Runes gleamed in the dim light.

All six.

The broken one—restored.

Silver perfectly inlaid into the ancient lattice, not a scratch out of place. A low hum filled the air, vibrating through the stone beneath their feet. The Mage-Gate wasn't dormant anymore.

It was alive.

"Wellsey," Aaron said slowly, "the gate is active."

"How?" she asked, stunned. "Could it have… malfunctioned? Some kind of mistake?"

"No. It's been repaired," Aaron said, pointing with his staff. "And none of us—not me, not Gideon, *no one*—knows how to do that. Or how to turn it on."

They stared at the gate in silence. The air seemed thicker now. Wellsey shifted uneasily, hugging her staff to her chest.

"What is it?" Aaron asked, watching her.

"A few times," she whispered, "I got this feeling—like I get back in Heerveen. When men watch me. When I know they're there, but they don't want to be seen. Someone has been watching us. Maybe this whole time. I should have told Gideon."

Aaron's blood simmered. His eyes swept the hall, searching every shadow, every alcove. No signs. Nothing obvious.

Then his gaze snapped back to the Mage-Gate.

He stepped toward it.

"What are you doing?" Wellsey called, alarmed.

"I have to see it up close," Aaron replied, breathless. "I have to."

He didn't wait for permission.

His boots scraped across the stone floor, breath quickening with each step. He reached the base of the ramp.

The Mage-Gate shuddered.

And then it whirred to life.

The portal in the middle spiraled open, swirling with distorted colors—perhaps a glimpse of the destination. Aaron put his foot on the ramp and ascended to the platform, heart pounding. He could go through… just for a second… just to see where it went.

A hand yanked him back with surprising force.

"Aaron! We don't know where it goes! Whoever's been watching us could still be here."

He went rigid. "The dungeons," he said. "Maybe they've been hiding there."

"And waiting for us to leave," she added. "So they could fix the Mage-Gate. But how do they know how to use it? To turn it on?"

"It has to be a wizard," Aaron said. "They've been spying on us, using magic to hide or hiding in the one place we haven't explored."

"The dungeons," Wellsey whispered.

"To hide from us, they must have magical knowledge and expertise. Only a wizard of great skill could do that."

"A wizard like that could have hurt us," Wellsey said. "He could have attacked at any time."

"Yet he didn't." Aaron paused to think, his gaze lingering on the humming Mage-Gate. "Instead of attacking us, he fixed the Elder Rune and activated the Mage-Gate. He was spying upon us all along, then was waiting for us to leave." His thoughts turned to Heather and the wizard she fought outside Druid's Glen. He couldn't ignore the logic, and that was the simplest explanation—it was the same wizard.

"We need to tell the others the Mage-Gate is active," Wellsey said. "We can be back here in an hour with Gideon and the others."

Aaron hesitated. "What if we peek through? In and out, a few seconds tops. It must function like a doorway."

"No," Wellsey said. "If there is a wizard waiting at the destination, he would make quick work of you. I doubt they'll be friendly."

Aaron bit his lip as he walked up the ramp. "He could still be in the dungeons, thinking we'll be gone for days. Maybe we should…"

"Aaron." Wellsey's voice was sharp as she pulled him to a stop. "We've already messed up by sneaking back here to go into the dungeons. Let's not follow one stupid decision with another. We must get our companions."

The air between them and the Mage-Gate crackled with a low droning noise.

Aaron opened his mouth to argue but stopped. She was right— they *should* turn back. But curiosity gnawed at him. This was a Mage-Gate comprised of ancient magic. It had to function like a door.

He kissed her quickly, grinning as he pulled back.

"Aaron…" Wellsey said, blushing. "What…?"

"I'm going."

"Aaron!" Wellsey hissed. "Are you insane?"

"Just one quick look!" Aaron grabbed her hand, and before she could stop him, he pulled her with him into the swirling colors.

The magic enveloped them, and they vanished.

Though the stillness was unsettling, Brak maintained his routine of watching Gideon from the battlements, half-swallowed by the virulent gold glory vines that choked the ruins. He had long since mastered the art of moving unseen—just as he had in Druid's Glen, where his arcane talents fooled the wild protections into thinking him a harmless creature. Here, too, he had become a shadow, a lowly crow by day, a watcher by night.

Direct observation proved difficult. The vines were too dense, and the druids too active. So he relied on scrying spells—finicky, unreliable things near the keep. The closer he cast to the Mage-Gate, the more erratic the visions became. He had adjusted his technique, repositioned himself, even changed the materials used in his divination bowls. It didn't matter.

A latent enchantment—certainly by design—was distorting the magic. A ward left by Mikal Yholl himself, perhaps. The thought intrigued him. If the interference was intentional, then the old Mage had feared what eyes might peer too closely at his secrets. And rightly so.

Still, the scrying had its uses. Combined with the occasional midnight prowl through the upper levels, Brak had learned more than enough. He knew their rhythms. Sooner or later, the druids would leave—either to resupply or to report their findings. That was when he would strike. Full access. No interruptions. No observers. Time to do his master's will.

The brittle stack of parchment tucked in his satchel supported his theory. Beneath the keep, in the dungeon levels, lay the molds, the patterns, and the strange silver-like alloy used to repair the broken Elder Rune. Not true silver—something older, ancient and alien, more receptive to infernal and celestial enchantment. That was why Mikal had built the Infernal Sanctum here, atop veins of buried power.

And fortune was with him. The druids had avoided the lower levels. Whatever they sensed, it had frightened them just enough to keep them cautious.

He had already dismantled the original wards at the dungeon entrance, painstakingly and in silence while they slept. In their place, he had woven subtle enchantments that mimicked the originals—perfectly, or near enough. None of the lesser druids would detect the change.

Not even Wilmund, who wore the mantle of Archdruid but lacked the instincts to match.

Only Gideon might see through it. The Grand Druid had a mind for hidden things.

But he wouldn't have time.

Brak scratched the stubble along his jaw, annoyed by its unevenness. He preferred to be clean-shaven—precise. Not out of vanity, but because it reflected discipline. Precision in the mind, precision in magic. His goatee had gone wild, and his mustache was beginning to curl. Another indignity he would endure for now. Soon, all of this would be behind him.

The wizard gathered his supplies and weapons, prepared for whatever guardians might linger in the dungeons. Undead were likely, but given Mikal's allegiance to the Nine Hells, Brak suspected devils and fiends might be bound here as well. He carried spells of flame and frost for infernal adversaries—and sunlight, in case the undead were there to challenge him.

He allowed himself a moment of righteous satisfaction. He had accomplished all this beneath Gideon's nose—breached the sanctum's outer wards, infiltrated the keep, and now stood ready to repair the Elder Rune. Soon, Mikal Yholl's secrets would be his to command.

Doubt was rare in Brak's mind, but teleporting within the Infernal Sanctum's reach gave him pause. The protective barrier surrounding the keep stretched for miles in a perfect sphere—Mage-crafted, enduring, and painfully effective. It repelled all magical travel, save for the Mage-Gates themselves. Ingenious. Everlasting.

He cast the spell.

The air around him shimmered and folded inward, and in the next instant, he stood within the dungeons—exactly where he had envisioned. Drawing his short sword, its cold white enchantment lit the space around him. With a word, he extended the spell's glow and pushed it ahead into the archway.

He stepped forward.

The protections, now attuned to him, parted like a curtain. He entered a long stone hallway, the walls carved in intricate bas relief— scenes of torment, domination, infernal conquest. War. Death.

As he moved deeper, dormant sconces flared to life on their own, shedding pale yellow light interspersed with flickers of white. The corridor stretched ahead, chill and utterly dry, as though the place had been sealed off from the world for centuries.

Brak smiled. He was certain—no one had walked these halls in an age.

He cast simple protections upon himself, uncertain of what lay ahead. As his gaze lingered on the devilish carvings along the walls, unease pricked at the edge of his thoughts. Still gripping his sword, he moved forward.

His light caught something—metal in the floor. He froze.

The glow spread through the gloom, revealing twin pentagrams inlaid into the stone floor, crafted from hammered gold. The air buzzed with quiet tension.

A trap.

Brak raised his hand and summoned a sword of glowing force, sending it sailing down the hallway beyond the pentagrams.

The response was immediate.

The air shimmered—distorted—and from the heart of each pentagram, portals tore open. A pair of towering Carverfiends emerged, their angular, skeletal forms radiating malice. Jagged spines flexed along their backs. Their whip-like tails struck the ground with audible cracks, stingers dripping venom that sizzled on the stone.

Brak didn't hesitate. A flick of his wrist, and a cone of frost erupted from his hand, the temperature plummeting with a thundercrack of cold. Ice surged across the pentagrams, engulfing the devils' limbs in rime. The spell wouldn't kill them—but it would slow them. The frost bit into their joints, seizing them mid-motion.

The fiend on the left snapped its jaws and strained forward, dragging frozen limbs across the slick stone. Too slow.

Brak's dancing sword struck first.

It flashed across the air with impossible speed and drove itself into the creature's chest, slipping between its rib-like plates. A strangled hiss escaped the fiend as its form convulsed, then ruptured into ichor and dust, banished back to its infernal realm.

The second Carverfiend shattered its icy shackles with a howl, swinging its black glaive in a wide arc. Brak sidestepped, his cloak billowing as the blade missed him by inches.

The creature lunged—but the dancing sword was faster.

It cleaved downward, splitting the fiend's skull from crown to jaw. The creature froze in place, then collapsed into a steaming pool of black filth.

Brak stepped through the silence that followed, the last hiss of magic fading from the air. He flicked his fingers, recalling the spectral sword to his side, its edge still gleaming with infernal gore.

Although he was accustomed to foul stenches—years of summoning demons had dulled his senses—the reek that filled this chamber sent him reeling.

He turned his face away and raised a sleeve to cover his nose and mouth, shuffling quickly toward a set of closed double doors. Behind him, the dancing sword clattered dutifully, less graceful than its master as it scraped against the wood trying to follow.

Brak shot it a glare and gestured sharply. The blade veered off down a side corridor.

The hallway beyond was no less foul but far more intriguing. The walls here were covered in detailed bas-relief—devilish carvings of infernal war. He paused, recognition blooming across his features.

There they were: towering Hellmaws, angular Carverfiends like the ones he had just dispatched, crystalline Frostbinders with cruel spears, chain-draped Lashbinders, and faceless Whisperspikes that whispered treason straight into the mind. In the background, swarms of Emberkin oozed across the battlefield like infernal larvae.

But opposite them—demons.

The mural depicted the Eternal Rift, the unending war between the Nine Hells and the Abyss. And though the devils were winning in this rendering, the depictions of their foes gave Brak pause.

He traced the infernal stone with reverent fingers, admiring the likenesses: hulking Throk'Gar, ape-shaped demons strong enough to tear a Hellmaw limb from limb; the scorpion-bodied Kravax, lethal and swift; gaunt, vulture-headed Voltogs with pincer talons, always among his favorites; and the gleaming emerald carapaces of the insectoid Zaskali, their sickle-bladed arms captured mid-swarm.

The field beneath them was strewn with the mangled forms of Drog'shar, Charn'Va, Maggoritch, Ur'thella, and Zulgosh—all rendered in exquisite detail, caught in frozen death.

Brak stared at them all, his breath slow and measured, and allowed himself a moment of cruel pride.

One day, he would turn that tide. The carving may show the devils triumphant, but the future belonged to those who could embrace the chaos.

He moved on.

The passage ended at a junction: a door straight ahead, and a darkened corridor to the right. Without hesitation, he chose the door, pushing it open just wide enough for the floating sword to pass through first.

A short hallway greeted him, leading to another pair of double doors, these carved in even greater detail. The same war raged across their surfaces, though here the craftsmanship was more refined— perhaps personal.

He placed a hand on the dry, cracked wood and pushed. The hinges groaned in protest, shedding flakes of rust and age to the floor.

Whatever lay beyond, it had been sealed for centuries.

The ghostly sword floated ahead of Brak, its pale blue glow casting long, flickering shadows across the chamber. Here, time had held its breath.

Lavish carpets stretched across the stone floor. Intricate tapestries clung to the walls, their woven threads still vibrant. Towering bookshelves brimmed with ancient tomes, scrolls, and records. A carved writing desk, several locked chests, and a high, canopied bed occupied the corners.

This was a sanctum. A vault of knowledge.

A place of answers.

As Brak stepped further in, the torchless sconces flared to life, exhaling eerie green flames. The room's shadows twisted and stretched—and then the sword's light struck something large.

And wrong.

A grotesque construct hunched at the chamber's heart. It was massive, its bulk stitched together from corpses—necrotic flesh patched in mismatched tones, knotted together with thick, blackened sutures. One leg was armored in human skin, the other scaled like a lizard's. Metal bolts jutted from its joints like spikes, anchoring muscle to bone. Despite its mass, it moved with an unnatural, pendulous grace.

Its face was worse.

A collage of stolen features sewn into one warped expression of suffering. One milky eye bulged lidless, the other sank deep into a recessed socket. Its mouth hung half open, lips chewed, a partial tongue writhing as if trying to form a word it didn't remember.

A stupid thing. Brak had seen similar abominations—slaved to commands, animated by blood, bone, or soul fragments. Not clever. Just dangerous.

The golem stirred.

It flexed thick fingers, the motion creaking like old leather dragged across wire. Its arm twitched. Then it moved—one ponderous step, then another. The impact trembled through the carpet and into the soles of Brak's boots.

Then it charged.

The sword struck first—blinding speed and deadly aim. The enchanted blade buried itself deep into the creature's torso.

It didn't even grunt.

The golem seized the blade with one enormous hand, lifted it effortlessly, and hurled it aside. The blade clanged off a bookcase, gouging the wood, then recovered its flight mid-air.

Brak swore under his breath and took two quick steps back. If it grabbed him, it would pulp his body in moments. That thing wasn't built to stop intruders. It was built to break them.

The golem swung a meaty arm. Brak ducked, barely—feeling the air rush past his head. The strike hit the desk behind him and shattered it in an explosion of splinters and steel fittings.

Time to rethink.

He circled, muttering under his breath. He needed to bind it. Blind it. Burn it. Or break its command tether—whatever soul anchor kept it upright.

His eyes scanned the chamber—looking for a rune, a glyph, a control rod. Anything.

If Mikal had built this thing, it wouldn't die by brute force. No, there would be a weakness. And Brak intended to find it before this stitched bastard found him.

Damn this stupid, lumbering thing.

With a sharp motion, Brak extended his free hand. A surge of fire burst from his palm, cascading over the golem's chest and shoulders. Flames licked across the patchwork skin, blackening it in uneven streaks.

It didn't stop.

The abomination charged through the blaze, swinging a massive fist like a battering ram.

Brak ducked backward, retreating toward the chamber door as the golem's strike obliterated a wooden chair, sending splinters skittering across the stone.

In the hallway now, Brak flicked his fingers, directing the ghostly sword. The enchanted blade surged forward, slashing across the construct's shoulder. It carved downward, severing the arm at the elbow with a wet, cracking snap. The limb tumbled to the floor in a heap of flesh and metal.

The golem didn't falter.

It turned its mangled body toward Brak, eyes hollow, and charged through the open doorway—unyielding, unthinking.

With another flick of his wrist, Brak summoned a second blast of fire. It struck the creature's head full-on. The flesh sizzled and split, stitched seams bursting open. One eye boiled in its socket, the other melting down its ruined cheek. The aged wooden door beside it caught fire, flames blooming across its surface.

Still, it came forward.

Brak gritted his teeth. It was too heavy, too solid. Fire alone wouldn't stop it quickly enough.

The dancing sword descended again from behind, driving through the creature's thick neck and punching out through its throat. The blade twisted, severing tendons and spinal cords alike. The head lolled to one side, still held on by necrotic strands.

The golem staggered.

It dropped to one knee, swaying—its remaining hand reaching out for balance. The gesture failed.

With a final, shuddering lurch, the construct collapsed. The impact rattled the floor. Dust billowed from the ruined carpet, mingling with a haze of ash and smoke. The stink of burnt flesh choked the air.

Brak stood over the corpse-heap, breath steady, eyes sharp, surveying the damage. Smoke curled toward the ceiling. The acrid stench of burnt flesh and old death clung to the air. The door was burning.

He flicked his fingers, sending a fan of frost over the flames, snuffing them out in a hiss of steam.

The wizard stepped over the smoldering corpse, brushing soot from his cloak. He touched the frozen door and it fell from its hinges, crashing onto the floor. He scanned the chamber. The books, the scrolls, the documents—Mikal's knowledge lay before him.

And Brak intended to take every secret for himself.

The magic enveloped Aaron and Wellsey, pulling them through space—and when they emerged on the other side, the cold hit them like a slap.

They stumbled onto the platform of another Mage-Gate, identical in shape and construction to the one they had left behind. Wind howled through shattered windows, driving sleet and freezing rain into the chamber. The air reeked of salt and decay.

Aaron's eyes adjusted to the dim light. He shivered as he spotted the piles of bones scattered across the floor.

"We're not alone," Wellsey whispered, her grip tightening around his hand.

Aaron swallowed hard, his gaze lingering on the skeletal remains. *What have we gotten ourselves into?*

They stood in a massive circular room—roughly one hundred sixty feet across—and it was deathly cold. The floor was set with gray granite, matching the walls both inside and out. Open windows with broken wooden sashes lined the chamber, admitting the full force of the storm. Rain and sleet blew in sideways, driven by savage winds.

To either side of the Mage-Gate, slate benches were set into the stonework, once intended for quiet observation or contemplation. The masonry was flawless, the craftsmanship ancient but still precise.

Directly ahead, sixty-five feet away, loomed the central staircase. It was wide and flanked by multiple sliding doors in various states of decay—some intact, others cracked or partially fallen from their frames.

Aaron glanced upward. Thick beams and trusses supported the pitched roof overhead. Though visibly weathered, the structure held. Rain trickled through small leaks, channeling into narrow culverts carved into the floor, feeding rusted iron drains. It was in far better condition than the roof of Mikal's ruined keep.

Aaron turned his attention to the windows—some shattered, others intact—and took a careful look at the outside world. Sleet and frozen rain battered the stone walls, driven sideways by howling winds. The storm blotted out any hint of sunlight. Cold clung to the air like a second skin.

To either side of the Mage-Gate, sections of the tower were sealed off behind massive double doors. As his eyes adjusted to the dimness, he saw piles of rubble and the remains of broken furniture—shattered crates, splintered barrels, collapsed shelving. Whatever had once filled this chamber was long since destroyed.

He descended the ramp, the cold pressing into him like a weight. He shivered. As he stepped clear of the Mage-Gate platform, soft lights flickered to life along the walls. Torchless sconces awakened—casting a dim but welcome glow to his left and right.

Navigating between the slate benches, he stepped carefully across the damp stone floor. It was slick in places, and he moved with caution. He reached the nearest window and wiped away the condensation with the sleeve of his cloak.

They were high—hundreds of feet above the ground, perched inside a tower that overlooked the world below. His estimate put it at four hundred feet, maybe more.

Far below, a violent ocean churned. Waves crested and crashed against jagged black rocks. The spray was lost in the distance, but he could feel its presence all the same. Near the shoreline, dense stands of white spruce trees crowded the landscape. It was a tangle of trunks, branches, and beds of old needles. No signs of civilization met his eye.

No smoke. No light from fires. No roads. Just wild, untouched land shrouded in mist and storm.

Wellsey followed him to the window, placed a hand on his shoulder, and said, "We should get back." She tapped her staff against the stone floor for emphasis.

Aaron nodded absently, still peering into the storm. "White spruce—native to coastal regions in the northwest…"

"Now," Wellsey cut in. "Back. Now."

He turned, his gaze snapping to the Mage-Gate still thrumming with active energy. Together, they walked toward the ramp.

Aaron slowed, a thought tugging at the edge of his mind.

Twelve symbols for destinations. Six Elder Runes. His father had said it was overkill. But what if—

"I figured it out!" he blurted. "I know why there are six Elder Runes! It's not just security—it's power distribution. You need one rune to activate the gate you're standing on. The other five? They power the destination. That's how you remotely activate the other end. That's it! That's it!"

The wind eased. The storm fell still for a breath, and in the sudden quiet, the Mage-Gate's low hum filled the space like a heartbeat.

"Let's go!" Wellsey begged. "Please, before something bad happens. Before the wizard finds us!"

Without another word, they ran up the ramp, gripping each other's hands. Together, they leapt into the swirling magic.

The world twisted.

A blast of dry, suffocating heat struck them the instant they emerged. Aaron stumbled, blinking against the sudden brightness pouring through shattered windows. The air was thick and hot. Dust clung to their skin.

He turned in place, his heart plummeting.

"This isn't the keep," he said. "We're somewhere else."

After plundering the bedroom, Brak pressed deeper into the dungeons, navigating corridors untouched by time. What he sought lay ahead.

A mine for the rare silvery alloy—Mikal's secret resource.

A crushing chamber where raw ore had once been processed.

A furnace, a refining crucible, and the original graphite molds.

According to Brak's journal, Mikal had been obsessively paranoid. He alone controlled the creation of Mage-Gates, hoarding the enchanted alloy and locking away the molds so that no one—Mage, artificer, or rival—could replicate his work. Even his most trusted subordinates had been kept in the dark, forced to rely on him to shape and inscribe the Elder Runes.

But now, all of it belonged to Brak.

He gathered the molds, consolidating them into a single crate for preservation. These weren't relics—they were power. With them, he could dictate the fate of the Mage-Gates, just as Mikal once had.

And with enough of the alloy, he could forge additional gates. He had the instructions. The schematics. The keys to empire.

Setting the crate aside, he selected the mold he needed most. A flick of his fingers summoned flame. The old furnace roared to life as Brak conjured a torrent of magical fire, feeding the crucible until the alloy softened and bubbled.

When the metal reached the proper consistency, he guided the glowing mixture into the mold with steady precision. Minutes passed as he watched it cool, his breath fogging in the stillness.

Then—sharp hiss, a frost cantrip sealed the cast.

Brak exhaled slowly and pulled his journal from his satchel. He had studied these pages for weeks, memorizing every precise step, every arcane detail. Now he whispered the enchantment, layering the lattice with energy, binding the silver's form to the function of the gate.

When the spell was complete, he examined the piece under flickering light—flawless.

He tucked the repaired lattice into his pack, alongside several untouched ingots scavenged from the shelves.

The mold had cooled enough now. Brak quenched it in water, steam curling around his fingers as he lifted it, testing its resilience.

It remained intact.

Perfect.

He hammered the crate shut and let out a muffled shout of victory.

He had the molds.

He had the knowledge.

He had the metal.

He alone controlled the keys to the Mage-Gates.

With these, he could repair any Elder Rune he encountered.

The activation sequence was committed to memory—etched into his thoughts as deeply as any spell.

Brak exhaled and hefted the crate, picturing his chosen hiding place in the keep's fortifications.

Now, he just had to wait for the fools above to leave.

And with any luck, they wouldn't notice the missing silver piece— or that, in the shadows beneath them, the Mage-Gate was already being restored.

Wellsey spun around, her staff raised. "What? How—?"

"We're somewhere else," Aaron muttered again, voice distant.

His mind raced, thoughts tangling in confusion and panic. *This doesn't make sense. We should have gone back to the keep...*

He forced a deep breath, willing himself to focus as they descended the ramp.

"What now?" Wellsey asked, clutching his arm. "We're stuck, aren't we? All because of your arrogance! Aaron, how are we going to get out of this place?"

"I'm sorry," he said. "I assumed... assumed it would lead back to the keep. I don't understand. It's not logical."

"You are *so* arrogant!" she snapped, fire flashing in her eyes.

Aaron took hold of her shoulder and waited. The storm behind her eyes slowly ebbed, just enough.

"I'm sorry I got us into this," he said. "But it may be my *arrogance* that gets us out."

"That doesn't make me feel any better," she hissed. "What do we do now?"

He didn't answer.

He was staring past her—at the tragedy unfolding in silence before them.

The circular room was identical in shape and size to the cold tower—one hundred sixty feet across—but this place was wrong. Utterly wrong.

Bones were everywhere.

Scattered across the floor in chaotic heaps. Stacked in corners like discarded firewood. Skulls grinned from the shadows, some human, others twisted with horns and fangs. Ribs jutted like broken teeth from shattered torsos.

Dried corpses clung to the edges of the room, still draped in scraps of faded clothing. Their skin was parchment-thin and stretched tight over brittle frames.

Five of them sat upright against the far wall, legs folded neatly beneath them like statues, throats slashed so deep Aaron could almost feel the blade himself. The wounds still gleamed in the low light—wet-looking, red-edged.

As though it had happened only yesterday.

Their final moments preserved. Their agony, waiting.

"They didn't just die here," Wellsey whispered, her voice trembling. "They were left here. Abandoned."

A lone body, perfectly preserved, lay between the Mage-Gate and the stairs. A knife jutted from its chest, the hilt angled as if placed, not thrown. Around the chamber, the tattered remnants of tents sagged against the stone. Whatever this place had been, it had become a tomb. Packs, sacks, crates, chests—dozens of them—sat piled in neat, orderly rows. Possessions meant to be carried. Meant to be saved.

"What happened here? Why are we here? Where is *here?*" Wellsey asked, her voice rising with each word.

Aaron turned to her, doing his best to remain calm. "I don't know. But I'll figure it out."

He stepped back toward the Mage-Gate.

"Aaron! Wait—"

He jumped into the portal without hesitation.

The cold slammed into him the moment he emerged, rain and sleet battering the stone walls once again. He descended the ramp, his boots splashing in shallow pools as he turned to examine the arch of the Mage-Gate.

Twelve glowing runes stared back—identical to the ones in the keep, save for two.

The one resembled an overlapping T and A was missing.

The other was entirely new: an I and S, fused together.

That one hadn't been there before.

IS—that had to be the master Mage-Gate in Mikal Yholl's keep. Which meant TA marked the Cold Tower.

He sprinted up the ramp and hurled himself into the swirling magic once more.

This time, the blast of heat nearly knocked him flat. He staggered on the sunbaked stone, blinking in the light. Dust and dry air coated his tongue as he reached the base of the ramp and turned back to the Mage-Gate.

There it was again—the missing rune.

This time, the symbol AA—two overlapping A's—was gone.

That was it.

Each Mage-Gate displayed all possible destinations except for itself.

TA was the Cold Tower.

AA was the Desert Tower.

IS was the master Mage-Gate in the keep.

"Aaron!" Wellsey called, sprinting down the ramp. "Don't do that again! What if you couldn't get back to me? We do this together. *Together!*"

"Sorry," he said. "I was curious."

He gestured to the gate. "The Mage-Gates are open to each other now, and I think they're identical—except each one is missing its own symbol. That's how I figured it out. Mikal's gate doesn't show IS—his own keep. So our wizard friend… whoever repaired that Elder Rune… they knew exactly what they were doing. They knew how to turn them on."

Wellsey gripped Aaron's arm, buried her head in his shoulder, and whispered, "How are we going to get back? Aaron, I'm *so* mad at you…"

"I need to think," he said, cutting her off gently. "We need to think. Either we figure out how to operate the Mage-Gate—unlikely—

or we find the wizard and convince him to send us back. That at least has *some* chance of success."

"That's a *terrible* plan. And where is he? Or she? Or *it?*"

Aaron didn't respond. His eyes scanned the room, absorbing the layout, the decay, the evidence of what had come before.

"Wellsey, what do you see here?" he asked quietly.

"I see camps," she said, her voice tight. "Hundreds of people. Dead a long time. That's what I see."

"This was a last stand," Aaron said. "A final hope. They gathered everything they had—packed their belongings, huddled by the Mage-Gate—and waited. This was supposed to be their escape."

"You're saying… they were waiting for someone to activate the gate?"

"Yes," he said, gesturing to the worn backpacks, the neatly stacked crates, the decayed tents. "They were ready. They were *prepared* to leave. But no one came."

"And you think it was Mikal Yholl they were waiting for?"

"Maybe. If he controlled the gates, he was probably the only one who *could* get them out." Aaron paused. "But this was around the time he was captured and executed. He couldn't save them. Or maybe… he chose not to."

Wellsey turned toward the shattered window and pointed. "That tells me the Mage-Gate *was* their only hope. Question is, why?"

Aaron nodded. "This place must've been isolated. Cut off. There may have been nowhere else to go."

Aaron stepped over the preserved bodies and approached a window, wiping the dust away with his sleeve. Outside, there was nothing but endless desert. At the edge of his vision, a smudge of black interrupted the horizon—something that might once have been civilization.

"I think there was a city here," he said quietly. "And it's been swallowed by the desert. Maybe hundreds of years ago… maybe more. If I had to guess, we're deep south of Pehrone, Flaux Smya—maybe even Scuria where the sand stretches forever. And I haven't seen a single tree."

"No green-speak. No rootwalk," Wellsey said. "Shades."

Aaron returned to her, gently gripping her shoulders and giving her a small, affectionate shake before pulling her into an embrace.

"I'm sorry," he said. "For being so arrogant. This isn't what I thought would happen."

"Well, what *are* we going to do?" she asked, her voice holding only a trace of anger now. "Can you really get us out of here? What about the wizard?"

"We need to figure out where he is," Aaron said. "Let's think this through. Step by step." He motioned to a nearby bench. "Come on. Let's sit."

They settled onto a slate bench, brushing away the dust. In front of them, the Mage-Gate pulsed softly with arcane energy.

Aaron pointed toward it. "He was hiding in the dungeons—probably watching us, waiting. Once we left for the village, that was his moment. He repaired the broken rune, then opened the Mage-Gate."

Wellsey nodded. "And he chose the cold tower as his destination."

"Why go there?" Aaron asked, his brow furrowing. The oppressive heat pressed in on him now and sweat beaded along his forehead.

"Well, maybe it wasn't a choice," she said. "Maybe those were the only two destinations available. But more likely… there's something he *needs* in each tower."

Aaron's expression sharpened. "And if he didn't find it in the cold tower… then he came here."

"To look for the next piece of whatever puzzle he's trying to solve."

"Right," Aaron said. "Which means he changed the destination of the Mage-Gate *after* visiting the cold tower. He's here now. Somewhere in this tower."

The thought settled heavily between them.

"Wellsey?" he asked, watching her face.

"I think you're right," she said. "The wizard is here. And we need to find him—before he finds us."

"I need to look outside again."

Aaron stood and crossed the room, taking care not to disturb the remains around them. He stepped over bones and preserved bodies, measuring each footfall. At the window, the late afternoon sun slanted in, casting long rays across the floor. He stared out across the wasteland.

No movement. Nothing alive.

In the distance, he thought he saw water—a lake or maybe the sea—but it could've been a trick of the heat. The land was covered in dunes. Faint impressions of roads still stretched across the sand, half-buried and useless. No one had traveled them in years. Maybe centuries. Yet the ruined city on the horizon remained, a dark smudge just visible. From this vantage, Aaron could pick out skeletal structures rising from the desert—what was left of a civilization.

"If the wizard's here," he said, "he must be in the levels below. This tower's huge—must be four hundred feet tall. That's at least twenty levels."

"Not counting what might lie beneath the main floor," Wellsey added. "Just like the keep."

Aaron nodded, still staring. "How did this tower even get here? There's nothing but desert in every direction. How do you build something like this? Gray granite like this would need to be quarried and hauled in—and there's no sign of a quarry."

"I'll tell you how it was built," Wellsey said. "Magic. Just like the keep. Same stonework, same precision. The cuts are perfect, fitted without mortar. Like dwarven craftsmanship—but I doubt any dwarf would've helped Mikal Yholl."

Aaron turned toward her. "The wizard knew exactly what he was doing. He repaired the Mage-Gate, then aligned it to this place. That wasn't random. It was deliberate."

"You think this is a trap?"

"Yes." Aaron's hands curled into fists. "I was so stupid. This was a trap."

"A trap for us?" Wellsey asked, her voice low beneath the hum of the still-active portal.

"He's the only one who knows how to operate the Mage-Gates," Aaron said. "He went from the keep to the cold tower—and then changed the destination to here. So if anyone follows him, they don't follow him at all. They get stuck."

"Well," Wellsey muttered, staring at the Mage-Gate, "it worked."

Aaron scanned the bones and debris scattered across the room. "Unless we find whatever he's after, we'll have no leverage—no way to convince him to send us back. Do you really think he's here, in the desert tower?"

"Yes, desert tower," Wellsey answered without hesitation. "I think he arrived at the cold tower, then opened a portal to this place and came through. He wouldn't have lingered."

"Makes sense," Aaron agreed.

"What should we do?" she asked.

"I think we should go back to the cold tower and see what's outside. There was ocean and forest, and it was cold—springtime in the north, maybe? I'm thinking it must be somewhere in the northwest? We can rootwalk from there, at least get away from this place."

"Or far northeast," Wellsey countered. "Same conditions up there, if not worse. The tower could be in either direction."

"True. Good point. We won't rule out the east or the north along the Sea of Ice."

Aaron pointed at the Mage-Gate. "Shall we? I'm not exactly looking forward to the cold."

"Aaron, this is not how I envisioned this day turning out."

He took her hand, kissed it, and flashed a playful grin. "Come on—look on the bright side. This'll make a great story for our grandchildren someday."

"You're assuming we'll live that long. We still have to get out of here."

"Details," he said with a shrug.

She rolled her eyes but couldn't hide her smile. "Let's survive today. *Then* we can argue about grandkids."

Brak passed the time poring over the faded journal, tracing each line of Mikal's meticulous process for constructing a Mage-Gate. Additional magic and rare materials were required—substances difficult to find, possibly irreplaceable. Still, in theory, he could replicate one in his hidden stronghold. It might take years, but the idea gnawed at him. Perhaps there were substitutes. Perhaps not.

His patience wore thin. The druids above were still scouring the city ruins, cataloging trinkets and chasing shadows. All the while, he longed to return to the treasure hoard beneath the keep—to dig deeper into Mikal's secrets, the real secrets, not the scraps these surface dwellers obsessed over.

But he knew better than to abandon his post. Not yet. Spying on the druids remained too important.

Brak stretched within the narrow confines of his hidden camp, joints cracking as he worked the stiffness from his limbs. He whispered an incantation, closing his eyes to direct the magic outward. Images flickered in his mind—distorted shapes, blurred edges. The voices came like whispers through water, muffled and indistinct.

He focused harder.

Then he narrowed the spell's reach, aiming it directly toward Gideon and his son, Aaron.

I will, because you asked me. But I'll bring it up in my own time. It may not be today or tomorrow. You'll be patient. Now—how about a day or two in the village? We need time away from this place.

Brak's focus intensified.

They were leaving. A day or two—just long enough. Time enough to fix the lattice. Time enough to open the Mage-Gate. Time enough to begin.

Returning, however… that would be the challenge. He would need another Mage-Gate—one still functional, one not under watch. If he was lucky, one that led deeper into Mikal's network of forgotten secrets.

That's not a bad idea.

Good. After a proper ale or two and restocking supplies, we'll give your theory the attention it deserves. Aaron… we're nearing the end of this expedition. And you know what we must do before we leave. We have to make sure the Mage-Gate can never be used—ever.

Brak's heart thumped.

The words cut through him—like the tip of a hot blade between his fingers. So that was their plan. Destroy it. Seal it. End it forever.

I understand the mission. But I can't help feeling we're locking a door without ever learning what's on the other side. Even if someone repaired the rune, they'd still need to know how to activate it. And that's not easy—it's practically impossible. So… when do we leave for the village?

For a moment Brak listened in disbelief, yet doubt filled him. Gideon was resourceful, and if there was a non-wizard who could figure out how to destroy or disable a Mage-Gate, it would be the Grand Druid.

And if Gideon got the chance, he would do it.

Soon. We'll go in pairs or threes. I've got assignments for everyone to gather supplies, and once that's done, we'll meet at The Stately Potato for a day or two of relaxation. We've earned it, that's for sure.

The spell dissipated, fading like mist in sunlight.

Brak moved at once. He strapped his pack tighter, fastened the satchel, and approached the crate of molds. For a moment, he hesitated. Part of him had considered leaving it behind—returning for it once the path was secure.

But now?

No. He would take everything. Gideon's intentions left no room for risk.

The moment the druids departed, he would complete the lattice, open the gate, and step through. His first destination—Thalraya.

Brak stood before the Mage-Gate, its towering arch humming with latent power. He ran a gloved hand over the cool, silver lattice, feeling the faint magical resonance thrumming beneath his fingertips. The Mages he so admired had forged these constructs—gateways of unimaginable power, binding distant locations with nothing more than will and design. They had wielded celestial and chaotic magic with terrifying precision, danced on the edges of forbidden truths, and bent the fabric of reality into obedient curves.

They had authored the *Librums*.

Brak glanced at the crate of molds at his feet. He had everything now. The final piece—the missing lattice—rested in his hand. The last step.

He climbed the ramp, slow and deliberate, each footfall echoing off the stone. Reaching the apex, he knelt, then pressed the silver segment into the gap where the Elder Rune had fractured.

The moment the lattice touched the broken rune, the entire structure shuddered.

The silver snapped into place with a magnetic jolt—no hammer, no spell, just a perfect, inevitable fit. An audible *click* echoed through the keep, followed by a surge of power.

A pulse of light surged outward, racing across the rune-carved stone, gold and silver bursting to life in a cascading wave.

Then—silence.

Brak exhaled.

A single utterance in an ancient tongue—one the mortal world had long since forgotten—awakened the gate. The Elder Runes shimmered in response, each sigil pulsing with magic as the gate reached outward, forging connections with its distant siblings. The void at its center swirled to life, distorting the air with ghostly hues—white fire, blue shadow, colorless light.

Brak stepped back, his eyes fixed on the runic symbols now flaring one by one along the archway. He knew them by heart. Each glyph marked a place of power—a name etched into history, or erased from it.

One symbol drew his attention more than the others: AB—Abyssal Bastion—his master's stronghold, buried deep beyond mortal reach. That was not his destination… not yet.

He noted the IS rune was missing, as expected. The Infernal Sanctum—the keep in which he stood—would never appear as a destination on its own gate.

His gaze swept across the others:

VS, SC, TK, WM, AM, HK, GB — the sanctums of the seven other Mages.

And then the last four:

TA, AA, VA, KA.

Thalraya. Aridaya. Virdaya. Kaldaraya.

Mikal's secrets. His private retreats.

Each a mystery wrapped in isolation, hidden behind layers of enchantment and silence.

Brak's mouth curled into a satisfied sneer.

These secret towers—Mikal's legacy—would now serve the brother he once betrayed.

The final insult.

And the first key to resurrection.

Each sigil was a tether to the ancient past—strongholds once ruled by near-godlike Mages, now tombs of power, knowledge, and death.

He longed to visit them all.

Plunder them.

Bend them to his will.

But his first destination was already chosen.

Thalraya.

One of Mikal's hidden towers. A place where his master, Ra-Joth, had buried a phylactery of terrible importance.

Somewhere within that hidden fortress, beneath centuries of wind-scoured ruin, lay a soul gem—one of several needed when his master returned to the Material Plane.

Brak raised his hand over the arch of runes. Each symbol flared to life as his palm passed, growing brighter as he hovered over Thalraya's sigil. With a sharp, decisive gesture, he closed his fist.

The selection locked.

The void at the gate's center twisted—then opened.

A glimpse of the destination flickered across its surface: a jagged tower of gray stone, beaten by sleet and wind, standing stubborn against the cold fury of the sea.

He tightened his cloak, gathered the crate and his pack, and stepped forward.

The sensation was disorienting. The world stretched—each nerve pulled thin, unraveling thread by thread—before snapping back into place.

The cold hit him like a hammer.

Brak drew a sharp breath, his lungs seizing at the sudden shift in climate. The wind tore through the seams of his cloak, icy fingers worming past every layer. Even his gloves did little to dull the bite.

The Mage-Gate had deposited him atop a weathered platform at the tower's peak.

The chamber was a ruin—a skeletal husk. Bones littered the stone floor, mingled with splinters of shattered furniture and the remains of something he couldn't quite identify.

So much for grandeur.

With a whispered phrase, he conjured a globe of warmth around himself, the air still bitter but tolerable now. He didn't plan to stay long. Just long enough to find the soul gem—and activate the next gate.

Brak ascended the ramp, boots scraping against frost-slick stone. He approached the arch of runes, heart quickening. Twelve symbols glimmered faintly before him.

His hand hovered, reaching toward the sigil he knew belonged to AB—the Abyssal Bastion, his master's lost fortress.

His fingers brushed the cold air. He spoke the command.

Nothing happened.

Brak frowned.

He swept his hand across the runes again, slower this time, commanding them with care. The glowing sigils remained fixed— unchanged, inert.

A cold dread settled over him.

No. That's not right.

He moved to deselect the current symbol—Aridaya—and tried to shift it. Nothing. The runes did not flicker, did not respond. They were locked.

Frozen? Malfunctioning? Or something worse?

With deliberate precision, he reset the sequence and once again selected Abyssal Bastion. The glyph acknowledged the command—it flared briefly—but it did not engage. The gate remained locked on Aridaya.

His hesitation was brief.

He stepped forward and into the swirling gate.

The heat struck him like a wall of fire.

It was a cruel inversion of Thalraya's biting cold. Here, the air baked every breath from his lungs. The sun glared down on endless dunes of sand, scorching the desolate landscape.

Before him lay death.

Preserved bodies littered the chamber—mummified, twisted into the shapes of starvation and surrender. Makeshift camps and burial mounds dotted the stone floor, the last relics of those who had believed salvation would come.

Brak climbed the ramp again, his cloak snapping in the hot wind. He moved to reset the Mage-Gate.

Again—nothing.

His jaw clenched. A muscle twitched in his cheek.

The symbol is locked.

He was trapped in a loop—shuttled between Thalraya and Aridaya. Nothing else.

The gate, now active, was no longer his to command.

A slow, simmering anger burned in his chest.

Mikal, you insufferable fool.

Even in death, the old Mage had ensured no one could travel beyond these two locations.

A trap.

Brak nearly uttered the command to shut down the Mage-Gate and restart it—but he hesitated.

Mikal was paranoid. What if he'd cursed the reset? What if deactivating the gate triggered another layer of his defenses?

No. He wouldn't take that risk. Not yet.

At least he had access to Thalraya—and what he came for—the soul gem.

Brak calmed himself and stepped through the swirling portal.

He was stuck—for now. But his mission remained. The phylactery was here, hidden in the cold tower. He would claim it, explore Aridaya, and when the time was right, he would find another way out.

He warded the stairwell leading deeper into the tower, crafting a spell that would whisper to him if the druids followed through the Mage-Gate.

Let them come.

They would be trapped in the same cycle.

Druids—bumbling fools who hugged trees and cured rot. A wizard would burn the forest and start anew.

With a final glance at the swirling portal, Brak turned and descended into the depths of Thalraya.

His next prize awaited.

Chapter Thirteen

∞

Battle of Druid's Glen

Gideon's arrival outside Lillia's grove did not go unnoticed. The forest—normally tranquil and empty—was teeming with activity. Soldiers, woodland knights, Elves, Fey-folk, and bound thralls moved in coordinated patrols, forming a living ring of watchful eyes. That alone set him on edge.

Why the heightened security?

Was it connected to the events in Druid's Glen?

A pair of guards—a Human and an Elf—approached, weapons drawn and wary. Though the sigil of The One Tree marked him as an ally, they didn't lower their guard. Further back, Gideon spotted pixies darting through the branches, likely hurrying to announce his presence to Lillia.

Good.

He stood still, raising his hands in a gesture of peace, giving the guards time to recognize him.

As they closed in, Gideon took in the changes around him. The settlement ahead had grown well beyond the modest village he remembered. Pathways and dwellings were woven into the rainforest itself, an elegant fusion of civilization and wildness. There was beauty in it—order carved into nature. Yet the humidity clung to his skin, and sweat gathered beneath his light armor.

In the heart of the grove, towering mahogany trees stretched a hundred feet skyward, their thick canopies interlacing to form a living dome. Lillia would be there, no doubt flanked by her advisors.

"I am Gideon Manawove, Grand Druid, Protector of Druid's Glen, and Head of the Druid Council," Gideon announced, his voice steady and commanding. "I seek an audience with Lillia. The matter is urgent."

The lead guard, a rugged man with sharp eyes, offered a curt, respectful nod.

"My name is Benji. Follow me."

Gideon fell into step without hesitation. Two more guards joined behind him, and together they transitioned from the soft forest floor onto a road of carefully laid flat stones. Wooden walkways flanked either side—likely to keep the mud at bay during the rainy season.

As they moved deeper into the grove, Gideon took in the scale of what had grown here. Residents paused to stare—men and women, Elves and Halflings, even a few wide-eyed children. Some of the children waved, and Gideon offered a gentle return gesture. But the adults pulled them back with wary glances, their eyes lingering on the unfamiliar stranger in their midst.

Shops and smithies lined the stone avenue, their signs modest but well-crafted. Taverns and trading stalls hummed with quiet commerce, while woodworkers and herbalists plied their trade in shaded alcoves. The scent of tanning hides and butchering was mercifully absent— Gideon guessed those places were farther out, beyond the residential boundaries. This was no longer a village.

It was a city.

Unprecedented.

The road widened into a green park—broad, serene, and deliberate. Lush grass grew in sweeping beds, and the trees were sculpted with the patient touch of a druid's hand. The balance between wild and tame was exacting. Perhaps too exacting.

Gideon's gaze swept across the manicured space, and a wry thought passed through him—he'd always disliked raking the leaves outside his own home. At some point, nature stopped looking natural.

Beyond the park rose the great mahogany trees, their enormous trunks arranged in a graceful semi-circle. Two woodland knights stood at the entrance, their sharp eyes tracking Gideon as he approached.

Inside the grove, Lillia stood atop a raised dais, where an ornately carved chair rested—not quite a throne, but close. Pixies flitted about her in constant motion, a buzz of wings and murmurs. To one side, her advisors huddled over a table strewn with parchment and maps.

Lillia's presence drew the eye. Her long green hair, adorned with fresh white hibiscus blooms, tumbled over one shoulder, revealing the curve of her perfect ear. Her skin glowed with the health of sun and soil. One hand settled on her hip, and she cocked it to the side, her bare shoulder catching the fading twilight.

Gideon's breath caught. *Shades*, why was a bare shoulder so intoxicating?

Her lips curled into a smile—playful, but edged with warning. "Gideon. What an unpleasant surprise. When my pixies said the Grand Druid had arrived, I assumed they were playing tricks on me."

"I have urgent business," he replied, voice tight with purpose. "This is no courtesy visit. What I bring affects you and your grove directly. You would be wise to listen."

Lillia's smile thinned. "In all my years on the Council, nothing has ever been *urgent*. Nature doesn't rush. Urgency comes only from outside the grove. Usually in the form of *you*."

"This is different," Gideon said, stepping closer. "I don't have time to pander to your whims. You will listen."

Her expression darkened. "You're being rude, Grand Druid. I could have you escorted out for that." At her side, the woodland knights shifted, their hands nearing their weapons.

Gideon didn't flinch. "Finola has kidnapped my daughter, Heather. And she means to take the leadership of the Council."

The knights froze. Lillia blinked, her posture changing subtly.

After a heartbeat, she waved the guards back with a flick of her wrist. "Go on," she said coolly. "I'm curious now."

Gideon exhaled, his anger contained for the moment. "If I don't act swiftly, Finola will kill my daughter. I need your help. *Now*."

Lillia tilted her head, considering. "Why should I help you? Perhaps it's time for a change in leadership. Finola seems a fine choice—more devoted to nature's harmony than you ever were."

Gideon resisted the urge to snap. "My standing is irrelevant. Heather is in danger, and I need allies—now."

"And you thought to come to me?" Lillia arched a brow, amused. "You should have gone to Nightshade. She's the one who licks your boots. The one who speaks to you when no one is looking."

With an effortless stride, Lillia ascended the dais and settled into the chair. "I've never understood why that fairy holds you in such high regard."

"I came to you because I don't have time to reach Nightshade," Gideon said, his tone steady. "You're one of the few who can cover great distances quickly. You are my only hope to stop this rebellion and save Heather."

Lillia waved her hand, dismissing the pixies, guards, and advisors. They vanished into the trees, leaving the two druids alone in the clearing.

"You'll have to choose, Gideon," Lillia said quietly. "I can help you save your daughter—or help you keep your place on the Council. But not both."

Gideon inhaled, the weight of her words settling on him. The humid air pressed against his lungs.

"I need you to alert Nightshade, Krik, and Buvic," Gideon said. "Tell them to meet me on the north side of Druid's Glen. Inform them in that order. Time is against us."

Lillia studied him, her expression unreadable. "Interesting. You've chosen your position over your daughter's life."

Gideon bristled. "No. I chose to fight for both."

With a grim nod, he recounted the events leading to this moment—the message from Finola, his trickery with DeCa, and his desperate journey here. He presented the talisman he'd taken from DeCa.

Lillia's delicate fingers traced the lacquered surface of the preserved leaf. "This is rare magic," she murmured. "I wonder what promises Finola made to acquire these."

"Or who she's in league with," Gideon said darkly. "If she's working with wizards, we're in deeper trouble than we realize."

Lillia pushed the talisman back toward him. "Keep it. It may speed you along your way. I'm sure you can figure out how to use it."

"I only need four more hops to reach Druid's Glen," Gideon said. "If you agree to alert the others, I'll leave immediately."

Lillia tapped her chin thoughtfully. "Very well. I'll deliver your message. But know this—I won't support or oppose whatever comes next. My grove stands apart." She paused. "And the Mage-Gate? Is it destroyed?"

"Not yet. I'll give you a full report after we deal with Finola."

Lillia gave a dismissive wave, her expression souring. "Then go. You are of no further use to me."

Gideon gave her a curt bow, stepped to the nearest mahogany tree, whispered the incantation, and touched the talisman. The tree responded, pulling him into its depths.

Once he was gone, Lillia whispered a word of power, and her skin hardened into bark—a protective layer of living armor.

Her advisors and guards returned, casting curious glances her way.

"Double the patrols," Lillia ordered. "No one enters or leaves the grove or the surrounding districts."

The woodland knights bowed and dispersed. Lillia turned to the hovering pixies.

"Bring me my belt, knife, pouch, bow, and quiver. Quickly."

The pixies zipped into the trees and returned moments later, laden with her gear. Lillia fastened the belt around her slim waist, slung the bow and quiver over her shoulder, and tied the knife to her hip.

"I won't be long," she murmured, placing a hand against the mahogany tree.

And with that, Lillia vanished into the green depths of the forest.

When Gideon arrived in the Needle Forest, the sun was low on the horizon, and dusk had begun to creep in, shrouding the small village in soft, crawling darkness. The twilight sky bled orange and violet through the towering canopy as he sprinted into the clearing, heart pounding. With any luck, he thought, he'd find Albic Fang preparing for supper.

In truth, Albic Fang was every bit Finola's equal in both rank and skill—an unspoken peer, barred from council affairs by the rigid structure of their order. Gideon allowed himself a fleeting thought: perhaps one day Albic Fang might relocate to the Midlands and take Finola's place. A sliver of hope—nothing more than a daydream in the middle of a storm.

But now was not the time for hope. Gideon was running on borrowed strength, and the adrenaline that had fueled his journey was beginning to wane. His muscles ached from the day's relentless pace, fatigue crawling in, heavy as stone, threatening to slow him.

He reached into his pouch, pulled out two druid berries, and chewed them. The burst of energy came fast—but not enough.

As the cottage came into view, the flicker of candlelight from within gave him a final push of resolve. He slowed just enough to catch his breath, then raised his fist and pounded on the door.

"Albic! It's Gideon! Open up!"

The moment stretched, every second steeped in dread. Gideon clenched his fists, ready to pound again—just as the door swung open.

Albic Fang loomed in the doorway like a figure from half-remembered legend. Nearly seven feet tall, all sinew and strength, his long, unkempt hair tumbled down in dark waves. His face was cragged and rough-hewn, framed by a beard that did nothing to soften him. His piercing green eyes gleamed, unreadable—filled with secrets, maybe, or threats best left unspoken. Even standing still, Albic radiated menace, like a predator waiting to strike.

"Gideon?" Albic rumbled, his voice a low grind of stone. "This is… unusual."

"I have no time for pleasantries," Gideon said, stepping forward. "Druid's Glen is under siege. Finola has taken Heather. She means to kill her unless I relinquish my title as Grand Druid. I need every druid you can gather. Every sword. We don't know how many enemies wait for us. We don't know what magic they'll bring. But make no mistake—people will die."

Albic stared at him, silent for a long heartbeat. Then a slow grin split through his beard—not warm, not kind, but feral.

"By Thatara," he said, almost laughing. "And here I was hoping for a quiet night." His chuckle rumbled deep in his chest. "Very well. I'll gather whoever's here."

"Take them to the north side of Druid's Glen. Stay hidden until you see Nightshade, Krik, or Buvic—any one of them. I'll use green-speak to keep you updated. Be careful—The One Tree will be guarded. If you have to tree-stride, use the tangle on the north side. The north side." He paused, letting the words settle. "When the time comes, strike fast. Don't expect allies inside the glen—it'll be Heather and me. I'll send a signal when the moment is right."

Albic gave a single nod, like it was just another assignment. "It'll be done. Now go."

Gideon didn't hesitate. He turned, sprinted toward the nearest tree, and vanished into the green.

Left alone on the doorstep, Albic Fang scratched his beard.

"Bloody hell," he muttered, shaking his head with a crooked grin.

It was near dusk, the shadows deepening around Druid's Glen as Gideon crept along the tangled forest perimeter. He resisted the urge to rootwalk directly to Heather. Moving too quickly, too recklessly, might alert the guards—and get them both killed.

Instead, he called upon the forest itself.

With a whispered incantation, he sent a silent plea through root and leaf, summoning the small creatures of the Glen. He promised them safety, though in his heart, he knew not all would return.

There was movement in the undergrowth. Squirrels. Hares. Rabbits. Hedgehogs. Voles. Chipmunks. They emerged one by one, drawn by the ancient call of the Grand Druid.

Gideon whispered an apology as they gathered at his feet. Then, eyes closed, he asked Thatara for forgiveness.

And with a heavy heart, he sent them scurrying into the tangle.

His form shifted as he whispered another incantation. Bark spread across his skin, curling over his limbs like natural armor. He drew his hunting knife, exhaled deeply, and pressed his palm to the tangle.

The spell took hold.

Roots and vines parted just enough to pull him through, slipping him between layers of ancient, living wood. He emerged on the far side, crouched low, motionless, straining to sense what lay beyond.

The air was heavy with tension.

Dozens of campfires dotted the glen, and torches lined the path like silent sentries. At least a hundred enemies—druids, soldiers, and mercenaries—were stationed here. Then he saw her.

Finola.

She stood near The One Tree, her stance composed, her expression cold. Power clung to her like a cloak. Rage surged through Gideon's blood, but he didn't move. He couldn't afford impulse.

Then the forest answered his earlier call.

The summoned creatures burst into the glen in a storm of confusion. Squirrels darted through tents, knocking over bundles of gear. Hares streaked between soldiers' legs. Warriors cursed and scrambled, drawing steel and cutting down anything that moved. Druids shouted spells to calm the chaos, but it only fed the panic.

Gideon remained hidden, scanning desperately.

There—Heather.

She lay bound in enchanted grasses near the base of the tree. Her body was limp, her form too still.

His breath caught.

Then—movement. A twitch of her arm. A shift in her shoulder.

Relief hit him like a wave. She was alive.

Steeling himself, Gideon crept forward and seized an unsuspecting warrior by the neck, sliding the hunting knife in with practiced precision. The man gave a soft, startled gasp—then went limp. Gideon eased the body to the ground, crouching low, every nerve alert.

Around him, the chaos was already waning. The summoned animals were being subdued—druids chanting, warriors regrouping. The window was closing. Fast.

They had to move now.

Gideon knelt beside Heather and whispered an incantation into the tangled grasses. A deep, silent tremor passed through the ground, like distant thunder without sound—and the enchanted vines released her.

He surged forward, lifting her into his arms.

She was light. Too light. The stink of sweat, urine, and fear clung to her skin. Her eyes were glassy with exhaustion or delirium—he couldn't tell which.

He turned.

Ahead stood The One Tree—but Gideon froze.

The sacred trunk had been ringed with barrels of oil, lashed tight to its base and stacked three high. Enough to burn the entire Glen to ash—perhaps the whole Needle Forest, if the fire wasn't contained.

Spears, sharp and deadly, surrounded the tree at a short distance, with their points turned toward The One Tree.

There would be no escape that way. No passage through the ring of spears.

His eyes snapped toward the council's table—not far.

Maybe… just maybe, they could reach it in time.

He crouched and set Heather gently on the ground, pressing the hunting knife into her trembling hand.

"We're going to escape," he whispered. "Stay low. Help is coming."

A voice rang out, sharp as a blade: "Gideon! Take him!"

He turned.

Finola.

Without hesitation, he slapped the beetle brooch pinned to his tunic. It cracked, and a chaotic swarm burst forth—beetles buzzing like a storm toward her.

Finola's hand snapped upward. Flames erupted from her fingers, a searing wall of fire that incinerated the swarm mid-flight. Blackened husks rained down like scorched snowflakes.

Gideon drew the crooked wand from his belt and leveled it in her direction.

Finola's eyes shifted—past him, to The One Tree. Its upper branches shimmered with a strange violet glow, pulsing like a beacon. The light spread upward, casting eerie hues into the darkening sky.

She raised her hand again.

"Intruders!" she bellowed.

Gideon moved to activate the wand—but his limbs seized. A cold tide swept over him, locking his joints, stealing his breath.

Paralyzed, he could only watch as enemy figures closed in around him.

And Heather.

Rough hands seized him, slamming him to the ground. His wand cracked in two with a fizzle of wasted magic.

One captor screamed as Heather drove the hunting knife into the back of his knee, twisting hard. He howled, collapsing to the dirt.

Before she could react, the second captor struck her hard across the jaw. Her body crumpled, limp and still.

Gideon's heart shattered.

He strained against the magic holding him, every nerve alight with panic, but his limbs remained frozen, bound by invisible cords.

Then came the sound—a faint, building buzz. The captors froze, hands tightening on their weapons.

Out of the darkness swept Nightshade.

Gone was the flowing white dress. She wore supple leather armor now, her long black hair tied back in a warrior's braid. A short blade pulsed green in her left hand. In her right, she held an acorn.

With a flick of her wrist, she hurled it.

It struck the captor square in the forehead and bounced to the earth beside Heather.

A heartbeat later, the ground exploded.

From the dirt erupted a *verdaleth*—fifteen feet of ancient bark and vengeance, its limbs gnarled and its amber eyes burning with purpose. It roared, a deep wooden groan like a tree splitting in a storm.

One massive arm swept outward, swatting the injured captor like a fly. The man sailed through the air, vanishing into the shadows beyond a distant campfire.

The *verdaleth* knelt, gently lifting Heather into its wooden arms. It cradled her with impossible tenderness, then turned and charged toward the edge of the glen.

Soldiers scattered.

Weapons bounced harmlessly from its bark-plated hide.

Flaming arrows streaked overhead—missiles of fire and fury.

But the *verdaleth* did not slow.

It would not stop.

Flaming arrows struck home, embedding in the *verdaleth's* side. It staggered, smoke curling from its bark, but it pressed on, shielding Heather from the worst of the blaze as the fire climbed its flanks.

Gideon turned toward Finola, fury seething in his chest. He whispered an incantation, fingers moving in tight, practiced motions— each one a curse aimed squarely at her.

Nightshade blinked into view with a flash of light. Her green blade slashed clean through the nearest enemy. Before the body hit the ground, she vanished again—reappearing closer to Finola, her eyes locked on the traitor.

Krik erupted from the base of The One Tree, bellowing like a storm given flesh. His great axe tore through the circle of spears, splinters and blood trailing every swing. Arrows whistled through the air, but he barreled forward, snarling, barkskin armor shrugging off the worst of the blows.

Then the ground answered the call of war.

Crystal spikes tore upward from the soil—jagged spears of gleaming stone. They impaled warriors mid-charge, flinging others aside like ragdolls. Finola was hurled from her stance, her back slamming against one of the rising spires with a sickening thud. She rolled, disoriented, struggling to regain her footing.

But the battlefield was shifting.

And not in her favor.

Gideon advanced, Nightshade flitting beside him, Krik charging in from the opposite side. Albic Fang emerged from the trees like a storm given form, his flaming scimitar painting the air in arcs of fire. Buvic surged forward, hurling crackling spells with both hands.

Finola's eyes darted, calculating. She saw it—the trap closing. Her plan was unraveling.

She raised her arms and spoke a final word of power.

A column of fire screamed from the heavens, tearing into the glen. The barrels lashed to The One Tree exploded in a blinding burst of flame and oil. Rivers of fire coursed outward, snaking through the roots and grass. Krik dove behind a crystal spire just in time, the flames licking across his cloak and searing the ends of his beard.

Gideon raised a wall of water, but it vanished in a hiss of steam the instant it met the blaze.

"It's lost!" Nightshade cried, her voice cutting sharp through the roar. "We need to get out—now!"

She vanished in a blink of light.

Gideon turned toward the fleeing *verdaleth*. "Retreat!" he bellowed. "Everyone, retreat!"

He ran, hurling spell after spell, wave after wave crashing over the flames. It wasn't enough. The fire had already won. The glen, once sacred, was devoured in flame.

As the inferno closed in, Gideon dove into the tangle. A blast of superheated air hurled him forward, flinging him out onto the forest floor like a broken twig.

He scrambled to his feet, turned back—and saw it.

A pillar of fire rising into the night sky where The One Tree should be.

The screams of friend and foe alike echoed through the burning glen, chilling Gideon's blood. The tangle blazed like a wall of hellfire, and the air reeked of scorched wood and burning flesh. Gideon stumbled backward, collapsing onto his back as the inferno surged forward, devouring everything in its path. Flames roared like wild beasts, consuming the sacred grove without mercy.

The fire snapped and hissed, climbing high into the night sky, casting flickering shadows that danced like phantoms across the battlefield.

He raised an arm to shield his face, squinting against the blinding heat as his mind struggled to catch up. The One Tree—countless centuries old—was a pyre now, a blazing monument to Finola's betrayal. Helpless rage clenched his heart. All the sacrifices, all the years of stewardship, reduced to smoke and ash.

He scrambled upright, tripping over twisted roots and fallen limbs—then froze.

The tangle was burning.

The great bramble wall, once an impenetrable shield protecting Druid's Glen, was now a death trap. Flames crawled hungrily across its thick vines, turning sanctuary into a prison.

Beyond it, screams tore through the night. Soldiers, druids, and forest beasts, all trapped between the tangle and the fire—dying in waves, their voices lost to the roar of the blaze.

It felt as if nature itself was rebelling—turned against itself by the very magic druids had sworn to protect and wield.

A sudden gust of wind sent the fire leaping forward like a living beast, forcing Gideon to retreat again. His thoughts raced. If the blaze broke past the glen's edge, it would sweep through the Needle Forest, devour Albic's grove, and roll on unchecked. Entire villages, towns— everything would burn. The region would be lost.

Just as despair threatened to take hold, a shimmering sphere of water formed in the air before him—rippling and luminous like a small moon. It hovered for only a breath before slamming into the tangle with a hiss like a dragon's exhale. Steam erupted in a blinding cloud.

Gideon coughed, fanning the hot mist from his face, and turned.

Nightshade hovered in the smoke, her silhouette framed by firelight. She moved like a dragonfly—blindingly fast, impossibly precise. Another sphere of water formed between her palms.

"Move!" she shouted over the roar. "More's coming!"

She hurled the second sphere, and it struck with another deafening splash, quenching more of the burning tangle. The scorched vines hissed and steamed, recoiling.

Without waiting for a reply, Nightshade conjured a third orb and flung it forward, a streak of blue against the churning orange glow—an unlikely savior, hurling salvation from the heart of the flames.

"We have to contain it!" Nightshade shouted. "The fire's too fast—we'll lose the entire forest if it spreads!"

Gideon nodded, dragging himself upright. Every muscle protested, his exhaustion clawing at him, but there was no time for rest. With a word of power, he summoned a wall of water from the soil itself, pulling moisture from deep in the earth. The wave crashed into the burning tangle, snuffing out a stretch of fire twenty feet wide.

"Keep working!" he called out.

Nightshade grinned, her wings a blur against the smoke-filled air. "About time you started pulling your weight, old man!" she quipped before vanishing again, streaking toward another blaze along the perimeter.

Gideon pressed on, summoning wall after wall of water. Each one slammed into the flames, steam rising in thick columns, hiss after hiss echoing into the night. For every fire they put down, another sparked to life, but the balance was shifting. The fire was losing ground.

His throat burned as he forced out another spell, coughing through the heat and smoke. He watched the water crash forward and sweep the flames aside, leaving behind blackened ground and embers.

For the first time, hope stirred in his chest. They might actually stop this.

When no more water would come, when his magic was spent, Gideon staggered back, chest heaving. The worst was out, but embers still glowed like malevolent eyes in the wreckage. If left alone, they'd reignite.

Nightshade zipped in beside him, her face grim now. "I'll find more druids—get them to mop up what's left," she said, scanning the battlefield. "You go. See to your daughter."

Gideon gave a weary nod, still catching his breath. "Thank you, Nightshade. I owe you everything."

"Don't make it a habit, Grand Druid," she said, and blinked away, vanishing into the dark forest to rally more help.

He turned toward the familiar path that led home. His lungs still burned with smoke, his limbs heavy with exhaustion—but none of it mattered. Only one thought drove him forward: *Heather.*

The forest path unfolded beneath his feet like memory made real. He knew every rise and dip, every curve, every stone and root. Even in the dark, he moved with purpose, his boots thudding softly against the earth as he ran.

Up ahead, a warm light glowed.

The lantern on the porch swayed gently in the breeze, casting golden light over the clearing. Relief struck him like a wave. Standing guard beside the porch was the towering figure of the *verdaleth*, still and solemn. Its bark was scorched along one flank, but it remained rooted and silent, giving no sign of pain.

Then he saw her.

Heather stood beside the *verdaleth*, her small frame silhouetted by the lantern's glow. The moment she saw him, she cried out, a sob catching in her throat, and sprinted across the mossy clearing.

"Father!" she cried, throwing herself into his arms.

Gideon caught her, pulling her in with a strength born of desperation and love. He held her close, his heart pounding, the weight of everything they'd endured crashing down at once. She trembled in his arms, clinging to him like a lifeline. He whispered soft reassurances, trying to quiet her sobs.

But when the tears came for him, he didn't stop them.

He let them fall.

"You're safe," he whispered, his voice hoarse. "I've got you. I've got you."

She buried her face into his shoulder, her breath hitching between sobs. "I thought… I thought I wouldn't make it."

"You're here now," he murmured, rubbing her back. "You're here with me. It's over."

Heather let out a shaky laugh through her tears. "I—I peed my trousers."

At that, Gideon couldn't help but laugh too—a deep, exhausted chuckle, raw and relieved. The absurdity of it, after all they'd endured, was the release they both needed.

She started laughing with him, the tension breaking at last. But then the laughter gave way to sobs again, and she clung to him tighter. Gideon kissed the top of her head, his heart overflowing with love and sorrow and joy all at once.

He glanced up at the *verdaleth*, which stood motionless but watchful, its presence a silent comfort.

"Thank you, friend," Gideon said in the druidic tongue, bowing his head toward the towering being.

The *verdaleth* gave a low, rumbling response—like the groan of a bending tree in the wind.

"Will you stay?" Gideon asked.

The *verdaleth* hesitated, then shook its massive head slowly. "My master calls," it rumbled. "But I will stay."

Gideon nodded. "You may go in peace when it is time. Thank you for watching over her."

The *verdaleth* gave a slow, creaking bow.

Heather sniffled and wiped her eyes with the back of her hand.

"You need a bath," she said, wrinkling her nose.

Gideon chuckled softly. "You first," he said. "Let's get inside."

He led her up the porch steps, lighting another lantern as they entered the house. The familiar smells of home greeted him—wood smoke, dried herbs, a faint trace of lavender and dampness. He made a mental note to clean up later; for now, all that mattered was Heather's safety and comfort.

"Fish," Heather said suddenly. "The trout—I caught two earlier. They're on the porch."

Gideon smiled. "Well then," he said, "looks like we're having trout for dinner."

He stepped back outside, collected the bucket, and gave the *verdaleth* another nod of thanks.

Inside, he cleaned the fish quickly and efficiently, the motions soothing in their familiarity. Heather fetched water for her bath, and together they worked in companionable silence to prepare a simple meal.

When the fish was sizzling in the skillet, Heather leaned against the counter and gave him a small, tired smile.

"I'm really glad you found me," she whispered.

Gideon reached over and brushed a strand of damp hair from her forehead. "Me too."

They ate standing over the skillet. And for the first time in what felt like forever, Gideon felt a flicker of hope. They had survived.

Whatever came next, they would face it together.

Soon, though, he would have to return to Druid's Glen—and the ruin waiting there.

When everything but the bones was gone, Heather went to bathe. The water wasn't deep, but it would be enough to get clean.

"I'll be outside. Call out if you need me," Gideon said.

"Won't take too long."

Gideon stepped out onto the porch, noting the smell of soot, ash, and the lingering taint of death in the air. It pained him to think how many had died—and for what? He pressed his nose to his sleeve, inhaling the smoke trapped in his clothing.

All at once, the weight of the day crashed through his veins, and he sank into his rocking chair for comfort. He tapped his side, felt for his pipe, and found it. Yes, he would have a smoke—in fact, he would have Great-Grandfather's blend, which he retrieved from the storage shed.

When he returned, Heather was dressed and standing beside the *verdaleth*.

"He says his master is calling for him to return," she said, patting the *verdaleth's* trunk. "He must leave."

Gideon spoke to the *verdaleth* in the druidic tongue, then asked Heather in the common tongue, "Did you understand what I said?"

Heather shook her head.

The *verdaleth* responded.

"I understood that," Heather said.

"You are a remarkable young lady. You certainly have your druidic ways with plants and animals."

The *verdaleth* boomed in protest.

"I stand corrected—you have your druidic ways with plants, *trees*, and animals."

The *verdaleth* gave a stiff bow, then turned and lumbered down the forest path. As it reached the halfway point, it shimmered and vanished, as though it had never been there at all.

"You need a bath too," Heather told her father.

"Later. Let's find Nightshade."

He lit his pipe and took a deep draw, savoring the familiar flavor of Great-Grandfather's blend.

"We need to hear what happened to you."

The search for survivors that evening proved futile. Inside Druid's Glen, the charred remains of friend and foe lay scattered across the blackened ground. Few things were recognizable—the occasional trinket, a twisted weapon, a scorched emblem. They would have to wait for morning light to properly search the ruins and account for the fallen. For now, darkness made the task impossible, and exhaustion pressed down on them all.

There was also the grim necessity of taking account of the living. One by one, those who remained drifted away from the ruined glen, returning to their homes or seeking refuge among the villagers. The visitors, weary and hollow-eyed, were welcomed into townsfolk's homes, with some taking shelter under Albic Fang's watch.

Gideon and Heather made their way to their house in silence, the only sounds the crunch of ash beneath their boots and the faint crackle of cooling embers from distant fires.

A darting figure zipped past them—a flicker of pale light in the shadows. Nightshade. She blinked in and out of sight, zigzagging ahead along the path.

When they reached the house, Gideon opened the door and ushered Heather inside. Nightshade followed them.

He guided Heather to a chair, then slid the wooden bolt into place. It was a simple barrier—easily bypassed by anyone determined enough—but it brought him a small, fleeting sense of peace.

Slumping into his chair, Gideon let the weariness settle over him like a heavy blanket. Every muscle in his body ached, and his mind churned like a storm that refused to quiet. He needed to send a message to Cedric about what had happened—but not tonight. The effort was more than he could summon.

He exhaled and glanced toward the countertop, where Nightshade was perched. The delicate fairy armor she wore looked almost like doll clothing, though it was stained with dried blood and other grim reminders of the night's battle. Her tiny, sheathed blade—so lethal just hours ago—now resembled a child's toy in the lamplight.

Nightshade rummaged through a small pouch at her hip and pulled out a chunk of honeycomb. Without ceremony, she bit into it, chewing eagerly as golden honey dripped down her chin. She licked her fingers clean, utterly unbothered by her audience—until she noticed the two Humans staring at her.

She paused, mid-lick, and arched a tiny eyebrow.

"What?" she said. "Fighting makes me hungry."

The fairy licked her fingers clean and narrowed her eyes on Heather. "What happened, my dear?"

Before she could answer, Gideon said, "Start from the days when we left. Leave nothing out—any detail may be crucial."

Heather began, telling her father how Finola hadn't liked being a babysitter, recounting the days up to Eric's birthday, his departure, then Finola's invitation to train.

Midstory, Nightshade's tiny nose wrinkled. She hovered above her seat, wings beating, sniffing the air.

"What is that smell?" the fairy asked, drifting toward the hallway. "It smells like... rot. Like decaying leaves."

Heather's eyes widened. She froze, the blood draining from her face. *Oh no.*

"Nightshade, wait!"

Heather scrambled to her feet, but Nightshade was already at the door to Aaron and Cedric's shared room. The fairy hovered in front of the wood, her tiny hands on her hips, a question forming at the corners of her mouth.

"Rotting leaves?" Gideon's voice was loud. He rose from his chair, exhaustion forgotten, and followed Nightshade to the door.

"Wait, Father—" Heather started, but she couldn't stop him. "I can explain."

Gideon pushed the door open. A wave of pungent, earthy decay hit him, and his eyes widened in horror.

The floor was covered in thigh-high piles of rotting leaves, their once-crisp edges now slimy and blackened. The mess had soaked into the bed, the rug, and the floorboards. The stench was thick enough to make Nightshade gag.

Heather braced herself. *I forgot. Completely forgot.* She watched as her father surveyed the scene, his sharp brown eyes narrowing into slits.

"Heather, what is this?"

"I…" Heather stammered, biting her lip. "It was… it was a prank." Her voice came out smaller than she intended.

"A prank?" Gideon turned, his voice a parental growl. "You call this a prank?"

"Well, at the time…" Heather's voice trailed off as she avoided his eyes. She couldn't think of a good excuse to justify the mess.

"You thought it was funny to pile leaves into your brother's room, knowing full well they would rot?" Gideon asked, voice sharp. "Explain yourself!"

Heather winced. "I—I didn't think about that part, Father. Before you left, Cedric made me the *Princess of the Pines*."

There was a pause. "I'm listening."

"Cedric put pinecones in my bed, my boots, my entire room. He said we were 'even.' From when I dumped him into the stream. It was a prank, so I wanted to get him back."

"And you had this bright idea to do this? To our home?"

"I thought you'd be home earlier," she answered. "The leaves… I forgot. I'm sorry. Pinecones are just as bad…"

"No, they aren't. Pinecones don't decay—*even a novice druid* knows this. Stop trying to justify this foolishness."

Heather dipped her head, defeated. "Sorry."

"'Sorry' isn't what I want to hear. Clean this up," Gideon ordered, pinching the bridge of his nose. He stepped back into the hallway, shaking his head. "All of it. And don't make me come back to check."

"Yes, Father," Heather mumbled, her cheeks burning as he walked away.

Nightshade fluttered nearby. "We can finish your story when you're done cleaning, *Princess of the Pines*."

Heather let out a frustrated groan, then went to get a bucket.

Chapter Fourteen

∞

Devastation

The next day arrived with bright spring sunshine and a glorious sunrise—though only those not too exhausted from the previous night stirred early enough to see it.

Gideon slept in, the warmth of sunlight rousing him from a deep, dreamless slumber. Taking advantage of the quiet, while Heather still slept, he made his way to the nearby stream to clean up.

The water was frigid, biting at his skin, but he braved it, scrubbing away the grime of battle. A simple warming spell and a change into a clean robe brought some comfort, though the ache in his muscles lingered. Bruises mottled his skin, and his magic reserves felt hollowed out, leaving him weary in both body and spirit.

After drying off, Gideon placed his hand on the rough bark of a nearby tree and murmured words of power, invoking plant-speak. He reached out, hoping to contact Wilmund's grove with a simple message.

Nothing. The connection failed, his magic falling into silence.

He tried again—this time reaching for a grove farther north. Still nothing.

Unease settled over him like a heavy shroud. He concentrated harder, this time sending a message to the plants near Albic Fang's residence.

After a long moment of tense waiting, a reply came—faint, but clear.

He exhaled in relief, though the concern clung to him, quiet and persistent.

With a renewed sense of urgency, Gideon returned to the house and gathered Heather for the day ahead. He handed her a spare knife and one of the old staves from the storage shed. His own weapons were secured, his staff steady in his hand.

Nightshade zipped along ahead of them, flitting back to wait before dashing off again. The little fairy was somehow clean, still clad in her tiny, bloodstained armor.

As they walked the forest path, the cool morning air carried the lingering taint of smoke and death. Each step closer to Druid's Glen weighed heavier on Gideon's heart. He knew what lay ahead would be difficult.

The protective tangle surrounding the glen was still partially intact, but even without touching it, Gideon could feel the truth. The magic wasn't dormant. It was dead.

"Heather," he said quietly, "you don't have to come with us. You'll see things—horrible things. Charred remains, bodies… Thatara knows what else."

"I want to," Heather said. "I need to."

"If it becomes too much—"

"I can handle it," she interrupted, her voice steady.

He nodded, though a part of him wished she would stay behind, safe from the horrors ahead.

They approached the ruins of Druid's Glen in silence, joining the gathering volunteers and druids already organizing the grim task of searching for survivors and identifying the dead. Several horse-drawn carts stood nearby, loaded with shovels, garden tools, and cloth masks to guard against the choking ash.

At the forefront stood Albic Fang, giving calm, precise instructions to the assembled workers. Gideon felt a glimmer of gratitude. Albic's leadership was a welcome relief, though Gideon knew he would have to address the group himself soon—his duty as Grand Druid was far from over.

The sight before him was more devastating than he had feared.

Druid's Glen—once a sanctuary of life and ancient magic—was now a wasteland. The soothing murmur of wind through leaves, the songs of birds and woodland creatures, had vanished, replaced by eerie silence.

The air was thick with the acrid scent of charred wood and loss—a bitter reminder of the senseless destruction wrought the night before.

The trees that once majestically ringed the glen were now blackened skeletons, their branches twisted and splintered by fire. What had been a lush carpet of moss and wildflowers was reduced to ash—a barren expanse scarred by intense heat.

The worst of the devastation lay at the heart of the glen, where the remains of The One Tree stood as a symbol of all that had been lost. Its mighty branches, once filled with crimson leaves that whispered secrets of the ages, were now nothing more than piles of cinders and charcoal.

Around the stump lay the shattered remnants of barrels—their contents, oil and fire, had fueled Finola's destruction. The once-protective canopy that had sheltered the glen was gone, leaving only an open, empty sky above.

And the magical tangle—the barrier that had guarded Druid's Glen for centuries—was dead, defeated by both fire and betrayal.

Gideon's distant gaze settled on the bare mound of dirt to the north—the hidden entrance to the Druid Histories, the library of knowledge tied to generations of his predecessors. Though scarred and damaged on the outside, he was confident the underground vault had survived the surface fire. *Haron Talathien* was deep enough in the earth to be insulated from the worst of the heat that had devastated the glen above.

He wanted to check the vault, to be sure. But now was not the time. That moment would come later, when he could properly assess the contents of *Haron Talathien* alone.

The silence was oppressive. The weight of loss pressed down on him, tightening around his chest with every breath—a pain no less sharp than when he had lost his beloved Emma.

He grabbed a white cloth from a nearby cart, folded it into a triangle, and tied it behind his neck to cover his nose and mouth. Heather followed suit, adjusting her mask with steady hands.

Without realizing it, Gideon took her hand. Together, they walked through the destruction, navigating the scorched remains toward the place where The One Tree had once stood in grandeur.

There, among the melted crystal spikes and scattered bones, Gideon saw the final remnants of the night's chaos: charred weapons, twisted and unidentifiable objects fused into molten globs.

No life stirred here. There would be no survivors.

Nightshade flitted above the blackened crystal shards, her wings buzzing softly. She hovered before Gideon, her usual lightheartedness dulled by sorrow. Her green eyes shimmered with sadness.

"Senseless," she whispered. "And for what? What did Finola think she would accomplish?"

Gideon shook his head, his voice low. "That's a question we'll have to answer—eventually."

For a moment, he stood in silence, watching as druids, soldiers, and villagers moved through the ruins. Some carried bodies. Others loaded the dead onto carts for burial. A few had paused near the blackened stump of The One Tree, staring in quiet disbelief. Drawn by the sight, they began to drift toward the center of the glen, their movements slow and reverent.

Gideon released Heather's hand and stepped forward. He laid his hands on the burnt stump, feeling the rough texture of what remained.

Nothing.

No magic. No lingering presence. Only lifeless wood—reduced to ash by treachery.

He wiped the soot from his hands onto his robes, pulled down the cloth from his face, and turned to face the gathering crowd.

"Gather round," he called, raising his voice so all could hear. "Gather round."

It took a moment for everyone to stop what they were doing and draw near, their footsteps soft in the ash. Gideon scanned their faces—marked by grief, exhaustion, and uncertainty. The weight of his role as Grand Druid settled on him. But he knew that words, no matter how difficult, needed to be spoken.

He took a slow, steady breath.

"Friends, we stand here amidst the ashes of our sacred tree—The One Tree—the very heart of Druid's Glen. It was more than a symbol of life and magic. It represented the deep connection between all living things.

"It may be gone, but the spirit of The One Tree lives on. It lives here," he pounded his chest, "right here.

"Today, we face the aftermath of destruction. But this is not the end. This is the beginning of our collective strength and resilience.

"We have witnessed the darkest side of conflict—death, and the devastation it brings. But from this darkness, light will rise. And that light will give us the strength to rebuild, to restore the land. We are the stewards of nature. And together, we will bring back what was lost.

"Look around you. This barren landscape makes my heart ache. But we must imagine what once was—the vibrant greenery, the red leaves of The One Tree, the songs of birds, the melodies of our forest kin. It is within our grasp.

"Today, with shovels in hand, carts to carry, and hearts filled with determination, we will cleanse this land—not only of ash, but of despair. Every action we take is a step toward healing—ourselves and the world around us.

"We must remember The One Tree, and the magic it gave us—its connection to distant lands, to places far beyond this glen.

"Together, we will breathe life back into Druid's Glen. And in doing so, we will restore the spirit of nature that will carry us forward.

"Thank you, my friends, for your unwavering dedication. Together, we will witness the rebirth of Druid's Glen."

A moment of silence followed. Then the crowd erupted into applause, building into a crescendo. Cheers rang through the glen, rising with new hope. Then, without delay, the gathered masses dispersed across the ruined clearing, ready to begin the work that awaited them.

Heather nudged her father. "That was amazing! I didn't know you could speak like that!"

Gideon thought back to his tense exchange with Hanlock Kull, remembering how he'd been forced to elevate his rhetoric to match the Judiciar's sharp tongue.

"I didn't know I could either," he admitted with a weary smile.

Nightshade blinked into view, her wings buzzing softly. "Smart. Very smart," she said. "But it won't work."

She perched briefly on Gideon's shoulder, then lifted off, hovering in front of him.

"Too bad Lillia, Aurora, and Wilmund didn't hear your speech— Lillia would've been livid. I'm sure Krik, Buvic, and Albic heard what you didn't say."

Gideon gave a tired shrug. "It was for me, if I'm honest. And for you," he added, looking pointedly at her.

"Nightshade, we both know in our hearts that this is where The One Tree belongs. It's been here for centuries—maybe longer—and it will remain here. I have a task for you. And for you, Heather."

They both waited, attentive.

"The One Tree is a total loss. It has to be regrown, and it may take years to restore its full magic. For that, we need acorns. There might be some here that survived the fire, though I'm not hopeful. But there's a chance the animals took some into the surrounding woods. We need to find them."

He turned to Nightshade. "You'll search the forest. If you find any, send word immediately. The acorns of The One Tree have a distinct black tip and are fat, not long."

Then to Heather: "I need you to ask the animals for help. Any squirrel, bird, or creature might've taken one. Have them bring any they have to us."

Both nodded and set off at once. Nightshade zipped ahead, her figure flickering in and out of view. Moments later, a host of fairies and pixies—brought with her from her homeland—appeared. With a wave of her hand, they scattered into the forest in search of the acorns.

Gideon watched them go, then whispered a silent prayer to Thatara, hoping they would succeed. He knew the battle for The One Tree wasn't over.

The other Archdruids would soon demand a share of the acorns, each eager to establish a new Druid's Glen in their own grove. According to the Council's ancient charter, the destruction of The One Tree triggered a competition among the groves to host the next sacred site. All it would take was the proper ritual and spells to plant an acorn—and in time, grow the new One Tree.

Krik, Buvic, and Albic Fang approached. Their expressions were grim, and Gideon could tell they hadn't been pleased by his spirited speech.

Albic and Buvic halted a few paces away, leaving Krik to continue forward. The imposing druid limped from a battle injury, but still carried himself with his usual daunting presence.

Gideon opened his arms in welcome, but Krik didn't respond.

"Just because you gave an inspiring speech to the masses," Krik said, voice heavy, "doesn't mean we'll stand by and let you decide where The One Tree should grow next. Thatara and the gods will determine that—not you, and certainly not your words."

"My intention was to rally everyone, not to dictate your choices," Gideon replied calmly. "You're right—each of you has the right to plant an acorn in your grove. That's the law of the council.

"Nightshade and Heather are already searching for acorns. If they find any, each of you will receive one." He paused, then added, glancing at Albic Fang, "Including you, Albic. You'll take Finola's place in the Midlands, and I'll see to it we find a suitable druid to fill your role here in the Needle Forest."

Krik studied him for a long moment, then gave a grudging nod. "For now."

"Good," Gideon said, with quiet finality. "Then let's get back to work."

He waved them away and turned back toward the blackened stump of The One Tree. The air still smelled of ash and soot, and the sight of it filled him with a profound sadness.

He retrieved his axe from where it rested against his pack and began chipping away at the charred wood.

Chunks of burnt bark flaked off with each swing, collecting at the base like dry, brittle leaves. It was a hopeless effort—he knew that. The intense heat had annihilated the tree, and the chances of finding a viable piece were slim.

Still, he kept swinging. There was always hope. A single sliver of living wood might be enough to restore what had been lost.

Each stroke of the axe felt like a small act of defiance, a refusal to accept the finality of The One Tree's destruction. The rhythmic *thunk-thunk* of the blade was oddly soothing—a way to channel grief into something tangible.

The sun climbed higher, casting long shadows across the ruined glen. In the distance, the sounds of shovels scraping dirt and carts rolling over ash drifted toward him.

The work had begun in earnest.

The midday meal was served outside Druid's Glen, and as the day wore on, more people arrived from Arboretum and the surrounding villages to lend their aid. Progress was steady, but the growing number of uncovered dead was disheartening. Gideon doubted anyone had survived—not even Finola. Yet with the remains so badly burned, it was impossible to tell one from another. Weapons, armor, and anything recognizable had been reduced to warped fragments.

Gideon drank from his waterskin, leaning against a nearby tree that had somehow survived the inferno. Down the trail, he spotted Heather approaching, a small basket tucked into the crook of her arm.

"What did you find?" he asked, taking another sip.

"Between Nightshade and me, we've found four that aren't damaged or half-eaten."

She held up the basket to reveal four plump acorns, each with the distinctive black tip.

Gideon let out a slow breath, the knot in his chest loosening slightly. "We'll need a few more if we can find them," he said. "One for each Archdruid."

"And one for you," she added with a smile.

"Yes, of course—one for me. How could I forget?"

"We'll find them," Heather said, her voice steady with quiet confidence. "I know it."

"I need to go back home for a bit," Gideon told her. "I want to see if I can reach your brothers. I fear the destruction of The One Tree has disrupted green-speak—and maybe root-walk too."

Heather's brow furrowed. "Are they in danger?"

"No," he assured her. "When I left them, they were lounging at The Stately Potato, enjoying a day of rest. Nothing to worry about. Stay here and keep looking for acorns. And have you spoken with Nightshade recently?"

Heather held up two acorns. "These are from her. She thinks there are more out there."

"Good. I'll be back soon to help."

He gave her shoulder a gentle squeeze, then set off down the path toward home, his strides long and purposeful. He resisted the urge to look back—Heather was strong, but the weight of everything that had happened would catch up to her soon enough.

As he walked, the air smelled fresher away from the burned-out glen, and a gentle breeze stirred the leaves. In the distance, he spotted his rocking chair swaying gently on the porch. Along the dirt trail, he noticed the unmistakable deep prints left behind by the *verdaleth*—massive impressions no natural creature could make. The sight brought a small smile to his lips, a reminder of the strange allies they had in the forest.

His path led him toward the stream, down the same game trail his children had once walked each morning. Not long ago—though it felt like an age—Heather had levered Cedric into the water with all the cunning of a mischievous fox. The memory brought a flicker of warmth, but it faded quickly. Too much had changed since then.

He reached the clear brook and veered upstream until he found a mighty white willow. Placing a hand on its smooth bark, he spoke words of power, invoking plant-speak. His magic reached out through the tree, seeking to connect with distant groves—but nothing.

He tried again, but the message fell short, just as before.

Frustrated but not surprised, he shifted to tree-stride.

A moment later, he slid out of a pine tree.

Deer grazed nearby, unbothered by his sudden arrival. Gideon scanned his surroundings and quickly realized he hadn't traveled nearly as far as intended. Instead of reaching Sonner, his chosen waypoint, he was only a fraction of the way there.

It would now take four more tree-strides to reach Sonner—and at least forty-eight hops to arrive at Wilmund's grove. What once took a day would now take several.

With a sigh, he returned to the pine and slipped back through the network of roots and branches until he emerged once more from the white willow.

He muttered a curse under his breath. If the loss of The One Tree had disrupted plant-speak and tree-stride so severely, long-distance travel was going to become a nightmare for druids.

He set off again toward home, following the familiar path. As he neared the house, his gaze narrowed.

Someone was sitting in his rocking chair, swaying with the breeze.

Lillia.

The dryad cast him a sharp glance, then rose from the chair. With effortless grace, she landed lightly on her feet, every movement deliberate and fluid. The belt slung low on her hips swayed with each step, and the pouch at her waist bounced with the rhythm of her walk. She slung her bow over one shoulder, the string slipping between her breasts. Her hair was pulled back—tight and practical—and the knife at her hip gleamed in its leather sheath. She was dressed for a fight.

Gideon quickened his pace to intercept her. His voice was cold, his words sharper still.

"Lillia, you are not welcome in my home. Leave. Now. Walk away in peace."

She stopped a few steps from him and gave a slow, knowing smile.

"Let's not play games, Gideon. You know why I'm here. And you're in no position to deny me."

Her gaze was unflinching, her confidence unsettling. She took a step closer.

"Give me what I want, and I'll leave when I'm good and ready. But first…"

She tapped the pouch at her waist with a soft *thunk*.

"We have other things to discuss."

Chapter Fifteen

∞

Shadows Beyond the Gate

Cedric found it odd that his father had left so suddenly after the messenger had arrived. It had to be something urgent from Druid's Glen—an emergency only Gideon could handle. He shrugged it off. Whatever it was, his father would deal with it and be back in no time.

The Stately Potato was still buzzing with activity, even this late, and Cedric savored the chance to relax with an ale. Supper had long passed, and it was nearing bedtime. He scanned the room, noting Aaron and Wellsey's absence, and told himself: just one more ale—then he'd go find out what they were up to.

He thought they made a good match, which brought his thoughts to Beatrice. She was a wonderful girl, full of surprises, and he couldn't wait to see her again. He figured the expedition wouldn't last much longer—not now that they'd explored nearly everything except the dungeons below the keep.

According to Gideon, the protections down there were impenetrable, save for the most experienced magic users.

Just as well. Cedric missed home—the familiarity of his father's cottage, the rolling meadows, his siblings. He missed Heather's sharp tongue and Eric's quiet brilliance. Eric was off on his own adventure in Ornst, but Cedric still wished he was here.

A yawn crept up on him, and he let it out with a sigh, his body heavy with the weariness of the past few weeks. A good night's sleep wouldn't hurt.

"Any news from Aaron?" Wilmund asked, coming over with a steaming cup of tea in hand.

"Not yet. What about Wellsey?" Cedric asked, straightening in his seat.

Wilmund shook his head. "No word from her either, but I'm not too worried. They're both sharp."

"They've probably lost track of time," Cedric said. "They do seem fond of each other."

"That may be," Wilmund said, though a flicker of concern crossed his features. "But this isn't a sprawling city with endless distractions—or trouble—for teenagers to get into."

He waved to Spider, who had been nursing an ale at a nearby table. The man drained his cup in a single gulp and ambled over, wiping foam from his scraggly beard.

"Can you track down Wellsey and Aaron? I'm sure they're still in town somewhere. A central spot should work for your divinations."

Spider nodded, tossed his empty mug on the counter, and headed for the door.

Cedric lifted his mug toward Wilmund. "May the wind ever be at your back."

"Hear, hear," Wilmund replied, raising his teacup.

Their glasses clinked with a satisfying chime, and both men took long pulls from their drinks.

The night air carried a chill as Spider left the warmth of The Stately Potato and made his way to the edge of the small city. He ventured toward a grove of trees, scanning the ground for what he needed.

After a brief search, he found a forked twig—a divination rod, as some called it. Satisfied, he tucked it under his arm and headed back into town.

Once he reached a shadowed alley, Spider whispered an incantation under his breath. The spell wound itself around the twig as he held it steady and began to walk, letting the magic guide him.

He traced a wide square through the streets, pacing slowly, his sharp eyes watching for any sign of the two missing teenagers.

Ten minutes passed without result. He had covered the heart of town and found no trace of them. A frown tugged at the corners of his mouth. It wasn't like them to vanish without a word.

Where could they have gone?

Spider returned to The Stately Potato, slipping the twig into his belt in case he needed it again. Inside, the barkeep was wiping down tables as the last few patrons shuffled out into the night.

He made his way to where Cedric and Wilmund still sat, both looking tired but still nursing their drinks.

"I couldn't find them," Spider said, holding up the twig for emphasis.

The two men exchanged glances, already guessing what spell he'd used.

"If they aren't in town," Wilmund asked quietly, "where else could they be?"

Cedric leaned forward, his elbows resting on the table. "Logically, it has to be the ruins or the camp outside the keep. I just… I don't see Aaron doing something like this. He's too smart. A rule follower. It doesn't make sense."

"Wellsey's no fool either," Wilmund added. "If they'd run into trouble in town, they would've sent for help. If Spider didn't sense them here, they've got to be at the camp or the ruins." He drummed his fingers on the table. "Still, it doesn't sit right. They're both clever. Why would they do something reckless?"

"Maybe smart plus smart equals dumb," Spider muttered, shrugging. "Both of them were obsessed with the dungeons beneath the keep. That much I know."

Cedric sighed and rubbed a hand over his face. "Aaron wouldn't be that reckless. But he's confident—too confident at times. Arrogant, even. Still… Gideon forbade anyone from messing with those dungeon protections. I can't imagine him going against that."

Wilmund folded his arms, thoughtful. "Gideon told me about Aaron's theory—using plant matter to bridge the protections. He thought they could rootwalk through the enchantments if they put something through the barrier first. Interesting idea. If they made a rope out of gold glory vines and threw it across, it could work. They'd be able to rootwalk a short distance through the protections."

Cedric hissed through his teeth, realization dawning. "He did it. That little idiot actually tried it."

He stood abruptly. "We're going back. Everyone. Gather the team. We'll take the supplies and head to base camp."

Spider raised a brow. "Wilmund and I can go. No need to ruin everyone else's evening. It's late, and they're probably bedding down by now."

Cedric shook his head. "No. If Aaron and Wellsey did something as reckless as going into the dungeons, we'll need every talent we have. We're all tired, but we don't have a choice. We endure."

The company, groggy and far from rested, pushed through the clinging coils of gold glory vines, their boots dragging over the cold stone path. The remnants of recently hacked vines marked a clear trail toward the keep's entrance—fresh and unsettling. Perhaps two foolish teenagers had forced their way through.

"Move," Wilmund ordered in a low voice, gripping his scythe.

They reached the double doors that were slightly ajar. With Sarif and Val lending their strength, the heavy doors creaked fully open, rusted hinges groaning under the weight.

As the doors swung wide, they froze—breath stolen by what greeted them inside.

"Shades," Wilmund hissed, his voice tight with disbelief.

There it was, to the left of the entryway: the Mage-Gate.

Alive.

Thrumming.

The entire room shimmered with arcane energy, the gate humming like an enormous, unseen heartbeat. Pulsing waves of magic radiated from the open portal, as if the air itself were alive. At its center, scintillating bands of color spiraled hypnotically—teal blues twisting into vibrant greens, then fading into molten golds. It was like staring into the eye of an everchanging storm.

"The runes…" Cedric whispered, his heart sinking into his stomach.

The silver piece that had been missing from the Elder Rune was now in place—whole and flawless. The circuit was complete, and the entire gate resonated with terrifying power, vibrating beneath their boots.

"Shades," Cedric said again, his voice hollower this time. "How did they figure out how to turn it on? How did they figure out how to fix it?"

"And why would they do such a thing?" Sarif muttered, his gaze locked on the spiraling magic.

Wilmund took a step forward, scythe in hand, his expression dark. "Agreed. How did they repair it? How did they activate it? And where does it lead?"

Aurora, standing beside Cedric, shook her head. "This is way beyond anything Aaron or Wellsey could've managed on their own. You know that."

"This is…" Cedric struggled for words. "They're smart, but this? You're right. This is far too advanced."

He scanned the darkened keep, noting the discarded cords of gold glory vines on the floor—dropped, no doubt, by Aaron and Wellsey.

"Look—the vines," Cedric said. "They must not have made it to the dungeons."

Wilmund's jaw tightened. "Chefera, Doud, Val, and Spider," he barked, "head to the dungeons. Check the protections. See if they've been breached. Report back—quickly."

The four moved to the back of the keep and descended the wide staircase without hesitation, disappearing into the shadows below. The remaining party members fanned out, calling Aaron and Wellsey's names into the dim recesses of the keep.

Their search yielded nothing. No footprints. No misplaced items. No hint that Aaron or Wellsey had passed through—aside from the dropped rope of vines.

"Why would they drop the vines here?" Cedric asked, crouching to examine them.

Wilmund eyed the Mage-Gate. "You don't think they went through?"

The swirling magic pulsed, relentless and rhythmic, vibrating in their chests like the beat of an ancient drum. Cedric stared at the gate, dread rising in his gut.

If Aaron and Wellsey had gone through it… why hadn't they come back?

He stepped toward the portal, his body moving before his mind could catch up. His heart pounded in his ears, as if the vortex itself were calling him forward. His hand trembled on his staff.

Just one step. Just one step through, and I can find them. If they're out there... they need me.

He lifted a boot toward the ramp.

Wilmund's hand clamped down on his shoulder—firm, steady. "No."

Cedric turned, frustration rising in his throat. "What if they went through? What if they're trying to come back right now?"

"We don't know that," Wilmund said. His grip tightened. "We can't afford to guess. Not with something this dangerous."

Cedric clenched his fists, swallowing the surge of emotions threatening to overwhelm him. "Maybe they'll come back through any moment," he said softly—more to himself than to anyone else.

A sudden clatter echoed from the staircase. They spun, weapons drawn—only to see Doud and Val emerge, breathless from their climb. Chefera and Spider followed close behind, their faces pale and drawn.

Chefera wiped sweat from her brow, her expression grim. "The protections are down," she said between gasps. "In their place were simple wards—alarms. I dispelled them."

She took a breath and continued. "We searched several chambers. A receiving hall with pentagrams. Devil residue everywhere. The place reeked of sulfur. Another room, touched by fire, held a dead protector."

"Protector?" Cedric asked, a sinking feeling settling in his chest.

Chefera gave a stiff nod. "A flesh golem. Hacked apart and burned." She met Cedric's gaze, her next words heavy with meaning. "There's no way Aaron or Wellsey defeated a golem. Someone else was there. Our companions didn't go into the dungeons."

"Then who *was* in the dungeons?" Cedric asked.

"I think whoever was down there has been there a while," Spider added. "We found a mine. Rock crushers. A melt shop. But no sign of Aaron or Wellsey."

"I think we should search the keep," Wilmund said. "Spread out. Look for clues. Garret, Doud—you two stay here and guard the gate."

The two mercenaries pulled their swords free in silent acknowledgment.

Cedric's heart pounded as thoughts spun faster. His worst fears began to take shape as he stared at the repaired Mage-Gate.

The wizard. The one in Druid's Glen.

Could it be?

Chefera and Cedric walked the battlements, the light from Cedric's staff blazing the way through the enclosed structure. Shadows fled before them in the cramped space designed for the keep's defense. The arrow slits and narrow openings above were choked with gold glory vines and tangle—some sections completely inundated.

It was slow going, but this was the only place they hadn't fully explored.

Cedric's boot crunched against brittle vines as he pushed deeper into the overgrown corridor. The air smelled of damp earth and decaying leaves, but the place felt… off. The gold glory vines here were twisted—unnaturally so—as if they had been coaxed into place rather than left to grow wild.

"I don't like this," Chefera muttered, gripping her knife. "These vines should've overtaken everything. They're too orderly."

Cedric agreed. Gaps showed between the thick tendrils— intentional spaces, as though the vines had been parted and arranged by a careful hand. His fingers tightened around his staff as he scanned the area, his sharp eyes catching a faint glimmer beneath the vine canopy, a pattern too regular to be natural.

"There," he whispered, nodding toward a patch of flattened vegetation.

He stepped forward and knelt, carefully pushing aside a dense tangle of vines to reveal a strange depression in the stone.

What they found was unmistakable—a hidden campsite.

There was no firepit, no discarded bones or food scraps like a common traveler might leave behind. Instead, a neatly woven mat of vines lay on the stone floor, its edges still fresh, as if recently used. At its center, a thin layer of cloth and padding suggested someone had been sleeping here—in secret.

Chefera crouched beside him, brushing her fingers over the arrangement. "This wasn't temporary. Whoever made this intended to stay a while. They were probably here the entire time we were."

Cedric's gaze drifted to a single wooden crate tucked against the battlement wall. His heart pounded as he eased it open. Inside were arranged supplies—parchment rolls, vials of ink, and a bundle of precisely wrapped tools.

He didn't know their exact purpose, but everything about the organization was meticulous. Deliberate.

"What the hell is all this?" he muttered.

Chefera had found a satchel nestled beneath a shallow overhang. Undoing the clasp, she rifled through the contents—blank parchment, rations, and vials of alchemical substances.

A chill crawled up his spine. This wasn't some random scavenger seeking shelter. Someone had been watching them. Studying them. Waiting for them to leave.

"Whoever was here knew exactly what they were doing," Chefera said, scanning the camp.

Cedric sheathed his sword and set his jaw. "We need to tell the others what we found—and what we think happened."

Without another word, they turned and hurried back toward the keep, leaving the eerie, abandoned camp behind.

"It was the wizard," Cedric whispered, his voice barely audible.

Wilmund turned sharply. "What wizard?"

Cedric's hands tightened around his staff. "There was a wizard near Druid's Glen—a spy that Heather and Lillia confronted. He must've followed us here, hidden in the battlements, then slipped into the dungeons right under our noses. He waited for us to leave so he could repair the Mage-Gate and activate it. He could've been here the entire time."

Wilmund exhaled, steadying himself. He tapped his scythe against the stone—*clink*—a dull sound that filled the uneasy silence.

"If the gate is open," he said, "this wizard knows something we don't. He's studied the Yholl brothers' magic—and he's opened the Mage-Gate with a purpose."

"But what purpose?" Garret asked. "What could he possibly want from the other side?"

"Relics. Artifacts. Ancient magic," Cedric answered. "It has to be connected to the Yholl brothers. Whatever this wizard's after, they're part of it."

Wilmund's expression darkened. "This is quicksand," he warned. "The more we try to fix this, the deeper we'll sink. If Aaron and Wellsey went through the gate, we may never get them back. We don't know what's on the other side. We don't even know *where* it leads."

Cedric squared his shoulders, resolve tightening across his face. "I'll go. I'll jump through, see what's there, and come right back. Simple."

"No," Wilmund said firmly. "This isn't simple. If it were, Aaron and Wellsey would've already come back."

"I'll go," Aurora offered, her weathered face calm. "If I can't come back through, I'll rootwalk away. I'll send word—somehow."

Wilmund shook his head. "This gate could connect to the other side of the world. Tree-striding back could take days."

Aurora coughed and shrugged. "Then we wait an hour. If they don't return, I go. That's not negotiable—Aaron and Wellsey could be in trouble."

Wilmund hesitated, then gave a slow nod. "One hour."

The group stood in tense silence, eyes fixed on the swirling portal.

The hum of the Mage-Gate thrummed in their chests like a warning—ancient, dangerous, and alive.

And they waited, mesmerized by the relic's call.

The storm outside had quieted to a low moan, with only the occasional gust of wind rattling through the cracks in the tower. No more sleet hammered the walls, but the bitter cold remained, leaching into every stone.

Aaron and Wellsey surveyed the scattered debris around them—broken benches, shattered trinkets, and remnants of a once-lived-in space buried under years of neglect. Aaron found a tattered blanket, stiff with age, and draped it over Wellsey's shoulders and her pack. He pulled on what must have once been a leather coat, though it was now hard as bark, and grimaced at the brittle sound it made.

"It's better than nothing," he muttered, flexing his arms inside the stiff sleeves. He slung on his pack and gripped his staff—it felt cold in his hand. The coat and pack together were bulky, restricting his movement.

"We need to get out of here," Wellsey whispered. "We might be able to rootwalk if we get to the outside."

"Maybe," Aaron said, though doubt tugged at him. "If the Mage-Gate isn't near any forests we know, our stride won't take us far—just as far as we can see."

"We have to try."

Aaron nodded, though the thought prickled at his intuition. *If the Mage-Gate took us to an island…*

"What do you think is behind those doors?" Wellsey asked, gesturing to the thick stone walls that divided this level of the tower.

Aaron frowned, mentally mapping the structure against the desert tower. "Half the level is walled off. Same layout as the other tower." He gave her a determined look.

"Let's find out. There might be something useful—or warmer clothes, at least."

He looked toward one of the tall, narrow windows, noting the faint light filtering in. "I wish the storm would break. If we could see the sun, we might be able to figure out where we are—maybe even what direction these towers lie in."

"Well, it was evening when we were in the desert tower," Wellsey said. "Sunset, probably."

"Which would mean this tower must be west of it," Aaron replied with a slow nod. "If it were east, it'd be night here by now." He rubbed his hands together, trying to warm his numb fingers. "There's no inland ocean, and it's cold so it must be northwest. If we were down south, it would be warm."

"Well, if we're on an island, tree-striding won't get us far." She gave him a grim smile. "Guess we'll find out."

They crossed the room toward the double doors to the left of the Mage-Gate. Their boots crunched on brittle wood and other debris—splinters of furniture, bits of smashed pottery, and personal belongings. A shattered mirror lay across the threshold, its broken glass glittering in the dim light.

Aaron reached the heavy doors and pressed his ear against the rough wood, straining to hear anything beyond. The silence was absolute.

He exchanged a look with Wellsey, then leaned in and shoved.

The ancient hinges groaned in protest—metal grinding against metal—until the door finally gave way with a harsh screech. Aaron winced at the sound, loud enough to carry.

They stepped into the shadowy space beyond.

As they crossed the threshold, magical lights flickered to life along the walls, casting a soft glow over the room. It looked like a barracks—rows of smashed beds, scattered clothing, and heaps of debris cluttered the floor.

The air was stale, heavy with a vile stench.

Aaron covered his nose with his sleeve.

"What is that smell?" Wellsey whispered, pressing a hand over her mouth.

Before Aaron could answer, something stirred at the far end of the room.

From the shadows, two pinpricks of red light began to glow.

"Shades," Aaron cursed.

The creature lunged from the shadows, its body twisted and dry like burned parchment. It snarled, limbs jerking as it barreled toward them—an undead ghoul, drawn to the noise and warmth of the living.

Wellsey's hand flew to the small crossbow at her hip. She squeezed the trigger as she raised it. The bolt struck true, sinking deep into the creature's shoulder.

The ghoul didn't slow. It tore through the debris in a frenzy, snarling with mindless wickedness.

Aaron summoned a ball of flame into his hand and hurled it at the oncoming monster. Fire splashed across its chest. The ghoul staggered, its flesh blackening as it burned—but still it came, flailing limbs centered on Wellsey.

Aaron brought his staff around in a wide arc, the impact cracking the ghoul's skull. It hit the ground in a heap but kept twitching, bony fingers scraping against the stone.

Wellsey was on it in an instant. Her scimitar flashed as she drove the blade into its chest again and again, until the red light in its eyes flickered out like dying embers.

"Well," Aaron muttered, catching his breath, "where there's one ghoul…"

"There are probably more," Wellsey finished, wiping her blade on the shredded remains of its clothes.

Aaron nodded. "We should head for the stairs. We can't waste time fighting our way through this level to see what's here."

"We have nothing to gain by staying," Wellsey agreed, casting a wary glance toward the darkened corners of the room. "We get outside—quietly."

Aaron whispered a word of power and held a pinch of bark between his fingers. His skin hardened to the texture of rough wood. Wellsey followed suit, and the faint scent of oak and pine filled the air around them.

"Shall we?" she asked, raising a brow.

Aaron gave a slow nod. They carefully shut the doors behind them and barred them with a splintered beam found on the floor.

"We go quietly."

After a few steps toward the stairs, he came to an abrupt halt. "We're fools," he said.

"What's wrong?"

Aaron dug through his pack and pulled out a stick of charcoal. It was typically used for spells, but it served other purposes—like writing.

He found a suitable piece of wood and wrote in neat, deliberate print:

We are going outside, heading for the trees so we can rootwalk. There are ghouls and possibly other undead. We suspect there is a wizard in the desert tower. The Mage-Gate is stuck in a loop between here and the desert tower, so there is no way back to the keep. We plan to get as far as we can away from here. —Aaron and Wellsey

He placed the message in clear view of the Mage-Gate.

Then they crept toward the stairs. The multiple doors lining the stairwell bore deep gouges—claw marks raked into the wood by restless undead.

Aaron reached the threshold first, his heart pounding as he peered into the shadows below.

Soft lights flickered to life, illuminating the winding steps with a faint, spectral glow. The light beckoned them downward.

Aaron gripped his staff tighter. "We move fast and quiet. No stopping."

Wellsey nodded, scimitar at the ready.

Together, they descended into the depths of the cold tower, the flickering lights casting long, shifting shadows along the stone walls.

Halfway down the tower, Brak worked as quickly as he dared. The air was stale and biting cold, his breath fogging in thin clouds. This level, once a cluster of resident apartments, lay in ruin. Wooden partitions jutted like broken ribs from the rubble, while shattered beams crisscrossed the floor like fractured bones. Few structures remained intact—most had been crushed by time, neglect, or violence.

Using a length of string to mark a perfect circle, Brak drew precise lines in white chalk, ensuring each curve was as flawless as possible. Cold sweat trickled down his back as he crouched to connect the final line, his movements quick but meticulous.

He withdrew a small vial of dark blood, unstoppered it, and poured it along the chalk outline. The coppery scent hung heavy in the frozen air.

Satisfied, Brak stepped inside the circle, careful not to smudge the chalk as he planted his feet firmly on the cold stone. His heart pounded in his chest. Even inside the protective boundary, summoning a powerful demon required exacting control—and this particular demon was… problematic.

He raised his hands and muttered words of power. His voice dropped into a harsh, grating cadence.

"Kozgokoth, ar'vak thul-zar," he spoke in the guttural Abyssal tongue: *Kozgokoth, I call you forth.*

Beyond the chalk circle, the air shimmered and twisted. The temperature plunged as a jagged rift tore open in space, belching a cloud of sulfur and rot.

From the tear stepped Kozgokoth.

He loomed—eight feet of muscled brutality, his broad, scaled chest heaving with unrestrained rage. His wings were half-spread, leathery membranes stretched taut between spiked joints, hinting at the power coiled within.

Jagged, charred scales covered his body, glistening like shards of obsidian in the dim light. Each scale was edged and irregular, giving him a fractured, menacing appearance. They drank in the light, as if absorbing it into the Abyss that formed his essence.

One side of his face was obscured by a cracked bone mask—the remnant of a greater devil he claimed to have slaughtered. The mask was grotesque, with one jagged horn broken at the base and hollow sockets that stared into nothingness.

The exposed side of his face was a ruin of blackened flesh, with one blood-red eye burning like coal beneath a heavy, protruding brow.

His clawed hands gripped a monstrous spear—blackened, jagged, warped and pitted as though forged in molten iron. The weapon was longer than a man was tall, its shaft engraved with Abyssal runes that pulsed with malevolent red light. The spearhead was serrated, wickedly curved, built not only to pierce but to tear flesh from bone with every thrust.

The demon snarled and lurched forward—only to slam into the invisible wall of the protective magic circle. Sparks danced along the boundary, and it snarled again, dragging its claws along the edge as if testing it for weakness.

"Druv'gar, vel'thak uthren?" Kozgokoth hissed, his voice a low rumble that reverberated through the broken walls. His red-on-black eyes gleamed with simmering hatred. *"Tuarik dal'vek morrahn. Vel drash, ur vakhaar."*

You dare summon me, mortal? One day, your walls will falter. And I will be waiting.

Brak's breath hitched as he translated, but he forced his expression to remain neutral. He knew better than to show fear—especially before this creature. The circle held. For now.

Kozgokoth, Brak projected telepathically, *there is a magical artifact within this tower. Can you sense it?*

The demon's wings twitched. His nostrils flared as he sniffed the air, body coiling with resentment.

No.

Brak clenched his fists, keeping his inner voice even. *Search the levels below. Find anything of power—an artifact, an ornate vial, perhaps made of glass. You'll know it when you see it. Bring it to me at once.*

Kozgokoth sneered, dragging the edge of his spear along the boundary in a slow, deliberate scrape. "*Vel druv'nak shorakh. Urvak taan ul'goroth, uthren?*"

There are many levels. Am I to delve into the deepest dungeons, mortal?

Brak gritted his teeth. Kozgokoth was stalling.

Do not test me, demon. Do as I command. Now.

The demon grinned, eyes gleaming with malevolent amusement. With a stretch of his wings, he turned toward the stairwell.

"*Vel'shar uthrik, zhur'kaan,*" he rumbled in the Abyssal tongue, stepping out of sight and vanishing down the stairs with a low, mocking laugh. The echo of leathery wings flapping faded into the gloom.

As you wish, summoner.

Brak exhaled slowly, trying to steady his racing heart.

Even outside the circle, Kozgokoth exuded an oppressive aura of malice—always probing for weakness. Brak knew the demon would seize any opportunity to turn on him.

Still within the protective circle, Brak crouched low and lit a small candle with a whispered word of power. Wax dripped onto the stone floor, anchoring it in place. It would burn for one hour—the same span Kozgokoth could remain bound to the Material Plane.

Brak sat cross-legged within the circle, closing his eyes to meditate. He focused on maintaining the summoning, keeping his will sharp and unyielding. The slightest lapse in concentration could grant Kozgokoth the space to disobey.

The hour stretched on, the cold seeping into his bones.

When the candle's flame sputtered low, Brak reached out telepathically, sending a command into the dark: *Kozgokoth, return to me. Now.*

Moments later, the demon emerged, rising from the stairwell like a shadow with wings. It landed with a heavy thud just outside the circle, its hulking form hunched in frustration.

Domonic blood dripped from scratches along its thighs. One wing hung limp, its membrane torn. The jagged tip of its spear glistened with gray, rotting ichor.

"*Vekhar ul'thrak varuun, uthren,*" Kozgokoth hissed. "*Nok'tul vel'drash thar'vak.*"

Hide behind your circle, mortal. It won't protect you forever.

Brak studied the demon's injuries. The stench of undead clung to it like smoke.

How many did you slay?

The demon sneered beneath his bone mask. *Countless. The dungeons are infested. But I could not reach what you seek. It lies deeper, far below the main levels.*

Brak frowned. *What else did you sense?*

The demon growled. *A great evil lurks in the depths. Ancient. Wicked. And it feels… familiar.*

The forked tongue flicked. "*Vel'kor jhaath, Ra-Joth.*"

Like your master, Ra-Joth.

Brak's stomach twisted. *Where exactly?*

Beneath layers of stone and filth. I could not reach it through the swarm of undead—and you called for my return.

Brak glanced at the candle. The wax was nearly gone.

Return to the Abyss.

Kozgokoth snarled, the edges of his mask curling in grotesque amusement. With a sound like tearing fabric, the demon vanished in a swirl of smoke—its laughter lingering long after it was gone.

Brak adjusted the straps of his pack and descended, stepping over the twitching remains of ghouls. Some still clung to undeath, their fingers spasming in mindless hunger. He dispatched one with a swift jab of his short blade, driving it between the ribs. The creature gurgled a moan before falling still.

The stairwell wound ever downward, past levels strewn with skeletal remains and shattered debris. Each step sent a dull ache through his legs, the weight of fatigue pressing against his endurance. The air grew heavier, thick with the stench of rot and the residue of lingering magic. He was overheating. A cool draft—any hint of open air—would have been a mercy.

At the next landing, a strange mist curled from the open threshold ahead, its eerie tendrils stretching across the floor. The scent of decay clung to it—unmistakable. Undead.

Brak peered into the chamber beyond. The remains of once-great doors lay splintered and scattered like discarded kindling. A vast hall stretched before him, its high ceiling lost to shadow.

Between rows of broken statues, ghouls and zombies wandered, their slack-jawed expressions vacant—until the scent of prey stirred them to life. At the far end, he spotted a breach in the wall where the creatures slithered in and out, free to roam under cover of the cursed storm.

Brak cursed under his breath. *That storm…* It cloaked the land in perpetual twilight, letting these wretches wander unchecked.

He stepped back, planting his feet on the stone. From his pouch he pulled out a thin thread of silk. With a sharp motion, he wove his hands through the air and spoke a word of power.

From his fingertips, thick strands of webbing erupted, expanding in a seamless cascade. The sticky mass stretched across the archway, sealing the path behind him in a silken barrier.

Any ghoul foolish enough to push through would be ensnared.

Satisfied, Brak pressed onward, descending two more levels until the stairs finally ended.

This was it.

The chamber before him lay empty—silent, still. He risked a little more light, murmuring an incantation that sent a soft glow radiating from his palm.

The illumination revealed a wide archway lined with faintly pulsing runes.

Mist drifted through the archway like a living thing, sluggish tendrils curling and twisting as if tasting the air. A chill rippled down Brak's spine.

This isn't ordinary magic. It is undead in origin.

The runes shimmered at his presence, their sigils familiar. He had seen markings like these before, deep within Mikal Yholl's dungeon—but these were different. Deeper. Older.

Brak exhaled.

They bore the unmistakable signature of Ra-Joth, Lich Lord of the Abyss.

His heart pounded. Whatever lay beyond this threshold was bound to his master's power. A relic of the past? A guardian? An ally?

Or all three?

He reached into his pouch and retrieved his spellbook, flipping quickly to the page he needed. His fingers traced the weaves of magic, and he began to unravel the wards with slow, deliberate precision.

The runes resisted. They hummed with latent energy, clinging to their bindings like a spider clutching its web.

Then—just as the final threads of magic began to loosen—a warning prickled at the edge of his mind.

Someone had come through the Mage-Gate.

Brak's breath stilled.

The wards across the stairs had been breached. There was only one explanation—they were moving. Fast. Heading deeper into the tower.

He clenched his jaw. *Gideon. It had to be.*

Time was slipping away.

Brak quickened his pace, pushing aside the tremor of unease crawling up his spine. The Grand Druid was getting closer by the minute.

And he had no intention of letting him catch up.

Chapter Sixteen

∞

Into the Depths

The farther they descended, the tighter Aaron's grip on his staff became—as if loosening it might cause everything around them to unravel. His breath misted in front of him, but the chill wasn't just from the wind outside. Just a few more levels, and they could reach the surface and tree-stride far from this cursed place.

They paused on a landing to catch their breath. This level of the tower was open and empty, save for a magic circle drawn in what looked like dried blood. A burnt-out candle sat nearby, melted into a dark puddle of wax.

"A magic circle," Aaron muttered. "Fresh."

"I thought the wizard was in the desert tower," Wellsey said, worry creeping into her voice.

"Maybe we were wrong," Aaron replied. "Maybe our logic was flawed."

"Should we go back? Up? Try the desert tower instead?"

"No trees there," Aaron said. "We have a better chance of tree-striding away from here than in the desert."

Wellsey eyed the circle. "Was it meant to keep something out—or keep something in?"

Aaron shook his head. "Either way, he must've gone deeper. Searching for whatever it is he wants."

She took a sip from her waterskin and passed it to him. "We're no match for that wizard if we run into him. Or the undead—unless we figure out a way to keep them off us. They don't like sunlight. That cursed storm is the only reason they're out at all."

"I don't know any spells strong enough to mimic sunlight," Aaron said, drinking before handing the waterskin back. "Let's keep going. We'll take it slow."

They moved down the stairs, the dim glow from the torchless sconces casting long, wavering shadows.

The smell of decay thickened with each step. They were forced to step over the dismembered corpses of the undead—the reek sharp, clinging, and unrelenting.

After descending several more flights, they reached a curious barrier—the exit was sealed by thick gray webs clinging to the walls like sinewy strands of muscle, glistening with moisture and reeking of rot and mildew.

Beyond the webbing, they could see ghouls and zombies milling about in what looked like an atrium.

"Why are these webs here?" Aaron whispered.

Wellsey examined the sticky mass, her gaze drifting to the undead beyond. "If the wizard went through, the undead would've followed. He must've put these webs up to keep them back."

"Which means he continued downward."

"We're close to the ground floor," she murmured, inching nearer to the barrier.

A ghoul noticed them. Its eyes gleamed with hunger as it let out a guttural snarl and charged. Several more followed, stumbling toward the web—but they became tangled in the sticky strands, snarling and thrashing. The zombies behind them lurched forward, undeterred by their trapped brethren.

"Well," Wellsey said, "webs burn."

"My thought exactly. Can you cast another web after I light this up?"

She nodded, reaching into her pouch. "Be ready."

Aaron extended his hand, muttering a word of power. Flame leapt from his palm and struck the web.

Fire roared through the sticky strands, catching the ghouls and igniting them in place.

The remaining undead hesitated—confused—while the zombies continued their sluggish advance through the smoke and fire.

"Now!"

Wellsey flung a handful of silvery strands into the air, conjuring another web that shot forward to entangle the next wave.

Aaron stepped in beside her and unleashed a fan of flame. The blaze engulfed the struggling undead, their moans and wails echoing through the atrium.

"Run! Look! A breach in the wall!"

Aaron darted left, Wellsey to the right, each skirting the flaming mass of thrashing ghouls as they sprinted toward the opening.

Mist and foul, decaying plant matter seeped in from outside. Aaron pushed through first, his staff held out before him as he forced his way over putrid vines and through the stench of rot.

The outside world greeted him with a bleak landscape—crumbling structures and twisted vegetation steeped in decay. To his right stretched a rocky shore, waves crashing hard against the stone.

Ahead, a cluster of dilapidated buildings lay slumped under layers of moss and mildew.

But to his left—a field of rotting grass led to a stand of white spruce. Salvation.

If they could reach those trees, they could tree-stride far from this cursed island.

He turned, hand outstretched for Wellsey—

But she wasn't there.

Mist, twisted roots, and the gaping hole in the tower wall yawned behind him. His heart lurched.

He ran back, eyes scanning frantically—

She was still inside the tower.

Collapsed. Surrounded by undead. Not moving.

A figure in gleaming golden armor fought beside her, wielding a shimmering blade. His shield was a blur, bashing back the ghouls while his sword cleaved through them.

When the last ghoul fell, the stranger banged his sword against his shield and turned to face Aaron.

"I have not seen a living soul in years," the warrior said, his voice like metal scraping over stone. "Time has no meaning here. But now— here you are... and another, within this tower."

Aaron took a cautious step forward, his gaze flicking nervously toward the staircase.

"Do not look upon me," the warrior warned, ducking behind his shield. "I was once known as Sir Aelion, lord of this island—before Mikal Yholl's unholy magic claimed it. This tower rose in a single day, and then later... came the undead. I have fought endless waves ever since. It feels like an eternity. I will fight until I have my revenge."

"Thank you for helping my friend," Aaron said, edging toward Wellsey. "We'll be on our way now."

As he bent to wake her, his eyes caught a glimpse of Sir Aelion's face—or what was left of it. Ghastly. Decayed. Somewhere between a corpse and a ghoul.

"Stay back," Aaron said, recoiling.

"I mean you no harm," Sir Aelion replied, his voice laced with bitterness. "The gods blessed my spirit. I roam this place to battle the undead. This body—" he gestured to his rotting form "—is but a vessel. My spirit is pure."

Aaron's gut twisted at the contradiction. "Good spirit or not, stay away."

Sir Aelion let out a tinny, haunting laugh. "I understand your fear. My vessel is loathsome, even to me. But know this," —his tone darkened— "I despise the undead as much as you do."

"Well, thank you," Aaron said, keeping his voice steady as he helped Wellsey to her feet. "But we must go. Mikal Yholl is dead, and your revenge… it's never coming."

"He saved me," Wellsey whispered, her voice weak. "The ghouls…"

Their exchange was cut short by a clatter from the stairs.

A swarm of squat, knuckle-walking demons poured into the chamber, their tentacled maws twitching as they scented fresh prey. Filthy pus and spores oozed from open wounds, and their claws scraped against stone with an unholy screech.

"Foul Maggoritch!" Sir Aelion growled. He slammed his sword against his shield and charged.

"Get outside!" he bellowed, cleaving through the oncoming horde.

Aaron pulled Wellsey toward the breach, where foul air mixed with the stench of decay. Outside, a mob of undead awaited—and in the distance, another horde advanced toward the tower, shrouded by the storm.

Together, they sprinted down the overgrown path toward the stand of white spruce.

Every step felt wrong, as though the forest itself were pulling away from them. The mist thickened, curling around their ankles, dragging at their heels.

At last, they reached the edge of the forest. The white spruces loomed ahead like silent sentinels.

Aaron grabbed a branch, Wellsey clutching his shoulder, panting beside him.

He whispered the incantation, his fingers brushing the bark—

And the tree pulled them in.

They twisted through the earth's lifeblood and vanished, flung far, far from the horrors of that cursed tower.

Brak, drained from unraveling the protections along the archway, paused only a moment to catch his breath. He whispered a string of foul words in the Abyssal tongue and, with a snap of his wrist, shattered a vial on the cold stone floor.

Seven squat, foul-smelling demons erupted—Maggoritch—hunched and leering, their breath thick with the stench of sulfur and rotted meat.

"Sek'var uthren," Brak commanded. *"Drav'korath."*

Find the humans. Destroy them.

The demons howled and scampered toward the stairs, claws scraping stone as they went. Brak knew the druids might overcome the lesser creatures—but that wasn't the point.

All he needed was time.

Between the Maggoritch and the undead, the druids would be delayed.

He reached into his pack and withdrew a thin strip of cured dragon meat—flesh from a young gold wyrm. Tearing off a chunk, he swallowed it whole.

A fiery warmth surged through him, as though the dragon's spirit roared from within the flesh.

The raw essence danced through his veins, sharpening his thoughts and banishing fatigue like a storm sweeping over dry plains. His fingertips buzzed with power—the residue of ancient strength.

Brak opened his spellbook, eyes scanning the pages, committing a handful of incantations to memory. He slung the pack over one shoulder, retrieved his glowing sword, and continued downward—deeper into the unknown.

He descended what felt like hundreds of steps.

At the base of the stairs, he entered a cavernous chamber carved from solid bedrock.

His blade's light stretched long shadows across towering rows of… furniture.

To his left: chairs, tables, and armoires—lined up neatly, as if in storage.

To his right: weapon stands, each displaying swords, shields, and suits of armor, arranged with military precision.

Enough to equip an army.

Brak stopped in place, holding his breath as he attuned his senses to the air.

The chamber was vast—far larger than his light could reach. He cast another illumination spell, one light on a nearby armoire, another on a set of armor. More of the chamber revealed itself: cavernous, silent.

Yet something hung in the air—a shift in pressure, a subtle warning.

His eyes locked on a black sphere embedded in the floor, half-buried in the stone.

Brak approached. It was a magical construct—clearly—but one far beyond his comprehension. He didn't recognize the weave.

A hum stirred in his skull. A buzz, faint at first, but steadily growing.

Then came a voice. Deep. Intrusive.

At last… a servant of the master. You have come to free me.

Brak's legs moved involuntarily, drawn closer to the sphere.

Two pinpricks of white light flared in the dark—eyes.

The blackness peeled away like smoke from bone, revealing a skeletal figure draped in tattered red robes, sashes of frayed silver still clinging to her wasted frame.

A lich.

Brak's pulse surged. He knew who this was—a relic of Dergan Yholl's dark past. One of the five legendary liches bound to serve his master, Ra-Joth. Their names were etched into memory.

This was… unexpected.

Na-Kerth, his master's eternal comrade—once known as the Mage Carick.

The others he only knew their undead lich names:

Nhok'naz.

Szighul.

Gaazheaz.

Hanzaghuz.

The voice curled through his thoughts like silk dipped in venom.

I was once called Enora… now I am Gaazheaz. Transformed. Preserved. Awaiting his call. We must finish what was started.

Brak froze. *Enora.*

The name struck like a blow. He remembered the stories—Mikal Yholl's consort. A Mage of immense skill and clarity.

Loyal.

Respected.

Creator of the *Librum Unfabrica. The Book of Dissolution.*

But this? This was not Mikal's doing.

This was Dergan's cruelty. His revenge. He had taken what his brother loved and twisted it—turned her into an eternal engine of undeath, locked away in a prison no one would think to search.

And the phylactery… hidden. Not in her grasp.

Brak's gaze swept the chamber beyond the sphere.

The black interior peeled back further, revealing a golden throne behind the lich, surrounded by overflowing chests of silver, platinum, and jewels. Closed armoires lined the walls. A bed with crumpled covers. A pillow still bearing the shape of a forgotten head.

Her *humanity*—stripped and replaced. Reforged in necrotic power, bound with the remnants of celestial magic from her Mage days.

Brak shivered.

One of these creatures could lay waste to the Material Plane.

But five under Ra-Joth's control?

Five would consume the world. Tear all boundaries asunder. Rip the Astral Veil.

And then? The Abyssal Lords would come—unhindered. A tide of ruin.

Brak looked up.

Shelves held countless glass containers—glowing, dim, swirling in endless color.

Souls.

The entire population of this island, perhaps more, harvested and preserved.

All to feed Gaazheaz.

He took a deliberate step back, forcing down the rising panic.

Gaazheaz leaned closer, her skeletal hand pressing against the inside of the sphere. Her pinprick eyes burned brighter.

Release me, she whispered, her voice sliding into his mind like a dagger, *and we will bring ruin to this world.*

Her gaze shifted past him, to the neatly arranged weapons, the stored furniture.

Wintermourne… is it intact? This place… my stronghold… I remember its bones, but not its breath. The tower rose too fast… he was angry. Mikal never meant for this…

Brak steadied himself, grounding in the present. "It is not my place to free you," he said aloud. "Perhaps one day. If my master requires it."

The lich tilted her head slowly—a gesture both regal and hollow.

Brak severed the mental tether with a sharp command.

The black sphere began to seal. Her eyes dimmed.

You are not his… not a Mage. I see the other in you… I see… rot… Abyss…

The pinpricks vanished.

Darkness swallowed the chamber.

He exhaled, the fog of Gaazheaz's presence clearing from his mind as his mission snapped back into focus.

The phylactery… not his master's.

Gaazheaz.

Brak stepped back, steadying himself.

For a long moment, he stood there, eyes fixed on the sealed black dome. His thoughts spun. He hadn't been sent to find Ra-Joth's phylactery—he'd been sent to find hers.

A mistake in assumption.

Ra-Joth must have hidden them—his lieutenants, his arsenal—until the time came to bring them together.

It was always about control.

And now Brak understood—not just this mission, but all those to come.

Excitement warred with dread.

There were five liches. Once Mages. Now imprisoned. Preserved. Waiting to lay waste to the Material Plane at his master's side.

Five liches.

Five soul gems.

Even possessing one would be perilous—akin to holding his master's severed hand, power and danger in equal measure.

Brak turned toward the uncharted side of the cavern.

His light spells pushed back the darkness, revealing a towering structure: brickwork twenty feet high, fifty feet wide. Seamless, except for three small, evenly spaced holes near the top.

A vault.

"The phylactery," he whispered, awe laced with greed.

He stepped forward, reaching for the weave of a detection spell—

But before he could study the vault further, a voice shattered the silence behind him.

"What do you want?"

Brak whirled, his hand tightening on the hilt of his sword.

A tall, elegant figure stood in the darkness, draped in a high-collared cloak of deep crimson velvet. His pale, angular features were beautiful in the way of predators—sharp, cold, and precise. Crimson eyes gleamed with restrained malice.

A vampire.

The source of the mist.

Brak clenched his jaw, forcing calm into his posture. "I've come on behalf of my master, Dergan Yholl, to retrieve the phylactery."

The vampire smiled—fangs flashing like ivory daggers.

"Then we serve the same master."

Brak relaxed slightly. "If that's true, then you understand why I'm here. Hand it over."

"I am called Aramastus," the vampire said. "Once a ruler of these lands. I have remained here… a very long time."

"I am Brak. Brak of the Dark Artifice. Binder of Demons."

Aramastus swept his cloak aside with theatrical grace, revealing a white shirt stained at the cuffs, its silver buttons dulled by age. His black trousers were embroidered with curling silver thread, and at his side hung a gem-encrusted longsword. His calf-high boots gleamed, polished to a mirror shine.

Then Brak noticed it—a gold medallion suspended from a fine chain around the vampire's neck. Odd in shape, intricate, not like any jewelry meant for display.

Aramastus lifted the medallion, held it for a moment, then unfastened it and extended it toward Brak.

Brak took it, frowning. The metal was warm—unnaturally so.

"That is not the phylactery," he said. "It would sense Gaazheaz. Her soul would scream from within."

"This," said Aramastus, "is merely the key to what you seek."

Brak's fingers closed around the medallion.

"What's in the vault?"

"A portal," Aramastus replied. "It connects to… other places. Other planes. I use it only to feed. There are no living things on this island."

Brak's gaze hardened, his voice cold. "Show me. I may be able to decipher its full workings."

Aramastus scoffed. "A simpleton could use the portal."

"Then let's be on our way—quickly."

"To enter the vault," Aramastus said, tapping an engraved ring on his index finger, "I must turn you to mist."

Brak's expression darkened.

"You'll pass through the holes near the top—one set leads to the outer chamber. I'll meet you there. But take care—there is a vault within the vault, and only I can guide you through the second set of apertures. Without my direction, you might be lost forever."

Brak stiffened as the vampire twisted the ring.

In the next breath, his body began to dissolve.

It was not a sudden shift, but a slow unraveling—thread by thread, the weave of his flesh unspooling. His weight fell away, bones and muscle loosening, his body becoming light, vaporous, undefined.

A wave of vertigo struck as his hands, arms, and legs ceased to exist—stopped *being* in any recognizable way—and he felt himself scatter, like vapor caught in a breeze.

He tried to hold onto some sense of himself, but it was impossible. His thoughts splintered into fragments, slipping through his mind like grains of sand through fingers that no longer existed.

I am Brak. I am Brak.

He repeated the thought like a lifeline, but even that began to fray.

There was no sight. No touch. No boundary.

He became blind and weightless—a drifting cloud of awareness adrift in a void. The familiar sensations of being upright, grounded, *contained* inside a body were gone.

Now there was only formlessness.

He could no longer tell where he ended or began—whether he floated or fell. There was no up, no down, only endless drift in every direction at once.

Move.

He willed himself forward, though "movement" felt like an afterthought, not a deliberate act.

He drifted toward the vault's openings, flowing like smoke through cracks in a door. The passage was both too fast and too slow—time stretched and compressed as though it, too, had lost its shape.

He felt his essence thread through the gaps, drawn along by the vampire's will—as if he were smoke caught in an invisible current.

The second set of holes greeted him with a cold, stagnant breath of air.

The vampire's presence brushed against him, nudging him forward like a breeze urging a lost cloud across the sky.

The second passage was smoother, but no less disorienting. He was weightless and heavy, stretched and condensed—each paradox twisting his sense of self into knots. He couldn't tell if he was being pulled forward or dragged backward through a dream.

And then, it ended.

The mist that was his body thickened, coiling into shape—bone, muscle, skin. His awareness slammed back into place with a sudden lurch, as if gravity had seized him and yanked him into reality.

Limbs he hadn't felt in what seemed like hours reformed in an awkward rush—heavy, sluggish, unfamiliar.

His skin prickled, nerves flaring like kindling catching fire.

His lungs expanded, sucking in a sharp breath that burned. Air flooded his chest—jarring after existing without breath—and he let it out in a ragged exhale, startled by how foreign it felt to breathe again.

He staggered, legs stiff, as if they'd forgotten their purpose.

He flexed his fingers. Joints popped. His skin felt too tight, too real. Cold air pressed against him like an unwelcome weight.

Every part of him tingled with residual discomfort, as though his body were still learning how to be real again.

Brak gave his head a sharp shake, trying to dispel the lingering fog from his thoughts. The transition had left him light-headed, his mind still reeling from the formless drift between states.

He took another breath—slow, deliberate—savoring the feel of air filling his lungs, grounding him.

His hands moved over his arms, his chest, confirming what instinct already told him: he was whole. He was back.

And yet, a part of him remained unsettled.

He couldn't forget how easily he had unraveled—how close he'd come to slipping into nothingness, thought and flesh dissolving into the void.

The vampire, unbothered by Brak's disquiet, moved through the chamber lighting candles one by one. The flickering glow revealed more of the vault's interior, casting long shadows across ancient stone.

Brak's attention, however, had already fixed on the object at the far end of the vault.

It stood like a sentinel—an oval structure as tall as a man, forged from gleaming silver untouched by time or tarnish. It rose from a base of polished stone, anchored to the floor like the root of a primeval tree.

The frame's surface curved upward in a perfect arc—elegant, seamless—a fusion of grace and permanence. It looked ancient, yet ahead of its time, as though forged by hands that had shaped realities, not tools.

The hands of his master.

The center of the oval resembled a mirror, but it held no reflection. No flicker of candlelight. No hint of Brak's face.

Instead, it showed only void.

It was like gazing into a pool of perfectly still water and finding no sky above it—no world, no self.

Only silence.

Only absence.

Brak took a cautious step closer.

The intricate runes etched along the outer frame stirred to life, glowing with a quiet intensity as if awakened by his presence. They pulsed softly, humming in unison like a hidden heartbeat—alive with ancient magic as old as a Mage-Gate or this tower, Thalraya.

The silver edges of the frame shimmered and rippled, enchantments layered deep within the metal. Though the runes were alien to him—looping curves, jagged slashes, cryptic sigils—his instincts rang clear.

This was no simple portal.

This was a gate—to places far beyond mortal understanding.

A relic of his master. A tool of great purpose.

Brak turned away, sharply, his gaze drawn toward the flicker of candlelight spilling from the vampire's chamber. He forced the silver oval from his thoughts—for now.

The adjoining room resembled a residence, though it felt more like a tomb dressed to resemble a memory.

At its center lay the heart of Aramastus' existence: a black-lacquered coffin, its hinged lid open like a waiting mouth.

The coffin's surface, once polished to a mirror sheen, had dulled over time. Faint scratches marred the lacquer—silent evidence of centuries of rising and resting.

Inside, the satin lining was frayed and discolored, the fabric worn thin by age and use. The edges were threadbare, and tufts of stuffing poked through small tears.

It was not a resting place.

It was a habit.

A ritual.

A reminder of what he was—and what he could never be again.

Around the coffin, the room stood in stark contrast—lavish, opulent, and meticulously arranged. It was as though the vampire clung to the last vestiges of dignity and refinement, even in the grip of endless servitude.

A small study nestled against one wall, centered around an ornate desk of dark mahogany. The surface was pristine—an inkwell, quill, and a few tightly rolled scrolls placed beside a neat stack of parchment. Every item was deliberate, positioned with obsessive precision. It spoke of a mind desperate for order amid ruin.

Across from the desk loomed a tall bookcase, its sagging shelves burdened with weight and time. The books' spines were cracked and faded, their titles long worn away. Pages curled and hung loose. Some volumes were warped, others dog-eared into oblivion.

Brak could tell: Aramastus had read them all.

Again and again.

A creature who devoured words the way others drank wine—seeking comfort in stories that could not dull the endless ache of immortality.

In one corner sat a dining table with two chairs—ornate, but mismatched, as if scavenged from different centuries. The table was set with a silver goblet and a dusty plate, untouched for years.

Lining the walls were carved cabinets, their contents sealed behind heavy locks. Small chests lay scattered across the floor, clasps shut, likely filled with gold, silver, and gemstones—the hoarded spoils of a life long since removed from need.

At the far end of the room, opposite the coffin, stood a tall display rack draped with a crimson cloak. Its edges were frayed, the fabric tattered, yet it still shimmered faintly with residual enchantment.

Beside it hung a longsword, polished and waiting. Its hilt was inlaid with gemstones; its blade remained sharp—ready for blood.

The vampire had cared for his weapons.

Time had eroded everything else.

Candles burned in wrought-iron holders scattered throughout the chamber, their flickering flames casting restless shadows along the stone walls.

The light was dim but warm—a strange juxtaposition to the cold truth of its occupant.

The space felt *lived in.*

Not just a crypt, but a home—one that had withered across centuries.

Every detail hinted at a once-proud existence now reduced to monotony and slow ruin.

And yet, despite the age and wear, the room exuded a quiet elegance, as if Aramastus had clung to the shreds of his humanity across endless years.

This was not the lair of a mindless predator.

It was the retreat of someone who had *lived, suffered,* and *endured* far beyond mortal comprehension.

Even in decay, there was beauty.

Even in ruin, there was purpose.

Brak's gaze lingered on the black lacquered coffin, imagining what it must be like to awaken alone, again and again, surrounded by relics from a world long vanished.

He thought he could almost feel the loneliness seeping from the vampire's belongings—silent witnesses to the cost of eternal life.

He exhaled slowly, a breath that trembled with both pity and dread.

This was no ordinary undead.

This was a creature who had endured the weight of centuries—waiting.

Waiting for him to arrive.

Brak let his pack slip from his shoulders. The relief was immediate. He gripped the back of a nearby chair, then sank into it with a grunt.

Across the room, the vampire dragged a chair across the stone floor and sat opposite him.

His face was sharp, chiseled—striking in its symmetry. Crimson eyes glinted with restrained hunger, and long jet-black hair cascaded over broad shoulders, framing a countenance both beautiful and vile.

"I must rest soon," Brak muttered. "I'm at the edge of my strength."

Aramastus did not blink. He did not move. He did not know exhaustion—yet he understood it.

Brak leaned back, exhaling. "Where does the portal lead?"

"To another portal," Aramastus replied. "The second gate connects to other planes—including the one where the phylactery is held."

Brak nodded slowly, feigning full comprehension. "You said you use it to feed."

"This portal leads to a place where humans dwell. I feed there… create thralls."

Aramastus's tone was matter-of-fact, as if discussing the weather.

"Our master did not want me thirsting so deeply that I would kill his messenger when he finally arrived—when *you* arrived."

He leaned forward slightly. "I am curious. What has happened?"

"Too much for one sitting," Brak said. "I've been sent to retrieve the phylactery of Gaazheaz, by order of Dergan Yholl."

The vampire nodded, slow and deliberate.

"In the final days before the fall, I was betrayed by Mikal. I chose Dergan—to subvert his brother, to serve a master who would not discard me. I am cursed to remain here, awaiting Dergan's word. Awaiting *you*."

The vampire smiled, dagger teeth bared.

Aramastus said, "We will retrieve the phylactery together."

Brak's eyes narrowed. "You assume too much."

His voice was quiet, but bitter. This was *his* task. And his alone.

"Do not insult me by questioning my prowess," Aramastus said, his tone a silken purr.

His crimson eyes flickered—amusement, perhaps. Or hunger.

"The phylactery lies in the Plane of Shadow. Alone, you will not last long. Together, we will succeed. We each have our reasons."

"I would not insult you by questioning your prowess," Brak said as he considered the vampire's offer. "Why do I need your… assistance?"

"Creatures of shadow will hunt you," Aramastus replied. "I am a creature of shadow. My thralls are creatures of shadow. We will fight shadows with shadows. Alone, you will not survive. You will fail without our protection."

Despite the unease coiling in his gut, Brak knew he had little choice.

"I will emerge alive from that portal with the phylactery intact. Do you understand?"

"Yes. Together, we will succeed," Aramastus murmured. "Your task and mine are aligned… until they are not."

Brak recognized the look in the vampire's eyes—cold, calculating. A predator biding its time.

The promise would hold only until it didn't.

"It's welcome, then," Brak said quietly.

He suppressed a yawn, fatigue pressing down like a physical weight. His shoulders sagged.

Aramastus rose and strode to his coffin, slipping inside with effortless grace.

"I will wake you in several hours," he said, fingers resting on the edge of the lid. "We'll retrieve my followers, then travel to the Plane of Shadow. Prepare yourself—it is a cold, dark place not meant for the living. Not meant for you."

The coffin shut with a soft, final *thud*.

Brak leaned back, his thoughts dimming.

Trust was a fragile thing—dangerous in the hands of predators.

But he needed Aramastus. For now.

He would rest, gather his strength—and when the time came, ensure that he, and he alone, walked away with the phylactery.

One step at a time. One betrayal at a time.

Brak closed his eyes.

Sleep claimed him at once.

PAUL HEISEL

Chapter Seventeen

∞

Allies in the Dark

The Mage-Gate thrummed with power, its swirling vortex crackling like a storm of fireflies. Cedric stood a few steps away, equal parts mesmerized and unnerved. Colors twisted and folded into one another, an endless spiral of motion that pulled at the edges of his mind.

He found himself staring too long, losing track of time as the hues shifted—sharpening into what looked like a distant image.

A tower of gray granite.

It flickered at the edge of his vision, teasing clarity—then dissolved back into the vortex.

It should have been beautiful.

All Cedric felt was dread.

Aaron and Wellsey hadn't returned.

He'd told himself—again and again—that Aaron was too smart to get trapped. If anyone could find a way back, it was him.

But it had been too long.

Sending Aurora through the gate was a risk. Wilmund had tried to sound confident in the plan, but Cedric could tell none of them truly believed it was safe.

The Mage-Gate didn't feel like a doorway.

It felt like a trap.

A one-way descent into something worse.

Wilmund's earlier warning echoed in Cedric's thoughts—quicksand. Every step to help might only drag them deeper.

They stood in silence now, each companion lost in their own unease.

The keep's stone walls pressed inward, cold even by daylight, colder now beneath the weight of nightfall.

Wilmund had ordered them to make camp in the main hall—close to the Mage-Gate. No one wanted to sleep far from it. Not with Aaron and Wellsey still missing. Not with Aurora preparing to vanish into the unknown.

They took turns on watch, eyes fixed on the swirling gate.

Waiting.

In case something—or someone—came through.

Cedric's eyes kept drifting to the swirling portal.

He stared even though it made him feel unsteady—like the longer he looked, the less real the ground beneath his feet became.

There—again. A flicker of the gray granite tower. Closer this time. Sharper.

Was that where Aaron and Wellsey had gone?

Were they trapped there?

"Time's up," Wilmund said softly.

The group gathered at the base of the ramp, offering quiet farewells as Aurora stepped forward.

Wilmund muttered a protective incantation, his hands brushing her shoulders. Her skin shimmered, hardening to a bark-like texture.

Spider followed with a spell of his own, casting a faint, translucent aura around her body—an extra layer of defense.

Cedric spoke before he could second-guess himself.

"Wait—can we try something?"

All eyes turned to him.

"What if we tie a rope around Aurora's waist?" he said quickly. "If something goes wrong, she can tug three times. We'll pull her back. It may not work… but it's worth a try."

Aurora shifted, clearly impatient, but gave a reluctant nod. "If it helps you sleep better, let's do it."

Wilmund gave a grim nod. He didn't protest—but the unease in his eyes was plain.

They worked quickly, tying the rope around Aurora's waist. She muttered under her breath about delays but didn't argue further.

"Go in, take a look, and come right back," Wilmund said. "If it all goes wrong, rootwalk out. Send us a message if you can. If not—three tugs, and we haul you back."

Aurora gave a final nod, turned, and ascended the ramp without hesitation.

She walked toward the Mage-Gate with steady, deliberate steps.

In an instant, the portal's swirling magic swallowed her whole.

Cedric gripped the rope, feeding it out as she vanished into the shimmering vortex.

For a heartbeat, everything was still.

No tug. No signal.

He felt tension rise in his chest like a tide. He clenched the rope tighter, ready to haul her back with everything he had.

Then—a twitch.

The rope jerked once—then went slack.

His breath caught.

He pulled. The rope came freely, hand over hand, offering no resistance.

No weight. No Aurora.

He hauled it in until the end lay at his feet, coiled like a dead serpent.

Then he saw it.

The rope had been severed.

Cleanly. Perfectly. No fraying. No tearing. Just a single, razor-cut edge.

Cedric stared, cold dread settling into his bones.

What could have done this?

His eyes flicked to the Mage-Gate, still swirling, still alive with energy.

Aurora was gone.

And there had been no signal.

He took a step forward, toward the gate—unable to help himself.

Wilmund's hand shot out, barring his path.

"Quicksand," the Archdruid said, voice low and grim. "If Aurora can't return, that's why Aaron and Wellsey didn't either. The gate must be one-way."

Cedric tore his shoulder away from Wilmund's grip. "We can't sit here. There has to be something we can do."

Wilmund took a deep breath, the words he wanted to say didn't come forth—it would only make things worse. His face was etched with grim resolve.

"We'll do something," he said. "But not blindly."

Wilmund turned to Chefera, who stood nearby.

"Cedric and Chefera—you'll head outside the keep's wards. Use green-speak to reach Gideon. It may take time, given the distance. Tell him everything—Aaron, Wellsey, Aurora. See if he can get a message back to us… or give instructions."

Cedric swallowed hard. He already knew how that conversation would go.

How was he supposed to tell his father that Aaron might be gone—lost forever?

Chefera rested a steady hand on his shoulder, reading his thoughts.

"Come on," she said gently. "It won't get easier if we wait."

Cedric nodded, a lump rising in his throat. "Agree. Let's get it over with."

He adjusted the strap of his pack, casting one last glance at the Mage-Gate.

The swirling portal pulsed in the dim light.

Every part of him screamed to act, to do something—anything—to help Aaron and Aurora.

But Wilmund's words echoed like a warning: *Quicksand.*

Forcing the situation might only pull them all under.

The best thing he could do now was follow orders. Get word to Gideon.

Find out what to do next. Find out when—*if*—he would return.

They moved out, slipping through the keep's wide doors and into the waiting dark.

As they passed beneath the shadowed arches, Cedric turned back for one last look.

The Mage-Gate still glowed, soft and silent in the heart of the ruined keep.

Aaron. Wellsey. Aurora.

They were out there somewhere.

And he had no idea how to bring them home.

The transportation through the Mage-Gate reminded Aurora of a less-queasy version of tree-stride—though it was still unsettling.

Rootwalking connected her to the living world, its rhythm and pulse, a symbiotic embrace.

This gate felt… void of life.

Devoid of meaning.

Without purpose.

The queasiness didn't matter much to her—her insides were always a mess these days.

She was dying.

No spell, no herb, no incantation could change that. Her body was betraying her, piece by piece.

The hardest part hadn't been accepting the truth.

It was saying goodbye.

She'd done it before leaving for the ruins of Mikal Yholl—said everything that needed saying to her family, knowing full well she might never return.

The cold air hit her the moment she arrived, sharp and biting, but she welcomed it.

It felt like home.

She'd been born in the far north, where snow and ice ruled most of the year.

The cold stirred memories—of hardy willows bent under frost, of spruce trees thick with scent, their sap dripping in the brief warmth of summer.

She would miss the hoarfrost! The beautiful hoarfrost!

This chill, for all its bite, was familiar.

And it was comforting.

Aurora found herself standing in a circular stone chamber—gray granite walls, smooth slate floors, and benches lining the edges.

Torchless sconces glowed along the walls, casting no heat, but enough light to reveal the central staircase winding downward.

She turned back toward the Mage-Gate, careful not to trip over the rope tied around her waist. Grasping it, she stepped back through the portal, expecting to reemerge in the keep.

Instead, a blast of hot air slammed into her, knocking the breath from her lungs.

She staggered, squinting against the heat, dragging the rope with her—until the end came loose in her hand.

Severed.

Perfectly sliced. No fray, no burn.

Aurora stared at it, unease twisting in her gut.

The room was nearly identical to the cold tower—same gray stone, same slate benches, same central stair.

But this one was suffocating.

The air was thick and stale, pressing close to her skin like wet cloth.

All around her were remnants of old camps—tattered tents slumped in ruin, crates upended, tools left unused.

Desiccated corpses littered the floor, mummified by heat and time.

They lay surrounded by the wreckage of their final days.

Behind her, the Mage-Gate hummed softly, its swirling magic pulsing with quiet menace.

"Shades," Aurora muttered, wiping sweat from her brow. Her clothes clung to her skin, damp and uncomfortable.

She crossed to one of the narrow windows, her boots scuffing lightly across the stone.

Through thick glass, she saw the sun sinking low on the horizon—casting the land in a wash of orange and deep violet.

Night was coming.

But it would bring no relief.

The heat would linger, festering like a fever within these walls.

She turned and stepped back into the Mage-Gate.

Relief hit her in a wave as the cold tower embraced her again.

She stepped off the ramp into the chill, the sconces glowing with their quiet light.

But the chamber was empty.

No sign of Aaron.

No sign of Wellsey.

Aurora cracked a smile when she saw the upright piece of wood.

Aaron's handwriting—neat, precise—told her exactly what she needed to know.

At the bottom of the message, an arrow pointed toward the path they'd taken.

She crossed the chamber to another window, wiping the fog from the glass.

Outside, the landscape came into focus—overgrown grasses, thorny tangles, and beyond them, a forest of white spruce. Trails snaked through the brush—not roads, but narrow paths, likely made by wildlife or—

Movement caught her eye.

Two figures sprinted side by side across the field, heading for the forest's edge.

Her heart leapt.

"Aaron!" she shouted. "Wellsey!"

They didn't hear her.

She watched them reach the trees—then vanish without slowing.

Tree-stride.

Aurora stepped back from the window, a wave of relief washing over her.

They were alive.

She had to follow—or at least send word. There had to be a way to coordinate. Escape was possible now.

Her nausea faded, replaced by something long absent: hope.

She kissed the rune-engraved ring on her finger and closed her eyes.

Center. Focus.

The air before her shimmered, bending like heat over stone, then twisting into a ripple of silver and blue.

A massive polar bear materialized—nearly ten feet tall on his hind legs, fur streaked with a soft, glow like the northern lights. His ice-blue eyes locked onto Aurora with a mix of affection and fierce loyalty.

The bear dropped to all fours, claws clicking against the stone floor. With a deep, rumbling growl, he nuzzled his massive head against her shoulder, nearly knocking her over.

"Aurora!" he rumbled, his voice like shifting glaciers. "It has been far too long since you summoned me!"

"I had no need until now, Harold," she whispered, placing a hand on his snout.

"But now I have great need. We must find my companions and guide them to safety. I saw them outside—running toward the forest. Two human teenagers. Their names are Aaron and Wellsey."

Harold sniffed the air, his massive nose twitching.

"I smell humans," he growled, "and the undead."

Aurora's grip on her staff tightened. "What else?"

The bear's fur bristled along his spine. "There is a stench of the Abyss," he snarled. "Demons are near."

"Where does the human trail lead?"

"Down the stairs, of course," Harold said, already padding toward the staircase. "No other place to go, my dear druid. I may be able to do many things, but flying isn't one of them."

His broad frame filled the stairwell entrance, claws clicking softly against stone as he began to descend.

Aurora adjusted her grip, steadying herself despite the dread curling in her gut.

"Ready?" Harold rumbled, glancing back over his shoulder.

Aurora nodded once. "Let's go."

She followed her faithful companion into the dark, her thoughts narrowed to a single purpose:

Find Aaron and Wellsey.

Get them out alive.

Aaron and Wellsey emerged from the tree-stride into an unfamiliar grove, the bitter taste of corruption still lingering on their tongues.

The white spruce trees around them appeared healthy, but the air carried that same taint they'd felt near Mikal Yholl's keep—an undercurrent of lasting sorcery that made Aaron's stomach churn.

Something was wrong.

All of it was wrong.

And this wasn't the mainland.

They were still trapped somewhere cold, still within reach of the tower's influence.

The spruce forest thinned ahead, giving way to a field of dark rocks scattered like bones across the frost-hardened earth.

Beyond the stone-strewn field, a handful of crumbling structures sagged beneath years of rot and weather. Farther still, Aaron spotted a broken spire on the distant rise—a lighthouse, split in two, its upper half collapsed inward like a snapped neck.

His heart kicked in his chest.

A lighthouse meant ships.

Ships meant boats.

Boats meant escape.

Hope surged.

He turned to Wellsey, who was already smiling—the same thought clearly dawning in her eyes.

"We might get off this island without magic," Aaron said, excitement threading through his voice. "If there's a lighthouse, there might be boats. Maybe we can sail back to the mainland."

"The forest must be too far from the mainland to connect with The One Tree," Wellsey said thoughtfully. "That's probably why the rootwalk didn't take us farther. I got that same bitter taste—maybe it's a warning from the barrier."

Aaron gave a grim nod. "Yeah. Lucky we didn't push harder. Wilmund said the barrier spits you out if you try to breach it with magic. And it's painful."

"Well, lucky for us, it spat us here without a scratch." She scanned the bleak horizon. "But what if there aren't any boats?"

"We'll find one—or fix what's left. We've got wood, and we know enough spells to patch things up. It'll be easier than staying here, that's for sure." He flashed her a grin. "Have faith."

"Well," she sighed, "faith's easier with fire and shelter. It's already freezing, and it'll only get worse after sunset."

Aaron placed a soft enchantment on his staff, casting a warm sphere of amber light. It hovered just above his shoulder, following them like a quiet sentinel.

Together, they left the white spruce forest behind, trudging toward the crumbled village and the broken lighthouse beyond.

Cold bit into Aaron's skin, not sharp but invasive, creeping into his bones like smoke into cloth. He shivered, debating the risk of lighting a fire. Undead hated flame, sure—but smoke and light could serve as a beacon, drawing worse things.

They kept moving.

He glanced over his shoulder, but the forest was too thick. The white spruces masked their trail completely. There was no sign of the tower.

"We'll scout it tomorrow in the daylight," Aaron muttered, more to himself than to Wellsey. "We'll get a better idea of where we are. I hope this storm passes."

As they approached the village, the relentless work of time and sea became more apparent. Bitter winds howled through the ruined structures, producing eerie groans and rattling the remains of shattered beams and broken windows. What might once have been a bustling fishing hamlet was now a corpse—half-swallowed by the earth.

The lighthouse, once a sentinel against treacherous waters, stood broken and hollow. Its lantern room had long since collapsed onto the jagged rocks below. Only the rusting frame remained, a crooked crown on a crumbling spire.

The nearby homes had fared no better. Roofs had caved in under decades of storms and neglect. Walls sagged inward like they were tired of standing. Rotting beams jutted out like ribs from the skeletons of old taverns, inns, and trading stalls.

Aaron slowed his pace, his gaze tracing the outlines of what once was. He could almost picture it—fishermen calling to one another as they hauled in nets, dockhands barking orders along a busy marina, travelers crowding into a warm inn like The Hound and Shrew back home.

The ghost of that life clung to the ruins, worn down by salt, wind, and time.

He thought of Cedric and his father, wondering if they'd discovered what had happened to him and Wellsey yet.

Then there was Heather. If they made it back, she'd tease him mercilessly about his little escapade.

Eric wouldn't say much—too serious, always thinking though.

And his father—Aaron cringed at the thought of the lecture waiting for him.

But that was fine. If they survived, he'd take that lecture without complaint.

They found a half-collapsed house that could serve as a lean-to. Its walls were still sturdy enough to block the worst of the wind. Inside, they cleared a small space and managed to coax a fire from the driest wood they could scavenge. It smoked more than it burned, offering little heat, but the flicker of flame brought comfort nonetheless.

Huddled together, they finished the last of their provisions. Tomorrow they'd need to forage—maybe fish, though Aaron doubted the sea would offer anything easily. The ocean here was violent, and the thought of trying to fish those waters made his stomach turn.

He tended to Wellsey's shallow wound, smearing a precious smear of druid-berry salve across it to stave off infection.

"What happened back there?" he asked softly once they were settled by the fire.

Wellsey leaned into him, drawing warmth from his side. She was quiet for a long moment, her gaze distant.

"One of the ghouls came out of nowhere. Knocked me down hard. I kept trying to get back up, but it was chaos… then Sir Aelion appeared. He cut through the ghouls—saved me." Her brow furrowed. "I think I hit my head. Everything after that is kind of a blur—until you were there."

Aaron's jaw tightened at the mention of Sir Aelion. "I don't trust him. If he hates the undead so much, why hasn't he dealt with them? Why wait until we show up to play the hero? He has another agenda."

"Well, we're far from the tower now," she murmured. "I doubt he'll find us out here."

Aaron nodded, though unease lingered. "Perhaps. If we were still close, I think we'd have seen more undead. This place seems… abandoned. I think we're safe, at least for tonight."

He kissed her forehead. "Get some rest. I'll take first watch. I'll wake you when it's your turn."

Wellsey yawned and closed her eyes, curling closer to his side.

Aaron sat quietly, holding her as she drifted to sleep. The warmth of her body against his brought a strange sense of peace, despite everything.

He knew he was falling in love with her.

Maybe he already had.

He imagined introducing her to his siblings, walking her through the Needle Forest, showing her The One Tree. He could picture it so clearly—Wellsey laughing with Eric and Heather, making memories in the village of Arboretum.

It was foolish to dream of such things now, with danger on every side.

But he couldn't help it.

Once Wellsey was asleep, Aaron adjusted her cloak to keep her warm, Aaron added more wood to the fire and stamped his feet to shake off the growing chill. Gripping his staff, he reignited its magical light and stepped out of the shelter. He needed to scout the area—just to be sure there were no surprises waiting in the dark.

He moved in a slow, careful square, tracing a path through the old marina, past the remains of an inn, and around what might once have been a small park. With each step, he scanned the shadows, keeping his staff raised to illuminate the way. The ruins around him held a tense stillness, as if they were holding their breath.

Three-quarters through his loop, he turned back toward the shelter—and froze.

The entrance was blocked.

Standing between him and Wellsey's sleeping form was the largest polar bear Aaron had ever seen.

Aurora flew down the spiraling staircase as fast as her legs would carry her, though it wasn't nearly fast enough—Harold was already well ahead. The massive polar bear moved with shocking speed, his great bulk seemingly weightless as he vaulted down the steps. She remembered a time he had outrun a bandit on horseback—much to the bandit's horror. Harold had won that race.

Now, the sounds of battle rose up to meet her—dull thuds, bone-snapping impacts, and the guttural mutterings of the undead. Aurora began whispering the first syllables of a spell, magic flaring at her fingertips, as she rounded the final bend—just in time to see Harold's hulking form crash through a doorway ahead.

She sprinted after him, her heart hammering, and burst into the statuary behind him.

The scene stopped her cold.

The chamber was swarming with undead—ghouls and zombies packed shoulder to shoulder, clawing at ancient statues, their foul limbs flailing with mindless hunger.

At the center of the chaos stood a warrior clad in radiant golden armor, his shield flashing in the low light as he fought. Each stroke of his blade was swift and brutal, each shield bash sent limbs snapping—but the tide pressed in, relentless and unending.

Then Harold roared.

The sound cracked through the statuary like an avalanche. He plowed into the horde, claws outstretched, scattering undead like broken dolls, smashing them into walls and statues, leaving carnage in his wake.

The polar bear crouched low, claws gouging deep furrows into the stone floor, then launched forward in a blur of muscle and fury. One swipe skewered a ghoul, the other impaled a zombie. With a thunderous crunch, Harold slammed them together, their brittle bones snapping like dry twigs. Then he leapt into the heart of the horde, flattening undead beneath his bulk, shredding others to ribbons with savage precision.

Aurora summoned her flaming scimitar, the blade igniting with a hiss of magic as she dove into the fray. Each swing of her weapon cleaved through rotted flesh and brittle bone, setting the undead ablaze. Ghouls shrieked and fell in heaps, their bodies collapsing into ash and charred sinew.

Beside her, the golden warrior gave no sign of acknowledgment — only fought, unrelenting. His sword glowed faintly with holy light, and his movements were relentless. Aurora fell into rhythm with him, cutting down enemies on his flank, their coordination effortless. The ground beneath her became a morass of mangled limbs, severed torsos, and twitching corpses slick with ash and gore.

Across the chamber, Harold carved a gory path of his own. His claws ripped through zombies like wet paper. A ghoul latched onto his flank—he whipped his head and hurled it across the room. It struck a stone pillar with a crunch, then slumped, lifeless.

Aurora released the flaming blade, letting it vanish in a swirl of embers. With a fluid motion, she raised both hands and cast a spell—threads of silver webbing shot outward, expanding in a lattice of magical strands. The remaining undead were snared where they stood, caught in the gleaming net.

Harold stalked the stragglers, jaws dripping, and ended them one by one with terrifying efficiency.

The golden warrior backed away from the webs, as though anticipating what would follow. Aurora summoned her flaming scimitar once more and slashed through the bindings. Fire erupted across the tangled strands, a roaring inferno that consumed the trapped undead in seconds.

When the flames died, only smoldering corpses remained.

Aurora and the warrior moved among the charred remains, finishing anything that dared twitch.

Harold trotted over, his radiant fur now streaked with gray matter and the black rot of the dead. He sniffed the warrior, then rose to his full height, towering above him like a god of judgment.

The golden warrior dropped to one knee. "I am Sir Aelion. Your intervention was timely—I was nearly overwhelmed."

Harold stepped in close, nose twitching, his ice-blue eyes narrowing to slits. "This warrior is not what he seems," the bear growled. "He is undead."

Aurora stepped back in one smooth motion, her flaming scimitar leveled. "Speak," she said, her voice sharp. "Or Harold will tear you in two."

Sir Aelion raised his hands slowly, palms open, though his gaze remained fixed on the massive bear. "I do not relish being torn apart," he said evenly, "but it would only inconvenience me. My spirit is eternal. I have no choice but to inhabit these vessels."

He stood with practiced calm, lowering his hands but making no move for his weapon. "This island was my home, once. Long before Mikal Yholl built the tower that shattered the land. The undead slaughtered my people, and I—cursed, or perhaps chosen—have fought them ever since. Centuries have passed. You are the first living beings I've seen in all that time."

Aurora narrowed her eyes. "Tell me about these living beings."

Sir Aelion nodded gravely. "There were three. One is still below— alive, last I saw. The other two escaped through a breach in the wall. Demons attacked. I held them off so the two druids could flee."

He pointed to the broken opening in the tower wall. "I helped them, if you must know."

Aurora's eyes narrowed. "What do you want in return?"

"I ask for nothing," Sir Aelion said. "For centuries I've battled the undead, trapped in this cursed form. I do not wish my fate upon anyone. I am one of the undying."

Aurora glanced at Harold. The bear rumbled low, a warning growl vibrating deep in his chest.

"Do you know the workings of the Mage-Gate?" she asked.

"I do not."

"Then how do you propose we leave this island?"

Sir Aelion gestured toward the breach in the wall. "A boat. We can repair one or build anew. The sea is calmer now—it's spring. We could reach the mainland in a matter of days."

"And you?" Aurora asked. "Will you come with us?"

"I cannot," Aelion said softly. "My spirit is bound to this island. I can never leave."

Aurora lowered the scimitar, her voice quiet but firm. "Harold."

The polar bear's ears twitched. "It is a vestige," he growled. "He twists the truth."

Aurora nodded and said, "Do what you must."

With a roar, Harold surged forward. His massive claws tore through Aelion's golden armor, ripping the undead body apart with brutal precision. Steel screeched, bone snapped, and rotten flesh was flung in gory arcs across the stone floor.

From the wreckage, a shadow burst forth—Aelion's spirit, a black, formless vestige. It howled as it surged toward Aurora, wrapping around her like a shroud of smoke and cold.

Aurora gasped, her knees buckling as the spirit pierced into her mind. It clawed through her thoughts, trying to root itself within her— seeking a vessel, a new body.

But Aurora's will was forged in both fire and frost. Gritting her teeth, she summoned every ounce of inner strength, forcing the invader back.

The vestige shrieked, writhing in frustration as it was cast out.

With one final, hollow wail, the spirit unraveled into drifting wisps and vanished into the shadows—banished, for now.

Aurora staggered, catching her breath. "Come, Harold—we need to move before it returns."

The polar bear shook undead gore from his fur with a grumble and lumbered toward the breach. Aurora followed, the steady light of her staff guiding their way.

Harold crossed the atrium, slipped through the broken wall, and set off down the path Aaron and Wellsey had taken. Aurora trailed behind, her legs heavy as the last traces of adrenaline drained from her system. Fatigue crept in, slow and sharp, but she forced herself forward. Sir Aelion's spirit was not gone—only scattered—and she knew better than to think it wouldn't return.

The darkness deepened with each step. Roots clawed across the trail. Stones lurked in shadow. Without the staff's glow, the forest would've swallowed them whole. The pale light spilled across Harold's fur ahead, catching the ethereal sheen that rippled across his back like a curtain of northern lights—his spectral pelt glowing faintly in the cursed air.

He came to a halt beside a white spruce tree, its lower branches bare. With an audible sigh, he rubbed his enormous head against the exposed trunk, fur catching in the bark.

"Ahhh," Harold rumbled, his voice rich with satisfaction. "White spruce hits the spot."

Aurora smiled despite everything. His contentment felt like a small island of peace amid so much loss. She approached the tree and laid her hand against the bark, pressing her fingers into its weathered grooves.

She whispered words of magic, her voice soft and precise, sending her intent outward through the tree's lifeblood. The spell laced itself into the bark and flowed into the roots, carried by plant-speak like invisible tendrils threading through the earth. Aurora closed her eyes, reaching deeper, waiting. Seconds turned to minutes. The silence stretched.

Her brow creased. *They have to be here.*

She pressed her palm harder to the trunk, pouring more focus into the connection—and then she felt it. A ripple, faint and fading, like the final note of a distant bell.

Residual magic. A signature. Aaron's greenstep.

Her eyes snapped open. "Harold," she whispered. "They're nearby. We're close."

The great bear lifted his head, nostrils flaring as he drew in deep, thoughtful breaths. His ears twitched once—then again. Without a word, he turned sharply toward the shoreline.

Aurora followed his gaze—and saw the tide.

From the rocks and crags beyond the trees came a flood of undead. Ghouls loped with jerking limbs and gnashing teeth, while zombies shambled in uneven ranks behind them, their rotting forms silhouetted in the moonlight. In the shadows, their eyes burned like coals—feral, hungering.

Harold roared, a thunderous cry that split the night. His radiant coat flared with magical light, gleaming like the aurora against the black tide. The ghouls snarled in reply and surged forward, faster now, emboldened by numbers and the scent of the living.

Harold met them head-on, charging with the fury of a storm. His claws slashed through bone and sinew, scattering bodies and tearing limbs from torsos. Ghouls screeched as they were flung aside. Zombies crumpled under his weight. But the swarm pressed in, crawling up his back, clawing at his sides—trying to drag him down beneath the crush of numbers.

Aurora raised her staff, magic pulsing through her fingertips. The air shimmered, charged with druidic power, and the ground responded. Grasses twisted to life. Vines erupted from the soil, snaring ankles and limbs, dragging undead down into the earth's grasp. The swarm screeched and flailed, caught in nature's merciless grip.

Harold thundered through the entanglement, each step crushing bone and severing limbs. Ghouls howled as he ripped them apart, their ruined bodies flung into the flaming grasses.

Still, the tide pressed forward.

Aurora gritted her teeth, spun her staff in a wide arc, and summoned a fan of fire. With a sweeping motion, she unleashed it—an inferno that raced along the woven grasses, devouring the trapped undead. Flames crackled through the night, rising high with every shriek that pierced the darkness. One by one, the ghouls fell— blackened husks collapsing into silence.

Ash swirled in the air as Aurora turned from the blaze and returned to the white spruce. Her hands trembled as she placed them on the trunk, drawing in the last threads of lingering magic. Aaron's tree-stride signature was there—barely. A fading echo.

"We must go now," she said, breath short from the exertion.

Harold's coat, once gleaming, was matted with blackened gore. He shook off what he could, then bounded forward with smooth, loping strides.

Aurora pressed her hand to the bark. Her voice was low but sure as she whispered the druidic word of passage. The forest opened to them, drawing them in like mist on the wind.

They emerged in a darker grove than expected—deep in the woods, not the edge. Trees loomed in every direction, their branches clutching at the stars. In the distance, the ocean called—its steady crash a whisper through the dark.

"It's darker than I expected," Aurora murmured. Her voice barely stirred the silence. "Can you smell them?"

Harold inhaled deeply, flaring his nostrils as he turned slowly in place. His head shifted toward the sea.

"I don't smell them," he said, his tone gruff with regret. "But I do smell the sea ahead." He sniffed again and grunted. "Maybe some seals."

Aurora chuckled. "You've earned a meal if you can find one, old friend." She shifted her grip on her staff, forcing her limbs to keep moving despite the growing heaviness that clung to her like a second skin. The forest pressed in around her—thick with the scent of rot and decay, the residue of too many deaths.

Halfway through the woods, her stride faltered. A sharp wave of nausea surged through her. She bent double, clutching her side as cold sweat prickled her brow.

"Not now," she breathed, teeth clenched against the pain. It was getting worse. She could feel it.

Harold turned, concern flickering in his pale blue eyes. But Aurora straightened and gave him a weak smile, forcing herself upright.

"I'm fine," she lied. "Lead the way."

The bear let out a low rumble of reluctance, but obeyed, padding ahead. His glowing coat cast a spectral light that danced across the trunks and underbrush, and for a time, Aurora followed that glow like a beacon. But it faded into the trees ahead—she couldn't keep up.

Then, the forest thinned. A clearing yawned open, and beyond it, a dim light moved among the broken remnants of a village.

Aurora squinted, hope flaring in her chest.

The glow sharpened—yes, a staff. A familiar shape.

"Aaron!" she cried, her voice cracking with relief.

The figure stopped and turned. His face lit with recognition.

"Aurora!" he called back. He ran toward her, joy and disbelief written across his face. "The polar bear—"

Aurora laughed softly, but it ended in a cough that shook her frame. She hunched, bracing against the pain, and when she straightened again, her voice was hoarse. "Don't worry about Harold," she said with a rasp. "He's a friend."

Aaron reached her side and glanced back toward the shelter. "Wellsey's safe—she's sleeping. We've been trying to figure out how to leave the island. Can you rootwalk out of here?"

Aurora nodded, though uncertainty clouded her eyes. "I can try. If there's a barrier, like the one at Mikal's keep…" She didn't finish the thought.

Aaron gave her a grateful smile, some of the weight lifting from his shoulders. "The polar bear… a friend?"

Aurora waved a hand, managing a smirk between coughs. "He won't harm either of you."

She coughed again, this time so hard it looked as though she might vomit. One hand clutched her ribs as she fought down the reflex, grimacing through the wave of pain. "Harold is his name," Aurora managed, her voice hoarse. "Are either of you hurt?"

Aaron exhaled, tension easing for the first time in hours. He stepped forward and pulled her into a quick embrace. She didn't resist—she returned it immediately. There was a grounding stillness in her presence, a calm that steadied him in ways even he didn't understand.

"We're fine now," Aaron said, his voice lighter. "Better now that you're here. Wellsey has a minor scratch."

Aurora gave a weak nod. "We'll figure out a plan." She met his gaze, her expression sharp despite her fatigue. "But first, I want to hear everything. Why did you go through the Mage-Gate? How did it activate?"

Aaron hesitated, scratching the back of his neck. "That's… mostly my fault. But let's wake Wellsey before I explain everything. You should hear it from both of us. The short version? We didn't activate the Mage-Gate—a wizard did."

Aurora's eyes narrowed. "We found his camp in the battlements at the keep. He explored the dungeons. He was watching us the whole time."

"We suspected," Aaron admitted. "But we weren't sure."

Aurora sighed. The pieces were falling together too quickly, each one more troubling than the last. As they approached the shelter, the fire inside had burned low, casting long shadows across the crumbled stone. To Aaron's quiet surprise, Wellsey wasn't startled in the least by Harold's looming presence. In fact, she appeared mildly amused.

The enormous bear was sprawled on the ground, utterly relaxed, his massive head nestled in Wellsey's lap. She scratched his neck with both hands, and Harold gave a deep, contented rumble in response.

Aaron chuckled. "I see you've made a new friend."

"Well, I see you have too," Wellsey shot back with a grin, leaping to her feet and throwing herself into Aurora's arms. She wrapped the Archdruid in a crushing hug. "I'm sorry you had to come after us."

Aurora returned the embrace, slightly winded but smiling. "I'd rather find you both safe than not at all."

"Well, we've got a problem," Wellsey said, stepping back with a frown. "We can't get off the island. The Mage-Gate is caught in some kind of loop."

Aurora sighed, rubbing her temple. "I might be able to rootwalk to the mainland—if it's close enough—or maybe to another island." She coughed hard, clenching a fist over her mouth. "But I don't have much confidence. The trees, this island, it's wrong."

Harold rumbled as he rolled onto all fours and gave a mighty shake, scattering dirt and flecks of undead gore from his fur. He lumbered a few paces away, rose onto his hind legs, and sniffed the air with slow, deliberate pulls.

"Nothing approaches," the bear announced in his deep, rolling voice. "We're safe. For now."

Aurora nodded. "Harold, keep watch while we talk."

The bear gave a solemn dip of his head and padded to the edge of the clearing, positioning himself between them and the woods. His radiant coat glowed faintly under the moonlight, a quiet beacon in the dark.

Aaron watched him go, curiosity stirring in his eyes. "What exactly is he? A familiar? An animal companion?"

Aurora hesitated.

It wasn't a question she answered lightly. Very few outside her grove—and fewer still beyond her family—knew the truth about Harold. But these two had earned more than just her trust. They had survived.

"Harold is… something more," Aurora said, turning her silver, rune-etched ring so they could see it. "He's a multi-planar being, bound to this ring. A king, where he comes from. I only summon him in times of great need." She smiled faintly. "He never complains and fights by my side until I release him. I can't begin to count how many undead he's slain to reach you—and he destroyed that spirit warrior. The vestige."

Wellsey's eyes widened. "Sir Aelion?"

Aurora nodded. "Yes."

"He helped us," Wellsey said quickly. "He fought off the undead so we could escape!"

"To serve his own agenda," Aaron said flatly. "Good riddance."

Aurora gave him a knowing look. "There's no such thing as a good spirit—at least, none I've ever known." She exhaled, weariness etched into every line of her face. "When Harold tore apart Sir Aelion's body, his spirit tried to invade me. Tried to make me his new host."

Aaron stiffened. "Did you—?"

"I resisted," Aurora said. "But he was desperate. If he gets another chance, he'll try to possess one of us again." She turned to the fire. "That's why we need to stay vigilant. Stoke those flames—undead don't like fire, and neither do vestiges."

She fixed Aaron and Wellsey with a stern gaze. "And you two? You're going to tell me everything—every embarrassing, reckless, or downright stupid thing that led us to this point. No skipping details."

Wellsey glanced at Aaron.

He gave a resigned chuckle.

"Well," Aaron muttered, "where do you want us to start?"

Aurora eased down beside the fire, its warm glow flickering across her drawn face. "From the beginning. And don't leave out anything you've seen or suspected about the wizard."

From the darkness, Harold gave a low rumble, ever-watchful while the three druids huddled together. The night pressed close—cold and unrelenting—but for now, they were safe. Together.

Chapter Eighteen

∞

Darker Paths, Darker Allies

Brak woke slowly, his mind clawing its way through the heavy fog of sleep. His dreams had been empty—just the way he preferred. Too many wizards had gone mad from wandering too far in dreams or peering into the hidden folds of magic. Brak knew better than to flirt with such dangers. Slipping too often between planes blurred the line between what was real and what was imagined—and once that line vanished, there was no coming back.

He forced the haze from his thoughts and surveyed the room.

The coffin beside him stood open, but Aramastus was gone. Brak felt neither fully rested nor particularly hungry, which told him he hadn't slept long. He reached for his waterskin and drank deeply, the cold bite of the water helping to steady his thoughts.

His gaze drifted to the portal. It glowed softly, swirling with layered shadows and shifting bands of energy. A moment later, Aramastus stepped through.

The vampire moved with unsettling ease, his steps almost soundless. Fresh blood stained his chin, and his red eyes gleamed with unnatural light. A slow smile curled across his face—hungry, amused.

"Did you rest well?" Aramastus asked.

Brak grunted and sat upright. "Well enough. We need to retrieve the phylactery. I don't have time to waste."

The vampire tilted his head, the motion slow and serpentine. "Time is ever a mortal's concern." He wiped the blood from his chin with an elegant sweep of his hand. "But yes, let us begin. I'll bring my thralls with me to the Plane of Shadow. And you? What will you summon?"

Brak considered the question.

Enough time had passed since his last summoning—he could call forth Kozgokoth again. A greater demon. A devastating ally, if unleashed. But summoning such a creature in the Plane of Shadow carried serious risk. Magic behaved unpredictably between worlds, and there would be no time for experiments. If his control faltered, even for a moment, they would all be doomed.

"I can summon a greater demon," Brak said at last. "He will tear through whatever stands in our way. I can also summon lesser demons, but only when the need is immediate—their presence is fleeting."

The vampire's pale lips curled. "An excellent ally." His voice carried a faint edge of mockery. "I will bring my spawn. They are tireless, well-adapted to shadow, and deadly in close quarters."

"You're certain you know where the phylactery is?"

"The Plane of Shadow mirrors the Material Plane in strange ways," Aramastus replied. "I feed in a castle carved into the mountainside—either the phylactery is hidden there or buried deeper within. I can't say what defenses we'll face... but they will be considerable."

Brak opened his pack and began sorting through its contents. Anything unnecessary would stay behind. Only the essentials—spell components, weapons, tools—would accompany him. The rest would remain in the vampire's lair, abandoned to dust if they failed.

He withdrew a bone scroll tube and gently unrolled the enchanted parchment inside. His fingers moved with care, reverence. The spell etched upon the page was a last resort—a single-use spell, potent enough to annihilate everything nearby within the Plane of Shadow... leaving only the caster and other living beings untouched.

Brak hoped it wouldn't come to that—but he was prepared if it did.

He re-rolled the parchment, slid it back into the bone tube, and secured it to his belt beside the vials of demon blood. His weapons—a short sword and a hunting knife, each marked with minor enchantments—were checked and sheathed.

From his pack, he retrieved a strip of leather, performed a swift series of gestures, and spoke a word of power. A ripple shimmered across his form as invisible armor settled over him—an arcane second skin, weightless but steadying. The enchantment anchored him, warded him, reminded him that he was not without defenses.

He flipped open his spellbook, scanning pages with trained precision, burning key incantations into memory. If magic faltered within the Plane of Shadow, there would be no second chances.

A shift in the portal's glow signaled Aramastus' return.

"My thralls are ready," the vampire said. His crimson eyes gleamed in the dim light. "They await your command."

Brak gave a curt nod and followed him through the shimmering portal.

The sensation was familiar—similar to the Mage-Gate, though on a smaller, more personal scale. Heat passed over him, subtle but strange, as the air thickened.

And then he was through.

They stood in a vacant cottage. The portal behind them still shimmered, a perfect replica of the one in the vampire's lair. Across the room, another stood silent—its frame dark, its magic dormant.

Two figures flanked the far portal. Vampire spawn—ashen-skinned, cold-eyed. Their stares locked on Brak, hungry and distrustful, red eyes glowing like coals in the dark.

The male spawn, Sablethorn, wore the tattered remnants of noble garb. A rotted cloak clung to his narrow shoulders, draping like dead skin. His once-handsome face had been twisted by undeath—too sharp, too smooth. His fingers had elongated into clawed talons that flexed in anticipation, like a predator denied its meal for too long.

The female, Veilstalker, flickered at the edge of sight—her body wrapped in shifting mist, her form never fully still. Her movements blurred, slipping between visibility and vanishing like smoke in wind. When she approached, her pale face flashed through the veil of shadow, her gleaming eyes fixed on Brak with predatory malice.

Aramastus stepped between them.

His voice, low and iron-hard, cut through the tension. "You will not harm Brak. No matter the circumstance. In my absence, you will obey his every command."

Veilstalker hissed, barely audible, but slinked backward without protest. She resumed her place near the portal, though her gaze never left Brak. He felt her animosity like a coiled serpent in the room— silent, but waiting.

Aramastus turned, gesturing toward the pair. "This is Sablethorn. He can rend stone like flesh. And Veilstalker—her speed and shifting form make her nearly impossible to detect, even by trained eyes. They guard the portal to the Plane of Shadow. Should we be separated, they will ensure you reach safety."

Brak's gaze moved between the two spawn, assessing rather than admiring. "Are they guarding the portal from things trying to enter… or escape?"

Aramastus gave a quiet, amused chuckle. "Both. The portal draws many unwelcome guests. The spawn's senses are tuned to its call. They'll know when something stirs."

Brak nodded, the flicker of suspicion never leaving his eyes. "You said the Plane of Shadow mirrors this place. I want to study the layout here first. The material version may give clues to what we're walking into."

The vampire's eyes narrowed, irritation flickering across his sharp features. "We do not have time. My thralls are waiting for us in the Plane of Shadow. They are in danger every moment they remain there. You will gain nothing by delaying."

Brak met his gaze without flinching. "We gain more by understanding the layout. The sooner you show me the material counterpart to the castle, the sooner we proceed—properly."

Aramastus hissed, his fangs bared in silent warning.

Brak didn't back down.

"Very well," the vampire growled, his voice laced with contempt. "Come, then. You'll see the folly in this."

He turned and stormed out of the cottage, and Brak followed into the cool night. A soft breeze stirred the dead leaves gathered at the threshold. Beyond the hedge-lined path, faint lights flickered from nearby cottages—some alive with murmured conversations, others silent and shuttered.

Brak's eyes drifted to the castle looming in the distance, its silhouette etched like a scar against the mountainside. Its towers caught the moonlight, casting long shadows across the valley. Massive. Ancient. Built into the stone itself.

It wasn't familiar.

"What is this place called?" Brak asked.

"Ravenview," Aramastus replied, the word sharp on his tongue. "The Lord of Ravenview rules from that fortress."

Brak studied the glowing stronghold. "How far?"

"An hour's walk," Aramastus muttered. "But it will gain you nothing."

Brak ignored the vampire's frustration. His mind was already mapping possible routes of escape for when he had the phylactery. If trapped here, he could journey east toward the mountains—though they were impassable—and then arc south around the edge of the continent to Ornst. Or head directly south to the coastal cities and find passage on a ship. Options for survival, just in case. Once he had the phylactery, teleporting long distances with it would be unwise.

"Let's go to the Plane of Shadow then," Brak said, relenting. "Tell me everything you know about the castle and the mountain. Leave nothing out."

Aramastus sneered but led the way back into the cottage. Once inside, they stepped through the portal and emerged into the Plane of Shadow.

The cold hit Brak like a wave. He shivered, pulling his cloak tighter. The air was dim, every surface cast in tones of gray and black. Shapes blurred together in the gloom, making it difficult to discern objects at a glance. As his eyes adjusted, he caught movement ahead—silent formations of vampire spawn, their pale eyes gleaming like coals in the dark. They drifted through the fog, shifting like mist given form.

Brak raised a hand and murmured an incantation. A small flame flickered to life at his fingertips—but it sputtered and died. He scowled. Just as he feared. Fire wouldn't serve here. He would rely on webs, protections, and other enchantments.

Aramastus moved through his thralls like a general among soldiers, issuing orders in a voice as hollow as the wind. The spawn obeyed without question, fanning out with eerie silence—predators at home in the dark.

Brak touched the medallion at his chest, feeling it vibrate softly. A strange pull gripped him—subtle but insistent—as if the artifact itself was guiding him forward.

"It's ahead," he murmured. "The castle. That's where it is."

Aramastus nodded, his crimson eyes gleaming. "Then we begin."

The vampire spawn slipped into the gloom ahead, silent as death. Brak followed, hand pressed to the medallion, its pulse aligning with the looming presence of the fortress on the horizon.

"Tell me everything about the castle," he said, his voice low, slicing through the cold.

With that, they marched into the deepening shadows.

It was nearing morning, but despite the promise of daylight, Aaron felt no relief. Fatigue pressed down on them, and their only solace was knowing the undead would retreat during the day. A few precious hours to search the village—maybe enough to find a seaworthy boat.

Wellsey looked better—an enormous relief. Whatever venom the undead carried hadn't taken hold of her.

Aurora had gone off to investigate the tree-stride network, undeterred by the reminder of a magical barrier. Harold, the polar bear, had vanished without explanation. Aurora hadn't said where he'd gone, or if he would return.

"I hope she can rootwalk," Wellsey murmured, kicking a loose rock off the edge of the pier. "I don't think we'll find a boat—at least, not one that floats."

"Agreed," Aaron said. "But she's still out there. Maybe that's a good sign—means she's making progress, right?"

They started with the marina.

What they found was a graveyard: shattered hulls rotting into the sand, fishing gear rusted into green-laced coils, torn nets snarled with seaweed, and buoys half-buried in brine and decay. The piers groaned beneath them, warped and half-collapsed, the planks jutting out like broken ribs. Beneath the boards, a sunken ship glistened with barnacles, half-swallowed by the tide.

Farther out, wrecks dotted the waves—masts shattered, hulls cracked open on the jagged reefs like the bones of an ancient leviathan.

Aaron rubbed the back of his neck. "This place is cursed. There's nothing here but ruin."

Wellsey gave him a sidelong glance. "And you thought we were going to sail across that?" She pointed toward the storm-lashed sea, just in time for a wave to crash against the rocks and explode in a spray of white foam.

Aaron recoiled at the size of it. "Alright. Maybe the raft was a stupid idea."

"Well," she muttered, scanning the shoreline, "it's starting to feel like our only option."

Aaron motioned toward the nearest intact structure—a squat, stone-walled building half-swallowed by debris. "Let's try that one. Looks like it might've been a repair shop. Maybe there's something useful inside."

Together they picked their way toward it. The lower walls still stood, their stones crusted with salt and streaked with green slime. The upper floors had long since caved in, the wood rotted into a tangle of beams and splinters that clogged the doorway.

They stepped through a jagged gap in the wall—and stopped.

The floor inside had collapsed, revealing a wide pit that dropped into a ruined basement. Below, stagnant water pooled in the corners, and splintered beams and soggy debris slumped in a heap. The air was thick with mildew and brine.

Aaron leaned forward, squinting at the stone lining the pit. "That's odd," he said. "Shouldn't the whole thing be flooded? We're right next to the sea."

Wellsey crouched beside him and brushed moss from a chunk of stone. "Yes… and these walls are fitted tight. Shouldn't this whole basement be full to the ceiling with seawater?"

Aaron nodded, eyes narrowing. "There must be a drain down there… or something even stranger."

"Or a hidden passage," Wellsey offered. "Old fishing towns sometimes built underground tunnels—to haul catch or hide contraband. Could be that."

Aaron let out a breath. "Only one way to find out. No rope… so we junk pile our way down."

The next several minutes were spent dragging debris—broken beams, splintered planks, and anything remotely stable—into the pit. They stacked the pieces into a crude, sagging ladder. Aaron tested the pile first, grimacing as the rotted wood shifted under his weight.

"Watch your step," he warned, descending carefully. He reached up to help Wellsey as she followed, the sludge-covered boards squelching beneath their boots.

At the far end of the basement, where the last of the murky water pooled, they found what they'd half expected—the faint outline of a doorframe, half-submerged in muck and time. The door itself was riddled with holes, as though deliberately perforated to drain.

Aaron muttered a low incantation. With a sweep of his hand, the water surged and congealed into blocks of ice that floated aside. The pool emptied, revealing the swollen, sagging door in full.

"Well," Wellsey said, drawing her axe with a grin, "let's see what they were trying to hide down here."

A few solid swings split the frame. Rotting wood gave way with a wet crack, and soon they had a gap wide enough to slip through.

Beyond lay a narrow tunnel. Cold air leaked out, stale and unmoving.

Aaron leaned closer, squinting into the dark. A chill ran down his spine. "We should wait for Aurora."

"Agreed," Wellsey said, lowering her axe and wiping sweat from her brow. "I'm done being reckless—even when it's not a magic doorway."

They climbed back out of the pit and settled near the entrance to wait. The blocks of ice in the basement had begun to melt, trickling water back toward the exposed doorway. Aaron tapped his fingers on his staff, nerves fraying. He kept glancing toward the forest, hoping to see movement.

At last, Aurora appeared, striding toward them from the trees.

Aaron stood. "Please tell me you found a way to rootwalk."

Aurora shook her head, her expression grim. "Tree-stride isn't working, neither is plant-speak. And it's not just the barrier. I think something's happened to the network of living things. It's like The One Tree... vanished."

Wellsey froze. "Vanished? What do you mean?"

Aurora coughed and pressed a hand to her chest until the pain faded. "The magic feels wrong. I've island-hopped before—tree to tree until I reached the mainland. But now... it's like The One Tree is simply gone. I think that's why Gideon was called back to Druid's Glen. Something terrible must have happened."

Aaron swore. "What could destroy The One Tree? And why?"

"Not accident," Aurora said wearily. "It's immune to blight. It would have to burn. Someone would have had to set it ablaze—and no enemy could breach the wards around Druid's Glen. It shouldn't be possible."

"If we can't use magic to leave," Wellsey said, her voice tight, "then we need to find a boat. Or make one. Before the undead find us."

Aurora managed a tired smile. "Let's start with that tunnel you found. Maybe it leads somewhere we can use."

Together, they climbed back down into the basement and squeezed through the splintered door. Aurora's staff lit the way, its glow revealing a narrow, stone-lined corridor. Water trickled along the floor, carrying bits of debris deeper into the darkness in a steady, silent current.

The passage opened into a series of forgotten chambers—long-abandoned rooms filled with rusted weapons, skeletal remains, and rotted furniture. One looked like a sanctuary, with a table and chairs still intact. Another had the remains of bunks, the frames collapsed, the mattresses reduced to moldering heaps.

They pressed farther down the passage. The water deepened around their ankles—cold, unmoving, as if something ancient refused to let it go. Aaron's eyes caught pale chalk-like lines high on the stone—marks of dried salt and embedded silt. He brushed his fingers along the crusted residue. Once, water had filled this corridor nearly to the ceiling.

Draining it no longer felt like a convenience. It felt like protection.

In the corridor's lowest point, a grated hole lay beneath the pooling water—an old drain, nearly lost to time. Its iron bars were warped and crusted with rust, clogged with rotting leaves and slick black sludge.

Aaron knelt beside it, hand hovering over the water's foul surface. He murmured a word of power, voice low and controlled, his fingers carving slow circles in the air.

A shimmer of magic gathered at his fingertips. With a flick of his wrist, the water stirred. A vortex formed—gentle at first, then tightening into a dark spiral. The drain gurgled as the column of water spun faster, drawing debris into its hungry mouth.

The stagnant pool drained away, leaving behind only streaks of mud and scattered silt clinging to the stone.

The air shifted—less damp, less heavy. The corridor no longer felt like a tomb about to drown them.

Whatever waited deeper in the passage, at least now it would come without warning.

With the drain cleared, Aaron felt they'd gained a small measure of safety—one they might desperately need before long.

Wellsey gave him a quick pat on the shoulder as they continued down the corridor.

At the far end, they came upon a rusted portcullis, its jagged bars warped and half-eaten by time. What had once been sturdy iron was now a brittle lattice of reddish corrosion, mottled and flaking like diseased skin.

Aaron lifted his staff and tapped one of the bars. It crumbled at the touch—fine shards of rusted metal hissing softly as they scattered across the damp stone. He pressed harder. The metal bent with a groan, shrieking faintly as ancient stress gave way.

"Well, it's weak enough," he muttered, eyeing the decayed barrier with rising confidence. Still, the shadows beyond the gate loomed heavy and unmoving, even Aurora's staff-light failing to breach their depth. Whatever lay past this point, the portcullis had done its job for centuries—keeping it sealed away.

He stepped closer, preparing to force a gap—

Aurora doubled over with a sudden, racking cough. Her body folded under the force of it, and Wellsey caught her just in time as she stumbled.

"Aurora!" Wellsey cried, alarm sharp in her voice.

The Archdruid waved her off weakly, trying to steady herself. "I'm fine—just—just give me a moment."

Aaron's expression hardened with worry. "Take her back," he said. "Let her rest in that room with the beds. I'll break through the gate."

Wellsey nodded and helped Aurora back down the passage. Once they were gone, Aaron conjured fire into his palms, channeling it toward the rusted gate. Flames hissed and danced across the corroded iron, sending up a thin veil of smoke that curled toward the ceiling— only to be whisked away by a faint draft drifting through the corridor.

He held the fire steady, hoping prolonged heat would weaken the portcullis further.

When Wellsey returned, they worked together—alternating bursts of heat and heavy blows. Each strike rang against the metal with a hollow clang, sending brittle flakes of rust showering down onto the damp stone floor. Gradually, they carved a gap wide enough to crawl through. The twisted remnants of the portcullis groaned in protest, each blow loosening it further, each movement shedding another gritty layer of iron dust.

Slipping through the jagged opening, they found the wheel mechanism on the far side—caked in rust, its frame buckled and brittle. Aaron placed both hands on the wheel and leaned in, feeling the resistance straining beneath his weight.

With a glance, Wellsey joined him. Together, they pushed.

The wheel shrieked as it turned, its rusted cogs grinding against themselves like old bones. The portcullis shuddered in response, lifting with agonizing reluctance. Then—with a final, metallic groan—the entire structure gave way. The topmost bars snapped from their mountings and the gate collapsed, crashing down in a heap. A storm of red dust erupted around them as the rusted iron disintegrated across the floor.

"Well," Aaron muttered, brushing rust from his hands, "at least we don't have to worry about closing it behind us."

Wellsey exhaled, but her gaze lingered on the shadows beyond the ruined threshold, wary and silent.

It opened into a vast, circular chamber. Gray granite columns ringed the walls like sentinels. Seven stone sarcophagi dotted the room, each positioned with deliberate symmetry to form a perfect circle around the center. These outer tombs were carved from the same cold granite as the chamber itself—weathered by time, yet still bearing intricate details preserved by the dry, unmoving air.

Each sarcophagus bore the bas-relief of a warrior—armored, dignified, and still—frozen in eternal vigil.

Aaron and Wellsey moved cautiously, their light casting long shadows that danced across the carved faces. Each tomb was distinct: subtle differences in armor and insignia hinted at the personalities and histories of the knights within. Some held swords crossed at the chest; others gripped shields adorned with faded crests—a lion, a falcon, a rearing stallion. Though time had worn them down, the carvings still radiated strength and dignity.

The inscriptions, though faint, remained legible in places. Aaron brushed dust from one with his fingertips and read softly:

HERE LIES COLINET OF THE FOREST

All the outer tombs seemed to defer to the sarcophagus at the chamber's heart.

Raised upon a low dais, the central tomb dominated the space—larger, darker, and far more elaborate. The knight carved into its lid lay with his hands resting on the hilt of a longsword that stretched the length of his body. The craftsmanship was breathtaking. Every detail—from the coiled locks of his hair to the precise etching on his armor—spoke of reverence so profound it bordered on worship.

The knight's face, though still in death, bore a serene expression that set him apart from the stoic visages of the others. His armor bore a crest—a phoenix rising from flame—rendered in such fine relief that Aaron almost expected the feathers to flutter. Around the knight's brow was a circlet, faint in the gloom, its surface etched with runes that shimmered faintly, as if the tomb still remembered power.

At the base of the sarcophagus, a bold inscription had been carved deep into the stone—its letters wide and enduring, meant to outlast centuries.

HERE LIES SIR AELION THE VALIANT, DEFENDER OF THE REALM. MAY HE REST IN ETERNAL PEACE.

Aaron felt a chill creep through him, the name settling like cold water down his spine.

Sir Aelion.

The same undead knight who had aided them—though clearly guided by motives beyond kindness. So this was where his body lay. Or had once lain.

The realization struck with grim clarity: if Sir Aelion's tomb was here, then his spirit—untethered and vengeful—was not bound to the earth by chance.

What else might linger in this crypt?

Wellsey's gaze swept the chamber, her voice hushed, barely a breath. "These knights… do you think they ever found peace? Or are they like him—trapped? Watching? Waiting?"

Aaron didn't answer right away. His eyes stayed fixed on the central sarcophagus, where the knight's serene face lay carved in stone. "I don't know," he said finally. "But we're not meant to be here."

They took a step back in unison, both feeling the pressure of the tomb grow heavier—like the carved stone warriors were watching, weighing them.

The shadows in the chamber pulsed, gathering at the edges, thickening.

"Shades," Aaron murmured. "Let's get out of here."

They turned to leave—

And Wellsey gasped.

A figure stood in their path.

Aurora.

But her eyes glowed with unnatural light, pale and cold.

The creatures that came at them from the shadows were like twisted echoes of life—silhouettes of men with hollow, smoldering eyes, and four-legged predators that moved like wolves but were forged from pure darkness. They had no scent, no sound beyond the whisper of their motion, yet they were relentless—charging at Brak and his undead escorts with eerie precision, as if driven by instinct older than memory.

Brak conserved his magic with discipline. Every spell he held in reserve might make the difference between success and failure. The medallion pulsed in his grip, beating in rhythm with his own heart—as if attuned to his lifeforce, amplifying both his fear and his focus. Whatever lay ahead would demand everything he had.

As they drew closer to the castle, Brak noted the unsettling distortions that marked this plane as something darker than a reflection. The trees were skeletal forms—twisted, misshapen, with branches like grasping claws. Not a single leaf adorned their limbs. They looked long-dead, their bark split like dried skin, their roots clawing into soil that felt more like ash than earth. There was no breeze, no birdsong—no trace of life at all. The only movement came from the shadows, swelling and ebbing like a slow, suffocating tide.

In this realm, he was the lone living thing—a warm pulse of breath and blood in a world of stillborn silence.

The castle loomed ahead, a monolithic void carved into the murk. Its stone walls were blackened and lightless, separated from the path by a deep chasm that ran the length of its outer wall. Where a moat might have existed in the Material Plane, here there was only a mass of thorn-choked vines—barbed and bloodless, yet writhing faintly, whispering in agitation. They moved without wind or touch, alive in a way that defied reason.

Brak slowed, his eyes narrowing.

This was no place for the living. But he had come too far to turn back.

The drawbridge was up, the portcullis down—a double barrier of impenetrable shadow and iron. Without a word, Aramastus dissolved into mist. His tall, lithe form unraveled in a swirl of gray vapor, nearly invisible against the gloom. The fog drifted across the chasm, seeping through narrow cracks in the gatehouse stone. Moments later, he reformed on the other side with eerie elegance.

A dull thud followed. Heavy chains groaned to life, and the drawbridge shuddered as it began to descend. With a thunderous crash, it slammed into place, spanning the chasm. Stone trembled beneath Brak's boots. A heartbeat later, the portcullis groaned upward, its jagged iron teeth grinding open, reluctant to yield.

The vampire spawn surged forward in silence—a flowing tide of undead, swift and purposeful. They poured across the drawbridge like a river of shadows, slipping into the gatehouse and spreading into the courtyard beyond.

Brak followed at a measured pace, the medallion pulsing harder now, its rhythm like a second heartbeat. It throbbed in his hand with every step, a beacon in the stillness, tugging him toward the castle walls and whatever secrets waited within.

Ahead, Brak caught sight of Aramastus ascending the grand staircase toward the keep's massive double doors, his crimson eyes gleaming with anticipation. The vampire spawn fanned out, taking positions on either side of the entrance. With a final heave, they flung open the heavy wooden doors, revealing a cavernous hall cloaked in gloom.

Brak reached the threshold just as the shadows stirred—drawn to his lifeforce and the pulsing magic of the medallion.

The darkness above descended in waves.

Shadow creatures poured forth—amorphous forms with elongated limbs and featureless faces, melting and reforming in an endless, liquid cycle. They dropped like smoke made solid, striking with limbs that moved faster than thought, slicing through the air with a hiss.

They fell upon the vampire spawn with vicious abandon.

But the spawn responded in kind. Twisted, pale figures moved with lethal grace, slipping between the shadow creatures with fangs and claws bared. The hall filled with the cacophony of snarls, shrieks, and rending flesh. For every spawn dragged down, another tore through the shadowy host, scattering their forms into drifting plumes of black smoke.

Slowly, the tide turned. The creatures were driven back, receding into the deeper dark corners of the hall, hissing as they withdrew.

Brak remained at the entrance, unmoving, his eyes drinking in every detail. Across the chamber, Aramastus turned. His sword, dark with ichor, glinted dully in the gloom. He met Brak's gaze and gave a single nod.

The way forward was clear—for now.

With a single gesture, Aramastus sent his thralls into the darkness. The vampire spawn melted into the gloom of the keep, becoming one with the shadows. Even with his enhanced vision, Brak struggled to track them. They vanished, indistinguishable from the shifting black— an unseen army of predators awaiting their master's call.

Unease stirred in his gut.

The hall fell silent again, save for the occasional whisper of fabric or the soft scrape of claws on stone. Brak felt the castle press in around him—its silence thick with the memory of old wars and the insatiable hunger of the dead.

He took a breath and stepped forward.

The medallion pulsed in his hand, its rhythm quickening as he crossed the threshold. Each beat felt stronger, deeper—no longer just a guide, but a tether pulling him onward. The phylactery was close. He could feel it, just beyond the next veil of shadow.

His fingers tightened around the golden disk, its warmth throbbing in time with his heartbeat. To hold it was to grip the thread of a destiny not entirely his own.

He glanced sideways at Aramastus. The vampire moved with quiet purpose, his lithe form gliding across the stone floor, crimson eyes fixed ahead—unblinking, unreadable.

They walked in silence, two predators—one living, one not—both drawn to the same prize.

"It's beyond the keep," Brak murmured, his voice a low whisper that didn't disturb the silence. "Deep in the mountain. I can't sense the exact place, but it calls me forward."

Aramastus gave a single nod. His face was stone, but a glint of anticipation burned in his crimson eyes. Without a word, he matched Brak's pace—his inhuman movements smooth, gliding. In contrast, Brak walked with measured caution, every step driven by instinct and calculation.

They passed through what had once been a great hall—a grotesque parody of nobility. The furniture scattered about—chairs, tables, benches—had warped into unnatural shapes, dark wood twisted into jagged angles. Carvings etched along the surfaces were cruel and leering, faces locked in sneers or screams, as if mocking the living for daring to enter.

Shadows clung to the corners, thick and watchful.

The medallion pulsed faster in Brak's grip. The phylactery was near. Its rhythm quickened with each step, syncing with his heartbeat, a steady, irresistible pull. His fingers closed tighter around it. The old magic sang through him now, ancient and urgent.

He allowed his thoughts to stray—just for a moment—to the druids he had left behind. Dawn would be breaking over their world by now—if they were still alive. Perhaps they had stumbled into

Gaazheaz's domain. Perhaps they'd fallen to some other thing that prowled the ruins. The thought stirred a flicker of cold amusement in him. If they perished, so much the better. Fewer complications when he returned.

Aramastus broke the silence. "Where is the medallion leading us?"

"Deeper," Brak said. "Into the mountain's heart."

They descended into the dungeons—a maze of damp stone and ancient cells, their iron bars eaten through by rust and time. At the end of one long corridor, Brak paused. His fingers traced a faint outline on the wall—too smooth, too regular to be natural stone.

A whispered incantation and a subtle motion of his hand, and the wall groaned open. Stone slid aside, revealing a narrow tunnel beyond. It was dark. Ancient. And waiting.

"This way," Brak instructed.

They entered the tunnel, where the air grew colder—heavy with an unnatural weight that pressed down on their shoulders. Brak strained his vision, but even his enhanced sight faltered here. The shadows were thicker, older, resisting the intrusion of light.

The walls were rough-hewn, the stone uneven and jagged beneath their feet. They picked their way carefully through the winding corridor, which twisted back on itself more than once before taking a sharp right and sloping steadily upward. The medallion throbbed with increasing intensity, each pulse stronger than the last—filling Brak with a growing urgency… and dread.

Then the tunnel opened into a vast cavern.

They stood on a ledge ten feet above the cavern floor, staring into a desolate expanse barely lit by the dull glow of Brak's magic. The air was thick with stillness, and every sound was swallowed by the darkness.

Stalactites loomed from the ceiling like ancient fangs, while stalagmites below thrust upward, worn smooth by the slow, patient erosion of centuries. To the left sprawled a chaotic heap of broken furniture, shattered wagons, and rotted barrels—a graveyard of the material world, abandoned and left to decay beneath the earth. Cobwebs blanketed the ruin like winding sheets.

Ahead, another mound caught Brak's eye.

Treasure chests—twisted open, overflowing with tarnished gold and cracked gemstones—piled in careless excess. The medallion in his hand flared hot, searing against his palm.

The phylactery was here.

Brak's pulse quickened, matching the medallion's rhythmic thrum. This was it—the culmination of his journey. Ahead lay the object he'd been sent to retrieve, the shard of Ra-Joth's dark legacy that would bring his master one step closer to return… and dominion.

"To the right," Brak murmured, pointing toward the yawning void that stretched into shadow. Shapes shifted in the gloom—unseen things, moving just beyond the edge of light. He dragged his gaze away and gestured to the mound of treasure. "It's down there. In the center."

Aramastus gave a slight tilt of his head, then raised one hand. Without a word, the vampire spawn moved. They flowed like oil down the slope, fanning out in tight clusters of four. Each group peeled away, probing corners and shadows with silent, ruthless efficiency. Their crimson eyes cut through the dark, scanning for traps or threats.

The cavern fell into an eerie hush.

Every scuff of claw on stone, every shuffle of boot or bone, echoed too loud in the stillness.

A disturbance rippled the cold air.

Not a sound at first—but a feeling. A pressure in the air. A vibration Brak felt in his teeth, his bones.

A gust howled from the right, sharp and sudden, sending rust and ash into the air in a spiraling cloud. Brak turned, instincts bristling.

He saw it—just a glimpse.

A hulking shadow, vast and coiled, blotting out even the darkness behind it.

With a roar that tore through the air, the creature surged forward.

It struck the ground like a falling star. Vampire spawn were flung aside, some crushed beneath the weight. Dust exploded outward as the beast unfolded—a massive, sinuous monster, blacker than the dark around it. A shadow dragon. Ten feet tall at the shoulders, its scales swallowed light. Its wings stretched thirty feet across, leathery spans edged in thorns, cloaking the cavern in living night.

The dragon's eyes blazed with a sickly green light—cold, calculating, and cruel. Its gaze swept the intruders like a predator appraising meat. Each step was fluid and lethal, claws grinding against the stone as it advanced with terrifying grace.

The vampire spawn scattered, instincts driving them apart—but not fast enough. The dragon's tail lashed out, a blur of muscle and shadow, and struck with the force of a siege engine. Two spawn were flung across the cavern, their bodies slamming into the stone with bone-splintering crunches before crumpling, motionless.

One of the spawn lunged, claws bared in a desperate strike.

The dragon turned and snatched it from the air in its massive jaws. There was a sickening snap, and the limp corpse was hurled into the dark like refuse.

Aramastus's remaining thralls regrouped, flanking the dragon, attempting to bury it in numbers. They surged from all sides, raking at its scales with tooth and claw.

But the dragon's hide drank the damage. Their slashes left no mark.

The beast reared back, its chest expanding. Brak's breath caught. He knew what was coming.

The dragon exhaled.

A roiling cone of darkness erupted from its maw—not smoke, not flame, but pure shadow, dense and writhing with tendrils of void. It slammed into the spawn like a wave. The front line was engulfed, their bodies swallowed whole.

Crushing pressure, coiling tendrils, then silence.

They were gone. Nothing remained but ash swirling in the black breath's wake.

Brak grit his teeth, heart hammering.

This was no beast. This was a manifestation of the plane itself—an apex predator of shadow, born to hunt the living. If he didn't act, Aramastus's forces would be shredded to nothing, and he would be next.

He reached into his satchel, fingers closing around the cool glass of a small vial—thick with the blood of his bound demon. Without hesitation, Brak hurled it to the stone. The vial shattered, and the viscous blood splattered in a wide arc, pooling at his feet.

Dark tendrils of energy rose from the stain, curling upward in a spiral of shadow and heat. The air grew heavy. A portal coalesced—an oily rift pulsing with malevolent light.

Brak drew a long breath, reached inward, and spoke the forbidden words in the guttural tongue of the Abyss. Each syllable twisted the air.

"*Kozgokoth*," he intoned, his voice deep, resonant, and full of power. "*Ar'vak thul-zar.*" *Kozgokoth, I call you forth.*

The portal shuddered, its edges flaring with unnatural light. A clawed hand reached through—then a horned head, its features masked in bone and scarred iron.

Kozgokoth emerged in full, rising from the breach like a titan of wrath. Eight feet tall, his obsidian-black flesh shimmered like cracked stone over molten blood. Every muscle flexed with violent tension. Jagged horns framed his mask, and from beneath it, two pits of black void burned with fury.

His abyssal spear pulsed pink, as if it drank pain.

Brak's mental command cut through the summoning tether.

Kill the dragon.

The demon's eyes blazed. He turned, hissed, and moved.

With terrifying speed, Kozgokoth charged. Each step thundered across the cavern. The shadow dragon turned, wings flaring, but it was too late.

Kozgokoth struck.

The spear drove deep into the beast's flank, slipping between the dragon's armored scales and tearing into the shadow-flesh beneath. A gout of black ichor hissed into the air, evaporating before it touched stone.

The dragon shrieked—an unholy sound that rippled through the cavern, shuddering stone and shadow alike.

The dragon turned, furious, its massive jaws snapping toward Kozgokoth.

But the demon moved with uncanny speed—sidestepping the strike and driving the butt of his spear into the beast's snout. The impact rang out like a thunderclap, echoing through the stone chamber.

Kozgokoth snarled and struck again, the spear's wicked tip slamming into the dragon's throat with brutal precision. The shadow beast shrieked, twisting away, its cry a chorus of hate and agony. It reared and bucked, thrashing with enough force to hurl vampire spawn from its back like dead leaves in a storm.

All around it, Aramastus's thralls renewed their assault, swarming the creature with tooth and claw, their pale faces twisted in glee. They clung to its wings and spine, stabbing down with rusted blades, trying to bring it low. But for every blow they landed, the dragon answered with savage force.

Its tail snapped outward—an eruption of muscle and shadow—catching three spawn mid-lunge and sending them hurtling into the cavern walls. They struck with wet, final sounds.

Kozgokoth took the blow squarely in the ribs, the force hurling him across the stone. He tumbled once, twice—then rolled to his feet, blood leaking between his teeth. He spat, grinned beneath his bone mask, and leveled his spear once more.

The dragon reared back, wings unfurling with a furious snap. It let out a final, baleful bellow, then beat the air with a thunderous crack and launched into the darkness. Its retreat was swift, the shadows swallowing it whole, leaving only the echo of its roar behind.

Brak exhaled, his heart pounding. He hadn't expected a creature of such power—and he knew it might return. For now, they had a fleeting reprieve.

Do you sense the phylactery? he asked, his thoughts sharp and insistent.

Kozgokoth, blood still trickling from shallow wounds, turned his burning gaze to Brak.

Yes, the word echoed in Brak's mind, thick with fury and hunger. *Go to it. Guard it.*

The demon moved without hesitation. His massive form crushed gold and splintered crates underfoot as he stepped forward. One powerful beat of his leathery wings carried him over the ruin and into the heart of the hoard. He landed atop a mound of glittering wreckage, jagged horns lowered, spear ready. The surviving vampire spawn crept closer, eyeing him with wary anticipation.

"Call off your minions," Brak said to Aramastus, voice low. "The demon loathes the undead as much as the living. And we must move quickly—the dragon *will* return."

Aramastus's crimson eyes flicked toward Brak with a flash of irritation, but he gave a sharp, silent command. The spawn melted back into the shadows, forming a loose perimeter around the treasure, watchful and poised.

With a fluid leap, Aramastus descended to the cavern floor. Brak followed, scrambling down the rocks, clutching the medallion against his chest. It burned against his skin—intense, urgent—until he pulled it free, holding it before him like a beacon. The medallion glowed a bright gray, pulsing in perfect rhythm with his heartbeat, drawing him toward a single point in the hoard where Kozgokoth stood sentinel.

"*Krah'noth*," Brak said, loud enough for the vampire to hear. "*Vel'darak." Step aside. Guard me.*

Kozgokoth shifted without a word, his hulking form retreating a few paces. His stance remained coiled, claws flexing against the stone as he took up position beside the mound, spear leveled and ready to strike at anything that came too close. His hateful eyes lingered on Aramastus and his vampire spawn.

Partially buried in broken chests and tarnished coins, Brak spotted the object he'd come for—a large black chest, its surface polished obsidian, cold and gleaming, inlaid with silver filigree that shimmered faintly in the cavern's gloom. The designs coiled like vines—or chains—around a central indentation, perfectly round, perfectly familiar.

Brak lifted the medallion, turned it once in his hand, and pressed it into the hollow. The etchings aligned with a subtle *click,* the metal sliding home with unnerving ease.

For a breath, nothing moved.

Then came the hiss of old seals breaking. The chest's lid creaked open, the sound dry and thin, as if reluctant to reveal its contents.

Inside, nestled in velvet, lay two objects.

A diamond the size of Brak's fist—dark, gleaming, and alive with a pulse that matched no mortal rhythm. It exuded power. Hunger. Awareness.

Beside it, a plain gold ring. Unadorned, but thrumming with latent magic.

Brak stared for a heartbeat too long.

He reached for the ring first, slipping it into a pouch on his belt. No time to test it now. The diamond was next—warm to the touch, its surface unnaturally smooth, as though it had been carved from stillness itself. He placed it into a hidden pocket sewn into the inner seam of his robes, where its weight pressed firm against his hip, real and impossible to ignore.

He closed the chest with care, retracted the medallion, and slipped it over his neck once more. The moment it touched his skin, he felt… nothing. Its magic was gone. It had served its purpose—and was now little more than a relic.

He removed it and handed both the chest and the medallion to Aramastus. "Keep these. We may have use for them again."

The vampire nodded, tucking the items under his arm with an efficiency Brak found reassuring. Together, they turned toward the exit, urgency pressing them forward.

"*Drath*," Brak ordered, then sent his thoughts to Kozgokoth: *Once we are through the castle, you will go ahead and clear the way of any shadow-spawn.*

Kozgokoth inclined his head, clearly irritated.

They made their way back up the slope—Brak climbing with effort while the vampire spawn vaulted ahead with speed and purpose. Aramastus carried the chest with grace, leaping to rejoin his minions. Kozgokoth lumbered behind them, his massive frame scraping the sides of the narrow tunnel as he forced his way through.

The shadow dragon will return. It will try to attack us as we make for the portal, Brak warned the demon. *If the vampire or his spawn show even a hint of aggression toward me, destroy the vampire first.*

The demon smiled beneath the bone mask. He rumbled his assent, his one functioning eye glinting with hungry malice as he watched the vampire spawn dart ahead, covering ground with supernatural ease. Brak, Aramastus, and Kozgokoth lagged behind.

Fatigue clawed at Brak—his limbs heavy, as though wading through quicksand. The unrelenting chill of the Plane of Shadow leeched his strength with every step.

They crossed the drawbridge, heading down the darkened avenue toward the faint outline of the town gates. The portal lay an hour's march beyond.

If they could quicken the pace, Brak thought, *they might reach it in half that time.*

But he wasn't sure he had the strength left to try. His eyes flicked to the swirling skies, half-expecting the dragon's silhouette to take shape above them at any moment.

Ahead, the vampire spawn moved with relentless, unholy purpose, setting the pace under Aramastus's silent command. The rhythm of Brak's heartbeat pounded in his ears, each pulse a grim reminder of his mortality. The phylactery's unnatural warmth pressed against his hip like a brand.

Then, without sound or warning, a massive shape dropped from the rooftops—a silent predator descending through the gloom.

The shadow dragon struck, talons outstretched—but Kozgokoth reacted instantly.

The demon surged forward, bracing his monstrous spear to meet the beast head-on. They collided with a thunderous impact that scattered the vampire spawn like leaves in a storm.

Aramastus dropped the chest, a snarl tearing from his lips as he drew his blade and blurred to the dragon's flank.

Brak steadied himself, spoke a word of power, and leveled a slender rod of glass at the creature. A bolt of lightning erupted from his hand, arcing through the darkness and slamming into the dragon's scaled side.

The beast convulsed, gray web-like energy crackling across its obsidian hide, illuminating the jagged edges of its scales.

With a furious roar, the dragon lashed out. Massive claws tore across the stone, narrowly missing Kozgokoth, who twisted aside with uncanny speed. He retaliated with a crushing blow to the dragon's snout, then drove his spear into its throat in a flurry of brutal thrusts.

The dragon reared back, gathering itself—then exhaled.

A cone of shadow-breath swept over Kozgokoth and the nearby spawn. Brak watched in horror as the demon's right wing dissolved, the dark energy devouring corded flesh until the limb hung limp and ruined at his side.

Kozgokoth, undeterred, tightened his grip on the spear and planted his feet with grim resolve.

Aramastus closed in, his longsword gleaming dully in the shadowed light. With undead strength, he drove the blade into the dragon's exposed side and twisted hard, forcing it deeper—past bone and scale—until it reached the lungs.

The beast screeched in agony, thrashing wildly, but the vampire spawn swarmed it, clawing and biting with relentless fury.

Grievously wounded, Kozgokoth saw his opening. Drawing on the last of his strength, he raised the spear high and drove it through the dragon's open maw—up through its skull and into the brain.

The creature shuddered, then collapsed in a final, deafening thud that sent dust and broken stones flying in all directions.

The spawn kept attacking until Aramastus raised a hand, commanding them to stop.

Brak stepped forward, the rush of adrenaline ebbing. His eyes went to Kozgokoth, assessing the damage. One arm hung limp, the wing beside it shredded—torn and useless.

How badly are you wounded? Brak asked in his mind.

Mortal, Kozgokoth replied, his voice a mocking rumble. *I will expire soon. Then you will not summon me again for quite some time, as I reform in the Abyss for countless years.* A dark, mirthless laugh echoed through Brak's thoughts.

I will send you back before it's too late. You can regenerate—

Not yet, the demon interrupted. *Not until I have my trophy.*

With a feral grin, Kozgokoth used the last of his strength to hack at the dragon's neck, sawing through scale and sinew with brutal strokes until the massive head was severed. He seized one of its horns with his remaining hand, a triumphant glint in his eye.

Then, before the demon could collapse, Brak summoned a shimmer of dark energy and cast him back to the Abyss.

Aramastus approached, crimson eyes gleaming with an unspoken question. "Your thrall—he will return? We may yet encounter other creatures that linger in shadow."

"He will return in time," Brak said curtly, offering no further explanation. Exhaustion pressed down on him; it took effort just to stay upright. "For now, your thralls will clear the path to the portal."

Aramastus nodded, his sharp features unreadable, and gestured to the spawn. With silent precision, they spread out—some melting into the shadows of the street, others leaping to the rooftops, their pale forms vanishing into the gloom.

They moved at a steady pace. Brak forced himself to match it, though every step was a struggle. His legs felt like lead, but he kept moving.

"Our master will be pleased," Brak said. "I'll tell him of your part in retrieving the phylactery. You performed flawlessly."

The vampire's lips curved into a chilling smile. "Certainly, he will be pleased with the result."

The journey back to the portal passed in a haze of tense silence and wary glances into the shadows. Brak's senses stayed taut, every footstep braced for an ambush that never came.

As they neared the outskirts of the town, the cottage and its gated compound emerged ahead, cloaked in the Plane of Shadow's perpetual twilight. Brak scanned the area, half-expecting Aramastus's spawn to lunge from the darkness and tear him apart.

But nothing moved.

His fingers drifted to the scroll case at his side, a flicker of doubt gnawing at him. He knew the spell inside might falter in this realm— but it was his only safeguard if Aramastus chose betrayal.

At the gate, the vampire turned, his face unreadable. "It is daytime on the Material Plane," he said. "My thralls will remain here until nightfall, when they can return to the village. There is not enough room inside the cottage or my vault for all of them. But come—we'll see you off soon enough."

Without waiting, Aramastus opened the cottage door and stepped inside, moving toward the portal.

Brak hesitated.

Dread coiled in his gut.

On the other side of that portal waited a vampire, two powerful spawn, and—very likely—his own doom.

The thought chilled him more than the Plane of Shadow ever had. He could picture it clearly: Aramastus draining him dry, turning him, binding him to eternal servitude.

His hand moved to the scroll tucked into his belt. He pulled it free, fingers trembling slightly as he unrolled the brittle parchment. *All I have to do is read it aloud,* he thought. He could feel the weight of the words even before he spoke them.

Now he understood why he'd kept the scroll in reserve. And now he knew what the ring was for—to let him escape the vampire's vault.

Steeling himself, he drew a deep breath, adjusted his grip on the scroll, and stepped through the portal.

Chapter Nineteen

∞

The Price of Possession

"I cannot return her to the living, yet she is not dead," said the voice from Aurora's mouth. It was a warped fusion—half Aurora's, half Sir Aelion's—rough and wavering, layered with the ghostly undertone of the vestige's spectral presence. Aurora's eyes had darkened, her expression hollow, as though her own spirit flickered dimly beneath the surface.

The vestige went on, "She is sick, but not beyond repair. I can hold her in this state—caught between life and death. But in time, she will expire unless we find a healer… or magic strong enough to mend what's broken."

"Release her!" Aaron shouted, fists clenched, his voice thick with grief and fury.

"She will live only if I possess her," Sir Aelion replied coldly. "If I release her, she dies."

"You're evil," Aaron spat. "Good spirits do not take the bodies of the unwilling. Let her go—let her soul be free. Do this, and we won't harm you."

"You harm me, you harm her—and any chance she has of survival," the vestige said. His voice filled the chamber with ice. "I will help one of you leave this island. The other will remain with me. That is the price. Decide who stays, and who goes."

Aaron's jaw tightened as he looked into the vacant, haunted eyes of the woman who had risked so much to save them. Aurora was trapped—her soul snared by a desperate spirit—and the choice before them was as cruel as it was impossible.

In the dim light of the chamber, Wellsey knelt beside Aurora and gently lowered her onto a cleared patch of cold stone. She brushed her hand over Aurora's short, gray hair, struggling to keep her voice steady.

"You just need some rest," Wellsey said. "This will pass. You'll be back on your feet in no time."

But Aurora, with a faint, weary smile, reached for the rune-etched ring on her left hand—the one used to summon Harold, her companion from another realm. She slipped it free and pressed it into Wellsey's palm, closing her fingers over it with surprising strength.

"You must connect with the ring," Aurora whispered. "Look at it. Feel its power. It will accept you, as it accepted me. When you have need of Harold… kiss the ring. He will come. He'll obey your command without question. He'll know I gave it to you freely."

Wellsey stared at the ring, eyes shining with unshed tears. In her hand, it felt warm—alive—pulsing in rhythm with her heartbeat.

"It's warm," she murmured.

"Then it's working," Aurora said softly. "Put it on."

With trembling fingers, Wellsey slid the ring onto her finger. At once, she felt it—an odd sensation, like a thread winding between her and a distant presence: silent, watchful, and immense.

She forced a smile, though her heart was breaking. "I'll be giving this back to you soon, Aurora. You're going to recover."

Aurora's eyelids fluttered as she drifted deeper into sleep. "Use it well," she whispered. "Wake me… soon."

Wellsey brought the ring to her lips and kissed it, her hand trembling as she summoned Harold. Silent tears slipped down her cheeks as the air thickened, crackling with unseen tension.

From a shimmering portal beside her, the massive polar bear emerged. His presence filled the burial chamber—majestic and haunting—casting a chill that froze the air around them.

Harold, towering nearly to the ceiling on his hind legs, gazed down at the scene before him. His intelligent eyes took in the mix of relief and sorrow on Wellsey's face, and the unnatural stillness in Aurora's.

For a long moment, he simply regarded her—his companion, his charge—as though willing her to wake. But he could feel it: the disturbance beneath her skin, the lingering shadow of Sir Aelion. Their bond, forged through years of loyalty and trust, was severed.

Wellsey's voice, thick with grief, barely rose above a whisper. "Harold… you must free Aurora from the vestige's grasp. From Sir Aelion's spirit. To do that… you must end her life. It's the only way."

The bear tilted his head, eyes narrowing with sorrow and resolve. He understood what she was asking. And he knew—it was a final act of love.

Aurora's eyes opened, locking with Harold's. Her expression shifted—strained, conflicted—as though she were fighting to break free, yet still bound.

"You will not harm me," she said, her voice a twisted blend of her own and Sir Aelion's spectral tone. "We are friends… companions."

Yet even as she spoke, her hand drifted to the hilt of her blade. The motion was hesitant, uncertain—betraying a deeper truth: she knew nothing she carried could stop the bear.

"There is no escape, spirit," Harold growled, his voice resonant with a power older and deeper than the stone walls around them. "Depart now, and you will be spared. Remain, and I will free her from your grasp… and tear you to shreds on the Ethereal Plane."

As he spoke, his form began to shimmer—growing translucent as he slipped into the spirit realm. Frost traced the stone beneath his paws. For an instant, he vanished… then reappeared on the Material Plane, solid once more. His breath curled in the frozen air. His eyes burned with quiet fury.

The spirit within Aurora flinched.

For a heartbeat, her true expression surfaced—flickers of sorrow… and acceptance. As if she knew her end had come.

Harold stepped closer, face-to-face now, his massive paw raised, claws glinting like ice.

The chamber held its breath.

Then—like a candle snuffed out—the eerie light in Aurora's eyes faded. Sir Aelion's spirit peeled away from her body, drifting back… and relinquished its hold.

The spectral figure of the knight, shimmering with frustration and resignation, hovered in the air before retreating into the shadows, vanishing into the Ethereal Plane.

Harold lowered his paw. His gaze softened as he gently gathered Aurora's frail body into his great forelimbs and laid her down on the cold stone.

She gasped—her eyes fluttering open, wide with fear and sudden, painful clarity.

"I'm so scared," she whispered, her voice barely audible. "I… I don't want to die."

Wellsey knelt beside her, taking her hand and holding it tightly. "We're here, Aurora. You're not alone. You've never been alone."

Aurora's gaze moved from Wellsey to Aaron, and then to Harold. Her expression eased. Her lips curved in the faintest smile. Her chest rose… and fell… one last time. Then her body stilled, her spirit slipping away like a breath on the wind.

A profound silence settled over the burial chamber, broken only by Harold's low, mournful groan as he nudged her still form with his snout.

The great polar bear let out a deep, sorrowful rumble, speaking not only to Wellsey and Aaron, but to the spirit of his departed friend.

"You were a great companion, Aurora," he said, his voice thick with grief. "We will honor your memory. You were a beacon of light in a world too often shrouded in darkness."

He lowered his head, voice soft and reverent. "In you, I found courage that inspired me to lead, kindness that humbled me, and strength that reminded me there is still good worth protecting. You showed me hope… even when despair surrounded us."

He turned to Wellsey and Aaron, his eyes dark and solemn. "She left an indelible mark on all who knew her. Her unwavering resolve and compassion were gifts to this world—gifts that live on in the lives she touched."

Looking back to Aurora, Harold continued, "Our time together was too brief… but the memories we forged—of verdant forests, mountain peaks, hidden groves—will remain with me, bound by magic and loyalty. You were more than a companion. You were a kindred spirit… a friend who showed me the beauty of this material world."

He let out a low, sorrowful groan, the sound echoing through the chamber with haunting resonance. "Farewell, Aurora. May your spirit find peace in the realms of light, where no shadow may reach you. And may your memory shine as a beacon of hope for all who follow your path."

The great bear turned to Wellsey, his voice hushed. "Send me back. I will carry her to my realm, where she will rest among heroes. She does not belong in this cold, forsaken place."

Wellsey, her face streaked with tears, gave a trembling nod and kissed the ring. "Harold," she whispered, her voice breaking, "return to your realm… and take her with you."

The air shimmered. With a faint, ethereal glow, Harold and Aurora vanished, leaving the chamber silent once more.

For a long time, Aaron and Wellsey stood motionless, eyes fixed on the place where their friend had been. At last, they turned to each other and embraced, finding what comfort they could in shared grief.

The weight of loss hung heavy around them. They knew they would have to face it—fully—and that soon, they'd need to find a way off this cursed island.

But not yet.

For now, they held each other, letting the sorrow come without resistance, mourning Aurora in silence… and honoring her with their tears.

Instantaneously, the spell erupted from the scroll as Brak strode through the gate. A sphere of light—bright as a miniature sun—flared into existence inside the cramped cottage, flooding every corner with searing brilliance.

The sunburst banished even the faintest shadow.

Sablethorn, the vampire spawn, screamed in agony, clawing at his face as his flesh sizzled under the relentless light.

Veilstalker flickered in and out of sight, the magic disrupting her unnatural camouflage as she darted for the closed door.

Aramastus stood ready in ambush—but his undead flesh began to wither before Brak's eyes, shriveling and burning as if doused in holy fire. He staggered, sword dropping, and lunged for the portal in a desperate bid to escape.

Brak anticipated it.

With a flick of his wrist, he redirected the vampire's path, slamming him into the doorframe. Aramastus let out a guttural snarl as the light intensified, searing through him until his form dissolved into mist, drifting helplessly toward the portal and the cold tower beyond.

The vampire spawn fared no better.

Reduced to shrieking shadows, their bodies crumbled to dust, leaving only scorched remnants on the stone floor.

Brak stepped forward, prodding the ashes with his sword, confirming the destruction. His eyes swept the room, now empty of enemies.

At last, he drew the mysterious ring from his pouch, holding it tightly in a clenched fist. He didn't trust it enough to wear—rings of this nature were often activated by a thought, a phrase, or mere contact. And this one, he suspected, would only work once.

He dared not try it on—not until he was inside the vault.

When he stepped through the portal, darkness swallowed him— deeper and more absolute than anything he'd encountered on the Plane of Shadow. His enhanced vision pierced the gloom, but it was like peering through layers of murky black glass.

In the center of the room lay an open coffin. Within, Aramastus's form was slowly reforming from mist—ashen bones knitting together, sinew and undead flesh reweaving themselves in a grotesque reversal of decay.

The sight turned Brak's stomach. He considered his options and concluded he had neither the means nor the time to destroy the vampire entirely. He could delay him—perhaps trap him for a while— but it wouldn't last. The spawn would return, or others would come to his aid.

He closed the lid of the coffin, sparing himself the rest of the horrific reconstruction, and turned his attention to the chamber.

Nothing here suggested a clear path to locating the other phylacteries he knew he had to collect.

Brak slipped the ring onto his finger.

The effect was immediate.

The world shifted to shades of gray. Temperature dissolved into a void—neither warm nor cold. He felt weightless, incorporeal, as though drifting beyond the reach of the physical realm.

With a thought, he moved forward, gliding through walls and stone with effortless grace.

Then he removed the ring—and solidness returned. He was once more grounded in the Material Plane.

A ring of etherealness, he realized. Invaluable for his search.

He removed it and placed it carefully into a secure pocket. Whether it would work again, he couldn't be sure—nor could he predict when he might need it next. Economy was paramount.

Fatigue clawed at him, but Brak pushed toward the staircase, keeping clear of the black dome that housed Gaazheaz's prison.

Even without looking, he felt her presence—the lich's gaze burning into him, her awareness crackling like a malevolent flame.

She knew he carried her soul gem.

He ignored her silent fury, focusing instead on his escape. He would ascend to the Mage-Gate, find a place to rest, and plan his next move: the desert tower and the search for more phylacteries.

As he climbed the winding staircase, Brak felt his strength ebbing. His limbs were leaden, each step harder than the last. By now, dawn must have broken outside, keeping the undead at bay. He estimated he was only minutes from sunlight.

The thought of resting under daylight's protective warmth brought some comfort. He had learned early on that the undead on this island reanimated at regular intervals—possibly every three days—sustained by an unseen necromantic curse. If his calculations were correct, the next reanimation could be imminent.

He tore off another strip of enchanted dragon jerky, feeling a surge of energy flood his limbs, and pressed on. At the top, he entered an adjacent chamber and quickly dispatched two lurking ghouls with precise streams of magical fire. They crumbled into ash with barely a sound, leaving him free to secure the room nearest the Mage-Gate.

The Mage-Gate loomed before him—a marvel of enchanted machinery, broken and now linked to only one other gate: the desert tower, Aridaya.

Brak cursed Mikal Yholl's convoluted sense of security. Perhaps twisted humor.

At first, he'd hoped to simply disable the gate, leaving the druids none the wiser to his presence or purpose. They lacked the knowledge to activate it, so he would've been confident walking away.

But the gate was locked into a cycle—an arcane mechanism connecting the two remote towers by a pattern even he couldn't decipher much less understand. It grated on him that Gideon intended to destroy the Mage-Gate in the keep. These two gates, locked to each other, were all but useless.

It was a setback—he didn't know the physical locations of the other Mage-Gates. More research would be needed, far more than he had already done.

His gaze swept over the runes adorning the gate's surface, pausing on the one he was certain represented the Infernal Sanctum. He muttered the word of power, clenched his fist, and tried to shift the destination from *AA* to *IS*. Still, the gate refused to respond.

It didn't matter if it changed.

By now, the druids would be guarding the Infernal Sanctum— awaiting his return.

Or perhaps they'd come through… and become trapped like the others.

Then, something at the edge of his vision caught his attention: a small plank of wood, propped with purpose among the debris. Scrawled across it was a message—from Aaron and Wellsey, members of the druid expedition.

They were outside, heading for the trees. Planning to rootwalk away. Tree-stride.

They knew he was here. Somehow, they had figured out the loop between the two towers.

Relief stirred in him—two fledgling druids had followed. But it was no guarantee others wouldn't step through after them.

Brak snatched up the piece of wood, erased the message with swipes of his sleeve, and tossed it into the rubble.

He had no more energy—barely enough to stagger into the secured room. With the last of his strength, he cast a ward across the doorway: a subtle web of magic that would alert him to any intruders.

He slumped against the wall, exhaling as exhaustion dragged him down like an anchor. Within seconds, he was asleep—slipping into a dreamless void, his mind shielded from intrusion.

The wizard's body lay still, his breath steady. The ring of etherealness remained tucked in its pocket; the soul gem lay secured in its pouch. For now, Brak was safe from the island's dangers.

But he knew—this was only a pause.

The desert tower, Aridaya, and its secrets awaited.

Perhaps another phylactery for him to collect.

Chapter Twenty

∞

Departure from Despair

"Where are they?" Lillia asked, her hand resting on her shapely hip, gaze fixed on Gideon with unyielding intensity.

"In the tobacco shed," Gideon replied, nodding toward the building. "You may take one of your choosing."

He led the dryad Archdruid around the side of his modest home, guiding her onto a narrow, well-worn path. Empty fields stretched out on either side—barren soil waiting for the season's planting.

His practiced eye caught the signs of neglect: stubborn weeds pushing through the earth, caterpillars clinging to the dry stalks of last year's crop. A quiet reminder of the labor still ahead. But today, other matters took precedence.

They reached the tobacco shed—a sturdy structure of interlocked logs with a steep roof and a long-dormant chimney. Its windowless walls bore the stains of many seasons. As he pulled open the heavy wooden door, a familiar thought returned: he really ought to install a lock—for peace of mind, if nothing else.

Inside, he cast a simple spell, and a soft, golden light spilled from a fixture hanging overhead.

The glow revealed neat rows of labeled bins, racks for curing tobacco, and a series of smaller rooms, each sealed behind closed doors. Gideon crossed to one of them, passing his hand over an acorn-shaped engraving to release the ward.

Within, he retrieved a small pine crate and brought it out, tipping it toward Lillia like an offering.

Nestled within were a dozen acorns, each wrapped in layers of white fabric to preserve them. The small orbs, compact beneath their protective sheaths, resembled tiny snowballs—innocent and unassuming. Yet each one held the power to reshape their world.

Gideon gave her a steady look. "Choose one. They're sealed with wax. I'd suggest melting it away slowly—boil it in water, then quench it in cool water. That'll keep the shell from cracking and damaging the seed within."

Lillia examined them one by one, her fingers lingering on the fabric as if she could feel the latent power beneath. At last, she selected one and tucked it carefully into the leather pouch at her waist.

Gideon made his own choices without ceremony, selecting three acorns before returning the crate to its place. He closed the door and passed his hand once more over the engraving, sealing it shut.

"You're offering these to the others?" Lillia asked, her tone edged with a faint challenge.

"I intend to give two to Wilmund and Aurora when I return to the Mage-Gate," he said. "Buvic, Albic, and Krik already have acorns gathered from the Needle Forest."

"And Nightshade?" Lillia's gaze sharpened. "Are you excluding her?"

"Nightshade declined," Gideon replied. "She wants Druid's Glen to remain here, in the Needle Forest. She doesn't want the burden—or visibility—of The One Tree within her borders." He arched an eyebrow. "I'm surprised you don't share the same sentiment."

Lillia's mouth tightened, but she sidestepped the remark. "When will you plant yours?"

"Soon," he said. "I'll clear the ashes from the old tree's resting place and plant it there. The remains of the previous One Tree will nourish the new."

A flicker of impatience crossed Lillia's face. Her voice sharpened. "What about the Mage-Gate? Did you destroy it?"

Gideon caught the acidity in her tone—she'd already assumed he'd failed.

"It's non-functional," he replied, calm but firm. "One of the Elder Runes is damaged. It would need repair to work—and even then, no one alive remembers how to operate it. That knowledge is lost to time. They left no instructions… or none we've found, at least." He paused, gaze steady. "You'll get a full report when I return. For now, I have a Glen to tend—and an acorn to plant."

Her green eyes narrowed, a gleam of challenge in them. "Tell me more about what you found. Unless, of course, you'd rather I go there myself?"

Gideon smiled. "You're bluffing. You won't go. You've made it abundantly clear how much you despise Mikal Yholl and his ilk. Going there would mean stepping closer to what you fear—Mages and relics best left buried. I think you know more about them than you let on."

Lillia scoffed, arching a brow. "Perhaps I'll go there to spite you."

"You're welcome to," he said mildly. "But I won't be there to greet you. I'll be here a few days. If you hurry, you might arrive and leave before I return. Then again…" He gave her a knowing look. "I doubt you'll stray far from your grove. You're eager to plant your acorn, aren't you?"

Her expression hardened. "I'll plant it in my grove," she said, voice steely. "And when The One Tree is established, I'll welcome you to the new Druid's Glen. As Grand Druid, you'll have the same rights as always." She paused, a smirk curling her lips. "Or perhaps you'll consider relocating your family… to be closer to The One Tree?"

Gideon shook his head, a note of finality in his voice. "Absolutely not. My home is here—no matter where The One Tree grows."

"Interesting." Her tone was laced with irony as she cast a glance toward the door. She gave a curt nod. "You have work to do. As do I." Without waiting for a reply, she turned and strode away—her figure moving with fluid, almost ethereal grace that drew the eye despite the tension still hanging between them.

Gideon watched her go, his breath held.

She reached the nearest tree and placed a hand on its bark. With a murmur of druidic words, she invoked tree-stride. Her form dissolved into the trunk and vanished, as though the forest itself had claimed her.

He lingered in the shed's doorway a moment longer, the faint scent of tobacco mixing with earth and memory—something deeper, older. A reminder of the roots they both served… and the ancient power they now risked nurturing.

Work on Druid's Glen took Gideon two full days—two days of clearing debris, removing rubble, and burying the bones of the fallen. By the time he finished, the sun was sinking low, casting the grove in a dim amber glow.

But his thoughts were already drifting ahead, toward the responsibilities waiting beyond this place. The Archdruids who had taken acorns to their own groves were likely nearing their destinations by now, enduring slow, wearisome travel in the absence of The One Tree's magic. Without its network to aid them, the distances stretched longer, heavier.

Albic Fang was tending to Finola's grove, salvaging what little remained. Gideon had left him with a warning—some of Finola's surviving followers might still be hiding among the locals, buried deep in plain sight. Caution was essential.

Finola's fate remained uncertain. Many bodies in the aftermath were too charred to identify, and her name had yet to be counted among the dead. The silence from Wilmund's grove was troubling, too. With plant-speak no longer carrying across great distances, the groves now stood isolated—each one its own island.

Gideon longed to return to his sons, Cedric and Aaron, to finish what they had begun. With the Mage-Gate now inoperative, it had become a matter of sealing it—enclosing the ancient mechanism in earth and stone, so that none could use it again.

A flicker of light in his peripheral vision pulled him from his thoughts.

He turned.

Through the twilight, a figure approached—lantern held high, her face illuminated by its warm glow.

It was Heather.

She had changed since the ordeal, carrying herself with a new, solemn maturity.

Finola's betrayal had left its mark, teaching her a harsh lesson in trust. In one hand, she carried a spare staff; at her waist hung a stout knife and a short blade. Her training with weapons was still rudimentary, but the resolve was there—clear in her eyes, steady in her steps.

Gideon had promised her training with sword and bow once things calmed. But even now, he could see it: a quiet resilience, a hunger to become strong—not just for herself, but for those she meant to protect.

"We want to be part of this," Heather said as she approached, her eyes reflecting the last light of the setting sun.

Gideon glanced past her and saw more figures emerging from the trees, each carrying a lantern. Druids, villagers, members of his order—gathering quietly, drawn to the grove by a shared understanding of what this moment meant.

He recognized many faces. The Poussins, with Beatrice still asking softly after Cedric. The Greenleafs—an Elven couple with their daughter and two adopted Human boys apprenticing as herbalists. The Oakhearts, stooped with age from years at the sawmill, but present nonetheless. The Silverstreams, Bennets, and Ellises—farmers, bakers, traders. From The Hound and Shrew came the Rousselles, and the Sunier family—leatherworkers by trade—stood with solemn expressions near the rear.

One by one, they formed a quiet ring around the heart of the glen. Gideon's druids took their places among them, a steady, protective presence woven into the crowd.

Gideon raised his hands, signaling for silence.

"I welcome all of you," he said formally, his voice carrying with calm authority. "I must ask for quiet… while we plant the acorn."

A murmur of acknowledgment rippled through the assembly, then faded into expectant stillness.

Gideon looked out over them, his gaze softening. "This gathering was unexpected—and yet… it feels right. In times like these, unity is our greatest strength." He drew a deep breath and began. "I will say a few words, and then we'll commit the acorn to the earth."

His voice dropped, taking on a reverent tone. "My fellow druids, my friends, members of our community… We stand here as guardians of the natural world, drawn to witness the rebirth of our sacred Druid's Glen. We bear the scars of destruction, but tonight, we gather to heal— to restore what has been lost."

The crowd listened, heads bowed, as Gideon continued, his words a balm to the wounded grove.

"It is my honor and privilege to preside over this ritual, which marks the renewal of life and our sacred bond with nature. But before we proceed, let us take a moment to honor Thatara, goddess of nature, whose spirit watches over this place."

All heads bowed in solemn homage.

"In the name of Thatara, we offer our prayers and praises," Gideon intoned. "We ask for her blessing upon this land, and upon all who dwell within it. May her wisdom guide us, her compassion strengthen us, and her grace be with us on this journey of renewal."

He glanced at the charred remnants scattered throughout the glen, a flicker of determination rising in his chest.

"As we stand among these ruins, let us not give in to despair. The forest endures. This acorn—gifted from The One Tree itself—is a symbol of rebirth. With humility, I will plant it here, invoking the ancient magic that flows through its veins."

Turning to Heather, Gideon handed her the acorn, letting her cradle it as though it were made of glass. The crowd watched in reverent silence as he took a spade and stepped to the center of the grove, carving a space in the earth to receive the seed.

When the hole was ready, he retrieved the acorn from Heather and lifted it high for all to see.

"May this acorn take root and flourish," he proclaimed. "May its branches reach for the sky, its roots anchor deep in the soil of our ancestors. May it grow strong, casting its sheltering canopy over this land, and bind all living things to this sacred place. May it bring peace."

With slow, practiced motion, Gideon traced a rune in the air above the acorn, whispering a druidic blessing:

> "In soil deep, with gentle care,
> We plant the acorn, green and fair.
> To Mother Earth, we make our plea,
> Grant life and growth—blessed be."

He placed the acorn in the ground and covered it with rich soil. Taking a waterskin, he sprinkled water over the freshly packed earth, then patted it down with the spade until the spot felt whole and complete.

Turning back to the crowd, he extended his hands.

"Let us renew our oath to protect and preserve the natural world. Let us pledge ourselves to harmony, to the beauty and diversity of life. Please—join hands with those beside you."

The villagers reached for one another, hand to hand, weaving together family and friend, druid and neighbor. Gideon took Heather's hand in his own, a simple gesture weighted with shared love and purpose.

"With our hearts joined, let us pray to Thatara that this sacred quest to restore Druid's Glen will succeed," Gideon said, his voice thick with emotion. "May her blessing guide us… and may the spirit of The One Tree give us strength."

A quiet energy filled the air—like the subtle hum of sap flowing through branches—an undercurrent of hope rippling outward from the acorn's resting place. Across the lands, in distant groves, other Archdruids would be planting their own acorns beneath the stars, invoking blessings of their own.

Gideon closed his eyes, offering up a silent plea: that Druid's Glen would be the one to thrive, that this place would remain the true heart of the druidic world.

As the ceremony drew to a close, the crowd began to disperse. Quiet conversations stirred like wind in tall grass as villagers turned back toward their homes and duties. Left behind were Gideon, Heather, and the druids gathered close around him.

Gideon turned to his followers. "I'll be leaving tomorrow morning," he said. "You'll need to guard this place carefully. I don't expect trouble, but after Finola's treachery, we can't afford to be complacent."

Heather stepped closer, her face tight with worry as she clutched at his robe. "I don't want you to go. I don't want to be here alone."

Gideon wrapped his arms around her, resting a reassuring hand on her shoulder. "You won't be here alone. You're coming with me."

Her eyes widened. "I am?"

"Yes. I need to get a message to Ornst—to see if Eric can stay at the library a while longer. He'll be safer there. He was supposed to come home in ten days, but… we may not be back by then."

She hesitated, then managed a small smile. "I'm going with you?"

Gideon nodded. "I won't leave you here, not while Finola's fate is uncertain. She could still be out there, plotting against us. I don't know what drove her to this, but…" He exhaled slowly, shaking his head. "Maybe we'll have time to figure it out on the road."

Heather nodded, her expression firming. "We'll have lots of time to talk," she echoed.

Gideon smiled softly and brushed a stray lock of hair from her face. "Yes, we will. Now go pack what you need for the journey. I'll be home soon."

She gave him one last, fierce hug, then turned and hurried toward their house, her lantern casting a warm glow as night settled in.

Gideon watched her go, heart swelling with pride—and a twinge of sorrow. This was the world he had hoped to build for his children: a world where The One Tree might protect them.

But as he glanced back at the mound of earth where he had planted the acorn, doubt stirred. He wondered if the forest—and the life it sheltered—would be enough to withstand what was coming.

It wasn't the ideal time—dusk was falling—but Brak refused to waste daylight waiting for more. The desert tower loomed ahead, silent and foreboding. He suspected it was devoid of life—and unlife—but the malevolence lingering in its stones made his skin crawl.

It was concerning and disconcerting.

Here, at last, he might search without constant harassment from ghouls. He could probe for signs of the remaining phylacteries without interference.

At least, he hoped so.

The Yholl brothers had proven anything but predictable. Yet in one thing, they were consistent: meticulous, malicious planning.

Through loyalty, deceit, and raw power, they had corrupted fellow Mages and turned them into liches.

Five liches.

Five beings who wielded both undeath and arcane mastery—a terrifying union. They weren't just seeking immortality. They were reshaping the Material Plane into a shadowed reflection of the Abyss. If they succeeded, the mortal world would fall into ruin and madness, ruled by demons—an ideal playground for their dark ambitions. Death beyond imagining. Chaos unbound. The Abyssal Lords would rule alongside the Lich Lords.

And he would be there at their side.

Brak of the Dark Artifice, Binder of Demons would join them.

He wondered what his new name would be once he ascended into immortality.

Steeling himself, Brak stepped through the Mage-Gate, trading the cool, musty air of Thalraya for the oppressive heat of Aridaya. The warmth hit him like a wall—stifling and unmoving.

Scattered across the floor were the tower's last inhabitants—corpses preserved in agonized postures, their death throes frozen into grotesque stillness. He moved among them, stepping over mummified limbs twisted in desperation.

In the corner, he found the pile of possessions he had left behind. He checked the crate of graphite molds—patterns for the Elder Runes of the Mage-Gate—and found it untouched. Satisfied, he turned toward the staircase, where torchless sconces glowed with pale, otherworldly light against the granite walls.

He descended into the depths below, ready to explore the lower levels—searching for any remnants of Mikal and Dergan's sinister legacy.

Before descending, he layered himself with protective enchantments, cast a ward in case the druids tried to follow him, and imbued his sword with bright light to augment the torchless sconces.

At a measured pace, he started down the stairs. The air grew cooler with each step, the silence pressing in around him. Preserved corpses and scattered rubble marked his path, but beyond those remnants, the tower felt abandoned… empty in a way that surpassed the absence of life.

Why had the residents stayed here, waiting for rescue that never came? he wondered. *Perhaps something roamed the desert beyond—deadly enough to trap them inside.*

Brak's knowledge of desert beasts was limited, and he couldn't afford the distraction now. Once his work here was done, he would teleport back to his stronghold and resume his efforts to free his master, Ra-Joth.

At least, that was the plan.

Teleporting with the phylactery was risky—he had already admitted that much to himself. Such an act might draw the attention of powerful beings, especially those attuned to the soul-bound currents of undeath. Yet the alternative was months of travel—exposed, vulnerable, and slow. He was likely weeks, perhaps a season, from his stronghold by conventional means, and the thought of slogging across wilderness and ruin-laced roads held no appeal.

He recalled the journey from *Château Saignoral,* hauling Ra-Joth's severed hand across Haddensack along broken trails until he reached Halstead. Weeks of evading patrols, scavengers, and bandits. Then up the winding mountain road to his remote keep.

He remembered seeing the old name in Elvish—*Vael'Aereth*—etched into the granite archway: weathered, cracked, and streaked with black mold. Below it, burned into the stone in jagged Abyssal script, was the new name: *Vhal'Araketh.* The Broken Eyrie.

But this was different. He had prepared more. He had grown stronger.

The risk remained—but so did the reward.

If he found nothing here, he would consider it.

He would weigh speed against secrecy… and decide whether the gamble was worth the gain.

But if he had two phylacteries?

He'd be on foot.

The lower level finally opened before him, revealing a broad archway etched with runes. Brak paused, feeling a flicker of anticipation. He half-expected an undead guardian waiting in the dark—a lich, a vampire, or perhaps a phylactery hidden within a layered dimension.

He cast a seeking spell, senses reaching outward to probe the gloom for traces of magic.

Nothing.

No wards. No enchantments. No latent power humming in the stone.

The runes on the archway were inert, their edges dulled with time. Whatever magic had once flowed through them had long since faded—if it had ever been invoked at all.

The air was stale. Lifeless.

Brak took a slow breath, grounding himself in the silence, and pressed onward—down the next flight of stairs beyond the arch.

He emerged into a cavernous chamber.

At once, he knew: it was empty.

His footsteps echoed against bare, smooth stone. The light from his blade cast long, angular shadows across granite walls that stretched on for hundreds of feet. There were no relics. No crypts. No clever illusions hiding secret vaults.

Only space. A hollow chamber carved from the bedrock, never finished. Never filled.

Whatever purpose this place had once served—it had been abandoned. Forgotten.

And it had nothing to offer him.

For a moment, he felt a pang of disappointment.

Another vampire might have been an obstacle—but at least it would have hinted at a greater purpose for this forsaken place. Yet despite the anticlimax, he was relieved. There was nothing here for the druids to discover. Nothing to tempt further exploration.

His task was simple now: retrieve the molds, deactivate the Mage-Gate, and seal this place off for good.

He turned back, ascending the stairs at a steady pace. By the time he reached the top, his breath was labored and sweat clung to his skin. He paused to rest, leaning against the granite wall before crossing to the crate he'd inspected earlier.

Inside were the graphite molds for the Elder Runes—six intricate templates once used to craft the Mage-Gate's core enchantments. He gathered them carefully, his mind already turning to the implications. With these molds, no one else could replicate the Yholl brothers' work. And if needed, he could reactivate a gate elsewhere—or forge one of his own.

From his pack, he retrieved a small, battered tome. The cover was cracked, its corners dog-eared. He flipped to a marked page, held the open book toward the Mage-Gate, and began to chant—speaking a word of power in a guttural, ancient tongue. With a flick of his wrist, he traced the Elder Runes in the air—precise, controlled.

The runes on the Mage-Gate flickered, then died. The surge of magic within it collapsed, its link severed not just here, but to the cold tower and Mikal Yholl's keep as well.

The Mage-Gate was now inert. A relic. Useless to anyone but him.

A grim smile tugged at the corner of his mouth as he imagined the druids' shock upon finding the closed portal. The two young ones who had entered the cold tower would now be trapped—surrounded by thousands of ghouls and zombies, with no hope of escape from the island. He doubted they could use their crude green-step to get to the coast, let alone to another island.

Even deactivated, he could still feel the residual magic—like a heartbeat under stone. It pulsed faintly, wrong.

He dared not teleport from here. A dormant Mage-Gate could still interfere with other spells, warping them with echoes of its ancient power.

He summoned an invisible servant to lift the crate, freeing his hands for travel.

With the magic here dormant, he felt a curious, chilling calm settle over him as he descended the endless staircase.

Exiting the tower, he stepped into the desert night. The air was heavy with warmth, and the vast expanse of sand shimmered beneath the full moon. Stars blazed across the sky—so bright, so clear—it felt as though he could reach out and touch them.

He doused the light on his sword and walked a hundred paces from the tower, scanning the dunes and rock clusters for movement.

Nothing stirred. The desert was still, blanketed in silence.

He took a long breath, letting the dry air fill his lungs. The fatigue clinging to him began to peel away, just slightly—replaced by a creeping sense of satisfaction.

He had done it. He'd found one. One of the five.

Four more to go.

The thought flared in his mind like a spark in dry kindling. He felt it in his chest: the rush of progress, the illusion of control. For the first time in weeks, his path felt clear. The other phylacteries would fall into place. He would find them. He would free Ra-Joth.

He would finish what the others could not.

Smiling faintly, he set his pack and the crate on the sand before him. The night air stirred his cloak, but still nothing moved. No ghouls. No spirits. No interference.

After a deep breath, he cast a ward on himself, hoping to shield the phylactery somewhat.

He invoked the enchantment, finishing with a word of power. The air shimmered.

In the blink of an eye, he vanished from the desert, leaving Aridaya—and its shadows—behind.

Aaron and Wellsey spent the rest of the day and night in the underground barracks adjacent to Sir Aelion's crypt, recovering and mourning the loss of their dear companion. Aurora's absence left a painful void—she had been their savior, their guide. Without her, the weight of responsibility pressed heavier with every hour.

They carried her supplies now, and the pouch of druid-berries would sustain them if it came to that. But her quiet strength was gone, and their path forward felt lonelier. At least Sir Aelion's spirit had not returned.

At dawn, they left the vault and followed the coastline. The storm had passed. The sky was clear and blue, the air brisk but no longer cruel. Sunshine touched the sea with warmth that did little to ease the chill in their hearts.

They walked hand in hand, saying little, their boots crunching over gravel and wind-smoothed rock. All around them, the island bore signs of ruin—collapsed towers in the distance, broken stonework overgrown with lichen, the long shadow of Mikal Yholl's forgotten ambition.

Far out in the bay, a whale breached—its immense body rising in slow majesty, water cascading from its flanks before it slammed back into the sea. A glittering plume erupted where it struck, catching the sunlight and spraying like shattered crystal.

They both stopped, stunned into stillness by the sheer, living beauty of it.

"Never see that in Druid's Glen," Aaron said quietly.

"Heerveen either," Wellsey replied, her voice soft with wonder.

They watched the ripples spread across the bay, a silent echo of something wild and free, untamed by death or magic.

Without the undead, this place could have been paradise.

"We should establish a second camp once we have a sense of the island's size," Aaron said at last, breaking the silence. He pointed toward a distant spire rising from the land. "The tower's that way, and the coast curves around here. Maybe there's a sheltered bay farther south—some kind of cove or marina where boats could be moored."

Wellsey twisted the rune-etched ring around her finger, her expression pensive. "We could summon Harold," she suggested. "He could help us search."

Aaron considered it, then shook his head. "Aurora only summoned him when she truly needed him. If we reach a point where we're out of options, then yes—but let's try to handle this ourselves first."

"Agreed," Wellsey said with a reluctant nod. "We'll explore for two more hours, then head back before dark. We've been lucky avoiding the undead, and I don't want to push that luck."

They continued south along the coast, stepping over sharp rocks and weaving through scattered stands of white spruce. After nearly an hour, a sheer wall of stone rose ahead, forcing them inland and into denser forest.

As they pushed through the undergrowth, Aaron's gaze caught on something in the distance—a structure piercing the canopy. A lighthouse, tall and weathered, rising above the trees.

"I want to see it up close," he said, a spark of excitement in his voice. "Wellsey—I've been so stupid. We can rootwalk! We should be establishing waypoints all over this island. That would let us move around so much faster, cut out hours of walking."

Wellsey grinned, her spirits lifted by his enthusiasm. "You're right. We've already set waypoints near the tower, the first marina, and by Sir Aelion's crypt. If we add one here, we'll have options no matter where we are on the island."

They moved closer to the lighthouse, memorizing the details of the area—the shape of the trees, the curve of the path, the nearby bay that shimmered in the afternoon light.

The bay was like a mirror, reflecting the pale sky, while the lighthouse loomed above them—a silent sentinel watching over calm waters. To the east, nestled along the shoreline, stood a village that appeared mostly intact, a stark contrast to the ruined marina they'd encountered earlier.

"I think I have enough details to rootwalk there," Aaron said, nodding toward a stand of white spruce near the rocks. "Do you?"

She nodded. "Let's do this. You go first. I'll follow in a few seconds."

Aaron placed his hand on the rough bark of a spruce and invoked the spell, feeling himself pulled into the vibrant network of the island's life force. A heartbeat later, he emerged near the lighthouse, the cool salt breeze brushing his face.

Moments later, Wellsey stepped out of a nearby tree, her hand still resting on the trunk as she steadied herself.

The lighthouse towered above them, weathered and scarred by centuries of wind and rain. Nearly as tall as the main tower, it rose defiantly into the sky, its stone walls a patchwork of grays and browns. The structure was ancient—older than anything they had yet seen on the island—and a silent testament to a time before Mikal Yholl's curse had taken hold.

Just as they began to appreciate the stillness, a shift in the breeze brought with it a sudden, stomach-turning stench.

The scent of decay and rot filled their nostrils, turning the sea air sour. Eyes watering, they covered their noses with their sleeves and turned toward the source. The wind carried the odor from the direction of the village.

They exchanged a grim look and moved toward the cluster of buildings near the marina, their steps quickening as the sun began to sink lower in the sky.

What they found stopped them cold.

The streets and alleys were choked with weeds and debris, the once-proud village reduced to hollow, crumbling shells. Deep grooves carved into the muddy ground marked the paths of countless undead—paths worn night after night, their feet trampling the earth into a morass of muck and filth.

From the shadowed alleys and collapsed doorways, twisted figures lingered. Zombies and ghouls, their grotesque forms huddled in heaps, lay dormant in the daylight—pressed into whatever darkness they could find, shrinking away from the sun.

Thousands upon thousands of undead crowded into the shadows, filling the air with the stench of rot and decay. Aaron and Wellsey stood on the outskirts, unwilling to venture any closer. Even in daylight, the village felt oppressive—its deathly silence a sinister promise of the horrors that would stir with the setting sun.

"We can't stay here much longer," Wellsey whispered. "I don't want to be anywhere near this place when they start moving. We must be wary of cloudy or stormy days. Only the sunlight has saved us."

Aaron nodded, eyes scanning the waterfront. "Agreed. Let's check the marina. If there's even one boat we can use, it could save us a lot of trouble."

The marina was in shambles.

Two half-collapsed piers jutted into the water like skeletal fingers, their boards warped and splintered. Beneath the surface, the remains of sunken vessels were clearly visible—charred hulls and tattered sails testament to their violent end. Aaron squinted, assessing the wreckage. Every ship looked like it had been deliberately burned before sinking. Even if they managed to pull one up, none of them would sail.

"I don't think anything here will float, let alone sail," he muttered, disheartened.

Wellsey tugged at his sleeve. "Then let's go. We'll come back tomorrow with a better plan. Right now, I want to be far from here before dark."

Aaron took her hand, guiding her along the mud-soaked path.

They both noticed the clumps of gray flesh scattered across the ground—chunks that had likely sloughed off the undead as they dragged themselves through the village. The sight made his stomach turn.

At last, they reached the relative safety of the white spruce trees at the village's edge. With one last wary glance at the horizon—where the sun was slipping toward its end—they invoked tree-stride. The familiar pull of the island's life force carried them away, back toward the underground vault where they felt safest.

That night, huddled together in silence, their thoughts turned to practical matters.

They would need a new strategy if they hoped to get off the island.

Wellsey clutched Aurora's rune-etched ring, her fingers brushing the intricate design as she thought of Harold. They were not out of options yet—but those options were narrowing with every passing day.

Chapter Twenty-One

∞

Mélange

The next day, with the sun blazing over the horizon, Aaron and Wellsey set out to ensure they could navigate the island in a full circuit. From the stand of white spruce near their refuge at the crypt, they could now jump to the rocky outcrop on the west side of the bay, reach the lighthouse to the east, and travel north to the tower—all by tree-stride. Though costly in magic, the entire loop took less than a minute.

Their spirits lifted. With this local network, they had newfound freedom—and a safety net.

They used tree-stride to arrive at the western curve of the bay, intent on finding a seaworthy boat. Scouring the marina, they saw many vessels, but most were broken, half-sunken, or thick with barnacles and sea life. Time and neglect had rendered them useless.

Though reluctant, Aaron stripped down and stepped into the bay, diving deep to investigate the cold waters. He was a strong swimmer—thanks to his life in the Needle Forest—and he cut through the chill with ease, driven by the fragile hope of escape.

The bay was oddly serene, the water crystal clear, as if enchanted. It formed a perfect semicircle, with shallow mooring areas giving way to deeper waters near the mouth, where larger ships might once have anchored.

In the deeper stretch, Aaron spotted a distorted, barnacle-covered skeleton of a ship resting ominously on the sandy floor.

"Anything?" Wellsey called from the shore, her hands cupped around her mouth.

Aaron surfaced and crossed his arms in an 'X'—their silent signal for *no*.

Though they were beyond the reach of the undead during daylight, they still preferred to keep their voices low.

After a fruitless search farther out, he turned east, swimming in long, lazy strokes to scan the depths below. The sunlight faded the farther he went, the water growing darker, the details hazy.

A flicker of unease crept over him.

He'd heard stories—of undead lurking in the depths, silent and still until disturbed. Of drowned revenants waiting for fools who swam alone.

Pushing the thought aside, Aaron continued. As he neared the shallows, something caught his eye—a boat, almost pristine, resting on the seabed. Painted white, it stood out sharply against the sand below, free of barnacles, seaweed, or signs of decay. It looked untouched by time.

The only flaw was a breach in the hull.

Excited, he waved to Wellsey.

"I found a boat! It looks intact!"

On shore, Wellsey jumped up and down, her joy breaking through the grimness of the day.

Aaron took a deep breath, dove again, and kicked his way toward the vessel. It was small, maybe ten feet long, with two oars, a broken mast, and an interior half-filled with silt. But something about it felt… off. Like it didn't belong here.

There was a stillness around it. A quiet wrongness.

Out of breath, he surfaced and swam back to shore.

"It's in nearly pristine condition," he said, panting as he reached her.

"Well that's suspicious," she said, frowning slightly. "Magic?"

"That's my guess," Aaron replied. "But we'll need a way to get it to the surface."

"I have an idea," she said, her eyes sparking. "Ice floats. What if we conjure ice underneath it?"

Aaron paused, considering. "Could work… though it'd have to fit perfectly. And I'm not sure I can cast spells effectively while swimming. It might take too long."

"Is the boat upright?"

"Yes, but why—"

She cupped her hands and mimed flipping something over. "Could you turn it upside down? If the hull's facing up, we could wedge the ice into the curve and let it lift naturally."

Aaron shook his head. "It's too heavy—even with both of us. I'm coming to shore. I need a breather."

He swam back, shivering, as Wellsey helped him dry off, brushing the water from his arms and shoulders with her hands.

They marked the boat's location, then used tree-stride to return to their base at the marina, where they built a small fire to warm up.

"If we make a net and attach it to the boat," Aaron mused, staring into the flames, "we could try to raise it with blocks of ice. Then we'd just need to push it to shore."

"Well, maybe we can scavenge some rope," Wellsey offered. "Or make it out of bark strips. My Da used to do that. Twisted them himself."

Aaron nodded, but his attention shifted as he noticed her fidgeting with the rune-etched ring on her finger—the one Aurora had given her. She froze mid-motion, then smacked her forehead.

"Harold could help us!" she exclaimed. "He could pull it up in no time. Polar bears love water!"

Aaron grinned. "I like the way you think. Should we try it today? We've still got a few hours of daylight."

"Well…" She hesitated. "Let's wait until morning. Even with Harold, I don't want to take any chances. Avoiding the undead is best."

"Fair." Aaron stood and stretched, his joints popping. "I'll forage in the forest. I saw black trumpet mushrooms and buckleberries growing near the ridge."

"Well, don't show me the trumpets," she said, shuddering. "Those things look like cursed sea slugs."

Aaron chuckled. "I'll make soup. You won't recognize it."

He reached toward the fire, letting the warmth soak into his fingers, then turned to her. "Alright. I'll be right back. If anything happens…"

"I'll summon Harold," she finished for him, her tone quiet but steady.

"Good. You'll probably be safer with him around anyway." He gave her shoulders a gentle shake, then kissed her forehead before invoking tree-stride and vanishing into the network of living things.

Left alone, Wellsey stared into the fire for a moment, then glanced down at the ring. She twisted it around her finger, her lips twitching into a grin.

"Harold, King of the Polar Bears," she muttered. "Our savior."

She burst out laughing, the sound bright and sudden in the stillness.

"Harold, you *will* be our hero."

Brak's attempted teleportation ended in agony.

The pain was excruciating—familiar in the worst way—and he cursed himself for not thinking it through.

From his toes to his fingertips, up his arms, across his chest and legs, a web of fire blazed through his nerves, locking his muscles in place. He could feel the sand beneath him, still warm from the day's heat, but he was paralyzed—trapped in his own pain.

He should have anticipated this.

The anti-magic shield surrounding Aridaya was identical to the one encircling Mikal Yholl's keep: a permanent barrier that blocked all forms of magical transport. The same, no doubt, would hold true for Thalraya.

The realization settled over him like a lead weight. The barrier around the tower likely stretched for miles—just as it did at the Infernal Sanctum—extending well beyond the structure itself. He would have to walk, perhaps four or five miles through the desert, before he reached its edge and could attempt teleportation again.

He clenched his teeth, fury tightening every muscle.

Worse, the magical backlash had drained him. The failed spell left his body wracked with pain, his strength sapped. He would be weak and aching for hours.

Slowly, he forced himself upright, muttering a protective enchantment to ward against any approach. He breathed deeply, focusing on restoring balance, on driving the pain back below the surface.

The desert stretched out before him—bleached bones scattered across the sands, the leathery shells of the dead preserved by the dry air. Something had doomed the tower's former inhabitants. A force, a presence, had kept them from fleeing into the desert.

Whatever it was… it might still be out there.

Why else would they have waited for an evacuation that never came?

Two hours later, Brak felt he could move again, though his muscles still trembled from the aftershock. The failed teleportation had drained him, but he couldn't afford to wait any longer.

He forced himself to his feet, chewing a strip of enchanted jerky to reclaim strength, then took a long pull from his waterskin. He estimated that, at a steady pace, he'd be beyond the barrier in another two hours—still under the cover of darkness. He wouldn't need light to escape, but he conjured a faint glow from his sword regardless, just enough to guide his steps.

Just a few miles, he told himself. *Just a few miles.*

The desert was dark and silent, the only illumination coming from a sickly moon low on the horizon. Its pale light barely touched the dunes around him. The path ahead was faint—what remained of a buried road, now mostly swallowed by time and shifting sands—but it was easier than braving the larger ridges flanking him.

As he walked, he tapped the pouch containing the soul gem, a habitual reassurance that it remained in his possession. Every step on the loose sand felt treacherous. He slowed his pace, wary of twisting an ankle in the uneven terrain.

At one point, his footing shifted oddly beneath him. He stopped and lowered the glow of his sword.

Beneath the sand, pale shapes waited.

He knelt and brushed the surface with his boot, pushing the grains aside—and revealed bones. Human bones, brittle and half-buried. The curve of a ribcage. A broken jaw. A single hand, fingers curled in a gesture that might once have been reaching.

He swept more sand away, uncovering skulls, femurs, ribs, and vertebrae—bleached and brittle from years beneath the desert sun.

Unease prickled at the back of his neck.

Muttering an incantation, he extended his hand and sent a gust of wind rushing forward. Sand scattered in a wide fan, revealing what lay beneath.

An endless field of bones stretched before him.

Tens of thousands had died here. Their remains lay in tangled heaps—interwoven, fractured, half-consumed by the earth—an ocean of white stretching as far as his conjured light could reach. A silent monument to despair.

The desert was quiet.

Too quiet.

Darkness draped over the land like a shroud, suffocating in its weight. The moonlight, dim as it was, barely touched the dunes. It felt weak. Distant. Almost afraid.

A chill skittered up Brak's spine.

Something was watching him.

He turned—and from the darkness, it emerged.

A creature of pure shadow and malice, towering and terrible, appeared at the edge of his vision. It was cloaked in impenetrable darkness, its form only half-discernible, like smoke held together by hate. Twin orbs of crimson flame burned in the void where eyes should be—ancient, insatiable, seething with loathing beyond understanding.

Brak's blood ran cold.

He knew this thing. From old tomes. From whispers. From nightmares.

A shadow-fiend.

It stood as tall as five men, its sinewy legs ending in hooved feet that crushed bones with each slow step. Muscles rippled beneath its cloak of blackness, barely seen, but felt—like the pressure of a storm gathering. Its arms were grotesquely long, each ending in four jagged claws that flexed with twitching malice.

At the center of its chest, a gaping maw pulsed—an abyssal wound, wide and fanged, radiating hunger that tugged at the edges of Brak's soul.

Behind its head, two twisted horns spiraled upward, jagged and uneven, casting warped shadows across the monster's face.

The silence deepened.

Brak's heart pounded.

He felt the weight of countless souls beneath his feet, as though each bleached bone whispered a warning—evidence of the destructive thing now standing before him.

The creature's gaze locked onto him.

And then it moved—gliding forward with chilling purpose.

Desperation overtook him.

Brak raised a pinch of sulfur, whispered a word of power, and thrust his hand forward. A fireball streaked into the night, colliding with the fiend's chest in a violent burst of flame. For a moment, the darkness lit up, harsh shadows flickering across the sand.

But as the fire faded, the shadow-fiend remained—unscathed. Untouched.

It moved faster.

Heart hammering, Brak reached into his pouch and shattered two vials of blood onto the sand. He spat a guttural incantation in the Abyssal tongue, the words torn from the depths of his training and terror.

The ground split.

Half a dozen squat, repulsive Maggoritch demons clawed their way into the world, followed by six more grotesque horrors—Zaskali, insectoid and glistening, with emerald carapaces and limbs like scythes.

Without hesitation, the demons lunged toward the shadow-fiend, shrieking with bloodlust.

It met them with terrifying ease.

Each swipe of its claws carved through flesh and carapace alike, dismembering the Maggoritch in sprays of ichor. The Zaskali took flight, launching themselves in a coordinated flurry—but the fiend swatted them from the air, shattering their armored bodies with bone-crunching precision.

One by one, they fell—banished in clouds of rotting vapor, leaving behind scorched sand and twisted bones.

Brak stood frozen, breath caught in his throat.

He had never faced anything like this.

This was death incarnate. An avatar of despair.

And it was still coming.

Panic gripped him like a vice. With a final, shaking incantation, he vanished—teleporting to the Mage-Gate at the top of the desert tower, the last place he could still call sanctuary.

He reappeared with a thud, crashing onto a stone bench and rolling hard onto the floor. Pain flared through his hip, but he ignored it, scrambling to his feet as the soft glow of the torchless sconces cut weakly through the dread clinging to him like a second skin.

The shadow-fiend was relentless.

He could feel it outside the tower—its hateful presence pressing against the walls, searching for him. Stalking.

Brak fled to the central staircase and collapsed onto the stone steps, wrapping his arms around himself as though he could hold the fear at bay. He curled into a ball, body shivering, breath ragged. Every heartbeat was a battle against panic. Each inhale felt too shallow, too tight.

Even through layers of thick granite, he could sense the fiend's dark energy—seeping inward, probing, tasting his life force.

He whispered words of shielding, spells of concealment and silence, burying his presence behind magical veils. He walled off his mind, locked his thoughts away, muttering protections with trembling lips.

But the fear still found him.

It clawed into his bones. Wrapped icy fingers around his spine.

This—this was why the tower's inhabitants had stayed. Why they had chosen to die inside rather than flee.

They must have known.

They must have known what waited out there in the dark—waiting to devour any soul foolish enough to cross the sands at night.

Brak pressed his back against the cold stone, teeth clenched, body shaking.

And then the realization came.

A whisper at first. Then a certainty.

If something this terrifying stalked the dunes by night…

What lived here by day?

The thought rooted deep, heavy and inescapable. A cold truth settling into his marrow:

Aridaya was not just cursed. It was a prison.

And he was trapped.

By the time morning arrived, Aaron and Wellsey had a plan.

They emerged from the shelter as sunlight spread across the marina, bringing warmth and dispelling the last of the lingering shadows.

Aaron chuckled softly as he watched Wellsey stride toward the white spruce forest. Her lips and the corners of her mouth were still stained from yesterday's buckleberries—a defiant reminder of her refusal to eat the black trumpet mushroom soup he'd so proudly prepared.

She looked like a mischievous child, and he couldn't help but smile at her stubbornness.

As they walked through the trees, they talked through the plan in hushed tones.

"Do you think Harold will be annoyed if we summon him to raise a boat?" Wellsey asked, biting her lip.

"It's an emergency," Aaron replied, trying to sound confident. "We'll explain it to him—I'm sure he'll understand."

She sighed. "I think *you* should do the talking."

Aaron raised an eyebrow. "You're the one with the ring."

"Yes, but *you're* better with words. And I don't want to be the one making a giant polar bear grumpy."

"Grumpy?" Aaron laughed. "Harold's a gentle soul. I'm sure he'll be fine." He paused, his grin turning sly. "How about we shake on it?"

Wellsey narrowed her eyes. After a tense game of rock-leaf-blade, she groaned in defeat.

"Fine," she muttered. "But if he growls at me, I'm blaming you."

Hand in hand, they made their way to the spruce trees, where they'd set their first waypoint.

As they stepped into the shadow of the lighthouse near the bay, Aaron paused. The sea stretched wide before them, waves crashing against jagged rocks, sunlight catching the spray like scattered jewels. He scanned the water, hoping to see another whale breach.

The rising sun cast a golden glow over everything. For a moment, he simply stood there, holding her hand.

The scene was peaceful. Serene. The kind of stillness that felt like a memory even as it happened.

A moment of quiet grace—on an island that had seen so much fear and death.

"I want to take you to Arboretum," Aaron said softly. "I want to show you my home—introduce you to my family. My little sister Heather would adore you, and my brother Eric… he'd want to know everything about you. The village is beautiful. We have fields, forests, rivers… and Druid's Glen, with The One Tree. I want you to see it."

"Well then," Wellsey replied with a shy smile, "I'd love to go." She paused, then added, "And if we're talking about the future… I'd like to take you to Grimmaw. It's wet and cold, yes, but it's where I grew up. I want you to meet my family too—my Ma, Da, and my sister Louise… They'd all love you."

Her voice softened as she leaned into him. "I used to dream about having my own grove someday. But maybe… maybe we could share it. Together."

He looked at her, surprised—and then pleased. "You'd want that? You'd want to be partners?"

"Well," she said, standing on her toes and kissing him, her lips sweet with the lingering taste of buckleberries, "I'd go anywhere with you, Aaron. But, if I'm being honest… I'd prefer somewhere warmer than Grimmaw. Maybe farther west, where the winters don't try to kill you."

"Farther west, nearer to the Needle Forest?" he mused. "I think I could get used to that."

"Well then," she said, a mischievous glint in her eyes, "is that *all* you have to say?"

Aaron looked into her eyes—and something inside him clicked into place.

He took her hand, brought it to his lips, and said simply, "I love you."

"I love you too," she whispered, her cheeks pink with emotion. She pressed her forehead to his, smiling. "And my only rule now is… don't ever leave me."

"Done," he said, pulling her close, holding her against him as her heartbeat settled into rhythm with his own. They stood together in that quiet moment, the world falling away—caught in the newness of their love and the fragile hope of a future together.

At last, Wellsey drew back with a laugh. "Alright, enough of that. Shall we summon Harold?"

"Yes—because nothing completes a romantic moment quite like summoning a giant undead-hating polar bear from another realm," Aaron said, grinning.

Wellsey laughed and kissed the ring, invoking the name of her companion.

Beside them, the air shimmered, and a portal opened with a soft rush of cold wind. Out stepped the massive polar bear, his thick coat gleaming with hints of blue and violet in the morning light. His ice-blue eyes sparkled when he saw them.

"Wellsey!" he boomed, his voice full of warmth. "Aaron!"

The playful bear dropped to all fours and lumbered toward them, nuzzling Wellsey's hip before giving Aaron a gentle shove that nearly knocked him off balance.

"Harold, it's wonderful to see you!" Wellsey said, laughing as she scratched his dense fur. "Thank you for coming. How are you? How's... Aurora?"

Harold's expression softened, and he lowered his massive head. "She rests peacefully in my realm. Thank you for allowing me to take her home."

He sniffed the air, his nose twitching at the faint, lingering scent of death. "And I see you're still on this cursed island."

"We found a sunken boat," Aaron said. "It's magical, we think— but too deep for us to raise alone. Could you... ?"

"Lead the way," Harold rumbled, rising to his full height with eager resolve.

They led Harold to the edge of the bay, pointing out where the boat lay submerged.

Without a word, the great bear crouched—and leapt. He arced through the air and plunged into the water with surprising grace. Moments later, the bow of the boat broke the surface, guided forward by Harold's immense strength. Slowly, deliberately, he brought it toward the shore, the magical vessel gliding as if weightless across the water.

Once it was grounded, Harold dove again, retrieving the broken mast and sail. He dropped them beside the boat as Aaron and Wellsey approached to inspect the hull.

It was in remarkable condition—pristine, untouched by rot or time.

"It is magical," Harold confirmed, sniffing along the wood. His nose twitched. "Mela… mela… melon?"

"What are you saying?" Wellsey asked, brow furrowed.

"There is a spoken word. A trigger. The enchantment recognizes it." Harold snorted. "My skill in such things is not what it once was. Give me a moment… Melang. Melang."

"Mélange?" Aaron guessed, eyebrow raised.

The boat shuddered.

With a creak and groan like wood stretching after centuries of sleep, the hull began to fold in on itself. Boards collapsed inward, reshaping with smooth, fluid motion until it became a small, intricately carved box.

Aaron picked it up and cracked it open, half-expecting to see a miniature boat inside. Instead, he found three objects nestled in the velvet-lined interior: a handful of gold coins, a delicate silver ring, and a single black feather.

With a grin, he placed the box at the water's edge and held his hands aloft like a stage magician. "Mélange!"

The box unfurled.

Wood expanded, reshaped, and rose from itself, the boat reforming in a swirl of light and motion until it was once more a fully rigged vessel—mast restored, sail billowing faintly, floating just off the shore.

"Harold, you're amazing," Wellsey said, beaming.

"I'll get the supplies," Aaron added. "You and Harold wait here."

With that, he turned and sprinted to the nearest spruce, placed his hand on the bark, and vanished with a whisper of magic.

Harold tilted his head, watching the tree for a moment before turning to Wellsey. "Where will you go?" the bear rumbled. "Do you know these lands well enough?"

"East, toward where the sun rises," Wellsey said. "No, I don't know these lands. Aurora told us the mainland lies in that direction, so that's where we'll go. We're hopeful we can find another island—one that lets us rootwalk to a grove we know."

She hesitated, glancing out over the water.

"But Aurora said something was wrong. The network of living things has been disrupted. We might have to sail for days before we can reach land we can actually use. Do you know anything about that? About what's affecting the network?"

The polar bear sniffed the air, then lifted his head and turned slowly, as if sensing something far away.

"It is a mystery to me," Harold said at last. "I do not travel through the living network, as druids do. I move from plane to plane, at will— or when summoned by the bearer of your ring. I travel without paths. I do not need The One Tree to find my way."

Wellsey was quiet for a moment, then asked, "Harold… would you serve anyone who had the ring?"

"I am bound to it," he said, his voice deep and certain. "But I have been fortunate. All my masters have been druids—wise, kind, and in service to the natural order. This ring has passed through Aurora's grove for centuries. Now it is yours to carry, and yours to call upon when needed. You are worthy of the magic you've been entrusted with. Use it well, and summon me when you have need."

She nodded slowly, her fingers brushing the ring.

"Are you… immortal?"

"I can be destroyed in this realm," Harold replied. "If that happens, I cannot return to you for many months—perhaps years. My body reforms around my spirit in my home plane, in my realm. Yes, my spirit is immortal. I cannot die in the way your kind understands death. I always return."

"Thank you for your help. We'll be leaving soon," Wellsey said. "Should I send you back?"

"I will swim alongside you for a time," Harold replied. "Until I know you're safe—and can operate the craft. Are you a sailor?"

Wellsey laughed. "No. I've been on rafts in the swamp near my home—that's about as close to boating as I've come. And I don't think Aaron knows what he's doing either."

"Then I'll stay with you for a while."

"I'd like that," she said warmly. "Harold, not only are you a noble beast… you're also a kind one."

Harold let out a great howl of pleasure, then nudged her playfully with his snout—so hard she tumbled backward into the sand.

They both burst into laughter, the kind that spilled out uncontrollably, catching and feeding on itself until it echoed through the bay.

Aaron returned to the clearing a moment later, confused by the scene before him. "What… happened?"

Neither of them could answer through the giggles.

Once their laughter faded, the three of them turned to the task at hand. They loaded the last of their supplies, adjusted the sail, and secured the gear. As Aaron and Wellsey stepped aboard, Harold gave them a long, knowing look—as if to say *I will be near, even when you cannot see me.*

Then, without a word, he slipped into the sea, his massive form cutting through the water with graceful ease.

They cast one last look back at the island—the place that had taken so much from them, and taught them even more.

Aaron reached for Wellsey's hand as the boat drifted into the open sea. For the first time in what felt like ages, they felt free.

And beside them, Harold swam silently, their guardian in the water, guiding them toward whatever waited in the east.

Chapter Twenty-Two

∞

In the Shadow of the Fiends

The morning was stuffy and hot, the sun rising steadily over the eastern horizon. Brak stood outside the tower, watching the first light spill across the desert, and felt a rare flicker of relief at the break of dawn.

Somewhere out there, the shadow-fiend was hidden—dormant now, waiting for nightfall. Perhaps it slept in a cave, a fissure in the earth, or an extra-dimensional hollow. Whatever its refuge, the creature would return with dusk.

Logic told him to walk away from the place he'd encountered it. Far away.

But the crate was still out there—the graphite molds abandoned in his panicked retreat. He had to go back.

His steps were heavy in the growing heat. The sand clung to his boots, already hot enough to sting. As he walked, Brak noted the faint signs of his flight the night before—scuffed footprints, broken crusts of wind-swept dunes, and bits of scattered debris from the crate.

The trail of bones stretched ahead, grotesque in the morning light—a bleached monument to the countless who had died under the fiend's reign.

He found the crate easily.

But the sight stopped him cold.

The wooden slats had been splintered, the contents crushed into dark powder. Pulverized graphite stained the sand like spilled ash. The molds were destroyed.

Brak stood motionless for a moment. Then rage overtook him.

He lashed out, kicking the wreckage with brutal force. Shards of wood and splinters of bone flew into the air, some catching the wind and scattering over the dunes.

Beyond him, the desert rolled on in all directions—an endless sea of heat and ruin. Far in the distance, a silhouette shimmered through the haze: the remains of a ruined city, mostly buried beneath the sands.

It was his best chance.

If he could reach the city, he might escape the anti-magic dome that enclosed the tower and its surroundings. He suspected the barrier extended for miles—like the one surrounding Mikal Yholl's keep—rendering any teleportation useless until he crossed its edge.

He reached into his robes and withdrew his worn compendium of spells, flipping it open with practiced fingers, scanning the pages for anything—anything—that could help him move faster across this cursed waste.

Nothing.

Brak sighed and resigned himself to the grueling trek.

He circled back to the tower to rest briefly, refilling his waterskin with a basic conjuration. Then he set out again, choosing what looked like the most stable path through the dunes.

It didn't last.

After several hundred feet, the sand began to shift beneath his boots—pulling, sliding, dragging him down. He staggered back, cursing, barely keeping his footing. This was no ordinary desert—this was a trap, shaped by the land itself. A curse woven into the terrain.

He tested other paths. Each proved just as treacherous.

There was no choice.

Grimly, he turned back to the trail of bones and continued toward the ruined city.

The sun climbed higher as he trudged forward, sweat dampening his robes, each step harder than the last. Black basalt structures rose from the dunes ahead—ruins of some long-dead civilization. He passed shattered archways, broken statues, and half-buried towers leaning like crooked teeth.

At last, he reached a central avenue—still partially intact—stretching through the heart of the city. It ran in a straight line toward the horizon, and with luck, it would carry him beyond the reach of the anti-magic dome.

He paused, took a slow swig from his waterskin, and stepped onto the ancient road.

Then he stopped.

There, etched into the sand crossing the avenue, was a strange series of indentations. He knelt to examine them.

Perfectly formed holes—each about three feet long—flanked by deep gouges. Tracks.

Something massive had passed this way.

The imprints followed an offset pattern down the avenue, too irregular for a beast on four legs, too large for anything human-sized. He couldn't tell if the creature had come from the city or gone into it.

Then, a glint caught his eye.

Through the rippling heat, he saw it—metal gleaming in the sun. A figure emerged from the haze.

It was bipedal. Hulking. A golem of tarnished metal, its limbs long and spindly, ending in tri-pronged pincers that clacked as it moved.

Brak stayed low, heart pounding, eyes locked on the advancing shape.

The construct was fifteen feet tall, its steel frame gleaming in the harsh sunlight. It moved with relentless, mechanical grace—every step calculated, every motion heavy with purpose.

Brak's breath caught.

This was no mere guardian. This was a weapon.

The golem broke into a gallop, joints clanking, its movements thundering across the ancient avenue as it closed in with terrifying speed.

Brak didn't hesitate.

He drew a crystal rod from his belt and fired a bolt of lightning. The energy arced through the air, striking the golem dead-on.

The construct barely reacted. The bolt dissipated across its frame like water on stone.

It came faster.

A panel in its chest snapped open—and began to glow. Red light gathered in the cavity, pulsing hotter, brighter.

Brak dove to the side as a beam of arcane energy erupted outward, scorching a molten trench into the sand. Heat rippled through the air.

He didn't wait for another.

Without a second thought, Brak invoked a teleportation spell.

In a flash, he vanished—just as the golem raised one massive pincer for its next strike.

He landed hard in the tower, hitting stone and narrowly missing the slate bench he'd nearly toppled over the night before. Air rushed from his lungs as he scrambled to his feet.

Still catching his breath, he rushed to the window and peered down.

The golem was there—pacing in circles near the edge of the city ruins, firing intermittent beams into the dunes. It searched for him, methodically. Patiently.

Brak's heart sank.

He was trapped.

There was no safe way out of the desert tower's anti-magic barrier.

He would have to return to the cold tower on the island and escape by sea. The alternative—returning to Mikal Yholl's keep—was equally unappealing, assuming he could even force the Mage-Gate to align with that destination. And if the druids were waiting for him there, he'd be overrun in seconds. Even his considerable magic would mean little against their combined power—and the raw brutality of their rangers.

Silently, he cursed Mikal Yholl for leaving him no easy path of retreat.

He opened the weathered book, recited the words of power, and activated the Mage-Gate. The destination was set to Thalraya. He tried to shift the alignment—force it somewhere else—but the sigil was frozen on the cold tower. Locked by Mikal's cruel design.

The portal stabilized, swirling with icy blue light. He stepped through.

Cold air hit him immediately—a sharp contrast to the oppressive heat of the desert. It was almost pleasant.

Brak paused at a window, watching the sunrise crest over the island. For a few hours, the undead would remain dormant in crypts and shadows. But inside the tower, it was different. There was no sunlight here. No protection.

He tried once more to change the Mage-Gate's destination—but it remained locked on Aridaya, the desert tower. Useless.

He deactivated the portal and turned to the next option.

There was only one path left: confront Aramastus and use the hidden portal in the vampire's crypt to reach Ravenview. From there, he could make his way back to his mountain stronghold.

Brak layered protective enchantments over himself—wards against claws, fangs, and dark magic. He summoned a lesser sunburst spell—not as devastating as the scroll's version, but enough to cause Aramastus real pain.

He descended the stairs.

And stopped.

There were far more undead in the tower than before—crowding the stairwell, shoulder to shoulder. Ghouls. Zombies. Restless and twitching in the gloom.

He hadn't expected this. Some force was drawing them inside.

Brak muttered a sharp command and conjured a thick web spell across the narrowest point of the stairs. Layered and sticky, it formed a dense barrier—enough to hold back the press of bodies, at least for now.

He stepped back, recalculating.

This was no longer a straight path to Aramastus.

Back on the top level, Brak steeled himself for the next step of his escape.

He closed his eyes and focused, visualizing every detail of Aramastus's crypt—the portal, the polished wood coffin, the carved furniture. He cast light upon his sword, held it high, and whispered the teleportation spell.

He appeared mere inches from his target.

The soft glow from his blade revealed the crypt's eerie interior—cold, silent, still. He took one step toward the portal.

A creak behind him stopped him cold.

Against better judgment, he turned.

Aramastus stood beside his coffin, fully reformed. Crimson eyes burned with hatred. His features were smooth and whole, but rage twisted them into something monstrous.

They locked eyes. The air thickened with unspoken threats.

Brak's hand lingered near the phylactery, tucked safely within his robes. When he spoke, his voice was cold and measured.

"I could have destroyed you while you were reforming," Brak said. "This time, I won't show mercy."

A snarl curled Aramastus's lip. "You dare stand in my way, wizard? I will not be so easily vanquished a second time."

"There won't be a third," Brak replied.

"Ra-Joth demands the phylactery," the vampire growled, voice like gravel grinding in stone. "Give it to me, and I'll let you leave unharmed. You're trapped here. That is why you've come—to use the portal."

"Ra-Joth chose me for this task," Brak said, his voice icy. "If you were truly loyal, you'd step aside."

Aramastus lunged, fangs bared.

Brak raised his hand and released a beam of searing sunlight. The arcane light slammed into Aramastus, scorching his flesh, sending the vampire reeling with a howl of pain. Smoke curled from his shoulders as skin blistered and peeled.

With another snarl, Aramastus lunged again.

This time, he met steel.

Brak drove the blade forward, catching him in the chest and driving him back, sparks flying as magicked steel met undead flesh.

Brak pressed his advantage, slamming his sunlight-infused fist into Aramastus's face. He watched with grim satisfaction as the vampire's flesh blistered and melted, revealing scorched bone beneath.

Aramastus staggered, let out a rasping hiss—and collapsed into mist, retreating to his coffin.

Brak didn't hesitate.

He tore apart a nearby chair, fashioning a crude stake, then drove it through the vampire's reformed chest, pinning him in place. With brutal precision, he severed the head, arms, and legs, dragging the dismembered remains to the corner of the crypt.

Then he set them ablaze.

The fire caught quickly, filling the crypt with thick, choking smoke. Brak turned away from the flames and retrieved Aramastus's sword from its resting place. It was a master-forged blade—well-balanced, finely crafted. He slid it into his belt. It might serve him yet.

With no time to waste, he stepped into the portal to Ravenview.

On the other side, two vampire spawn were waiting.

He raised his hand and blasted them with twin jets of fire. They shrieked, bodies igniting, stumbling back into the shadows.

Brak sprinted for the cottage's door and flung it open—sunlight pouring in behind him like a divine weapon.

The spawn recoiled from the rays, hissing, vanishing into the darkness.

Outside, Brak took a deep breath of clean air.

He reached for the phylactery, fingers closing around its shape beneath his robes. Still there. Still safe.

Closing his eyes, he visualized his stronghold—*Vhal'Araketh*—its cold stone halls and lonely mountain spires.

He spoke the final word and vanished in a flash of magic.

Whether his work had been enough… whether the path ahead would be clear… he did not know.

But at least, for now, he was free of this cursed place.

Chapter Twenty-Three

∞

A Worthy Bargain

Beyond the bay, the waters were anything but calm. The *Mélange* bucked and pitched with each rising swell, testing Aaron and Wellsey's strength and resolve. The craft, a marvel of magic—sturdy and resilient—still demanded a sailor's skill neither of them possessed. Every gust of wind, every twist of current, brought a fresh challenge.

The jib swung around again, striking Aaron in the shoulder and nearly knocking him overboard.

"Hold steady!" Wellsey shouted, her voice tight with effort as she gripped the tiller, knuckles white, trying to keep the boat on course. The sky above was a cloudless azure, the air crisp and salted—but the wind was ceaseless, offering little comfort.

Grimacing, Aaron reset the sail, wrestling the ropes with numb fingers until it finally caught. The boat lurched forward as it found the current, picking up speed.

"You got it!" Wellsey called from the stern, her smile a brief flash of encouragement amid the chaos.

Aaron rubbed his sore shoulder and nodded. "Yes. Finally. I think I've figured it out."

He glanced over the side.

Harold swam alongside them, effortlessly keeping pace with his powerful strokes, his great white form slicing through the water like a living myth. It was a strange comfort, knowing he was there.

They were headed east, toward the rising sun—toward the promise of mainland shores or another island where tree-stride might connect them to safer lands.

Behind them, the cursed island shrank into the distance. Aaron frowned. The dark tower—once a stark silhouette against the sky—was now gone, obscured by haze or magic. As if the island itself had chosen to vanish.

Just another mystery to leave behind.

The rhythm of sailing was rough at first, but after half an hour, the chaos began to settle. The wind became a pattern. The boat found its pace.

"Wellsey," Aaron said, glancing down at the water. "I think we should let Harold go. There's nothing more he can do for us out here."

She nodded, reluctant but resigned. "Agreed. He's done enough for us already."

Aaron leaned over the side of the boat, waiting until Harold breached the surface. When the polar bear's head appeared, his fur slick with seafoam, Aaron called out, "Thanks, Harold. You've helped us more than we can say. We're going to be all right from here—so we're sending you home."

Harold paused, treading water with slow, powerful strokes. His gaze met theirs—warm, paternal.

"Take care, young ones," he said. "Remember Aurora's spirit, and honor her properly when you reach your lands."

"We will," Aaron promised.

Harold turned to Wellsey. "Be cautious in the days ahead. If ever you need me, the ring will call."

"Thank you, Harold," she said softly, her voice thick with emotion. "Take care of yourself. You may return home."

With a final nod, Harold shimmered—his massive form dissolving in a froth of bubbles and light, leaving only ripples in the water where he had been.

Wellsey twisted the ring on her finger, staring down at it as the waves rocked the *Mélange*. "I hope we don't need to summon him again," she murmured.

"Me too," Aaron said, giving her a small, reassuring smile. "That would mean we're safe—that we don't need help."

They fell into silence, each lost in thought as the boat cut its steady path through the endless waves. They took turns manning the tiller and adjusting the sail, learning the quirks of the *Mélange* together, growing more confident with each passing hour.

Behind them, the sun began to dip toward the horizon, casting golden light across the water. They both paused to watch it—their first sunset free from danger. Serene, quiet, and warm.

A stark contrast to the haunted island they had left behind.

As darkness fell, they secured the sail, tying it off along with the tiller to keep the boat on a steady course. Aaron cast a light spell on the mainsail, turning it into a glowing beacon—faint but visible, a small comfort in the vast, empty sea.

At last, they huddled together beneath the starry sky, the steady rocking of the *Mélange* lulling them toward sleep.

The night stretched on, silent but for the rhythmic whisper of waves against the hull.

And there, beneath a canopy of stars, Aaron and Wellsey found a fragile but welcome peace.

"Ahoy!"

Aaron stirred, blinking groggily in the dim pre-dawn light, the call of an unfamiliar voice drifting across the waves. He gently peeled Wellsey from their shared warmth, nudging her awake with a quiet touch.

"Hello!" he called back, his voice rough with sleep.

He squinted toward the sound—and there, not far off, loomed a hulking ship. Lanterns lined its railings, casting a golden glow across the water. Faces peered down from the deck, and as his eyes adjusted, he caught sight of a familiar banner: the dark green flag of the Free Duchy of Canter, rippling in the sea breeze.

Relief flickered through him—tempered by caution. The Duchy was generally friendly, but at sea, protocol was unclear.

"We need help!" he shouted. "We're lost at sea!"

"Aye," came the reply, the voice of a sailor carrying clearly over the water. "We'll come about and bring you aboard."

Aaron braced himself against the rocking boat. "Who are you?" he called, his tone edged with wariness.

"This is the merchant ship *Duquesne*, flying under the banner of the Free Duchy of Canter. Home port's Ornst—around the southern horn." A pause. "And who might you be?"

Aaron glanced at Wellsey. She nodded faintly.

"I'm Aaron Manawove," he answered. "Druid of the Needle Forest. And this is Wellsey Oggery, druid of the groves far to the east in Faustron. We were stranded on an island. This craft was our only chance to escape certain death."

"Aye, a fine-looking craft indeed," the sailor called back. "We'll get you aboard and winch it up after. Captain's resting till morning, but you'll meet him at breakfast. Name's Gilly—first mate."

"Thank you, Gilly," Aaron replied, genuine relief in his voice.

Deckhands tossed down ropes, and with some maneuvering, they brought the *Mélange* alongside the larger vessel. A swaying rope ladder was lowered, and they lashed their packs into a cargo basket, which the crew hauled up with ease. After removing the *Mélange*'s mast, they helped secure it with the other longboats tied along the side.

"Welcome aboard," Gilly said with a nod. "Not kind seas to be out in a boat that size. We've had trouble finding favorable winds ourselves, and that's with a full crew."

"Where are you headed?" Aaron asked.

"Caliss. We're running down from Pelt with a hold full of merchandise. Good trade—weather permitting."

"It hasn't been stormy," noted a nearby sailor.

"Aye," Gilly replied with a crooked grin. "Avoiding storms is one thing. Finding wind's another. Come on, let's get you settled. The captain will talk payment in the morning—if you can't pay, we'll be putting you and your little boat back in the sea."

Aaron gave a respectful nod. "Understood. Thank you."

Gilly led them below deck and guided them to a narrow cabin tucked near the crew quarters.

"Captain's Allard Leighton," he said over his shoulder. "Well-known in these waters—for his bravery, if not his kindness. I'll let the night watch know we've extra guests. The captain'll want a word with you in the morning. Stories travel fast—tales of islands and towers, secrets and undead." He gave them a meaningful look. "Folk are listening."

"Thank you again," Aaron said.

"Yes, we're grateful," Wellsey added softly.

Gilly handed over a lantern with a flickering candle. "Mind that flame. Fire on a ship is a deadly thing."

Wellsey nodded and murmured an incantation. The flame winked out, replaced by a steady glow of conjured light. "Safer," she said with a faint smile.

The cabin was cramped and low-ceilinged, forcing them both to stoop. Two narrow bunks lined the walls, each with a lumpy mattress barely thick enough to soften the boards beneath. A small porthole offered a sliver of starlit sea, and a crooked table stood in the corner, cluttered with mismatched plates and dented tin cups.

Aaron gave a tired grin. "The outside bunk will be cooler. I'll take it—you're always cold."

They unstrapped their gear, stacking their soft leather armor and staves in the corner. Bedrolls were laid over the thin mattresses for what little extra comfort they could provide.

After a brief, weary kiss goodnight, they wriggled into place, adjusting to the creaking beds. Wellsey draped a cloth over the lantern, dimming the glow to a gentle hum.

"If we make it to Caliss," Aaron said quietly, "we should be able to rootwalk back to Arboretum." There was hope in his voice, however cautious.

"Well… we may not be able to," Wellsey whispered in return. "Aurora said something's wrong with the network of living things. Even if we reach Caliss, it could be a long walk. And that's only to your home…"

She hesitated.

"My grove's on the far side of the world."

Aaron sighed, running a hand over his face. "If we can't rootwalk, we'll have to find work until we can afford transport or horses. Whatever coin I have left is probably going toward our passage on this ship. And we'll need to figure out how to retrieve the *Mélange* without anyone seeing us. I'll think of something."

"We should also decide what to tell the captain tomorrow," Wellsey murmured, worry edging her voice. "What if he asks too many questions?"

"We'll keep it simple," Aaron said, thinking aloud. "We were part of a druid expedition. Got separated by a magical trap—a portal. We ended up stranded on an island filled with undead, including a cursed knight named Sir Aelion. We found the boat in a ruined marina and sailed, hoping to reach the mainland."

He paused, then added firmly, "We say nothing about the Mage-Gate. Nothing about Aurora, or the wizard. And definitely nothing about Harold."

Wellsey nodded, though her hand drifted to the ring on her finger. She twisted it anxiously, eyes flicking down as if the magic might betray her.

"I think you should keep the ring," she whispered, glancing up. "You'd be a better caretaker."

Aaron gave a quiet laugh. "Harold likes you. I doubt he'd take orders from me the same way. Keep it—you're the right one to wear it."

"I don't feel safe," she admitted, her voice barely audible. "I know it sounds silly…"

"It isn't silly." Aaron reached beneath his tunic and removed his simple necklace—its pendant a polished stone set in silver. "Here. Put this on."

He leaned across and draped it over her head.

"It's enchanted for protection. My father gave it to me when I first left for the Mage-Gate."

As the pendant settled against her chest, Wellsey exhaled. A small smile tugged at her lips, and the tension in her face eased.

"Thank you," she said softly. "I do feel safer now."

"Good." Aaron pulled the thin blanket up to his chin. "Now sleep. I can barely keep my eyes open."

Wellsey made a quiet sound of agreement, but her reply faded into silence. Before either could say more, they were already slipping into sleep—deep and dreamless, the kind only exhaustion could bring—lulled by the ship's steady sway and the hush of the sea outside their cabin walls.

Gilly woke them at dawn, rapping briskly on the cabin door. Sunlight streamed through the porthole, half-obscured by ropes and rigging, casting shifting patterns of shadow across the cramped room.

Aaron and Wellsey blinked the sleep from their eyes, rose slowly, and gathered their things. They followed Gilly up to the main deck, squinting as the brightness struck them full in the face.

Above, the deck bustled with movement. Sailors moved with practiced purpose—adjusting lines, coiling ropes, and resecuring cargo. The sharp scent of salt and tar hung in the morning air.

Gilly led them aft, toward the stern, and ushered them into the captain's quarters.

Where the crew's quarters had been plain and practical, Captain Leighton's day cabin radiated quiet wealth. Rich mahogany paneling lined the walls, and polished brass fixtures gleamed wherever the morning light struck. The scent of varnished wood mingled with a faint trace of pipe smoke, old but comforting.

At the center of the room stood a broad oak table dressed in fine linen. Platters of fresh fruit, soft cheeses, and golden pastries were laid out with precise care. Three delicate glasses stood beside a crystal decanter filled with amber liquid that caught the light like fire.

Captain Leighton sat at the head of the table, scanning a stack of papers. He looked up as they entered, his face weathered but sharp, framed by a neatly trimmed beard. His piercing blue eyes held the quiet authority of a man long at sea—and unaccustomed to surprises.

When Gilly stepped aside, the captain rose smoothly to greet them, a warm smile touching his features—welcoming, but measured.

"Ah, young travelers!" the captain said, his voice steeped in the authority of long command. "Gilly didn't mention how young you both are. Please, be welcome at my table. I am Captain Allard Leighton."

"Aaron Manawove," Aaron said, offering a respectful nod.

"Wellsey Oggery," she added, dipping her head politely.

"Gilly, refreshments for our guests, if you would."

The first mate moved swiftly, pouring drinks with a sailor's economy, while Captain Leighton gestured for them to sit. Once they had taken their seats across from him, the captain leaned back, folding his hands, his gaze measuring.

"Now then," he began, "I trust you slept well in the guest quarters? I understand you're seeking passage to Caliss. So tell me—what brings two young druids aboard my ship, drifting alone in a small craft on open water?"

Aaron took a breath, measured and steady. "We were part of a druidic expedition investigating a ruin," he said carefully. "Wellsey and I got separated from the others and stumbled through a portal. We didn't realize it was one-way until it was too late. When we emerged, we were on an island—far from where we began, with no means of return."

Captain Leighton's brow arched. "And where exactly is this ruin you speak of?"

"In Faustron," Wellsey answered. "Not far from Kaalnaes. That whole region is rich with old elven sites. Some date back to the founding of the groves—it's a place where magic runs deep."

Aaron picked up the thread. "The island we reached… it was cursed. We found an ancient tower riddled with undead—ghouls, zombies, worse. We barely survived. A spirit who called himself Sir Aelion helped us at first, or so we thought. In the end, he was something darker. We had to destroy him."

Leighton's expression darkened as he listened, his sharp eyes narrowing with thought. "A malevolent spirit, you say?" He lifted his glass in a small, solemn gesture. "May the Guardian watch over us and guide us through treacherous waters."

Aaron mirrored the motion, recognizing the invocation to Qhesin, god of the sea and its creatures. "May Thatara protect us," he added quietly, invoking the goddess of nature.

They drank. The port burned its way down Aaron's throat—nutty, sweet, and far stronger than he expected. Across the table, Wellsey coughed mid-sip, her cheeks flushing pink.

"A little strong for me," she said, recovering quickly. "Pardon me."

Captain Leighton chuckled, clearly amused. "An acquired taste. This is a fine port wine—crafted for long voyages and longer storms." He held up his glass again, watching the light play through the amber liquid. "Do you know why they call it 'port'?"

Aaron and Wellsey both shook their heads.

"Years ago," the captain said, settling comfortably into the tale, "wine spoiled too easily at sea. So the vintners fortified it with brandy to keep it from turning. The brandy halted the fermentation, kept the sugars in place, and left us with this—sweet, strong, and enduring." He took another sip. "Rather like sailors, wouldn't you say?"

Aaron smiled faintly, but the warmth in the room thinned as Leighton set his glass down and returned to the matter at hand.

"Now then. This island of yours. It must lie nearby—if you made it to us in that little vessel."

"Close enough," Wellsey replied. "The island was overrun. Thousands of undead, swarming the ruins. The seas were wild, but there was one quiet bay where we found the boat. We saw no living souls—just wreckage and the dead."

Leighton's brow rose, his lips twitching in faint skepticism. "Thousands of undead, you say? And the two of you survived?" He gave a slow shake of his head, not unkindly. "I've heard tall tales in every port, but this might be the tallest yet."

Aaron met his gaze. "Every word we've spoken is true. We survived because we had to. And now… we're just grateful someone found us."

Captain Leighton studied him for a long moment, his gaze unblinking. Then he eased back in his chair and gestured toward the table.

"Well, eat up. It's a long sail to Caliss, and I daresay you've earned a proper breakfast. We've other passengers aboard—merchants out of Pelt. You're welcome to join them after you've eaten."

"Thank you," Aaron said, the gratitude in his voice sincere.

He and Wellsey reached for the platters, filling their plates with sliced oranges, hard cheese, and buttery pastries. After days of dried rations, trumpet mushroom soup, and raw buckleberries, the fresh flavors felt like a feast. For a moment, neither of them spoke.

Leighton watched them with a faint smile, then leaned forward, hands clasped. "Now. To business."

The warmth in the room dimmed.

"Passage to Caliss isn't free," the captain went on. "Standard fare is twenty gold per person. But given the state of the sea—and our route—I'll have to add five more each. Fifty total."

Aaron's stomach turned. He kept his expression even.

Across the table, Wellsey had paused mid-bite. Her eyes met his, wide with worry.

"So… fifty gold," Aaron repeated, forcing calm into his tone. "Perhaps we could work off part of that fare. We're druids—our skills might be useful."

Leighton raised a brow. "Ah. So you don't have the coin." He gave a dry chuckle. "Tree-lovers like you don't exactly blend in with a working crew. But… I might find a task or two you could handle. Won't shave much off, but it'd help."

Aaron looked to Wellsey. The exchange between them was silent, mutual, resolved.

"What if we offered a trade?" he said.

The captain leaned back slightly, intrigued. "I'm listening."

"Our boat," Wellsey said. Her voice was firm. "It's not an ordinary craft."

Leighton's expression shifted—skepticism giving way to mild curiosity. "Aye, it's a handsome thing. But you're saying it's worth fifty gold?"

"It's worth more," Aaron said. "The boat has… properties a man of the sea might find useful. I propose a trade—our craft, *Mélange*, in exchange for safe passage to Caliss for both of us, and two horses when we arrive."

The captain let out a hearty laugh, shaking his head in disbelief. "Two horses as well? That's a steep price for a little boat. You're telling me this craft of yours is worth two hundred gold?"

"Indeed," Aaron said, calm and sure. "And I can show you why. But I'll need your word—if you accept the trade, you'll honor it."

Captain Leighton's smile faded, replaced by something harder and more measured. "I'm no welcher, lad. If your boat is worth what you say, you'll have your passage and your horses. But if not—tomorrow, you're back in that little vessel."

"Agreed," Aaron said, extending his hand.

The captain took it in a firm, weathered grip, sealing the deal without another word.

With the terms settled, Aaron and Wellsey eased back into their chairs, the tension unwinding from their shoulders. They returned to their breakfast, savoring every bite—the juicy orange slices, the creamy cheese, the warm, flaky pastries. Each mouthful was a quiet celebration, a reminder of safety, of civilization, of survival.

They had escaped the island of the undead.

Now came the next trial—outwitting the sharp eyes and sharper instincts of Captain Allard Leighton.

Outside, the sky stretched wide and blue, the wind blowing steady from the west. The *Duquesne* sliced through the waves on her southerly course, her dark wooden hull gleaming against the endless backdrop of sea and sky.

Captain Leighton led Aaron and Wellsey to the port side, where their small craft—the *Mélange*—was lashed securely. As they reached the railing, a sudden spray from the ocean surged up and over the deck, misting them in a veil of saltwater that sparkled in the morning sun.

Aaron leaned over the rail. The little white craft looked impossibly small beside the *Duquesne*, its painted hull a bright contrast against the ship's weathered wood and the rolling sea beneath.

Captain Leighton crossed his arms. "All right, lad. Show me what makes this boat worth two horses and safe passage."

Aaron nodded and took a breath. "Stand back, if you would. I'll need a little space."

Leighton, Gilly, and Wellsey took a step back, watching him with measured curiosity. Aaron extended his hand over the rail, palm open, fingers slightly trembling.

"*Mélange*," he said, his voice low and steady.

For a heartbeat, there was only wind and the hiss of waves.

Then came a sound like wind chimes in a storm—metallic clicks and soft whirrs, rising in tempo as the *Mélange* began to shift. Its sleek hull folded in on itself, panels sliding and compressing, the entire craft reshaping with fluid, deliberate precision. The air shimmered faintly with arcane resonance, the magic palpable, pulsing in rhythm with the sea's song.

Captain Leighton stiffened, his brow furrowing as he gripped the rail. Gilly's jaw dropped. Even Wellsey, who had witnessed the transformation before, couldn't help the small smile of satisfaction that tugged at her lips.

In moments, the vessel was no more. In its place hovered a smooth, carved box no larger than a loaf of bread, gleaming faintly with residual enchantment. It floated upward, unbound by rope or hand, and settled gently into Aaron's waiting palm.

Aaron held it, feeling the pulse of magic in the compacted vessel, and tapped it affectionately as if it were a loyal companion.

Captain Leighton let out a low whistle. "Well, I'll be damned. I've seen all sorts of magic on the seas, but never anything like that." He looked Aaron up and down with renewed respect. "You druids are full of surprises, aren't you?"

Aaron gave a modest nod, slipping the box into his pack. "It was a gift—a relic from another druid. It saved our lives."

Leighton shook his head, still visibly astonished. "A deal is a deal, lad," he said, a grudging smile breaking through. "You've earned your passage. And when we reach Caliss, two horses will be waiting for you."

Aaron met the captain's gaze, his own eyes steady. "Thank you, Captain. We're in your debt."

"Seems to me," Leighton replied with a smirk, "you're the one with the treasure worth something. Don't go flashing that trick around too often, or someone might take a fancy to it."

Aaron's expression turned serious. "I understand, Captain. The *Mélange* is precious to us. We'll keep it safe."

Captain Leighton gave a short nod, his face returning to its usual stoic look of command. "Good. Now, if you'll excuse me, I've a ship to run." He looked to Gilly, giving a nod. "See that they're settled with the other passengers."

As Captain Leighton strode back across the deck, Gilly motioned for Aaron and Wellsey to follow. He flashed them an impressed grin as they walked away from the rail.

"Now I see why the captain agreed to the trade," Gilly said. "A clever bit of magic, that is. You'll be the talk of the crew for days. You're safe here but be mindful if you catch my meaning."

Aaron gave a rueful chuckle. "Understood. Not exactly what we intended, but… I suppose it's better than being set adrift."

"Well," Wellsey murmured as she squeezed his hand, "we're one step closer to home."

The *Duquesne* continued on her way, sails billowing as she rode the steady wind southward. Behind them, distant islands faded from view, replaced by the open sea and the promise of a fresh start.

The next day, Aaron and Wellsey roamed the deck, familiarizing themselves with the layout of the ship. The *Duquesne* was a massive vessel, built to transport heavy cargo, yet its two masts held steady, catching the wind and propelling them southward at a good pace.

"That was a great idea to trade the boat," Aaron said, leaning against the railing. "I was thinking the same thing."

"Well, I worry that we overpaid," Wellsey replied. "That magic boat is worth more than passage on this ship—and two horses."

"We had to do it. Don't worry, I'll empty the contents before we hand it over. There were some coins, a ring, and a strange feather that feels… magical. We'll figure that out once we're on shore."

Wellsey nodded, gazing out over the waves. "You know, being on the ocean isn't so bad. I thought we'd be battered by storms and monstrous waves. This is almost… refreshing."

Aaron chuckled. "It's an experience we'll never forget. So—Needle Forest first?"

She nodded. "As soon as we're close enough to rootwalk, we'll sell the horses and head home." She hesitated, then added, "I wonder what happened with The One Tree."

Aaron sighed. "Like Aurora said, it must have been damaged. She mentioned my father left in a hurry—it must have been a huge problem. Albic Fang and Finola are there, so it had to be bad if they couldn't handle it. There was also this wizard… he managed to get past the protections of Druid's Glen. I wonder if he's involved."

Wellsey's brow furrowed. "Could it be the same wizard we chased into the Mage-Gate?"

Aaron nodded slowly. "I think so. He was spying on the Druid Council on the day they discussed the Mage-Gate."

"Well," she said, "he must have spied on Wilmund's grove too—or my own. Maybe he has allies or informants among the druids, or he's using other magical methods to gather information."

"If he has spies, that's more dangerous." Aaron's expression darkened. "We need to warn Wilmund and my father."

"Well, when we're back, we'll tell them everything." She paused. "Do you call your father 'Gideon' or 'Da'?"

Aaron smiled. "Father, most of the time. 'Gideon' when we're on druid business." He tilted his head. "Isn't 'Da' an Ornst term?"

"My family's roots are in Ornst, though we've been in Faustron for generations. My grandparents still speak High Ornst—but not me."

"Not even the curse words?" Aaron teased.

Wellsey laughed. "Especially not the curse words!"

They shared a laugh, Aaron slipping his arm around her waist as she leaned against his shoulder.

Suddenly, a shout broke the moment.

"Ship on the horizon!" The lookout's voice rang from the crow's nest. "Three-mast frigate, coming from the west! All sails unfurled!"

The deck sprang to life. Sailors scrambled, manning rigging and securing lines. Aaron and Wellsey hugged the railing to stay out of the way.

From high above, the lookout called again, sharper this time. "Deck movement! Looks like they're preparing for conflict!"

Gilly appeared at their side, urgency in his voice. "Get below and get your things. If we're boarded, you may need to help us fight."

"Who's on that ship?" Aaron asked.

"Don't know," Gilly said. "It's a three-mast frigate—fast enough to chase us down if they're not friendly. Captain'll try to outmaneuver them, but we'll be in for a fight if they catch up."

"We'll help defend the ship," Wellsey offered. "We may be druids, but we can still be useful."

The lookout shouted again. "Three-mast ship, turning toward us! Flying Canter colors!"

"It's a ruse, it has to be," Gilly muttered. "That's the Black Storm." His voice rose in alarm. "Black Storm!" he hollered.

The two words sent a ripple of fear through the crew. The Black Storm was notorious—a mercenary outfit of thieves, assassins, and cutthroats who took contracts to kill, steal, and terrorize. When they turned to piracy, they were known for leaving no survivors.

The deck was orderly chaos.

"Bells!" Gilly shouted, signaling the threat.

Sailors dashed to their stations, shouting over one another as they readied the ship's defenses.

At the helm, Captain Leighton held a glass jar with an unhinged lid, from which gusts of wind howled forth, filling the sails and propelling the *Duquesne* forward with a sudden burst of speed.

Aaron and Wellsey emerged from below. "Tell us what to do," Aaron said, ready for anything.

Gilly hesitated, then gave a sharp nod. "Stay close. But don't cast spells unless I say. Once they know you're spellcasters, you'll be their first targets."

Behind them, the approaching frigate raised a black flag—its sigil a demonic skull crowned in flames, a snake coiled within a triangle.

"Arrogant bastards," Gilly spat.

A blinding flash erupted from the bow of the enemy ship. Bolts of lightning cracked across the sky, striking the *Duquesne's* main sail. The mast shuddered. Wood exploded in splinters. Sparks rained down across the deck.

"Down!" Gilly roared, dragging Aaron and Wellsey to the planks.

Debris scattered. Smoke choked the air as sailors scrambled to clear the smoldering remains of the sail.

"That's the *Magistrate*," Gilly growled, helping them up. "Pride of the Black Storm fleet. This isn't ordinary piracy."

"Aye," said Captain Leighton, pale but resolute. "They're not here for gold. They're here for someone. Either us—or the passengers below."

Aaron and Wellsey exchanged a glance. They remembered seeing the strange family traveling aboard.

The *Magistrate* loomed closer. On its bow stood a cloaked figure— face obscured by shadow. Beside him, a tall, broad-shouldered man gazed across the water, his icy blue eyes cold and unyielding.

"Prepare to be boarded!" the man called. "I am Captain Lynford Sutherland of the Black Storm. Surrender now, or my wizard Vortigern will incinerate your ship."

Captain Leighton stepped forward, unflinching. "You come any closer," he warned, "and neither of us will make it home."

"Perhaps," Captain Sutherland replied coolly, "but we have ways of crippling your ship. Prepare to be boarded."

The *Magistrate* closed in. Grappling hooks whistled through the air, latching onto the *Duquesne's* rails with sharp metallic thuds.

Aaron and Wellsey exchanged a desperate glance.

"If you can hinder their ship, the time is now," Gilly urged.

"I'll take the bow," Aaron said. "You set fire to the stern."

They whispered incantations, casting flickers of flame onto the *Magistrate's* deck in two places. Fire bloomed, licking up ropes and planks, sending up black smoke.

Vortigern raised his arms in answer. From the darkening sky above, a torrent of hail and ice descended. Shards of jagged frost battered the *Duquesne*, tearing through rigging and sails, coating the deck in a treacherous sheen of ice and sleet.

The ship lurched and slowed.

The *Magistrate* came alongside, its deck swarming. Pirates scrambled to smother the fires even as others hurled more hooks and dropped gangplanks across the gap. In a matter of moments, they boarded.

The Black Storm crew moved with brutal precision—overpowering resistance, seizing weapons, forcing the *Duquesne's* sailors to their knees.

Captain Sutherland crossed onto the deck, cloak billowing behind him. Vortigern followed, his hood still shadowing his face.

Sutherland approached Captain Leighton, his tone cold. "You should have surrendered. This could have been avoided."

"You have what you want," Leighton replied tightly. "Take our cargo and leave."

Sutherland's eyes drifted to Aaron and Wellsey. "I'm curious about these two... passengers."

Aaron stepped forward, keeping his tone even. "We were stranded on an island. Captain Leighton agreed to take us to port. We're passengers—nothing more."

A sudden commotion from amidships drew every gaze. The Black Storm pirates were forcing a family of four toward the helm. The father, tall and broad-shouldered, moved with restrained fury, his piercing eyes fixed on Sutherland. Beside him, his wife clutched their two children tightly, her face pale but resolute.

"Porthos Vernier," Captain Sutherland said, his voice heavy with contempt. "Trying to slip away unnoticed, are we?"

Vernier held the captain's gaze, his voice hard as stone. "I'm guilty only of seeking the truth. If you must take someone, take me—but leave my family out of this."

Sutherland's eyes narrowed. "A noble sentiment. But I think your entire family will be coming with us."

He turned to Leighton, gesturing toward Aaron and Wellsey. "And the druids. They've meddled more than enough."

"They're not part of this," Captain Leighton growled, his jaw tight.

Sutherland shrugged, unconcerned. "Then I'll sink your ship and leave your crew to the sharks. Or perhaps Vortigern can give them a proper fiery sendoff."

Aaron gave a faint nod to Wellsey and hefted his pack. His voice was low as he squeezed his staff. "We'll go. Just leave the others alone."

Sutherland smiled thinly. "How generous."

He turned to his men. "Get them aboard. We're done here."

The Black Storm pirates seized the Verniers and flanked Aaron and Wellsey, marching them toward the *Magistrate* as the *Duquesne* drifted in their wake—wounded, silent, and slowly disappearing into the morning haze.

True to his word, Captain Sutherland left the *Duquesne* to her own fate.

Aaron watched the crippled ship drift into the distance, hoping Captain Leighton and his crew could make the necessary repairs and sail to safety. The *Magistrate*, sleek and swift, now plowed steadily northward with its prize—a druid, a druidess, and an unfortunate family of four who were clearly the pirates' true targets.

Aaron and Wellsey stood near the aft rail by the helm, trying to take in their surroundings while feigning cooperation.

Wellsey leaned in and whispered, "I hope you have a plan."

"I do," Aaron murmured, "but we'll have to talk later. Vortigern's coming."

The *Magistrate*'s sinister wizard approached, his narrow frame draped in the dark robes of the Wizards of Arcana. He gestured to two nearby sailors, who stepped forward to relieve Aaron and Wellsey of their weapons, including their staves.

"Very clever, you two," Vortigern sneered. "Now tell me—what spell did you use to set our deck on fire?"

Aaron and Wellsey exchanged a glance.

"It's a simple cantrip," Aaron replied. "We use it to start campfires. It's more for convenience than combat."

"Convenience or not, it was effective," Vortigern said, his eyes narrowing as he extended a hand. "Now, your packs."

Reluctantly, Aaron handed his over, the *Mélange* hidden inside. He could only hope Vortigern wouldn't recognize the boat for what it truly was.

Vortigern rummaged through the contents, his long fingers quick and methodical, until he uncovered the small box. He held it up with a bemused expression. "What's this? A trinket?"

"Just a keepsake," Aaron answered quickly. "From home."

Vortigern shot him a suspicious glance—but before he could respond, something else caught his eye. A feather had tumbled from the box during his search. He reached down, plucked it from the deck, and held it up to the light, studying it closely.

"This," he said, stroking the feather between his fingers, "this is what I felt… interesting." His eyes flicked to Aaron. "You won't be needing it."

"It's just a feather," Aaron insisted, trying to keep the desperation out of his voice.

"Indeed. Just a feather," Vortigern murmured, sliding it into his pocket without another glance. He snapped Aaron's pack shut and tossed it back. Aaron caught it, grateful the wizard hadn't figured out the *Mélange* hidden within.

Satisfied, Vortigern produced two slender silver bracelets from the folds of his robe. "Put out your wrists."

Aaron and Wellsey complied. With a sharp word of power, the bracelets clamped into place, tightening around their skin and growing heavier with a faint hum.

"These are anti-magic restraints," Vortigern said, flashing a twisted grin. "If you try to cast a spell, it will backfire. Painfully." His brow arched. "Feel free to test it, if you don't believe me."

Aaron stared down at the bracelet, then raised his fingers slightly, driven by a mix of curiosity and defiance. He attempted to spark the faintest ember.

Agony lanced through his body—searing pain that shot from his wrist through his arms and chest, dropping him to his knees with a strangled cry.

Wellsey grabbed his shoulder, steadying him as he doubled over, gasping. Vortigern chuckled darkly.

"You are as stupid as you look. I told you it would hurt."

"Not stupid," Aaron rasped. "Just… curious."

Pleased with himself, Vortigern gestured to two sailors. "Take them below."

The sailors dragged Aaron to his feet and led them below deck, down into the *Magistrate*'s brig. The air grew colder and damper with each step, thick with mildew and the weight of despair.

The brig was dim and cramped. Two prisoners already occupied cells—slumped figures in tattered clothes, their eyes hollow, their hope long gone. There was no sign of the Vernier family.

Aaron's stomach tightened.

Vortigern halted before a narrow cell near the hull—barely wide enough for two thin pallets and a sliver of floor. "This one," he said curtly.

"We don't lock the cells here," Vortigern said, his voice dry. "But the door to the brig is bolted tight. Stay in your cell, and you might make it to Stormkeep in one piece." He held out a hand. "Now—your spell books."

They complied, handing over their small tomes. Vortigern flipped through the pages with visible disinterest, his lip curling at the simple diagrams and inked notes. With a scoff, he tossed the books back at them.

"Useless," he muttered. "To me—and now, to you." He tapped his wrist, indicating the restraints.

Without another word, he turned and strode away. The iron door groaned shut behind him, followed by the sharp screech of the locking mechanism.

Aaron waited a long moment, listening for footsteps. When he was certain they were alone, he leaned back against the wall and stared at the dull silver band circling his wrist.

"Well," he muttered. "This complicates things."

"Are you all right?" Wellsey asked, watching him with quiet concern.

"Yeah," he said, wincing. "Lesson learned. These restraints are real."

"What's the plan?" she whispered. "Our magic's useless like this."

"True," Aaron said, tugging absently at the bracelet. "But we still have the *Mélange*. It's still in the pack, and they didn't figure out what it is."

"Well, even if we escape with it, they'll catch us for sure," Wellsey said softly. "What about Harold?"

Aaron reached out, gently massaging her shoulders, his voice a low murmur. "That's a great idea."

They exchanged a determined look, the weight of the moment settling between them. If they were going to escape, it would take every bit of their courage—and a miracle or two.

Chapter Twenty-Four

∞

Seeds of Corruption

Heather and Gideon strolled down the cobbled streets of Kaalnaes, the late afternoon sun casting long, angled shadows. The air smelled faintly of wood smoke, and around them, townsfolk moved at an unhurried pace—chatting, laughing, exchanging goods. Heather took it all in: the narrow alleys crowded with merchant carts, the weathered faces of passersby, and the tall timbered buildings leaning close like old friends sharing secrets. After days of hopping from forest to forest via tree-stride, the earthy smells and grounded bustle of town life felt almost foreign.

As they neared The Double Weasel—a shabby tavern wedged between a cooper's shop and a smithy—Gideon chuckled to himself. Heather caught the sound and glanced at him, curious. "What's funny?"

"Just remembering my last time here," Gideon said, a glint in his eye. "Let's just say I had to outwit a certain Judiciar. You never know who you'll run into in a place like this."

Heather's gaze lingered on a pair of men loitering near the tavern's entrance, their faces half-hidden beneath worn hats. "What was he like—the Judiciar?"

"Duke Graystone?" Gideon's tone sharpened slightly. "A slippery man with a sharper tongue than most. Not someone to cross lightly." He nodded toward the tavern. "Let's talk about it inside. Not all ears here are friendly."

They stepped into The Double Weasel. The air inside was thick with the scent of stale ale and roasted meat. It was mid-afternoon, and most of the tables were filled—woodcutters and laborers sipping weak beer and picking at cold lunches. The hum of quiet conversation filled the room, punctuated now and then by the clink of a tankard or the scrape of a stool.

Gideon chose a table near the window, where he could watch both the street and the room with equal ease. Heather, her legs aching from days of travel, dropped into her chair and awkwardly fiddled with her short sword.

"Unbuckle it and lean it against the wall," Gideon said, hiding a smile as he settled in across from her.

She did as instructed, then rubbed her temples. "My head hurts."

"You're hungry," he replied, raising a hand to catch the barkeep's attention. The barkeep—a stocky, middle-aged man with a deeply furrowed brow—recognized Gideon at once and hurried over.

"Ah, welcome back, sir!" the barkeep said, a little too eagerly. "Any friend of Duke Graystone is always welcome here."

Gideon raised an eyebrow. "Friend? Hardly. I'd call us professional rivals at best."

"Understood, understood," the barkeep said quickly, his tone turning more cautious. "What can I get for you? We've still got venison soup, and the meat pies just came out of the oven."

At the mention of meat pies, both Heather and Gideon perked up, exclaiming in unison, "Meat pies!"

The barkeep grinned at their enthusiasm. "And drinks? Ale?"

Gideon nodded. "Two ales. Equal measure."

The barkeep bustled off, and Heather turned to her father, curiosity in her eyes. "So, this Duke Graystone—you debated him?"

"Debated, yes. He was ready to interrogate me, maybe even detain me, until I changed his mind over a drink. He's not someone to underestimate. If you ever meet him, keep your wits sharp."

Heather smirked. "How did you change his mind?"

"With Papa's brandy," Gideon said with a wink. "Let's call it… strategic hospitality and a touch of luck. Peak Estate, of course."

Her face brightened. "I miss Papa and Mama," she murmured, a wistful look passing over her features. "It feels like I haven't seen them in ages."

Gideon's expression softened. "When we get back, we'll visit them. All of us."

He motioned to the beetle-shaped brooch pinned to his chest. "Think Papa will remember this?"

"Of course!" Heather laughed, recalling the old story. "The beetles chased him all over until he finally let you marry Mother!"

They both chuckled, the warmth of the memory lingering between them. Gideon took a moment to study his daughter—so much of Emma in her features, her posture, the light in her eyes. He murmured a quiet prayer to Thatara, feeling the goddess's presence like a breeze through leaves, grateful for his family and for Heather's safe return from all she had faced. The goddess of nature, like Emma, was never far from his thoughts.

When their meal arrived, they eagerly dug into the flaky meat pies, steam billowing out as they cracked open the golden crust. Heather took a cautious sip of her ale and immediately wrinkled her nose.

"It tastes like metal," she muttered.

Gideon frowned, tasting his own. "I noticed that too. Could be their brewing equipment—or maybe the water's bad. They don't have the clean springs of Arboretum."

Heather pushed her mug aside, still grimacing, but perked up as Gideon began spinning stories from his younger days.

"You know," he said, grinning, "before I met your mother, I used to brew my own ale. Not that it was any good. I called it *Gideon's Timid Toasted Toad Stout.*"

Heather burst out laughing. "Was it actually toasted?"

"No, not in the slightest. I just thought the name was funny." He laughed, eyes gleaming with mischief. "Naming it was the best part. Made it sound clever enough that folks might ignore the fact it tasted like swamp water. Slimy swamp water. On a hot day."

She shook her head and stuck out her tongue. "Yuck."

Gideon chuckled, eyeing his mug with mock suspicion. He mused, not for the first time, that an ale-brewing contest might make a fine family project one day.

Heather took another cautious sip of her metallic ale, then grinned mischievously. "How about *Dryad's Bare Butt Ale?* That's what I'd name mine."

Gideon nearly choked, snorting a mouthful of ale through his nose as he burst into laughter. He grabbed his sleeve to wipe his face, still grinning. "Your brothers would love that one. They'd demand you make a whole cask."

They savored the rest of their meal in companionable silence, watching the tavern slowly fill with patrons as the day wore on. The low murmur of conversation blended with the occasional burst of laughter or clink of tankards. Outside, shadows stretched longer on the cobbled street.

At last, as the barkeep cleared their plates, Heather's expression shifted—her easy smile fading to something more serious.

"Do you think Finola's still alive?" Heather asked quietly.

Gideon's face grew somber. "There's no proof she perished in the fire. Some of the bodies we recovered were her followers… but there's no telling if she was among them."

Heather considered this, her jaw tight. "If she's still out there, she'll try again to take over. Destroying The One Tree was… insane. I still don't understand why she'd do it."

Gideon's expression darkened. He shook his head, as if some long-buried suspicion had resurfaced. "You know… it's possible she didn't care about becoming Grand Druid at all. What if her goal all along was to destroy The One Tree so she could plant her own acorn somewhere? Create her own Druid's Glen—and seize control of the Druid Council that way?"

Heather's eyes widened. "She'd have control over everything."

Gideon nodded. "If Thatara chooses her acorn to replace The One Tree… she could found her own druidic circle. A rival council that answers only to her. But having control over The One Tree doesn't assure her of power."

Heather clenched her fists. "If she controls The One Tree, maybe she could manipulate druid travel and communication. Maybe she's figured something out."

Gideon reached across the table and placed a comforting hand over hers. "We'll pray to Thatara that she chooses our acorn instead. Her wisdom will guide us. A single tree will retain the magic… and we'll know soon enough if Druid's Glen begins to form naturally."

Heather took a deep breath, her resolve firm. "And if it doesn't?"

"Then we'll fight, Heather," Gideon said quietly, a steely edge in his voice. "As druids have fought before, to protect Thatara's will."

The tavern owner returned, asked if they needed anything else, and nodded politely as Gideon placed a silver piece on the table. Heather made a half-hearted attempt to finish her ale, but after a sip, she wrinkled her nose and slid the tankard over to her father, who finished it with a shrug.

"Come on," he said, rising from his seat. "Let's go find your brothers. One rootwalk should bring us close to their camp. We'll walk the rest of the way."

Heather buckled her short sword at her side, slung her pack over one shoulder, and followed her father into the twilight streets of Kaalnaes—her heart heavy with questions, but steadied by purpose.

Despite her injury, Finola endured the agony left by the destruction of The One Tree. Burns marred the left side of her body and face, and her left hand remained nearly useless—stiff, swollen, and slow to heal.

The moment replayed endlessly in her mind—the kegs of oil igniting, the blast wave melting everything in its path. Even now, she could feel the heat on her skin, smell the scorched oil and flesh, hear the screams of her followers.

In her good hand, she clutched the defunct coin—her salvation in the fire. She kept it clenched at all times, unwilling to let it go.

Since the inferno, she had refused to look into a mirror or glimpse her reflection in water. Her hair had been singed to uneven stubble, and one of her followers had shaved her head clean. She could only imagine how monstrous she must look.

Ointments and salves covered her wounds, soothing the rawest patches. Elixirs of Tidall and healing spells had helped, but only to a point. The pain lingered. She groaned softly as she swung her legs over the side of the bed and eased her feet into heavy leather slippers— thick-soled, suitable for the outdoors.

A knock came at the door. It opened a moment later to reveal a burly man in black robes, his deep cowl shadowing his face.

"He has arrived," he said.

Finola stood up gingerly. "I will meet him in Boxfait Glade," she said. "Tell Comrade I will be there shortly."

The guard nodded and departed, shutting the door behind him.

She limped toward the dresser, bracing herself against the ache that flared with every shift of her left side. A blanket had been draped over the mirror—her own doing—and now, with reluctant hands, she pulled it free and tossed it onto the bed.

Her heart sank at the sight that met her.

Once a woman of ethereal beauty and poise, she now bore the scars of her own making. The left side of her body was a ruin of blistered, healing flesh—a permanent mark of the fire she had set upon The One Tree. Her hand trembled at rest, nearly useless, her fingers curled like a wilted leaf. Every step, every breath sent new waves of pain radiating up her arm and shoulder.

Worst of all was her hair. Once long and silken, it had been singed down to stubble. Where it hadn't burned, it had been shaved, uneven and coarse. She barely recognized the woman in the mirror—scarred, hollow-eyed, and stripped of every illusion of grace.

A sharp pang of regret gripped her.

This was the cost of ambition. It had etched itself into her flesh, carved away the person she had once been. She looked away, her vision blurring as grief twisted in her chest. She could not bear to face what she had become—not yet.

She grabbed the fox mask and carefully fitted it over her face, then reached for her black robe. Her left arm resisted, the pain sharp and immediate, but she gritted her teeth and forced it through the sleeve. The cowl followed, drawn up over her head with trembling fingers.

It had to be this way. Her injuries were too severe to shapeshift into her fox form. Recovery would take time, and even then, her body would never be the same. Her beauty—once a weapon as sharp as any blade—had been irreversibly marred.

Was it worth it?

She didn't know how many Archdruids had survived the fire. No doubt, new acorns had already been planted across the world. She had a head start, but in the grand rhythm of the cosmos, that meant little. What mattered was which seed took hold first, which acorn rooted into the living network. She was counting on that logic—that the first to root would become *The One Tree*.

And if she was right, it would be hers. Not just *a* One Tree, but *her* One Tree—reborn under the banner of the Shadow Circle, a sacred weapon to subvert civilization from its roots.

On her writing desk lay an ancient tome, its cracked leather cover dulled with age, but its spine still gleaming with gold arcane sigils. *The Shadowmaster's Testament*—part autobiography, part doctrine, part magical treatise—passed down through generations of her order. It could only be read by moonlight, its words inked in true shadow.

The tome had led her to another volume, buried at the bottom of a forgotten chest amid other relics of power: *Arcane Eclipse: The Point of Balance.*

Her time in recovery had not been wasted. She had devoured its contents, slowly unraveling its layered spells. Three in particular stood out—but they required components and assistance she could not summon alone. For that, she needed the Wizards of Arcana. She needed Comrade.

Finola tapped the cover of *The Shadowmaster's Testament*, then turned toward the door, her resolve sealed beneath the fox's mask.

She emerged from her cabin, a modest structure nestled among the pine trees of the deep forest. Their camp lay far from any town or trade road—hidden from the reach of kings and common folk alike.

This place was simply known as Shadow Grove.

Remote, tangled, and treacherous, the land was a snarl of undergrowth and ancient roots, impassable on foot or horseback. Towering pine trees dominated the landscape, their trunks thick as towers, their limbs knit together in a shadowed canopy that choked out the sun. These were old trees—sentinels of an older world—and their presence lent the grove a silence that felt half sacred, half haunted.

The small village within consisted of wooden cabins and structures built for the needs of those who served the Shadow Circle. Here, they lived apart from civilization, self-sufficient and devout, thriving in the wilds they revered and defended.

Here, under the dark boughs of the forest, the Shadow Circle plotted.

Their purpose was clear: to erode the reach of civilization, to unmake the cities, the keeps, the roads—to return the world to wildness.

At the grove's heart was Boxfait Glade—the place of gathering, judgment, and doctrine. The glade was ringed by gnarled trees, their trunks carved with ancient runes that shimmered faintly when the moon was high. The forest floor was layered thick with needles, swept clear only at the center, where the bonfire pit lay dormant.

Even now, the glade chilled her.

The rune-marked trees stood close, unnaturally so, their bark warped and blackened, coated in blotches of cancerous fungi. They were part of the ritual. They were shaped by the magic of the Circle, their scars a byproduct of power and sacrifice.

And there, beside the bonfire pit, stood the execution tree.

A grim reminder of failure. Of what happened to those who strayed, who faltered. The bark there was scorched and twisted, the rope still hanging limp, swaying slightly in the still air.

Finola paused at the edge of the glade, her gaze on the ring of trees.

This was the cost. This was the creed. And she had made her choice.

As she walked, followers acknowledged their leader with respectful bows and clenched-fist salutes to their chests. Two of her Archdruids—Squirrel and Wolf—stood near the cords of wood stacked for the central bonfire, speaking in hushed tones. At her approach, they fell silent, turning to watch her pass.

She wasn't sure what lingered in their eyes—disdain, disgust, or admiration.

Comrade waited alone, as always, flanked by the guards stationed near the execution tree. He wore the ceremonial robes of the Wizards of Arcana—flowing, expensive, and woven with magic—reserved only for the most accomplished of their order. Even at rest, they shimmered faintly in the light, as if reacting to the presence of unseen arcane forces.

He looked taller than she remembered. Then again, her senses had not been reliable since the fire. Every step brought fresh pain; every shift of her body a reminder of what she had lost.

As instructed, he wore a mask.

This was their first meeting in daylight—a choice he had insisted upon. Finola found herself wondering if the wizard feared the night, or the secrets that stirred in the deep forest after dusk.

She pressed forward, the stiff edges of her fox mask scraping against her ruined skin. The scent of her own blood seeped past the salves and bandages, mingling with the pines. It sickened her.

She endured the agony in silence, gritting her teeth—only for her jaw to throb in protest.

At last, she exhaled a breath she hadn't realized she was holding and spoke, voice steady despite the pain.

"Comrade. Welcome again to Boxfait Glade."

He inclined his head. "An interesting name. Boxfait, if I recall correctly, is derived from the High Ornst phrase for *promising fate*." He paused, eyes unreadable behind the mask. "Now… tell me what happened in Druid's Glen."

"It was a success," she said, though the weight of her disfigured face made it feel like failure. "The One Tree has been destroyed, crippling the network of living things and severing long-range communication and travel. Plant-speak and tree-stride are now severely limited. Druids—shadow and otherwise—can still move through the world, but only across short distances. We are encumbered."

Comrade tilted his head. "Curious. That consequence is… unexpected, given your stated desire to restore nature. I suspect this was your plan all along—not to seize The One Tree, but to destroy it. Plans within plans."

"There are times when you must burn a forest to begin anew," she said. "The Druid Council has been destabilized—for now. But they will recover. In time, they'll take action… and that may lead them here." She turned slightly, gesturing toward the trees. "Come. Walk with me. I have something to show you."

They passed through Boxfait Glade and onto a narrow path that wound between ancient pine trunks. Each step was marked by the soft crunch of fallen needles beneath their boots. For a time, they walked in silence.

Comrade moved ahead, his stride quick and effortless, but when he noticed her lagging, he slowed.

"You are injured?" he asked, his tone oddly sincere.

"Those who survived didn't escape unscathed. We lost many in the assault—more still to the fire. Few of my druids have returned. But with the network crippled, I suspect some are simply delayed. I'll take full inventory in the coming weeks."

"How bad are your injuries?"

Finola paused, weighing the question and its intent. "They will heal. In time, my strength will return."

"Have you lost your ability to shapechange?" he asked. "I've only seen you in fox form."

She hesitated, sensing the test beneath his words. He was measuring her weakness, perhaps even calculating its value.

"My injuries are temporary," she replied. "When my body mends, so too will my other gifts. My mind remains sharp—my will, intact. If that is your concern."

"My concerns are for the Wizards of Arcana, and our objectives," he said coolly. "If you are too weak to lead, then step aside until you are healed."

"Do not test my resolve," Finola snapped, her voice rising with anger.

Comrade didn't reply.

He wasn't sure whether to admire Fox for her sacrifice and resilience—or to file it away with the rest of the lunacy he often attributed to these useful zealots. What once had been a far-fetched notion, whispered among the more reckless members of their order— *What if we disrupted nature's protections? What might be uncovered?*—had now become reality.

And it was the druids who had done it.

The Shadow Circle, of all groups, had burned the very fabric of their own tradition to ashes. The network that cloaked and protected ancient relics was failing, and now, with The One Tree destroyed, long-hidden artifacts would be exposed—artifacts the Wizards of Arcana could seize for their own ends.

The irony wasn't lost on him.

"I'm not testing your resolve," Comrade said after a pause. "I am evaluating. None of our operatives returned with you. It's a disappointing loss of life. Tell me honestly—were you the sole survivor?"

"I'm certain others survived," Finola said. "As I told you, travel is hindered. If any make it back, it will be a welcome surprise."

Comrade's eyes narrowed. "I wonder how *you* managed to escape so easily."

"Why does that matter?" Finola replied, her voice tense.

"It matters," Comrade said, his tone turning sharp, "because you were in the heart of a fortified grove, surrounded by the most powerful druids in the realm. And yet—here you stand. Not unscathed, no, but alive." His gaze lingered on her burned features. "Luck only stretches so far, Fox. I'd like to know how you achieved it."

Finola's eyes narrowed behind her fox mask. "You doubt my abilities?"

"Oh, not at all," he said, a hidden smirk playing at the corners of his mouth. "But even the most capable of us have limits."

She hesitated, feeling the weight of the defunct coin clenched in her good hand. She could lie—but the Wizards of Arcana had their ways of uncovering truth, and withholding would only sharpen his curiosity.

With a reluctant sigh, she extended her hand and opened her fingers, revealing the tarnished, time-worn coin resting in her palm.

"A Coin of Recollection," she said, her tone edged with defiance. "I used it to escape."

Comrade's eyes widened slightly before he caught himself. He stepped closer, peering at the coin without touching it, as though proximity alone might implicate him in some forbidden practice. "Those were outlawed decades ago. The method of their creation was erased from the archives. Who sold this to you?"

Finola's fingers curled slowly around the coin. "I don't reveal my sources—even to allies."

"You do understand the risk," he said, voice low and deliberate. "Whoever provided this knows who you are. That knowledge could become... inconvenient."

"Not if they value their life," she replied. "My intermediaries are loyal. My identity is layered in enough secrecy to keep even you guessing. And now, you're the only one who knows about the coin. I trust you'll keep that knowledge to yourself."

Comrade's gaze lingered on her, thoughtful, calculating. "That remains to be seen," he said at last. "But my interests are best served by your survival, Fox." His voice softened, edged with mockery. "For now."

The path ended in a massive clearing where ancient trees had once stood—trunks felled, stumps removed. Whether by the sweat of labor or the art of magic, it was difficult to tell.

The space opened before them: vast, circular, and raw, bordered by dense forest on all sides. The soil had been freshly tilled, a great expanse of turned earth dark as dusk and damp with promise. At its center, a smaller plot had been marked out—its surface rich and even darker, as if pulsing with latent potential.

They walked in silence, their steps sinking into the soft ground until they reached the hallowed section at the clearing's heart.

"I have replanted The One Tree," Finola said at last, her voice both grim and filled with quiet hope. "If Thatara smiles upon us, this will become The One Tree—ours to nurture, ours to control. Druid's Glen will belong to the Shadow Circle. And with it, we will wield the power to slow the spread of civilization itself."

She let the words settle before continuing. "It may take a year or two before it flourishes. Until then, I've unbalanced nature. But balance will return—whether through me or another druid. Whatever plans you have, make haste. We may have two years, but in the service of chaos, I suggest you act as if we have only two months."

Comrade's expression darkened beneath his mask. A frown creased his brow. "You told us the disruption would last a year," he said, his voice sharp with suspicion. "You've not been honest."

"The One Tree, once it takes hold, will begin the process of reattaching its roots to the network of living things," she said, her gaze fixed on the tiny sapling before them. "But it will remain fragile—weak—unable to fully establish itself for perhaps a year or more. In a matter of months, however, the roots of this tree—or another acorn planted elsewhere—may begin to reach into the network and assert dominance."

Comrade pondered her words in silence, feeling the weight of what was at stake.

The destruction of The One Tree had sent ripples through the natural world, shattering the ancient balance it had once maintained. That upheaval had created cracks in the foundation of druidic magic—

cracks through which opportunity now leaked. Arcane artifacts, long buried and concealed by The One Tree's far-reaching influence, might now surface. Energies once suppressed would awaken, lighting the path for the Wizards of Arcana to follow.

He also considered the fractured state of the druidic orders—their inability to communicate across distance, their sudden isolation. United, they had been formidable. Now, scattered and muted, they posed less of a threat. A forest divided was easier to burn.

"You summoned me," Comrade said at last, his voice calm and precise. "Was it merely to show me this sapling and your garden, or is there something more?"

Finola gestured to the tree. "You see this sapling, don't you? It symbolizes new life—a rebirth, not only for the Shadow Circle, but for the world we seek to shape. Destroying The One Tree came at a high cost, yes. But it was necessary. And now, to see this through, we need your magic."

Comrade rubbed his chin, studying the frail little sapling. It would be so easy to uproot it. To destroy it.

"We are not purveyors of druidic magic," he said at last, his tone skeptical. "We cannot accelerate its growth or force it to bind with the network of living things. I am not yet convinced the Wizards of Arcana have a role to play in this endeavor."

"We have uncovered a Ritual of Rootbinding," Finola replied, her gaze narrowing. "It's old. We need wizards to complete it."

Comrade's eyes widened slightly behind his mask—intrigued, but cautious. "Ancient spells to bind nature itself," he murmured. "And you expect us to perform this ritual?"

"A manuscript," she offered. "*Arcane Eclipse: The Point of Balance.* From it, you may transcribe what spells you wish."

His interest sharpened, though his skepticism held firm. "A generous offer. One that must come with... conditions."

"Two more requests," she said before he could continue. "We must anchor The One Tree in the Plane of Shadow."

His head tilted. "And the third?"

"There is a formula for an ichor of corruption," she said, lowering her voice to a whisper. "A substance potent enough to alter the essence of The One Tree. If it works, it will grant the tree powers unseen in nature. But we need rare and volatile components."

Comrade was quiet for a long moment, weighing the enormity of what she proposed. "This is no small request. Why should we take such a risk? What's in it for us?"

"As I said," Finola replied, "you may transcribe the spells from the tome."

He raised an eyebrow. "And I'm to trust the value of this tome without seeing it?"

"You may look," she said coolly. "But not touch."

He gave a slow nod, accepting the terms for now. For both of them, the cost of betrayal was ruin—but the reward could reshape the world.

They walked back through Boxfait Glade, the towering trees standing like ancient sentinels around them, and entered Finola's residence—a modest cabin bearing quiet signs of its owner's pain and persistence. She gestured for Comrade to sit at the small wooden table where she took her meals. From a nearby shelf, she retrieved an ancient tome and laid it before him with reverence. Another, she held close to her chest, almost protectively.

Comrade leaned in, eyes narrowing with curiosity. He traced the faded lettering on the cracked spine and read aloud, "*Arcane Eclipse: The Point of Balance.*" He looked up at her, unmistakable intrigue flickering in his gaze.

Finola opened the tome carefully, as if afraid it might crumble in her hands. She pointed to the first intricate diagram—a convergence of druidic runes and arcane symbols. Her finger hovered over the faded lines. "This is the Ritual of Rootbinding. It's designed to bind The One Tree's roots deeper into the network, making its connection to the natural flow nearly impossible to sever. But it needs arcane stabilization to hold."

Comrade scanned the page with practiced precision. The structure was familiar—an enchantment he'd seen before in other forms—but this one bore a dangerous volatility. Dark magic braided with natural currents. A single miscast or lapse in focus could backfire catastrophically, flooding the caster's veins with wild, untamed energy.

No wonder the druids distrusted arcane interference, he thought.

Still, he wasn't concerned. The Wizards of Arcana had trained for spells far more treacherous. "A fascinating piece of work," he murmured. "Nothing beyond our capacity—though rarely have we attempted anything on this scale. Ambitious, yes. But not impossible."

Finola turned the page, her tone more grave. "Here—the Shadow Anchor. It will tether The One Tree to the Plane of Shadow, cloaking it from all but the most trained druidic perception. To the uninitiated, it will look like a withered, dying husk. A trick of perception… to keep it hidden."

Comrade's interest sharpened, though he hid it behind a mask of cool detachment. He saw at a glance the danger in the ritual. Anchoring anything—let alone a living entity—to the Plane of Shadow was an undertaking few dared attempt. It demanded exact timing, power, and coordination, with no margin for error. One slip, and the tree could rot from the inside out… taking anyone nearby with it.

But that was a risk worth taking.

Only lesser wizards feared the unknown. To Comrade, this was the sort of endeavor that separated the truly skilled from mere practitioners.

"Complicated," he said with a small, arrogant smile. "But feasible, if done by experts."

Finally, Finola turned to the last page. She hesitated, her fingers hovering over a formula etched in twisting runes and dark, precise instructions.

"And this," she said, her voice dropping to a near whisper, "is the Ichor of Corruption. A potent elixir meant to be poured over The One Tree's roots, forcing it to spread blight through the network. We have some of the ingredients, but others remain elusive."

Comrade's gaze lingered on the list—petrified kraken ink, powdered fey bone, dryad's tears. Each was rare, unstable, and notoriously dangerous to handle. The mixture would pulse with dark energy, potent enough to rewrite the tree's purpose… or unravel the very ground beneath it.

A single misstep could turn the entire forest into a wasteland, he realized with a flicker of unease—then dismissed it.

Or the place it is brewed…

For a lesser wizard, this would be a suicidal endeavor. But Comrade's pride surged at the thought of wielding such dangerous magic.

"It's rare to see druidic magic wielded with such… ambition," he said, his voice thick with admiration, tempered by a simmering sense of superiority. "But the ichor recipe—this is no minor feat. Are you certain your druids can manage it?"

Finola met his gaze. "Our druids will handle their part. But we need the expertise of wizards to harness the full power of these spells—and ensure they don't spiral out of control. We need your experts to find the last few ingredients and brew the potion."

Comrade inclined his head, a surge of satisfaction rising in his chest. *Of course they need us*, he thought, his eyes gleaming behind the mask. This alliance wasn't merely mutual benefit—it was proof of the Wizards of Arcana's superiority. The druids might wield raw magic, but only mastery of the arcane could bring such volatile rituals to life without catastrophe.

"Very well. I will present this to my superiors," he said, his voice laced with confidence. "I think they'll find your proposal… intriguing."

Finola nodded slowly, masking the flicker of doubt that troubled her as she held Comrade's gaze. She was all too aware of the risks she was taking by entrusting him with this knowledge.

Comrade might present himself as an ally, but the Wizards of Arcana were opportunists—known for their self-serving agendas. Would he return as promised? Or take the spells, the ichor formula, and vanish, leaving her—and the Shadow Circle—bereft of the power they'd sacrificed so much to gain?

The thought chilled her, and for a moment, her injuries throbbed, as if to remind her of everything she had already endured for this mission. Handing him copies of the spells, rather than the original tome, had been a calculated choice—one she hoped would keep him tethered to the alliance.

But as she watched him, a shadow of suspicion lingered in her mind.

How much of her trust was real, and how much was merely desperation?

#

Finola was resting, the time spent with Comrade having taken its toll. Every breath felt heavy, the pain in her side an ever-present reminder of what she had sacrificed. Still, she allowed herself a flicker of satisfaction—a confidence that the Wizards of Arcana were now intrigued enough to assist in shaping The One Tree and making it stronger, different, malleable to their needs.

It would become a weapon of the Shadow Circle, to be wielded in ways other druids had never dared to dream.

Not without cost, of course.

For a fleeting moment, she wondered if this path was stripping away the last remnants of the woman she had once been. But regret was a luxury she could no longer afford. There was no return to her former life—none. It was a necessary price, one she was willing to pay to ensure The One Tree flourished under her influence.

After finishing a meager meal, Finola thumbed through the pages of *Arcane Eclipse*.

The worn tome held within it a power and knowledge that still eluded her grasp—rituals, spells, forces she had yet to master, let alone dare to cast. Each incantation felt like a door, one that could swing open to greatness… or collapse into madness. The intricacies of the gestures, the delicacy of each movement, the exact words of power—it was all too advanced for the uninitiated.

Each spell was a dare even to the most seasoned druids—a quiet testament that their understanding was but a shadow of what their forebearers once held, in an age when druids were more than guardians of the wild. Finola had begun to grasp just how much had been lost. She saw patterns others missed, traced echoes of intent older than the Circle itself. The *Arcane Eclipse* was more than a spellbook—it was a relic of memory, of purpose.

And some pages went deeper still. They hinted at relics beyond spells—a puzzle woven through the ink, written not in riddle but in reverence. Clues meant for those who still walked with the trees, who remembered the roots of the world. To others, they might read as metaphor. But to her, they were maps.

She had once thought such a discovery would bring wonder, excitement—vindication. But her instincts held. It filled her instead with dread. Like falling from a cliff, an inevitable plunge into the unknown, the kind that cannot be undone. No flight, no turning back. Only the fall—and the truth that waits at the bottom.

She stood still, cold to her bones, and for the first time in years, Finola shivered.

This remnant… this path she had seen… was not one she would willingly walk.

If all else failed, she might have no choice.

And when that time came, she would not walk it alone—she would not dare walk it alone.

Her gaze drifted to the chest at the foot of her bed—its lock unyielding, its contents potent. More archives rested within, tomes she had yet to fully explore.

From the Shadows, Power Emerges.
Bound by Darkness, Freed by Will.
Betrayer's Knowledge.
Blood and Branch.
Corruption Creation.
The Pact.

Each had its place—each existed to teach, to strengthen, to shape the Shadowmaster into one who could bend nature itself.

A knock at the door broke her musing, and a guard stepped inside. "He has returned," he said, his voice flat.

Finola slipped on her fox mask, wincing as the movement pulled at her damaged skin. With deliberate slowness, she rose from her desk, her left arm hanging useless at her side, her body aching with every step. She limped toward the door, her shadow stretching long across the walls of the dim room.

She greeted Comrade with a nod as he stepped inside. The door shut behind him with a heavy thud, sealing them away from prying eyes.

"I have promising news," Comrade began, his voice muffled by his mask. "Perhaps we can sit at the table."

Finola gestured for him to proceed, and they gathered at the small, battered table. She eased herself down, her right hand braced against the wood for balance while her left remained limp at her side—a constant reminder of her frailty.

"We have decided it is worth the attempt," Comrade said evenly, though his eyes gleamed with excitement. "We will assist you with the rituals and brew the ichor of corruption. In return, we require a full copy of *Arcane Eclipse*—and access to study The One Tree."

Finola's gaze sharpened behind the mask.

Granting access to The One Tree was no small concession. It introduced risk—too much, perhaps. Letting the Wizards observe it directly could expose vulnerabilities, betray the true extent of its power, or worse, tempt them to seize control.

But as their collaboration deepened, such entanglements were becoming inevitable.

"I cannot guarantee The One Tree will permit a non-druid to study it," she said, her tone edged with warning. "The tree is attuned to Archdruids. It may reject you—and that choice lies beyond my influence."

"Will you agree to it in principle?" Comrade pressed, his eagerness seeping through the calm cadence of his voice. She could hear his breathing quicken beneath the mask.

"In principle, yes. But it's no guarantee," she replied. "Not like the spells and potion you're guaranteeing in exchange for the copy of the manuscript."

Satisfied, Comrade nodded and unslung his satchel.

He placed it on the table and carefully removed the rolled pages she had lent him. Handing them back with practiced precision, he then produced a scroll tube—its surface etched with glowing runes and stamped with the insignia of the Wizards of Arcana.

He uncorked it and drew out a parchment, unfurling it across the tabletop.

The edges of the scroll were trimmed in gold leaf, and a lattice of silver script danced across the page in delicate, spellbound elegance. At the bottom, two signature lines awaited. At the center, stamped in gold, was the seal of the Wizards of Arcana: a pentacle ringed with elemental glyphs.

Comrade pushed it toward her.

"A contract?" Finola's voice dripped with disdain.

"Yes," Comrade replied. "A binding agreement between us. It outlines our duties and obligations—including access to The One Tree, in principle. If either party fails to uphold the terms… the consequences will be severe. I'm willing to risk my life for this. Are you?"

Finola took the parchment and began to read.

The terms were clear. The Wizards of Arcana would offer magical assistance—contributing to the rituals that would suppress the spread of civilization and aid in the crafting of the ichor of corruption. They would provide clandestine support to fortify the Shadow Circle's dominion.

In return, they demanded a full transcription of *Arcane Eclipse*, along with continued cooperation in their future searches for lost relics and forbidden artifacts. The agreement would expire only when The One Tree reestablished itself within the network of living things—though access to study it would persist beyond that point.

Finola read each clause twice, her gaze sharp behind the mask. She hunted for veiled contingencies, hidden pitfalls buried in elegant language. Comrade was clever, and the Wizards of Arcana were infamous for exploiting alliances—not honoring them.

As far as she could tell, there was no deceit hidden within the flowing script—no veiled traps or arcane snares. She found herself surprised by the clarity of the terms and appreciated the clause defining an end to their mutual obligations.

"You understand," Finola said, her tone cautious, "that if my One Tree doesn't take root as *The One Tree*, it will not become the heart of the network. There is a chance it will fail. If that happens, you'll have nothing to study."

"We understand," Comrade replied, his gaze steady. "Regardless of which tree takes root, it will be some time before any of them reattach to the network."

Finola eyed him a moment longer, weighing his words. Then she sighed, the sound thin and brittle. "Quill?" she asked, her voice laced with sarcasm.

Without a word, Comrade reached into his robe and withdrew a long, black feather. He jabbed the quill into his fingertip, drawing a single bead of blood, and handed it to her.

"Must I prick myself as well?" she asked, the mask distorting her voice.

"No," Comrade said. "My blood will suffice. But you must sign your true name. *Fox* will not do."

Finola took the feather and dipped it into the crimson drop now resting on the parchment.

She hesitated only a moment, then scrawled her name across the bottom of the contract. The blood shimmered in the candlelight as it dried, the letters binding her to the arcane seal.

Comrade followed suit, pricking his finger again and signing with a smooth, practiced flourish: *Xekius*.

The parchment shimmered faintly, then stilled. The contract was sealed.

Finola's burns itched fiercely beneath the robes. The mask felt like a hot brand against her damaged skin. She was certain a fever was settling into her bones, her body beginning to rebel against the demands she placed upon it.

But none of it mattered. A new moon was approaching, and when it rose, she would demand the first two spells be cast—Rootbinding and Shadow Anchor—with her druids standing ready to fulfill their part of the ritual.

The One Tree would soon be theirs, reshaped through the combined power of druids and wizards. Finola knew the Wizards of Arcana saw the Shadow Circle as little more than useful zealots, but this alliance—this painful, treacherous path—was the only way forward. They would destroy the nature civilization relied upon in order to save what mattered most.

"The new moon approaches," she said, her voice tight with resolve. "Be prepared to join us for the Rootbinding and Shadow Anchor rituals."

Comrade gave a slight nod, his gaze drifting toward the ceiling as though already calculating logistics. "I will need additional wizards for the Shadow Infusion," he said, correcting her with maddening calm.

"Infusion?" she asked, narrowing her eyes.

"The arcane spell, while often translated as *anchor*, is in fact *infusion*. It will infuse the Plane of Shadow into your tree."

"But will it have the same effect?"

Comrade bowed slightly. "Yes. The tree will be anchored to the Plane of Shadow. I trust that is acceptable?"

"It is necessary," Finola replied, her voice low, final. "But do not forget—we can bring down your towers."

"Spare me the threats," Comrade said, his voice suddenly weary. "We are in this too deeply to turn back now."

He tapped the edge of the table with two fingers. "We'll honor our end of the bargain. Expect us at the new moon—hopefully with the potion complete. I will contact you if I have questions."

Finola nodded, her movements slow and deliberate as she reached up and pushed back her cowl. She removed the fox mask, wincing as the cool air met her scarred skin, tugging at the half-healed wounds beneath.

Across the table, Xekius removed his cloth mask, revealing his face in kind.

"Outside this cabin, we wear our masks," she said, her voice quiet but firm. "I will regain my strength—and my ability to shapechange— in time."

Xekius regarded her with unreadable eyes. There was a flicker of pity there, perhaps respect. Her face was no longer the visage of ethereal beauty it had once been—now it was harder, wounded but unbowed. Yet her eyes, sharp and burning with defiant will, remained unchanged.

Without a word, Xekius rolled up the contract and slid it back into his satchel. Then he stood, gave a shallow bow, and spoke a single word of power.

Magic coiled around him, spiraling up like smoke. In a breath, he vanished, leaving behind only a faint shimmer in the air.

As the magic faded, so did the warmth in the room. The light felt dimmer, the walls closer. Alone once more, Finola sat in silence, her gaze lingering on the space where Xekius had stood.

The Wizards of Arcana would honor their contract—until it no longer suited them. She had no illusions about that.

With a groan, she pushed herself to her feet. Her entire body ached, her side throbbed in time with her heartbeat, but she had one task left before she would allow herself to rest.

She needed to see The One Tree.

She needed to know it was still there—that all of this suffering had not been in vain.

Painfully, she made her way toward Boxfait Glade. The gray hush of evening had begun to settle over the forest, the sky pale and empty above the trees. The air was cool and sharp with the scent of pine. Without her mask, she felt exposed, vulnerable... but also relieved. She could breathe more freely.

Even if she knew that anyone who looked upon her now would recoil in horror.

As she approached the central glade, a commotion caught her attention.

Warriors, guards, and druids stood clustered tightly around a figure in the clearing, their low murmurs thick with tension. Finola did not hasten her pace—every step was measured, labored—but her presence alone caused the group to part as she neared.

At the center stood a man restrained by two guards, his clothes in tatters, his face bruised and bloodied.

"DeCa?" Finola's voice carried clearly through the glade, quiet yet unmistakable. Her gaze narrowed, recognition dawning. "We thought you were dead. It is... good to see you alive."

DeCa strained against the guards, trying to shrug them off, but his strength was gone. His face bore the unmistakable imprint of Gideon's staff—a deep bruise that had not healed cleanly, evidence of both magic and force.

"I was tricked by Gideon," he spat, his voice ragged with humiliation. "He overpowered me—magic, brute force, both. I returned as quickly as I could, but something's wrong. The network of living things... it feels broken."

Finola's expression hardened, her voice flat. "The One Tree is dead."

A hush fell over the gathering.

She stepped forward, her injured side stiff, every movement a battle. "We have replanted it—*here*, in our grove. If it takes root and flourishes, then The One Tree will be ours. It will belong to the Shadow Circle, not *Taldras Arbo Solien*."

Her eyes locked onto him.

"Where is your talisman?"

DeCa faltered. His head dropped slightly, a flicker of shame passing over his battered features. "Gideon took it."

A silence followed. Heavy. Final.

He had failed her. And in the Shadow Circle, failures were not tolerated. Every weak link endangered the whole. Every loose end threatened to unravel the web she had so carefully spun.

Her face was unreadable beneath the mask—but those closest to her had seen this before.

That stillness meant judgment was coming, and mercy was never part of it.

A surge of anger flared within Finola, heat rising beneath her skin. The salves covering her burns felt as if they were melting into her flesh, pooling at her collar and soaking into the fabric of her robe. The loss of the talisman was not merely an inconvenience—it was evidence. A vulnerability they could not afford.

"Then it was a success?" DeCa asked, hope threading his voice.

Finola's lips twisted into a grimace. "Relatively speaking," she replied. "But as you can see, I am not the Grand Druid. Not yet." Her voice cooled, sharpened. "And I can't help but think your failure played a role in this debacle."

She raised her good hand and flicked her fingers once.

"We do not tolerate failure."

"No!" DeCa screamed, his voice ragged with terror.

The guards struck him hard in the gut. As he doubled over, they forced a gag into his mouth and slipped a black bag over his head. Rope bound his wrists, and a noose was brought and cinched tight around his neck. Without ceremony, they dragged him to the execution tree—its twisted branches already heavy with the scars of past betrayals—and hanged him.

His body jerked once, twice, and then stilled.

Finola turned away, her gaze already shifting toward the heart of the clearing.

She walked with purpose, each step drawing her closer to the sapling that symbolized all they had sacrificed to obtain. Her body screamed with every movement, yet she pressed forward.

Despite her resolve, a quiet truth gnawed at the edge of her mind: nature was fickle, and she was only mortal. She had dared to meddle in divine forces. She had cast the dice—but only Thatara could decide the outcome.

Finola would pray. She would beg for Thatara's favor. And she would hope that their gamble would pay off.

Taldras Morilenn would rise.

As the new power in the world.

- 432 -

Chapter Twenty-Five

∞

Through the Veil

Cedric was walking back from the base camp with Chefera, troubled by his continued inability to use plant-speak or tree-stride for long distances. Ever since his father left, it was as if the network of living things had simply… vanished. No matter how he tried, the connection refused to open beyond the range of a short walk.

Once inside the magic barrier, he invoked tree-stride and whisked them to a wooded area just outside the keep. Ahead, the mass of golden glory vines writhed gently in the breeze. The protective vines were beautiful to behold, but even their familiar shimmer couldn't shake the unease that had settled in his chest. The wizard had hidden in there once—had spied on them.

Chefera watched him, sensing his worry. "What does it mean if we can't tree-stride like before?" she asked. "How will we get back home?"

Cedric flexed his hands, a hollow ache pressing against his ribs. The One Tree was more than a network for travel and speech—it was the living heart of their world. A constant, like the breath of the forest itself. Without it, he felt like a leaf cut loose from the branch, adrift in the wind.

"My only conclusion is something's happened to The One Tree," he said, his voice tight. "That must be why Gideon was recalled to Druid's Glen so urgently. I'm worried for him. Losing the connection… it could mean an attack. Or a takeover of Druid's Glen." He paused, realization striking hard and fast. "Heather! My sister Heather is there. Alone." His voice caught. "Shades, I didn't even think of that."

Chefera placed a reassuring hand on his arm, her cleric's calm grounding him. "Don't lose heart, Cedric," she said, her voice serene. "Thatara's watchful gaze is with your father and sister—and with Aaron, Wellsey, and Aurora too. Thatara protects the faithful. We're seldom alone, even when we feel we are."

"I do have faith," Cedric replied, the words tasting bitter. "I just feel helpless. Like I should be doing something."

They approached the keep, bypassing the virulent, protective vines and stepping into the courtyard. Their camp was undisturbed—quiet, just as they had left it. The keep's doors stood slightly ajar, and inside, Wilmund was near the Mage-Gate, relaxed but alert.

Spider lay nearby, eyes half-closed yet watchful.

Val, Sarif, Doud, and Garret were gathered farther off, speaking in hushed tones.

Cedric approached, the frustration bubbling out of him.

"Something's wrong with The One Tree," he said. "We tried green-speak and rootwalk—nothing works. I can only rootwalk a mile or two, maybe a little farther, but nothing long-range. Anything beyond that just… fails. If we're right, it would take us four days to reach the Needle Forest, even using our combined efforts. The network isn't functioning."

"Four days?" Wilmund asked, his expression darkening. "Is that why Gideon had to leave so suddenly?"

"I can only assume that's the reason. There must have been a threat to The One Tree, and he had to go." Cedric's voice softened as he grappled with the implications. "But what concerns me—now that I've had a moment to think—is why he didn't take us with him. He must have known we'd want to help."

Wilmund's face remained calm, but he took a steadying breath, his gaze drifting across the anxious expressions of his companions. Then, in a voice edged with quiet authority, he said, "We'll understand things when he returns. Perhaps he couldn't take you."

Cedric's heart twisted at the thought. "That would mean the threat was to him, not us… but my sister…" The words came out as a whisper. He tried not to picture Heather standing alone in their home, surrounded by unknown danger. A knot of dread tightened in his stomach.

"Gideon can take care of himself—and your sister," Wilmund said, though his gaze softened with understanding. "You're not the only one with family to worry about. He'll do whatever it takes to protect her."

Cedric nodded, though the worry refused to leave him. "If we're lucky, it'll only be four or five days before he's back."

He turned toward the Mage-Gate. "Any change?"

Wilmund shook his head. "No change. We'll keep watching it until Gideon returns."

Cedric felt the restlessness rise again, a wave of helpless urgency. "I feel like we should go through and at least help them. If they're in danger, we don't have much time."

His eyes lingered on the Mage-Gate, its shimmering surface reflecting eerie, shifting light. There was something almost sinister about it—a sensation that prickled at the back of his neck. And yet, part of him was drawn to it, as if the portal whispered promises of answers just out of reach.

Wilmund held up a hand, his expression turning stern. "Everyone stays here. For all we know, stepping into that is instant death, or it leads to an inescapable prison. For all we know, Aaron, Wellsey, and Aurora are trapped or dead. We wait until we have facts to act on, not emotions."

He held Cedric's gaze, then lowered his hand. As he did, Wilmund's own hand brushed against the small dagger at his belt—a habit he'd recently developed.

But this time, he recoiled from it as though it had burned him.

Cedric noticed the reflex and felt a surge of unease. Wilmund was always calm, the steady heart of their order. If he was struggling to find peace, then perhaps the situation was graver than Cedric had feared.

The room fell silent, each of them wrestling with their own worries and suspicions. Cedric looked around, taking in the tense faces of his companions and the foreboding presence of the Mage-Gate. Despite Wilmund's reassurances, he couldn't shake the feeling that something was terribly, irreversibly wrong.

Two days passed, and tension thickened among the group as they kept their vigil over the Mage-Gate. Patience frayed with each passing hour, and the hope for Aaron, Wellsey, and Aurora's return dwindled to a fragile thread.

Cedric spent much of the time practicing staff forms, occasionally sparring with the Stairwell rangers. He'd always considered himself proficient—but their skill with blades was humbling. They moved with lethal precision, every feint a trap, every strike a lesson in inadequacy.

By the end of each session, Cedric knew he'd have to rely on spells to keep his distance if he ever faced one of them in earnest. And even then, he wasn't sure it would be enough.

They were just as deadly with a bow.

His respect for their prowess grew—but so did his unease, drawing him back toward the keep, toward the Mage-Gate… and Wilmund.

Inside, he found the dark druid standing near the portal, leaning heavily on his scythe. Wilmund looked drawn, his skin sallow in the cold, eerie glow. The faint hum of arcane energy vibrated in Cedric's bones—a low discomfort he couldn't shake.

"You don't look well," Cedric said softly. "How are you feeling?"

Wilmund looked up. His eyes were glassy, hollow with fatigue. "Not well at all," he murmured. "I think… being near the Mage-Gate is affecting me. I can't explain it, but I feel sick. Not myself."

Cedric hesitated, his grip tightening on his staff. "Then maybe we should step away from it," he said gently. "A few days at The Stately Potato could do us all good. If our friends come back through, they'll find us. But staying here—if it's harming you—is a risk we don't need to take."

Wilmund didn't seem to hear him.

His gaze remained fixed on the Mage-Gate, eyes reflecting the arcane shimmer. Slowly, almost unconsciously, he stepped toward it, his fingers drifting to the dagger at his waist. His expression shifted— awed, almost reverent.

"What a wonder of the ancient world," he murmured, his voice deepening with strange intensity. "We must open our minds to the vast wonders that lie beyond. This is a conduit to forgotten places, where magic flowed like a mighty river… an age of marvels and mysteries, shaped by the hands of mortal gods—the Mages."

He lifted a hand toward the pulsing archway. "This relic stands as a testament to their ambition—and a warning. Beyond it lie realms steeped in legend, strongholds and towers hidden in distant mountains, deserts, and shadowed woods… places where dreams and nightmares intertwine. Together, we could journey into the heart of magic itself— and uncover truths no one has seen in a thousand years."

Cedric felt a chill run down his spine.

Wilmund's voice had changed—distant, detached, as if something else were speaking through him.

He stepped up beside the older druid, placing a firm hand on his shoulder.

"Wilmund," he said, keeping his tone steady, "please, listen to me. I understand the allure of this place, but we can't risk losing more of us. Think of Aaron, Wellsey, and Aurora—they stepped through, and they haven't returned. No matter how wondrous it seems, we can't forget how dangerous it is."

Wilmund blinked, as if waking from a trance. His eyes turned to Cedric, suddenly brimming with unshed tears.

"You're right," he whispered, voice cracking. "I don't know what came over me. I feel... sick... so sick."

The Mage-Gate gave a low, guttural rumble. The hum of arcane energy vanished, and its glow faded to dull, inert stone.

Wilmund clutched his chest, gasped in agony, and collapsed to his knees. His face twisted in pain—and then he slumped forward, unconscious.

The entire group was growing increasingly impatient and uneasy. With each hour that passed, the Mage-Gate remained cold and inert—a silent monument to their frustration. Every time they looked to the portal, hope for Aaron, Wellsey, and Aurora withered a little more.

They felt helpless.

Needing space, Cedric took a long walk outside, the cool air doing little to calm the turmoil in his chest. There had to be something— anything—they could do.

When he returned to the keep, Wilmund was still on the floor, ghostly pale and motionless. Chefera knelt beside him, her hands aglow with healing magic.

Wilmund stirred with a groan, and Cedric rushed to help him sit up. "Take it slow," he said, steadying the older druid. "You were unconscious for hours."

"Rest has brought me clarity," Wilmund rasped. His voice was weak, but resolute. "If we're going to save them, we need to find a way to activate the Mage-Gate. We must."

"That's impossible," Cedric replied, trying not to let frustration slip into despair. "We don't have the knowledge, the magic—there are no instructions. We've scoured this keep and found nothing. I think the wizard shut it down from the other side, sealing it. Maybe it served his purpose, and he doesn't intend to come back."

"He knew we were here," Wilmund muttered, eyes drifting toward the lifeless gate. "He didn't want to face us."

Cedric tightened his grip to steady him as Wilmund swayed on his feet. "Are you sure you're all right?"

Wilmund nodded slowly. "Better. The nausea's easing since the Mage-Gate powered down. But we still need to turn it back on. Maybe the lower dungeons… the room full of tomes and scrolls. It's the one place we haven't searched thoroughly. There might be a clue we missed."

Cedric hesitated, then drew a slow breath. "It's possible," he said. "But we go in together. No more wandering alone. We'll bring everything up from the dungeons and study it as a team. Is that understood?"

Wilmund nodded, though his eyes were distant. "A sensible approach, yes… though every moment we delay, your family—and our friends—face whatever fate lies beyond that gate."

Cedric's fists clenched. "First, we rest," he said firmly. "Four hours. Away from this place. We're all worn thin, especially you, Wilmund. You need time to clear your head and regain your strength."

He cast a glance around at the others, reading the exhaustion in their postures, the tension in their silence. "We'll reconvene outside. Follow me."

Four hours later, they roused Wilmund from a deep, uneasy slumber. Together, they descended into the keep's dungeons, each carrying a weapon or staff lit with soft magical light. The corridors were dimly illuminated by torchless sconces, their pale glow barely enough to see by—just enough to cast long, wavering shadows that danced alongside the flickers from their spells. As they moved deeper, the combined light revealed grotesque bas-reliefs carved into the stone walls—scenes of torture and war rendered with unsettling precision, as if the stone itself still remembered every scream.

They moved with careful steps, bypassing two pentagrams embedded in the floor as they made their way toward the dusty bedchamber lined with ancient tomes, scrolls, and manuscripts. Working in tense silence, they gathered every document they could find, filling sacks with books, loose pages, and brittle scrolls for transport back to the surface.

It took four grueling hours of hauling and sorting before everything was laid out in their makeshift study area.

They organized the materials by type, creating piles of tomes, bound books, scrolls, and scattered parchments. Each pile had two people assigned to it, scanning for anything written in a language they could read. Texts they couldn't decipher were set aside, reserved for anyone with broader knowledge.

Chefera looked up from a stack of scrolls, frustration clear in her expression. "Even if we find something, how will we know it's what we need? Are we even sure what we're looking for?"

Cedric sighed, setting aside another undecipherable volume. "Anything mentioning the Mage-Gate or bearing symbols like the ones on the portal. It's tedious, but it's all we can do."

"We could be at this for a decade and still miss it," she muttered. "It would've been easier to follow the wizard through the portal and make him explain how it works. Too bad that chance is long gone."

Cedric grunted in agreement, flipping through another book filled with strange, swirling script. "Maybe. But a wizard powerful enough to operate the Mage-Gate would likely be beyond our ability to handle. We can only hope our companions managed to avoid him."

As they worked, Cedric couldn't shake his unease. Wilmund seemed different—changed. Since the Mage-Gate had gone dark, the Archdruid's demeanor had shifted from cautious vigilance to something more erratic… almost obsessive. Cedric had caught him more than once muttering under his breath or staring at the inert portal with a strange gleam in his eye. It wasn't the Wilmund he knew.

After a while, Cedric crossed the room to where Wilmund and Spider were sorting through scrolls. "Have you found anything promising?"

Wilmund barely looked up, his fingers trembling slightly as he set aside a scroll. "Nothing yet. Mostly spell inscriptions. Some may prove useful later. But for the Mage-Gate… nothing. Unless we bring wizards here, we may never find the answer."

Cedric frowned. "There's no need to activate it. The Mage-Gates were likely tied to places within our own lands. All we need is for Aaron, Wellsey, or Aurora to get a message to us. Once the network of living things is stable again, they might be able to contact us."

Wilmund's gaze turned distant. "Yes… perhaps. But think of the possibilities, Cedric. These gates were built in the age of the Mages. They might lead to the places where their power was strongest. Just imagine what lies beyond—what knowledge awaits."

There was a reverence in his voice that made Cedric's skin prickle. He straightened and met Wilmund's gaze. "Knowledge can wait. We're here to find our friends and family—nothing more."

Wilmund pulled out a weathered journal, thumbing through pages filled with diagrams and cramped script. "I've compiled records of the Mages' names and supposed strongholds," he said. "Dergan Yholl's fortress was said to be subterranean, hidden beneath a mountain range. And there's mention of another Mage-Gate deep in the southern deserts, somewhere beyond Pehrone."

Cedric leaned in, studying the scrawled notes. A strange unease stirred in his chest. "Nine Mages… but the Mage-Gate has twelve symbols. If their reach spanned that many regions, their empire must've been enormous." He glanced toward the inert portal. "I wish we had a map to compare against."

Wilmund gave a faint smile—wistful, almost boyish. "It would be a grand thing, wouldn't it? To trace their path, to walk the ruins of a forgotten age…"

Cedric pulled his gaze away. The Mage-Gate's allure had burrowed deep into Wilmund—deeper than he'd realized. He turned to the others, his voice firm. "We've done enough for today. Let's rest, eat, and regroup in the morning."

As they packed away scrolls and tomes, Cedric cast one last glance at Wilmund. The Archdruid looked worn thin—his face gaunt, dark circles etched beneath hollow eyes. Though his words still sounded measured, Cedric saw what now lingered behind them: not wisdom, but hunger. A growing obsession that, if left unchecked, might consume him.

Three days had passed with no meaningful progress. The group was weary and discouraged, having sifted through scrolls and tomes until the words blurred together without yielding anything of value about the Mage-Gate. Each day felt more like an exercise in futility, and each night, as they sat around the fire, their hope for Aaron, Wellsey, and Aurora dimmed a little further.

That evening, Cedric sat outside his tent, staring into the darkness as he smoked his pipe. The sun had long since vanished, leaving only the hush of starlight, and the campfire had burned down to low, pulsing embers. He let the smoke curl lazily into the air, his thoughts drifting—his father, Heather, the fate of their friends.

Val, one of the Stairwell rangers, settled beside him without a word, eyes following the slow dance of smoke into the sky.

"That a good pipe blend?" Val asked.

Cedric nodded. "It is. You carry one?"

Val gave a faint smile and shook his head. "Don't partake. It reminds me of my Papa, though. He was a ranger. And my Da."

Cedric caught the phrasing. "From Ornst, then?"

"A long time back. I think most folks come out of Ornst, whether they stay or not. It's the beating heart of civilization around here." He paused, eyes distant. "Though it's not as peaceful as it used to be. Leskaré's got a firm grip on it now."

Cedric drew slowly from his pipe, letting the words settle. "I've heard of Leskaré. Smugglers. Thieves."

"Not only thieves," Val said, his voice low, touched with warning. "They've got a network that runs deeper than most know. Not as bloody as the Black Storm, but clever—and just as dangerous. They've infiltrated courts, guilds, markets. And they hate the Stairwell. Always watching for us. Always waiting." He sighed. "Ornst is one of the few places we're not welcomed with open arms."

Cedric nodded slowly. "Sounds like your responsibilities stretch far beyond the wilds. You're policing cities, too."

Val shrugged. "Where law bends, the Stairwell straightens it."

Cedric looked down at the glowing bowl of his pipe. "I don't envy you. Our charge as druids is simpler—protect nature, maintain balance."

Val gave a short chuckle. "Balance," he echoed. "Hard thing to find these days."

"The Stairwell… you take care of everything."

"Sometimes it feels that way," Val said with a soft chuckle. "We've got treaties with dukes, earls, barons—each one tangled in its own mess of politics. There's corruption in our ranks too, and bureaucracy slows everything down. And sometimes, we just don't have the numbers."

Cedric exhaled a long stream of smoke. "Well, at least you work together. Druids… not so much. We stick to our own groves and territories. This expedition is the exception, not the rule."

Val gave him a thoughtful look. "You know, we could use more druids in the Stairwell. Someone with your skills would be a real asset."

Cedric laughed quietly, shaking his head. "I appreciate that. But my path leads elsewhere."

"Had to ask." Val stood and stretched, his gaze drifting toward the tents. "The mercenaries are on first watch. They'll wake me later. You should try to get some rest."

"Not far behind you," Cedric said, tapping the ashes from his pipe.

When he finally slipped into his tent and closed his eyes, he could only hope that tomorrow would bring answers instead of more questions.

A noise woke him—faint, but insistent. Cedric blinked, the fog of sleep clinging to his thoughts, and slowly became aware of a presence in his tent. Light bloomed softly as he sat up, squinting to see Chefera standing over him, her face tight with concern.

"Wake up," she whispered. "Wilmund, Spider, Doud, and Garret are gone."

Cedric's mind struggled to process her words. "Gone?"

"No one woke Val or Sarif for their watch. When they finally stirred on their own, they found the others missing. Their supplies are gone too—everything but their tents."

Cedric threw on his druid robes and stepped out into the dead of night. Chefera led him to the fire circle, where Val and Sarif were hastily gearing up, grim-faced and quiet.

"We won't be able to track them properly until dawn," Val said, tightening the straps on his pack. "We could try with enchanted light, but daylight will give us the trail. Sarif and I will find them."

"Where would they go?" Cedric muttered, more to himself than to anyone else.

Chefera shook her head. "Your guess is as good as mine."

Cedric cast light on his staff, sweeping it across the quiet camp. Seven tents dotted the courtyard, and a quick scan confirmed only four were now occupied. He ducked into the storage tent and checked the scrolls, tomes, and scattered papers. Everything was untouched, exactly where they'd left it.

He emerged, striding back to Val and Sarif, who were now fully armed and alert.

"Did either of you hear or see anything strange?" Cedric asked.

Val frowned, shaking his head. "Nothing. It's like they vanished."

Cedric's brow furrowed. His mind reeled, trying to make sense of it. "If it was personal, they would have told us. If they sensed danger, they would have raised the alarm. No… they must've discovered something about the Mage-Gate."

"That's why we stopped yesterday," Chefera said. "Wilmund seemed… different. Maybe he found what he was looking for and didn't want to keep searching with us."

"Then he might have figured out how to activate the Mage-Gate." Cedric's face darkened. "But why keep it from us?"

The four companions exchanged uneasy glances, eyes drifting toward the keep looming in the shadows. Its massive doors stood barely visible in the gloom, the carvings of Mikal Yholl's reign etched deep into the ancient wood—twisted, arcane patterns that whispered of a darker time.

They approached cautiously, stopping just short of the entrance. Val and Sarif braced themselves, pushing hard against the doors, but they didn't budge. Cedric felt the wrongness settle over him like a heavy fog—an aching certainty that their companions were beyond those doors, unreachable.

"Stand back," Chefera said, murmuring a spell. A soundless ripple of force struck the wood, but the doors remained unmoved.

Val and Sarif tried again, muscles straining. "It's no use," Val panted, stepping back. "It's physically barred. From the inside."

Cedric stepped forward, raising his voice. "Wilmund! Open the doors! Let us in!"

Silence.

"If he's locked us out," Val muttered, eyeing the keep's dark windows, "we'll have to go in from above. Second floor's climbable—unless you've got magic that can help?"

"Climbing is safest," Cedric said. "You and Sarif get inside and unbar the doors if you can. But assume nothing. If they're not themselves, don't trust them. Don't... kill them."

Val and Sarif nodded grimly and moved into position, securing grappling hooks and ropes to scale the stone face. Cedric stepped back and began casting, his skin becoming rough like bark. Chefera whispered her own spell, her expression hardening as the familiar glow of warding light wrapped around her fingers.

As the rangers disappeared over the ledge, Cedric tightened his grip on his staff, heart pounding. Whatever they found beyond those walls, he knew one thing for certain—Wilmund and the others weren't the same. And if the Mage-Gate had taken hold of them, it might not let them go.

The evening stars shone above, casting a pale, haunting light over the keep. Wilmund—no, *Exon*—stood before the ancient structure, marveling at its silent grandeur. Now he understood why Mikal Yholl had chosen this place. It was inaccessible, self-sufficient, and isolated—a fortress meant to outlast the ages.

Exon found himself impressed, though he knew his own stronghold had once rivaled this one. While the Infernal Sanctum was buried deep and secret, Gatebreaker, his keep, had stood on the edge of a living empire. A stone avenue stretched from the great city of Lyrom to its gates, lined with immaculate towers, reverent shrines, great libraries, and schools dedicated to knowledge. All of it devoted to him.

To Exon.

To the Mage.

A cool breeze swept across his face. He closed his eyes and breathed it in.

He had a face.

He had hands.

Thanks to the ingenious Mage-Core, an invention of Mikal's infinite and insightful magic, he was whole again.

After centuries of bodiless entrapment, the feel of flesh—of Wilmund's calloused fingers, the subtle tension in muscle and sinew—was intoxicating.

He flexed his fingers slowly, marveling at the strength he could channel through bone and blood. There was power in this body, both old and new.

With renewed purpose, he strode toward the keep. The Mage-Gate awaited, and with it, the next stage of his plan. Quietly, he began to speak the ancient words, arcane syllables flowing like silk from his lips, each one binding strands of ambient magic into a lattice of will and control.

He repeated the incantation, stronger with each utterance, until he felt the enchantment tighten, ready to ensnare.

From the shadows, Doud emerged—the sellsword who had accompanied them on this expedition.

Exon met his eyes, let the moment stretch, then released the spell.

The net of magic snapped around Doud's mind like a vice.

And the first thread of control was drawn taut.

"I will need you to protect me without fail," Exon intoned, his voice layered with command and subtle power. "Eliminate any threat. Go to your tent and pack your things. We are going home."

Doud nodded once. "Yes," he said, his voice flat, eyes glazed. Then he turned and walked away, unaware of the spell's grip closing around his mind like iron bands.

Exon allowed himself a slow smile, pleased by the ease of the ensnarement. But as he turned to cast again, the toll of the magic became undeniable. His shoulders sagged. Each invocation drained him more than expected.

It had been too long since he'd shaped magic through muscle and breath. He had forgotten the toll it took on a body—this body. He couldn't bind them all. Perhaps one more.

He followed Doud to his tent, where Garret sat unstrapping his boots. Exon raised his hand. The enchantment loosed with a silent pulse, flowing like mist across the space and coiling around Garret's will.

"I will need you to protect me without fail," he repeated, softer this time, his breath beginning to catch. "Eliminate any threat. Pack your things. You, Doud, and I are going on a splendid journey. We're going home."

Garret nodded, already moving.

Staggering slightly, Exon ducked out into the cool night. His strength was flagging, his limbs leaden. One more—he could manage one more.

Not Cedric. His will was too strong, too guarded.

Not Chefera. The cleric's divine protections would resist him and possibly break his hold.

That left Spider.

Spider, the odd one. Loyal. Quiet. Curious. His magic was strange and instinctive—a hybrid of arcane and nature, not unlike the kind Exon had once dabbled in himself. And more importantly, Spider didn't question authority. Not if it wore the right mask.

Exon slipped into Spider's tent.

The young man was coiled under his blanket, half-asleep, eyes fluttering open as Exon sat beside him.

"Archdruid?" Spider asked groggily.

Exon smiled, drawing the spell to his lips.

"Don't mind me," Exon said. "I'm going to pray for a bit."

"Just keep it down," Spider muttered, closing his eyes.

Exon began the incantation, forcing the words through gritted teeth as the strain mounted. He could feel Wilmund's body resisting—muscles tightening, breath shortening, heart laboring—but he pushed through. With the final words, the web of magic settled over Spider, binding him.

"I will need you to protect me without fail," Exon commanded, his voice heavy with magic. "Eliminate any threat. Doud and Garret are your allies. Pack your things for a splendid journey. We are going home."

Spider's eyes flickered, his brow furrowing in confusion. "What are you talking about?" he whispered, clutching his head.

A splitting pain ripped through him, and he fell to his knees, blood trickling from his ears. Exon narrowed his eyes, furious at the resistance.

"If you resist," he said, "you will die. Eventually. Pack your things. We are leaving."

After a moment, Spider nodded weakly and began gathering his belongings, his movements slow and measured.

Satisfied, Exon allowed himself a moment of rest—but the exertion had taken its toll. He reached up, wiping away a thick trickle of blood from his nose with the back of his hand. His heart pounded like a war drum inside his chest, each beat a jarring pulse of pain. For a moment, he thought it might tear free from his ribs.

He leaned against the tent frame, swallowing down the nausea rising in his throat.

Too much. Too fast.

But they were his now. His guardians.

And soon, he would reclaim what was his.

Deep in the night, a weary but resolute Exon led his three enthralled companions through the gates of the keep. They barred the doors with thick planks of wood, then Exon pressed a trembling hand against the frame and murmured a sealing phrase. The locking spell flickered to life—weak, but sufficient. He had nothing left.

He guided them onward, drawn by the pulse of arcane energy that still hummed through the stone bones of the ruin. Each step brought them closer to the Mage-Gate, and as it came into view, Exon's expression shifted. Satisfaction. Possession.

He climbed the ramp slowly, reverently. His voice fell into the cadence of an ancient tongue, each syllable threading through the air like silk woven from memory. The language curled into the silence, reawakening the slumbering portal.

The Elder Runes along the arch shimmered and ignited, one by one, until the keep trembled with power. A deep vibration pulsed beneath their feet, as though the very earth remembered.

Exon raised his gaze to the twelve runes etched above the gate—symbols that once marked the limits of the world.

He recognized them all. Especially the four sanctums he and Mikal had crafted in secret, hidden from the others.

TA. AA. VA. KA.

Their experiments.

Four societies, each unique, each a marvel—or a cruelty—of design.

He, Enora, and Mikal had visited them often, stepping through the Mage-Gate to observe their progress like gods peering into seed-realms. They watched, studied, even interfered. Sometimes subtly. Other times not. Ozumonar had joined them on occasion, though always reluctantly. He preferred the shadows of his fortress, *Achivum Maledictum*, where every hallway was lined with spells of suspicion and control. Exon couldn't help but wonder what had become of Oz—if he had survived, or if his caution had ultimately undone him.

Thalraya—an island bound by the old feudal codes. Lords ruled with lineage and sword, their dominions carved into gentle valleys and misty highlands. The society was elegant in its simplicity: duty, loyalty, and service. Crops bloomed in three seasons, but in winter, when the winds from the north howled and ice sealed the harbors, starvation loomed. The Mages had once destroyed the grain stores in mid-autumn, curious to see if the people would rebel or submit. Some turned to cannibalism. Others built shrines of bone and prayed for deliverance. One lord declared himself the true heir to the gods and was struck down by lightning—not by divine wrath, but by Enora's spell.

Aridaya—a desert kingdom along the Brisdosa River, a marvel of irrigation and order. Here, civilization flourished in the sand. Tens of thousands worked in harmony, harvesting dates, barley, and lotus-root. The people worshipped the Mages as divine avatars, crafting temples of marble and obsidian where high priests chanted oaths to their unseen rulers. There were no kings—only councils, elected by merit and age. It was a self-governing system, a curiosity to Mikal, who secretly despised the absence of hierarchy. Once, they poisoned the river upstream to see if the society would crumble. It did not. The people adapted, learned to distill water from the air, and built underground reservoirs. Mikal had grumbled for weeks afterward.

Virdaya—lush, humid, and alive with enchantment. This was a realm of altered Fey, creatures once wild and chaotic, now reshaped by the Mages' will. Nymphs became priests. Dryads were bound to trees far from their kin. Pixies served as scribes and record-keepers. The society was layered in ritual and arcane ceremony, its structure delicate and strange. The Mages had embedded subtle compulsions in the people's minds—suggestions, really—to see how deeply order could root in chaos. Sometimes they reversed the spells mid-century just to watch the societal collapse and confusion. Once, a Fey queen tore her own wings off in protest. Exon found it exhilarating.

Kaldaraya— frozen for most of the year, its inhabitants were resilient, austere, and endlessly practical. Situated in the northern wastes, it was a society ruled not by kings or councils, but by stewards who believed their true rulers would one day return. A people shaped by hardship and forged in myth. They worshipped the absent monarchs in silence, building monuments of ice, waiting with a faith colder than the land itself. The Mages would visit only in summer, when the snows receded and daylight stretched for nearly a day without end. Once, they salted the soil and brought blight to the stored seed. Half the population perished, but the stewards rebuilt, calling it a trial from the gods. Mikal wept from laughter.

Each society had been a living thesis—proof of what magic and manipulation could do. But centuries had passed. Civilization adapts. Memory fades.

And now, Exon was eager to see what had endured.

In the air, he traced the four runes etched into the stone of the Mage-Gate arch:

TA. AA. VA. KA.

Thalraya. Aridaya. Virdaya. Kaldaraya.

Their experiments.

Their dominions.

Their legacy.

Enora… He wondered—had Mikal saved her, as he had saved him, Exon? Had he infused her essence into a vessel, securing her for resurrection as he had done for himself with a Mage-Core?

Where would he have hidden her Mage-Core?

Could it be found?

The Mage-Gate pulsed before him, its runes alive with power, urging him to choose. Memories cascaded over him—triumphs and betrayals, love and fury—all the final thoughts he'd known before his soul, mind, and essence were sealed into the Mage-Core.

From that instant onward, nothing more would reach him. Time would move, but he would not.

AB — Abyssal Bastion — Dergan Yholl. Traitor. Demon-bound filth. The greatest threat to them all.

VS — Veilspire — Opianne. Her neutrality was her flaw. It killed her in the end: he was sure of it.

SC — Shadowfang Citadel — Carick. Dergan's lackey. A snake in service to the Abyss. Also traitor.

TK — Tower of Knekora — Utaz. Quiet, reclusive, his dominion cloaked in the endless forest, but too close to Dergan's sanctum for his liking. Another who watched but did not act.

WM — Wintermourne — Enora. Friend. Ally. Lethal and beautiful. He dared to hope he could find her Mage-Core.

AM — Achivium Maledictum — Ozumonar. Reclusive genius. Rarely seen. Often feared.

HK — Hollowkeep — Striviar. An enigma, neither friend nor foe.

GB — Gatebreaker — His own citadel. The jewel of southeastern Troasia. And Lyrom—his city. His people.

And then the last four—the secret experiments:

TA — Thalraya.

AA — Aridaya.

VA — Virdaya.

KA — Kaldaraya.

He focused on one: GB.

His domain. His fortress. His throne.

Gatebreaker.

Exon's lips parted in the first true smile he'd felt in centuries. With a final invocation, he wove the ancient words and poured what strength remained into the spell. The Mage-Gate responded, the twelve runes blazing like stars as the interior whirled to life, revealing a shimmering portal into his past—his future.

The sight filled him with awe. He would return. He would reclaim Gatebreaker. Lyrom would rise again, and with it, his name.

A shockwave of magic rippled through the keep.

He stiffened.

The wards on the doors collapsed, melting away with a soft hiss of displaced power.

Only the wooden bars remained.

Outside, the voices grew louder. Urgent. Closer.

Exon turned toward the Mage-Gate one final time, the swirling colors promising legacy, dominion, and glory.

"What are you doing?" Spider gasped, his voice ragged as he clutched his head in pain. Blood trickled from his nose and ears, and his eyes filled with sudden, terrible clarity. "You're… you're not Wilmund."

Exon's eyes narrowed. A flicker of irritation crossed his face. "Idiot," he muttered.

He strode forward and brought the butt of his scythe down hard against Spider's temple. The impact dropped him in a heap, unconscious.

"A waste of magic," Exon said, his voice low with disdain.

Turning back to the Mage-Gate, he extended an unsteady hand toward the portal, breath shallow, heart hammering from overexertion.

"You two," he ordered, pointing to Doud and Garret, "go through. If it is safe, return. If not—make it safe."

Without hesitation, the two warriors obeyed, weapons in hand, vanishing into the swirling vortex.

Exon stood alone before the glowing arch, the colors of the portal reflecting in his eyes. A faint, satisfied smile came to his lips.

Soon, he thought, *Gatebreaker will be mine again. And from there—*
The world.

The rangers moved like shadows, silent as wind through pine. Though stone and torchless sconces had replaced branches and moonlight, they descended the stairs of the keep with the same caution they'd use tracking prey through the forest. Every step was deliberate. Every sense, sharpened.

Below, arcane energy pulsed like a heartbeat.

The Mage-Gate crackled, its swirling colors throwing ghostly blues and purples across the chamber. In that strange light, Spider lay in a crumpled heap, motionless.

And pacing before the gate, like a big cat caged too long, stood Wilmund.

Doud and Garret were gone.

"Stay where you are," the man said. His voice was Wilmund's, but not. It carried a weight, a command sharper than anything they'd heard from him before. "Come no closer."

Val raised his hands slowly in a show of peace, though every muscle in his body stayed taut. Hidden behind him, Sarif nocked an arrow in silence, the bowstring barely whispering as he drew.

"I only want to talk," Val said, keeping his voice low and calm. "What happened here, Wilmund? Why is Spider on the ground?"

Wilmund glanced at the druid's prone form. "He started bleeding. Eyes. Ears. Nose. Nothing you can fix."

There was no sympathy in his voice—just cold detachment.

Val's stomach twisted. "Put the scythe down," he said, taking a slow step forward. "Step away from the Mage-Gate."

Wilmund's hand twitched, gripping his scythe tighter.

For a moment, it looked like he might comply—but then his eyes flickered with something dangerous.

In one sudden motion, he turned and sprinted toward the Mage-Gate, his scythe glinting in the eerie light.

Sarif's arrow streaked past Val's ear, piercing Wilmund's shoulder below the collarbone, causing him to lurch forward. Another arrow whizzed through the air, striking him in the upper back.

Wilmund staggered but kept crawling forward, dragging himself toward the swirling portal. Before a third arrow could land, he vanished into the shimmering vortex.

Val didn't hesitate. He sprinted to the Mage-Gate and dove through, disappearing in a flash of light. Sarif immediately turned and sprinted to the doors, wrenching them open to let Cedric and Chefera inside.

Cedric's eyes went wide as he took in the scene. "The Mage-Gate—Wilmund activated it!"

Sarif shook his head, expression grim. "I'm not so sure that was Wilmund. His voice sounded… off, and he hurt Spider. Whatever is going on, it's not right."

Chefera was already kneeling beside Spider, her face drawn with concern. She placed her hands on his head, murmuring a healing incantation. Soft light radiated from her palms, and the bleeding from Spider's eyes, nose, and ears slowed, though he remained unconscious, his breathing shallow and labored.

"Val followed Wilmund through the Mage-Gate. I'm sure Doud and Garret are with him on the other side," Sarif said. "We can't just leave him there alone."

Cedric nodded, the decision already made. "We're going in. Chefera, stay here with Spider. Tend to him and guard the gate."

Chefera nodded, her expression resolute. "Be careful. I don't know what kind of magic is at work here, but it's dark and twisted."

Without another word, Cedric and Sarif leapt through the Mage-Gate, their vision warping as the portal swallowed them whole.

The sensation was disorienting—a lurching, twisting pull that mimicked rootwalking but felt harsher, colder, as if the magic itself was reluctant to carry them.

When they emerged on the other side, they found themselves in the dim, dust-choked interior of a vast, ancient keep. Only the glow of the Mage-Gate lit the shadowed hall.

Val was locked in combat, surrounded by the glint of steel.

Wilmund lay writhing on the ground nearby, a bloody trail marking his crawl. Arrows jutted from his back, and a deep gash in his leg soaked his robes with blood. His face was contorted in agony and fury.

Doud and Garret, eyes glazed and weapons drawn, closed in on Val with unnatural, measured steps—puppets moving on unseen strings.

Sarif charged without hesitation, clashing blades with Garret in a brutal flurry that echoed through the hall. Steel rang out, sharp and sudden, throwing leaping shadows against the ancient walls.

Cedric raised his staff and muttered an incantation, each word deliberate and forceful. With a final gesture, he thrust his palm forward, and Wilmund's body seized. He froze in place, limbs locked, blood pouring from his wounded leg to pool beneath him. His wide, blazing eyes burned—not just with hatred, but with helpless fury, as he realized he couldn't stop the tide of blood.

Turning back to the fray, Cedric spotted an opening and murmured an incantation, focusing on Doud.

The mercenary's sword flared with heat, glowing red, then smoking. Doud screamed and dropped it, his hands blistering from the heat. Val seized the moment, slashing a near-mortal blow that sent him staggering back.

Sarif, seeing the opportunity, disengaged and circled around, helping Val corner Garret. Steel clashed as they drove him back—until Cedric swung his staff and cracked it hard against Garret's jaw. Dazed, Garret stumbled. Sarif closed in, knocking the sword from his hands and raising his blade for a killing strike.

"No!" Cedric shouted, raising his hand. "They're enchanted—bewitched! We don't have to kill them. Drag them back through the Mage-Gate!"

A rasping voice interrupted.

"You… will… never… get back…"

They turned to see Wilmund still bleeding out on the floor, his voice distorted and guttural.

He began to chant in a harsh, ancient tongue, each word twisted with dark magic. Trembling fingers reached toward the Mage-Gate, manipulating the runes.

Cedric's eyes went wide. "He's changing the destination—or shutting it down! Run! Now!"

Together, Cedric, Sarif, and Val bolted for the portal, abandoning the mercenaries.

Behind them, the chant quickened. The Mage-Gate's hum faltered, pulsing erratically as the portal flickered.

They leapt through.

The transition hit like a blow—harder than before. Cedric stumbled on landing, falling hard on the stone steps. Sarif and Val skidded to a halt, spinning just in time to see the portal's light dim and collapse in on itself.

Silence fell.

Only their ragged breathing remained as they stared at the dormant stone ring.

The Mage-Gate was dormant, dashing their hopes of finding their companions.

Epilogue Part One

∞

Liraelth's Gambit

Excerpts from the Recovered Translations of Scribe Superior Halric Danorin.

Compiled over two decades of research within the Ornst Library, Haddensack Imperial Library, and Second Scriptorium of Khaalndra in western Thariel.

"It is said a rogue Elf took it upon himself to secure all Elven knowledge once it became apparent the Mages and Hexenfold were closing in. This ritual, lost to the ages, is rumored to have worked.

Whispers call it the Gambit Rooted in Silence—Vael'Thaldrien, they say in the old tongue. No one speaks of the cost."

 —SS HD, RH 254

"A name whispered in legends is Suriharon. Most assume it to be a hidden city, a tower, a vault… but the deeper I dig, the more I suspect it is not a place at all. The original texts call it 'the Wellspring of Remembrance.'

One solitary passage mentions it to be 'a living vessel, chosen not born, into whom the Weave of Thought is poured.' If true, it would change the very foundation of Elven history.

This has been debated exhaustively: is Suriharon a place or a person?"

 —SS HD, RH 263

"There is mention—tattered and incomplete—of a blade forged not by divine will but in opposition to it. It is said to have been drawn from star-ore and sanctified in Elven flame. A cruel blasphemy by ancient standards.

They called it Thauren'dal — the literal translation is 'Song-Ender.' Its edge, it is written, holds 'the weight of denial.' Even now, demons shudder at its name. Some say the one who forged it disappeared in the same year Suriharon emerged. There are whispers the blade is powerful enough to slay a god."

 —SS HD, RH 274

The following account was assembled from the collective writings of Scribe Superior Halric Danorin. Given the gaps in knowledge of what happened to the Elves after the Sundering and the fall of the Mages, many facts, conversations, and descriptions have been *imagined* by the author—who, by all measures, was the most authoritative source of Elven history prior to his death.

I t was a fortified city deep within the forests of eastern Stenga, near the borders of Jeclan. A marvel of Elven design, it stood as a testament to what could be accomplished when nature, stonework, and magic lived in harmony. The avenues were paved in interlocking stone, fired in ancient kilns, and interspersed with granite and sun-kissed sandstone quarried from the eastern cliffs.

Vael'Araneth was its name.

Its buildings rose with elegance—swooping curves, domes of copper-green patina, and thick forest-stone columns that bore the weight of time without effort. Homes and halls were woven into the trees themselves, elevated dwellings suspended in canopies, linked by wooden bridges that creaked like songs in the wind. The forest was not disrupted—it was embraced.

The city did more than thrive—it led. It was the beating heart of the Elven world, where knowledge, history, and magic converged in the great library called *Talarion*, the Archive of the First Root.

Some called it the Vault of Root and Memory. To the workers, it was simply the Rootvault. In ancient ballads, The Deep Grove. Among the soldiers, it was The Vault.

Vael'Araneth was founded during the Quiet Age of Expansion, and from it, the Elves spread outward—seeding colonies and forest-holds across the east and north of the known world.

At its center stood *Elaril*, the God-Tree. Neither myth nor metaphor, it was a living divine gift, its roots believed to reach into the marrow of the world. In a sacred glen open to the sky, the druids tended to its needs, guided by rites older than song.

On this windswept day, Liraelth walked among the autumn leaves, his long white hair trailing behind him. Though not the eldest of the Elves, he had witnessed centuries—the rise of the Mages, the spread of Hexenfold, the slow unraveling of balance. He had felt the change, *anticipated it…* and now, quietly, was beginning to answer it.

Liraelth was often dismissed as eccentric. He was left alone to conduct his experiments, to haul strange stones from rivers, to whisper to trees, to conjure spells in the dead of night. Many of his ventures ended in failure—but those that succeeded changed lives. He had developed spells to stave off famine, forged weapons of renown, and weaved wards that still protected Elven borders to this day.

So no one stopped him when he visited *Elaril*, nor when he took pieces of its bark—a familiar sight, now wrapped gently by druids in linen to protect the tree from illness or rot. They muttered, but they tolerated him. He had, after all, earned the right to fail.

That day, the wind stirred sharply through the glen. Leaves flared red and gold against the pale blue sky, and the acorns fell heavy to the grass. The druids moved quickly, gathering them with reverent care.

As Liraelth knelt to pray, the wind tore through the glen again, shaking the fiery canopy. More acorns fell. The druids scrambled to gather them.

One nearby paused and asked with a sideways glance, "Why is it you only visit on the windiest of days, Master Liraelth?"

Liraelth smiled faintly, not looking up. "Because the air is cleaner," he said. "Easier to think."

Liraelth knelt before the tree, bowing his head in prayer. He murmured quietly to Thatara and Allisa, the twin Human and Elven patrons of nature and memory. Then, silently, his hand slipped to the grass and retrieved a single acorn that the druids had missed.

Without comment, he tucked it deep into the folds of his robes.

Rising—stiffly—he accepted a druid's arm for balance.

"I need bark," he said plainly. "Perhaps you can manage a few strips for me? My hands aren't as steady as they once were."

The druid gave a knowing nod and approached *Elaril* with care. With a small curved knife, he peeled away a long ribbon of bark—dark outside, silver-veined within—and rolled it gently before handing it to Liraelth.

"You must tell me Master Liraelth," the druid said. "Are you forging another weapon? One that will turn the tide of war?"

Liraelth chuckled. "No." He patted the druid's shoulder. "But it will save the Elven people."

The druid laughed in kind.

He turned from the glen, staff in hand, bark under one arm, the acorn hidden. He walked with purpose now, each step deliberate. He carried with him two pieces of a desperate plan—keys not to conquest, but to preservation.

Although outwardly his residence resembled a hut fit for a hermit, Liraelth's home was anything but humble inside. The space was clean, ordered, and strangely soothing—a sanctuary of quiet purpose. Few outside of *Tal'Serandor*, the Council of Elders, knew that beneath this modest dwelling lay an expansive laboratory and workshop, carved deep into the roots of the hill.

He had long wrestled with guilt for never taking an apprentice—no one to pass on his knowledge, his failures, his triumphs. But what he now intended could only be done in solitude. Another mind would question. Another voice might plead. He could not afford either.

Liraelth shuffled forward, the sacred acorn gripped tightly in one hand, clenched as though letting go might shatter the world beneath his feet. It was cool in the deep reaches of the cellar—quiet, still, untouched.

He approached a door he hadn't opened in nearly a decade. The air behind it felt forgotten, and for a moment, so did he.

He lifted the latch and pushed the door open. Lantern light spilled inside.

The floors, walls, and ceiling were lined in pristine whitewood, sealed with resin, untouched by age. The planks still gave off the faint scent of freshly split timber. Along the left-hand wall stood a long bench—and atop it, a box of black ironwood, heavy and matte, cut from trees that grew where sunlight never reached.

It was cool. The perfect place to begin.

He hooked the lantern to a rusted iron bracket and approached the bench. With slow care, he unlatched the ironwood box. The sides fell open on sturdy, hinged braces, collapsing outward to form a flat ritual platform. The lid was removed and set aside.

The base of the box gleamed—a sheet of flawless obsidian, polished to a glass-like sheen.

From his robe he withdrew a diamond-tipped etching tool. His hand trembled as he bent over the glass. He began to carve.

His heart thudded harder with each line. Though he doubted, though he feared, he knew: a terrible sacrifice was the only path left to preserve the soul of his people.

Sweat beaded on his brow. It stung his eyes. He wiped it away with his sleeve and carved on.

When he finished the pentagram, he stepped back, chest heaving.

The symbol felt alive—pulsing, watching.

It was infernal, drawn from the language of devils, a shape not meant to be born in this world. It was a conduit to the Nine Hells, a gate that drew energy from places he had never dared name aloud.

He doubled over, one hand braced on the bench, revulsion rising in his throat.

But he wasn't finished.

He took a chisel, enchanted it with a word of fire, and pressed its glowing tip to the inner faces of the box's walls and lid. On each surface—five in all—he burned replicas of the pentagram, precisely inscribed, until all six internal planes mirrored the same terrible shape.

When he finished, the air began to hum. Low, resonant. Like a breath held too long.

He placed the fat white acorn into the center of the obsidian base, exactly within the etched lines.

From his robe he withdrew a scroll tube, sealed long ago. He unfurled the parchment—weathered, spotted, older than memory.

He read the incantation aloud.

Infernal words burned his throat as he spoke. The taste of ash filled his mouth. His teeth ached.

The scroll turned to dust between his fingers.

The lantern dimmed.

The air went still.

The cold sank into his bones.

Before he could falter, he closed the box—sealing the acorn of the God-Tree within a prison of infernal geometry. The lid clicked into place, muffling the energy radiating from within.

He placed both hands on the *Vael'Noctharin*, closed his eyes, and whispered:

"Forgive me. Understand me. There is no other way."

Since closing the *Vael'Noctharin*, Liraelth had not dared open it.

He'd felt its hum each time he entered the laboratory—a low throb of infernal energy, pulsing faintly from beneath the ironwood lid. Though he tried to ignore it, the box whispered of its contents, of what it had become. Still, he had left it untouched. He was reluctant to see the corrupted seed. But now… the time was near.

On the far side of the room, a modest cauldron waited, half-buried in shadow. Inside it lay ash gathered from the fallen—not taken in ceremony, but stolen from grief.

Over many months, Liraelth had visited battlefields, slipping through the aftermath of slaughter. At each funeral pyre, he knelt quietly, scooping a single spoonful of Elven remains from the charred ground. One thousand Elves. A thousand deaths. Reduced and measured. The ash filled the volume of two waterskins.

He thought often of their faces—not the ones he'd known, but the ones he'd imagined. Yet it wasn't the ash that haunted him most. It was the other component.

Blood of the innocent.

He had wandered among the sick and the dying. Tended to the feeble. Whispered comfort to those beyond healing. And while they slept or struggled, he drew from them what he needed. He told himself it was mercy. That their lives would serve a greater good.

It had to be this way.

He was the only one who could save the Elven people.

With steady hands, he poured the dark, viscous blood into the cauldron of ash. The mixture hissed and thickened, forming a paste the color of old rust, malleable like clay.

He approached the *Vael'Noctharin*.

Even sealed, the ironwood box radiated heatless pressure. The pulse of contained blasphemy. It crawled along his skin.

He unlatched the hinges, and the box unfolded like a flower of darkness.

Where once had rested a pure, pale acorn, there was now something shriveled and black—twisted, veined with red. It looked more like a desiccated fruit than a seed of the God-Tree. No druid would have recognized it. No forest would have claimed it.

Liraelth donned a glove and lifted it gently.

He rolled it in the thick paste, shaping a sphere around the seed. It was almost too large to fit. The clay hissed where it touched the twisted core, but it held. Once formed, he took the bark strips from *Elaril*, softened and darkened by age, and wrapped them carefully around the sphere, binding it in layers.

He placed it back into the *Vael'Noctharin*, exactly at the center of the etched pentagram.

With trembling hands, he closed the box.

The energy locked into place like a breath drawn and never exhaled.

It would take months for the next transformation to begin.

For now, he would rest.

He would return to *Elaril*, pray for forgiveness, and—should this one fail—collect another acorn.

Spring passed into summer, and Liraelth checked the *Vael'Noctharin* daily for signs of change.

As the days shortened and the scent of dry leaves returned to the wind, troubling news arrived. The war with the Mages had worsened. Elven cities and ancient groves had been reduced to ash, sacred rivers diverted, children lost. The only reprieve came from the Fey uprisings, whose collective magic and mischief harried the Mage-legions and stalled their advance.

It was not a victory. But it was proof.

The Mages could be defeated.

They could bleed.

They could fail.

As the land drew breath, the weary rested and the Elves reinforced their wards and war-lines. To Liraelth, it felt like a gift of time—short-lived, but precious.

And then the day came.

He stepped into the laboratory and stopped cold. The cool cellar air that had always greeted him was gone. Heat rolled across the floor like breath from a buried furnace. The *Vael'Noctharin* sat on its bench, smoldering. Thin ribbons of smoke curled from the ironwood joints, blackening the whitewood walls and ceiling in long, trailing fingers.

He raised the lantern, heart thudding. The box pulsed—not with light, but with pressure, as though something inside was breathing.

He whispered a spell of shielding and moved closer. He unlatched the box.

The sides fell away.

Inside, the bark wrap was blackened, charred and curling away from the thing it once protected. The sphere of ash and blood had hardened into something dark red and solid—its surface spiderwebbed with cracks. The interior walls of the ironwood box were scored with claw marks, as if something had tried to escape.

Liraelth stared in silence, hands trembling.

Then it pulsed.

Not a sound—just a sensation. Like thunder without a voice. The pressure in the air shifted.

It pulsed again.

And cracked.

With a sharp, brittle noise, the sphere split down the center, falling into two perfect halves. A hiss escaped into the air like a final breath.

Nestled within the broken shell was a seed—bloated, veined, and glistening. It no longer resembled an acorn. It was mottled black and white, streaked with pulsing red threads like blood vessels. The surface twitched faintly, like a muscle. It looked more like a heart than anything that should have grown from *Elaril*.

An evil thing.

A corrupted thing.

He reached for it with a gloved hand.

The moment his fingers touched it, he felt it—awareness. The seed was alive. Not in a natural way. Not with breath or spirit. But something worse. Something *watching*.

He wrapped it in linen, carefully, slowly.

Then placed it into a pouch and sealed it tight.

It wasn't unusual for Liraelth to be seen loitering in the gardens near *Talarion*. The old sage had tended the plants and trees surrounding the great archive for years—sometimes absentmindedly, sometimes with great care.

The archive itself stood before him like a monolith of knowledge, all stone and grandeur. Scholars came and went through its arched doors. The guards stationed outside did not watch for mischief, but for anything *odd*—things that didn't belong.

Liraelth waved to them with a faint smile as he stepped over the granite benches and entered the gardens. He skirted the edge of the building, then slipped between two thick hedges.

Behind them lay a secluded ring of miniature trees, arranged like a pocket forest around a still pond. The little grove was a living model— tiny white rock paths wound between trees trimmed to resemble their towering counterparts. Small benches dotted the area, and carved figurines—gifts from children and artisans—sat nestled in mossy corners.

At the grove's center was an empty clearing.

Liraelth stepped carefully, mindful not to crush anything underfoot. He reached the center and knelt, retrieving a small bronze spade from his robe.

He worked the soil—chopping, loosening, mixing. He sprinkled yellow sulfur into the earth, turning it until the powder was fully integrated.

From a pouch at his belt, he withdrew bleached white finger bones, placing them into a pentagram. He overlapped the joints with precision, then pressed the shape beneath the soil.

He carved a small hole in the center and reached into his robe.

The corrupted seed, now wrapped in linen, rested in his palm. He dropped it into the hole and covered it with a thin layer of earth, pressing it down gently with both love and loathing.

"New tree for the miniature forest?"

The voice made his heart leap, but his face showed no surprise.

"Yes, Seghnor," he answered smoothly. "It will be like *Elaril*, both in form and shape. I just hope it doesn't grow too tall."

He stood and dusted his hands on his already work-stained robe. As he stepped back across the miniature grove, lifting his hem to avoid disturbing the display, he stumbled.

A hand caught his elbow.

"Many thanks," Liraelth said, steadying himself.

Seghnor nodded. "Have you always tended this part of the gardens?"

"I have," Liraelth replied. "This miniature representation of the *Elaril* glen has been a passion of mine."

"I noticed."

Liraelth glanced sideways. "And what else have you noticed?"

"You come here often," Seghnor said. "You care for these trees like your own children. Your visits are never too long or too short. If I didn't know better, I'd think you were up to something."

Liraelth laughed. "Ever observant, young elf. I *am* always up to something. But it's always for the good of our people. You focus on guarding *Talarion*. Let me focus on saving what can still be saved."

"Guarding The Vault is my duty," Seghnor replied. "Watching you is a necessity."

"You're too clever for your own good," Liraelth said with a smile. "Watch your ambition, Seghnor. I'll remember this. And when I call upon you to assist with a mission for *Tal'Serandor*, you won't refuse me."

"Nor will I," Seghnor said. "Return to your hut. I'll watch over your garden as part of my duties. No one will disturb what grows here—or the tree you've planted."

He escorted Liraelth to the path with quiet dignity.

The elder paused and turned.

"Seghnor, learn all you can about combat. You'll need it before long. And when time permits, come to my hut. You'll need a proper weapon—one I forged for a worthy hand. And a worthy mind."

"I will," Seghnor said.

Liraelth tightened the sash of his robes and hurried down the path, his sandals soft against the moss-worn stone.

"Tell me," Liraelth said, voice low and steady as he drew the cloth back from the blade. "What do you see?"

Seghnor stared, momentarily breathless.

"I've never seen the like," he murmured. "It's a wonder."

"It is called *Thalas'Inariel*," Liraelth replied.

"*Song of the Last Flame*," Seghnor translated under his breath, brow furrowed in reverence.

"*Lightpiercer* is what I call it," Liraelth said, a wry smile creasing the corners of his mouth. "The last light before the dark."

The blade shimmered faintly in the forge light—forged of silver-steel alloy, its length veined with sky-gold that caught no glint, only the suggestion of old fire. The fuller was inlaid with Elder Runes, and the crossguard curled like the folded wings of a falcon in flight. At its pommel sat a gemstone shaped like a seed—red as blood, yet seeming to pulse with hidden breath.

Etched along the blade's flat were five runes, sharp and ancient:

Courage in Combat

Fortitude

Angelic Power

Precision

Bind To

"It bears many properties," Liraelth said quietly, "but their true meanings are not for me to explain. You must uncover them yourself. A sword, after all, is not just a weapon—it is a song. And every song must be *sung*, not *read*."

Seghnor reached for it. The moment his hand wrapped around the grip, a pulse of warmth rushed up his arm—not scalding, but purposeful, as if testing his spirit.

It felt light in the hand, yet solid, anchored. Its edge looked endless—as if sharpness was not a feature but a law it obeyed. It vibrated faintly, as though it knew it had been chosen.

"Carry it with you always," Liraelth said, stepping back. "Learn its touch, its weight. Its silence and song. When you have truly bound with it, *Thalas'Inariel* will suffer no other wielder. It will remember only you."

Seghnor looked up, reverent. "This is an incredible gift. I don't know that I deserve it."

"You put up with my mutterings. You don't help with my secret work, but you don't report it either. You've shown patience, and above all, you've shown loyalty. That is no small thing. You are a friend I can rely on, and that… is rarer than steel."

He met Seghnor's gaze, and there was something heavier in his voice now.

"Remember this, Seghnor. There may come a day when I ask you to carry that blade into the very maw of the Nine Hells."

Seghnor scoffed, half-laughing. "You always were dramatic, old elf. But if that day comes—" he lifted the sword in salute, "—I will follow you."

"You've said it in the presence of *Thalas'Inariel*," Liraelth warned, though not unkindly. "It will remember your words. Keep it well."

Seghnor turned the blade, studying the pommel gem. "This stone… it's unlike any ruby I've ever seen."

"It is not a ruby," Liraelth said cryptically. "It is the heart of the forest, cut and bound by elven spells. When our people are at peace, it will shine green. But now—"

"It is red," Seghnor finished. "And you think you have the key to turning it green?"

"I do," Liraelth whispered. "But the road is long, and full of shadow. We must wait for an arcane sign—from Allisa, perhaps. Or Halamar, if he sees fit to bless fools like us."

He reached forward, his voice now low and earnest.

"Until then, stay the course. Stay true to what must be done."

"What *must* be done?" Seghnor asked, the question a challenge.

"You'll know. But not today." Liraelth folded the cloth beside the empty pedestal. "Stay your curiosity. If you chase the answers too soon, it may drive you mad. Learn the blade. Become one with it. Then return to me—not as you are now, but as a warrior."

Seghnor bowed, sword in hand. "I will."

Deep in the night, with darkness pressed thick around him, Liraelth moved with cautious, deliberate steps through the garden paths. Starlight shimmered above, guiding his sharp elven sight as he slipped past granite benches and hedges toward the miniature grove. He paused, tilting his head skyward.

A streak of light tore across the sky, brief and beautiful—a falling star, its sparks devoured by the void above.

The sapling in the grove had grown for nearly two years, a perfect miniature echo of *Elaril*, the God-Tree. Through druidic craft and infernal binding, Liraelth had stunted its physical growth, halting its rise—but not its reach.

He knew that below, its roots had burrowed deep, stretching silently across sacred earth, touching veins of old magic. The time was coming. He could feel it.

"When the day becomes dark as night, and for a moment, the world is motionless."

He didn't believe it was a riddle. It was prophecy. It was an eclipse.

Though no astrologer, Liraelth had divined its approach. He had read it in tree rings, in the spin of clouds, in the fading patterns of constellations. It was close.

When the sky darkened, and the corrupted tree bathed in unlight, the *Oathroot—Vael'Virelen*—would awaken, completing the tether between the sapling and the divine roots of *Elaril*.

Then, a vessel could be chosen.

He didn't know if he had the strength to bear the burden.

Once, he thought he might.

Now… he wasn't sure.

The old Elf knelt in the dark, interlaced his fingers, and rested his chin upon them, staring into the heart of the little grove. He prayed— to Halamar, god of wild nature, and to Allisa, guardian of knowledge and the Weave.

He needed their blessing.

He needed their wisdom.

He needed their permission to do the unthinkable.

The world was unraveling.

The Mages had pierced through Thariel, driving refugees west. Even shattered Human settlements had sent their displaced to *Vael'Araneth*, where suspicion festered. Resources dwindled. Riots broke out in shadowed streets.

This was exactly what the Mages wanted.

And in the east, Hexenfold—with their stolen children and necrotic magic—had turned the forests to ash even as they wounded the Mages. The Elves were trapped between fires.

"I have not seen you here at night," came a voice.

Liraelth didn't look up. "Sometimes the gods only listen when the world is asleep. Then, they can hear clearly."

Seghnor stepped forward. "I do not sleep much since becoming one with *Thalas'Inariel*," he murmured. "I train. I learn. Sleep feels like wasted time."

Liraelth turned to him, eyes narrowing. "You have learned the blade's nature, yet you haven't come to see me. What offense have I committed?"

"None," Seghnor said. "It hasn't been the right time. You've been busy saving our people. I see you visiting the council. You don't need my interruptions."

"I need your assistance," Liraelth said. "Help me up—I'd see your eyes more clearly."

Seghnor stepped forward and lifted the elder Elf easily, strong hands gripping Liraelth's forearms. The old Elf stood, unsteady.

"You've grown stronger," Liraelth said, noting the ease with which Seghnor moved him.

"And faster. And wiser. I cannot be defeated in combat."

Moonlight kissed Seghnor's face. Liraelth saw it then—the change.

His form was lean, carved by training. Light armor clung to a warrior's frame. *Thalas'Inariel* sat at his hip, and knives, bow, and quiver adorned him like ornaments of war. His eyes—bright, intelligent—had turned sharp with purpose.

"Yet you remain here, guarding *Talarion*. Why not the front lines?"

"Few know what I am now," Seghnor said. "But soon, all will. Those who guard the Vault will be called to war."

"Is it battle you seek?"

Seghnor smiled faintly, resting a hand on Liraelth's shoulder. "No. I seek victory. I want to help *you* win this war. If that's what you need—say so."

Liraelth looked into his eyes and saw no hesitation. "What I must ask… is strange. But you must trust me. It is for our people. For our legacy. There will be sacrifice. Perhaps death."

"What must I do?" Seghnor asked without fear. "I'm ready."

"You aren't ready," Liraelth said. "No one is." He paused, voice a whisper. "What must be done, I cannot do. I lack the strength."

"Then tell me what *must* be done," Seghnor said, sharper now. "Stop being cryptic."

"In three months, during the *Vaer'Halamarien*, the eclipse will come. When it does, the tree in that grove will manifest its heart—*Vael'Virelen*, the *Oathroot*. It will bind to a willing vessel and awaken the connection to *Elaril*. That vessel will carry the soul of our people. *You*, Seghnor."

"Me?" Seghnor said, stunned. "What does it mean?"

"It means that in time, you will forget who you are. But in exchange, you will become *everyone*. *Everything*. You will become the Wellspring of Remembrance."

"*Suriharon?*" he whispered. "That's a legend. A place where all elven knowledge is stored."

"It is not a place," Liraelth said. "It is a person. It is *you*. I was never strong enough to bear it. But you… you may be."

Silence fell across the garden.

No wind stirred.

No insects trilled.

The stars burned above them like silent witnesses.

"What must I do?"

"Accept the *Oathroot*. Then, we must journey to Hexenfold."

Seghnor bristled at the name. "*Talthrien Mor'vany* is a pit of evil. No one returns from the Dreadwood."

"We must speak with their leaders," Liraelth said. "Direct their fire against the Mages. We cannot survive trapped between them both. If we survive that… we begin the preservation. You will become our memory."

"*Suriharon*," Seghnor repeated, this time with weight.

"Are you with me?" Liraelth asked, his voice trembling. "We are our people's only hope."

"I will meet you here during *Vaer'Halamarien*," Seghnor said. "When the day becomes dark, I will take the *Oathroot*. And then… we walk into the darkness."

"We leave moments after, once the rite is complete. You'll be my guardian. I'll need three more to come with us—willing to die."

"I will find them," Seghnor said, placing a hand on the hilt of his sword. "And if we must die, *many songs will be sung.*"

Liraelth nodded, solemn and proud.

"Remember," he said, "this is for our people."

"I will not forget."

Vaer'Halamarien—The Day of Halamar's Gaze.

The hut was quiet in the dawn's soft light. No birds sang. No wind stirred the canopy. Liraelth stood alone in the low-walled chamber he had called home for countless decades.

He stood before one of his oldest creations—a moon-shaped carving hanging on the wall. It had been one of his first endeavors as a young Elf, a boy's effort to turn wonder into something permanent.

In his hand, he held perhaps the last key Seghnor would ever need. It wasn't an explanation. It was instruction—how to secure the knowledge of the Elves, how to become *Suriharon*, how to ensure they were never truly forgotten.

The scroll tube was smooth, sealed with wards keyed to *Thalas'Inariel.* Inside, the note was written in silverleaf ink—visible only in moonlight, or under the soft glow of *Lightpiercer.*

He stooped low, feeling the stiffness in his knees, the quiet ache in his spine. Movements that had once been graceful were now measured. *Time consumes all things,* he thought.

With care, he lifted a floorboard designed for just such secrets and nestled the scroll into the hollow beneath.

Seghnor would find it.

Liraelth straightened with effort, reaching out to brush his fingers along the moon carving one last time. Then he turned to gather his pack and strapped it to his shoulders.

It felt heavier than it should have.

He took one last look around.

The hearth was cold. The herb bundles that once filled the room with forest scent now hung brittle and dry from the beams. On the table by the door lay a folded note—ink still faintly glistening, as if he'd hesitated even after writing it.

He stared at it for a long while.

Then he stepped forward, picked it up, read it again, and returned it gently to the table. Whoever found it would understand his wishes.

His last wishes.

He took his walking stick—gnarled and twisted, capped with a glinting stone—and slid a pair of slender knives into the folds of his cloak. He would not use or need them. His path lay in older magic.

Then he stepped outside. And for a long moment, he simply stood there, gazing across the garden paths and flowering hedges.

There was no ceremony.

Only silence.

He walked slowly through the city he had once helped shape.

Epilogue Part Two

∞

Suriharon

In *Vael'Araneth*, the Celebration of Halamar was in full bloom. Elves adorned in green and gold filled the terraces, singing beneath the ancient spires and trees as old as the world. Laughter echoed around the fountains. Druids danced in spirals, whispering prayers to the living world.

And above them all, the sky began to change.

First came the hush.

Then, the wind.

A shadow crept over the land like a veil drawn across the sun. Voices faltered. The warmth faded. Even the birds grew silent.

Eyes turned upward.

From the towers of *Talarion* to the vaulted halls of the city, unease stirred. The eclipse had been marked by astronomers and loremasters—but to fall on this day, during the sacred celebration of *Vaer'Halamarien*, was an ill omen. Even the elders grew pale.

Among the common folk, panic whispered.

Some wept. Others fell to their knees. Druids called for calm, but the birds did not sing. The insects did not chirp.

The Elven world was holding its breath.

At the miniature grove, Liraelth waited.

Seghnor stood beside him, dressed for war but calm.

The sapling—just a slender tree with black-veined silver bark and delicate crimson leaves—began to move.

At first, it was subtle. The branches tilted unnaturally. Then they twitched. Elongated. Coiled.

"Shades…" Seghnor whispered.

The limbs writhed like tentacles, reaching toward him. Thin strands of darkness and fire, black-rooted and red-tipped, snaked through the air like blood-scenting serpents.

Liraelth said nothing.

The eclipse had reached its peak.

Darkness fell like a veil.

"When the day becomes dark as night, and for a moment, the world is motionless…"

The roots pulsed. A low thrum filled the air. The *Oathroot* was awake.

Seghnor stepped forward and knelt in the grove.

One tendril lashed out, coiling around his left arm. Then another. And another. Like living veins, they wound up his forearm, wrapping tight.

The pressure was immediate.

He clenched his teeth.

The tendrils burned.

Red light ignited along their lengths. Flames licked across his skin—but the fire did not consume. It *merged.* It *bound.*

The tendrils seared into his flesh, becoming sinew, becoming blood.

Seghnor bowed his head, enduring in silence.

Liraelth stepped back, watching, unmoving.

The agony was immense. His breath came ragged. His hand trembled. But still, he did not scream.

The branches left behind marks—black and red lines, barklike veins reaching from wrist to elbow.

When the last tendril snapped free and sank into his arm, the tree stilled. Its movement ceased. Its branches returned to their natural posture.

The eclipse waned.

The air moved again.

And Seghnor rose, steam rising from his skin, his eyes alight with something more than understanding.

Liraelth nodded, eyes wet and unreadable.

"Come," he said. "They are waiting."

#

At the edge of the city, beneath a low archway carved in the image of twin falcons, three Elves waited—armed, armored, cloaked in shadow.

They did not speak as Seghnor and Liraelth approached.

"We leave now," Liraelth said. "The path ahead is darker than any forest. But there is light enough to walk it."

Seghnor turned to glance back—toward the city, the gardens, the hut.

They would return.

He believed that.

He touched the burning lines on his arm.

"I'm ready."

Liraelth gave a solemn nod.

But the voice inside him whispered,

I'm not.

They moved beneath boughs as dusk approached, the waning sunlight dappled and broken by branches tangled like skeletal fingers. The forest had grown silent over the last three days—no birds, no wind. The kind of silence that felt chosen.

Seghnor rode ahead of the others, one hand resting lightly on the hilt of *Thalas'Inariel.* His eyes were sharp, always scanning. Even in stillness, his mind remained in motion.

They were at the fringe now—the edge of the cousin forests, where Elven blood still lingered in the trees but was fading fast. Beyond lay the blight: the true wild of Dreadwood, where Hexenfold's roots had taken hold.

Behind them, Liraelth rode cloaked and quiet, barely speaking since morning. He looked leaner. Diminished. As if the closer they came, the thinner the old Elf became.

Seghnor's gaze swept the shadows.

They were being followed.

The Human guards were easy to sense—clumsy in the forest, yet likely well-trained in open combat. But something else moved with them. Not seen. Only *felt*.

The witches and warlocks of Hexenfold.

Sorcerers first. Deadly even without their magic.

Cloaked in power.

And *Thalas'Inariel* could feel them too.

He narrowed his eyes as the gates of the city came into view.

Towering walls loomed ahead, carved from black volcanic stone, etched with runes so old they seemed to hum. The gates were massive iron constructs adorned with the sigils of Malgareth—a black iron chain entwined around a crimson eye.

They emerged from the trees—those who had shadowed them. The Human guards took up a loose formation behind two figures who stepped forward: a witch and a warlock, standing at the path in apparent welcome.

Weapons remained sheathed. But they blocked the road.

The witch removed her cowl.

Dark ringlets framed a face smooth as porcelain, her emerald eyes bright against her pale skin. She radiated poise. Unnatural beauty. A mask that blinked far too little.

Ritual blades. Curved, ceremonial. Not made for defense. Staves etched with downward-pointing sigils—they drew power from beneath, from the Nine Hells.

Seghnor steadied his horse with a hand to her neck.

"We've been expecting you," the witch said, her voice melodic and unnervingly warm.

"You've been following us for an hour," Seghnor replied. "Your men are not born of the forest."

"No," she said. "But they are born of shadow. And shadows are *everywhere*. The forest is not."

The warlock pulled back his own hood. Rugged. Handsome. Days of stubble trimmed to perfection. His skin was flawless, his grey eyes glinting with confidence… or mischief.

"I'd welcome you properly," he said, "but you seem too clever to believe such things."

"Welcome or not, we've come to treat with Hexenfold," Liraelth said before Seghnor could speak.

"Then come," the witch said, turning. "You will not be hindered at our gates."

The city beyond was an unnatural marvel.

Thirteen avenues, like spokes in a wheel, each one vanishing into a different domain of dark study. Though ancient, the city thrummed faintly with new life—like an old beast beginning to stir again.

As they passed through the gates, another emissary stepped forward.

She wore robes of glossy black and crimson, high-collared and embroidered with infernal script. Her golden hair cascaded over her shoulders, framing a face so symmetrical it seemed unnatural. Her eyes were wide and crystalline blue.

"Honored guests," she said, voice smooth as poured wine. "The Circle of Thirteen welcomes your presence. You will be escorted to your chambers."

Seghnor didn't like how she said *"guests."*

Still, he gave a nod.

They passed dark towers and streets lit by everburning embers. The walls whispered. The trees here didn't sway—they *leaned,* unnaturally still. Magic clung to the air like damp wool.

Their horses were taken and stabled. Then they walked—on foot, through the heart of Maldrithar—to where Covenhold loomed.

Seghnor felt it beneath his feet: a hum through the stones, not of life or warmth, but a vibration that came from beneath. It made his stomach turn.

Their quarters were stone—bare, but warm. Food was delivered—delicacies, even by Elven standards. Seghnor only pretended to eat.

The earth here was wrong.

The air, heavy with the scent of brimstone and rot, was wrong.

Even the water, drawn from deep underground, tasted of stillness and old metal.

Whatever grew in this place, whatever was harvested or hunted—it was nourished by corruption.

And so, it too would be corrupted.

Seghnor set his plate aside. Hunger was better than poison.

When the food was cleared and they were left alone, Liraelth finally spoke.

"Our journey isn't over yet," he said. "We'll be taken before their council to negotiate. It won't be easy. But we must endure—for our people."

Seghnor touched the hilt of his blade. The magic within comforted him.

This was an evil place.

A place they were not meant to be.

The knock came like a whisper—three slow, deliberate taps.

Seghnor opened the door.

A cloaked figure stood beyond the threshold, tall and indistinct. The hood masked all features, and the voice that followed was soft, genderless, eerily calm.

"You are to be brought to our most sacred place. For negotiations. Bring no weapons. Leave your burdens here."

Silence stretched.

Seghnor stepped forward, the air tense around him.

"No."

The figure tilted its head, birdlike. "The rite—"

"I said no."

He turned to the others, voice clipped and steady.

"Gear up. Full kit. Weapons ready. We're not walking into the dark unarmed."

His eyes met Liraelth's across the dim chamber.

The old Elf said nothing—only nodded, slow and weary.

"You heard him," Liraelth murmured.

They were taken from the heart of the city, past stone towers and quiet watchfires, to a dense woodland that clung to the edges of Maldrithar like a wound refusing to heal. The trees here were twisted and ancient, their branches clawing skyward like the hands of the damned.

At the woodland's heart, they reached a clearing where wild magic gathered thick as fog—pooling like molten silver in the air, drifting between the roots of a colossal, timeworn tree. Beneath those roots lay the source: the Veilrift.

Its surface shimmered like liquid moonlight, rippling with an otherworldly calm. But beneath the silvery glow, a crimson pulse beat slow and steady—like embers burning in the depths, alive with infernal heat.

From the shadows, witches and warlocks emerged. They moved in silence, cloaked in robes of midnight black and blood-red, their garments woven with infernal script. The sigils on their sleeves glowed faintly, casting their faces in flickering hues.

"You must drink of the waters," their escort said, voice serene, gesturing toward the Veilrift.

Seghnor's hand moved to the hilt of his blade.

Thalas'Inariel pulsed in warning.

Not of treachery here.

But of peril elsewhere.

Distant.

Watching.

Waiting… for them.

He shifted his stance, ready to draw.

Then a hand reached out—weathered, calm, firm—and stilled him.

"It is the only way," Liraelth said, voice low but certain. "You must follow."

The old Elf stepped forward without hesitation. Kneeling at the edge of the Veilrift, he dipped his hand into the molten pool and cupped the glowing liquid.

He drank.

A heartbeat passed.

The air shimmered around him—his form fading at the edges, turning translucent.

Then, without a word, Liraelth vanished.

Crossing into the Nine Hells was not merely a shift of realm—it was a rupture.

The instant Seghnor's essence breached the Veilrift, the world contorted.

Air thickened into poison—sulfur and scorched iron—filling his lungs with weight instead of breath. Heat bled into his veins, threading through muscle like molten metal. Pressure crashed inward, distorting his senses, folding space around his thoughts.

Shadows moved without light. Space trembled with wrongness. Time staggered—seconds dragged, stretched thin as sinew, yet everything rushed past in a blur of dread.

This place did not welcome.

It knew them.

Then came the sound.

A whisper at first—disjointed murmurs behind thought—then screams. Distant and immediate, countless and close. Beneath the shrieking rose the grind of infernal gears, the hiss of unseen monstrosities, and the rattle of chains too heavy for mortal hands.

Kel'Durmor, the Ninth Plane, was alive. It measured them—not with eyes, but with the weight of law woven into the very stone.

And it was watching.

They stood upon a jagged outcropping of basalt, cracked and smoldering, rising from a plain of ash and bone. Beneath their feet the rock pulsed, slow and heavy, like the heart of a buried titan.

Across the valley loomed the Fortress of Chains—a citadel wrought not by hand but through torment. Its black walls were mortared with soul-ash, its towers crowned by spinning girdles of living chain that groaned and shrieked with each revolution. Chains stretched across the sky like strands of fate—some anchored to nothing, others hung like nooses from unseen heights.

The weight of obligation was tangible.

Here, every broken oath had echo. Every kept vow had a price.

Then the air stilled.

From the haze, he arrived.

Malgareth did not walk. He simply was.

A gaunt silhouette cloaked in shadowed robes, draped in the tattered remains of shattered pacts. His crown was forged of iron thorns; his eyes twin furnaces burning with crimson judgment. He said nothing—he didn't need to.

Chains stirred.

The Veilrift behind them flared.

"One among you seeks the bond. One among you has brought the price," the voice intoned—not from lips, but from within bone, beneath skin, everywhere at once.

Then the sky ruptured.

Ur'Belreth descended, vast wings spread wide, as if a star were falling with purpose. Clad in obsidian and crimson plate, she bore the sigil of Malgareth across her helm—the crimson eye bound in chain. At her side hung the *Chain of Judgment*, thick as a tree trunk, every link etched with infernal truths.

She landed hard, stone cracking beneath her feet. A dozen Hellmaws flanked her—fiends in spiked armor, trailing flame from their mouths and dragging molten furrows with every step.

Seghnor's hand tightened on *Thalas'Inariel*.

The sword began to hum—alive, alert.

Ur'Belreth's voice rolled forth like a thousand whispered commands:

"You seek salvation. But here, salvation is earned. You will be judged. You will be claimed."

"I know the price," Liraelth said, placing a hand on Seghnor's shoulder to steady him.

"Then the pact is made," Malgareth intoned.

Ur'Belreth unfurled a scroll, its infernal runes writhing like worms in oil. She sliced her claw across the air, and Liraelth's finger bled freely. He stepped forward and pressed it to the parchment.

The pact curled in on itself and streaked toward the Fortress of Chains in a line of burning ash.

"You will be the vessel," Ur'Belreth said. "Untouchable. Protected. But after one thousand years and one day, you will be mine."

Malgareth's shadow lifted a hand.

The three companions turned to ash, weapons clattering on the basalt.

Liraelth turned to Seghnor as he looked on in horror. "It is the only way."

He vanished like smoke.

The vision of Malgareth flickered and was gone.

"One thousand years, elf," Ur'Belreth said. "Then the pact will be fulfilled."

Seghnor drew his blade in defiance.

"Thalas'Inariel, voraé na'thalan!"

The sword blazed with white-hot radiance.

The Hellmaws recoiled, their flesh seared by holy light. Even Ur'Belreth faltered, a shimmer of pain running through her as the sword's glow struck her armored foot and left it smoking.

The blade carved light through the air—pure, defiant.

A wave of divine force blasted through the Hellmaws, tossing them aside or rending them in half.

A chain descended like a judgment, but when it struck *Thalas'Inariel,* it cracked with a sound like the sundering of mountains.

Ur'Belreth roared.

Then came more devils—*Thulven Gaathir* led by a towering *Gaathrak Vorn.* From the fields, *Kel'Saevren* and *Mor'Kelthurra* poured forth, screaming and charging.

Seghnor shattered Ur'Belreth's chain weapon with a swing of his blade.

Still more *Narthtunel* surged from the citadel.

"Take him," she hissed.

He was outnumbered, overwhelmed.

Yet he remembered:

Untouchable. Protected.

The sword pulled him—urged retreat.

Seghnor turned and sprinted for the Veilrift. He passed through.

The sulfurous air gave way to night-cooled wind. His sword still shone, the glow spilling across the gathered witches and warlocks.

Before he could act, a black ribbon of necrotic force lashed around him.

It drained him—soul first.

With a cry, he severed it with a sweeping arc of holy fire.

More ribbons came. He fought on, blade flaring with each strike—until they wrapped around him like a cocoon.

He fell, thrashing.

The last thing he saw was her face—porcelain skin, black ringlets, and those emerald eyes that saw far too much.

"He should be dead," the witch muttered as the final ribbons of necrotic energy unraveled and faded into the soil.

She knelt beside Seghnor, her blade drawn, its edge poised over his throat. But as she pressed the point to his skin, her eyes narrowed.

There, just above his collarbone, was a brand—faint but unmistakable. A crimson eye bound in chains, burned into the flesh with infernal permanence.

She recoiled as if struck. "This one bears the mark," she said. Her voice had lost its edge. She sheathed the blade with a hiss of reluctance. "He has made a pact."

A warlock stepped closer, his expression darkening. "Then he is not ours to kill. Place him beyond the gates with his horse. Let the master claim what is his in due time."

The witch hesitated, then nodded.

None dared touch the marked—for Malgareth's will was law, and his reach eternal.

Even the damned stepped aside, fearing to draw his gaze..

Seghnor awoke sore, drained… confused.

He should have been dead.

Instead, he found himself propped against a tree, the morning sun warming his face. Nearby, a soft whinny drew his gaze—his horse, waiting faithfully.

In the near distance, the heart of Hexenfold still loomed. Too close. Far too close.

There was no time to delay.

He rose stiffly, every bone aching, and climbed into the saddle. The sun streamed behind him as he turned west.

It had been Liraelth's plan all along.

To sacrifice himself—and the others—so Seghnor could live.

So the Elves could live.

But at what cost?

Take him!

The command echoed still.

The pact had been signed. Why then had Ur'Belreth moved to claim him? Wasn't he protected? Invulnerable? Untouchable—for a thousand years?

His grip tightened on the reins.

"You must fly like an eagle," he whispered to his steed. "There is no time to waste."

He spurred the horse forward and fled the edges of Dreadwood, the rising sun casting his shadow long behind him.

Seghnor didn't bother to wash, rest, or even catch his breath. Dust-caked, sweat-stained, and weary from his journey across the wilds, he stepped through the door of Liraelth's hut.

It looked untouched.

Dust motes swirled in the light filtering through the shutters. Everything was in its place—too perfectly. And on the central table lay a folded note, sealed with wax… the seal already broken.

Someone had been here.

He lifted the parchment, his fingers smudging the edges.

I, Liraelth, hereby bequeath this abode and all my possessions to Seghnor. Upon his return, this and all that was mine shall be his.

Beneath it was a second notation, written in a firmer, less graceful hand.

Understood. If you or Seghnor do not return within one year, this will become community property. —Council of Elders

He set the notes aside with a grim nod. The hut was his now. No more barracks. No more shared walls and whispered suspicions. Just this quiet place… and the burden it carried.

Seghnor unshouldered his pack and stripped away his gear, leaning *Thalas'Inariel* carefully against the far wall. It still pulsed faintly, as if the sword knew the next step would matter.

He was sure Liraelth had left him something more. A final truth. Instructions. Guidance for the impossible task ahead. So much had been sacrificed—Liraelth, the others, their innocence. Now Seghnor had to become what the pact demanded.

He had to become *Suriharon*.

The hut was small but layered in secrets. Seghnor began methodically—checking under tables, sliding open drawers, feeling behind old wall hangings and decorative carvings. Many spots seemed likely, even clever… but yielded nothing.

Then he paused before a wooden carving mounted on the wall— an etched moon surrounded by faint rays. One of Liraelth's favorite symbols. He'd spoken of it often, too often, as if it carried meaning others failed to grasp.

Seghnor lifted it from its mount, turning it over in his hands. No obvious seams. No hollow center. But just as he began to set it back, something caught his eye.

Barely visible, etched in the grain of the wood, were delicate words: *To those who walk in shadowlight, speak not your question aloud.*

He froze.

Moonlight.

And *Thalas'Inariel.*

He returned the carving to its place and moved back across the room. As he shifted his weight, a quiet creak betrayed a loose board beneath his foot. He crouched, slid the plank aside, and there it was:

A scroll tube. Not plain, but adorned with faintly glowing runes. Purpose-made, set into a hidden recess.

He lifted it carefully. The metal was warm to the touch. The cap vibrated as he twisted it open.

Inside was a single sheet of parchment.

Blank.

Of course.

It would be hours before moonrise. Until then, the message would remain hidden.

He resealed the tube and set it gently on the table beside *Thalas'Inariel,* then began to unpack. The hut—his new home—was quiet, but not peaceful. The weight of destiny hung in the air like a sword poised above his heart.

Whatever came next, it would begin soon.

Washed clean of dust and ash, Seghnor emerged from the hut in robes of green and gold. They were simple, ceremonial in cut but humble in design—Liraelth's colors. Across his chest hung a thin sash bearing the mark of the moon, and at his hip, strapped securely to a leather belt, hung *Thalas'Inariel.*

The blade felt heavier than usual. Not in weight, but in meaning.

The night air met him like a balm, cool and crisp beneath the stars. A few villagers stood nearby, drawn by torchlight or curiosity. Some waved in greeting, expecting the familiar gait of Liraelth. But it was not the elder they saw—it was Seghnor, taller, broader, tempered by unseen forces. Liraelth, who had left nearly a season ago, was not the one who had returned.

He walked past them with a calm nod, saying nothing.

The path to *Talarion*—the Archive of the First Root—was short, but he walked it with purpose. The two guards outside its sacred gates bowed their heads as he approached. They did not stop him.

The moon hung high and full above the ancient grove. It bathed the world in silver, casting elongated shadows across the glade. Seghnor paused beside the miniature tree—the very sapling that had gifted him the *Oathroot.* He touched a hand to its bark, offering a silent word of thanks.

Then, with a soft hiss, he unsheathed *Thalas'Inariel.*

The blade caught the moonlight and came alive, its runes gleaming faintly, as if remembering the pact that had been struck. As the sword was raised, the scroll tube at his side trembled. He unstoppered it, and the parchment within shimmered as moonlight spilled over its surface.

Words bloomed across the page like ink guided by unseen hands.

Seghnor,

Undoubtedly you have many questions. But be warned—those answers may not bring the peace you seek.

To save our people, and the legacy of our knowledge, I had to find a way to make Suriharon a person, not a place. This was the only way.

Our collective knowledge is stored in Talarion—the Archive of the First Root. You must absorb the words by touching each scroll, book, or tome. In time, you will become attuned to the Archive, and the knowledge of our ancestors will seek you out. One day, you will no longer need to touch the texts at all. They will come to you.

Eventually, you must travel. Seek out other repositories—forgotten vaults, hidden caches, and allied sanctuaries. I have made arrangements. Certain volumes will be delivered to you: teachings on our ancient magic, lost techniques in metal shaping, and the harmony we once shared with the natural world.

I do not know how long it will take before you truly become Suriharon—the Living Memory of the Elves.

I'm sorry I placed this burden on you. I had hoped to bear it myself. But I was not strong enough.

—Liraelth

Seghnor let the scroll fall to his side, heart pounding with the weight of it all.

He had not just returned to *Talarion*. He had returned to become something far older, far greater than himself.

He looked once more to the moonlit grove, then turned and stepped through the archway into the Archive, where thousands of years of knowledge waited for him.

Years Later

Seghnor rose with the dawn each day, though time no longer held meaning. Morning and night blurred into a rhythm of purpose—eat, train, absorb. His body remained honed through daily swordplay; his mind, taxed and reshaped by *Talarion's* endless offerings.

The Archive of the First Root groaned beneath the weight of knowledge. Thousands of tomes had passed through his hands. He had developed a method: touch, pause, absorb. The queue within him—unseen, unfelt—sorted and indexed the knowledge with growing speed.

After two years, even proximity triggered the transference. Shelves whispered to him now. Scrolls unrolled themselves. Books exhaled dust and language as he passed, imprinting into his soul without touch.

His face grew leaner. His robes hung loose despite constant meals. The warmth in his voice faded. He no longer laughed. He no longer visited the outer groves. He no longer remembered his sister's face.

Elven artisans brought entire vaults from distant lands. Hidden caches from ruined towers. Forbidden works, entrusted to no one else. The druids wove protective wards around *Talarion*—not to keep others out, but to keep what he was becoming contained. He never left the archive without cause. He dared not.

By the third year, he stopped speaking unless necessary. His dreams were full of symbols and histories. Names that did not belong to him circled through his thoughts—high scholars long dead, generals of forgotten wars, sages who spoke languages lost before his people learned to write.

And then, in the fourth year, he found his journal again.

Journal of Seghnor, Fourth Year, Day 112

I wrote my name just now and stared at it for minutes.

It felt wrong. Not the spelling. Not the ink. Just… wrong. Like it belonged to someone else.

I remember a place with white flowers. I don't know where. A girl laughed there once. She had silver rings. Maybe they were mine. Maybe I gave them to her. I can't recall her face.

Liraelth. That name still burns in my chest. I don't know if I loved him or hated him for what he made me become. Perhaps both. Perhaps neither. His voice is gone from my memory, but not our purpose.

I am not sad. Not anymore. The sadness passed like weather—there, then gone, then forgotten. But I do fear.

What happens when I no longer need this journal? When the part of me that remembers how to miss someone is gone? Will I still be Seghnor?

Or just the shell he left behind to carry this burden?

The sky has been wrong for days. The wind carries a heat I've never felt here before. Talarion is uneasy.

I will not sleep tonight.

Though I do not need sleep.

Fog crept low through the grasslands outside *Vael'Araneth*, curling in ghostlike waves at the forest's edge. In the hush of dawn, a small herd of deer grazed beneath the whispering boughs, their ears twitching at distant sounds. For a moment, all was still.

Then—the air rippled.

A distortion shimmered in the mist, like heat rising from stone. Without a sound, a cloaked figure stepped from the void. His silhouette was long and lean, outlined in shadow, the hem of his robe smoldering where it brushed the earth.

He paused. Inhaled. Spoke a single word in a tongue lost to all but the ancient dead. A veil of shimmering warding magic rippled over him, wrapping his form in faint, flickering light.

Then he walked.

Each footfall pressed into the moss with quiet deliberation. Burned glyphs smoldered in his wake—symbols of forgotten power etched in red and black. Beneath his step, the roots of the forest recoiled and hissed—unwilling to grant him passage, yet powerless to stop him.

The deer fled in silence, driven by an instinct older than memory.

With every step toward the city, the veil between realms thinned. Trees bent away. Stones trembled in their beds.

There was risk in such exposure.

But the reward—was worth it.

The convergence of planes had begun. And with it, an opportunity. The disruption would grant him access to what the Elves had buried. Hidden. Forgotten. Protected by arrogance and magic.

His brother. So brilliant. So foolish.

In his great wisdom, Mikal had meddled too deeply with the spaces between—twisting the Astral Veil, tampering with the laws that governed planar travel, soul projection, and the dreams of the divine.

And yet, for all his celestial brilliance, his brother had made a critical error chasing his riddles.

He would take what was needed. Claim the secret so no one would be enticed or swayed by it.

He was the *brilliant* one.

And this would begin the next phase of his design.

Eternal life.

Eternal unlife.

The elven city had shifted around him—quietly, respectfully—after his return. To spare him the burden of distance, *Tal'Serandor* had consecrated a new sparring circle just beyond the miniature grove, near enough that he could rise from sleep, train, and enter the *Talarion* within a single breath of morning.

He was already in the ring when the first light broke over the trees.

His opponent came fast—one of the younger guards, skilled, confident. He led with a sweeping cut that should have forced a retreat.

Seghnor didn't yield. He slipped inside the arc and struck his opponent's blade aside, turning his shoulder to unbalance him. A second blow disarmed the guard entirely, sending the wooden practice sword skidding across the stone.

Seghnor nodded toward the discarded blade.

The Elf picked up the blade and went at him twice more.

And twice more the guard ended sprawled in the dust, breath ragged, sweat pouring down his temples.

"You can't be beaten," the Elf said with admiration, grinning through exhaustion.

Seghnor gazed at him.

He said, "Let's hope you're correct."

Seghnor turned from the circle and passed through the grove in silence. The miniature oak tree greeted him with its gentle hush, the low rustle of leaves like a pulse in the morning stillness. Beyond it, only a few paces away, stood *Talarion*.

The Archive's stone doors opened without touch, responding to his presence alone.

Inside, breakfast was waiting on a low table: bread, dried fruit, and steaming tea. He gave the tray no more than a glance. Hunger had become irrelevant.

The knowledge nourished him.

Seghnor stood before the cart, where ancient scrolls whispered across the ages. As he reached out his hand, the *Oathroot* pulsed beneath his sleeve, glowing faintly through the fabric. Veins of silver and green lit his arm, and when his fingers brushed the wood of the first tome, the knowledge unraveled in light.

The scrolls trembled. Threads of memory—incantations, lineages, treaties, and techniques—spilled from them like spun thread, drawn into the root that had bound itself to his flesh.

He did not move.

Did not blink.

He took his seat, a chair worn from years of use. The cushions molded to his body as he settled in. The attendants brought him tome after tome.

One book passed. Then a second. Then a hundred.

The transfer was clean, seamless. No need to read. No need to comprehend. The *Oathroot* did it all, feeding the collected wisdom of his people directly into the deep well of his mind.

Then, without warning, the light wavered.

A breathless silence filled the chamber.

His eyes flew open.

"We're under attack."

The breach began with silence.

A tremor passed through the roots of the forest like distant thunder—unnoticed by all but the oldest trees. Then came the rupture. A jagged tear ripped open the air itself, split wide by the Shatterfront as it tore into the Material Plane. From that wound surged a tide of chaos.

Tharozh-Kel, the Maw Render, emerged first—his massive, ape-like frame steaming with the heat of the Abyss. Bone spines jutted from his shoulders, and his maw hung perpetually open, teeth grinding even in silence. Behind him came his horde.

The Throk'Gar surged forth—hulking demons with four corded arms and hides like cracked obsidian. Their tusked jaws jutted wide as they slammed their fists together, shedding flakes of ash with every movement. Clubs and maces swung in eager arcs, demolishing all in reach.

The Charn'Va crawled beside them, shrouded in living shadow. Their mottled, gray-blue flesh pulsed with twitching movement—not just their too-many limbs, but the half-formed faces embedded in their torsos, each whispering in a different, maddening tongue. Bloated leeches clung to their backs, pulsing with stolen blood.

They came as hunger made flesh. And the world before them would burn.

They flooded the forest like locusts, a writhing wave of destruction. Deer scattered from the grove—but none escaped. Sundered mid-stride, their bodies were tossed like straw. Trees ignited where Abyssal claws raked bark, or shattered into splinters from thunderous blows.

The rift behind them pulsed and belched waves of distortion as the planes collided. The demons stormed the outer woods in a frenzy—smashing huts, rending earth, shrieking in glee. They had not expected to reach the Material Plane, but now that they had, they gave themselves over to ruin.

Then a second surge tore the air.

Ur'Belmirez stepped through with grace and malice. A tall Ur'Devil with dark bronze skin and a crown of curled horns, she bore a glaive inscribed in infernal script that shimmered with heat.

Hellmaws flanked her—towering juggernauts of brute metal and flesh, armored in mismatched plate. Their glowing eyes swept the field in assessment. Maces and cleavers dragged behind them, scoring the ground.

The devils paused at their master's command, analyzing.

The Eternal Rift—once sealed between the Nine Hells and the Abyss—had spilled into the mortal world.

Ur'Belmirez inhaled.

"Elven land," she hissed. Her furnace eyes narrowed toward *Vael'Araneth*, where the forest thinned into towers and walkways. The pale sun was beginning to rise, dimmed behind gray clouds.

"The marked one… he's here."

Then came the Carverfiends—sleek, bone horrors with exposed spines and carved bone plating. Their bodies bore etched infernal glyphs—names of the damned inscribed in jagged script across their ribs, skulls, and limbs. Symbols glowed faintly, burning like embers in the morning gloom. Their hooked, twin-bladed swords spun in wide arcs as they took flight, wings buzzing like hornets. Their segmented tails lashed and stabbed—each one tipped with black venom.

The demons paid them no heed. Chaos had no use for tactics. They smashed elven structures, defiled ancient trees, and struck down anyone who fled.

The devils moved as one—precise, unrelenting. They advanced in tight formations, their weapons rising and falling with brutal economy. Ur'Belmirez shot ahead, her glaive decapitating a Throk'Gar before it could turn. The demon collapsed into a pool of steaming black slime.

They cut through the elven outskirts like a blade through silk. Demon, Elf—it mattered not. All fell. Families were executed without pause. Trees that had stood for centuries collapsed beneath infernal fire and iron.

Where the demons surged wild, the devils pressed forward like a tide of knives.

As battle swelled, Ur'Belmirez pointed her glaive toward the heart of the city.

"Find him," she growled to her Hellmaws. "The one who escaped my sister's chains."

The gates of *Vael'Araneth* stood wide.

Civilians fled inward—mothers clutching children, the wounded borne on stretchers, elders supported by younger kin. Arrows streaked overhead in a steady arc, their silver-tipped heads glowing faintly as they found purchase in demon flesh. The outer barricades had fallen. Flames consumed the sacred forests. Screams echoed through the glades.

Then—silence.

Elven blades met Hell-forged iron and Abyssal steel. The line buckled.

From the southern flank, thunder came.

A mounted charge erupted from the broken treeline—elven cavalry in gleaming scale and forest cloaks, galloping forward with spears leveled and curved swords drawn. Their steeds tore across the ruins of shattered glades with reckless speed. Behind them came foot soldiers, rallying from watch posts and narrow trails, forming around the last defensive bastion.

From the high wall, an officer called out:

"Telar i'vanyali! Halta nor!"

Defend the roots! Hold the line!

A volley answered him. Dozens more demons fell—some still writhing, others collapsing into smoke and ichor. The devils pressed onward, methodical and relentless. Carverfiends leapt branch to branch, slashing down fleeing archers with cruel precision. Hellmaws roared as their spiked maces shattered the front ranks.

Still, the Elves surged forward.

Then—through smoke and haze beyond the eastern rise—he came.

A lone rider.

The figure cut through the ruin like a blade of wind, his cloak streaming behind him, green and gold catching the dawn. Silver hair trailed like flame. His sword burned.

Thalas'Inariel pulsed with radiant fury, a trail of white fire unfurling in its wake. The *Oathroot* along his arm glowed in rhythm—veins of living magic wrapping from wrist to shoulder like roots lit from within.

Seghnor.

A cheer rose from the elven ranks. From towers and ramparts, from shieldmaidens and scouts, from the wounded who could no longer stand. His name was not screamed. It was spoken—clear, full-throated, defiant.

'Seghnor! *Suriharon!*"

The ancient tongue rippled through the trees like wind before a storm.

Demons flinched.

Devils snarled, recoiling from the purity of the words.

Carverfiends hissed as the infernal script etched in their bones smoked and blackened in protest.

Seghnor charged. His mount flew like a storm wind. He cleaved a Hellmaw as he passed—*Thalas'Inariel* slicing through armor and sinew, leaving a gaping wound that flared with silver flame.

He did not slow. He did not speak.

But the tide was vast.

The ground quaked. *Throk'Gar* surged ahead, four-armed brutes swinging obsidian clubs. *Charn'Va* slithered between them, whispering and gnashing. Claws reached. Teeth snapped.

They dragged his horse down.

The beast fell with a shriek, swallowed by a crush of fiendish bodies.

Seghnor rose from the fall, silent.

Surrounded. Hemmed in by shadow and bone. Clawed limbs lashed toward him.

None touched him.

They died on elven steel and sacred light.

At the edge of the fray stood Ur'Belmirez, her glaive poised to strike.

The one who escaped.

Seghnor lifted *Thalas'Inariel.*

The *Oathroot* flared—bright and blinding with both infernal and elven magic.

"Thalas'Inariel, voraé na'thalan!"

Holy fire surged outward in a sweeping arc.

Demons ignited in silver flame. Screams pierced the canopy. Devils staggered, blinded. Dozens fell—vaporized mid-charge.

Ur'Belmirez reeled. Her bronze skin blackened, her infernal glaive shattered the ground as she fell to one knee.

Around Seghnor, a ring of scorched earth widened.

Purified of the filth.

He stood at its center—unbent, alight with fury.

He stepped toward the Ur'Devil, the sword glowing white-hot, its edge dripping with starfire.

The wind died.

For a moment, all was still—flames frozen mid-flicker, ash drifting as if time itself had paused. A cheer began to rise from the elven lines, a trembling cry of hope carried from ramparts and ruined fields.

Then the world tore open again.

The rift split wide behind Seghnor in a rush of sulfur and shadow. Chains slithered out first, writhing like serpents tasting the air. Then came the Hellmaws—not with swords or maces, but bearing shackles of infernal iron, each link forged to hold the damned. They lumbered forward in silence, eyes burning low, the ground cracking beneath their weight.

And behind them stepped Ur'Belreth.

Writhed in chains that coiled like living things, her presence silenced the field. Where her younger sister was elegant and hungry, Ur'Belreth was vast and inevitable. One of her chains dragged behind her, shortened at the end—the wound left by *Thalas'Inariel* still seared into its last few links.

Though her mind had already issued the command, she pointed toward the Elf in the center of the scorched earth.

The Hellmaws surged. Chains snapped through the air, whistling like broken flutes. Seghnor met them head-on. His blade danced through the assault, cleaving two devils in quick succession—black ichor spraying the battlefield. The *Oathroot* flared along his arm, radiant and infernal tendrils of living magic crackling with every strike.

But there were too many.

More chains lashed toward him. He cut one, then another, but they coiled back, reforming like snakes that refused to die. In the distance, Ur'Belmirez fled toward the rift, limping, scorched, her glaive left behind in the ash. The rift swallowed her and she was gone.

Seghnor turned, readying himself for the next wave—when the first chain struck.

It caught his wrist, locking with a burning hiss. He roared, tried to tear free, but more followed. One around his ankle. Another across his chest. A fourth around his sword arm. The radiant blade faltered, flickering under the weight of binding magic.

Still, he did not fall.

He dragged the devils forward with every step, pulling them from their feet as he advanced on Ur'Belreth.

The *Oathroot* burned hot along his skin.

Then her chain came—a massive iron serpent, etched with infernal runes.

It struck his blade.

Thalas'Inariel flew from his grasp, skidding across the stone and vanishing into the mist and ruin.

Seghnor shouted, straining against the bindings, but it was too late.

Chains snapped tight, dragging him back.

Ur'Belreth stepped forward, her expression cold.

"We will see," she said, her voice low and final, "how defiant you are… in Vel'Karuun."

The Hellmaws dragged him into the rift.

And the light was gone.

The chaos outside did not touch him.

Nor did it bother him.

He embraced chaos.

Order took too much energy to maintain—energy spent overcoming entropy was a waste.

Dergan Yholl moved through the heart of *Vael'Araneth* like a ghost, cloaked and warded so heavily that the ground smoked beneath his steps. Where his boots landed, grass hissed and blackened—not from flame, but from the raw planar energy leeching from his vessel. He was no longer of one realm.

He was of all.

He strode without urgency, yet every step spoke of inevitability.

The garden beside the archives remained untouched—one of the few spaces spared from flame or blood. At its center stood the miniature god-tree, the sacred seedling tended for years by Liraelth's hands.

Dergan paused. Radiant and infernal magic both pulsed from the roots.

Devils.

The allies of his brother, Mikal.

Without ceremony, he reached forward, gripped the slender trunk with one gloved hand, and tore it from the soil.

The tree screamed.

The earth cracked in protest. Roots split and curled, grasping for lost sanctity. The tree gave one final cry—its magic flared in desperation, then guttered out like a snuffed lamp. He dropped it behind him, already forgotten.

Had they been wise, they would've anchored it in the Plane of Shadow. Then, even he—a godlike Mage—would not have been able to uproot it.

The nearby archivists and guards turned toward the disruption. Despite the chaos, they'd remained at their post.

Dergan didn't raise his voice.

"You two. Come with me. You will protect me now."

Their eyes glazed. Words of protest died in their throats. Compelled by magic deeper than command, they fell in behind him without question.

Before the archivists could speak, Dergan flicked his fingers.

They clutched their chests and fell to the stone.

Dead.

Hearts burst.

He led the guards not into the archive but to a squat, crumbling structure half-buried in ivy and shadow. Its doors bore no sigils, no runes, no titles. A building forgotten by all but the highest echelon of elven memory.

Dergan turned to the guards.

"Kill anyone who approaches."

They nodded and drew their blades.

He raised his hand. A beam of green fire arced from his fingers— thin, precise.

The outer door dissolved to dust. No explosion. No sound. Just absence.

Ivy curled and withered, as if catching flame, dissolving into blackened ash.

He stepped through.

Inside, the dark waited. With a snap of his fingers, cold green light flared from the corners of the chamber, pulsing with his heartbeat. A corridor stretched ahead, its walls carved with bas-relief: forest kin, gods beside Elves, sacred trees untouched by time. Elven runes shimmered between the scenes, some interlaced with the deeper, older glyphs of the Elder Speech.

Elder Runes.

Something even he, as a near god, respected.

At the corridor's end stood a sealed archway glowing with layered wards.

Ancient.

Impenetrable.

He approached without hesitation.

Threads of magic snaked through the air—snares designed to blind, to burn, to banish.

Dergan raised both hands. He whispered syllables not spoken since the forming of the Material Plane. His fingers traced symbols in the air—precise, surgical. One by one, the wards unraveled.

Not broken.

Dismissed.

Had they woven even one Elder Rune into the defense, it might've taken him hours. Maybe a full day.

But they hadn't.

These Elves, creatures, were not worthy of existence. They didn't deserve to breathe in his presence.

The golden seal dimmed and folded inward.

Beyond lay a domed vault, carved of stone. Silent.

At its center, upon a pedestal of living wood and woven crystal, rested the blade feared by all creation.

Thauren'dal.

The Song Ender.

The Godkiller.

It shimmered—not with reflected light, but with memory. Its edge bore no rust, no stain—only the stillness of perfect violence, bound in form.

The metal was not of this world.

Dergan reached for it.

The moment his fingers touched the hilt, the vault fell away.

A star screamed.

He saw the sky torn open by a burning meteor, its descent a wound carved across the heavens. Mountains groaned. Forests bowed. The heavens cracked. The stone fell, crashing into the earth with divine force—its impact split the land and buried itself in the roots of the world.

Liraelth.

His face swam into view—resolute, alone. The Elf dragged the fallen star in silence. Fire trailed his steps. His hands bled starlight.

A forge rose in secret on the Elemental Crucible, an outer plane filled with fire, water, earth, and air.

The mold born of Elemental Earth.

The metal melted by Elemental Fire.

He sang the blade into being. The great hammer fell once for every line of the blade. Each strike bent both celestial law and root-song into perfect unity.

Then it was quenched by Elemental Water.

Finally, sharpened by Elemental Air.

When it was done, the forest wept.

The blade *lived.*

Its unseen eye opened—aware. Watching. Waiting.

Liraelth knew the truth.

It was too powerful for any mortal—Human or Elf.

He sealed it. Locked it behind warded stone. Buried its true name. No one would wield it.

The vision snapped shut.

Dergan stood alone once more, breath ragged. His grip had not loosened.

He conjured a brand of emerald fire and burned a word into the hilt.

Quickling.

A private joke. A title no one else deserved.

The blade vanished into the folds of his robe—its weight unnatural, like carrying a sealed storm.

He turned to leave.

The guards stood silent.

Two more gestures. Two more burst hearts.

Dergan strode to the Archive of the First Root—*Talarion*—and raised his hand.

He had to be certain. The name *Thauren'dal* could not survive.

A green ray shredded the doors, reducing them to dust.

Another flick of his fingers, and a sphere of flame flew into the center of the ancient archive and library.

Screams. Then silence.

The explosion rocked the foundation.

Talarion folded in on itself—books, tomes, scrolls, and memory—all erased in a tower of fire and ash.

Dergan whispered a command. Magic coiled around him like a shroud.

He vanished, transported to the edge of his sanctum—beyond the reach of all wards.

The convergence collapsed, the Eternal Rift retreating to where it belonged. The lingering devils and demons fought on, even as their masters withdrew to continue the endless war where the Nine Hells and the Abyss entwined.

The elven forces, though decimated, pressed in from all sides, surrounding the infernal and abyssal beasts. They showed no mercy. Fires were contained and extinguished. The wounded and dead were tended in silence.

Upon the field where Seghnor once stood, the earth lay scorched. Not far from the body of his horse, the blade *Thalas'Inariel* gleamed amid the ash. On the day it had turned the tide—yet there was no joy. Seghnor was gone, along with thousands of others.

An Elf reached down and grasped the hilt, the deep red gem a swirl of slow color.

He dropped it with a hiss, flexing his hand as if burned.

"No other may hold *Thalas'Inariel*," someone said.

An elder approached, his brow streaked with ash, his eyes sunken with sorrow.

"We must secure it—for Seghnor's return," he murmured.

"Where shall we put it?" asked another. She glanced toward the shattered skyline. "*Talarion* is gone. We have no vault worthy of this blade."

The elder didn't answer. He removed his cloak, wrapped the sword with care, and cradled it as one might a newborn.

"Where will you take it?" the younger Elf asked.

"Home," said the elder.

\#

The hut stood as Seghnor had left it.

The elder moved to the back wall and descended into the hidden cellar. The stone pavers beneath his feet felt crooked, as if the battle above had unsettled them. At the last chamber, deep in the earth, he unwrapped the blade.

With a grimace, he took it in both hands, ignoring the pain, and drove it down into the ground.

Thalas'Inariel flared—briefly—its glow warm and pulsing, as if in thanks.

Then it dimmed. Silent again.

The elder withdrew, sealing the door behind him.

This was the end of his people.

He knew it.

Here ends Book Two of the Keeper of the Deer series:

The One Tree

Heather and Gideon will return in Book Three:

Keeper

Follow our heroes as they navigate treacherous waters, regrow The One Tree, and vie for control of the Druid Council. Heather will endure her druid trials—her life changed forever.

Dramatis Personae

A

Aaron Manawove — Second eldest son of Gideon and Emma Manawove, apprentice druid from the Needle Forest. Known for his intelligence.

Abigail von Schule — Youngest daughter of Xavier von Schule, bright and quick-witted. *(deceased)*

Alden Fairmont — Ornst nobleman, known for his prowess judging wines and hosting cotillions. Reportedly kidnapped and being held for ransom by the Black Storm.

Aurora — Archdruid of the northern cold wastes, The Circle of Whitewake, *Thenvora*, member of the Druid Council.

B

Bastien — Cult leader of the Maw of Darkness, a branch of the Pale Dominion, follower of the Demon Prince of Undeath.

Bella von Schule — Eldest daughter of Xavier von Schule.

Brak — Grim, calculating wizard with command over Abyssal forces. Follower of Ra-Joth, Lich Lord of the Abyss. Risking soul and sanity to serve his master.

Buvic — Archdruid of the northwest regions, The Circle of Frosthall, *Taldras Thal'Korrin*, known for being aloof and clumsy.

C

Cedric Manawove — Eldest son of Gideon and Emma Manawove, apprentice druid from the Needle Forest. Known for his way with nature.

Chefera — Priestess of Thatara, companion to Gideon investigating the Mage-Gate.

Chilcott — Also known as "Puzzle Boy," runs errands for Leskaré, ally and friend to Radcliffe von Schule.

Comrade (Xekius) — Wizard of Arcana, ally to the Shadow Circle and emissary.

D

Doud — Mercenary fighter who works with Wilmund, brother of Garret.

Duwy — Black Storm representative, operating in Ornst.

E

Emma Manawove — Wife of Gideon, mother of Cedric, Aaron, Eric, and Heather. *(deceased)*

Eric Manawove —Youngest son of Gideon and Emma. Known for his love of the written word.

F

Finola — Archdruid of the Midlands. The Circle of Heartwood, *Taldras Telvarin,* known for her combat prowess and intelligence.

Florence — Housemaid at *Château Saignoral.*

Fox — Archdruid of the Shadow Circle, *Taldras Morilenn.* Known for her leadership and uncompromising drive to ruin civilization.

G

Gabrielle — Governess to the von Schule children, known for her stunning beauty.

Garret — Mercenary fighter who works with Wilmund, brother of Doud.

Gideon Manawove — Grand Druid, leader of The Circle, *Taldras Arbo Solien,* commander of Druid's Glen, protector of The One Tree.

H

Hadley — Horse-master at Château Saignoral, also known as "Hadley the Pillager." *(deceased)*

I

Ilimitar — Archdruid of Thariel and forests to the east of Druid's Glen, representing the Elves, The Greenwood Circle, *Elarien Taldras.*

J

Jamie — Young stable hand at *Château Saignoral;* friend to Radcliffe.

Justine von Schule - Matron of the von Schule family, wife of Xavier. *(deceased)*

K
Killigrew — Longtime friend and business partner of Xavier von Schule.
Krik — Archdruid of the western areas, known as the Barbarian Druid, The Ironwood Circle, *Gorvan'dar*. Known for his battle, eating, and drinking prowess.

L
Lanny Zeh — Former business partner of Xavier von Schule and ranking member of Leskaré. Father of Radcliffe.
Lillia — Archdruid of the south. A dryad who commands The Circle of Stillgrove, *Taldras Vael'Thira*, known for her stunning beauty and not wearing clothes. Ever.
Liraelth — Elder Elf, crafter of wondrous elven artifacts. *(deceased)*

M
Marie von Schule — Middle daughter of Xavier von Schule.
Merrow Keff — Renown scholar from the *Library of Gilded Thought*. *(deceased?)*

N
Nightshade — Archdruid of the Fey. Fairy druid of The Circle of Veilwood, *Taldras Shal'Vaerith*. An ancient creature, longest serving member of the Druid Council.

R
Radcliffe von Schule — Stepson of Xavier von Schule. True father is Lanny Zeh. Known as Rad.
Robert Ruud — Young nobleman of Ornst, known to have admired Abigail.
Rosamund — Young woman who used to work as a prostitute at The Sweet Hatchet. Love interest of Radcliffe von Schule.

S

Sarif — Ranger of the Stairwell. Member of the expedition to investigate the Mage-Gate.

Seghnor — Elf entrusted with the knowledge of the Elves, friend and companion of Liraelth.

Spider — Apprentice druid, follower of Wilmund, member of the expedition to investigate the Mage-Gate.

T

Tristin von Schule — Eldest son of Xavier von Schule, heir to *Château Saignoral.*

V

Val — Ranger of the Stairwell. Member of the expedition to investigate the Mage-Gate.

W

Wellsey — Apprentice druid, follower of Wilmund, member of the expedition to investigate the Mage-Gate.

Wilkins — Household valet to the von Schule family; precise and formal.

Wilmund — Archdruid of the vast eastern lands. Also known as the Dark Druid because of his clothing and favorite weapon, a scythe. Leader of The Circle of Farreach, *Taldras Sol'Vareth,* discoverer of the Mage-Gate.

X

Xavier von Schule — Master of *Château Saignoral,* powerful and calculating.

Xekius (Comrade) — Wizard of Arcana, ally to the Shadow Circle and emissary.

The Shadow Circle (Identities Uknown)

Deer — Calm, measured voice who warns of reckless action and emphasizes control over corruption.

Fox — Central figure and leader of the Shadow Circle.

Hawk — Pragmatic and strategic, patient and precise. Like Squirrel, wants to strike from the shadows.

Polar Bear — Stoic, calculating. Motivation is preservation of the Shadow Circle.

Squirrel — Master at spying, cunning, wants to strike from the shadows at their enemies.

Wild Boar — Impatient, aggressive, wants immediate action against civilization despite the consequences.

Wolf — Cautious, strategic, wants to understand the enemy before striking to ensure long-term survival.

Timeline

Era	Years Ago	Key Themes
Primordial Age	???–4000	Wild magic, flourishing of ancient races.
Age of the Bloodlords	4000–3000	Human dynasties thrive; coexistence with elder races.
The Bloodletting	~3000	Collapse of Bloodlords; chaos, wars, ruin.
Age of Quiet Expansion	3000–1100	Gradual rebuilding; early libraries; cautious magic.
Rise of the Mages	1100–1000	Mage domination, obsessive chronicling of knowledge.
Sundering	~1000	Mage downfall; global collapse.
Age of Recovery	1000–700	Survival, preservation of knowledge.
Age of Rising Kingdoms	700–300	Human duchies rise; Elves retreat into isolation.
Reign of Haddensack	300–Present	Human stabilization; ancient secrets stir anew.

"The Timeline was never meant to be linear. It is a wound that bleeds in both directions. As we learn more, these wounds heal… or reopen."
—Scholar Merrow Keff, in defiance of several edicts circa AR64

"If the Timeline is sacred, someone should tell the past to stop changing."
—Scholar Vindrel Hoss, in a letter to Merrow Keff, circa AR64

Undead

Summarized from the treatises commissioned by Xavier von Schule. *A Treatise on the Undead: Characteristics and Known Environments*
A Treatise on the Undead: A Compendium of Fiends

General observation taken from the treatises: all undead shun sunlight, as it is deadly to them in extended exposure.

B
Blightghouls – Ghouls with toxic spores, variant of a ghoul, fungal in origin, highly contagious. Will hide in groups during the daylight.

D
Dread wolves – Undead beasts, fast and powerful, often found near vampire lairs, eyes glow red, claws poisonous.

G
Ghosts – Remnants of profound trauma, not aggressive unless provoked, may be reasoned with, exist in the Ethereal Plane and can cross over into Material Plane.
Ghouls – Undead warriors, mindless servants, agile and quick, can climb, hunt all living things, follow instructions of their master. Will hide in groups during the daylight, but will brave the sunlight if provoked.

L
Liches – Undead wizards or magi, bound to phylacteries, destruction of physical form does not end them. Dangerous planners, near immortals. Perfected by the Mages.

M
Mummies – Desiccated undead, tied to unholy rituals practiced upon the living, carry curses, best to avoid. Often found in tombs.

S

Shadow-fiends – Giant extraplanar undead, extremely rare, used as guardian-hunters, vengeful, survivors, cataclysmic??? Only suspected vulnerability is sunlight.

Shadows – Vitality draining entities, may be controlled with wards or runes, susceptible to holy or consecrated light.

Skeletons – Animated bones, mindless warriors, controlled by necromancers, often massed to overrun the living. Only undead able to survive daylight for a few hours.

Specters – Vengeful incorporeal spirits, drawn to places of violent death.

U

Umbrals – Intelligent shadow-born undead, stronger than ghosts or specters, maybe necromantic spell casters or soul-drainers. Often created by liches to collect souls to feed their hunger.

V

Vestiges – Location-bound spirits, seek living or undead hosts, undying, extremely difficult to destroy, exist in the Ethereal and Material Planes. Often thought of as neither good or evil. A living host allows them to move in sunlight.

Vampires – Cunning, intelligent, blood-feeding, retains intellect and spellcasting, master manipulators, used at times as forever guardians. Create their own vampire spawn and dread wolves, avoid sunlight (deadly to them). Vampires can have necromancer abilities to create ghouls and blightghouls.

Vampire spawn - stealthy undead, corrupted victims of vampires, skulk in ruins, hunt at night, avoid sunlight (deadly to them).

W

Will-o'-wisps – Lure travelers to ruin, feed on fear, appear in regions where there has been ancient death or tragedy, often found in deep forests and known to hunt Fey.

Wraiths – Powerful spirits, often can command lesser undead, often born from rituals, avoid direct confrontation. Difficult to destroy.

Wights – Intelligent undead, often bound to ancient oaths and burial grounds, possess martial skill and will, dangerous in small numbers. Can wield weapons.

Z
Zombies – Rotting corpses, mindless but relentless, decay slows reactions, carry disease. Mildly resistant to sunlight.

Planes of Existence

The following planes represent the major known realms of reality. Though countless hidden or theoretical planes may exist beyond mortal understanding, these are the planes most scholars agree upon—mapped, named, and feared in equal measure.

Plane	Description
Astral Veil	Plane of thought, memory, and soul travel. Connects all planes and reflects the dreams of gods and mortals alike. Can also be called The Void.
Divine Realms	Homes of the gods, split into domains of Light, Nature, Knowledge, War, and Death. Each reflects the virtues or vices of its divine patrons.
Elemental Crucible	Unified elemental realm with four chaotic regions of raw Earth, Air, Fire, and Water
Ethereal Plane	A ghostly echo of the Material Plane, filled with mist and intangible echoes. Used by spirits and certain forms of magic.
Material Plane	Mortal realm, physical world where most mortal civilizations exist and history unfolds. The primary nexus of reality where natural laws hold strongest sway.
Nine Hells	Hierarchical realm of devils organized into nine distinct layers, each ruled by archdevils. A plane of strict order twisted toward evil ends.
Plane of Shadow	Mirrored Material Plane, twisted by darkness and negative energy. Reality here is fluid and mutable, with shadows taking on substance and form.
The Abyss	Realm of chaos, madness, and ruin. Home to demons and the raw forces of destruction.

The Infernals: Archdevils of the Nine Hells

Plane	Plane Name	Ruler (Archdevil)	Enforcer (Ur'Devil)	Notes
1	Vhal'Zaruun	Zarkhul	Ur'Belmirez	Border bastion, perpetual warfront with the Abyss
2	Draz'Khareth	Malveris	Ur'Thalor	Labyrinthine politics and backstabbing
3	Tor'Sivareth	Vexarion	Ur'Sinadra	False redemption becomes eternal chains
4	Zhul'Tharezz	Kelivrax	Ur'Terelis	Minds break in unending introspection
5	Shar'Ghalor	Vashtorak	Ur'Neress	Regret is weapon, memory is coin
6	Mal'Vokrenn	Tharnaxis	Ur'Kelroth	Pain refined into perfection
7	Rav'Embereth	Syrrik	Ur'Daelith	The end of hope, the beginning of void
8	Urz'Velgrith	Krelzahar	Ur'Maziel	Obedience forged by pact and punishment
9	Kel'Durmor	Malgareth	Ur'Belreth	Malgareth's seat of power

The Infernals: Abyssal Rulers

Layer Name	Ruler (Great Demon)	Title	Notes
Carrion Deep	Gurh'Naaz	Maw That Consumes	Border layer, perpetual warfront with the Nine Hells
Ember Howl	Rhal'Zurrek	The Infernal Howler	Firestorms, madness, infernal beasts
Hollow Requiem	En'Mavhul	The Ghost King	Silence, spectral echoes
Iron Spiral	Mekh'Varuun	Architect of Chains	Endless metal labyrinth, rust
Noxblight Vale	Ith'Quareth	Lord of the Spores	Poison, corrupted nature, fungus
Screaming Depths	Uthu'Maresh	Leviathan of the Drowned	Water, drowning, isolation
The Bleeding Wastes	Vaz'Gaath	Demon Prince of Undeath	Undeath, rot, skeletal legions, undead
The Crucible Coil	Drak'Vorul	The Flesh Artisan	Fleshforges, stitched horrors
The Sepulcher of Unbeing	Ra-Joth	Lich Lord of the Abyss	Abandoned prison
Thirsting Sands	Zael'Thune	The Bone Queen	Deserts of glass and bone
Webbed Catacombs	Vesha'Tar	Mother Queen of Spiders	Spiders, silk-choked ruins
The Crimson Feast	Zai'Vethra	Demon Prince of Decadence	Indulgence and pleasures of the flesh.

The Infernals: Known Devils

Name	Type	Description
Hellmaws	Greater Fiend	Generals, enforcers, towering devils. Thickly muscled and armored. Leathery wings.
Carverfiends	Greater Fiend	Torturers, executioners. Skeletal, long limbs with armored plates etched with names of the damned.
Frostbinders	Lesser Fiend	Inquisitors, insectoid, blue-white carapaces, breath freezes steel.
Ur'Belreth	Ur'Devil	Imposing devil, bat wings, armored, wielding Chain of Judgment. Rules with Malgareth.
Ur'Belmirez	Ur'Devil	Second in command of Carrion Deep. Sister of Ur'Belreth. Imposing devil with bronze skin. Led an incursion into the Material Plane.

The Infernals: Known Demons

Name	Type	Description
Throk'Gar	Ape Demon	Hulking demon with four muscular arms, tusked jaw, and cracked infernal hide.
Charn'Va	Beast Demon	Mottled skin, too many limbs, half-formed faces on torso; leeches ride its body.
Maggoritch	Beast Demon	Squat, bloated thing oozing fungus and spores, tentacle maw, cloud of infectious gas. Fodder.
Zaskali	Beast Demon	Tall, lithe, insectoid creature with sickle-bladed arms and glistening emerald carapace.
Kozgokoth	Greater Demon	Eight-foot war demon with cracked bone mask, dark wings, and a serrated spear. Bound by Brak.
Tharozh-Kel	Greater Demon	Massive demon with bone spines and a gaping maw. Led an Abyssal incursion.

Pantheon

The gods of Humankind are the most widely worshipped, their influence extending across nearly all races. While certain beings—such as the Mages or Malgareth—have ascended to near-divine power, they are not included here, as they are not true gods.

God	Domain – Influences	Symbol	Description
Origin Species of the God – Human			
Dhusyn	Nature, Trickery - Weather and Crops	Stalk of Grain	God of nature and trickery.
Ehnos	War - War and Warriors	Armored Fist	Patron of warriors and champions.
Gaeyar	Knowledge, Life - Smiths and Healing	Hammer	Patron of smiths and healers.
Oris	War - Battle	Crossed Swords	Delights in suffering and destruction.
Ozotl	Light - Sun, Light, Warmth	Sun	Bringer of sun, light, and warmth.
Qhabin	Life, Death - Life and Death	Black Star next to a White Star	Arbiter of existence and oblivion.
Qhesin	Nature, Tempest - Ocean and Sea Creatures	Wave	Dominion over oceans and sea creatures.
Sidros	Knowledge - Speech and Writing	Unfurled Scroll	Keeper of speech and writing.
Synas	Nature - Mountains and Peaks	Mountain Peak	Dominion over mountains and towering peaks.
Taanh	Life - Rivers and Livestock	Foot Bridge	Guardian of rivers and livestock.
Thatara	Nature - Nature and Forests	The One Tree	Guardian of forests and forest creatures.

God	Domain – Influences	Symbol	Description
Tidall	Life - Medicine and Healing	Mistletoe	Healer and protector of the sick and injured.
Unara	Knowledge, Life - Arts, Travel, Commerce	Hand with a Coin	Patron of arts, travel, and commerce.
Untos	Knowledge - Magic	Staff	Master of magic and arcane secrets.
Origin Species of the God – Elves			
Allisa	Knowledge - Magic	Staff	Mistress of magic and arcane lore.
Galaeron	War - War and Warriors	Bow and Quiver	Patron of warriors and defenders
Halamar	Nature - Nature and Forests	Spruce Tree	Guardian of forests and spirits.
Syvis	Life - Healing	Chamomile Flower	Healer and caretaker of the sick and wounded.
Tsarra	Knowledge - Dance and Songs	Lute	Muse of music and dance.
Origin Species of the God – Dwarf			
Kidoum	Nature, Life - Stone, Growth, Balance	A blooming tree rooted in stone	Guardian of caverns and stone.
Nomunli	War, Forge, Knowledge - Craft, Battle, Endurance	An anvil split by an axe	Patron of forge-fires and war.
Thradmir	Trickery, Wealth - Trade, Contracts, Wealth	A scale weighed by a hammer	Presides over bargains, ledgers, and contracts.

Mages

Of celestial origin, the Mages first emerged upon the Material Plane at the will of the gods. Though not deities themselves, they wielded unfathomable power—magic interwoven with the very fabric of the planes. With it, they bent the world to their will, waging wars of domination against all intelligent life. Yet even as they brought ruin, their obsession with recording knowledge endured. From their conquests rose countless tomes, chronicles, and vaults of lore—the very foundations of the great libraries that remain.

Name	Gender	Affiliation	Stronghold (Mage-Gate Symbol)
Dergan Yholl	Male	Dergan	Abyssal Bastion (AB)
Mikal Yholl	Male	Mikal	Infernal Sanctum (IS)
Opianne	Female	None	Veilspire (VS)
Carick	Male	Dergan	Shadowfang Citadel (SC)
Utaz	Male	None	Tower of Knekora (TK)
Enora	Female	Mikal	Wintermourne (WM)
Ozumonar	Male	Mikal	Achivum Maledictum AM)
Striviar	Male	None	Hollowkeep (HK)
Exon	Male	Mikal	Gatebreaker (GB)

"The Mages did not fall. They rose—higher than gods, in their own estimation—until the rest of us were insects in their way. Power made them indifferent, then curious, then cruel. And when they finally saw the end coming, they called it inevitable… and congratulated themselves for preparing for it."
— Merrow Keff, On Tyrants Cloaked in Flame, AR65

Elvish Dictionary

While Elvish encompasses many ancient dialects, all share a common root. Though spellings and pronunciations may vary, the core meanings remain consistent across regions and traditions.

Elvish Term	Common Translation	Context/Usage
Elar'andoré na Tharaniel araneth	"The proper place for Elaril to watch over our people."	Original name of the known lands given by the Elves.
Elarandor Or *Elrandor*	"The land overseen by Elaril."	Original name of the lands shortened by Humans. Also used is Eldor, Tora, and Randor by various people. 'EA' is used by cartographers.
Vael'Araneth	"Sanctified Throne" or "Rooted High Place"	Name of the great Elven city, cultural and magical capital.
Talarion	"Archive of the First Root"	Name of the great library in Vael'Araneth; also called the Rootvault or Deep Grove.
Tal'Serandor	"The Rooted Circle of Elders"	The ruling Council of Elders in Elven society.
Elaril	"The God-Tree"	Sacred, sentient tree located at the heart of Vael'Araneth. Predecessor of The One Tree.
Vael'Noctharin	"Root of Becoming in Darkness"	The ritual box used to contain and corrupt the sacred acorn with innocent blood and ashes of the fallen.
Thauren'dal	"The Song-Ender"	True Elvish name of the Godkiller blade.
Vaernil Harondras	"The Memory of the Deep Roots"	A sacred Elvish chronicle containing histories of the ancient druids and early Grove Wars.
Nuin'Kelharon	"Songs of the Hidden Grove"	A poetic text containing secret druidic rites and

Elvish Term	Common Translation	Context/Usage
		encoded passages on natural magic.
Arbo	"Tree"	Use in combination with other words.
Vael'Arboras'Doralien	"The sanctified passage through the lifeblood of the trees."	Full ceremonial Elvish phrase for the druidic magic known in Common as tree-stride. Used in rituals, songs, and sacred contexts.
Arb'Doralien	"Root-passage."	Contracted Elvish form. Used in common elven speech. Humans shortened further into *Tree-stride, Greenstep,* or *Rootwalk.*
Aras'Lir	"Song of leaf."	Elven term for plant-speak, green-speak, or root-tongue. *Leafsong.*
Elarien Taldras	"The Greenwood Circle"	The druid circle representing the Elves.
Vaer'Elaril'Thalien	"The Root of Elaril That Is Everywhere"	The One Tree
Arboras Taldorien	"Druid's Glen"	The original name of Druid's Glen as given by the Elves.
Taldras Arbo Solien	"Circle of Tree Light"	The original name of The Circle, designating where The One Tree is located. Gathering or collection of druids.
Lathren vëa taldorin	"May his leaves rot inward."	An Elven insult.
Talthrien Mor'vany	"The Forest of Black Remembrance."	Commonly known as the Dreadwood.
Narthtunel	"Devils"	Refers to anything infernal that is not a demon.
Zaurgorith	"Demons"	Demons and their infernal ilk.
Haron Talathien	"Memory of the Rooted Place"	The vault underneath Druid's Glen where the

Elvish Term	Common Translation	Context/Usage
		druid histories are kept secure.
Narae'loth taldren vaerun	"Do not stir the roots that drink in silence"	A reference to don't disturb things that are at rest.
Verdaleth	"Green guardian" or "verdant protector"	Reference to a living tree often summoned by Fey.
Taldras Morilenn	"Circle of Darkness" "Circle of Shadows"	Where the Shadow Circle rules to subvert civilization.
Vael'Thaldrien	"Gambit Rooted in Silence"	Liraelth's attempt to save all the Elven knowledge.
Thalas'Inariel	"Song of the Last Flame"	Seghnor's magnificent holy blade, also known as *Lightpiercer*.
Vael'Virelen	"The Oathroot"	A magical intertwining of infernal and radiant magic that came from the god-tree's seed and integrated with Seghnor.
Vaer'Halamarien	"The Rite of Halamar" "Sanctified Celebration of Halamar"	A time of the year where the Elves celebrate Halamar, god of nature.
Thalas'Inariel, voraé na'thalan!	"Lightpiercer, stand with me."	Activation phrase in battle for Seghnor's sword.
Telar i'vanyali! Halta nor!	"Defend the roots, hold the line!"	Yelled from the battlements by Elvish commanders.
Gaathrak Vorn	"Burning Tyrant"	Hellmaws.
Thulven Gaathir	"Scribe of Pain"	Carverfiends
Kel'Saevren	"Judges of Ice and Order"	Frostbinders
Mor'Kelthurra	"Chain-Lord of Suffering"	Lashbinders
Vernithil	"Voice in the Thorns"	Whisperspikes
Gaulthrim	"Ash-Spawn"	Emberkin

www.ingramcontent.com/pod-product-compliance
Lightning Source LLC
Chambersburg PA
CBHW022011300726
48970CB00003B/836